Saga Six Pack 6

Saga Six Pack 6

By

Hélène Adeline Guerber

Henry Rider Haggard

Snorri Sturluson

Charles W. Whistler

Laurence Marcellus Larson

Enhanced Media
2016

Saga Six Pack 6

Harald Harfager's Saga by Snorri Sturluson. From *The Heimskringla: or, Chronicle of the kings of Norway*. Translated by Samuel Laing. First published in 1844.

Saga of Hakon Herdebreid ("Hakon the Broad-Shouldered") by Snorri Sturluson. From *The Heimskringla: or, Chronicle of the kings of Norway*. Translated by Samuel Laing. First published in 1844.

Eric Brighteyes by Henry Rider Haggard. First published in 1890.

A Thane of Wessex by Charles W. Whistler. First published in 1896.

The Valkyrs by Hélène Adeline Guerber. From *Myths of the Norsemen: From the Eddas and Sagas*. First published in 1909.

The Elves by Hélène Adeline Guerber. From *Myths of the Norsemen: From the Eddas and Sagas*. First published in 1909.

Canute the Great and the Rise of Danish Imperialism during the Viking Age by Laurence Marcellus Larson. First published in 1912.

Saga Six Pack 6. Published by Enhanced Media, 2016.

Enhanced Media Publishing
Los Angeles, CA.

First Printing: 2016.

ISBN-13: 978-1530091614

ISBN-10: 1530091616

Contents

Harald Harfager's Saga by Snorri Sturluson 7
Saga of Hakon Herdebreid (Hakon the Broad-Shouldered) by Snorri Sturluson 31
Eric Brighteyes by H. Rider Haggard 45
A Thane of Wessex by Charles W. Whistler 237
The Valkyrs by Hélène Adeline Guerber 352
The Elves by Hélène Adeline Guerber 357
Canute the Great by Laurence Marcellus Larson 360

Harald Harfager's Saga by Snorri Sturluson

From *Heimskringla, The Chronicle of the Kings of Norway*

Harald was but ten years old when he succeeded his father (Halfdan the Black). He became a stout, strong, and comely man, and withal prudent and manly. His mother's brother, Guthorm, was leader of the hird, at the head of the government, and commander ('hertogi') of the army. After Halfdan the Black's death, many chiefs coveted the dominions he had left. Among these King Gandalf was the first; then Hogne and Frode, sons of Eystein, king of Hedemark; and also Hogne Karuson came from Ringerike. Hake, the son of Gandalf, began with an expedition of 300 men against Vestfold, marched by the main road through some valleys, and expected to come suddenly upon King Harald; while his father Gandalf sat at home with his army, and prepared to cross over the fiord into Vestfold. When Duke Guthorm heard of this he gathered an army, and marched up the country with King Harald against Hake. They met in a valley, in which they fought a great battle, and King Harald was victorious; and there fell King Hake and most of his people. The place has since been called Hakadale. Then King Harald and Duke Guthorm turned back, but they found King Gandalf had come to Vestfold. The two armies marched against each other, and met, and had a great battle; and it ended in King Gandalf flying, after leaving most of his men dead on the spot, and in that state he came back to his kingdom. Now when the sons of King Eystein in Hedemark heard the news, they expected the war would come upon them, and they sent a message to Hogne Karuson and to Herse Gudbrand, and appointed a meeting with them at Ringsaker in Hedemark.

After the battle King Harald and Guthorm turned back, and went with all the men they could gather through the forests towards the Uplands. They found out where the Upland kings had appointed their meeting-place, and came there about the time of midnight, without the watchmen observing them until their army was before the door of the house in which Hogne Karuson was, as well as that in which Gudbrand slept. They set fire to both houses; but King Eystein's two sons slipped out with their men, and fought for a while, until both Hogne and Frode fell. After the fall of these four chiefs, King Harald, by his relation Guthorm's success and powers, subdued Hedemark, Ringerike, Gudbrandsdal, Hadeland, Thoten, Raumarike, and the whole northern part of Vingulmark. King Harald and Guthorm had thereafter war with King Gandalf, and fought several battles with him; and in the last of them King Gandalf was slain, and King Harald took the whole of his kingdom as far south as the river Raum.

King Harald sent his men to a girl called Gyda, daughter of King Eirik of Hordaland, who was brought up as foster-child in the house of a great bonde in Valdres. The king wanted her for his concubine; for she was a remarkably handsome girl, but of high spirit withal. Now when the messengers came there, and delivered their errand to the girl, she answered, that she would not throw herself away even to take a king for her husband, who had no greater kingdom to rule over than a few districts.

"And methinks," said she, "it is wonderful that no king here in Norway will make the whole country subject to him, in the same way as Gorm the Old did in Denmark, or Eirik at Upsala."

The messengers thought her answer was dreadfully haughty, and asked what she thought would come of such an answer; for Harald was so mighty a man, that his invitation was good enough for her. But although she had replied to their errand differently from what they wished, they saw no chance, on this occasion, of taking her with them against her will; so they prepared to return. When they were ready, and the people followed them out, Gyda said to the messengers, "Now tell to King Harald these my words. I will only agree to be his lawful wife upon the condition that he shall first, for my sake, subject to himself the whole of Norway, so that he may rule over that kingdom as freely and fully as King Eirik over the Swedish dominions, or King Gorm over Denmark; for only then, methinks, can he be called the king of a people."

Now came the messengers back to King Harald, bringing him the words of the girl, and saying she was so bold and foolish that she well deserved that the king should send a greater troop of people for her, and inflict on her some disgrace. Then answered the king, "This girl has not spoken or done so much amiss that she should be punished, but rather she should be thanked for her words. She has reminded me," said he, "of something which it appears to me wonderful I did not think of before. And now," added he, "I make the solemn vow, and take God to witness, who made me and rules over all things, that never shall I clip or comb my hair until I have subdued the whole of Norway, with scat(1), and duties, and domains; or if not, have died in the attempt." Guthorm thanked the king warmly for his vow; adding, that it was royal work to fulfil royal words.

(1) Scat was a land-tax, paid to the king in money, malt, meal, or flesh-meat, from all lands.

After this the two relations gather together a great force, and prepare for an expedition to the Uplands, and northwards up the valley (Gudbrandsdal), and north over Dovrefjeld; and when the king came down to the inhabited land he ordered all the men to be killed, and everything wide around to be delivered to the flames. And when the people came to know this, they fled every one where he could; some down the country to Orkadal, some to Gaulardal, some to the forests. But some begged for peace, and obtained it, on condition of joining the king and becoming his men. He met no opposition until he came to Orkadal. There a crowd of people had assembled, and he had his first battle with a king called Gryting. Harald won the victory, and King Gryting was made prisoner, and most of his people killed. He took service himself under the king, and swore fidelity to him. Thereafter all the people in Orkadal district went under King Harald, and became his men.

King Harald made this law over all the lands he conquered, that all the udal property should belong to him; and that the bondes, both great and small, should pay him land dues for their possessions. Over every district he set an earl to judge according to the law of the land and to justice, and also to collect the land dues and the fines; and for this each earl received a third part of the dues, and services, and fines, for the support of his table and other expenses. Each earl had under him four or more herses, each of whom had an estate of twenty marks yearly income bestowed on him and was bound to support twenty men-at-arms, and the earl sixty men, at their own expenses. The king had increased the land dues and burdens so much, that each of his earls had greater power and income than the kings had before; and when that became known at Throndhjem, many great men joined the king and took his service.

It is told that Earl Hakon Grjotgardson came to King Harald from Yrjar, and brought a great crowd of men to his service. Then King Harald went into Gaulardal, and had a great battle, in which he slew two kings, and conquered their dominions; and these were Gaulardal district and Strind district. He gave Earl Hakon Strind district to rule over as earl. King Harald then proceeded to Stjoradal, and had a third battle, in which he gained the victory, and took that district also. There upon the Throndhjem people assembled, and four kings met together with their troops. The one ruled over Veradal, the second over Skaun, third over the Sparbyggja district, and the fourth over Eyin Idre (Inderoen); and this latter had also Eyna district. These four kings marched with their men against King Harald, but he won the battle; and some of these kings fell, and some fled. In all, King Harald fought at the least eight battles, and slew eight kings, in the Throndhjem district, and laid the whole of it under him.

North in Naumudal were two brothers, kings,—Herlaug and Hrollaug; and they had been for three summers raising a mound or tomb of stone and lime and of wood. Just as the work was finished, the brothers got the news that King Harald was coming upon them with his army. Then King Herlaug had a great quantity of meat and drink brought into the mound, and went into it himself, with eleven companions, and ordered the mound to be covered up. King Hrollaug, on the contrary, went upon the summit of the mound, on which the kings were wont to sit, and made a throne to be erected, upon which he seated himself. Then he ordered feather-beds to be laid upon the bench below, on which the earls were wont to be seated, and threw himself down from his high seat or throne into the earl's seat, giving himself the title of earl. Now Hrollaug went to meet King Harald, gave up to him his whole kingdom, offered to enter into his service, and told him his whole proceeding. Then took King Harald a sword, fastened it to Hrollaug's belt, bound a shield to his neck, and made him thereupon an earl, and led him to his earl's seat; and therewith gave him the district Naumudal, and set him as earl over it (A.D. 866).

King Harald then returned to Throndhjem, where he dwelt during the winter, and always afterwards called it his home. He fixed here his head residence, which is called Lade. This winter he took to wife Asa, a daughter of Earl Hakon Grjotgardson, who then stood in great favour and honour with the king. In spring the king fitted out his ships. In winter he had caused a great frigate (a dragon) to be built, and had it fitted-out in the most splendid way, and brought his house-troops and his berserks on board. The forecastle men were picked men, for they had the king's banner. From the stem to the mid-hold was called rausn, or the fore-defence; and there were the berserks. Such men only were received into King Harald's house-troop as were remarkable for strength, courage, and all kinds of dexterity; and they alone got place in his ship, for he had a good choice of house-troops from the best men of every district. King Harald had a great army, many large ships, and many men of might followed him. Hornklofe, in his poem called *Glymdrapa*, tells of this; and also that King Harald had a battle with the people of Orkadal, at Opdal forest, before he went upon this expedition.

"O'er the broad heath the bowstrings twang,
While high in air the arrows sang.
The iron shower drives to flight
The foeman from the bloody fight.
The warder of great Odin's shrine,
The fair-haired son of Odin's line,
Raises the voice which gives the cheer,
First in the track of wolf or bear.
His master voice drives them along
To Hel—a destined, trembling throng;
And Nokve's ship, with glancing sides,
Must fly to the wild ocean's tides.—
Must fly before the king who leads
Norse axe-men on their ocean steeds."

King Harald moved out with his army from Throndhjem, and went southwards to More. Hunthiof was the name of the king who ruled over the district of More. Solve Klofe was the name of his son, and both were great warriors. King Nokve, who ruled over Raumsdal, was the brother of Solve's mother. Those chiefs gathered a great force when they heard of King Harald, and came against him. They met at Solskel, and there was a great battle, which was gained by King Harald (A.D. 867). Hornklofe tells of this battle:—

"Thus did the hero known to fame,
The leader of the shields, whose name
Strikes every heart with dire dismay,
Launch forth his war-ships to the fray.
Two kings he fought; but little strife
Was needed to cut short their life.
A clang of arms by the sea-shore,—
And the shields' sound was heard no more."

The two kings were slain, but Solve escaped by flight; and King Harald laid both districts under his power. He stayed here long in summer to establish law and order for the country people, and set men to rule them, and keep them faithful to him; and in autumn he prepared to return northwards to Throndhjem. Ragnvald Earl of More, a son of Eystein Glumra, had the summer before become one of Harald's men; and the king set him as chief over these two districts, North More and Raumsdal; strengthened him both with men of might and bondes, and gave him the help of ships to defend the coast against enemies. He was called Ragnvald the Mighty, or the Wise; and people say both names suited him well. King Harald came back to Throndhjem about winter.

The following spring (A.D. 868) King Harald raised a great force in Throndhjem, and gave out that he would proceed to South More. Solve Klofe had passed the winter in his ships of war, plundering in North More, and had killed many of King Harald's men; pillaging some places, burning others, and making great ravage; but sometimes he had been, during the winter, with his friend King Arnvid in South More. Now when he heard that King Harald was come with ships and a great army, he gathered people, and was strong in men-at-arms; for many thought they had to take vengeance of King Harald. Solve Klofe went southwards to Firdafylke (the Fjord district), which King Audbjorn ruled over, to ask him to help, and join his force to King Arnvid's and his own.

"For," said he, "it is now clear that we all have but one course to take; and that is to rise, all as one man, against King Harald, for we have strength enough, and fate must decide the victory; for as to the other condition of becoming his servants, that is no condition for us, who are not less noble than Harald. My father thought it better to fall in battle for his kingdom, than to go willingly into King Harald's service, or not to abide the chance of weapons like the Naumudal kings."

King Solve's speech was such that King Audbjorn promised his help, and gathered a great force together and went with it to King Arnvid, and they had a great army. Now, they got news that King Harald was come from the north, and they met within Solskel. And it was the custom to lash the ships together, stem to stem; so it was done now. King Harald laid his ship against King Arnvid's, and there was the sharpest fight, and many men fell on both sides. At last King Harald was raging with anger, and went forward to the fore-deck, and slew so dreadfully that all the forecastle men of Arnvid's ship were driven aft of the mast, and some fell. Thereupon Harald boarded the ship, and King Arnvid's men tried to save themselves by flight, and he himself was slain in his ship. King Audbjorn also fell; but Solve fled. So says Hornklofe:—

"Against the hero's shield in vain
The arrow-storm fierce pours its rain.
The king stands on the blood-stained deck,
Trampling on many a stout foe's neck;
And high above the dinning stound
Of helm and axe, and ringing sound
Of blade and shield, and raven's cry,
Is heard his shout of 'Victory!'"

Of King Harald's men, fell his earls Asgaut and Asbjorn, together with his brothers-in-law, Grjotgard and Herlaug, the sons of Earl Hakon of Lade. Solve became afterwards a great sea-king, and often did great damage in King Harald's dominions.

After this battle (A.D. 868) King Harald subdued South More; but Vemund, King Audbjorn's brother, still had Firdafylke. It was now late in harvest, and King Harald's men gave him the counsel not to proceed south-wards round Stad. Then King Harald set Earl Ragnvald over South and North More and also Raumsdal, and he had many people about him. King Harald returned to Throndhjem. The same winter (A.D. 869) Ragnvald went over Eid, and southwards to the Fjord district. There he heard news of King Vemund, and came by night to a place called Naustdal, where King Vemund was living in guest-quarters. Earl Ragnvald surrounded the house in which they were quartered, and burnt the king in it, together with ninety men. The came Berdlukare to Earl Ragnvald with a complete armed long-ship, and they both returned to More. The earl took all the ships Vemund had, and all the goods he could get hold of. Berdlukare proceeded north to Throndhjem to King Harald, and became his man; and dreadful berserk he was.

The following spring (A.D. 869) King Harald went southwards with his fleet along the coast, and subdued Firdafylke. Then he sailed eastward along the land until he came to Vik; but he left Earl Hakon Grjotgardson behind, and set him over the Fjord district. Earl Hakon sent word to Earl Atle Mjove that he should leave Sogn district, and be earl over Gaular district, as he had been before, alleging that King Harald had given Sogn district to him. Earl Atle sent word that he would keep both Sogn district and Gaular district, until he met King Harald. The two earls quarreled about this so long, that both gathered troops. They met at Fialar, in Stavanger fiord, and had a great battle, in which Earl Hakon fell, and Earl Atle got a mortal wound, and his men carried him to the island of Atley, where he died. So says Eyvind Skaldaspiller:—

> "He who stood a rooted oak,
> Unshaken by the swordsman's stroke,
> Amidst the whiz of arrows slain,
> Has fallen upon Fjalar's plain.
> There, by the ocean's rocky shore,
> The waves are stained with the red gore
> Of stout Earl Hakon Grjotgard's son,
> And of brave warriors many a one."

King Harald came with his fleet eastward to Viken and landed at Tunsberg, which was then a trading town. He had then been four years in Throndhjem, and in all that time had not been in Viken. Here he heard the news that Eirik Eymundson, king of Sweden, had laid under him Vermaland, and was taking scat or land-tax from all the forest settlers; and also that he called the whole country north to Svinasund, and west along the sea, West Gautland; and which altogether he reckoned to his kingdom, and took land-tax from it. Over this country he had set an earl, by name Hrane Gauzke, who had the earldom between Svinasund and the Gaut river, and was a mighty earl. And it was told to King Harald that the Swedish king said he would not rest until he had as great a kingdom in Viken as Sigurd Hring, or his son Ragnar Lodbrok, had possessed; and that was Raumarike and Vestfold, all the way to the isle Grenmar, and also Vingulmark, and all that lay south of it. In all these districts many chiefs, and many other people, had given obedience to the Swedish king. King Harald was very angry at this, and summoned the bondes to a Thing at Fold, where he laid an accusation against them for treason towards him. Some bondes defended themselves from the accusation, some paid fines, some were punished. He went thus through the whole district during the summer, and in harvest he did the same in Raumarike, and laid the two districts under his power. Towards winter he heard that Eirik king of Sweden was, with his court, going about in Vermaland in guest-quarters.

King Harald takes his way across the Eid forest eastward, and comes out in Vermaland, where he also orders feasts to be prepared for himself. There was a man by name Ake, who was the greatest of the bondes of Vermaland, very rich, and at that time very aged. He sent men to King Harald, and invited him to a feast, and the king promised to come on the day appointed. Ake invited also King Eirik to a feast, and appointed the same day. Ake had a great feasting hall, but it was old; and he made a new hall, not less than the old one, and had it ornamented in the most splendid way. The new hall he had hung with new hangings, but the old had only its old ornaments. Now when the kings came to the feast, King Eirik with his court was taken into the old hall; but Harald with his followers into the new. The same difference was in all the table furniture, and King Eirik and his men had the old-fashioned vessels and horns, but all gilded and splendid; while King Harald and his men had entirely new vessels and horns adorned with gold, all with carved figures, and shining like glass; and both companies had the best of liquor. Ake the bonde had formerly been King Halfdan the Black s man. Now when daylight came, and the feast was quite ended, and the kings made themselves ready for their journey, and the horses were saddled, came Ake before King Harald, leading in his hand his son Ubbe, a boy of twelve years of age, and said, "If the goodwill I have shown to thee, sire, in my feast, be worth thy friendship, show it hereafter to my son. I give him to thee now for thy service." The king thanked him with many agreeable words for his friendly entertainment, and promised him his full friendship in return. Then Ake brought out great presents, which he gave to the king, and they gave each other thereafter the parting kiss. Ake went next to the Swedish king, who was dressed and ready for the road, but not in the best humour. Ake gave to him also good and valuable gifts; but the king answered only with few words, and mounted his horse. Ake followed the king on the road and talked with him. The road led through a wood which was near to the house; and when Ake came to the wood, the king said to him, "How was it that thou madest such a difference between me and King Harald as to give him the best of everything, although thou knowest thou art my man?"

"I think," answered Ake, "that there failed in it nothing, king, either to you or to your attendants, in friendly entertainment at this feast. But that all the utensils for your drinking were old, was because you are now old; but King Harald is in the bloom of youth, and therefore I gave him the new things. And as to my being thy man, thou art just as much my man."

On this the king out with his sword, and gave Ake his deathwound. King Harald was ready now also to mount his horse, and desired that Ake should be called. The people went to seek him; and some ran up the road that King Eirik had taken, and found Ake there dead. They came back, and told the news to King Harald, and he bids his men to be up, and avenge Ake the bonde. And away rode he and his men the way King Eirik had taken, until they came in sight of each other. Each for himself rode as hard as he could, until Eirik came into the wood which divides Gautland and Vermaland. There King Harald wheels about, and returns to Vermaland, and lays the country under him, and kills King Eirik's men wheresoever he can find them. In winter King Harald returned to Raumarike, and dwelt there a while.

King Harald went out in winter to his ships at Tunsberg, rigged them, and sailed away eastward over the fiord, and subjected all Vingulmark to his dominion. All winter he was out with his ships, and marauded in Ranrike; so says Thorbjorn Hornklofe:—

"The Norseman's king is on the sea,
Tho' bitter wintry cold it be.—
On the wild waves his Yule keeps he.
When our brisk king can get his way,
He'll no more by the fireside stay
Than the young sun; he makes us play
The game of the bright sun-god Frey.
But the soft Swede loves well the fire
The well-stuffed couch, the doway glove,
And from the hearth-seat will not move."

The Gautlanders gathered people together all over the country. In spring, when the ice was breaking up, the Gautlanders drove stakes into the Gaut river to hinder King Harald with his ships from coming to the land. But King Harald laid his ships alongside the stakes, and plundered the country, and burnt all around; so says Hornklofe:—

"The king who finds a dainty feast,
For battle-bird and prowling beast,
Has won in war the southern land
That lies along the ocean's strand.
The leader of the helmets, he
Who leads his ships o'er the dark sea,
Harald, whose high-rigged masts appear
Like antlered fronts of the wild deer,
Has laid his ships close alongside
Of the foe's piles with daring pride."

Afterwards the Gautlanders came down to the strand with a great army, and gave battle to King Harald, and great was the fall of men. But it was King Harald who gained the day. Thus says Hornklofe:—

"Whistles the battle-axe in its swing
O'er head the whizzing javelins sing,
Helmet and shield and hauberk ring;
The air-song of the lance is loud,
The arrows pipe in darkening cloud;
Through helm and mail the foemen feel
The blue edge of our king's good steel
Who can withstand our gallant king?
The Gautland men their flight must wing."

King Harald went far and wide through Gautland, and many were the battles he fought there on both sides of the river, and in general he was victorious. In one of these battles fell Hrane Gauzke; and then the king took his whole land north of the river and west of the Veneren, and also Vermaland. And after he turned back therefrom, he set Duke Guthorm as chief to defend the country, and left a great force with him. King Harald himself went first to the Uplands, where he remained a while, and then proceeded northwards over the Dovrefjeld to Throndhjem, where he dwelt for a long time. Harald began to have children. By Asa he had four sons. The eldest was Guthorm. Halfdan the Black and Halfdan the White were twins. Sigfrod was the fourth. They were all brought up in Throndhjem with all honour.

News came in from the south land that the people of Hordaland and Rogaland, Agder and Thelemark, were gathering, and bringing together ships and weapons, and a great body of men. The leaders of this were Eirik king of Hordaland; Sulke king of Rogaland, and his brother Earl Sote: Kjotve the Rich, king of Agder, and his son Thor Haklang; and from Thelemark two brothers, Hroald Hryg and Had the Hard. Now when Harald got certain news of this, he assembled his forces, set his ships on the water, made himself ready with his men, and set out southwards along the coast, gathering many people from every district. King Eirik heard of this when he same south of Stad; and having assembled all the men he could expect, he proceeded southwards to meet the force which he knew was coming to his help from the east. The whole met together north of Jadar, and went into Hafersfjord, where King Harald was waiting with his forces. A great battle began, which was both hard and long; but at last King Harald gained the day. There King Eirik fell, and King Sulke, with his brother Earl Sote. Thor Haklang, who was a great berserk, had laid his ship against King Harald's, and there was above all measure a desperate attack, until Thor Haklang fell, and his whole ship was cleared of men. Then King Kjotve fled to a little isle outside, on which there was a good place of strength. Thereafter all his men fled, some to their ships, some up to the land; and the latter ran southwards over the country of Jadar. So says Hornklofe, viz.:—

"Has the news reached you?—have you heard

Of the great fight at Hafersfjord,
Between our noble king brave Harald
And King Kjotve rich in gold?
The foeman came from out the East,
Keen for the fray as for a feast.
A gallant sight it was to see
Their fleet sweep o'er the dark-blue sea:
Each war-ship, with its threatening throat
Of dragon fierce or ravenous brute (1)
Grim gaping from the prow; its wales
Glittering with burnished shields, (2) like scales
Its crew of udal men of war,
Whose snow-white targets shone from far
And many a mailed spearman stout
From the West countries round about,
English and Scotch, a foreign host,
And swordsmen from the far French coast.
And as the foemen's ships drew near,
The dreadful din you well might hear
Savage berserks roaring mad,
And champions fierce in wolf-skins clad, (3)
Howling like wolves; and clanking jar
Of many a mail-clad man of war.
Thus the foe came; but our brave king
Taught them to fly as fast again.
For when he saw their force come o'er,
He launched his war-ships from the shore.
On the deep sea he launched his fleet
And boldly rowed the foe to meet.
Fierce was the shock, and loud the clang
Of shields, until the fierce Haklang,
The foeman's famous berserk, fell.
Then from our men burst forth the yell
Of victory, and the King of Gold
Could not withstand our Harald bold,
But fled before his flaky locks
For shelter to the island rocks.
All in the bottom of the ships
The wounded lay, in ghastly heaps;
Backs up and faces down they lay
Under the row-seats stowed away;
And many a warrior's shield, I ween
Might on the warrior's back be seen,
To shield him as he fled amain
From the fierce stone-storm's pelting rain.

> The mountain-folk, as I've heard say,
> Ne'er stopped as they ran from the fray,
> Till they had crossed the Jadar sea,
> And reached their homes—so keen each soul
> To drown his fright in the mead bowl."

(1) The war-ships were called dragons, from being decorated with the head of a dragon, serpent, or other wild animal; and the word 'draco' was adopted in the Latin of the Middle Ages to denote a ship of war of the larger class. The snekke was the cutter or smaller war-ship. (2) The shields were hung over the side-rails of the ships. (3) The wolf-skin pelts were nearly as good as armour against the sword.

After this battle King Harald met no opposition in Norway, for all his opponents and greatest enemies were cut off. But some, and they were a great multitude, fled out of the country, and thereby great districts were peopled. Jemtaland and Helsingjaland were peopled then, although some Norwegians had already set up their habitation there. In the discontent that King Harald seized on the lands of Norway, the out-countries of Iceland and the Farey Isles were discovered and peopled. The Northmen had also a great resort to Hjaltland (Shetland Isles) and many men left Norway, flying the country on account of King Harald, and went on viking cruises into the West sea. In winter they were in the Orkney Islands and Hebrides; but marauded in summer in Norway, and did great damage. Many, however, were the mighty men who took service under King Harald, and became his men, and dwelt in the land with him.

When King Harald had now become sole king over all Norway, he remembered what that proud girl had said to him; so he sent men to her, and had her brought to him, and took her to his bed. And these were their children: Alof—she was the eldest; then was their son Hrorek; then Sigtryg, Frode, and Thorgils. King Harald had many wives and many children. Among them he had one wife, who was called Ragnhild the Mighty, a daughter of King Eirik, from Jutland; and by her he had a son, Eirik Blood-axe. He was also married to Svanhild, a daughter of Earl Eystein; and their sons were Olaf Geirstadaalf, Bjorn and Ragnar Rykkil. Lastly, King Harald married Ashild, a daughter of Hring Dagson, up in Ringerike; and their children were, Dag, Hring, Gudrod Skiria, and Ingigerd. It is told that King Harald put away nine wives when he married Ragnhild the Mighty. So says Hornklofe:—

> "Harald, of noblest race the head,
> A Danish wife took to his bed;
> And out of doors nine wives he thrust,—
> The mothers of the princes first.
> Who 'mong Holmrygians hold command,
> And those who rule in Hordaland.
> And then he packed from out the place
> The children born of Holge's race."

King Harald's children were all fostered and brought up by their relations on the mother's side. Guthorm the Duke had poured water over King Harald's eldest son and had given him his own name. He set the child upon his knee, and was his foster-father, and took him with himself eastward to Viken, and there he was brought up in the house of Guthorm. Guthorm ruled the whole land in Viken and the Uplands, when King Harald was absent.

King Harald heard that the vikings, who were in the West sea in winter, plundered far and wide in the middle part of Norway; and therefore every summer he made an expedition to search the isles and out-skerries on the coast. Wheresoever the vikings heard of him they all took to flight, and most of them out into the open ocean. At last the king grew weary of this work, and therefore one summer he sailed with his fleet right out into the West sea. First he came to Hjaltland (Shetland), and he slew all the vikings who could not save themselves by flight. Then King Harald sailed southwards, to the Orkney Islands, and cleared them all of vikings. Thereafter he proceeded to the Sudreys (Hebrides), plundered there, and slew many vikings who formerly had had men-at-arms under them. Many a battle was fought, and King Harald was always victorious. He then plundered far and wide in Scotland itself, and had a battle there. When he was come westward as far as the Isle of Man, the report of his exploits on the land had gone before him; for all the inhabitants had fled over to Scotland, and the island was left entirely bare both of people and goods, so that King Harald and his men made no booty when they landed. So says Hornklofe:—

"The wise, the noble king, great
Whose hand so freely scatters gold,
Led many a northern shield to war
Against the town upon the shore.
The wolves soon gathered on the sand
Of that sea-shore; for Harald's hand
The Scottish army drove away,
And on the coast left wolves a prey."

In this war fell Ivar, a son of Ragnvald, Earl of More; and King Harald gave Ragnvald, as a compensation for the loss, the Orkney and Shetland isles, when he sailed from the West; but Ragnvald immediately gave both these countries to his brother Sigurd, who remained behind them; and King Harald, before sailing eastward, gave Sigurd the earldom of them. Thorstein the Red, a son of Olaf the White and of Aud the Wealthy, entered into partnership with him; and after plundering in Scotland, they subdued Caithness and Sutherland, as far as Ekkjalsbakke. Earl Sigurd killed Melbridge Tooth, a Scotch earl, and hung his head to his stirrup-leather; but the calf of his leg were scratched by the teeth, which were sticking out from the head, and the wound caused inflammation in his leg, of which the earl died, and he was laid in a mound at Ekkjalsbakke. His son Guthorm ruled over these countries for about a year thereafter, and died without children. Many vikings, both Danes and Northmen, set themselves down then in those countries.

After King Harald had subdued the whole land, he was one day at a feast in More, given by Earl Ragnvald. Then King Harald went into a bath, and had his hair dressed. Earl Ragnvald now cut his hair, which had been uncut and uncombed for ten years; and therefore the king had been called Lufa (i.e., with rough matted hair). But then Earl Ragnvald gave him the distinguishing name—Harald Harfager (i.e., fair hair); and all who saw him agreed that there was the greatest truth in the surname, for he had the most beautiful and abundant head of hair.

Earl Ragnvald was King Harald's dearest friend, and the king had the greatest regard for him. He was married to Hild, a daughter of Rolf Nefia, and their sons were Rolf and Thorer. Earl Ragnvald had also three sons by concubines,—the one called Hallad, the second Einar, the third Hrollaug; and all three were grown men when their brothers born in marriage were still children Rolf became a great viking, and was of so stout a growth that no horse could carry him, and wheresoever he went he must go on foot; and therefore he was called Rolf Ganger. He plundered much in the East sea. One summer, as he was coming from the eastward on a Viking's expedition to the coast of Viken, he landed there and made a cattle foray. As King Harald happened, just at that time, to be in Viken, he heard of it, and was in a great rage; for he had forbid, by the greatest punishment, the plundering within the bounds of the country. The king assembled a Thing, and had Rolf declared an outlaw over all Norway. When Rolf's mother, Hild heard of it she hastened to the king, and entreated peace for Rolf; but the king was so enraged that here entreaty was of no avail. Then Hild spake these lines:—

"Think'st thou, King Harald, in thy anger,
To drive away my brave Rolf Ganger
Like a mad wolf, from out the land?
Why, Harald, raise thy mighty hand?
Why banish Nefia's gallant name-son,
The brother of brave udal-men?
Why is thy cruelty so fell?
Bethink thee, monarch, it is ill
With such a wolf at wolf to play,
Who, driven to the wild woods away
May make the king's best deer his prey."

Rolf Ganger went afterwards over sea to the West to the Hebrides, or Sudreys; and at last farther west to Valland, where he plundered and subdued for himself a great earldom, which he peopled with Northmen, from which that land is called Normandy. Rolf Ganger's son was William, father to Richard, and grandfather to another Richard, who was the father of Robert Longspear, and grandfather of William the Bastard, from whom all the following English kings are descended. From Rolf Ganger also are descended the earls in Normandy. Queen Ragnhild the Mighty lived three years after she came to Norway; and, after her death, her son and King Harald's was taken to the herse Thorer Hroaldson, and Eirik was fostered by him.

King Harald, one winter, went about in guest-quarters in the Uplands, and had ordered a Christmas feast to be prepared for him at the farm Thoptar. On Christmas eve came Svase to the door, just as the king went to table, and sent a message to the king to ask if he would go out with him. The king was angry at such a message, and the man who had brought it in took out with him a reply of the king's displeasure. But Svase, notwithstanding, desired that his message should be delivered a second time; adding to it, that he was the Fin whose hut the king had promised to visit, and which stood on the other side of the ridge. Now the king went out, and promised to go with him, and went over the ridge to his hut, although some of his men dissuaded him. There stood Snaefrid, the daughter of Svase, a most beautiful girl; and she filled a cup of mead for the king. But he took hold both of the cup and of her hand. Immediately it was as if a hot fire went through his body; and he wanted that very night to take her to his bed. But Svase said that should not be unless by main force, if he did not first make her his lawful wife. Now King Harald made Snaefrid his lawful wife, and loved her so passionately that he forgot his kingdom, and all that belonged to his high dignity. They had four sons: the one was Sigurd Hrise; the others Halfdan Haleg, Gudrod Ljome and Ragnvald Rettilbeine. Thereafter Snaefrid died; but her corpse never changed, but was as fresh and red as when she lived. The king sat always beside her, and thought she would come to life again. And so it went on for three years that he was sorrowing over her death, and the people over his delusion. At last Thorleif the Wise succeeded, by his prudence, in curing him of his delusion by accosting him thus:—"It is nowise wonderful, king, that thou grievest over so beautiful and noble a wife, and bestowest costly coverlets and beds of down on her corpse, as she desired; but these honours fall short of what is due, as she still lies in the same clothes. It would be more suitable to raise her, and change her dress." As soon as the body was raised in the bed all sorts of corruption and foul smells came from it, and it was necessary in all haste to gather a pile of wood and burn it; but before this could be done the body turned blue, and worms, toads, newts, paddocks, and all sorts of ugly reptiles came out of it, and it sank into ashes. Now the king came to his understanding again, threw the madness out of his mind, and after that day ruled his kingdom as before. He was strengthened and made joyful by his subjects, and his subjects by him and the country by both.

After King Harald had experienced the cunning of the Fin woman, he was so angry that he drove from him the sons he had with her, and would not suffer them before his eyes. But one of them, Gudrod Ljome, went to his foster-father Thjodolf of Hvin, and asked him to go to the king, who was then in the Uplands; for Thjodolf was a great friend of the king. And so they went, and came to the king's house late in the evening, and sat down together unnoticed near the door. The king walked up and down the floor casting his eye along the benches; for he had a feast in the house, and the mead was just mixed. The king then murmured out these lines:—

"Tell me, ye aged gray-haired heroes,
Who have come here to seek repose,
Wherefore must I so many keep
Of such a set, who, one and all,
Right dearly love their souls to steep,
From morn till night, in the mead-bowl?"

Then Thjodolf replies:—
"A certain wealthy chief, I think,
Would gladly have had more to drink
With him, upon one bloody day,
When crowns were cracked in our sword-play."

Thjodolf then took off his hat, and the king recognised him, and gave him a friendly reception. Thjodolf then begged the king not to cast off his sons; "for they would with great pleasure have taken a better family descent upon the mother's side, if the king had given it to them." The king assented, and told him to take Gudrod with him as formerly; and he sent Halfdan and Sigurd to Ringerike, and Ragnvald to Hadaland, and all was done as the king ordered. They grew up to be very clever men, very expert in all exercises. In these times King Harald sat in peace in the land, and the land enjoyed quietness and good crops.

When Earl Ragnvald in More heard of the death of his brother Earl Sigurd, and that the vikings were in possession of the country, he sent his son Hallad westward, who took the title of earl to begin with, and had many men-at-arms with him. When he arrived at the Orkney Islands, he established himself in the country; but both in harvest, winter, and spring, the vikings cruised about the isles plundering the headlands, and committing depredations on the coast. Then Earl Hallad grew tired of the business, resigned his earldom, took up again his rights as an allodial owner, and afterwards returned eastward into Norway. When Earl Ragnvald heard of this he was ill pleased with Hallad, and said his son were very unlike their ancestors. Then said Einar, "I have enjoyed but little honour among you, and have little affection here to lose: now if you will give me force enough, I will go west to the islands, and promise you what at any rate will please you—that you shall never see me again." Earl Ragnvald replied, that he would be glad if he never came back; "For there is little hope," said he, "that thou will ever be an honour to thy friends, as all thy kin on thy mother's side are born slaves." Earl Ragnvald gave Einar a vessel completely equipped, and he sailed with it into the West sea in harvest. When he came to the Orkney Isles, two vikings, Thorer Treskeg and Kalf Skurfa, were in his way with two vessels. He attacked them instantly, gained the battle, and slew the two vikings. Then this was sung:—

"Then gave he Treskeg to the trolls,
Torfeinar slew Skurfa."

He was called Torfeinar, because he cut peat for fuel, there being no firewood, as in Orkney there are no woods. He afterwards was earl over the islands, and was a mighty man. He was ugly, and blind of an eye, yet very sharp-sighted withal.

Duke Guthorm dwelt principally at Tunsberg, and governed the whole of Viken when the king was not there. He defended the land, which, at that time, was much plundered by the vikings. There were disturbances also up in Gautland as long as King Eirik Eymundson lived; but he died when King Harald Harfager had been ten years king of all Norway.

After Eirik, his son Bjorn was king of Svithjod for fifty years. He was father of Eirik the Victorious, and of Olaf the father of Styrbjorn. Guthorm died on a bed of sickness at Tunsberg, and King Harald gave his son Guthorm the government of that part of his dominions and made him chief of it.

When King Harald was forty years of age many of his sons were well advanced, and indeed they all came early to strength and manhood. And now they began to take it ill that the king would not give them any part of the kingdom, but put earls into every district; for they thought earls were of inferior birth to them. Then Halfdan Haleg and Gudrod Ljome set off one spring with a great force, and came suddenly upon Earl Ragnvald, earl of More, and surrounded the house in which he was, and burnt him and sixty men in it. Thereafter Halfdan took three long-ships, and fitted them out, and sailed into the West sea; but Gudrod set himself down in the land which Ragnvald formerly had. Now when King Harald heard this he set out with a great force against Gudrod, who had no other way left but to surrender, and he was sent to Agder. King Harald then set Earl Ragnvald's son Thorer over More, and gave him his daughter Alof, called Arbot, in marriage. Earl Thorer, called the Silent, got the same territory his father Earl Ragnvald had possessed.

Halfdan Haleg came very unexpectedly to Orkney, and Earl Einar immediately fled; but came back soon after about harvest time, unnoticed by Halfdan. They met and after a short battle Halfdan fled the same night. Einar and his men lay all night without tents, and when it was light in the morning they searched the whole island and killed every man they could lay hold of. Then Einar said "What is that I see upon the isle of Rinansey? Is it a man or a bird? Sometimes it raises itself up, and sometimes lies down again." They went to it, and found it was Halfdan Haleg, and took him prisoner.

Earl Einar sang the following song the evening before he went into this battle:—

"Where is the spear of Hrollaug? where
Is stout Rolf Ganger's bloody spear!
I see them not; yet never fear,
For Einar will not vengeance spare
Against his father's murderers, though
Hrollaug and Rolf are somewhat slow,
And silent Thorer sits add dreams
At home, beside the mead-bowl's streams."

Thereafter Earl Einar went up to Halfdan, and cut a spread eagle upon his back, by striking his sword through his back into his belly, dividing his ribs from the backbone down to his loins, and tearing out his lungs; and so Halfdan was killed. Einar then sang:—

"For Ragnvald's death my sword is red:
Of vengeance it cannot be said
That Einar's share is left unsped.

So now, brave boys, let's raise a mound,—
Heap stones and gravel on the ground
O'er Halfdan's corpse: this is the way
We Norsemen our scat duties pay."

Then Earl Einar took possession of the Orkney Isles as before. Now when these tidings came to Norway, Halfdan's brothers took it much to heart, and thought that his death demanded vengeance; and many were of the same opinion. When Einar heard this, he sang:—

"Many a stout udal-man, I know,
Has cause to wish my head laid low;
And many an angry udal knife
Would gladly drink of Eina's life.
But ere they lay Earl Einar low,—
Ere this stout heart betrays its cause,
Full many a heart will writhe, we know,
In the wolf's fangs, or eagle's claws."

King Harald now ordered a levy, and gathered a great force, with which he proceeded westward to Orkney; and when Earl Einar heard that King Harald was come, he fled over to Caithness. He made the following verses on this occasion:—

"Many a bearded man must roam,
An exile from his house and home,
For cow or horse; but Halfdan's gore
Is red on Rinansey's wild shore.
A nobler deed—on Harald's shield
The arm of one who ne'er will yield
Has left a scar. Let peasants dread
The vengeance of the Norsemen's head:
I reck not of his wrath, but sing,
'Do thy worst!—I defy thee, king!—'"

Men and messages, however, passed between the king and the earl, and at last it came to a conference; and when they met the earl submitted the case altogether to the king's decision, and the king condemned the earl Einar and the Orkney people to pay a fine of sixty marks of gold. As the bondes thought this was too heavy for them to pay, the earl offered to pay the whole if they would surrender their udal lands to him. This they all agreed to do: the poor because they had but little pieces of land; the rich because they could redeem their udal rights again when they liked. Thus the earl paid the whole fine to the king, who returned in harvest to Norway. The earls for a long time afterwards possessed all the udal lands in Orkney, until Sigurd son of Hlodver gave back the udal rights.

While King Harald's son Guthorm had the defence of Viken, he sailed outside of the islands on the coast, and came in by one of the mouths of the tributaries of the Gaut river. When he lay there Solve Klofe came upon him, and immediately gave him battle, and Guthorm fell. Halfdan the White and Halfdan the Black went out on an expedition, and plundered in the East sea, and had a battle in Eistland, where Halfdan the White fell.

Eirik, Harald's son, was fostered in the house of the herse Thorer, son of Hroald, in the Fjord district. He was the most beloved and honoured by King Harald of all his sons. When Eirik was twelve years old, King Harald gave him five long-ships, with which he went on an expedition,—first in the Baltic; then southwards to Denmark, Friesland, and Saxland; on which expedition he passed four years. He then sailed out into the West sea and plundered in Scotland, Bretland, Ireland, and Valland, and passed four years more in this way. Then he sailed north to Finmark, and all the way to Bjarmaland, where he had many a battle, and won many a victory. When he came back to Finmark, his men found a girl in a Lapland hut, whose equal for beauty they never had seen. She said her name was Gunhild, and that her father dwelt in Halogaland, and was called Ozur Tote. "I am here," she said, "to learn sorcery from two of the most knowing Fins in all Finmark, who are now out hunting. They both want me in marriage. They are so skilful that they can hunt out traces either upon the frozen or the thawed earth, like dogs; and they can run so swiftly on skees that neither man nor beast can come near them in speed. They hit whatever they take aim at, and thus kill every man who comes near them. When they are angry the very earth turns away in terror, and whatever living thing they look upon then falls dead. Now ye must not come in their way; but I will hide you here in the hut, and ye must try to get them killed." They agreed to it, and she hid them, and then took a leather bag, in which they thought there were ashes which she took in her hand, and strewed both outside and inside of the hut. Shortly after the Fins came home, and asked who had been there; and she answered, "Nobody has been here." "That is wonderful," said they, "we followed the traces close to the hut, and can find none after that." Then they kindled a fire, and made ready their meat, and Gunhild prepared her bed. It had so happened that Gunhild had slept the three nights before, but the Fins had watched the one upon the other, being jealous of each other. "Now," she said to the Fins, "come here, and lie down one on each side of me." On which they were very glad to do so. She laid an arm round the neck of each and they went to sleep directly. She roused them up; but they fell to sleep again instantly, and so soundly the she scarcely could waken them. She even raised them up in the bed, and still they slept. Thereupon she too two great seal-skin bags, and put their heads in them, and tied them fast under their arms; and then she gave a wink to the king's men. They run forth with their weapons, kill the two Fins, and drag them out of the hut. That same night came such a dreadful thunder-storm that they could not stir. Next morning they came to the ship, taking Gunhild with them, and presented her to Eirik. Eirik and his followers then sailed southwards to Haloga-land and he sent word to Ozur Tote, the girl's father, to meet him. Eirik said he would take his daughter in marriage, to which Ozur Tote consented, and Eirik took Gunhild and went southwards with her (A.D. 922).

When King Harald was fifty years of age many of his sons were grown up, and some were dead. Many of them committed acts of great violence in the country, and were in discord among themselves. They drove some of the king's earls out of their properties, and even killed some of them. Then the king called together a numerous Thing in the south part of the country, and summoned to it all the people of the Uplands. At this Thing he gave to all his sons the title of king, and made a law that his descendants in the male line should each succeed to the kingly title and dignity; but his descendants by the female side only to that of earl. And he divided the country among them thus:—Vingulmark, Raumarike, Vestfold and Thelamark, he bestowed on Olaf, Bjorn, Sigtryg, Frode, and Thorgils. Hedemark and Gudbrandsdal he gave to Dag, Hring, and Ragnar. To Snaefrid's sons he gave Ringerike, Hadeland, Thoten, and the lands thereto belonging. His son Guthorm, as before mentioned, he had set over the country from Glommen to Svinasund and Ranrike. He had set him to defend the country to the East, as before has been written. King Harald himself generally dwelt in the middle of the country, and Hrorek and Gudrod were generally with his court, and had great estates in Hordaland and in Sogn. King Eirik was also with his father King Harald; and the king loved and regarded him the most of all his sons, and gave him Halogaland and North More, and Raumsdal. North in Throndhjem he gave Halfdan the Black, Halfdan the White, and Sigrod land to rule over. In each of these districts he gave his sons the one half of his revenues, together with the right to sit on a high-seat,—a step higher than earls, but a step lower than his own high-seat. His king's seat each of his sons wanted for himself after his death, but he himself destined it for Eirik. The Throndhjem people wanted Halfdan the Black to succeed to it. The people of Viken, and the Uplands, wanted those under whom they lived. And thereupon new quarrels arose among the brothers; and because they thought their dominions too little, they drove about in piratical expeditions. In this way, as before related, Guthorm fell at the mouth of the Gaut river, slain by Solve Klofe; upon which Olaf took the kingdom he had possessed. Halfdan the White fell in Eistland, Halfdan Haleg in Orkney. King Harald gave ships of war to Thorgils and Frode, with which they went westward on a viking cruise, and plundered in Scotland, Ireland, and Bretland. They were the first of the Northmen who took Dublin. It is said that Frode got poisoned drink there; but Thorgils was a long time king over Dublin, until he fell into a snare of the Irish, and was killed.

Eirik Blood-axe expected to be head king over all his brothers and King Harald intended he should be so; and the father and son lived long together. Ragnvald Rettilbeine governed Hadaland, and allowed himself to be instructed in the arts of witchcraft, and became an area warlock. Now King Harald was a hater of all witchcraft. There was a warlock in Hordaland called Vitgeir; and when the king sent a message to him that he should give up his art of witchcraft, he replied in this verse:—

"The danger surely is not great
From wizards born of mean estate,
When Harald's son in Hadeland,
King Ragnvald, to the art lays hand."

But when King Harald heard this, King Eirik Blood-axe went by his orders to the Uplands, and came to Hadeland and burned his brother Ragnvald in a house, along with eighty other warlocks; which work was much praised.

Gudrod Ljome was in winter on a friendly visit to his foster-father Thjodolf in Hvin, and had a well-manned ship, with which he wanted to go north to Rogaland. It was blowing a heavy storm at the time; but Gudrod was bent on sailing, and would not consent to wait. Thjodolf sang thus:—

"Wait, Gudrod, till the storm is past,—
Loose not thy long-ship while the blast
Howls over-head so furiously,—
Trust not thy long-ship to the sea,—
Loose not thy long-ship from the shore;
Hark to the ocean's angry roar!
See how the very stones are tost
By raging waves high on the coast!
Stay, Gudrod, till the tempest's o'er—
Deep runs the sea off the Jadar's shore."

Gudrod set off in spite of what Thjodolf could say: and when they came off the Jadar the vessel sunk with them, and all on board were lost.

King Harald's son, Bjorn, ruled over Vestfold at that time, and generally lived at Tunsberg, and went but little on war expeditions. Tunsberg at that time was much frequented by merchant vessels, both from Viken and the north country, and also from the south, from Denmark, and Saxland. King Bjorn had also merchant ships on voyages to other lands, by which he procured for himself costly articles, and such things as he thought needful; and therefore his brothers called him Farman (the Seaman), and Kaupman (the Chapman). Bjorn was a man of sense and understanding, and promised to become a good ruler. He made a good and suitable marriage, and had a son by his wife, who was named Gudrod. Eirik Blood-axe came from his Baltic cruise with ships of war, and a great force, and required his brother Bjorn to deliver to him King Harald's share of the scat and incomes of Vestfold. But it had always been the custom before, that Bjorn himself either delivered the money into the king's hands, or sent men of his own with it; and therefore he would continue with the old custom, and would not deliver the money. Eirik again wanted provisions, tents, and liquor. The brothers quarrelled about this; but Eirik got nothing and left the town. Bjorn went also out of the town towards evening up to Saeheim. In the night Eirik came back after Bjorn, and came to Saeheim just as Bjorn and his men were seated at table drinking. Eirik surrounded the house in which they were; but Bjorn with his men went out and fought. Bjorn, and many men with him, fell. Eirik, on the other hand, got a great booty, and proceeded northwards. But this work was taken very ill by the people of Viken, and Eirik was much disliked for it; and the report went that King Olaf would avenge his brother Bjorn, whenever opportunity offered. King Bjorn lies in the mound of Farmanshaug at Saeheim.

King Eirik went in winter northwards to More, and was at a feast in Solve, within the point Agdanes; and when Halfdan the Black heard of it he set out with his men, and surrounded the house in which they were. Eirik slept in a room which stood detached by itself, and he escaped into the forest with four others; but Halfdan and his men burnt the main house, with all the people who were in it. With this news Eirik came to King Harald, who was very wroth at it, and assembled a great force against the Throndhjem people. When Halfdan the Black heard this he levied ships and men, so that he had a great force, and proceeded with it to Stad, within Thorsbjerg. King Harald lay with his men at Reinsletta. Now people went between them, and among others a clever man called Guthorm Sindre, who was then in Halfdan the Black's army, but had been formerly in the service of King Harald, and was a great friend of both. Guthorm was a great skald, and had once composed a song both about the father and the son, for which they had offered him a reward. But he would take nothing; but only asked that, some day or other, they should grant him any request he should make, which they promised to do. Now he presented himself to King Harald, brought words of peace between them, and made the request to them both that they should be reconciled. So highly did the king esteem him, that in consequence of his request they were reconciled. Many other able men promoted this business as well as he; and it was so settled that Halfdan should retain the whole of his kingdom as he had it before, and should let his brother Eirik sit in peace. After this event Jorun, the skald-maid, composed some verses in *Sendibit* ("The Biting Message"):—

"I know that Harald Fairhair
Knew the dark deed of Halfdan.
To Harald Halfdan seemed
Angry and cruel."

Earl Hakon Grjotgardson of Hlader had the whole rule over Throndhjem when King Harald was anywhere away in the country; and Hakon stood higher with the king than any in the country of Throndhjem. After Hakon's death his son Sigurd succeeded to his power in Throndhjem, and was the earl, and had his mansion at Hlader. King Harald's sons, Halfdan the Black and Sigrod, who had been before in the house of his father Earl Hakon, continued to be brought up in his house. The sons of Harald and Sigurd were about the same age. Earl Sigurd was one of the wisest men of his time, and married Bergljot, a daughter of Earl Thorer the Silent; and her mother was Alof Arbot, a daughter of Harald Harfager. When King Harald began to grow old he generally dwelt on some of his great farms in Hordaland; namely, Alreksstader or Saeheim, Fitjar, Utstein, or Ogvaldsnes in the island Kormt. When Harald was seventy years of age he begat a son with a girl called Thora Mosterstang, because her family came from Moster. She was descended from good people, being connected with Kare (Aslakson) of Hordaland; and was moreover a very stout and remarkably handsome girl. She was called the king's servant-girl; for at that time many were subject to service to the king who were of good birth, both men and women. Then it was the custom, with people of consideration, to choose with great care the man who should pour water over their children, and give them a name. Now when the time came that Thora, who was then at Moster, expected her confinement, she would to King Harald, who was then living at Saeheim; and she went northwards in a ship belonging to Earl Sigurd. They lay at night close to the land; and there Thora brought forth a child upon the land, up among the rocks, close to the ship's gangway, and it was a man child. Earl Sigurd poured water over him, and called him Hakon, after his own father, Hakon earl of Hlader. The boy soon grew handsome, large in size, and very like his father King Harald. King Harald let him follow his mother, and they were both in the king's house as long as he was an infant.

At this time a king called Aethelstan had taken the Kingdom of England. He was called victorious and faithful. He sent men to Norway to King Harald, with the errand that the messengers should present him with a sword, with the hilt and handle gilt, and also the whole sheath adorned with gold and silver, and set with precious jewels. The ambassador presented the sword-hilt to the king, saying, "Here is a sword which King Athelstan sends thee, with the request that thou wilt accept it." The king took the sword by the handle; whereupon the ambassador said, "Now thou hast taken the sword according to our king's desire, and therefore art thou his subject as thou hast taken his sword." King Harald saw now that this was an insult, for he would be subject to no man. But he remembered it was his rule, whenever anything raised his anger, to collect himself, and let his passion run off, and then take the matter into consideration coolly. Now he did so, and consulted his friends, who all gave him the advice to let the ambassadors, in the first place, go home in safety.

The following summer King Harald sent a ship westward to England, and gave the command of it to Hauk Habrok. He was a great warrior, and very dear to the king. Into his hands he gave his son Hakon. Hank proceeded westward in England, and found King Athelstan in London, where there was just at the time a great feast and entertainment. When they came to the hall, Hauk told his men how they should conduct themselves; namely, that he who went first in should go last out, and all should stand in a row at the table, at equal distance from each other; and each should have his sword at his left side, but should fasten his cloak so that his sword should not be seen. Then they went into the hall, thirty in number. Hauk went up to the king and saluted him, and the king bade him welcome. Then Hauk took the child Hakon, and set it on the king's knee. The king looks at the boy, and asks Hauk what the meaning of this is. Hauk replies, "Herald the king bids thee foster his servant-girl's child." The king was in great anger, and seized a sword which lay beside him, and drew it, as if he was going to kill the child. Hauk says, "Thou hast borne him on thy knee, and thou canst murder him if thou wilt; but thou wilt not make an end of all King Harald's sons by so doing." On that Hauk went out with all his men, and took the way direct to his ship, and put to sea,—for they were ready,—and came back to King Harald. The king was highly pleased with this; for it is the common observation of all people, that the man who fosters another's children is of less consideration than the other. From these transactions between the two kings, it appears that each wanted to be held greater than the other; but in truth there was no injury, to the dignity of either, for each was the upper king in his own kingdom till his dying day.

King Athelstan had Hakon baptized, and brought up in the right faith, and in good habits, and all sorts of good manners, and he loved Hakon above all his relations; and Hakon was beloved by all men. He was henceforth called Athelstan's foster-son. He was an accomplished skald, and he was larger, stronger and more beautiful than other men; he was a man of understanding and eloquence, and also a good Christian. King Athelstan gave Hakon a sword, of which the hilt and handle were gold, and the blade still better; for with it Hakon cut down a mill-stone to the centre eye, and the sword thereafter was called the Quernbite. Better sword never came into Norway, and Hakon carried it to his dying day.

When King Harald was eighty years of age (A.D. 930) he became very heavy, and unable to travel through the country, or do the business of a king. Then he brought his son Eirik to his high-seat, and gave him the power and command over the whole land. Now when King Harald's other sons heard this, King Halfdan the Black also took a king's high-seat, and took all Throndhjem land, with the consent of all the people, under his rule as upper king. After the death of Bjorn the Chapman, his brother Olaf took the command over Vestfold, and took Bjorn's son, Gudrod, as his foster-child. Olaf's son was called Trygve; and the two foster-brothers were about the same age, and were hopeful and clever. Trygve, especially, was remarkable as a stout and strong man. Now when the people of Viken heard that those of Hordaland had taken Eirik as upper king, they did the same, and made Olaf the upper king in Viken, which kingdom he retained. Eirik did not like this at all. Two years after this, Halfdan the Black died suddenly at a feast in Throndhjem and the general report was that Gunhild had bribed a witch to give him a death-drink. Thereafter the Throndhjem people took Sigrod to be their king.

King Harald lived three years after he gave Eirik the supreme authority over his kingdom, and lived mostly on his great farms which he possessed, some in Rogaland, and some in Hordaland. Eirik and Gunhild had a son on whom King Harald poured water, and gave him his own name, and the promise that he should be king after his father Eirik. King Harald married most of his daughters within the country to his earls, and from them many great families are descended. Harald died on a bed of sickness in Hogaland (A.D. 933), and was buried under a mound at Haugar in Karmtsund. In Haugesund is a church, now standing; and not far from the churchyard, at the north-west side, is King Harald Harfager's mound; but his grave-stone stands west of the church, and is thirteen feet and a half high, and two ells broad. One stone was set at head and one at the feet; on the top lay the slab, and below on both sides were laid small stones. The grave, mound, and stone, are there to the present day. Harald Harfager was, according to the report of men of knowledge, or remarkably handsome appearance, great and strong, and very generous and affable to his men. He was a great warrior in his youth; and people think that this was foretold by his mother's dream before his birth, as the lowest part of the tree she dreamt of was red as blood. The stem again was green and beautiful, which betokened his flourishing kingdom; and that the tree was white at the top showed that he should reach a grey-haired old age. The branches and twigs showed forth his posterity, spread over the whole land; for of his race, ever since. Norway has always had kings.

King Eirik took all the revenues (A.D. 934), which the king had in the middle of the country, the next winter after King Harald's decease. But Olaf took all the revenues eastward in Viken, and their brother Sigrod all that of the Throndhjem country. Eirik was very ill pleased with this; and the report went that he would attempt with force to get the sole sovereignty over the country, in the same way as his father had given it to him. Now when Olaf and Sigrod heard this, messengers passed between them; and after appointing a meeting place, Sigrod went eastward in spring to Viken, and he and his brother Olaf met at Tunsberg, and remained there a while. The same spring (A.D. 934), King Eirik levied a great force, and ships and steered towards Viken. He got such a strong steady gale that he sailed night and day, and came faster than the news of him. When he came to Tunsberg, Olaf and Sigrod, with their forces, went out of the town a little eastward to a ridge, where they drew up their men in battle order; but as Eirik had many more men he won the battle. Both brothers, Olaf and Sigrod, fell there; and both their grave-mounds are upon the ridge where they fell. Then King Eirik went through Viken, and subdued it, and remained far into summer. Gudrod and Trygve fled to the Uplands. Eirik was a stout handsome man, strong, and very manly,—a great and fortunate man of war; but bad-minded, gruff, unfriendly, and silent. Gunhild, his wife, was the most beautiful of women,—clever, with much knowledge, and lively; but a very false person, and very cruel in disposition. The children of King Eirik and Gunhild were, Gamle, the oldest; then Guthorm, Harald, Ragnfrod, Ragnhild, Erling, Gudrod, and Sigurd Sleva. All were handsome, and of manly appearance (1).

(1) Of Eirik, his wife, and children, see the following sagas.

Saga of Hakon Herdebreid (Hakon the Broad-Shouldered) by Snorri Sturluson

From *Heimskringla, The Chronicle of the Kings of Norway*

This saga describes the feud between Hakon Sigurdson and his uncle Inge. The only skald quoted is Einar Skulason.

Hakon, King Sigurd's son, was chosen chief of the troop which had followed King Eystein, and his adherents gave him the title of king. He was ten years old. At that time he had with him Sigurd, a son of Halvard Hauld of Reyr, and Andreas and Onund, the sons of Simon, his foster-brothers, and many chiefs, friends of King Sigurd and King Eystein; and they went first up to Gautland. King Inge took possession of all the estates they had left behind, and declared them banished. Thereafter King Inge went to Viken, and was sometimes also in the north of the country. Gregorius Dagson was in Konungahella, where the danger was greatest, and had beside him a strong and handsome body of men, with which he defended the country.

The summer after (A.D. 1158) Hakon came with his men, and proceeded to Konungahella with a numerous and handsome troop. Gregorius was then in the town, and summoned the bondes and townspeople to a great Thing, at which he desired their aid; but he thought the people did not hear him with much favour, so he did not much trust them. Gregorius set off with two ships to Viken, and was very much cast down. He expected to meet King Inge there, having heard he was coming with a great army to Viken. Now when Gregorius had come but a short way north he met Simon Skalp, Haldor Brynjolfson, and Gyrd Amundason, King Inge's foster-brothers. Gregorius was much delighted at this meeting, and turned back with them, being all in one body, with eleven ships. As they were rowing up to Konungahella, Hakon, with his followers, was holding a Thing without the town, and saw their approach; and Sigurd of Reyr said, "Gregorius must be fey to be throwing himself with so few men into our hands." Gregorius landed opposite the town to wait for King Inge, for he was expected, but he did not come. King Hakon put himself in order in the town, and appointed Thorliot Skaufaskalle, who was a viking and a robber, to be captain of the men in the merchant ships that were afloat in the river; and King Hakon and Sigurd were within the town, and drew up the men on the piers, for all the townspeople had submitted to King Hakon.

Gregorius rowed up the river, and let the ship drive down with the stream against Thorliot. They shot at each other a while, until Thorliot and his comrades jumped overboard; and some of them were killed, some escaped to the land. Then Gregorius rowed to the piers, and let a gangway be cast on shore at the very feet of Hakon's men. There the man who carried his banner was slain, just as he was going to step on shore. Gregorius ordered Hal, a son of Audun Halson, to take up the banner, which he did, and bore the banner up to the pier. Gregorius followed close after him, held his shield over his head, and protected him as well as himself. As soon as Gregorius came upon the pier, and Hakon's men knew him, they gave way, and made room for him on every side. Afterwards more people landed from the ships, and then Gregorius made a severe assault with his men; and Hakon's men first moved back, and then ran up into the town. Gregorius pursued them eagerly, drove them twice from the town, and killed many of them. By the report of all men, never was there so glorious an affair as this of Gregorius; for Hakon had more than 4000 men, and Gregorius not full 400. After the battle, Gregorius said to Hal Audunson, "Many men, in my opinion, are more agile in battle than ye Icelanders are, for ye are not so exercised as we Norwegians; but none, I think, are so bold under arms as ye are." King Inge came up soon after, and killed many of the men who had taken part with Hakon; made some pay heavy fines, burnt the houses of some, and some he drove out of the country, or treated otherwise very ill. Hakon fled at first up to Gautland with all his men; but the winter after (A.D. 1159), he proceeded by the upper road to Throndhjem, and came there before Easter. The Throndhjem people received him well, for they had always served under that shield. It is said that the Throndhjem people took Hakon as king, on the terms that he should have from Inge the third part of Norway as his paternal heritage. King Inge and Gregorius were in Viken, and Gregorius wanted to make an expedition against the party in the north; but it came to nothing that winter, as many dissuaded from it.

King Hakon left Throndhjem in spring with thirty ships nearly; and some of his men sailed before the rest with seven ships, and plundered in North and South More. No man could remember that there ever before had been plundering between the two towns (Bergen and Nidaros). Jon the son of Halkel Huk collected the bondes in arms, and proceeded against them; took Kolbein Ode prisoner, killed every woman's son of them in his ship. Then they searched for the others, found them all assembled in seven ships, and fought with them; but his father Halkel not coming to his assistance as he had promised, many good bondes were killed, and Jon himself was wounded. Hakon proceeded south to Bergen with his forces; but when he came to Stiornvelta, he heard that King Inge and Gregorius had arrived a few nights before from the east at Bergen, and therefore he did not venture to steer thither. They sailed the outer course southwards past Bergen, and met three ships of King Inge's fleet, which had been outsailed on the voyage from the east. On board of them were Gyrd Amundason, King Inge's foster-brother, who was married to Gyrid a sister of Gregorius, and also lagman Gyrd Gunhildson, and Havard Klining. King Hakon had Gyrd Amundason and Havard Klining put to death; but took lagman Gyrd southwards, and then proceeded east to Viken.

When King Inge heard of this he sailed east after them, and they met east in the Gaut river. King Inge went up the north arm of the river, and sent out spies to get news of Hakon and his fleet; but he himself landed at Hising, and waited for his spies. Now when the spies came back they went to the king, and said that they had seen King Hakon's forces, and all his ships which lay at the stakes in the river, and Hakon's men had bound the stems of their vessels to them. They had two great Eastcountry trading vessels, which they had laid outside of the fleet, and on both these were built high wooded stages (castles). When King Inge heard the preparations they had made, he ordered a trumpet to call a House-thing of all the men; and when the Thing was seated he asked his men for counsel, and applied particularly to Gregorius Dagson, his brother-in-law Erling Skakke, and other lendermen and ship-commanders, to whom he related the preparations of Hakon and his men.

Then Gregorius Dagson replied first, and made known his mind in the following words:—"Sometimes we and Hakon have met, and generally they had the most people; but, notwithstanding, they fell short in battle against us. Now, on the other hand, we have by far the greatest force; and it will appear probable to the men who a short time ago lost gallant relations by them, that this will be a good occasion to get vengeance, for they have fled before us the greater part of the summer; and we have often said that if they waited for us, as appears now to be the case, we would have a brush with them. Now I will tell my opinion, which is, that I will engage them, if it be agreeable to the king's pleasure; for I think it will go now as formerly, that they must give way before us if we attack them bravely; and I shall always attack where others may think it most difficult."

The speech was received with much applause, and all declared they were ready to engage in battle against Hakon. Then they rowed with all the ships up the river, until they came in sight of each other, and then King Inge turned off from the river current under the island. Now the king addressed the lendermen again, and told them to get ready for battle. He turned himself especially to Erling Skakke, and said, what was true, that no man in the army had more understanding and knowledge in fighting battles, although some were more hot. The king then addressed himself to several of the lendermen, speaking to them by name; and ended by desiring that each man should make his attack where he thought it would be of advantage, and thereafter all would act together.

Erling Skakke replied thus to the king's speech: "It is my duty, sire, not to be silent; and I shall give my advice, since it is desired. The resolution now adopted is contrary to my judgment; for I call it foolhardy to fight under these circumstances, although we have so many and such fine men. Supposing we make an attack on them, and row up against this river-current; then one of the three men who are in each half room must be employed in rowing only, and another must be covering with the shield the man who rows; and what have we then to fight with but one third of our men? It appears to me that they can be of little use in the battle who are sitting at their oars with their backs turned to the enemy. Give me now some time for consideration, and I promise you that before three days are over I shall fall upon some plan by which we can come into battle with advantage."

It was evident from Erling's speech that he dissuaded from an attack; but, notwithstanding, it was urged by many who thought that Hakon would now, as before, take to the land. "And then," said they, "we cannot get hold of him; but now they have but few men, and we have their fate in our own hands."

Gregorius said but little; but thought that Erling rather dissuaded from an attack that Gregorius's advice should have no effect, than that he had any better advice to give.

Then said King Inge to Erling, "Now we will follow thy advice, brother, with regard to the manner of attacking; but seeing how eager our counsellors are for it, we shall make the attack this day."

Erling replied, "All the boats and light vessels we have should row outside the island, and up the east arm of the river, and then down with the stream upon them, and try if they cannot cut them loose from the piles. Then we, with the large ships, shall row from below here against them; and I cannot tell until it be tried, if those who are now so furiously warm will be much brisker at the attack than I am."

This counsel was approved by all. There was a ness stretched out between their fleet and Hakon's, so that they could not see each other. Now when Hakon and his men, who had taken counsel with each other in a meeting, saw the boat-squadron rowing down the river, some thought King Inge intended to give them battle; but many believed they did not dare, for it looked as if the attack was given up; and they, besides, were very confident, both in their preparations and men. There were many great people with Hakon: there were Sigurd of Reyr, and Simon's sons; Nikolas Skialdvarson; Eindride, a son of Jon Mornef, who was the most gallant and popular man in the Throndhjem country; and many other lendermen and warriors. Now when they saw that King Inge's men with many ships were rowing out of the river, Hakon and his men believed they were going to fly; and therefore they cut their land-ropes with which they lay fast at the piles, seized their oars, and rowed after them in pursuit. The ships ran fast down with the stream; but when they came further down the river, abreast of the ness, they saw King Inge's main strength lying quiet at the island Hising. King Inge's people saw Hakon's ships under way, and believed they were coming to attack them; and now there was great bustle and clash of arms, and they encouraged each other by a great war-shout. Hakon with his fleet turned northwards a little to the land, where there was a turn in the bight of the river, and where there was no current. They made ready for battle, carried land-ropes to the shore, turned the stems of their ships outwards, and bound them all together. They laid the large East-country traders without the other vessels, the one above, the other below, and bound them to the long-ships. In the middle of the fleet lay the king's ship, and next to it Sigurd's; and on the other side of the king's ship lay Nikolas, and next to him Endride Jonson. All the smaller ships lay farther off, and they were all nearly loaded with weapons and stones.

Then Sigurd of Reyr made the following speech: "Now there is hope that the time is come which has been promised us all the summer, that we shall meet King Inge in battle. We have long prepared ourselves for this; and many of our comrades have boasted that they would never fly from or submit to King Inge and Gregorius, and now let them remember their words. But we who have sometimes got the toothache in our conflicts with them, speak less confidently; for it has happened, as all have heard, that we very often have come off without glory. But, nevertheless, it is now necessary to fight manfully, and stand to it with steadiness; for the only escape for us is in victory. Although we have somewhat fewer men than they, yet luck determines which side shall have the advantage, and God knows that the right is on our side. Inge has killed two of his brothers; and it is obvious to all men that the mulct he intends to pay King Hakon for his father's murder is to murder him also, as well as his other relations, which will be seen this day to be his intent. King Hakon desired from the beginning no more of Norway than the third part, which his father had possessed, and which was denied him; and yet, in my opinion, King Hakon has a better right to inherit after his father's brother, King Eystein, than Inge or Simon Skalp, or the other men who killed King Eystein. Many of them who would save their souls, and yet have defiled their hands with such bloody deeds as Inge has done, must think it a presumption before God that he takes the name of king; and I wonder God suffers such monstrous wickedness as his; but it may be God's will that we shall now put him down. Let us fight then manfully, and God will give us victory; and, if we fall, will repay us with joys unspeakable for now allowing the might of the wicked to prevail over us. Go forth then in confidence, and be not afraid when the battle begins. Let each watch over his own and his comrade's safety, and God protect us all." There went a good report abroad of this speech of Sigurd, and all promised fairly, and to do their duty. King Hakon went on board of the great East-country ship, and a shield-bulwark was made around him; but his standard remained on the long-ship in which it had been before.

Now must we tell about King Inge and his men. When they saw that King Hakon and his people were ready for battle, and the river only was between them, they sent a light vessel to recall the rest of the fleet which had rowed away; and in the meantime the king waited for them, and arranged the troops for the attack. Then the chiefs consulted in presence of the army, and told their opinions; first, which ships should lie nearest to the enemy; and then where each should attack.

Gregorius spoke thus: "We have many and fine men; and it is my advice, King Inge, that you do not go to the assault with us, for everything is preserved if you are safe. And no man knows where an arrow may hit, even from the hands of a bad bowman; and they have prepared themselves so, that missiles and stones can be thrown from the high stages upon the merchant ships, so that there is less danger for those who are farthest from them. They have not more men than we lendermen can very well engage with. I shall lay my ship alongside their largest ship, and I expect the conflict between us will be but short; for it has often been so in our former meetings, although there has been a much greater want of men with us than now." All thought well of the advice that the king himself should not take part in the battle.

Then Erling Skakke said, "I agree also to the counsel that you, sire, should not go into the battle. It appears to me that their preparations are such, that we require all our precaution not to suffer a great defeat from them; and whole limbs are the easiest cured. In the council we held before to-day many opposed what I said, and ye said then that I did not want to fight; but now I think the business has altered its appearance, and greatly to our advantage, since they have hauled off from the piles, and now it stands so that I do not dissuade from giving battle; for I see, what all are sensible of, how necessary it is to put an end to this robber band who have gone over the whole country with pillage and destruction, in order that people may cultivate the land in peace, and serve a king so good and just as King Inge who has long had trouble and anxiety from the haughty unquiet spirit of his relations, although he has been a shield of defence for the whole people, and has been exposed to manifold perils for the peace of the country." Erling spoke well and long, and many other chiefs also; and all to the same purpose—all urging to battle. In the meantime they waited until all the fleet should be assembled. King Inge had the ship Baekisudin; and, at the entreaty of his friends, he did not join the battle, but lay still at the island.

When the army was ready they rowed briskly against the enemy, and both sides raised a war-shout. Inge's men did not bind their ships together, but let them be loose; for they rowed right across the current, by which the large ships were much swayed. Erling Skakke laid his ship beside King Hakon's ship, and ran the stem between his and Sigurd's ship, by which the battle began. But Gregorius's ship swung upon the ground, and heeled very much over, so that at first she could not come into the battle; and when Hakon's men saw this they laid themselves against her, and attacked Gregorius's ship on all sides. Ivar, Hakon Mage's son, laid his ship so that the stems struck together; and he got a boat-hook fastened on Gregorius, on that part of his body where the waist is smallest, and dragged him to him, by which Gregorius stumbled against the ship's rails; but the hook slipped to one side, or Gregorius would have been dragged over-board. Gregorius, however, was but little wounded, for he had on a plate coat of armour. Ivar called out to him, that he had a "thick bark." Gregorius replied, that if Ivar went on so he would "require it all, and not have too much." It was very near then that Gregorius and his men had sprung overboard; but Aslak Unge threw an anchor into their ship, and dragged them off the ground. Then Gregorius laid himself against Ivar's ship, and they fought a long while; but Gregorius's ship being both higher sided and more strongly manned, many people fell in Ivar's ship, and some jumped overboard. Ivar was so severely wounded that he could not take part in the fight. When his ship was cleared of the men, Gregorius let Ivar be carried to the shore, so that he might escape; and from that time they were constant friends.

When King Inge and his men saw that Gregorius was aground, he encouraged his crew to row to his assistance. "It was," he said, "the most imprudent advice that we should remain lying here, while our friends are in battle; for we have the largest and best ship in all the fleet. But now I see that Gregorius, the man to whom I owe the most, is in need of help; so we must hasten to the fight where it is sharpest. It is also most proper that I should be in the battle; for the victory, if we win it, will belong to me. And if I even knew beforehand that our men were not to gain the battle, yet our place is where our friends are; for I can do nothing if I lose the men who are justly called the defence of the country, who are the bravest, and have long ruled for me and my kingdom." Thereupon he ordered his banner to be set up, which was done; and they rowed across the river. Then the battle raged, and the king could not get room to attack, so close lay the ships before him. First he lay under the East-country trading ship, and from it they threw down upon his vessel spears, iron-shod stakes, and such large stones that it was impossible to hold out longer there, and he had to haul off. Now when the king's people saw that he was come they made place for him, and then he laid alongside of Eindride Jonson's ship. Now King Hakon's men abandoned the small ships, and went on board the large merchant vessels; but some of them sprang on shore. Erling Skakke and his men had a severe conflict. Erling himself was on the forecastle, and called his forecastlemen, and ordered them to board the king's ship; but they answered, this was no easy matter, for there were beams above with an iron comb on them. Then Erling himself went to the bow, and stayed there a while, until they succeeded in getting on board the king's ship: and then the ship was cleared of men on the bows, and the whole army gave way. Many sprang into the water, many fell, but the greater number got to the land. So says Einar Skulason:—

"Men fall upon the slippery deck—
Men roll off from the blood-drenched wreck;
Dead bodies float down with the stream,
And from the shores witch-ravens scream.
The cold blue river now runs red
With the warm blood of warriors dead,
And stains the waves in Karmt Sound
With the last drops of the death-wound.

"All down the stream, with unmann'd prow,
Floats many an empty long-ship now,
Ship after ship, shout after shout,
Tell that Kign Hakon can't hold out.
The bowmen ply their bows of elm,
The red swords flash o'er broken helm:
King Hakon's men rush to the strand,
Out of their ships, up through the land."

Einar composed a song about Gregorius Dagson, which is called the Riversong. King Inge granted life and peace to Nikolas Skialdvarson when his ship was deserted, and thereupon he went into King Inge's service, and remained in it as long as the king lived. Eindride Jonson leaped on board of King Inge's ship when his own was cleared of men, and begged for his life. King Inge wished to grant it; but Havard Klining's son ran up, and gave him a mortal wound, which was much blamed; but he said Eindride had been the cause of his father's death. There was much lamentation at Eindride's death, but principally in the Throndhjem district. Many of Hakon's people fell here, but not many chiefs. Few of King Inge's people fell, but many were wounded. King Hakon fled up the country, and King Inge went north to Viken with his troops; and he, as well as Gregorius, remained in Viken all winter (A.D. 1160). When King Inge's men, Bergliot and his brothers, sons of Ivar of Elda, came from the battle to Bergen, they slew Nickolas Skeg, who had been Hakon's treasurer, and then went north to Throndhjem.

King Hakon came north before Yule, and Sigurd was sometimes home at Reyr; for Gregorius, who was nearly related to Sigurd, had obtained for him life and safety from King Inge, so that he retained all his estates. King Hakon was in the merchant-town of Nidaros in Yule; and one evening in the beginning of Yule his men fought in the room of the court, and in this affray eight men were killed, and many were wounded. The eighth day of Yule, King Hakon's man Alf Rode, son of Ottar Birting, with about eighty men, went to Elda, and came in the night unexpectedly on the people, who were very drunk, and set fire to the room; but they went out, and defended themselves bravely. There fell Bergliot, Ivar's son, and Ogmund, his brother, and many more. They had been nearly thirty altogether in number. In winter died, north in the merchant-town, Andres Simonson, King Hakon's foster-brother; and his death was much deplored. Erling Skakke and Inge's men, who were in Bergen, threatened that in winter they would proceed against Hakon and his men; but it came to nothing. Gregorius sent word from the east, from Konungahella, that if he were so near as Erling and his men, he would not sit quietly in Bergen while Hakon was killing King Inge's friends and their comrades in war north in the Throndhjem country.

King Inge and Gregorius left the east in spring, and came to Bergen; but as soon as Hakon and Sigurd heard that Inge had left Viken, they went there by land. When King Inge and his people came to Bergen, a quarrel arose between Haldor Brynjolfson and Bjorn Nikolason. Bjorn's house-man asked Haldor's when they met at the pier, why he looked so pale.

He replied, because he had been bled.

"I could not look so pale if I tried, at merely being bled."

"I again think," retorted the other, "that thou wouldst have borne it worse, and less manfully." And no other beginning was there for their quarrel than this. Afterwards one word followed another, till from brawling they came to fighting. It was told to Haldor Brynjolfson, who was in the house drinking, that his house-man was wounded down on the pier and he went there immediately. But Bjorn's house-men had come there before, and as Haldor thought his house-man had been badly treated, he went up to them and beat them; and it was told to Bjorn Buk that the people of Viken were beating his house-men on the pier. Then Bjorn and his house-men took their weapons, hurried down to the pier, and would avenge their men; and a bloody strife began. It was told Gregorius that his relation Haldor required assistance, and that his house-men were being cut down in the street; on which Gregorius and his men ran to the place in their armour. Now it was told Erling Skakke that his sister's son Bjorn was fighting with Gregorius and Haldor down on the piers, and that he needed help. Then he proceeded thither with a great force, and exhorted the people to stand by him; saying it would be a great disgrace never to be wiped out, if the Viken people should trample upon them in their own native place. There fell thirteen men, of whom nine were killed on the spot, and four died of their wounds, and many were wounded. When the word came to King Inge that Gregorius and Erling were fighting down on the piers, he hastened there, and tried to separate them; but could do nothing, so mad were they on both sides. Then Gregorius called to Inge, and told him to go away; for it was in vain to attempt coming between them, as matters now stood. He said it would be the greatest misfortune if the king mixed himself up with it; for he could not be certain that there were not people in the fray who would commit some great misdeed if they had opportunity. Then King Inge retired; and when the greatest tumult was over, Gregorius and his men went to Nikolas church, and Erling behind them, calling to each other. Then King Inge came a second time, and pacified them; and both agreed that he should mediate between them.

When King Inge and Gregorius heard that King Hakon was in Viken, they went east with many ships; but when they came King Hakon fled from them, and there was no battle. Then King Inge went to Oslo, and Gregorius was in Konungahella.

Soon after Gregorius heard that Hakon and his men were at a farm called Saurby, which lies up beside the forest. Gregorius hastened there; came in the night; and supposing that King Hakon and Sigurd would be in the largest of the houses, set fire to the buildings there. But Hakon and his men were in the smaller house, and came forth, seeing the fire, to help their people. There Munan fell, a son of Ale Uskeynd, a brother of King Sigurd Hakon's father. Gregorius and his men killed him, because he was helping those whom they were burning within the house. Some escaped, but many were killed. Asbjorn Jalda, who had been a very great viking, escaped from the house, but was grievously wounded. A bonde met him, and he offered the man money to let him get away; but the bonde replied, he would do what he liked best; and, adding that he had often been in fear of his life for him, he slew him. King Hakon and Sigurd escaped, but many of their people were killed. Thereafter Gregorius returned home to Konungahella. Soon after King Hakon and Sigurd went to Haldor Brynjolfson's farm of Vettaland, set fire to the house, and burnt it. Haldor went out, and was cut down instantly with his house-men; and in all there were about twenty men killed. Sigrid, Haldor's wife, was a sister of Gregorius, and they allowed her to escape into the forest in her night-shift only; but they took with them Amunde, who was a son of Gyrd Amundason and of Gyrid Dag's daughter, and a sister's son of Gregorius, and who was then a boy about five years old.

When Gregorius heard the news he took it much to heart, and inquired carefully where they were. Gregorius set out from Konungahella late in Yule, and came to Fors the thirteenth day of Yule, where he remained a night, and heard vespers the last day of Yule, which was a Saturday, and the holy Evangel was read before him. When Gregorius and his followers saw the men of King Hakon and Sigurd, the king's force appeared to them smaller than their own. There was a river called Befia between them, where they met; and there was unsound ice on the river, for there went a stream under the ice from it. King Hakon and his men had cut a rent in the ice, and laid snow over it, so that nobody could see it. When Gregorius came to the ice on the river the ice appeared to him unsound, he said; and he advised the people to go to the bridge, which was close by, to cross the river. The bonde-troops replied, that they did not know why he should be afraid to go across the ice to attack so few people as Hakon had, and the ice was good enough. Gregorius said it was seldom necessary to encourage him to show bravery, and it should not be so now. Then he ordered them to follow him, and not to be standing on the land while he was on the ice, and he said it was their council to go out upon the dangerous ice, but he had no wish to do so, or to be led by them. Then he ordered the banner to be advanced, and immediately went out on the ice with the men. As soon as the bondes found that the ice was unsound they turned back. Gregorius fell through the ice, but not very deep, and he told his men to take care. There were not more than twenty men with him, the others having turned back. A man of King Hakon's troop shot an arrow at Gregorius, which hit him under the throat, and thus ended his life. Gregorius fell, and ten men with him. It is the talk of all men that he had been the most gallant lenderman in Norway that any man then living could remember; and also he behaved the best towards us Icelanders of any chief since King Eystein the Elder's death. Gregorius's body was carried to Hofund, and interred at Gimsey Isle, in a nunnery which is there, of which Gregorius's sister, Baugeid, was then the abbess.

Two bailiffs went to Oslo to bring the tidings to King Inge. When they arrived they desired to speak to the king: and he asked, what news they brought.

"Gregorius Dagson's death," said they.

"How came that misfortune?" asked the king.

When they had told him how it happened, he said, "They gave advice who understood the least."

It is said he took it so much to heart that he cried like a child. When he recovered himself he said, "I wanted to go to Gregorius as soon as I heard of Haldor's murder; for I thought that Gregorius would not sit long before thinking of revenge. But the people here would think nothing so important as their Yule feasts, and nothing could move them away; and I am confident that if I had been there, he would either have proceeded more cautiously, or I and Gregorius would now have shared one lodging. Now he is gone, the man who has been my best friend, and more than any other has kept the kingdom in my hands; and I think it will be but a short space between us. Now I make an oath to go forth against Hakon, and one of two things shall happen: I shall either come to my death, or shall walk over Hakon and his people; and such a man as Gregorius is not avenged, even if all were to pay the penalty of their lives for him."

There was a man present who replied, "Ye need not seek after them, for they intend to seek you."

Kristin, King Sigurd's daughter and King Inge's cousin, was then in Oslo. The king heard that she intended going away. He sent a message to her to inquire why she wished to leave the town.

She thought it was dangerous and unsafe for a female to be there. The king would not let her go. "For if it go well with me, as I hope, you will be well here; and if I fall, my friends may not get leave to dress my body; but you can ask permission, and it will not be denied you, and you will thereby best requite what I have done for you."

On Saint Blasius' day (February 3, 1161), in the evening, King Inge's spies brought him the news that King Hakon was coming towards the town. Then King Inge ordered the war-horns to call together all the troops up from the town; and when he drew them up he could reckon them to be nearly 4000 men. The king let the array be long, but not more than five men deep. Then some said that the king should not be himself in the battle, as they thought the risk too great; but that his brother Orm should be the leader of the army. The king replied, "I think if Gregorius were alive and here now, and I had fallen and was to be avenged, he would not lie concealed, but would be in the battle. Now, although I, on account of my ill health, am not fit for the combat as he was, yet will I show as good will as he would have had; and it is not to be thought of that I should not be in the battle."

People say that Gunhild, who was married to Simon, King Hakon's foster-brother, had a witch employed to sit out all night and procure the victory for Hakon; and that the answer was obtained, that they should fight King Inge by night, and never by day, and then the result would be favourable. The witch who, as people say, sat out was called Thordis Skeggia; but what truth there may be in the report I know not.

Simon Skalp had gone to the town, and was gone to sleep, when the war-shouts awoke him. When the night was well advanced, King Inge's spies came to him, and told him that King Hakon and his army were coming over the ice; for the ice lay the whole way from the town to Hofud Isle.

Thereupon King Inge went with his army out on the ice, and he drew it up in order of battle in front of the town. Simon Skalp was in that wing of the array which was towards Thraelaberg; and on the other wing, which was towards the Nunnery, was Gudrod, the king of the South Hebudes, a son of Olaf Klining, and Jon, a son of Svein Bergthor Buk. When King Hakon and his army came near to King Inge's array, both sides raised a war-shout. Gudrod and Jon gave King Hakon and his men a sign, and let them know where they were in the line; and as soon as Hakon's men in consequence turned thither, Gudrod immediately fled with 1500 men; and Jon, and a great body of men with him, ran over to King Hakon's army, and assisted them in the fight. When this news was told to King Inge, he said, "Such is the difference between my friends. Never would Gregorius have done so in his life!" There were some who advised King Inge to get on horseback, and ride from the battle up to Raumarike; "where," said they, "you would get help enough, even this very day." The king replied, he had no inclination to do so. "I have heard you often say, and I think truly, that it was of little use to my brother, King Eystein, that he took to flight; and yet he was a man distinguished for many qualities which adorn a king. Now I, who labour under so great decrepitude, can see how bad my fate would be, if I betook myself to what proved so unfortunate for him; with so great a difference as there is between our activity, health, and strength. I was in the second year of my age when I was chosen king of Norway, and I am now twenty-five; and I think I have had misfortune and sorrow under my kingly dignity, rather than pleasure and peaceful days. I have had many battles, sometimes with more, sometimes with fewer people; and it is my greatest luck that I have never fled. God will dispose of my life, and of how long it shall be; but I shall never betake myself to flight."

Now as Jon and his troop had broken the one wing of King Inge's array, many of those who were nearest to him fled, by which the whole array was dispersed, and fell into disorder. But Hakon and his men went briskly forwards; and now it was near daybreak. An assault was made against King Inge's banner, and in this conflict King Inge fell; but his brother Orm continued the battle, while many of the army fled up into the town. Twice Orm went to the town after the king's fall to encourage the people, and both times returned, and went out again upon the ice to continue the battle. Hakon's men attacked the wing of the array which Simon Skalp led; and in that assault fell of King Inge's men his brother-in-law, Gudbrand Skafhogson. Simon Skalp and Halvard Hikre went against each other with their troops, and fought while they drew aside past Thraelaberg; and in this conflict both Simon and Halvard fell. Orm, the king's brother, gained great reputation in this battle; but he at last fled. Orm the winter before had been contracted with Ragna, a daughter of Nikolas Mase, who had been married before to King Eystein Haraldson; and the wedding was fixed for the Sunday after Saint Blasius's mass, which was on a Friday. Orm fled east to Svithjod, where his brother Magnus was then king; and their brother Ragnvald was an earl there at that time. They were the sons of Queen Ingerid and Henrik Halte, who was a son of the Danish king Svein Sveinson. The princess Kristin took care of King Inge's body, which was laid on the stone wall of Halvard's church, on the south side without the choir. He had then been king for twenty-three years (A.D. 1137-1161). In this battle many fell on both sides, but principally of King Inge's men. Of King Hakon's people fell Arne Frirekson. Hakon's men took all the feast and victuals prepared for the wedding, and a great booty besides.

Then King Hakon took possession of the whole country, and distributed all the offices among his own friends, both in the towns and in the country. King Hakon and his men had a meeting in Halvard's church, where they had a private conference concerning the management of the country. Kristin the princess gave the priest who kept the church keys a large sum of money to conceal one of her men in the church, so that she might know what Hakon and his counsellors intended. When she learnt what they had said, she sent a man to Bergen to her husband Erling Skakke, with the message that he should never trust Hakon or his men.

It happened at the battle of Stiklestad, as before related, that King Olaf threw from him the sword called Hneiter when he received his wound. A Swedish man, who had broken his own sword, took it up, and fought with it. When this man escaped with the other fugitives he came to Svithjod, and went home to his house. From that time he kept the sword all his days, and afterwards his son, and so relation after relation; and when the sword shifted its owner, the one told to the other the name of the sword and where it came from. A long time after, in the days of Kirjalax the emperor of Constantinople, when there was a great body of Varings in the town, it happened in the summer that the emperor was on a campaign, and lay in the camp with his army. The Varings who had the guard, and watched over the emperor, lay on the open plain without the camp. They changed the watch with each other in the night, and those who had been before on watch lay down and slept; but all completely armed. It was their custom, when they went to sleep, that each should have his helmet on his head, his shield over him, sword under the head, and the right hand on the sword-handle. One of these comrades, whose lot it was to watch the latter part of the night, found, on awakening towards morning, that his sword was gone. He looked after it, and saw it lying on the flat plain at a distance from him. He got up and took the sword, thinking that his comrades who had been on watch had taken the sword from him in a joke; but they all denied it. The same thing happened three nights. Then he wondered at it, as well as they who saw or heard of it; and people began to ask him how it could have happened. He said that his sword was called Hneiter, and had belonged to King Olaf the Saint, who had himself carried it in the battle of Stiklestad; and he also related how the sword since that time had gone from one to another. This was told to the emperor, who called the man before him to whom the sword belonged, and gave him three times as much gold as the sword was worth; and the sword itself he had laid in Saint Olaf's church, which the Varings supported, where it has been ever since over the altar. There was a lenderman of Norway while Harald Gille's sons, Eystein, Inge, and Sigurd lived, who was called Eindride Unge; and he was in Constantinople when these events took place. He told these circumstances in Norway, according to what Einar Skulason says in his song about King Olaf the Saint, in which these events are sung.

It happened once in the Greek country, when Kirjalax was emperor there, that he made an expedition against Blokumannaland. When he came to the Pezina plains, a heathen king came against him with an innumerable host. He brought with him many horsemen, and many large waggons, in which were large loop-holes for shooting through. When they prepared for their night quarters they drew up their waggons, one by the side of the other, without their tents, and dug a great ditch without; and all which made a defence as strong as a castle. The heathen king was blind. Now when the Greek king came, the heathens drew up their array on the plains before their waggon-fortification. The Greeks drew up their array opposite, and they rode on both sides to fight with each other; but it went on so ill and so unfortunately, that the Greeks were compelled to fly after suffering a great defeat, and the heathens gained a victory. Then the king drew up an array of Franks and Flemings, who rode against the heathens, and fought with them; but it went with them as with the others, that many were killed, and all who escaped took to flight. Then the Greek king was greatly incensed at his men-at-arms; and they replied, that he should now take his wine-bags, the Varings. The king says that he would not throw away his jewels, and allow so few men, however bold they might be, to attack so vast an army. Then Thorer Helsifig, who at that time was leader of the Varings replied to the king's words, "If there was burning fire in the way, I and my people would run into it, if I knew the king's advantage required it." Then the king replied, "Call upon your holy King Olaf for help and strength." The Varings, who were 450 men, made a vow with hand and word to build a church in Constantinople, at their own expense and with the aid of other good men, and have the church consecrated to the honour and glory of the holy King Olaf; and thereupon the Varings rushed into the plain. When the heathens saw them, they told their king that there was another troop of the Greek king's army come out upon the plain; but they were only a handful of people. The king says, "Who is that venerable man riding on a white horse at the head of the troop?" They replied, "We do not see him." There was so great a difference of numbers, that there were sixty heathens for every Christian man; but notwithstanding the Varings went boldly to the attack. As soon as they met terror and alarm seized the army of the heathens, and they instantly began to fly; but the Varings pursued, and soon killed a great number of them. When the Greeks and Franks who before had fled from the heathens saw this, they hastened to take part, and pursue the enemy with the others. Then the Varings had reached the waggon-fortification, where the greatest defeat was given to the enemy. The heathen king was taken in the flight of his people, and the Varings brought him along with them; after which the Christians took the camp of the heathens, and their waggon-fortification.

Eric Brighteyes by H. Rider Haggard

INTRODUCTION

Eric Brighteyes is a romance founded on the Icelandic Sagas. "What is a saga?" "Is it a fable or a true story?" The answer is not altogether simple. For such sagas as those of Burnt Njal and Grettir the Strong partake both of truth and fiction: historians dispute as to the proportions. This was the manner of the saga's growth: In the early days of the Iceland community—that republic of aristocrats—say, between the dates 900 and 1100 of our era, a quarrel would arise between two great families. As in the case of the Njal Saga, its cause, probably, was the ill doings of some noble woman. This quarrel would lead to manslaughter. Then blood called for blood, and a vendetta was set on foot that ended only with the death by violence of a majority of the actors in the drama and of large numbers of their adherents. In the course of the feud, men of heroic strength and mould would come to the front and perform deeds worthy of the iron age which bore them. Women also would help to fashion the tale, for good or ill, according to their natural gifts and characters. At last the tragedy was covered up by death and time, leaving only a few dinted shields and haunted cairns to tell of those who had played its leading parts.

But its fame lived on in the minds of men. From generation to generation skalds wandered through the winter snows, much as Homer may have wandered in his day across the Grecian vales and mountains, to find a welcome at every stead, because of the old-time story they had to tell. Here, night after night, they would sit in the ingle and while away the weariness of the dayless dark with histories of the times when men carried their lives in their hands, and thought them well lost if there might be a song in the ears of folk to come. To alter the tale was one of the greatest of crimes: the skald must repeat it as it came to him; but by degrees undoubtedly the sagas did suffer alteration. The facts remained the same indeed, but around them gathered a mist of miraculous occurrences and legends. To take a single instance: the account of the burning of Bergthorsknoll in the Njal Saga is not only a piece of descriptive writing that for vivid, simple force and insight is scarcely to be matched out of Homer and the Bible, it is also obviously true. We feel as we read, that no man could have invented that story, though some great skald threw it into shape. That the tale is true, the writer of "Eric" can testify, for, saga in hand, he has followed every act of the drama on its very site. There he who digs beneath the surface of the lonely mound that looks across plain and sea to Westman Isles may still find traces of the burning, and see what appears to be the black sand with which the hands of Bergthora and her women strewed the earthen floor some nine hundred years ago, and even the greasy and clotted remains of the whey that they threw upon the flame to quench it. He may discover the places where Fosi drew up his men, where Skarphedinn died, singing while his legs were burnt from off him, where Kari leapt from the flaming ruin, and the dell in which he laid down to rest—at every step, in short, the truth of the narrative becomes more obvious. And yet the tale has been added to, for, unless we may believe that some human beings are gifted with second sight, we cannot accept as true the prophetic vision that came to Runolf, Thorstein's son; or that of Njal who, on the evening of the onslaught, like Theoclymenus in the Odyssey, saw the whole board and the meats upon it "one gore of blood."

Thus, in the Norse romance now offered to the reader, the tale of Eric and his deeds would be true; but the dream of Asmund, the witchcraft of Swanhild, the incident of the speaking head, and the visions of Eric and Skallagrim, would owe their origin to the imagination of successive generations of skalds; and, finally, in the fifteenth or sixteenth century, the story would have been written down with all its supernatural additions.

The tendency of the human mind—and more especially of the Norse mind—is to supply uncommon and extraordinary reasons for actions and facts that are to be amply accounted for by the working of natural forces. Swanhild would have needed no "familiar" to instruct her in her evil schemes; Eric would have wanted no love-draught to bring about his overthrow. Our common experience of mankind as it is, in opposition to mankind as we fable it to be, is sufficient to teach us that the passion of one and the human weakness of the other would suffice to these ends. The natural magic, the beauty and inherent power of such a woman as Swanhild, are things more forceful than any spell magicians have invented, or any demon they are supposed to have summoned to their aid. But no saga would be complete without the intervention of such extraneous forces: the need of them was always felt, in order to throw up the acts of heroes and heroines, and to invest their persons with an added importance. Even Homer felt this need, and did not scruple to introduce not only second sight, but gods and goddesses, and to bring their supernatural agency to bear directly on the personages of his chant, and that far more freely than any Norse sagaman. A word may be added in explanation of the appearances of "familiars" in the shapes of animals, an instance of which will be found in this story. It was believed in Iceland, as now by the Finns and Eskimo, that the passions and desires of sorcerers took visible form in such creatures as wolves or rats. These were called "sendings," and there are many allusions to them in the Sagas.

Another peculiarity that may be briefly alluded to as eminently characteristic of the Sagas is their fatefulness. As we read we seem to hear the voice of Doom speaking continually. "Things will happen as they are fated": that is the keynote of them all. The Norse mind had little belief in free will, less even than we have today. Men and women were born with certain characters and tendencies, given to them in order that their lives should run in appointed channels, and their acts bring about an appointed end. They do not these things of their own desire, though their desires prompt them to the deeds: they do them because they must. The Norns, as they name Fate, have mapped out their path long and long ago; their feet are set therein, and they must tread it to the end. Such was the conclusion of our Scandinavian ancestors—a belief forced upon them by their intense realisation of the futility of human hopes and schemings, of the terror and the tragedy of life, the vanity of its desires, and the untravelled gloom or sleep, dreamless or dreamfull, which lies beyond its end.

Though the Sagas are entrancing, both as examples of literature of which there is but little in the world and because of their living interest, they are scarcely known to the English-speaking public. This is easy to account for: it is hard to persuade the nineteenth century world to interest itself in people who lived and events that happened a thousand years ago. Moreover, the Sagas are undoubtedly difficult reading. The archaic nature of the work, even in a translation; the multitude of its actors; the Norse sagaman's habit of interweaving endless side-plots, and the persistence with which he introduces the genealogy and adventures of the ancestors of every unimportant character, are none of them to the taste of the modern reader.

"Eric Brighteyes" therefore, is clipped of these peculiarities, and, to some extent, is cast in the form of the romance of our own day, archaisms being avoided as much as possible. The author will be gratified should he succeed in exciting interest in the troubled lives of our Norse forefathers, and still more so if his difficult experiment brings readers to the Sagas—to the prose epics of our own race. Too ample, too prolix, too crowded with detail, they cannot indeed vie in art with the epics of Greece; but in their pictures of life, simple and heroic, they fall beneath no literature in the world, save the Iliad and the Odyssey alone.

I

HOW ASMUND THE PRIEST FOUND GROA THE WITCH

There lived a man in the south, before Thangbrand, Wilibald's son, preached the White Christ in Iceland. He was named Eric Brighteyes, Thorgrimur's son, and in those days there was no man like him for strength, beauty and daring, for in all these things he was the first. But he was not the first in good-luck.

Two women lived in the south, not far from where the Westman Islands stand above the sea. Gudruda the Fair was the name of the one, and Swanhild, called the Fatherless, Groa's daughter, was the other. They were half-sisters, and there were none like them in those days, for they were the fairest of all women, though they had nothing in common except their blood and hate.

Now of Eric Brighteyes, of Gudruda the Fair and of Swanhild the Fatherless, there is a tale to tell.

These two fair women saw the light in the self-same hour. But Eric Brighteyes was their elder by five years. The father of Eric was Thorgrimur Iron-Toe. He had been a mighty man; but in fighting with a Baresark,[*] who fell upon him as he came up from sowing his wheat, his foot was hewn from him, so that afterwards he went upon a wooden leg shod with iron. Still, he slew the Baresark, standing on one leg and leaning against a rock, and for that deed people honoured him much. Thorgrimur was a wealthy yeoman, slow to wrath, just, and rich in friends. Somewhat late in life he took to wife Saevuna, Thorod's daughter. She was the best of women, strong in mind and second-sighted, and she could cover herself in her hair. But these two never loved each other overmuch, and they had but one child, Eric, who was born when Saevuna was well on in years.

[*] *The Baresarks were men on whom a passing fury of battle came; they were usually outlawed.*

The father of Gudruda was Asmund Asmundson, the Priest of Middalhof. He was the wisest and the wealthiest of all men who lived in the south of Iceland in those days, owning many farms and, also, two ships of merchandise and one long ship of war, and having much money out at interest. He had won his wealth by viking's work, robbing the English coasts, and black tales were told of his doings in his youth on the sea, for he was a "red-hand" viking. Asmund was a handsome man, with blue eyes and a large beard, and, moreover, was very skilled in matters of law. He loved money much, and was feared of all. Still, he had many friends, for as he aged he grew more kindly. He had in marriage Gudruda, the daughter of Björn, who was very sweet and kindly of nature, so that they called her Gudruda the Gentle. Of this marriage there were two children, Björn and Gudruda the Fair; but Björn grew up like his father in youth, strong and hard, and greedy of gain, while, except for her wonderful beauty, Gudruda was her mother's child alone.

The mother of Swanhild the Fatherless was Groa the Witch. She was a Finn, and it is told of her that the ship on which she sailed, trying to run under the lee of the Westman Isles in a great gale from the north-east, was dashed to pieces on a rock, and all those on board of her were caught in the net of Ran[*] and drowned, except Groa herself, who was saved by her magic art. This at the least is true, that, as Asmund the Priest rode down by the sea-shore on the morning after the gale, seeking for some strayed horses, he found a beautiful woman, who wore a purple cloak and a great girdle of gold, seated on a rock, combing her black hair and singing the while; and, at her feet, washing to and fro in a pool, was a dead man. He asked whence she came, and she answered:

"Out of the Swan's Bath."

[*] *The Norse goddess of the sea.*

Next, he asked her where were her kin. But, pointing to the dead man, she said that this alone was left of them.

"Who was the man, then?" said Asmund the Priest.
She laughed again and sang this song:—
Groa sails up from the Swan's Bath,
Death Gods grip the Dead Man's hand.
Look where lies her luckless husband,
Bolder sea-king ne'er swung sword!
Asmund, keep the kirtle-wearer,
For last night the Norns were crying,
And Groa thought they told of thee:

Yea, told of thee and babes unborn.

"How knowest thou my name?" asked Asmund.
"The sea-mews cried it as the ship sank, thine and others—and they shall be heard in story."
"Then that is the best of luck," quoth Asmund; "but I think that thou art fey."
"Ay," she answered, "fey and fair."
"True enough thou art fair. What shall we do with this dead man?"
"Leave him in the arms of Ran. So may all husbands lie."
They spoke no more with her at that time, seeing that she was a witchwoman. But Asmund took her up to Middalhof, and gave her a farm, and she lived there alone, and he profited much by her wisdom.

Now it chanced that Gudruda the Gentle was with child, and when her time came she gave a daughter birth—a very fair girl, with dark eyes. On the same day, Groa the witchwoman brought forth a girl-child, and men wondered who was its father, for Groa was no man's wife. It was women's talk that Asmund the Priest was the father of this child also; but when he heard it he was angry, and said that no witchwoman should bear a bairn of his, howsoever fair she was. Nevertheless, it was still said that the child was his, and it is certain that he loved it as a man loves his own; but of all things, this is the hardest to know. When Groa was questioned she laughed darkly, as was her fashion, and said that she knew nothing of it, never having seen the face of the child's father, who rose out of the sea at night. And for this cause some thought him to have been a wizard or the wraith of her dead husband; but others said that Groa lied, as many women have done on such matters. But of all this talk the child alone remained and she was named Swanhild.

Now, but an hour before the child of Gudruda the Gentle was born, Asmund went up from his house to the Temple, to tend the holy fire that burned night and day upon the altar. When he had tended the fire, he sat down upon the cross-benches before the shrine, and, gazing on the image of the Goddess Freya, he fell asleep and dreamed a very evil dream.

He dreamed that Gudruda the Gentle bore a dove most beautiful to see, for all its feathers were of silver; but that Groa the Witch bore a golden snake. And the snake and the dove dwelt together, and ever the snake sought to slay the dove. At length there came a great white swan flying over Coldback Fell, and its tongue was a sharp sword. Now the swan saw the dove and loved it, and the dove loved the swan; but the snake reared itself, and hissed, and sought to kill the dove. But the swan covered her with his wings, and beat the snake away. Then he, Asmund, came out and drove away the swan, as the swan had driven the snake, and it wheeled high into the air and flew south, and the snake swam away also through the sea. But the dove drooped and now it was blind. Then an eagle came from the north, and would have taken the dove, but it fled round and round, crying, and always the eagle drew nearer to it. At length, from the south the swan came back, flying heavily, and about its neck was twined the golden snake, and with it came a raven. And it saw the eagle and loud it trumpeted, and shook the snake from it so that it fell like a gleam of gold into the sea. Then the eagle and the swan met in battle, and the swan drove the eagle down and broke it with his wings, and, flying to the dove, comforted it. But those in the house ran out and shot at the swan with bows and drove it away, but now he, Asmund, was not with them. And once more the dove drooped. Again the swan came back, and with it the raven, and a great host were gathered against them, and, among them, all of Asmund's kith and kin, and the men of his quarter and some of his priesthood, and many whom he did not know by face. And the swan flew at Björn his son, and shot out the sword of its tongue and slew him, and many a man it slew thus. And the raven, with a beak and claws of steel, slew also many a man, so that Asmund's kindred fled and the swan slept by the dove. But as it slept the golden snake crawled out of the sea, and hissed in the ears of men, and they rose up to follow it. It came to the swan and twined itself about its neck. It struck at the dove and slew it. Then the swan awoke and the raven awoke, and they did battle till all who remained of Asmund's kindred and people were dead. But still the snake clung about the swan's neck, and presently snake and swan fell into the sea, and far out on the sea there burned a flame of fire. And Asmund awoke trembling and left the Temple.

Now as he went, a woman came running, and weeping as she ran.

"Haste, haste!" she cried; "a daughter is born to thee, and Gudruda thy wife is dying!"

"Is it so?" said Asmund; "after ill dreams ill tidings."

Now in the bed-closet off the great hall of Middalhof lay Gudruda the Gentle and she was dying.

"Art thou there, husband?" she said.

"Even so, wife."

"Thou comest in an evil hour, for it is my last. Now hearken. Take thou the new-born babe within thine arms and kiss it, and pour water over it, and name it with my name."

This Asmund did.

"Hearken, my husband. I have been a good wife to thee, though thou hast not been all good to me. But thus shalt thou atone: thou shalt swear that, though she is a girl, thou wilt not cast this bairn forth to perish, but wilt cherish and nurture her."

"I swear it," he said.

"And thou shalt swear that thou wilt not take the witchwoman Groa to wife, nor have anything to do with her, and this for thine own sake: for, if thou dost, she will be thy death. Dost thou swear?"

"I swear it," he said.

"It is well; but, husband, if thou dost break thine oath, either in the words or in the spirit of the words, evil shall overtake thee and all thy house. Now bid me farewell, for I die."

He bent over her and kissed her, and it is said that Asmund wept in that hour, for after his fashion he loved his wife.

"Give me the babe," she said, "that it may lie once upon my breast."

They gave her the babe and she looked upon its dark eyes and said:

"Fairest of women shalt thou be, Gudruda—fair as no woman in Iceland ever was before thee; and thou shalt love with a mighty love—and thou shalt lose—and, losing, thou shalt find again."

Now, it is said that, as she spoke these words, her face grew bright as a spirit's, and, having spoken them, she fell back dead. And they laid her in earth, but Asmund mourned her much.

But, when all was over and done, the dream that he had dreamed lay heavy on him. Now of all diviners of dreams Groa was the most skilled, and when Gudruda had been in earth seven full days, Asmund went to Groa, though doubtfully, because of his oath.

He came to the house and entered. On a couch in the chamber lay Groa, and her babe was on her breast and she was very fair to see.

"Greeting, lord!" she said. "What wouldest thou here?"

"I have dreamed a dream, and thou alone canst read it."

"That is as it may be," she answered. "It is true that I have some skill in dreams. At the least I will hear it."

Then he unfolded it to her every word.

"What wilt thou give me if I read thy dream?" she said.

"What dost thou ask? Methinks I have given thee much."

"Yea, lord," and she looked at the babe upon her breast. "I ask but a little thing: that thou shalt take this bairn in thy arms, pour water over it and name it."

"Men will talk if I do this, for it is the father's part."

"It is a little thing what men say: talk goes by as the wind. Moreover, thou shalt give them the lie in the child's name, for it shall be Swanhild the Fatherless. Nevertheless that is my price. Pay it if thou wilt."

"Read me the dream and I will name the child."

"Nay, first name thou the babe: for then no harm shall come to her at thy hands."

So Asmund took the child, poured water over her, and named her.

Then Groa spoke: "This lord, is the reading of thy dream, else my wisdom is at fault: The silver dove is thy daughter Gudruda, the golden snake is my daughter Swanhild, and these two shall hate one the other and strive against each other. But the swan is a mighty man whom both shall love, and, if he love not both, yet shall belong to both. And thou shalt send him away; but he shall return and bring bad luck to thee and thy house, and thy daughter shall be blind with love of him. And in the end he shall slay the eagle, a great lord from the north who shall seek to wed thy daughter, and many another shall he slay, by the help of that raven with the bill of steel who shall be with him. But Swanhild shall triumph over thy daughter Gudruda, and this man, and the two of them, shall die at her hands, and, for the rest, who can say? But this is true—that the mighty man shall bring all thy race to an end. See now, I have read thy rede."

Then Asmund was very wroth. "Thou wast wise to beguile me to name thy bastard brat," he said; "else had I been its death within this hour."

"This thou canst not do, lord, seeing that thou hast held it in thy arms," Groa answered, laughing. "Go rather and lay out Gudruda the Fair on Coldback Hill; so shalt thou make an end of the evil, for Gudruda shall be its very root. Learn this, moreover: that thy dream does not tell all, seeing that thou thyself must play a part in the fate. Go, send forth the babe Gudruda, and be at rest."

"That cannot be, for I have sworn to cherish it, and with an oath that may not be broken."

"It is well," laughed Groa. "Things will befall as they are fated; let them befall in their season. There is space for cairns on Coldback and the sea can shroud its dead!"

And Asmund went thence, angered at heart.

II

HOW ERIC TOLD HIS LOVE TO GUDRUDA IN THE SNOW ON COLDBACK

Now, it must be told that, five years before the day of the death of Gudruda the Gentle, Saevuna, the wife of Thorgrimur Iron-Toe, gave birth to a son, at Coldback in the Marsh, on Ran River, and when his father came to look upon the child he called out aloud:

"Here we have a wondrous bairn, for his hair is yellow like gold and his eyes shine bright as stars." And Thorgrimur named him Eric Brighteyes.

Now, Coldback is but an hour's ride from Middalhof, and it chanced, in after years, that Thorgrimur went up to Middalhof, to keep the Yule feast and worship in the Temple, for he was in the priesthood of Asmund Asmundson, bringing the boy Eric with him. There also was Groa with Swanhild, for now she dwelt at Middalhof; and the three fair children were set together in the hall to play, and men thought it great sport to see them. Now, Gudruda had a horse of wood and would ride it while Eric pushed the horse along. But Swanhild smote her from the horse and called to Eric to make it move; but he comforted Gudruda and would not, and at that Swanhild was angry and lisped out:

"Push thou must, if I will it, Eric."

Then he pushed sideways and with such good will that Swanhild fell almost into the fire of the hearth, and, leaping up, she snatched a brand and threw it at Gudruda, firing her clothes. Men laughed at this; but Groa, standing apart, frowned and muttered witch-words.

"Why lookest thou so darkly, housekeeper?" said Asmund; "the boy is bonny and high of heart."

"Ah, he is bonny as no child is, and he shall be bonny all his life-days. Nevertheless, she shall not stand against his ill luck. This I prophesy of him: that women shall bring him to his end, and he shall die a hero's death, but not at the hand of his foes."

And now the years went by peacefully. Groa dwelt with her daughter Swanhild up at Middalhof and was the love of Asmund Asmundson. But, though he forgot his oath thus far, yet he would never take her to wife. The witchwife was angered at this, and she schemed and plotted much to bring it about that Asmund should wed her. But still he would not, though in all things else she led him as it were by a halter.

Twenty full years had gone by since Gudruda the Gentle was laid in earth; and now Gudruda the Fair and Swanhild the Fatherless were women too. Eric, too, was a man of five-and-twenty years, and no such man had lived in Iceland. For he was strong and great of stature, his hair was yellow as gold, and his grey eyes shone with the light of swords. He was gentle and loving as a woman, and even as a lad his strength was the strength of two men; and there were none in all the quarter who could leap or swim or wrestle against Eric Brighteyes. Men held him in honour and spoke well of him, though as yet he had done no deeds, but lived at home on Coldback, managing the farm, for now Thorgrimur Iron-Toe, his father, was dead. But women loved him much, and that was his bane—for of all women he loved but one, Gudruda the Fair, Asmund's daughter. He loved her from a child, and her alone till his day of death, and she, too, loved him and him only. For now Gudruda was a maid of maids, most beautiful to see and sweet to hear. Her hair, like the hair of Eric, was golden, and she was white as the snow on Hecla; but her eyes were large and dark, and black lashes drooped above them. For the rest she was tall and strong and comely, merry of face, yet tender, and the most witty of women.

Swanhild also was very fair; she was slender, small of limb, and dark of hue, having eyes blue as the deep sea, and brown curling hair, enough to veil her to the knees, and a mind of which none knew the end, for, though she was open in her talk, her thoughts were dark and secret. This was her joy: to draw the hearts of men to her and then to mock them. She beguiled many in this fashion, for she was the cunningest girl in matters of love, and she knew well the arts of women, with which they bring men to nothing. Nevertheless she was cold at heart, and desired power and wealth greatly, and she studied magic much, of which her mother Groa also had a store. But Swanhild, too, loved a man, and that was the joint in her harness by which the shaft of Fate entered her heart, for that man was Eric Brighteyes, who loved her not. But she desired him so sorely that, without him, all the world was dark to her, and her soul but as a ship driven rudderless upon a winter night. Therefore she put out all her strength to win him, and bent her witcheries upon him, and they were not few nor small. Nevertheless they went by him like the wind, for he dreamed ever of Gudruda alone, and he saw no eyes but hers, though as yet they spoke no word of love one to the other.

But Swanhild in her wrath took counsel with her mother Groa, though there was little liking between them; and, when she had heard the maiden's tale, Groa laughed aloud:

"Dost think me blind, girl?" she said; "all of this I have seen, yea and foreseen, and I tell thee thou art mad. Let this yeoman Eric go and I will find thee finer fowl to fly at."

"Nay, that I will not," quoth Swanhild: "for I love this man alone, and I would win him; and Gudruda I hate, and I would overthrow her. Give me of thy counsel."

Groa laughed again. "Things must be as they are fated. This now is my rede: Asmund would turn Gudruda's beauty to account, and that man must be rich in friends and money who gets her to wife, and in this matter the mind of Björn is as the mind of his father. Now we will watch, and, when a good time chances, we will bear tales of Gudruda to Asmund and to her brother Björn, and swear that she oversteps her modesty with Eric. Then shall Asmund be wroth and drive Eric from Gudruda's side. Meanwhile, I will do this: In the north there dwells a man mighty in all things and blown up with pride. He is named Ospakar Blacktooth. His wife is but lately dead, and he has given out that he will wed the fairest maid in Iceland. Now, it is in my mind to send Koll the Half-witted, my thrall, whom Asmund gave to me, to Ospakar as though by chance. He is a great talker and very clever, for in his half-wits is more cunning than in the brains of most; and he shall so bepraise Gudruda's beauty that Ospakar will come hither to ask her in marriage; and in this fashion, if things go well, thou shalt be rid of thy rival, and I of one who looks scornfully upon me. But, if this fail, then there are two roads left on which strong feet may travel to their end; and of these, one is that thou shouldest win Eric away with thine own beauty, and that is not little. All men are frail, and I have a draught that will make the heart as wax; but yet the other path is surer."

"And what is that path, my mother?"

"It runs through blood to blackness. By thy side is a knife and in Gudruda's bosom beats a heart. Dead women are unmeet for love!"

Swanhild tossed her head and looked upon the dark face of Groa her mother.

"Methinks, with such an end to win, I should not fear to tread that path, if there be need, my mother."

"Now I see thou art indeed my daughter. Happiness is to the bold. To each it comes in uncertain shape. Some love power, some wealth, and some—a man. Take that which thou lovest—I say, cut thy path to it and take it; else shall thy life be but a weariness: for what does it serve to win the wealth and power when thou lovest a man alone, or the man when thou dost desire gold and the pride of place? This is wisdom: to satisfy the longing of thy youth; for age creeps on apace and beyond is darkness. Therefore, if thou seekest this man, and Gudruda blocks thy path, slay her, girl—by witchcraft or by steel—and take him, and in his arms forget that thine own are red. But first let us try the easier plan. Daughter, I too hate this proud girl, who scorns me as her father's light-of-love. I too long to see that bright head of hers dull with the dust of death, or, at the least, those proud eyes weeping tears of shame as the man she hates leads her hence as a bride. Were it not for her I should be Asmund's wife, and, when she is gone, with thy help—for he loves thee much and has cause to love thee—this I may be yet. So in this matter, if in no other, let us go hand in hand and match our wits against her innocence."

Now, Koll the Half-witted went upon his errand, and the time passed till it lacked but a month to Yule, and men sat indoors, for the season was dark and much snow fell. At length came frost, and with it a clear sky, and Gudruda, ceasing from her spinning in the hall, went to the woman's porch, and, looking out, saw that the snow was hard, and a great longing came upon her to breathe the fresh air, for there was still an hour of daylight. So she threw a cloak about her and walked forth, taking the road towards Coldback in the Marsh that is by Ran River. But Swanhild watched her till she was over the hill. Then she also took a cloak and followed on that path, for she always watched Gudruda.

Gudruda walked on for the half of an hour or so, when she became aware that the clouds gathered in the sky, and that the air was heavy with snow to come. Seeing this she turned homewards, and Swanhild hid herself to let her pass. Now flakes floated down as big and soft as fifa flowers. Quicker and more quick they came till all the plain was one white maze of mist, but through it Gudruda walked on, and after her crept Swanhild, like a shadow. And now the darkness gathered and the snow fell thick and fast, covering up the track of her footsteps and she wandered from the path, and after her wandered Swanhild, being loath to show herself. For an hour or more Gudruda wandered and then she called aloud and her voice fell heavily against the cloak of snow. At the last she grew weary and frightened, and sat down upon a shelving rock whence the snow had slipped away. Now, a little way behind was another rock and there Swanhild sat, for she wished to be unseen of Gudruda. So some time passed, and Swanhild grew heavy as though with sleep, when of a sudden a moving thing loomed upon the snowy darkness. Then Gudruda leapt to her feet and called. A man's voice answered:

"Who passes there?"

"I, Gudruda, Asmund's daughter."

The form came nearer; now Swanhild could hear the snorting of a horse, and now a man leapt from it, and that man was Eric Brighteyes.

"Is it thou indeed, Gudruda!" he said with a laugh, and his great shape showed darkly on the snow mist.

"Oh, is it thou, Eric?" she answered. "I was never more joyed to see thee; for of a truth thou dost come in a good hour. A little while and I had seen thee no more, for my eyes grow heavy with the death-sleep."

"Nay, say not so. Art lost, then? Why, so am I. I came out to seek three horses that are strayed, and was overtaken by the snow. May they dwell in Odin's stables, for they have led me to thee. Art thou cold, Gudruda?"

"But a little, Eric. Yea, there is place for thee here on the rock."

So he sat down by her on the stone, and Swanhild crept nearer; for now all weariness had left her. But still the snow fell thick.

"It comes into my mind that we two shall die here," said Gudruda presently.

"Thinkest thou so?" he answered. "Well, I will say this, that I ask no better end."

"It is a bad end for thee, Eric: to be choked in snow, and with all thy deeds to do."

"It is a good end, Gudruda, to die at thy side, for so I shall die happy; but I grieve for thee."

"Grieve not for me, Brighteyes, worse things might befall."

He drew nearer to her, and now he put his arms about her and clasped her to his bosom; nor did she say him nay. Swanhild saw and lifted herself up behind them, but for a while she heard nothing but the beating of her heart.

"Listen, Gudruda," Eric said at last. "Death draws near to us, and before it comes I would speak to thee, if speak I may."

"Speak on," she whispers from his breast.

"This I would say, then: that I love thee, and that I ask no better fate than to die in thy arms."

"First shalt thou see me die in thine, Eric."

"Be sure, if that is so, I shall not tarry for long. Oh! Gudruda, since I was a child I have loved thee with a mighty love, and now thou art all to me. Better to die thus than to live without thee. Speak, then, while there is time."

"I will not hide from thee, Eric, that thy words are sweet in my ears."

And now Gudruda sobs and the tears fall fast from her dark eyes.

"Nay, weep not. Dost thou, then, love me?"

"Ay, sure enough, Eric."

"Then kiss me before we pass. A man should not die thus, and yet men have died worse."

And so these two kissed, for the first time, out in the snow on Coldback, and that first kiss was long and sweet.

Swanhild heard and her blood seethed within her as water seethes in a boiling spring when the fires wake beneath. She put her hand to her kirtle and gripped the knife at her side. She half drew it, then drove it back.

"Cold kills as sure as steel," she said in her heart. "If I slay her I cannot save myself or him. Let us die in peace, and let the snow cover up our troubling." And once more she listened.

"Ah, sweet," said Eric, "even in the midst of death there is hope of life. Swear to me, then, that if by chance we live thou wilt love me always as thou lovest me now."

"Ay, Eric, I swear that and readily."

"And swear, come what may, that thou wilt wed no man but me."

"I swear, if thou dost remain true to me, that I will wed none but thee, Eric."

"Then I am sure of thee."

"Boast not overmuch, Eric: if thou dost live thy days are all before thee, and with times come trials."

Now the snow whirled down faster and more thick, till these two, clasped heart to heart, were but a heap of white, and all white was the horse, and Swanhild was nearly buried.

"Where go we when we die, Eric?" said Gudruda; "in Odin's house there is no place for maids, and how shall my feet fare without thee?"

"Nay, sweet, my May, Valhalla shuts its gates to me, a deedless man; up Bifrost's rainbow bridge I may not travel, for I do not die with byrnie on breast and sword aloft. To Hela shall we go, and hand in hand."

"Art thou sure, Eric, that men find these abodes? To say sooth, at times I misdoubt me of them."

"I am not so sure but that I also doubt. Still, I know this: that where thou goest there I shall be, Gudruda."

"Then things are well, and well work the Norns.[*] Still, Eric, of a sudden I grow fey: for it comes upon me that I shall not die to-night, but that, nevertheless, I shall die with thy arms about me, and at thy side. There, I see it on the snow! I lie by thee, sleeping, and one comes with hands outstretched and sleep falls from them like a mist—by Freya, it is Swanhild's self! Oh! it is gone."

[*] The Northern Fates.

"It was nothing, Gudruda, but a vision of the snow—an untimely dream that comes before the sleep. I grow cold and my eyes are heavy; kiss me once again."

"It was no dream, Eric, and ever I doubt me of Swanhild, for I think she loves thee also, and she is fair and my enemy," says Gudruda, laying her snow-cold lips on his lips. "Oh, Eric, awake! awake! See, the snow is done."

He stumbled to his feet and looked forth. Lo! out across the sky flared the wild Northern fires, throwing light upon the darkness.

"Now it seems that I know the land," said Eric. "Look: yonder are Golden Falls, though we did not hear them because of the snow; and there, out at sea, loom the Westmans; and that dark thing is the Temple Hof, and behind it stands the stead. We are saved, Gudruda, and thus far indeed thou wast fey. Now rise, ere thy limbs stiffen, and I will set thee on the horse, if he still can run, and lead thee down to Middalhof before the witchlights fail us."

"So it shall be, Eric."

Now he led Gudruda to the horse—that, seeing its master, snorted and shook the snow from its coat, for it was not frozen—and set her on the saddle, and put his arm about her waist, and they passed slowly through the deep snow. And Swanhild, too, crept from her place, for her burning rage had kept the life in her, and followed after them. Many times she fell, and once she was nearly swallowed in a drift of snow and cried out in her fear.

"Who called aloud?" said Eric, turning; "I thought I heard a voice."

"Nay," answers Gudruda, "it was but a night-hawk screaming."

Now Swanhild lay quiet in the drift, but she said in her heart:

"Ay, a night-hawk that shall tear out those dark eyes of thine, mine enemy!"

The two go on and at length they come to the banked roadway that runs past the Temple to Asmund's hall. Here Swanhild leaves them, and, climbing over the turf-wall into the home meadow, passes round the hall by the outbuildings and so comes to the west end of the house, and enters by the men's door unnoticed of any. For all the people, seeing a horse coming and a woman seated on it, were gathered in front of the hall. But Swanhild ran to that shut bed where she slept, and, closing the curtain, threw off her garments, shook the snow from her hair, and put on a linen kirtle. Then she rested a while, for she was weary, and, going to the kitchen, warmed herself at the fire.

Meanwhile Eric and Gudruda came to the house and there Asmund greeted them well, for he was troubled in his heart about his daughter, and very glad to know her living, seeing that men had but now begun to search for her, because of the snow and the darkness.

Now Gudruda told her tale, but not all of it, and Asmund bade Eric to the house. Then one asked about Swanhild, and Eric said that he had seen nothing of her, and Asmund was sad at this, for he loved Swanhild. But as he told all men to go and search, an old wife came and said that Swanhild was in the kitchen, and while the carline spoke she came into the hall, dressed in white, very pale, and with shining eyes and fair to see.

"Where hast thou been, Swanhild?" said Asmund. "I thought certainly thou wast perishing with Gudruda in the snow, and now all men go to seek thee while the witchlights burn."

"Nay, foster-father, I have been to the Temple," she answered, lying. "So Gudruda has but narrowly escaped the snow, thanks be to Brighteyes yonder! Surely I am glad of it, for we could ill spare our sweet sister," and, going up to her, she kissed her. But Gudruda saw that her eyes burned like fire and felt that her lips were cold as ice, and shrank back wondering.

III

HOW ASMUND BADE ERIC TO HIS YULE-FEAST

Now it was supper-time and men sat at meat while the women waited upon them. But as she went to and fro, Gudruda always looked at Eric, and Swanhild watched them both. Supper being over, people gathered round the hearth, and, having finished her service, Gudruda came and sat by Eric, so that her sleeve might touch his. They spoke no word, but there they sat and were happy. Swanhild saw and bit her lip. Now, she was seated by Asmund and Björn his son.

"Look, foster-father," she said; "yonder sit a pretty pair!"

"That cannot be denied," answered Asmund. "One may ride many days to see such another man as Eric Brighteyes, and no such maid as Gudruda flowers between Middalhof and London town, unless it be thou, Swanhild. Well, so her mother said that it should be, and without doubt she was foresighted at her death."

"Nay, name me not with Gudruda, foster-father; I am but a grey goose by thy white swan. But these shall be well wed and that will be a good match for Eric."

"Let not thy tongue run on so fast," said Asmund sharply. "Who told thee that Eric should have Gudruda?"

"None told me, but in truth, having eyes and ears, I grew certain of it," said Swanhild. "Look at them now: surely lovers wear such faces."

Now it chanced that Gudruda had rested her chin on her hand, and was gazing into Eric's eyes beneath the shadow of her hair.

"Methinks my sister will look higher than to wed a simple yeoman, though he is large as two other men," said Björn with a sneer. Now Björn was jealous of Eric's strength and beauty, and did not love him.

"Trust nothing that thou seest and little that thou hearest, girl," said Asmund, raising himself from thought: "so shall thy guesses be good. Eric, come here and tell us how thou didst chance on Gudruda in the snow."

"I was not so ill seated but that I could bear to stay," grumbled Eric beneath his breath; but Gudruda said "Go."

So he went and told his tale; but not all of it, for he intended to ask Gudruda in marriage on the morrow, though his heart prophesied no luck in the matter, and therefore he was not overswift with it.

"In this thing thou hast done me and mine good service," said Asmund coldly, searching Eric's face with his blue eyes. "It had been said if my fair daughter had perished in the snow, for, know this: I would set her high in marriage, for her honour and the honour of my house, and so some rich and noble man had lost great joy. But take thou this gift in memory of the deed, and Gudruda's husband shall give thee another such upon the day that he makes her wife," and he drew a gold ring off his arm.

Now Eric's knees trembled as he heard, and his heart grew faint as though with fear. But he answered clear and straight:

"Thy gift had been better without thy words, ring-giver; but I pray thee to take it back, for I have done nothing to win it, though perhaps the time will come when I shall ask thee for a richer."

"My gifts have never been put away before," said Asmund, growing angry.

"This wealthy farmer holds the good gold of little worth. It is foolish to take fish to the sea, my father," sneered Björn.

"Nay, Björn, not so," Eric answered: "but, as thou sayest, I am but a farmer, and since my father, Thorgrimur Iron-Toe, died things have not gone too well on Ran River. But at the least I am a free man, and I will take no gifts that I cannot repay worth for worth. Therefore I will not have the ring."

"As thou wilt," said Asmund. "Pride is a good horse if thou ridest wisely," and he thrust the ring back upon his arm.

Then people go to rest; but Swanhild seeks her mother, and tells her all that has befallen her, nor does Groa fail to listen.

"Now I will make a plan," she says, "for these things have chanced well and Asmund is in a ripe humour. Eric shall come no more to Middalhof till Gudruda is gone hence, led by Ospakar Blacktooth."

"And if Eric does not come here, how shall I see his face? for, mother, I long for the sight of it."

"That is thy matter, thou lovesick fool. Know this: that if Eric comes hither and gets speech with Gudruda, there is an end of thy hopes; for, fair as thou art, she is too fair for thee, and, strong as thou art, in a way she is too strong. Thou hast heard how these two love, and such loves mock at the will of fathers. Eric will win his desire or die beneath the swords of Asmund and Björn, if such men can prevail against his might. Nay, the wolf Eric must be fenced from the lamb till he grows hungry. Then let him search the fold and make spoil of thee, for, when the best is gone, he will desire the good."

"So be it, mother. As I sat crouched behind Gudruda in the snow at Coldback, I had half a mind to end her love-words with this knife, for so I should have been free of her."

"Yes, and fast in the doom-ring, thou wildcat. The gods help this Eric, if thou winnest him. Nay, choose thy time and, if thou must strike, strike secretly and home. Remember also that cunning is mightier than strength, that lies pierce further than swords, and that witchcraft wins where honesty must fail. Now I will go to Asmund, and he shall be an angry man before to-morrow comes."

Then Groa went to the shut bed where Asmund the Priest slept. He was sitting on the bed and asked her why she came.

"For love of thee, Asmund, and thy house, though thou dost treat me ill, who hast profited so much by me and my foresight. Say now: wilt thou that this daughter of thine, Gudruda the Fair, should be the light May of yonder long-legged yeoman?"

"That is not in my mind," said Asmund, stroking his beard.

"Knowest thou, then, that this very day your white Gudruda sat on Eric's lap in the snow, while he fondled her to his heart's content?"

"Most likely it was for warmth. Men do not dream on love in the hour of death. Who saw this?"

"Swanhild, who was behind, and hid herself for shame, and therefore she held that these two must soon be wed! Ah, thou art foolish now, Asmund. Young blood makes light of cold or death. Art thou blind, or dost thou not see that these two turn on each other like birds at nesting-time?"

"They might do worse," said Asmund, "for they are a proper pair, and it seems to me that each was born for each."

"Then all goes well. Still, it is a pity to see so fair a maid cast like rotten bait upon the waters to hook this troutlet of a yeoman. Thou hast enemies, Asmund; thou art too prosperous, and there are many who hate thee for thy state and wealth. Were it not wise to use this girl of thine to build a wall about thee against the evil day?"

"I have been more wont, housekeeper, to trust to my own arm than to bought friends. But tell me, for at the least thou art far-seeing, how may this be done? As things are, though I spoke roughly to him last night, I am inclined to let Eric Brighteyes take Gudruda. I have always loved the lad, and he will go far."

"Listen, Asmund! Surely thou hast heard of Ospakar Blacktooth—the priest who dwells in the north?"

"Ay, I have heard of him, and I know him; there is no man like him for ugliness, or strength, or wealth and power. We sailed together on a viking cruise many years ago, and he did things at which my blood turned, and in those days I had no chicken heart."

"With time men change their temper. Unless I am mistaken, this Ospakar wishes above all to have Gudruda in marriage, for, now that everything is his, this alone is left for him to ask—the fairest woman in Iceland as a housewife. Think then, with Ospakar for a son-in-law, who is there that can stand against thee?"

"I am not so sure of this matter, nor do I altogether trust thee, Groa. Of a truth it seems to me that thou hast some stake upon the race. This Ospakar is evil and hideous. It were a shame to give Gudruda over to him when she looks elsewhere.

Knowest thou that I swore to love and cherish her, and how runs this with my oath? If Eric is not too rich, yet he is of good birth and kin, and, moreover, a man of men. If he take her good will come of it."

"It is like thee, Asmund, always to mistrust those who spend their days in plotting for thy weal. Do as thou wilt: let Eric take this treasure of thine—for whom earls would give their state—and live to rue it. But I say this: if he have thy leave to roam here with his dove the matter will soon grow, for these two sicken each to each, and young blood is hot and ill at waiting, and it is not always snow-time. So betroth her or let him go. And now I have said."

"Thy tongue runs too fast. The man is quite unproved and I will try him. To-morrow I will warn him from my door; then things shall go as they are fated. And now peace, for I weary of thy talk, and, moreover, it is false; for thou lackest one thing—a little honesty to season all thy craft. What fee has Ospakar paid thee, I wonder. Thou at least hadst never refused the gold ring to-night, for thou wouldst do much for gold."

"And more for love, and most of all for hate," Groa said, and laughed aloud; nor did they speak more on this matter that night.

Now, early in the morning Asmund rose, and, going to the hall, awoke Eric, who slept by the centre hearth, saying that he would talk with him without. Then Eric followed him to the back of the hall.

"Say now, Eric," he said, when they stood in the grey light outside the house, "who was it taught thee that kisses keep out the cold on snowy days?"

Now Eric reddened to his yellow hair, but he answered: "Who was it told thee, lord, that I tried this medicine?"

"The snow hides much, but there are eyes that can pierce the snow. Nay, more, thou wast seen, and there's an end. Now know this—I like thee well, but Gudruda is not for thee; she is far above thee, who art but a deedless yeoman."

"Then I love to no end," said Eric; "I long for one thing only, and that is Gudruda. It was in my mind to ask her in marriage of thee to-day."

"Then, lad, thou hast thy answer before thou askest. Be sure of one thing: if but once again I find thee alone with Gudruda, it is my axe shall kiss thee and not her lips."

"That may yet be put to the proof, lord," said Eric, and turned to seek his horse, when suddenly Gudruda came and stood between them, and his heart leapt at the sight of her.

"Listen, Gudruda," Eric said. "This is thy father's word: that we two speak together no more."

"Then it is an ill saying for us," said Gudruda, laying her hand upon her breast.

"Saying good or ill, so it surely is, girl," answered Asmund. "No more shalt thou go a-kissing, in the snow or in the flowers."

"Now I seem to hear Swanhild's voice," she said. "Well, such things have happened to better folk, and a father's wish is to a maid what the wind is to the grass. Still, the sun is behind the cloud and it will shine again some day. Till then, Eric, fare thee well!"

"It is not thy will, lord," said Eric, "that I should come to thy Yule-feast as thou hast asked me these ten years past?"

Now Asmund grew wroth, and pointed with his hand towards the great Golden Falls that thunder down the mountain named Stonefell that is behind Middalhof, and there are no greater water-falls in Iceland.

"A man may take two roads, Eric, from Coldback to Middalhof, one by the bridle-path over Coldback and the other down Golden Falls; but I never knew traveller to choose this way. Now, I bid thee to my feast by the path over Golden Falls; and, if thou comest that way, I promise thee this: if thou livest I will greet thee well, and if I find thee dead in the great pool I will bind on thy Hell-shoes and lay thee to earth neighbourly fashion. But if thou comest by any other path, then my thralls shall cut thee down at my door." And he stroked his beard and laughed.

Now Asmund spoke thus mockingly because he did not think it possible that any man should try the path of the Golden Falls.

Eric smiled and said, "I hold thee to thy word, lord; perhaps I shall be thy guest at Yule."

But Gudruda heard the thunder of the mighty Falls as the wind turned, and cried "Nay, nay—it were thy death!"

Then Eric finds his horse and rides away across the snow.

Now it must be told of Koll the Half-witted that at length he came to Swinefell in the north, having journeyed hard across the snow. Here Ospakar Blacktooth had his great hall, in which day by day a hundred men sat down to meat. Now Koll entered the hall when Ospakar was at supper, and looked at him with big eyes, for he had never seen so wonderful a man. He was huge in stature—his hair was black, and black his beard, and on his lower lip there lay a great black fang. His eyes were small and narrow, but his cheekbones were set wide apart and high, like those of a horse. Koll thought him an ill man to deal with and half a troll,[*] and grew afraid of his errand, since in Koll's half-wittedness there was much cunning—for it was a cloak in which he wrapped himself. But as Ospakar sat in the high seat, clothed in a purple robe, with his sword Whitefire on his knee, he saw Koll, and called out in a great voice:

[*] An able-bodied Goblin.

"Who is this red fox that creeps into my earth?"

For, to look at, Koll was very like a fox.

"My name is Koll the Half-witted, Groa's thrall, lord. Am I welcome here?" he answered.

"That is as it may be. Why do they call thee half-witted?"

"Because I love not work overmuch, lord."

"Then all my thralls are fellow to thee. Say, what brings thee here?"

"This lord. It was told among men down in the south that thou wouldst give a good gift to him who should discover to thee the fairest maid in Iceland. So I asked leave of my mistress to come on a journey and tell thee of her."

"Then a lie was told thee. Still, I love to hear of fair maids, and seek one for a wife if she be but fair enough. So speak on, Koll the Fox, and lie not to me, I warn thee, else I will knock what wits are left there from that red head of thine."

So Koll took up the tale and greatly bepraised Gudruda's beauty; nor in truth, for all his talk, could he praise it too much. He told of her dark eyes and the whiteness of her skin, of the nobleness of her shape and the gold of her hair, of her wit and gentleness, till at length Ospakar grew afire to see this flower of maids.

"By Thor, thou Koll," he said, "if the girl be but half of what thou sayest, her luck is good, for she shall be wife to Ospakar. But if thou hast lied to me about her, beware! for soon there shall be a knave the less in Iceland."

Now a man rose in the hall and said that Koll spoke truth, for he had seen Gudruda the Fair, Asmund's daughter, and there was no maid like her in Iceland.

"I will do this now," said Blacktooth. "To-morrow I will send a messenger to Middalhof, saying to Asmund the Priest that I purpose to visit him at the time of the Yule-feast; then I shall see if the girl pleases me. Meanwhile, Koll, take thou a seat among the thralls, and here is something for thy pains," and he took off the purple cloak and threw it to him.

"Thanks to thee, Gold-scatterer," said Koll. "It is wise to go soon to Middalhof, for such a bloom as this maid does not lack a bee. There is a youngling in the south, named Eric Brighteyes, who loves Gudruda, and she, I think, loves him, though he is but a yeoman of small wealth and is only twenty-five years old."

"Ho! ho!" laughed great Ospakar, "and I am forty-five. But let not this suckling cross my desire, lest men call him Eric Holloweyes!"

Now the messenger of Ospakar came to Middalhof, and his words pleased Asmund and he made ready a great feast. And Swanhild smiled, but Gudruda was afraid.

IV

HOW ERIC CAME DOWN GOLDEN FALLS

Now Ospakar rode up to Middalhof on the day before the Yule-feast. He was splendidly apparelled, and with him came his two sons, Gizur the Lawman and Mord, young men of promise, and many armed thralls and servants. Gudruda, watching at the women's door, saw his face in the moonlight and loathed him.

"What thinkest thou of him who comes to seek thee in marriage, foster-sister?" asked Swanhild, watching at her side.

"I think he is like a troll, and that, seek as he will, he shall not find me. I had rather lie in the pool beneath Golden Falls than in Ospakar's hall."

"That shall be proved," said Swanhild. "At the least he is rich and noble, and the greatest of men in size. It would go hard with Eric were those arms about him."

"I am not so sure of that," said Gudruda; "but it is not likely to be known."

"Comes Eric to the feast by the road of Golden Falls, Gudruda?"

"Nay, no man may try that path and live."

"Then he will die, for Eric will risk it."

Now Gudruda thought, and a great fire burned in her heart and shone through her eyes. "If Eric dies," she said, "on thee be his blood, Swanhild—on thee and that dark mother of thine, for ye have plotted to bring this evil on us. How have I harmed thee that thou shouldst deal thus with me?"

Swanhild turned white and wicked-looking, for passion mastered her, and she gazed into Gudruda's face and answered: "How hast thou harmed me? Surely I will tell thee. Thy beauty has robbed me of Eric's love."

"It would be better to prate of Eric's love when he had told it thee, Swanhild."

"Thou hast robbed me and therefore I hate thee, and therefore I will deliver thee to Ospakar, whom thou dost loath—ay and yet win Brighteyes to myself. Am I not also fair and can I not also love, and shall I see thee snatch my joy? By the Gods, never! I will see thee dead, and Eric with thee, ere it shall be so! but first I will see thee shamed!"

"Thy words are ill-suited to a maiden's lips, Swanhild! But of this be sure: I fear thee not, and shall never fear thee. And one thing I know well that, whether thou or I prevail, in the end thou shalt harvest the greatest shame, and in times to come men shall speak of thee with hatred and name thee by ill names. Moreover, Eric shall never love thee; from year to year he shall hate thee with a deeper hate, though it may well be that thou wilt bring ruin on him. And now I thank thee that thou hast told me all thy mind, showing me what indeed thou art!" And Gudruda turned scornfully upon her heel and walked away.

Now Asmund the Priest went out into the courtyard, and meeting Ospakar Blacktooth, greeted him heartily, though he did not like his looks, and took him by the hand and led him to the hall, that was bravely decked with tapestries, and seated him by his side on the high seat. And Ospakar's thralls brought good gifts for Asmund, who thanked the giver well.

Now it was supper time, and Gudruda came in, and after her walked Swanhild. Ospakar gazed hard at Gudruda and a great desire entered into him to make her his wife. But she passed coldly by, nor looked on him at all.

"This, then, is that maid of thine of whom I have heard tell, Asmund? I will say this: fairer was never born of woman."

Then men ate and Ospakar drank much ale, but all the while he stared at Gudruda and listened for her voice. But as yet he said nothing of what he came to seek, though all knew his errand. And his two sons, Gizur and Mord, stared also at Gudruda, for they thought her most wonderfully fair. But Gizur found Swanhild also fair.

And so the night wore on till it was time to sleep.

On this same day Eric rode up from his farm on Ran River and took his road along the brow of Coldback till he came to Stonefell. Now all along Coldback and Stonefell is a steep cliff facing to the south, that grows ever higher till it comes to that point where Golden River falls over it and, parting its waters below, runs east and west—the branch to the east being called Ran River and that to the west Laxà—for these two streams girdle round the rich plain of Middalhof, till at length they reach the sea. But in the midst of Golden River, on the edge of the cliff, a mass of rock juts up called Sheep-saddle, dividing the waters of the fall, and over this the spray flies, and in winter the ice gathers, but the river does not cover it. The great fall is thirty fathoms deep, and shaped like a horseshoe, of which the points lie towards Middalhof. Yet if he could but gain the Sheep-saddle rock that divides the midst of the waters, a strong and hardy man might climb down some fifteen fathoms of this depth and scarcely wet his feet.

Now here at the foot of Sheep-saddle rock the double arches of waters meet, and fall in one torrent into the bottomless pool below. But, some three fathoms from this point of the meeting waters, and beneath it, just where the curve is deepest, a single crag, as large as a drinking-table and no larger, juts through the foam, and, if a man could reach it, he might leap from it some twelve fathoms, sheer into the spray-hidden pit beneath, there to sink or swim as it might befall. This crag is called Wolf's Fang.

Now Eric stood for a long while on the edge of the fall and looked, measuring every thing with his eye. Then he went up above, where the river swirls down to the precipice, and looked again, for it is from this bank that the dividing island-rock Sheep-saddle must be reached.

"A man may hardly do this thing; yet I will try it," he said to himself at last. "My honour shall be great for the feat, if I chance to live, and if I die—well, there is an end of troubling after maids and all other things."

So he went home and sat silent that evening. Now, since Thorgrimur Iron-Toe's death, his housewife, Saevuna, Eric's mother, had grown dim of sight, and, though she peered and peered again from her seat in the ingle nook, she could not see the face of her son.

"What ails thee, Eric, that thou sittest so silent? Was not the meat, then, to thy mind at supper?"

"Yes, mother, the meat was well enough, though a little undersmoked."

"Now I see that thou art not thyself, son, for thou hadst no meat, but only stock-fish—and I never knew a man forget his supper on the night of its eating, except he was distraught or deep in love."

"Was it so?" said Brighteyes.

"What troubles thee, Eric?—that sweet lass yonder?"

"Ay, somewhat, mother."

"What more, then?"

"This, that I go down Golden Falls to-morrow, and I do not know how I may come from Sheep-saddle rock to Wolf's Fang crag and keep my life whole in me; and now, I pray thee, weary me not with words, for my brain is slow, and I must use it."

When she heard this Saevuna screamed aloud, and threw herself before Eric, praying him to forgo his mad venture. But he would not listen to her, for he was slow to make up his mind, but, that being made up, nothing could change it. Then, when she learned that it was to get sight of Gudruda that he purposed thus to throw his life away, she was very angry and cursed her and all her kith and kin.

"It is likely enough that thou wilt have cause to use such words before all this tale is told," said Eric; "nevertheless, mother, forbear to curse Gudruda, who is in no way to blame for these matters."

"Thou art a faithless son," Saevuna said, "who wilt slay thyself striving to win speech with thy May, and leave thy mother childless."

Eric said that it seemed so indeed, but he was plighted to it and the feat must be tried. Then he kissed her, and she sought her bed, weeping.

Now it was the day of the Yule-feast, and there was no sun till one hour before noon. But Eric, having kissed his mother and bidden her farewell, called a thrall, Jon by name, and giving him a sealskin bag full of his best apparel, bade him ride to Middalhof and tell Asmund the Priest that Eric Brighteyes would come down Golden Falls an hour after mid-day, to join his feast; and thence go to the foot of the Golden Falls, to await him there. And the man went, wondering, for he thought his master mad.

Then Eric took a good rope, and a staff tipped with iron, and, so soon as the light served, mounted his horse, forded Ran River, and rode along Coldback till he came to the lip of Golden Falls. Here he stayed a while till at length he saw many people streaming up the snow from Middalhof far beneath, and, among them, two women who by their stature should be Gudruda and Swanhild, and, near to them, a great man whom he did not know. Then he showed himself for a space on the brink of the gulf and turned his horse up stream. The sun shone bright upon the edge of the sky, but the frost bit like a sword. Still, he must strip off his garments, so that nothing remained on him except his sheepskin shoes, shirt and hose, and take the water. Now here the river runs mightily, and he must cross full thirty fathoms of the swirling water before he can reach Sheep-saddle, and woe to him if his foot slip on the boulders, for certainly he must be swept over the brink.

Eric rested the staff against the stony bottom and, leaning his weight on it, took the stream, and he was so strong that it could not prevail against him till at length he was rather more than half-way across and the water swept above his shoulders. Now he was lifted from his feet and, letting the staff float, he swam for his life, and with such mighty strokes that he felt little of that icy cold. Down he was swept—now the lip of the fall was but three fathoms away on his left, and already the green water boiled beneath him. A fathom from him was the corner of Sheep-saddle. If he may grasp it, all is well; if not, he dies.

Three great strokes and he held it. His feet were swept out over the brink of the fall, but he clung on grimly, and by the strength of his arms drew himself on to the rock and rested a while. Presently he stood up, for the cold began to nip him, and the people below became aware that he had swum the river above the fall and raised a shout, for the deed was great. Now Eric must begin to clamber down Sheep-saddle, and this was no easy task, for the rock is almost sheer, and slippery with ice, and on either side the waters rushed and thundered, throwing their blinding spray about him as they leapt to the depths beneath. He looked down, studying the rock; then, feeling that he grew afraid, made an end of doubt and, grasping a point with both hands, swung himself down his own length and more. Now for many minutes he climbed down Sheep-saddle, and the task was hard, for he was bewildered with the booming of the waters that bent out on either side of him like the arc of a bow, and the rock was very steep and slippery. Still, he came down all those fifteen fathoms and fell not, though twice he was near to falling, and the watchers below marvelled greatly at his hardihood.

"He will be dashed to pieces where the waters meet," said Ospakar, "he can never gain Wolf's Fang crag beneath; and, if so it be that he come there and leaps to the pool, the weight of water will drive him down and drown him."

"It is certainly so," quoth Asmund, "and it grieves me much; for it was my jest that drove him to this perilous adventure, and we cannot spare such a man as Eric Brighteyes."

Now Swanhild turned white as death; but Gudruda said: "If great heart and strength and skill may avail at all, then Eric shall come safely down the waters."

"Thou fool!" whispered Swanhild in her ear, "how can these help him? No troll could live in yonder cauldron. Dead is Eric, and thou art the bait that lured him to his death!"

"Spare thy words," she answered; "as the Norns have ordered so it shall be."

Now Eric stood at the foot of Sheep-saddle, and within an arm's length the mighty waters met, tossing their yellow waves and seething furiously as they leapt to the mist-hid gulf beneath. He bent over and looked through the spray. Three fathoms under him the rock Wolf's Fang split the waters, and thence, if he can come thither, he may leap sheer into the pool below. Now he unwound the rope that was about his middle, and made one end fast to a knob of rock—and this was difficult, for his hands were stiff with cold—and the other end he passed through his leathern girdle. Then Eric looked again, and his heart sank within him. How might he give himself to this boiling flood and not be shattered? But as he looked, lo! a rainbow grew upon the face of the water, and one end of it lit upon him, and the other, like a glory from the Gods, fell full upon Gudruda as she stood a little way apart, watching at the foot of Golden Falls.

"Seest thou that," said Asmund to Groa, who was at his side, "the Gods build their Bifrost bridge between these two. Who now shall keep them asunder?"

"Read the portent thus," she answered: "they shall be united, but not here. Yon is a Spirit bridge, and, see: the waters of Death foam and fall between them!"

Eric, too, saw the omen and it seemed good to him, and all fear left his heart. Round about him the waters thundered, but amidst their roar he dreamed that he heard a voice calling:

"Be of good cheer, Eric Brighteyes; for thou shalt live to do mightier deeds than this, and in guerdon thou shalt win Gudruda."

So he paused no longer, but, shortening up the rope, pulled on it with all his strength, and then leapt out upon the arch of waters. They struck him and he was dashed out like a stone from a sling; again he fell against them and again was dashed away, so that his girdle burst. Eric felt it go and clung wildly to the rope and lo! with the inward swing, he fell on Wolf's Fang, where never a man has stood before and never a man shall stand again. Eric lay a little while on the rock till his breath came back to him, and he listened to the roar of the waters. Then, rising on his hands and knees, he crept to its point, for he could scarcely stand because of the trembling of the stone beneath the shock of the fall; and when the people below saw that he was not dead, they raised a great shout, and the sound of their voices came to him through the noise of the waters.

Now, twelve fathoms beneath him was the surface of the pool; but he could not see it because of the wreaths of spray. Nevertheless, he must leap and that swiftly, for he grew cold. So of a sudden Eric stood up to his full height, and, with a loud cry and a mighty spring, bounded out from the point of Wolf's Fang far into the air, beyond the reach of the falling flood, and rushed headlong towards the gulf beneath. Now all men watching held their breath as his body travelled, and so great is the place and so high the leap that through the mist Eric seemed but as a big white stone hurled down the face of the arching waters.

He was gone, and the watchers rushed down to the foot of the pool, for there, if he rose at all, he must pass to the shallows. Swanhild could look no more, but sank upon the ground. The face of Gudruda was set like a stone with doubt and anguish. Ospakar saw and read the meaning, and he said to himself: "Now Odin grant that this youngling rise not again! for the maid loves him dearly, and he is too much a man to be lightly swept aside."

Eric struck the pool. Down he sank, and down and down—for the water falling from so far must almost reach the bottom of the pool before it can rise again—and he with it. Now he touched the bottom, but very gently, and slowly began to rise, and, as he rose, was carried along by the stream. But it was long before he could breathe, and it seemed to him that his lungs would burst. Still, he struggled up, striking great strokes with his legs.

"Farewell to Eric," said Asmund, "he will rise no more now."

But just as he spoke Gudruda pointed to something that gleamed, white and golden, beneath the surface of the current, and lo! the bright hair of Eric rose from the water, and he drew a great breath, shaking his head like a seal, and, though but feebly, struck out for the shallows that are at the foot of the pool. Now he found footing, but was swept over by the fierce current, and cut his forehead, and he carried that scar till his death. Again he rose, and with a rush gained the bank unaided and fell upon the snow.

Now people gathered about him in silence and wondering, for none had known so great a deed. And presently Eric opened his eyes and looked up, and found the eyes of Gudruda fixed on his, and there was that in them which made him glad he had dared the path of Golden Falls.

V

HOW ERIC WON THE SWORD WHITEFIRE

Now Asmund the priest bent down, and Eric saw him and spoke:

"Thou badest me to thy Yule-feast, lord, by yonder slippery road and I have come. Dost thou welcome me well?"

"No man better," quoth Asmund. "Thou art a gallant man, though foolhardy; and thou hast done a deed that shall be told of while skalds sing and men live in Iceland."

"Make place, my father," said Gudruda, "for Eric bleeds." And she loosed the kerchief from her neck and bound it about his wounded brow, and, taking the rich cloak from her body, threw it on his shoulders, and no man said her nay.

Then they led him to the hall, where Eric clothed himself and rested, and he sent back the thrall Jon to Coldback, bidding him tell Saevuna, Eric's mother, that he was safe. But he was somewhat weak all that day, and the sound of waters roared in his ears.

Now Ospakar and Groa were ill pleased at the turn things had taken; but all the others rejoiced much, for Eric was well loved of men and they had grieved if the waters had prevailed against his might. But Swanhild brooded bitterly, for Eric never turned to look on her.

The hour of the feast drew on and, according to custom, it was held in the Temple, and thither went all men. When they were seated in the nave of the Hof, the fat ox that had been made ready for sacrifice was led in and dragged before the altar on which the holy fire burned. Now Asmund the Priest slew it, amid silence, before the figures of the Gods, and, catching its blood in the blood-bowl, sprinkled the altar and all the worshippers with the blood-twigs. Then the ox was cut up, and the figures of the almighty Gods were anointed with its molten fat and wiped with fair linen. Next the flesh was boiled in the cauldrons that were hung over fires lighted all down the nave, and the feast began.

Now men ate, and drank much ale and mead, and all were merry. But Ospakar Blacktooth grew not glad, though he drank much, for he saw that the eyes of Gudruda ever watched Eric's face and that they smiled on each other. He was wroth at this, for he knew that the bait must be good and the line strong that should win this fair fish to his angle, and as he sat, unknowingly his fingers loosed the peace-strings of his sword Whitefire, and he half drew it, so that its brightness flamed in the firelight.

"Thou hast a wondrous blade there, Ospakar!" said Asmund, "though this is no place to draw it. Whence came it? Methinks no such swords are fashioned now."

"Ay, Asmund, a wondrous blade indeed. There is no other such in the world, for the dwarfs forged it of old, and he shall be unconquered who holds it aloft. This was King Odin's sword, and it is named Whitefire. Ralph the Red took it from King Eric's cairn in Norway, and he strove long with the Barrow-Dweller[*] before he wrenched it from his grasp. But my father won it and slew Ralph, though he had never done this had Whitefire been aloft against him. But Ralph the Red, being in drink when the ships met in battle, fought with an axe, and was slain by my father, and since then Whitefire has been the last light that many a chief's eyes have seen. Look at it, Asmund."

[*] The ghost in the cairn.

Now he drew the great sword, and men were astonished as it flashed aloft. Its hilt was of gold, and blue stones were set therein. It measured two ells and a half from crossbar to point, and so bright was the broad blade that no one could look on it for long, and all down its length ran runes.

"A wondrous weapon, truly!" said Asmund. "How read the runes?"

"I know not, nor any man—they are ancient."

"Let me look at them," said Groa, "I am skilled in runes." Now she took the sword, and heaved it up, and looked at the runes and said, "A strange writing truly."

"How runs it, housekeeper?" said Asmund.

"Thus, lord, if my skill is not at fault:—

"Whitefire is my name—
Dwarf-folk forged me—
Odin's sword was I—
Eric's sword was I—
Eric's sword shall I be—
And where I fall there he must follow me."

Now Gudruda looked at Eric Brighteyes wonderingly, and Ospakar saw it and became very angry.

"Look not so, maiden," he said, "for it shall be another Eric than yon flapper-duck who holds Whitefire aloft, though it may very well chance that he shall feel its edge."

Now Gudruda bit her lip, and Eric burned red to the brow and spoke:

"It is ill, lord, to throw taunts like an angry woman. Thou art great and strong, yet I may dare a deed with thee."

"Peace, boy! Thou canst climb a waterfall well, I gainsay it not; but beware ere thou settest up thyself against my strength. Say now, what game wilt thou play with Ospakar?"

"I will go on holmgang with thee, byrnie-clad or baresark,[*] and fight thee with axe or sword, or I will wrestle with thee, and Whitefire yonder shall be the winner's prize."

[*] To a duel, usually fought, in mail or without it, on an island—"holm"—within a circle of hazel-twigs.

"Nay, I will have no bloodshed here at Middalhof," said Asmund sternly. "Make play with fists, or wrestle if ye will, for that were great sport to see; but weapons shall not be drawn."

Now Ospakar grew mad with anger and drink—and he grinned like a dog, till men saw the red gums beneath his lips.

"Thou wilt wrestle with me, youngling—with me whom no man has ever so much as lifted from my feet? Good! I will lay thee on thy face and whip thee, and Whitefire shall be the stake—I swear it on the holy altar-ring; but what hast thou to set against the precious sword? Thy poor hovel and its lot of land shall be all too little."

"I set my life on it; if I lose Whitefire let Whitefire slay me," said Eric.

"Nay, that I will not have, and I am master here in this Temple," said Asmund. "Bethink thee of some other stake, Ospakar, or let the game be off."

Now Ospakar gnawed his lip with his black fang and thought. Then he laughed aloud and spoke:

"Bright is Whitefire and thou art named Brighteyes. See now: I set the great sword against thy right eye, and, if I win the match, it shall be mine to tear it out. Wilt thou play this game with me? If thy heart fails thee, let it go; but I will set no other stake against my good sword."

"Eyes and limbs are a poor man's wealth," said Eric: "so be it. I stake my right eye against the sword Whitefire, and we will try the match to-morrow."

"And to-morrow night thou shalt be called Eric One-eye," said Ospakar—at which some few of his thralls laughed.

But most of the men did not laugh, for they thought this an ill game and a worst jest.

Now the feast went on, and Asmund rose from his high seat in the centre of the nave, on the left hand looking down from the altar, and gave out the holy toasts. First men drank a full horn to Odin, praying for triumph on their foes. Then they drank to Frey, asking for plenty; to Thor, for strength in battle; to Freya, Goddess of Love (and to her Eric drank heartily); to the memory of the dead; and, last of all, to Bragi, God of all delight. When this cup was drunk, Asmund rose again, according to custom, and asked if none had an oath to swear as to some deed that should be done.

For a while there was no answer, but presently Eric Brighteyes stood up.

"Lord," he said, "I would swear an oath."

"Set forth the matter, then," said Asmund.

"It is this," quoth Eric. "On Mosfell mountain, over by Hecla, dwells a Baresark of whom all men have ill knowledge, for there are few whom he has not harmed. His name is Skallagrim; he is a mighty man and he has wrought much mischief in the south country, and brought many to their deaths and robbed more of their goods: for none can prevail against him. Still, I swear this, that, when the days lengthen, I will go up alone against him and challenge him to battle, and conquer him or fall."

"Then, thou yellow-headed puppy-dog, thou shalt go with one eye against a Baresark with two," growled Ospakar.

Men took no heed of his words, but shouted aloud, for Skallagrim had plagued them long, and there were none who dared to fight with him any more. Only Gudruda looked askance, for it seemed to her that Eric swore too fast. Nevertheless he went up to the altar, and, taking hold of the holy ring, he set his foot on the holy stone and swore his oath, while the feasters applauded, striking their cups upon the board.

And after that the feast went merrily, till all men were drunk, except Asmund and Eric.

Now Eric went to rest, but first he rubbed his limbs with the fat of seals, for he was still sore with the beating of the waters, and they must needs be supple on the morrow if he would keep his eye. Then he slept sound, and rose strong and well, and going to the stream behind the stead, bathed, and anointed his limbs afresh. But Ospakar did not sleep well, because of the ale that he had drunk. Now as Eric came back from bathing, in the dark of the morning, he met Gudruda, who watched for his coming, and, there being none to see, he kissed her often; but she chided him because of the match that he had made with Ospakar and the oath that he had sworn.

"Surely," she said, "thou wilt lose thine eye, for this Ospakar is a giant, and strong as a troll; also he is merciless. Still, thou art a mighty man, and I shall love thee as well with one eye as with two. Oh! Eric, methought I should have died yesterday when thou didst leap from Wolf's Fang! My heart seemed to stop within me."

"Yet I came safely to shore, sweetheart, and well does this kiss pay for all I did. And as for Ospakar, if but once I get these arms about him, I fear him little, or any man, and I covet that sword of his greatly. But we can talk more certainly of these things to-morrow."

Now Gudruda clung to him and told him all that had befallen, and of the doings and words of Swanhild.

"She honours me beyond my worth," he said, "who am in no way set on her, but on thee only, Gudruda."

"Art thou so sure of that, Eric? Swanhild is fair and wise."

"Ay and evil. When I love Swanhild, then thou mayest love Ospakar."

"It is a bargain," she said, laughing. "Good luck go with thee in the wrestling," and with a kiss she left him, fearing lest she should be seen.

Eric went back to the hall, and sat down by the centre hearth, for all men slept, being still heavy with drink, and presently Swanhild glided up to him, and greeted him.

"Thou art greedy of deeds, Eric," she said. "Yesterday thou camest here by a path that no man has travelled, to-day thou dost wrestle with a giant for thine eye, and presently thou goest up against Skallagrim!"

"It seems that this is true," said Eric.

"Now all this thou doest for a woman who is the betrothed of another man."

"All this I do for fame's sake, Swanhild. Moreover, Gudruda is betrothed to none."

"Before another Yule-feast is spread, Gudruda shall be the wife of Ospakar."

"That is yet to be seen, Swanhild."

Now Swanhild stood silent for a while and then spoke: "Thou art a fool, Eric—yes, drunk with folly. Nothing but evil shall come to thee from this madness of thine. Forget it and pluck that which lies to thine hand," and she looked sweetly at him.

"They call thee Swanhild the Fatherless," he answered, "but I think that Loki, the God of Guile, was thy father, for there is none to match thee in craft and evil-doing, and in beauty one only. I know thy plots well and all the sorrow that thou hast brought upon us. Still, each seeks honour after his own manner, so seek thou as thou wilt; but thou shalt find bitterness and empty days, and thy plots shall come back on thine own head—yes, even though they bring Gudruda and me to sorrow and death."

Swanhild laughed. "A day shall dawn, Eric, when thou who dost hate me shalt hold me dear, and this I promise thee. Another thing I promise thee also: that Gudruda shall never call thee husband."

But Eric did not answer, fearing lest in his anger he should say words that were better unspoken.

Now men rose and sat down to meat, and all talked of the wrestling that should be. But in the morning Ospakar repented of the match, for it is truly said that ale is another man, and men do not like that in the morning which seemed well enough on yester eve. He remembered that he held Whitefire dear above all things, and that Eric's eye had no worth to him, except that the loss of it would spoil his beauty, so that perhaps Gudruda would turn from him. It would be very ill if he should chance to lose the play—though of this he had no fear, for he was held the strongest man in Iceland and the most skilled in all feats of strength—and, at the best, no fame is to be won from the overthrow of a deedless man, and the plucking out of his eye. Thus it came to pass that when he saw Eric he called to him in a big voice:

"Hearken, thou Eric."

"I hear thee, thou Ospakar," said Eric, mocking him, and people laughed; while Ospakar grinned angrily and said, "Thou must learn manners, puppy. Still, I shall find no honour in teaching thee in this wise. Last night we made a match in our cups, and I staked my sword Whitefire and thou thine eye. It would be bad that either of us should lose sword or eye; therefore, what sayest thou, shall we let it pass?"

"Ay, Blacktooth, if thou fearest; but first pay thou forfeit of the sword."

Now Ospakar grew very mad and shouted, "Thou wilt indeed stand against me in the ring! I will break thy back anon, youngster, and afterwards tear out thine eye before thou diest."

"It may so befall," answered Eric, "but big words do not make big deeds."

Presently the light came and thralls went out with spades and cleared away the snow in a circle two rods across, and brought dry sand and sprinkled it on the frozen turf, so that the wrestlers should not slip. And they piled the snow in a wall around the ring.

But Groa came up to Ospakar and spoke to him apart.

"Knowest thou, lord," she said, "that my heart bodes ill of this match? Eric is a mighty man, and, great though thou art, I think that thou shalt lout low before him."

"It will be a bad business if I am overthrown by an untried man," said Ospakar, and was troubled in his mind, "and it would be evil moreover to lose the sword. For no price would I have it so."

"What wilt thou give me, lord, if I bring thee victory?"

"I will give thee two hundred in silver."

"Ask no questions and it shall be so," said Groa.

Now Eric was without, taking note of the ground in the ring, and presently Groa called to her the thrall Koll the Half-witted, whom she had sent to Swinefell.

"See," she said, "yonder by the wall stand the wrestling shoes of Eric Brighteyes. Haste thee now and take grease, and rub the soles with it, then hold them in the heat of the fire, so that the fat sinks in. Do this swiftly and secretly, and I will give thee three pennies."

Koll grinned, and did as he was bid, setting back the shoes just as they were before. Scarcely was the deed done when Eric came in, and made himself ready for the game, binding the greased shoes upon his feet, for he feared no trick.

Now everybody went out to the ring, and Ospakar and Eric stripped for wrestling. They were clad in tight woollen jerkins and hose, and sheep-skin shoes were on their feet.

They named Asmund master of the game, and his word must be law to both of them. Eric claimed that Asmund should hold the sword Whitefire that was at stake, but Ospakar gainsaid him, saying that if he gave Whitefire into Asmund's keeping, Eric must also give his eye—and about this they debated hotly. Now the matter was brought before Asmund as umpire, and he gave judgment for Eric, "for," he said, "if Eric yield up his eye into my hand, I can return it to his head no more if he should win; but if Ospakar gives me the good sword and conquers, it is easy for me to pass it back to him unharmed."

Men said that this was a good judgment.

Thus then was the arm-game set. Ospakar and Eric must wrestle thrice, and between each bout there would be a space while men could count a thousand. They might strike no blow at one another with hand, or head, or elbow, foot or knee; and it should be counted no fall if the haunch and the head of the fallen were not on the ground at the self-same time. He who suffered two falls should be adjudged conquered and lose his stake.

Asmund called these rules aloud in the presence of witnesses, and Ospakar and Eric said that should bind them. Ospakar drew a small knife and gave it to his son Gizur to hold.

"Thou shalt soon know, youngling, how steel tastes in the eyeball," he said.

"We shall soon know many things," Eric answered.

Now they drew off their cloaks and stood in the ring. Ospakar was great beyond the bigness of men and his arms were clothed with black hair like the limbs of a goat. Beneath the shoulder joint they were almost as thick as a girl's thigh. His legs also were mighty, and the muscles stood out upon him in knotty lumps. He seemed a very giant, and fierce as a Baresark, but still somewhat round about the body and heavy in movement.

From him men looked at Eric.

"Lo! Baldur and the Troll!" said Swanhild, and everybody laughed, since so it was indeed; for, if Ospakar was black and hideous as a troll, Eric was beautiful as Baldur, the loveliest of the Gods. He was taller than Ospakar by the half of a hand and as broad in the chest. Still, he was not yet come to his greatest strength, and, though his limbs were well knit, they seemed but as a child's against the limbs of Ospakar. But he was quick as a cat and lithe, his neck and arms were white as whey, and beneath his golden hair his bright eyes shone like spears.

Now they stood face to face, with arms outstretched, waiting the word of Asmund. He gave it and they circled round each other with arms held low. Presently Ospakar made a rush and, seizing Eric about the middle, tried to lift him, but with no avail. Thrice he strove and failed, then Eric moved his foot and lo! it slipped upon the sanded turf. Again Eric moved and again he slipped, a third time and he slipped a third time, and before he could recover himself he was full on his back and fairly thrown.

Gudruda saw and was sad at heart, and those around her said that it was easy to know how the game would end.

"What said I?" quoth Swanhild, "that it would go badly with Eric were Ospakar's arms about him."

"All is not done yet," answered Gudruda. "Methinks Eric's feet slipped most strangely, as though he stood on ice."

But Eric was very sore at heart and could make nothing of this matter—for he was not overthrown by strength.

He sat on the snow and Ospakar and his sons mocked him. But Gudruda drew near and whispered to him to be of good cheer, for fortune might yet change.

"I think that I am bewitched," said Eric sadly: "my feet have no hold of the ground."

Gudruda covered her eyes with her hand and thought. Presently she looked up quickly. "I seem to see guile here," she said. "Now look narrowly on thy shoes."

He heard, and, loosening his shoe-string, drew a shoe from his foot and looked at the sole. The cold of the snow had hardened the fat, and there it was, all white upon the leather.

Now Eric rose in wrath. "Methought," he cried, "that I dealt with men of honourable mind, not with cheating tricksters. See now! it is little wonder that I slipped, for grease has been set upon my shoes—and, by Thor! I will cleave the man who did it to the chin," and as he said it his eyes blazed so dreadfully that folk fell back from him. Asmund took the shoes and looked at them. Then he spoke:

"Brighteyes tells the truth, and we have a sorry knave among us. Ospakar, canst thou clear thyself of this ill deed?"

"I will swear on the holy ring that I know nothing of it, and if any man in my company has had a hand therein he shall die," said Ospakar.

"That we will swear also," cried his sons Gizur and Mord.

"This is more like a woman's work," said Gudruda, and she looked at Swanhild.

"It is no work of mine," quoth Swanhild.

"Then go and ask thy mother of it," answered Gudruda.

Now all men cried aloud that this was the greatest shame, and that the match must be set afresh; only Ospakar bethought him of that two hundred in silver which he had promised to Groa, and looked around, but she was not there. Still, he gainsaid Eric in the matter of the match being set afresh.

Then Eric cried out in his anger that he would let the game stand as it was, since Ospakar swore himself free of the shameful deed. Men thought this a mad saying, but Asmund said it should be so. Still, he swore in his heart that, even if he were worsted, Eric should not lose his eye—no not if swords were held aloft to take it. For of all tricks this seemed to him the very worst.

Now Ospakar and Eric faced each other again in the ring, but this time the feet of Eric were bare.

Ospakar rushed to get the upper hold, but Eric was too swift for him and sprang aside. Again he rushed, but Eric dropped and gripped him round the middle. Now they were face to face, hugging each other like bears, but moving little. For a time things went thus, while Ospakar strove to lift Eric, but in nowise could he stir him. Then of a sudden Eric put out his strength, and they staggered round the ring, tearing at each other till their jerkins were rent from them, leaving them almost bare to the waist. Suddenly, Eric seemed to give, and Ospakar put out his foot to trip him. But Brighteyes was watching. He caught the foot in the crook of his left leg, and threw his weight forward on the chest of Blacktooth. Backward he went, falling with the thud of a tree on snow, and there he lay on the ground, and Eric over him.

Then men shouted "A fall! a fair fall!" and were very glad, for the fight seemed most uneven to them, and the wrestlers rolled asunder, breathing heavily.

Gudruda threw a cloak over Eric's naked shoulders.

"That was well done, Brighteyes," she said.

"The game is still to play, sweet," he gasped, "and Ospakar is a mighty man. I threw him by skill, not by strength. Next time it must be by strength or not at all."

Now breathing-time was done, and once more the two were face to face. Thrice Ospakar rushed, and thrice did Eric slip away, for he would waste Blacktooth's strength. Again Ospakar rushed, roaring like a bear, and fire seemed to come from his eyes, and the steam went up from him and hung upon the frosty air like the steam of a horse. This time Eric could not get away, but was swept up into that great grip, for Ospakar had the lower hold.

"Now there is an end of Eric," said Swanhild.

"The arrow is yet on the bow," answered Gudruda.

Blacktooth put out his might and reeled round and round the ring, dragging Eric with him. This way and that he twisted, and time on time Eric's leg was lifted from the ground, but so he might not be thrown. Now they stood almost still, while men shouted madly, for no such wrestling had been known in the southlands. Grimly they hugged and strove: forsooth it was a mighty sight to see. Grimly they hugged, and their muscles strained and cracked, but they could stir each other no inch.

Ospakar grew fearful, for he could make no play with this youngling. Black rage swelled in his heart. He ground his fangs, and thought on guile. By his foot gleamed the naked foot of Eric. Suddenly he stamped on it so fiercely that the skin burst.

"Ill done! ill done!" folk cried; but in his pain Eric moved his foot.

Lo! he was down, but not altogether down, for he did but sit upon his haunches, and still he clung to Blacktooth's thighs, and twined his legs about his ankles. Now with all his strength Ospakar strove to force the head of Brighteyes to the ground, but still he could not, for Eric clung to him like a creeper to a tree.

"A losing game for Eric," said Asmund, and as he spoke Brighteyes was pressed back till his yellow hair almost swept the sand.

Then the folk of Ospakar shouted in triumph, but Gudruda cried aloud:

"Be not overthrown, Eric; loose thee and spring aside."

Eric heard, and of a sudden loosed all his grip. He fell on his outspread hand, then, with a swing sideways and a bound, once more he stood upon his feet. Ospakar came at him like a bull made mad with goading, but he could no longer roar aloud. They closed and this time Eric had the better hold. For a while they struggled round and round till their feet tore the frozen turf, then once more they stood face to face. Now the two were almost spent; yet Blacktooth gathered up his strength and swung Eric from his feet, but he found them again. He grew mad with rage, and hugged him till Brighteyes was nearly pressed to death, and black bruises sprang upon the whiteness of his flesh. Ospakar grew mad, and madder yet, till at length in his fury he fixed his fangs in Eric's shoulder and bit till the blood spurted.

"Ill kissed, thou rat!" gasped Eric, and with the pain and rush of blood, his strength came back to him. He shifted his grip swiftly, now his right hand was beneath the fork of Blacktooth's thigh and his left on the hollow of Blacktooth's back. Twice he lifted—twice the bulk of Ospakar rose from the ground—a third mighty lift—so mighty that the wrapping on Eric's forehead burst, and the blood streamed down his face—and lo! great Blacktooth flew in air. Up he flew, and backward he fell into the bank of snow, and was buried there almost to the knees.

VI

HOW ASMUND THE PRIEST WAS BETROTHED TO UNNA

For a moment there was silence, for all that company was wonderstruck at the greatness of the deed. Then they cheered and cheered again, and to Eric it seemed that he slept, and the sound of shouting reached him but faintly, as though he heard through snow. Suddenly he woke and saw a man rush at him with axe aloft. It was Mord, Ospakar's son, mad at his father's overthrow. Eric sprang aside, or the blow had been his bane, and, as he sprang, smote with his fist, and it struck heavily on the head of Mord above the ear, so that the axe flew from his hand, and he fell senseless on his father in the snow.

Now swords flashed out, and men ringed round Eric to guard him, and it came near to the spilling of blood, for the people of Ospakar gnashed their teeth to see so great a hero overthrown by a youngling, while the southern folk of Middalhof and Ran River rejoiced loudly, for Eric was dear to their hearts.

"Down swords," cried Asmund the priest, "and haul yon carcass from the snow."

This then they did, and Ospakar sat up, breathing in great gasps, the blood running from his mouth and ears, and he was an evil sight to see, for what with blood and snow and rage his face was like the face of the Swinefell Goblin.

But Swanhild spoke in the ear of Gudruda:

"Here," she said, looking at Eric, "we two have a man worth loving, foster-sister."

"Ay," answered Gudruda, "worth and well worth!"

Now Asmund drew near and before all men kissed Eric Brighteyes on the brow.

"In sooth," he said, "thou art a mighty man, Eric, and the glory of the south. This I prophesy of thee: that thou shalt do deeds such as have not been done in Iceland. Thou hast ill been served, for a knave unknown greased thy shoes. Yon swarthy Ospakar, the most mighty of all men in Iceland, could not overthrow thee, though, like a wolf, he fastened his fangs in thee, and, like a coward, stamped upon thy naked foot. Take thou the great sword that thou hast won and wear it worthily."

Now Eric took snow and wiped the blood from his brow. Then he grasped Whitefire and drew it from the scabbard, and high aloft flashed the war-blade. Thrice he wheeled it round his head, then sang aloud:

"Fast, yestermorn, down Golden Falls,
Fared young Eric to thy feast,
Asmund, father of Gudruda—
Maid whom much he longs to clasp.
But to-day on Giant Blacktooth
Hath he done a needful deed:
Hurling him in heaped-up snowdrift;
Winning Whitefire for his wage."

And again he sang:

"Lord, if in very truth thou thinkest
Brighteyes is a man midst men,
Swear to him, the stalwart suitor,
Handsel of thy sweet maid's hand:
Whom, long loved, to win, down Goldfoss
Swift he sped through frost and foam;
Whom, to win, to troll-like Ogre,
He, 'gainst Whitefire, waged his eye."

Men thought this well sung, and turned to hear Asmund's answer, nor must they wait long.

"Eric," he said, "I will promise thee this, that if thou goest on as thou hast begun, I will give Gudruda in marriage to no other man."

"That is good tidings, lord," said Eric.

"This I say further: in a year I will give thee full answer according as to how thou dost bear thyself between now and then, for this is no light gift thou askest; also that, if ye will it, you twain may now plight troth, for the blame shall be yours if it is broken, and not mine, and I give thee my hand on it."

Eric took his hand, and Gudruda heard her father's words and happiness shone in her dark eyes, and she grew faint for very joy. And now Eric turned to her, all torn and bloody from the fray, the great sword in his hand, and he spoke thus:

"Thou hast heard thy father's words, Gudruda? Now it seems that there is no great need of troth-plighting between us two. Still, here before all men I ask thee, if thou dost love me and art willing to take me to husband?"

Gudruda looked up into his face, and answered in a sweet, clear voice that could be heard by all:

"Eric, I say to thee now, what I have said before, that I love thee alone of all men, and, if it be my father's wish, I will wed no other whilst thou dost remain true to me and hold me dear."

"Those are good words," said Eric. "Now, in pledge of them, swear this troth of thine upon my sword that I have won."

Gudruda smiled, and, taking great Whitefire in her hand, she said the words again, and, in pledge of them, kissed the bright blade.

Then Eric took back the war-sword and spoke thus: "I swear that I will love thee, and thee only, Gudruda the Fair, Asmund's daughter, whom I have desired all my days; and, if I fail of this my oath, then our troth is at an end, and thou mayst wed whom thou wilt," and in turn he put his lips upon the sword, while Swanhild watched them do the oath.

Now Ospakar was recovered from the fight, and he sat there upon the snow, with bowed head, for he knew well that he had won the greatest shame, and had lost both wife and sword. Black rage filled his heart as he listened, and he sprang to his feet.

"I came hither, Asmund," he said, "to ask this maid of thine in marriage, and methinks that had been a good match for her and thee. But I have been overthrown by witchcraft of this man in a wrestling-bout, and thereby lost my good sword; and now I must seem to hear him betrothed to the maid before me."

"Thou hast heard aright, Ospakar," said Asmund, "and thy wooing is soon sped. Get thee back whence thou camest and seek a wife in thine own quarter, for thou art unfit in age and aspect to have so sweet a maid. Moreover, here in the south we hold men of small account, however great and rich they be, who do not shame to seek to overcome a foe by foul means. With my own eyes I saw thee stamp on the naked foot of Eric, Thorgrimur's son; with my own eyes I saw thee, like a wolf, fasten that black fang of thine upon him—there is the mark of it; and, as for the matter of the greased shoes, thou knowest best what hand thou hadst in it."

"I had no hand. If any did this thing, it was Groa the Witch, thy Finnish bedmate. For the rest, I was mad and know not what I did. But hearken, Asmund: ill shall befall thee and thy house, and I will ever be thy foe. Moreover, I will yet wed this maid of thine. And now, thou Eric, hearken also: I will have another game with thee. This one was but the sport of boys; when we meet again—and the time shall not be long—swords shall be aloft, and thou shalt learn the play of men. I tell thee that I will slay thee, and tear Gudruda, shrieking, from thy arms to be my wife! I tell thee that, with yonder good sword Whitefire, I will yet hew off thy head!"—and he choked and stopped.

"Thou art much foam and little water," said Eric. "These things are easily put to proof. If thou willest it, to-morrow I will come with thee to a holmgang, and there we may set the twigs and finish what we have begun to-day."

"I cannot do that, for thou hast my sword; and, till I am suited with another weapon, I may fight no holmgang. Still, fear not: we shall soon meet with weapons aloft and byrnie on breast."

"Never too soon can the hour come, Blacktooth," said Eric, and turning on his heel, he limped to the hall to clothe himself afresh. On the threshold of the men's door he met Groa the Witch.

"Thou didst put grease upon my shoes, carline and witch-hag that thou art," he said.

"It is not true, Brighteyes."

"There thou liest, and for all this I will repay thee. Thou art not yet the wife of Asmund, nor shalt be, for a plan comes into my head about it."

Groa looked at him strangely. "If thou speakest so, take heed to thy meat and drink," she said. "I was not born among the Finns for nothing; and know, I am still minded to wed Asmund. For thy shoes, I would to the Gods that they were Hell-shoon, and that I was now binding them on thy dead feet."

"Oh! the cat begins to spit," said Eric. "But know this: thou mayest grease my shoes—fit work for a carline!—but thou mayest never bind them on. Thou art a witch, and wilt come to the end of witches; and what thy daughter is, that I will not say," and he pushed past her and entered the hall.

Presently Asmund came to seek Eric there, and prayed him to be gone to his stead on Ran River. The horses of Ospakar had strayed, and he must stop at Middalhof till they were found; but, if these two should abide under the same roof, bloodshed would come of it, and that Asmund knew.

Eric said yea to this, and, when he had rested a while, he kissed Gudruda, and, taking a horse, rode away to Coldback, bearing the sword Whitefire with him, and for a time he saw no more of Ospakar.

When he came there, his mother Saevuna greeted him as one risen from the dead, and hung about his neck. Then he told her all that had come to pass, and she thought it a marvellous story, and sorrowed that Thorgrimur, her husband, was not alive to know it. But Eric mused a while, and spoke.

"Mother," he said, "now my uncle Thorod of Greenfell is dead, and his daughter, my cousin Unna, has no home. She is a fair woman and skilled in all things. It comes into my mind that we should bid her here to dwell with us."

"Why, I thought thou wast betrothed to Gudruda the Fair," said Saevuna. "Wherefore, then, wouldst thou bring Unna hither?"

"For this cause," said Eric; "because it seems that Asmund the Priest wearies of Groa the Witch, and would take another wife, and I wish to draw the bands between us tighter, if it may befall so."

"Groa will take it ill," said Saevuna.

"Things cannot be worse between us than they are now, therefore I do not fear Groa," he answered.

"It shall be as thou wilt, son; to-morrow we will send to Unna and bid her here, if it pleases her to come."

Now Ospakar stayed three more days at Middalhof, till his horses were found, and he was fit to travel, for Eric had shaken him sorely. But he had no words with Gudruda and few with Asmund. Still, he saw Swanhild, and she bid him to be of good cheer, for he should yet have Gudruda. For now that the maid had passed from him the mind of Ospakar was set in winning her. Björn also, Asmund's son, spoke words of good comfort to him, for he envied Eric his great fame, and he thought the match with Blacktooth would be good. And so at length Ospakar rode away to Swinefell with all his company; but Gizur, his son, left his heart behind.

For Swanhild had not been idle this while. Her heart was sore, but she must follow her ill-nature, and so she had put out her woman's strength and beguiled Gizur into loving her. But she did not love him at all, and the temper of Asmund the Priest was so angry that Gizur dared not ask her in marriage. So nothing was said of the matter.

Now Unna came to Coldback, to dwell with Saevuna, Eric's mother, and she was a fair and buxom woman. She had been once wedded, but within a month of her marriage her husband was lost at sea, this two years gone. At first Gudruda was somewhat jealous of this coming of Unna to Coldback; but Eric showed her what was in his mind, and she fell into the plan, for she hated and feared Groa greatly, and desired to be rid of her.

Since this matter of the greasing of Eric's wrestling-shoes great loathing of Groa had come into Asmund's mind, and he bethought him often of those words that his wife Gudruda the Gentle spoke as she lay dying, and grieved that the oath which he swore then had in part been broken. He would have no more to do with Groa now, but he could not be rid of her; and, notwithstanding her evil doings, he still loved Swanhild. But Groa grew thin with spite and rage, and wandered about the place glaring with her great black eyes, and people hated her more and more.

Now Asmund went to visit at Coldback, and there he saw Unna, and was pleased with her, for she was a blithe woman and a bonny. The end of it was that he asked her in marriage of Eric; at which Brighteyes was glad, but said that he must know Unna's mind. Unna hearkened, and did not say no, for though Asmund was somewhat gone in years, still he was an upstanding man, wealthy in lands, goods, and moneys out at interest, and having many friends. So they plighted troth, and the wedding-feast was to be in the autumn after hay-harvest. Now Asmund rode back to Middalhof somewhat troubled at heart, for these tidings must be told to Groa, and he feared her and her witchcraft. In the hall he found her, standing alone.

"Where hast thou been, lord?" she asked.

"At Coldback," he answered.

"To see Unna, Eric's cousin, perchance?"

"That is so."

"What is Unna to thee, then, lord?"

"This much, that after hay-harvest she will be my wife, and that is ill news for thee, Groa."

Now Groa turned and grasped fiercely at the air with her thin hands. Her eyes started out, foam was on her lips, and she shook in her fury like a birch-tree in the wind, looking so evil that Asmund drew back a little way, saying:

"Now a veil is lifted from thee and I see thee as thou art. Thou hast cast a glamour over me these many years, Groa, and it is gone."

"Mayhap, Asmund Asmundson—mayhap, thou knowest me; but I tell thee that thou shalt see me in a worse guise before thou weddest Unna. What! have I borne the greatest shame, lying by thy side these many years, and shall I live to see a rival, young and fair, creep into my place with honour? That I will not while runes have power and spells can conjure the evil thing upon thee. I call down ruin on thee and thine—yea and on Brighteyes also, for he has brought this thing to pass. Death take ye all! May thy blood no longer run in mortal veins anywhere on the earth! Go down to Hela, Asmund, and be forgotten!" and she began to mutter runes swiftly.

Now Asmund turned white with wrath. "Cease thy evil talk," he said, "or thou shalt be hurled as a witch into Goldfoss pool."

"Into Goldfoss pool?—yea, there I may lie. I see it!—I seem to see this shape of mine rolling where the waters boil fiercest—but thine eyes shall never see it! Thy eyes are shut, and shut are the eyes of Unna, for ye have gone before!—I do but follow after," and thrice Groa shrieked aloud, throwing up her arms, then fell foaming on the sanded floor.

"An evil woman and a fey!" said Asmund as he called people to her. "It had been better for me if I had never seen her dark face."

Now it is to be told that Groa lay beside herself for ten full days, and Swanhild nursed her. Then she found her sense again, and craved to see Asmund, and spoke thus to him:

"It seems to me, lord, if indeed it be aught but a vision of my dreams, that before this sickness struck me I spoke mad and angry words against thee, because thou hast plighted troth to Unna, Thorod's daughter."

"That is so, in truth," said Asmund.

"I have to say this, then, lord: that most humbly I crave thy pardon for my ill words, and ask thee to put them away from thy mind. Sore heart makes sour speech, and thou knowest well that, howsoever great my faults, at least I have always loved thee and laboured for thee, and methinks that in some fashion thy fortunes are the debtor to my wisdom. Therefore when my ears heard that thou hadst of a truth put me away, and that another woman comes an honoured wife to rule in Middalhof, my tongue forgot its courtesy, and I spoke words that are of all words the farthest from my mind. For I know well that I grow old, and have put off that beauty with which I was adorned of yore, and that held thee to me. 'Carline' Eric Brighteyes named me, and 'carline' I am—an old hag, no more! Now, forgive me, and, in memory of all that has been between us, let me creep to my place in the ingle and still watch and serve thee and thine till my service is outworn. Out of Ran's net I came to thee, and, if thou drivest me hence, I tell thee that I will lie down and die upon thy threshold, and when thou sinkest into eld surely the memory of it shall grieve thee."

Thus she spoke and wept much, till Asmund's heart softened in him, and, though with a doubting mind, he said it should be as she willed.

So Groa stayed on at Middalhof, and was lowly in her bearing and soft of speech.

VII

HOW ERIC WENT UP MOSFELL AGAINST SKALLAGRIM THE BARESARK

Now Atli the Good, earl of the Orkneys, comes into the story.

It chanced that Atli had sailed to Iceland in the autumn on a business about certain lands that had fallen to him in right of his mother Helga, who was an Icelander, and he had wintered west of Reyjanes. Spring being come, he wished to sail home, and, when his ship was bound, he put to sea full early in the year. But it chanced that bad weather came up from the south-east, with mist and rain, so he must needs beach his ship in a creek under shelter of the Westman Islands.

Now Atli asked what people dwelt in these parts, and, when he heard the name of Asmund Asmundson the Priest, he was glad, for in old days he and Asmund had gone many a viking cruise together.

"We will leave the ship here," he said, "till the weather clears, and go up to Middalhof to stay with Asmund."

So they made the ship snug, and left men to watch her; but two of the company, with Earl Atli, rode up to Middalhof.

It must be told of Atli that he was the best of the earls who lived in those days, and he ruled the Orkneys so well that men gave him a by-name and called him Atli the Good. It was said of him that he had never turned a poor man away unsuccoured, nor bowed his head before a strong man, nor drawn his sword without cause, nor refused peace to him who prayed it. He was sixty years old, but age had left few marks on him, except that of his long white beard. He was keen-eyed, and well-fashioned of form and face, a great warrior and the strongest of men. His wife was dead, leaving him no children, and this was a sorrow to him; but as yet he had taken no other wife, for he would say: "Love makes an old man blind," and "When age runs with youth, both shall fall," and again, "Mix grey locks and golden and spoil two heads." For this earl was a man of many wise sayings.

Now Atli came to Middalhof just as men sat down to meat and, hearing the clatter of arms, all sprang to their feet, thinking that perhaps Ospakar had come again as he had promised. But when Asmund saw Atli he knew him at once, though they had not met for nearly thirty years, and he greeted him lovingly, and put him in the high seat, and gave place to his men upon the cross-benches. Atli told all his story, and Asmund bade him rest a while at Middalhof till the weather grew clearer.

Now the Earl saw Swanhild and thought the maid wondrous fair, and so indeed she was, as she moved scornfully to and fro in her kirtle of white. Soft was her curling hair and deep were her dark blue eyes, and bent were her red lips as is a bow above her dimpled chin, and her teeth shone like pearls.

"Is that fair maid thy daughter, Asmund," asked Atli.

"She is named Swanhild the Fatherless," he answered, turning his face away.

"Well," said Atli, looking sharply on him, "were the maid sprung from me, she would not long be called the 'Fatherless,' for few have such a daughter."

"She is fair enough," said Asmund, "in all save temper, and that is bad to cross."

"In every sword a flaw," answers Atli; "but what has an old man to do with young maids and their beauty?" and he sighed.

"I have known younger men who would seem less brisk at bridals," said Asmund, and for that time they talked no more of the matter.

Now, Swanhild heard something of this speech, and she guessed more; and it came into her mind that it would be the best of sport to make this old man love her, and then to mock him and say him nay. So she set herself to the task, as it ever was her wont, and she found it easy. For all day long, with downcast eyes and gentle looks, she waited upon the Earl, and now, at his bidding, she sang to him in a voice soft and low, and now she talked so wisely well that Atli thought no such maid had trod the earth before. But he checked himself with many learned saws, and on a day when the weather had grown fair, and they sat alone, he told her that his ship was bound for Orkney Isles.

Then, as though by chance, Swanhild laid her white hand in his, and on a sudden looked deep into his eyes, and said with trembling lips, "Ah, go not yet, lord!—I pray thee, go not yet!"—and, turning, she fled away.

But Atli was much moved, and he said to himself: "Now a strange thing is come to pass: a fair maid loves an old man; and yet, methinks, he who looks into those eyes sees deep waters," and he beat his brow and thought.

But Swanhild in her chamber laughed till the tears ran from those same eyes, for she saw that the great fish was hooked and now the time had come to play him.

For she did not know that it was otherwise fated.

Gudruda, too, saw all these things and knew not how to read them, for she was of an honest mind, and could not understand how a woman may love a man as Swanhild loved Eric and yet make such play with other men, and that of her free will. For she guessed little of Swanhild's guilefulness, nor of the coldness of her heart to all save Eric; nor of how this was the only joy left to her: to make a sport of men and put them to grief and shame. Atli said to himself that he would watch this maid well before he uttered a word to Asmund, and he deemed himself very cunning, for he was wondrous cautious after the fashion of those about to fall. So he set himself to watching, and Swanhild set herself to smiling, and he told her tales of warfare and of daring, and she clasped her hands and said:

"Was there ever such a man since Odin trod the earth?" And so it went on, till the serving-women laughed at the old man in love and the wit of her that mocked him.

Now upon a day, Eric having made an end of sowing his corn, bethought himself of his vow to go up alone against Skallagrim the Baresark in his den on Mosfell over by Hecla. Now, this was a heavy task: for Skallagrim was held so mighty among men that none went up against him any more; and at times Eric thought of Gudruda, and sighed, for it was likely that she would be a widow before she was made a wife. Still, his oath must be fulfilled, and, moreover, of late Skallagrim having heard that a youngling named Eric Brighteyes had vowed to slay him singlehanded, had made a mock of him in this fashion. For Skallagrim rode down to

Coldback on Ran River and at night-time took a lamb from the fold. Holding the lamb beneath his arm, he drew near to the house and smote thrice on the door with his battle-axe, and they were thundering knocks. Then he leapt on to his horse and rode off a space and waited. Presently Eric came out, but half clad, a shield in one hand and Whitefire in the other, and, looking, by the bright moonlight he saw a huge black-bearded man seated on a horse, having a great axe in one hand and the lamb beneath his arm.

"Who art thou?" roared Eric.

"I am called Skallagrim, youngling," answered the man on the horse. "Many men have seen me once, none have wished to see me twice, and some few have never seen aught again. Now, it has been echoed in my ears that thou hast vowed a vow to go up Mosfell against Skallagrim the Baresark, and I am come hither to say that I will make thee right welcome. See," and with his axe he cut off the lamb's tail on the pommel of his saddle: "of the flesh of this lamb of thine I will brew broth and of his skin I will make me a vest. Take thou this tail, and when thou fittest it on to the skin again, Skallagrim will own a lord," and he hurled the tail towards him.

"Bide thou there till I can come to thee," shouted Eric; "it will spare me a ride to Mosfell."

"Nay, nay. It is good for lads to take the mountain air," and Skallagrim turned his horse away, laughing.

Eric watched Skallagrim vanish over the knoll, and then, though he was very angry, laughed also and went in. But first he picked up the tail, and on the morrow he skinned it.

Now the time was come when the matter must be tried, and Eric bade farewell to Saevuna his mother, and Unna his cousin, and girt Whitefire round him and set upon his head a golden helm with wings on it. Then he found the byrnie which his father Thorgrimur had stripped, together with the helm, from that Baresark who cut off his leg—and this was a good piece, forged of the Welshmen—and he put it on his breast, and taking a stout shield of bull's hide studded with nails, rode away with one thrall, the strong carle named Jon.

But the women misdoubted them much of this venture; nevertheless Eric might not be gainsayed.

Now, the road to Mosfell runs past Middalhof and thither he came. Atli, standing at the men's door, saw him and cried aloud: "Ho! a mighty man comes here."

Swanhild looked out and saw Eric, and he was a goodly sight in his war-gear. For now, week by week, he seemed to grow more fair and great, as the full strength of his manhood rose in him, like sap in the spring grass, and Gudruda was very proud of her lover. That night Eric stayed at Middalhof, and sat hand in hand with Gudruda and talked with Earl Atli. Now the heart of the old viking went out to Eric, and he took great delight in him and in his strength and deeds, and he longed much that the Gods had given him such a son.

"I prophesy this of thee, Brighteyes," he cried: "that it shall go ill with this Baresark thou seekest—yes, and with all men who come within sweep of that great sword of thine. But remember this, lad: guard thy head with thy buckler, cut low beneath his shield, if he carries one, and mow the legs from him: for ever a Baresark rushes on, shield up."

Eric thanked him for his good words and went to rest. But, before it was light, he rose, and Gudruda rose also and came into the hall, and buckled his harness on him with her own hands.

"This is a sad task for me, Eric!" she sighed, "for how do I know that Baresark's hands shall not loose this helm of thine?"

"That is as it may be, sweet," he said; "but I fear not the Baresark or any man. How goes it with Swanhild now?"

"I know not. She makes herself sweet to that old Earl and he is fain of her, and that is beyond my sight."

"I have seen as much," said Eric. "It will be well for us if he should wed her."

"Ay, and ill for him; but it is to be doubted if that is in her mind."

Now Eric kissed her soft and sweet, and went away, bidding her look for his return on the day after the morrow.

Gudruda bore up bravely against her fears till he was gone, but then she wept a little.

Now it is to be told that Eric and his thrall Jon rode hard up Stonefell and across the mountains and over the black sand, till, two hours before sunset, they came to the foot of Mosfell, having Hecla on their right. It is a grim mountain, grey with moss, standing alone in the desert plain; but between it and Hecla there is good grassland.

"Here is the fox's earth. Now to start him," said Eric.

He knows something of the path by which this fortress can be climbed from the south, and horses may be ridden up it for a space. So on they go, till at length they come to a flat place where water runs down the black rocks, and here Eric drank of the water, ate food, and washed his face and hands. This done, he bid Jon tend the horses—for hereabouts there is a little grass—and be watchful till he returned, since he must go up against Skallagrim alone. And there with a doubtful heart Jon stayed all that night. For of all that came to pass he saw but one thing, and that was the light of Whitefire as it flashed out high above him on the brow of the mountain when first Brighteyes smote at foe.

Eric went warily up the Baresark path, for he would keep his breath in him, and the light shone redly on his golden helm. High he went, till at length he came to a pass narrow and dark and hedged on either side with sheer cliffs, such as two armed men might hold against a score. He peered down this path, but he saw no Baresark, though it was worn by Baresark feet. He crept along its length, moving like a sunbeam through the darkness of the pass, for the light gathered on his helm and sword, till suddenly the path turned and he was on the brink of a gulf that seemed to have no bottom, and, looking across and down, he could see Jon and the horses more than a hundred fathoms beneath. Now Eric must stop, for this path leads but into the black gulf. Also he was perplexed to know where Skallagrim had his lair. He crept to the brink and gazed. Then he saw that a point of rock jutted from the sheer face of the cliff and that the point was worn with the mark of feet.

"Where Baresark passes, there may yeoman follow," said Eric and, sheathing Whitefire, without more ado, though he liked the task little, he grasped the overhanging rock and stepped down on to the point below. Now he was perched like an eagle over the dizzy gulf and his brain swam. Backward he feared to go, and forward he might not, for there was nothing but air. Beside him, growing from the face of the cliff, was a birch-bush. He grasped it to steady himself. It bent beneath his clutch, and then he saw, behind it, a hole in the rock through which a man could creep, and down this hole ran footmarks.

"First through air like a bird; now through earth like a fox," said Eric and entered the hole. Doubling his body till his helm almost touched his knee he took three paces and lo! he stood on a great platform of rock, so large that a hall might be built on it, which, curving inwards, cannot be seen from the narrow pass. This platform, that is backed by the sheer cliff, looks straight to the south, and from it he could search the plain and the path that he had travelled, and there once more he saw Jon and the horses far below him.

"A strong place, truly, and well chosen," said Eric and looked around. On the floor of the rock and some paces from him a turf fire still smouldered, and by it were sheep's bones, and beyond, in the face of the overhanging precipice, was the mouth of a cave.

"The wolf is at home, or was but lately," said Eric; "now for his lair;" and with that he walked warily to the mouth of the cave and peered in. He could see nothing yet a while, but surely he heard a sound of snoring?

Then he crept in, and, presently, by the red light of the burning embers, he saw a great black-bearded man stretched at length upon a rug of sheepskins, and by his side an axe.

"Now it would be easy to make an end of this cave-dweller," thought Eric; "but that is a deed I will not do—no, not even to a Baresark—to slay him in his sleep," and therewith he stepped lightly to the side of Skallagrim, and was about to prick him with the point of Whitefire, when! as he did so, another man sat up behind Skallagrim.

"By Thor! for two I did not bargain," said Eric, and sprang from the cave.

Then, with a grunt of rage, that Baresark who was behind Skallagrim came out like a she-bear robbed of her whelps, and ran straight at Eric, sword aloft. Eric gives before him right to the edge of the cliff. Then the Baresark smites at him and Brighteyes catches the blow on his shield, and smites at him in turn so well and truly, that the head of the Baresark flies from his shoulders and spins along the ground, but his body, with outstretched arms yet gripping at the air, falls over the edge of the gulf sheer into the water, a hundred fathoms down. It was the flash that Whitefire made as it circled ere it smote that Jon saw while he waited in the dell upon the mountain side. But of the Baresark he saw nothing, for he passed down into the great fire-riven cleft and was never seen more, save once only, in a strange fashion that shall be told. This was the first man whom Brighteyes slew.

Now the old tale tells that Eric cried aloud: "Little chance had this one," and that then a wonderful thing came to pass. For the head on the rock opened its eyes and answered:

"Little chance indeed against thee, Eric Brighteyes. Still, I tell thee this: that where my body fell there thou shalt fall, and where it lies there thou shalt lie also."

Now Eric was afraid, for he thought it a strange thing that a severed head should speak to him.

"Here it seems I have to deal with trolls," he said; "but at the least, though he speak, this one shall strike no more," and he looked at the head, but it answered nothing.

Now Skallagrim slept through it all and the light grew so dim that Eric thought it time to make an end this way or that. Therefore, he took the head of the slain man, though he feared to touch it, and rolled it swiftly into the cave, saying, "Now, being so glib of speech, go tell thy mate that Eric Brighteyes knocks at his door."

Then came sounds as of a man rising, and presently Skallagrim rushed forth with axe aloft and his fellow's head in his left hand. He was clothed in nothing but a shirt and the skin of Eric's lamb was bound to his chest.

"Where now is my mate?" he said. Then he saw Eric leaning on Whitefire, his golden helm ablaze with the glory of the passing sun.

"It seems that thou holdest somewhat of him in thine hand, Skallagrim, and for the rest, go seek it in yonder rift."

"Who art thou?" roared Skallagrim.

"Thou mayest know me by this token," said Eric, and he threw towards him the skin of that lamb's tail which Skallagrim had lifted from Coldback.

Now Skallagrim knew him and the Baresark fit came on. His eyes rolled, foam flew to his lips, his mouth grinned, and he was awesome to see. He let fall the head, and, swinging the great axe aloft, rushed at Eric. But Brighteyes is too swift for him. It would not be well to let that stroke fall, and it must go hard with aught it struck. He springs forward, he louts low and sweeps upwards with Whitefire. Skallagrim sees the sword flare and drops almost to his knee, guarding his head with the axe; but Whitefire strikes on the iron half of the axe and shears it in two, so that the axe-head falls to earth. Now the Baresark is weaponless but unharmed, and it would be an easy task to slay him as he rushes by. But it came into Eric's mind that it is an unworthy deed to slay a swordless man, and this came into his mind also, that he desired to match his naked might against a Baresark in his rage. So, in the hardihood of his youth and strength, he cast Whitefire aside, and crying "Come, try a fall with me, Baresark," rushed on Skallagrim.

"Thou art mad," yells the Baresark, and they are at it hard. Now they grip and rend and tear. Ospakar was strong, but the Baresark strength of Skallagrim is more than the strength of Ospakar, and soon Brighteyes thinks longingly on Whitefire that he has cast aside. Eric is mighty beyond the might of men, but he can scarcely hold his own against this mad man, and very soon he knows that only one chance is left to him, and that is to cling to Skallagrim till the Baresark fit be passed and he is once more like other men. But this is easier to tell of than to do, and presently, strive as he will, Eric is on his back, and Skallagrim on him. But still he holds the Baresark as with bands of iron, and Skallagrim may not free his arms, though he strive furiously. Now they roll over and over on the rock, and the gloom gathers fast about them till presently Eric sees that they draw near to the brink of that mighty rift down which the severed head of the cave-dweller has foretold his fall.

"Then we go together," says Eric, but the Baresark does not heed. Now they are on the very brink, and here as it chances, or as the Norns decree, a little rock juts up and this keeps them from falling. Eric is uppermost, and, strive as he will, Skallagrim may not turn him on his back again. Still, Brighteyes' strength may not endure very long, for he grows faint, and his legs slip slowly over the side of the rift till now he clings, as it were, by his ribs and shoulder-blades alone, that rub against the little rock. The light dies away, and Eric thinks on sweet Gudruda and makes ready to die also, when suddenly a last ray from the sun falls on the fierce face of Skallagrim, and lo! Brighteyes sees it change, for the madness goes out of it, and in a moment the Baresark becomes but as a child in his mighty grip.

"Hold!" said Skallagrim, "I crave peace," and he loosed his clasp.

"Not too soon, then," gasped Eric as, drawing his legs from over the brink of the rift, he gained his feet and, staggering to his sword, grasped it very thankfully.

"I am fordone!" said Skallagrim; "come, drag me from this place, for I fall; or, if thou wilt, hew off my head."

"I will not serve thee thus," said Eric. "Thou art a gallant foe," and he put out his hand and drew him into safety.

For a while Skallagrim lay panting, then he gained his hands and knees and crawled to where Eric leaned against the rock.

"Lord," he said, "give me thy hand."

Eric stretched forth his left hand, wondering, and Skallagrim took it. He did not stretch out his right, for, fearing guile, he gripped Whitefire in it.

"Lord," Skallagrim said again, "of all men who ever were, thou art the mightiest. Five other men had not stood before me in my rage, but, scorning thy weapon, thou didst overcome me in the noblest fashion, and by thy naked strength alone. Now hearken. Thou hast given me my life, and it is thine from this hour to the end. Here I swear fealty to thee. Slay me if thou wilt, or use me if thou wilt, but I think it will be better for thee to do this rather than that, for there is but one who has mastered me, and thou art he, and it is borne in upon my mind that thou wilt have need of my strength, and that shortly."

"That may well be, Skallagrim," said Eric, "yet I put little trust in outlaws and cave-dwellers. How do I know, if I take thee to me, that thou wilt not murder me in my sleep, as it would have been easy for me to do by thee but now?"

"What is it that runs from thy arm," asked Skallagrim.

"Blood," said Eric.

"Stretch out thine arm, lord."

Eric did so, and the Baresark put his lips to the scratch and sucked the blood, then said:

"In this blood of thine I pledge thee, Eric Brighteyes! May Valhalla refuse me and Hela take me; may I be hunted like a fox from earth to earth; may trolls torment me and wizards sport with me o' night; may my limbs shrivel and my heart turn to water; may my foes overtake me, and my bones be crushed across the doom-stone—if I fail in one jot from this my oath that I have sworn! I will guard thy back,

I will smite thy enemies, thy hearthstone shall be my temple, thy honour my honour. Thrall am I of thine, and thrall I will be, and whiles thou wilt we will live one life, and, in the end, we will die one death."

"It seems that in going to seek a foe I have found a friend," said Eric, "and it is likely enough that I shall need one. Skallagrim, Baresark and outlaw as thou art, I take thee at thy word. Henceforth, we are master and man and we will do many a deed side by side, and in token of it I lengthen thy name and call thee Skallagrim Lambstail. Now, if thou hast it, give me food and drink, for I am faint from that hug of thine, old bear."

VIII

HOW OSPAKAR BLACKTOOTH FOUND ERIC BRIGHTEYES AND SKALLAGRIM LAMBSTAIL ON HORSE-HEAD HEIGHTS

Now Skallagrim led Eric to his cave and fed the fire and gave him flesh to eat and ale to drink. When he had eaten his fill Eric looked at the Baresark. He had black hair streaked with grey that hung down upon his shoulders. His nose was hooked like an eagle's beak, his beard was wild and his sunken eyes were keen as a hawk's. He was somewhat bent and not over tall, but of a mighty make, for his shoulders must pass many a door sideways.

"Thou art a great man," said Eric, "and it is something to have overcome thee. Now tell me what turned thee Baresark."

"A shameful deed that was done against me, lord. Ten years ago I was a yeoman of small wealth in the north. I had but one good thing, and that was the fairest housewife in those parts—Thorunna by name—and I loved her much, but we had no children. Now, not far from my stead is a place called Swinefell, and there dwells a mighty chief named Ospakar Blacktooth; he is an evil man and strong——

Eric started at the name and then bade Skallagrim take up the tale.

"It chanced that Ospakar saw my wife Thorunna and would take her, but at first she did not listen. Then he promised her wealth and all good things, and she was weary of our hard way of life and hearkened. Still, she would not go away openly, for that had brought shame on her, but plotted with Ospakar that he should come and take her as though by force. So it came about, as I lay heavily asleep one night at Thorunna's side, having drunk somewhat too deeply of the autumn ale, that armed men seized me, bound me, and haled me from my bed. There were eight of them, and with them was Ospakar. Then Blacktooth bid Thorunna rise, clothe herself and come to be his May, and she made pretence to weep at this, but fell to it readily enough. Now she bound her girdle round her and to it a knife hung.

"'Kill thyself, sweet,' I cried: 'death is better than shame.'

"'Not so, husband,' she answered. 'It is true that I love but thee; yet a woman may find another love, but not another life,' and I saw her laugh through her mock tears. Now Ospakar rode in hot haste away to Swinefell and with him went Thorunna, but his men stayed a while and drank my ale, and, as they drank, they mocked me who was bound before them, and little by little all the truth was told of the doings of Ospakar and Thorunna my housewife, and I learned that it was she who had planned this sport. Then my eyes grew dark and I drew near to death from very shame and bitterness. But of a sudden something leaped up in my heart, fire raged before my eyes and voices in my ears called on to war and vengeance. I was Baresark—and like hay bands I burst my cords. My axe hung on the wainscot. I snatched it thence, and of what befell I know this alone, that, when the madness passed, eight men lay stretched out before me, and all the place was but a gore of blood.

"'Then I drew the dead together and piled drinking tables over them, and benches, and turf, and anything else that would burn, and put cod's oil on the pile, and fired the stead above them, so that the tale went abroad that all these men were burned in their cups, and I with them.

"'But I took the name of Skallagrim and swore an oath against all men, ay, and women too, and away I went to the wood-folk and worked much mischief, for I spared few, and so on to Mosfell. Here I have stayed these five years, awaiting the time when I shall find Ospakar and Thorunna the harlot, and I have fought many men, but, till thou camest up against me, none could stand before my might."

"A strange tale, truly," said Eric; "but now hearken thou to a stranger, for of a truth it seems that we have not come together by chance," and he told him of Gudruda and the wrestling and of the overthrow of Blacktooth, and showed him Whitefire which he won out of the hand of Ospakar.

Skallagrim listened and laughed aloud. "Surely," he said, "this is the work of the Norns. See, lord, thou and I will yet smite this Ospakar. He has taken my wife and he would take thy betrothed. Let it be! Let it be! Ah, would that I had been there to see the wrestling—Ospakar had never risen from his snow-bed. But there is time left to us, and I shall yet see his head roll along the dust. Thou hast his goodly sword and with it thou shalt sweep Blacktooth's head from his shoulders—or perchance that shall be my lot," and with this Skallagrim sprang up, gnashing his teeth and clutching at the air.

"Peace," said Eric. "Blacktooth is not here. Save thy rage until it can run along thy sword and strike him."

"Nay, not here, nor yet so far off, lord. Hearken: I know this Ospakar. If he has set eyes of longing on Gudruda, Asmund's daughter, he will not rest one hour till he have her or is slain; and if he has set eyes of hate on thee—then take heed to thy going and spy down every path before thy feet tread it. Soon shall the matter come on for judgment and even now Odin's Valkyries[*] choose their own."

[*] The "corse-choosing sisters" who were bidden by Odin to single out those warriors whose hour had come to die in battle and win Valhalla.

"It is well, then," said Eric.

"Yea, lord, it is well, for we two have little to fear from any six men, if so be that they fall on us in fair fight. But I do not altogether like thy tale. Too many women are mixed up in it, and women stab in the back. A man may deal with swords aloft, but not with tricks, and lies, and false women's witchery. It was a woman who greased thy wrestling soles; mayhap it will be a woman that binds on thy Hell-shoes when all is done—ay! and who makes them ready for thy feet."

"Of women, as of men," answered Eric, "there is this to be said, that some are good and some evil."

"Yes, lord, and this also, that the evil ones plot the ill of their evil, but the good do it of their blind foolishness. Forswear women and so shalt thou live happy and die in honour—cherish them and live in wretchedness and die an outcast."

"Thy talk is foolish," said Eric. "Birds must to the air, the sea to the shore, and man must to woman. As things are so let them be, for they will soon seem as though they had never been. I had rather kiss my dear and die, if so it pleases me to do, than kiss her not and live, for at the last the end will be one end, and kisses are sweet!"

"That is a good saying," said Skallagrim, and they fell asleep side by side and Eric had no fear.

Now they awoke and the light was already full, for they were weary and their sleep had been heavy.

Hard by the mouth of the cave is a little well of water that gathers there from the rocks above and in this Eric washed himself. Then Skallagrim showed him the cave and the goodly store of arms that he had won from those whom he had slain and robbed.

"A wondrous place, truly," said Eric, "and well fitted to the uses of such a chapman as thou art; but, say, how didst thou find it?"

"I followed him who was here before me and gave him choice—to go, or to fight for the stronghold. But he needs must fight and that was his bane, for I slew him."

"Who was that, then," asked Eric, "whose head lies yonder?"

"A cave-dweller, lord, whom I took to me because of the lonesomeness of the winter tide. He was an evil man, for though it is good to be Baresark from time to time, yet to dwell with one who is always Baresark is not good, and thou didst a needful deed in smiting his head from him—and now let it go to find its trunk," and he rolled it over the edge of the great rift.

"Knowest thou, Skallagrim, that this head spoke to me after it had left the man's shoulders, saying that where its body fell there I should fall, and where it lay there I should lie also?"

"Then, lord, that is likely to be thy doom, for this man was foresighted, and, but the night before last, as we rode out to seek sheep, he felt his head, and said that, before the sun sank again, a hundred fathoms of air should link it to his shoulders."

"It may be so," answered Eric. "I thought as I lay in thy grip yonder that the fate was near. And now arm thyself, and take such goods as thou needest, and let us hence, for that thrall of mine who waits me yonder will think thou hast been too mighty for me."

Skallagrim went to the edge of the rift and searched the plain with his hawk eyes.

"No need to hasten, lord," he said. "See yonder rides thy thrall across the black sand, and with him goes thy horse. Surely he thought thou camest no more down the path by which thou wentest up, and it is not thrall's work to seek Skallagrim in his lair and ask for tidings."

"Wolves take him for a fool!" said Eric in anger. "He will ride to Middalhof and sing my death-song, and that will sound sadly in some ears."

"It is pleasant, lord," said Skallagrim, "when good tidings dog the heels of bad, and womenfolk can spare some tears and be little poorer. I have horses in a secret dell that I will show thee, and on them we will ride hence to Middalhof—and there thou must claim peace for me."

"It is well," said Eric; "now arm thyself, for if thou goest with me thou must make an end of thy Baresark ways, or keep them for the hour of battle."

"I will do thy bidding, lord," said Skallagrim. Then he entered the cave and set a plain black steel helm upon his black locks, and a black chain byrnie about his breast. He took the great axe-head also and fitted to it the half of another axe that lay among the weapons. Then he drew out a purse of money and a store of golden rings, and set them in a bag of otter skin, and buckled it about him. But the other goods he wrapped up in skins and hid behind some stones which were at the bottom of the cave—purposing to come another time and fetch them.

Then they went forth by that same perilous path which Eric had trod, and Skallagrim showed him how he might pass the rock in safety.

"A rough road this," said Eric as he gained the deep cleft.

"Yea, lord, and, till thou camest, one that none but wood-folk have trodden."

"I would tread it no more," said Eric again, "and yet that fellow thief of thine said that I should die here," and for a while his heart was heavy.

Now Skallagrim Lambstail led him by secret paths to a dell rich in grass, that is hid in the round of the mountain, and here three good horses were at feed. Then, going to a certain rock, he brought out bits and saddles, and they caught the horses, and, mounting them, rode away from Mosfell.

Now Eric and his henchman Skallagrim the Baresark rode four hours and saw nobody, till at length they came to the brow of a hill that is named Horse-Head Heights, and, crossing it, found themselves almost in the midst of a score of armed men who were about to mount their horses.

"Now we have company," said Skallagrim.

"Yes, and bad company," answered Eric, "for yonder I spy Ospakar Blacktooth, and Gizur and Mord his sons, ay and others. Down, and back to back, for they will show us little gentleness."

Then they sprang to earth and took their stand upon a mound of rising ground—and the men rode towards them.

"I shall soon know what thy fellowship is worth," said Eric.

"Fear not, lord," answered Skallagrim. "Hold thou thy head and I will hold thy back. We are met in a good hour."

"Good or ill, it is likely to be a short one. Hearken thou: if thou must turn Baresark when swords begin to flash, at the least stand and be Baresark where thou art, for if thou rushest on the foe, my back will be naked and I must soon be sped."

"It shall be as thou sayest, lord."

Now men rode round them, but at first they did not know Eric, because of the golden helm that hid his face in shadow.

"Who are ye?" called Ospakar.

"I think that thou shouldst know me, Blacktooth," Eric answered, "for I set thee heels up in the snow but lately—or, at the least, thou wilt know this," and he drew great Whitefire.

"Thou mayest know me also, Ospakar," cried the Baresark. "Skallagrim, men called me, Lambstail, Eric Brighteyes calls me, but once thou didst call me Ounound. Say, lord, what tidings of Thorunna?"

Now Ospakar shook his sword, laughing. "I came out to seek one foe, and I have found two," he cried. "Hearken, Eric: when thou art slain I go hence to burn and kill at Middalhof. Shall I bear thy head as keepsake from thee to Gudruda? For thee, Ounound, I thought thee dead; but, being yet alive, Thorunna, my sweet love, sends thee this," and he hurled a spear at him with all his might.

But Skallagrim catches the spear as it flies and hurls it back. It strikes right on the shield of Ospakar and pierces it, ay and the byrnie, and the shoulder that is beneath the byrnie, so that Blacktooth was made unmeet for fight, and howled with pain and rage.

"Go, bid Thorunna draw that splinter forth," says Skallagrim, "and heal the hole with kisses."

Now Ospakar, writhing with his hurt, shouts to his men to slay the two of them, and then the fight begins.

One rushes at Eric and smites at him with an axe. The blow falls on his shield, and shears off the side of it, then strikes the byrnie beneath, but lightly. In answer Eric sweeps low at him with Whitefire, and cuts his leg from under him between knee and thigh, and he falls and dies.

Another rushes in. Down flashes Whitefire before he can smite, and the carle's shield is cloven through. Then he chooses to draw back and fights no more that day.

Skallagrim slays a man, and wounds another sore. A tall chief with a red scar on his face comes at Brighteyes. Twice he feints at the head while Eric watches, then lowers the sword beneath the cover of his shield, and sweeps suddenly at Eric's legs. Brighteyes leaps high into the air, smiting downward with Whitefire as he leaps, and presently that chief is dead, shorn through shoulder to breast.

Now Skallagrim slays another man, and grows Baresark. He looks so fierce that men fall back from him.

Two rush on Eric, one from either side. The sword of him on the right falls on his shield and sinks in, but Brighteyes twists the shorn shield so strongly that the sword is wrenched from the smiter's hand. Now the other sword is aloft above him, and that had been Eric's bane, but Skallagrim glances round and sees it about to fall. He has no time to turn, but dashes the hammer of his axe backward. It falls full on the swordsman's head, and the head is shattered.

"That was well done," says Eric as the sword goes down.

"Not so ill but it might be worse," growls Skallagrim.

Presently all men drew back from those two, for they have had enough of Whitefire and the Baresark's axe.

Ospakar sits on his horse, his shield pinned to his shoulder and curses aloud.

"Close in, you cowards!" he yells, "close in and cut them down!" but no man stirs.

Then Eric mocks them. "There are but two of us," he says, "will no man try a game with me? Let it not be sung that twenty were overcome of two."

Now Ospakar's son Mord hears, and he grows mad with rage. He holds his shield aloft and rushes on. But Gizur the Lawman does not come, for Gizur was a coward.

Skallagrim turns to meet Mord, but Eric says:—

"This one for me, comrade," and steps forward.

Mord strikes a mighty blow. Eric's shield is all shattered and cannot stay it. It crashes through and falls full on the golden helm, beating Brighteyes to his knee. Now he is up again and blows fall thick and fast. Mord is a strong man, unwearied, and skilled in war, and Eric's arms grow faint and his strength sinks low. Mord smites again and wounds him somewhat on the shoulder.

Eric throws aside his cloven shield and, shouting, plies Whitefire with both arms. Mord gives before him, then rushes and smites; Eric leaps aside. Again he rushes and lo! Brighteyes has dropped his point, and it stands a full span through the back of Mord, and instantly that was his bane.

Now men rush to their horses, mount in hot haste and ride away, crying that these are trolls whom they have to do with here, not men. Skallagrim sees, and the Baresark fit takes him sore. With axe aloft he charges after them, screaming as he comes. There is one man, the same whom he had wounded. He cannot mount easily, and when the Baresark comes he still lies on the neck of his horse. The great axe wheels on high and falls, and it is told of this stroke that it was so mighty that man and horse sank dead beneath it, cloven through and through. Then the fit leaves Skallagrim and he walks back, and they are alone with the dead and dying.

Eric leans on Whitefire and speaks:

"Get thee gone, Skallagrim Lambstail!" he said; "get thee gone!"

"It shall be as thou wilt, lord," answered the Baresark; "but I have not befriended thee so ill that thou shouldst fear for blows to come."

"I will keep no man with me who puts my word aside, Skallagrim. What did I bid thee? Was it not that thou shouldst have done with the Baresark ways, and where thou stoodest there thou shouldst bide? and see: thou didst forget my word swiftly! Now get thee gone!"

"It is true, lord," he said. "He who serves must serve wholly," and Skallagrim turned to seek his horse.

"Stay," said Eric; "thou art a gallant man and I forgive thee: but cross my will no more. We have slain several men and Ospakar goes hence wounded. We have got honour, and they loss and the greatest shame. Nevertheless, ill shall come of this to me, for Ospakar has many friends and will set a law-suit on foot against me at the Althing, and thou didst draw the first blood."

"Would that the spear had gone more home," said Skallagrim.

"Ospakar's time is not yet," answered Eric; "still, he has something by which to bear us in mind."

IX: HOW SWANHILD DEALT WITH GUDRUDA

Now Jon, Eric's thrall, watched all night on Mosfell, but saw nothing except the light of Whitefire as it smote the Baresark's head from his shoulders. He stayed there till daylight, much afraid; then, making sure that Eric was slain, Jon rode hard and fast for Middalhof, whither he came at evening.

Gudruda was watching by the women's door. She strained her eyes towards Mosfell to catch the light gleaming on Eric's golden helm, and presently it gleamed indeed, white not red.

"See," said Swanhild at her side, "Eric comes!"

"Not Eric, but his thrall," answered Gudruda, "to tell us that Eric is sped."

They waited in silence while Jon galloped towards them.

"What news of Brighteyes?" cried Swanhild.

"Little need to ask," said Gudruda, "look at his face."

Now Jon told his tale and Gudruda listened, clinging to the door post. But Swanhild cursed him for a coward, so that he shrank before her eyes.

Gudruda turned and walked into the hall and her face was like the face of death. Men saw her, and Asmund asked why she wore so strange a mien. Then Gudruda sang this song:

"Up to Mosfell, battle eager,
Rode helmed Brighteyen to the fray.
Back from Mosfell, battle shunning.
Slunk yon coward thrall I ween.
Now shall maid Gudruda never
Know a husband's dear embrace;
Widowed is she—sunk in sorrow,
Eric treads Valhalla's halls!"

And with this she walked from the stead, looking neither to the right nor to the left.

"Let the maid be," said Atli the Earl. "Grief fares best alone. But my heart is sore for Eric. It should go ill with that Baresark if I might get a grip of him."

"That I will have before summer is gone," said Asmund, for the death of Eric seemed to him the worst of sorrows.

Gudruda walked far, and, crossing Laxà by the stepping stones, climbed Stonefell till she came to the head of Golden Falls, for, like a stricken thing, she desired to be alone in her grief. But Swanhild saw her and followed, coming on her as she sat watching the water thunder down the mighty cleft. Presently Swanhild's shadow fell athwart her, and Gudruda looked up.

"What wouldst thou with me, Swanhild?" she asked. "Art thou come to mock my grief?"

"Nay, foster-sister, for then I must mock my own. I come to mix my tears with thine. See, we loved Eric, thou and I, and Eric is dead. Let our hate be buried in his grave, whence neither may draw him back."

Gudruda looked upon her coldly, for nothing could stir her now.

"Get thee gone," she said. "Weep thine own tears and leave me to weep mine. Not with thee will I mourn Eric."

Swanhild frowned and bit her lip. "I will not come to thee with words of peace a second time, my rival," she said. "Eric is dead, but my hate that was born of Eric's love for thee lives on and grows, and its flower shall be thy death, Gudruda!"

"Now that Brighteyes is dead, I would fain follow on his path: so, if thou listest, throw the gates wide," Gudruda answered, and heeded her no more.

Swanhild went, but not far. On the further side of a knoll of grass she flung herself to earth and grieved as her fierce heart might. She shed no tears, but sat silently, looking with empty eyes adown the past, and onward to the future, and finding no good therein.

But Gudruda wept as the weight of her loss pressed in upon her—wept heavy silent tears and cried in her heart to Eric who was gone—cried to death to come upon her and bring her sleep or Eric.

So she sat and so she grieved till, quite outworn with sorrow, sleep stole upon her and she dreamed. Gudruda dreamed that she was dead and that she sat nigh to the golden door that is in Odin's house at Valhalla, by which the warriors pass and repass for ever. There she sat from age to age, listening to the thunder of ten thousand thousand tramping feet, and watching the fierce faces of the chosen as they marched out in armies to do battle in the meads. And as she sat, at length a one-eyed man, clad in gleaming garments, drew near and spoke to her. He was glorious to look on, and old, and she knew him for Odin the Allfather.

"Whom seekest thou, maid Gudruda?" he asked, and the voice he spoke with was the voice of waters.

"I seek Eric Brighteyes," she answered, "who passed hither a thousand years ago, and for love of whom I am heart-broken."

"Eric Brighteyes, Thorgrimur's son?" quoth Odin. "I know him well; no brisker warrior enters at Valhalla's doors, and none shall do more service at the coming of grey wolf Fenrir.[*] Pass on and leave him to his glory and his God."

[*] *The foe destined to bring destruction on the Norse gods.*

Then, in her dream, she wept sore, and prayed of Odin by the name of Freya that he would give Eric to her for a little space.

"What wilt thou pay, then, maid Gudruda?" said Odin.

"My life," she answered.

"Good," he said; "for a night Eric shall be thine. Then die, and let thy death be his cause of death." And Odin sang this song:

"Now, corse-choosing Daughters, hearken
To the dread Allfather's word:
When the gale of spears' breath gathers
Count not Eric midst the slain,

Till Brighteyen once hath slumbered,
Wedded, at Gudruda's side—
Then, Maidens, scream your battle call;
Whelmed with foes, let Eric fall!"

And Gudruda awoke, but in her ears the mighty waters still seemed to speak with Odin's voice, saying:

"Then, Maidens, scream your battle call;
Whelmed with foes, let Eric fall!"

She awoke from that fey sleep, and looked upwards, and lo! before her, with shattered shield and all besmeared with war's red rain, stood gold-helmed Eric. There he stood, great and beautiful to see, and she looked on him trembling and amazed.

"Is it indeed thou, Eric, or is it yet my dream?" she said.

"I am no dream, surely," said Eric; "but why lookest thou thus on me, Gudruda?"

She rose slowly. "Methought," she said, "methought that thou wast dead at the hand of Skallagrim." And with a great cry she fell into his arms and lay there sobbing.

It was a sweet sight thus to see Gudruda the Fair, her head of gold pillowed on Eric's war-stained byrnie, her dark eyes afloat with tears of joy; but not so thought Swanhild, watching. She shook in jealous rage, then crept away, and hid herself where she could see no more, lest she should be smitten with madness.

"Whence camest thou? ah! whence camest thou?" said Gudruda. "I thought thee dead, my love; but now I dreamed that I prayed Odin, and he spared thee to me for a little."

"Well, and that he hath, though hardly," and he told her all that had happened, and how, as he rode with Skallagrim, who yet sat yonder on his horse, he caught sight of a woman seated on the grass and knew the colour of the cloak.

Then Gudruda kissed him for very joy, and they were happy each with each—for of all things that are sweet on earth, there is nothing more sweet than this: to find him we loved, and thought dead and cold, alive and at our side.

And so they talked and were very glad with the gladness of youth and love, till Eric said he must on to Middalhof before the light failed, for he could not come on horseback the way that Gudruda took, but must ride round the shoulder of the hill; and, moreover, he was spent with toil and hunger, and Skallagrim grew weary of waiting.

"Go!" said Gudruda; "I will be there presently!"

So he kissed her and went, and Swanhild saw the kiss and saw him go.

"Well, lord," said Skallagrim, "hast thou had thy fill of kissing?"

"Not altogether," answered Eric.

They rode a while in silence.

"I thought the maid seemed very fair!" said Skallagrim.

"There are women less favoured, Skallagrim."

"Rich bait for mighty fish!" said Skallagrim. "This I tell thee: that, strive as thou mayest against thy fate, that maid will be thy bane and mine also."

"Things foredoomed will happen," said Eric; "but if thou fearest a maid, the cure is easy: depart from my company."

"Who was the other?" asked the Baresark—"she who crept and peered, listened, then crept back again, hid her face in her hands, and talked with a grey wolf that came to her like a dog?"

"That must have been Swanhild," said Eric, "but I did not see her. Ever does she hide like a rat in the thatch, and as for the wolf, he must be her Familiar; for, like Groa, her mother, Swanhild plays much with witchcraft. Now I will away back to Gudruda, for my heart misdoubts me of this matter. Stay thou here till I come, Lambstail!" And Eric turns and gallops back to the head of Goldfoss.

When Eric left her, Gudruda drew yet nearer to the edge of the mighty falls, and seated herself on their very brink. Her breast was full of joy, and there she sat and let the splendour of the night and the greatness of the rushing sounds sink into her heart. Yonder shone the setting sun, poised, as it were, on Westman's distant peaks, and here sped the waters, and by that path Eric had come back to her. Yea, and there on Sheep-saddle was the road that he had trod down Goldfoss; and but now he had slain one Baresark and won another to be his thrall, and they two alone had smitten the company of Ospakar, and come thence with honour and but little harmed. Surely no such man as Eric had ever lived—none so fair and strong and tender; and she was right happy in his love! She stretched out her arms towards him whom but an hour gone she had thought dead, but who had lived to come back to her with honour, and blessed his beloved name, and laughed aloud in her joyousness of heart, calling:

"Eric! Eric!"

But Swanhild, creeping behind her, did not laugh. She heard Gudruda's voice and guessed Gudruda's gladness, and jealousy arose within her and rent her. Should this fair rival like to take her joy from her?

"Grey Wolf, Grey Wolf! what sayest thou?"

See, now, if Gudruda were gone, if she rolled a corpse into those boiling waters, Eric might yet be hers; or, if he was not hers, yet Gudruda's he could never be.

"Grey Wolf, Grey Wolf! what is thy counsel?"

Right on the brink of the great gulf sat Gudruda. One stroke and all would be ended. Eric had gone; there was no eye to see—none save the Grey Wolf's; there was no tongue to tell the deed that might be done. Who could call her to account? The Gods! Who were the Gods? What were the Gods? Were they not dreams? There were no Gods save the Gods of Evil—the Gods she knew and communed with.

"Grey Wolf, Grey Wolf! what is thy rede?"

There sat Gudruda, laughing in the triumph of her joy, with the sunset-glow shining on her beauty, and there, behind her, Swanhild crept—crept like a fox upon his sleeping prey.

Now she is there—

"I hear thee, Grey Wolf! Back to my breast, Grey Wolf!"

Surely Gudruda heard something? She half turned her head, then again fell to calling aloud to the waters:

"Eric! beloved Eric!—ah! is there ever a light like the light of thine eyes—is there ever a joy like the joy of thy kiss?"

Swanhild heard, and her springs of mercy froze. Hate and fury entered into her. She rose upon her knees and gathered up her strength:

"Seek, then, thy joy in Goldfoss," she cried aloud, and with all her force she thrust.

Gudruda fell a fathom or more, then, with a cry, she clutched wildly at a little ledge of rock, and hung there, her feet resting on the shelving bank. Thirty fathoms down swirled and poured and rolled the waters of the Golden Falls. A fathom above, red in the red light of evening, lowered the pitiless face of Swanhild. Gudruda looked beneath her and saw. Pale with agony she looked up and saw, but she said naught.

"Let go, my rival; let go!" cried Swanhild: "there is none to help thee, and none to tell thy tale. Let go, I say, and seek thy marriage-bed in Goldfoss!"

But Gudruda clung on and gazed upwards with white face and piteous eyes.

"What! art thou so fain of a moment's life?" said Swanhild. "Then I will save thee from thyself, for it must be ill to suffer thus!" and she ran to seek a rock. Now she finds one and, staggering beneath its weight to the brink of the gulf, peers over. Still Gudruda hangs. Space yawns beneath her, the waters roar in her ears, the red sky glows above. She sees Swanhild come and shrieks aloud.

Eric is there, though Swanhild hears him not, for the sound of his horse's galloping feet is lost in the roar of waters. But that cry comes to his ears, he sees the poised rock, and all grows clear to him. He leaps from his horse, and even as she looses the stone, clutches Swanhild's kirtle and hurls her back. The rock bounds sideways and presently is lost in the waters.

Eric looks over. He sees Gudruda's white face gleaming in the gloom. Down he leaps upon the ledge, though this is no easy thing.

"Hold fast! I come; hold fast!" he cries.

"I can no more," gasps Gudruda, and one hand slips.

Eric grasps the rock and, stretching downward, grips her wrist; just as her hold loosens he grips it, and she swings loose, her weight hanging on his arm.

Now he must needs lift her up and that with one hand, for the ledge is narrow and he dare not loose his hold of the rock above. She swings over the great gulf and she is senseless as one dead. He gathers all his mighty strength and lifts. His feet slip a little, then catch, and once more Gudruda swings. The sweat bursts out upon his forehead and his blood drums through him. Now it must be, or not at all. Again he lifts and his muscles strain and crack, and she lies beside him on the narrow ledge!

All is not yet done. The brink of the cleft is the height of a man above him. There he must lay her, for he may not leave her to find aid, lest she should wake and roll into the chasm. Loosing his hold of the cliff, he turns, facing the rock, and, bending over Gudruda, twists his hands in her kirtle below the breast and above the knee. Then once more Eric puts out his might and draws her up to the level of his breast, and rests. Again with all his force he lifts her above the crest of his helm and throws her forward, so that now she lies upon the brink of the great cliff. He almost falls backward at the effort, but, clutching the rock, he saves himself, and with a struggle gains her side, and lies there, panting like a wearied hound of chase.

Of all trials of strength that ever were put upon his might, Eric was wont to say, this lifting of Gudruda was the greatest; for she was no light woman, and there was little to stand on and almost nothing to cling to.

Presently Brighteyes rose and peered at Gudruda through the gloom. She still swooned. Then he gazed about him—but Swanhild, the witchgirl, was gone.

Then he took Gudruda in his arms, and, leading the horse, stumbled through the darkness, calling on Skallagrim. The Baresark answered, and presently his large form was seen looming in the gloom.

Eric told his tale in few words.

"The ways of womankind are evil," said Skallagrim; "but of all the deeds that I have known done at their hands, this is the worst. It had been well to hurl the wolf-witch from the cliff."

"Ay, well," said Eric; "but that song must yet be sung."

Now dimly lighted of the rising moon by turns they bore Gudruda down the mountain side, till at length, utterly fordone, they saw the fires of Middalhof.

X

HOW ASMUND SPOKE WITH SWANHILD

Now as the days went, though Atli's ship was bound for sea, she did not sail, and it came about that the Earl sank ever deeper in the toils of Swanhild. He called to mind many wise saws, but these availed him little: for when Love rises like the sun, wisdom melts like the mists. So at length it came to this, that on the day of Eric's coming back, Atli went to Asmund the Priest, and asked him for the hand of Swanhild the Fatherless in marriage. Asmund heard and was glad, for he knew well that things went badly between Swanhild and Gudruda, and it seemed good to him that seas should be set between them. Nevertheless, he thought it honest to warn the Earl that Swanhild was apart from other women.

"Thou dost great honour, earl, to my foster-daughter and my house," he said. "Still, it behoves me to move gently in this matter. Swanhild is fair, and she shall not go hence a wife undowered. But I must tell thee this: that her ways are dark and secret, and strange and fiery are her moods, and I think that she will bring evil on the man who weds her. Now, I love thee, Atli, were it only for our youth's sake, and thou art not altogether fit to mate with such a maid, for age has met thee on thy way. For, as thou wouldst say, youth draws to youth as the tide to the shore, and falls away from eld as the wave from the rock. Think, then: is it well that thou shouldst take her, Atli?"

"I have thought much and overmuch," answered the Earl, stroking his grey beard; "but ships old and new drive before a gale."

"Ay, Atli, and the new ship rides, where the old one founders."

"A true rede, a heavy rede, Asmund; yet I am minded to sail this sea, and, if it sink me—well, I have known fair weather! Great longing has got hold of me, and I think the maid looks gently on me, and that things may yet go well between us. I have many things to give such as women love. At the least, if thou givest me thy good word, I will risk it, Asmund: for the bold thrower sometimes wins the stake. Only I say this, that, if Swanhild is unwilling, let there be an end of my wooing, for I do not wish to take a bride who turns from my grey hairs."

Asmund said that it should be so, and they made an end of talking just as the light faded.

Now Asmund went out seeking Swanhild, and presently he met her near the stead. He could not see her face, and that was well, for it was not good to look on, but her mien was wondrous wild.

"Where hast thou been, Swanhild?" he asked.

"Mourning Eric Brighteyes," she made answer.

"It is meeter for Gudruda to mourn over Eric than for thee, for her loss is heavy," Asmund said sternly. "What hast thou to do with Eric?"

"Little, or much; or all—read it as thou wilt, foster-father. Still, all wept for are not lost, nor all who are lost wept for."

"Little do I know of thy dark redes," said Asmund. "Where is Gudruda now?"

"High is she or low, sleeping or perchance awakened: naught reck I. She also mourned for Eric, and we went nigh to mingling tears—near together were brown curls and golden," and she laughed aloud.

"Thou art surely fey, thou evil girl!" said Asmund.

"Ay, foster-father, fey: yet is this but the first of my feydom. Here starts the road that I must travel, and my feet shall be red ere the journey's done."

"Leave thy dark talk," said Asmund, "for to me it is as the wind's song, and listen: a good thing has befallen thee—ay, good beyond thy deserving."

"Is it so? Well, I stand greatly in need of good. What is thy tidings, foster-father?"

"This: Atli the Earl asks thee in marriage, and he is a mighty man, well honoured in his own land, and set higher, moreover, than I had looked for thee."

"Ay," answered Swanhild, "set like the snow above the fells, set in the years that long are dead. Nay, foster-father, this white-bearded dotard is no mate for me. What! shall I mix my fire with his frost, my breathing youth with the creeping palsy of his age? Never! If Swanhild weds she weds not so, for it is better to go maiden to the grave than thus to shrink and wither at the touch of eld. Now is Atli's wooing sped, and there's an end."

Asmund heard and grew wroth, for the matter seemed strange to him; nor are maidens wont thus to put aside the word of those set over them.

"There is no end," he said; "I will not be answered thus by a girl who lives upon my bounty. It is my rede that thou weddest Atli, or else thou goest hence. I have loved thee, and for that love's sake I have borne thy wickedness, thy dark secret ways, and evil words; but I will be crossed no more by thee, Swanhild."

"Thou wouldst drive me hence with Groa my mother, though perchance thou hast yet more reason to hold me dear, foster-father. Fear not: I will go—perhaps further than thou thinkest," and once more Swanhild laughed, and passed from him into the darkness.

But Asmund stood looking after her. "Truly," he said in his heart, "ill deeds are arrows that pierce him who shot them. I have sowed evilly, and now I reap the harvest. What means she with her talk of Gudruda and the rest?"

Now as he thought, he saw men and horses draw near, and one man, whose helm gleamed in the moonlight, bore something in his arms.

"Who passes?" he called.

"Eric Brighteyes, Skallagrim Lambstail, and Gudruda, Asmund's daughter," answered a voice; "who art thou?"

Then Asmund the Priest sprang forward, most glad at heart, for he never thought to see Eric again.

"Welcome, and thrice welcome art thou, Eric," he cried; "for, know, we deemed thee dead."

"I have lately gone near to death, lord," said Eric, for he knew the voice; "but I am hale and whole, though somewhat weary."

"What has come to pass, then?" asked Asmund, "and why holdest thou Gudruda in thy arms? Is the maid dead?"

"Nay, she does but swoon. See, even now she stirs," and as he spake Gudruda awoke, shuddering, and with a little cry threw her arms about the neck of Eric.

He set her down and comforted her, then once more turned to Asmund:

"Three things have come about," he said. "First, I have slain one Baresark, and won another to be my thrall, and for him I crave thy peace, for he has served me well. Next, we two were set upon by Ospakar Blacktooth and his fellowship, and, fighting for our hands, have wounded Ospakar, slain Mord his son, and six other men of his following."

"That is good news and bad," said Asmund, "since Ospakar will ask a great weregild[*] for these men, and thou wilt be outlawed, Eric."

[*] The penalty for manslaying.

"That may happen, lord. There is time enough to think of it. Now there are other tidings to tell. Coming to the head of Goldfoss I found Gudruda, my betrothed, mourning my death, and spoke with her. Afterwards I left her, and presently returned again, to see her hanging over the gulf, and Swanhild hurling rocks upon her to crush her."

"These are tidings in truth," said Asmund—"such tidings as my heart feared! Is this true, Gudruda?"

"It is true, my father," answered Gudruda, trembling. "As I sat on the brink of Goldfoss, Swanhild crept behind me and thrust me into the gulf. There I clung above the waters, and she brought a rock to hurl upon me, when suddenly I saw Eric's face, and after that my mind left me and I can tell no more."

Now Asmund grew as one mad. He plucked at his beard and stamped on the ground. "Maid though she be," he cried, "yet shall Swanhild's back be broken on the

Stone of Doom for a witch and a murderess, and her body hurled into the pool of faithless women, and the earth will be well rid of her!"

Now Gudruda looked up and smiled: "It would be ill to wreak such a vengeance on her, father," she said; "and this would also bring the greatest shame on thee, and all our house. I am saved, by the mercy of the Gods and the might of Eric's arm, and this is my counsel: that nothing be told of this tale, but that Swanhild be sent away where she can harm us no more."

"She must be sent to the grave, then," said Asmund, and fell to thinking. Presently he spoke again: "Bid yon man fall back, I would speak with you twain," and Skallagrim went grumbling.

"Hearken now, Eric and Gudruda: only an hour ago hath Atli the Good asked Swanhild of me in marriage. But now I met Swanhild here, and her mien was wild. Still, I spoke of the matter to her, and she would have none of it. Now, this is my counsel: that choice be given to Swanhild, either that she go hence Atli's wife, or take her trial in the Doom-ring."

"That will be bad for the Earl then," said Eric. "Methinks he is too good a man to be played on thus."

"Bairn first, then friend," answered Asmund.

"Now I will tell thee something that, till this hour, I have hidden from all, for it is my shame. This Swanhild is my daughter, and therefore I have loved her and put away her evil deeds, and she is half-sister to thee, Gudruda. See, then, how sore is my straight, who must avenge daughter upon daughter."

"Knows thy son Björn of this?" asked Eric.

"None knew it till this hour, except Groa and I."

"Yet I have feared it long, father," said Gudruda, "and therefore I have also borne with Swanhild, though she hates me much and has striven hard to draw my betrothed from me. Now thou canst only take one counsel, and it is: to give choice to Swanhild of these two things, though it is unworthy that Atli should be deceived, and at the best little good can come of it."

"Yet it must be done, for honour is often slain of heavy need," said Asmund. "But we must first swear this Baresark thrall of thine, though little faith lives in Baresark's breast."

Now Eric called to Skallagrim and charged him strictly that he should tell nothing of Swanhild, and of the wolf that he saw by her, and of how Gudruda was found hanging over the gulf.

"Fear not," growled the Baresark, "my tongue is now my master's. What is it to me if women do their wickedness one on another? Let them work magic, hate and slay by stealth, so shall evil be lessened in the world."

"Peace!" said Eric; "if anything of this passes thy lips thou art no longer a thrall of mine, and I give thee up to the men of thy quarter."

"And I cleave that wolf's head of thine down to thy hawk's eyes; but, otherwise, I give thee peace, and will hold thee from harm, wood-dweller as thou art," said Asmund.

The Baresark laughed: "My hands will hold my head against ten such mannikins as thou art, Priest. There was never but one man who might overcome me in fair fight and there he stands, and his bidding is my law. So waste no words and make not niddering threats against greater folk," and he slouched back to his horse.

"A mighty man and a rough," said Asmund, looking after him; "I like his looks little."

"Natheless a strong in battle," quoth Eric; "had he not been at my back some six hours gone, by now the ravens had torn out these eyes of mine. Therefore, for my sake, bear with him."

Asmund said it should be so, and then they passed on to the stead.

Here Eric stripped off his harness, washed, and bound up his wounds. Then, followed by Skallagrim, axe in hand, he came into the hall as men made ready to sit at meat. Now the tale of the mighty deeds that he had done, except that of the saving of Gudruda, had gone abroad, and as Brighteyes came all men rose and with one voice shouted till the roof of the great hall rocked:

"Welcome, Eric Brighteyes, thou glory of the south!"

Only Björn, Asmund's son, bit his hand, and did not shout, for he hated Eric because of the fame that he had won.

Brighteyes stood still till the clamour died, then said:

"Much noise for little deeds, brethren. It is true that I overthrew the Mosfell Baresarks. See, here is one," and he turned to Skallagrim; "I strangled him in my arms on Mosfell's brink, and that was something of a deed. Then he swore fealty to me, and we are blood-brethren now, and therefore I ask peace for him, comrades—even from those whom he has wronged or whose kin he has slain. I know this, that when thereafter we stood back to back and met the company of Ospakar Blacktooth, who came to slay us—ay, and Asmund also, and bear away Gudruda to be his wife—he warred right gallantly, till seven of their band lay stiff on Horse-Head Heights, overthrown of us, and among them Mord, Blacktooth's son; and Ospakar himself went thence sore smitten of this Skallagrim. Therefore, for my sake, do no harm to this man who was Baresark, but now is my thrall; and, moreover, I beg the aid and friendship of all men of this quarter in those suits that will be laid against me at the Althing for these slayings, which I hereby give out as done by my hand, and by the hand of Skallagrim Lambstail, the Baresark."

At these words all men shouted again; but Atli the Earl sprang from the high seat where Asmund had placed him, and, coming to Eric, kissed him, and, drawing a gold chain from his neck, flung it about the neck of Eric, crying:

"Thou art a glorious man, Eric Brighteyes. I thought the world had no more of such a breed. Listen to my bidding: come thou to the earldom in Orkneys and be a son to me, and I will give thee all good gifts, and, when I die, thou shalt sit in my seat after me."

But Eric thought of Swanhild, who must go from Iceland as wife to Atli, and answered:

"Thou doest me great honour, Earl, but this may not be. Where the fir is planted, there it must grow and fall. Iceland I love, and I will stay here among my own people till I am driven away."

"That may well happen, then," said Atli, "for be sure Ospakar and his kin will not let the matter of these slayings rest, and I think that it will not avail thee much that thou smotest for thine own hand. Then, come thou and be my man."

"Where the Norns lead there I must follow," said Eric, and sat down to meat. Skallagrim sat down also at the side-bench; but men shrank from him, and he glowered on them in answer.

Presently Gudruda entered, and she seemed pale and faint.

When he had done eating, Eric drew Gudruda on to his knee, and she sat there, resting her golden head upon his breast. But Swanhild did not come into the hall, though ever Earl Atli sought her dark face and lovely eyes of blue, and he wondered greatly how his wooing had sped. Still, at this time he spoke no more of it to Asmund.

Now Skallagrim drank much ale, and glared about him fiercely; for he had this fault, that at times he was drunken. In front of him were two thralls of Asmund's; they were brothers, and large-made men, and they watched Asmund's sheep upon the fells in winter. These two also grew drunk and jeered at Skallagrim, asking him what atonement he would make for those ewes of Asmund's that he had stolen last Yule, and how it came to pass that he, a Baresark, had been overthrown of an unarmed man.

Skallagrim bore their gibes for a space as he drank on, but suddenly he rose and rushed at them, and, seizing a man's throat in either hand, thrust them to the ground beneath him and nearly choked them there.

Then Eric ran down the hall, and, putting out his strength, tore the Baresark from them.

"This then is thy peacefulness, thou wolf!" Eric cried. "Thou art drunk!"

"Ay," growled Skallagrim, "ale is many a man's doom."

"Have a care that it is not thine and mine, then!" said Eric. "Go, sleep; and know that, if I see thee thus once more, I see thee not again."

But after this men jeered no more at Skallagrim Lambstail, Eric's thrall.

XI

HOW SWANHILD BID FAREWELL TO ERIC

Now all this while Asmund sat deep in thought; but when, at length, men were sunk in sleep, he took a candle of fat and passed to the shut bed where Swanhild slept alone. She lay on her bed, and her curling hair was all about her. She was awake, for the light gleamed in her blue eyes, and on a naked knife that was on the bed beside her, half hidden by her hair.

"What wouldst thou, foster-father?" she asked, rising in the couch. Asmund closed the curtains, then looked at her sternly and spoke in a low voice:

"Thou art fair to be so vile a thing, Swanhild," he said. "Who now would have dreamed that heart of thine could talk with goblins and with were-wolves—that those eyes of thine could bear to look on murder and those white hands find strength to do the sin?"

She held up her shapely arms and, looking on them, laughed. "Would that they had been fashioned in a stronger mould," she said. "May they wither in their woman's weakness! else had the deed been done outright. Now my crime is as heavy upon me and nothing gained by it. Say what fate for me, foster-father—the Stone of Doom and the pool where faithless women lie? Ah, then might Gudruda laugh indeed, and I will not live to hear that laugh. See," and she gripped the dagger at her side: "along this bright edge runs the path to peace and freedom, and, if need be, I will tread it."

"Be silent," said Asmund. "This Gudruda, my daughter, whom thou wouldst have foully done to death, is thine own sister, and it is she who, pitying thee, hath pleaded for thy life."

"I will naught of her pity who have no pity," she answered; "and this I say to thee who art my father: shame be on thee who hast not dared to own thy child!"

"Hadst thou not been my child, Swanhild, and had I not loved thee secretly as my child, be sure of this, I had long since driven thee hence; for my eyes have been open to much that I have not seemed to see. But at length thy wickedness has overcome my love, and I will see thy face no more. Listen: none have heard of this shameful deed of thine save those who saw it, and their tongues are sealed. Now I give thee choice: wed Atli and go, or stand in the Doom-ring and take thy fate."

"Have I not said, father, while death may be sought otherwise, that I will never do this last? Nor will I do the first. I am not all of the tame breed of you Iceland folk—other and quicker blood runs in my veins; nor will I be sold in marriage to a dotard as a mare is sold at a market. I have answered."

"Fool! think again, for I go not back upon my word. Wed Atli or die—by thy own hand, if thou wilt—there I will not gainsay thee; or, if thou fearest this, then anon in the Doom-ring."

Now Swanhild covered her eyes with her hands and shook the long hair about her face, and she seemed wondrous fair to Asmund the Priest who watched. And as she sat thus, it came into her mind that marriage is not the end of a young maid's life—that old husbands have been known to die, and that she might rule this Atli and his earldom and become a rich and honoured woman, setting her sails in such fashion that when the wind turned it would fill them. Otherwise she must die—ay, die shamed and leave Gudruda with her love.

Suddenly she slipped from the bed to the floor of the chamber, and, clasping the knees of Asmund, looked up through the meshes of her hair, while tears streamed from her beautiful eyes:

"I have sinned," she sobbed—"I have sinned greatly against thee and my sister. Hearken: I was mad with love of Eric, whom from a child I have turned to, and Gudruda is fairer than I and she took him from me. Most of all was I mad this night when I wrought the deed of shame, for ill things counselled me—things that I did not call; and oh, I thank the Gods—if there are Gods—that Gudruda died not at my hand. See now, father, I put this evil from me and tear Eric from my heart," and she made as though she rent her bosom—"I will wed Atli, and be a good housewife to

107

him, and I crave but this of Gudruda: that she forgive me her wrong; for it was not done of my will, but of my madness, and of the driving of those whom my mother taught me to know."

Asmund listened and the springs of his love thawed within him. "Now thou dost take good counsel," he said, "and of this be sure, that so long as thou art in that mood none shall harm thee; and for Gudruda, she is the most gentle of women, and it may well be that she will put away thy sin. So weep no more, and have no more dealings with thy Finnish witchcraft, but sleep; and to-morrow I will bear thy word to Atli, for his ship is bound and thou must swiftly be made a wife."

He went out, bearing the light with him; but Swanhild rose from the ground and sat on the edge of the bed, staring into the darkness and shuddering from time to time.

"I shall soon be made his wife," she murmured, "who would be but one man's wife—and methinks I shall soon be made a widow also. Thou wilt have me, dotard—take me and thy fate! Well, well; better to wed an Earl than to be shamed and stretched across the Doom-stone. Oh, weak arms that failed me at my need, no more will I put trust in you! When next I wound, it shall be with the tongue; when next I strive to slay, it shall be by another's hand. Curses on thee, thou ill counseller of darkness, who didst betray me at the last! Is it for this that I worshipped thee and swore the oath?"

The morning came, and at the first light Asmund sought the Earl. His heart was heavy because of the guile that his tongue must practise, and his face was dark as a winter dawn.

"What news, Asmund?" asked Atli. "Early tidings are bad tidings, so runs the saw, and thy looks give weight to it."

"Not altogether bad, Earl. Swanhild gives herself to thee."

"Of her own will, Asmund?"

"Ay, of her own will. But I have warned thee of her temper."

"Her temper! Little hangs to a maid's temper. Once a wife and it will melt in softness like the snow when summer comes. These are glad tidings, comrade, and methinks I grow young again beneath the breath of them. Why art thou so glum then?"

"There is something that must yet be told of Swanhild," said Asmund. "She is called the Fatherless, but, if thou wilt have the truth, why here it is for thee—she is my daughter, born out of wedlock, and I know not how that will please thee."

Atli laughed aloud, and his bright eyes shone in his wrinkled face. "It pleases me well, Asmund, for then the maid is sprung from a sound stock. The name of the Priest of Middalhof is famous far south of Iceland; and never that Iceland bred a comelier girl. Is that all?"

"One more thing, Earl. This I charge thee: watch thy wife, and hold her back from witchcraft and from dealings with evil things and trolls of darkness. She is of Finnish blood and the women of the Finns are much given to such wicked work."

"I set little store by witchwork, goblins and their kin," said Atli. "I doubt me much of their power, and I shall soon wean Swanhild from such ways, if indeed she practise them."

Then they fell to talking of Swanhild's dower, and that was not small. Afterwards Asmund sought Eric and Gudruda, and told them what had come to pass, and they were glad at the news, though they grieved for Atli the Earl. And when Swanhild met Gudruda, she came to her humbly, and humbly kissed her hand, and with tears craved pardon of her evil doing, saying that she had been mad; nor did Gudruda withhold it, for of all women she was the gentlest and most forgiving. But to Eric, Swanhild said nothing.

The wedding-feast must be held on the third day from this, for Atli would sail on that same day, since his people wearied of waiting and his ship might lie bound no longer. Blithe was Atli the Earl, and Swanhild was all changed, for now she seemed the gentlest of maids, and, as befitted one about to be made a wife, moved through the house with soft words and downcast eyes. But Skallagrim, watching her, bethought him of the grey wolf that he had seen by Goldfoss, and this seemed not well to him.

"It would be bad now," he said to Eric, as they rode to Coldback, "to stand in yon old earl's shoes. This woman's weather has changed too fast, and after such a calm there'll come a storm indeed. I am now minded of Thorunna, for she went just so the day before she gave herself to Ospakar, and me to shame and bonds."

"Talk not of the raven till you hear his croak," said Eric.

"He is on the wing, lord," answered Skallagrim.

Now Eric came to Coldback in the Marsh, and Saevuna his mother and Unna, Thorod's daughter, the betrothed of Asmund, were glad to welcome him; for the tidings of his mighty deeds and of the overthrow of Ospakar and the slaying of Mord were noised far and wide. But at Skallagrim Lambstail they looked askance. Still, when they heard of those things that he had wrought on Horse-Head Heights, they welcomed him for his deed's sake.

Eric sat two nights at Coldback, and on the second day Saevuna his mother and Unna rode thence with their servants to the wedding-feast of Swanhild the Fatherless. But Eric stopped at Coldback that night, saying that he would be at Middalhof within two hours of sunrise, for he must talk with a shepherd who came from the fells.

Saevuna and her company came to Middalhof and was asked, first by Gudruda, then by Swanhild, why Brighteyes tarried. She answered that he would be there early on the morrow. Next morning, before it was light, Eric girded on Whitefire, took horse and rode from Coldback alone, for he would not bring Skallagrim, fearing lest he should get drunk at the feast and shed some man's blood.

It was Swanhild's wedding-day; but she greeted it with little lightsomeness of heart, and her eyes knew no sleep that night, though they were heavy with tears.

At the first light she rose, and, gliding from the house, walked through the heavy dew down the path by which Eric must draw near, for she desired to speak with him. Gudruda also rose a while after, though she did not know this, and followed on the same path, for she would greet her lover at his coming.

Now three furlongs or more from the stead stood a vetch stack, and Swanhild waited on the further side of this stack. Presently she heard a sound of singing come from behind the shoulder of the fell and of the tramp of a horse's hoofs. Then she

109

saw the golden wings of Eric's helm all ablaze with the sunlight as he rode merrily along, and great bitterness laid hold of her that Eric could be of such a joyous mood on the day when she who loved him must be made the wife of another man.

Presently he was before her, and Swanhild stepped from the shadow of the stack and laid her hand upon his horse's bridle.

"Eric," she said humbly and with bowed head, "Gudruda sleeps yet. Canst thou, then, find time to hearken to my words?"

He frowned and said: "Methinks, Swanhild, it would be better if thou gavest thy words to him who is thy lord."

She let the bridle-rein drop from her hands. "I am answered," she said; "ride on."

Now pity stirred in Eric's heart, for Swanhild's mien was most heavy, and he leaped down from his horse. "Nay," he said, "speak on, if thou hast anything to tell me."

"I have this to tell thee, Eric; that now, before we part for ever, I am come to ask thy pardon for my ill-doing—ay, and to wish all joy to thee and thy fair love," and she sobbed and choked.

"Speak no more of it, Swanhild," he said, "but let thy good deeds cover up the ill, which are not small; so thou shalt be happy."

She looked at him strangely, and her face was white with pain.

"How then are we so differently fashioned that thou, Eric, canst prate to me of happiness when my heart is racked with grief? Oh, Eric, I blame thee not, for thou hast not wrought this evil on me willingly; but I say this: that my heart is dead, as I would that I were dead. See those flowers: they smell sweet—for me they have no odour. Look on the light leaping from Coldback to the sea, from the sea to Westman Isles, and from the Westman crown of rocks far into the wide heavens above. It is beautiful, is it not? Yet I tell thee, Eric, that now to my eyes howling winter darkness is every whit as fair. Joy is dead within me, music's but a jangled madness in my ears, food hath no savour on my tongue, my youth is sped ere my dawn is day. Nothing is left to me, Eric, save this fair body that thou didst scorn, and the dreams which I may gather from my hours of scanty sleep, and such shame as befalls a loveless bride."

"Speak not so, Swanhild," he said, and clasped her by the hand, for, though he loathed her wickedness, being soft-hearted and but young, it grieved him to hear her words and see the anguish of her mind. For it is so with men, that they are easily moved by the pleading of a fair woman who loves them, even though they love her not.

"Yea, I will speak out all my mind before I seal it up for ever. See, Eric, this is my state and thou hast set this crown of sorrow on my brows: and thou comest singing down the fell, and I go weeping o'er the sea! I am not all so ill at heart. It was love of thee that drove me down to sin, as love of thee might otherwise have lifted me to holiness. But, loving thee as thou seest, this day I wed a dotard, and go his chattel and his bride across the sea, and leave thee singing on the fell, and by thy side her who is my foe. Thou hast done great deeds, Brighteyes, and still greater shalt thou do; yet but as echoes they shall reach my ears. Thou wilt be to me as one dead, for it is Gudruda's to bind the byrnie on thy breast when thou goest forth to war, and hers to loose the winged helm from thy brow when thou returnest, battle-worn and conquering."

Now Swanhild ceased, and choked with grief; then spoke again:

"So now farewell; doubtless I weary thee, and—Gudruda waits. Nay, look not on my foolish tears: they are the heritage of woman, of naught else is she sure! While I live, Eric, morn by morn the thought of thee shall come to wake me as the sun wakes yon snowy peak, and night by night thy memory shall pass as at eve he passes from the valleys, but to dawn again in dreams. For, Eric, 'tis thee I wed to-day—at heart I am thy bride, thine and thine only; and when shalt thou find a wife who holds thee so dear as that Swanhild whom once thou knewest? So now farewell! Yes, this time thou shalt kiss away my tears; then let them stream for ever. Thus, Eric! and thus! and thus! do I take farewell of thee."

And now she clung about his neck, gazing on him with great dewy eyes till things grew strange and dim, and he must kiss her if only for her love and tender beauty's sake. And so he kissed, and it chanced that as they clung thus, Gudruda, passing by this path to give her betrothed greeting, came upon them and stood astonished. Then she turned and, putting her hands to her head, fled back swiftly to the stead, and waited there, great anger burning in her heart; for Gudruda had this fault, that she was very jealous.

Now Eric and Swanhild did not see her, and presently they parted, and Swanhild wiped her eyes and glided thence.

As she drew near the stead she found Gudruda watching.

"Where hast thou been, Swanhild?" she said.

"To bid farewell to Brighteyes, Gudruda."

"Then thou art foolish, for doubtless he thrust thee from him."

"Nay, Gudruda, he drew me to him. Hearken, I say, thou sister. Vex me not, for I go my ways and thou goest thine. Thou art strong and fair, and hitherto thou hast overcome me. But I am also fair, and, if I find space to strike in, I also have a show of strength. Pray thou that I find not space, Gudruda. Now is Eric thine. Perchance one day he may be mine. It lies in the lap of the Norns."

"Fair words from Atli's bride," mocked Gudruda.

"Ay, Atli's bride, but never Atli's love!" said Swanhild, and swept on.

A while after Eric rode up. He was shamefaced and vexed at heart, because he had yielded thus to Swanhild's beauty, and been melted by her tender words and kissed her. Then he saw Gudruda, and at the sight of her all thought of Swanhild passed from him, for he loved Gudruda and her alone. He leapt down from his horse and ran to her. But, drawn to her full height, she stood with dark flashing eyes and fair face set in anger.

Still, he would have greeted her loverwise; but she lifted her hand and waved him back, and fear took hold of him.

"What now, Gudruda?" he asked, faltering.

"What now, Eric?" she answered, faltering not. "Hast seen Swanhild?"

"Yea, I have seen Swanhild. She came to bid farewell to me. What of it?"

"What of it? Why 'thus! and thus! and thus!' didst thou bid farewell to Atli's bride. Ay, 'thus and thus,' with clinging lips and twined arms. Warm and soft was thy farewell kiss to her who would have slain me, Brighteyes!"

"Gudruda, thou speakest truth, though how thou sawest I know not. Think no ill of it, and scourge me not with words, for, sooth to say, I was melted by her grief and the music of her talk."

"It is shame to thee so to speak of her whom but now thou heldest in thine arms. By the grief and the music of the talk of her who would have murdered me thou wast melted into kisses, Eric!—for I saw it with these eyes. Knowest thou what I am minded to say to thee? It is this: 'Go hence and see me no more;' for I have little wish to cleave to such a feather-man, to one so blown about by the first breath of woman's tempting."

"Yet, methinks, Gudruda, I have withstood some such winds. I tell thee that, hadst thou been in my place, thyself hadst yielded to Swanhild and kissed her in farewell, for she was more than woman in that hour."

"Nay, Eric, I am no weak man to be led astray thus. Yet she is more than woman—troll is she also, that I know; but less than man art thou, Eric, thus to fall before her who hates me. Time may come when she shall woo thee after a stronger sort, and what wilt thou say to her then, thou who art so ready with thy kisses?"

"I will withstand her, Gudruda, for I love thee only, and this is well known to thee."

"Truly I know thou lovest me, Eric; but tell me of what worth is this love of man that eyes of beauty and tongue of craft may so readily bewray? I doubt me of thee, Eric!"

"Nay, doubt me not, Gudruda. I love thee alone, but I grew soft as wax beneath her pleading. My heart consented not, yet I did consent. I have no more to say."

Now Gudruda looked on him long and steadfastly. "Thy plight is sorry, Eric," she said, "and this once I forgive thee. Look to it that thou givest me no more cause to doubt thee, for then I shall remember how thou didst bid farewell to Swanhild."

"I will give none," he answered, and would have embraced her; but this she would not suffer then, nor for many days after, for she was angry with him. But with Swanhild she was still more angry, though she said nothing of it. That Swanhild had tried to murder her, Gudruda could forgive, for there she had failed; but not that she had won Eric to kiss her, for in this she had succeeded well.

XII

HOW ERIC WAS OUTLAWED AND SAILED A-VIKING

Now the marriage-feast went on, and Swanhild, draped in white and girt about with gold, sat by Atli's side upon the high seat. He was fain of her and drew her to him, but she looked at him with cold calm eyes in which hate lurked. The feast was done, and all the company rode to the sea strand, where the Earl's ship lay at anchor. They came there, and Swanhild kissed Asmund, and talked a while with Groa, her mother, and bade farewell to all men. But she bade no farewell to Eric and to Gudruda.

"Why sayest thou no word to these two?" asked Atli, her husband.

"For this reason, Earl," she answered, "because ere long we three shall meet again; but I shall see Asmund, my father, and Groa, my mother, no more."

"That is an ill saying, wife," said Atli. "Methinks thou dost foretell their doom."

"Mayhap! And now I will add to my redes, for I foretell thy doom also: it is not yet, but it draws on."

Then Atli bethought him of many wise saws, but spoke no more, for it seemed to him this was a strange bride that he had wed.

They hauled the anchor home, shook out the great sail, and passed away into the evening night. But while land could still be seen, Swanhild stood near the helm, gazing with her blue eyes upon the lessening coast. Then she passed to the hold, and shut herself in alone, and there she stayed, saying that she was sick, till at length, after a fair voyage of twenty days, they made the Orkney Islands.

But all this pleased Atli wondrous ill, yet he dared not cross her mood.

Now, in Iceland the time drew on when men must ride to the Althing, and notice was given to Eric Brighteyes of many suits that were laid against him, in that he had brought Mord, Ospakar's son, to his death, dealing him a brain or a body or a marrow wound, and others of that company. But no suits were laid against Skallagrim, for he was already outlaw. Therefore he must go in hiding, for men were out to slay him, and this he did unwillingly, at Eric's bidding. Asmund took up Eric's case, for he was the most famous of all lawmen in that day, and when thirteen full weeks of summer were done, they two rode to the Thing, and with them a great company of men of their quarter.

Now, men go up to the Lögberg, and there came Ospakar, though he was not yet healed of his wound, and all his company, and laid their suits against Eric by the mouth of Gizur the Lawman, Ospakar's son. The pleadings were long and cunning on either side; but the end of it was that Ospakar brought it about, by the help of his friends—and of these had many—that Eric must go into outlawry for three years. But no weregild was to be paid to Ospakar and his men for those who had been killed, and no atonement for the great wound that Skallagrim Lambstail gave him, or for the death of Mord, his son, inasmuch as Eric fought for his own hand to save his life.

The party of Ospakar were ill pleased at this finding, and Eric was not over glad, for it was little to his mind that he should sail a-warring across the seas, while Gudruda sat at home in Iceland. Still, there was no help for the matter.

Now Ospakar spoke with his company, and the end of it was that he called on them to take their weapons and avenge themselves by their own might. Asmund and Eric, seeing this, mustered their army of freemen and thralls. There were one hundred and five of them, all stout men; but Ospakar Blacktooth's band numbered a hundred and thirty-three, and they stood with their backs to the Raven's Rift.

"Now I would that Skallagrim was here to guard my back," said Eric, "for before this fight is done few will left standing to tell its tale."

"It is a sad thing," said Asmund, "that so many men must die because some men are now dead."

"A very sad thing," said Eric, and took this counsel. He stalked alone towards the ranks of Ospakar and called in a loud voice, saying:

"It would be grievous that so many warriors should fall in such a matter. Now hearken, you company of Ospakar Blacktooth! If there be any two among you who will dare to match their might against my single sword in holmgang, here I, Eric Brighteyes, stand and wait them. It is better that one man, or perchance three men, should fall, than that anon so many should roll in the dust. What say ye?"

Now all those who watched called out that this was a good offer and a manly one, though it might turn out ill for Eric; but Ospakar answered:

"Were I but well of my wound I alone would cut that golden comb of thine, thou braggart; as it is, be sure that two shall be found."

"Who is the braggart?" answered Eric. "He who twice has learned the weight of this arm and yet boasts his strength, or I who stand craving that two should come against me? Get thee hence, Ospakar; get thee home and bid Thorunna, thy leman, whom thou didst beguile from that Ounound who now is named Skallagrim Lambstail the Baresark, nurse thee whole of the wound her husband gave thee. Be sure we shall yet stand face to face, and that combs shall be cut then, combs black or golden. Nurse thee! nurse thee! cease thy prating—get thee home, and bid Thorunna nurse thee; but first name thou the two who shall stand against me in holmgang in Oxarà's stream."

Folk laughed aloud while Eric mocked, but Ospakar gnashed his teeth with rage. Still, he named the two mightiest men in his company, bidding them take up their swords against Brighteyes. This, indeed, they were loth to do; still, because of the shame that they must get if they hung back, and for fear of the wrath of Ospakar, they made ready to obey his bidding.

Then all men passed down to the bank of Oxarà, and, on the other side, people came from their booths and sat upon the slope of All Man's Raft, for it was a new thing that one man should fight two in holmgang.

Now Eric crossed to the island where holmgangs are fought to this day, and after him came the two chosen, flourishing their swords bravely, and taking counsel how one should rush at his face, while the other passed behind his back and spitted him, as woodfolk spit a lamb. Eric drew Whitefire and leaned on it, waiting for the word, and all the women held him to be wondrous fair as, clad in his byrnie and his golden helm, he leaned thus on Whitefire. Presently the word was given, and Eric, standing not to defend himself as they deemed he surely would, whirled Whitefire round his helm and rushed headlong on his foes, shield aloft.

The great carles saw the light that played on Whitefire's edge and the other light that burned in Eric's eyes, and terror got hold of them. Now he was almost come, and Whitefire sprang aloft like a tongue of flame. Then they stayed no more, but, running one this way and one that, cast themselves into the flood and swam for the river-edge. Now from either bank rose up a roar of laughter, that grew and grew, till it echoed against the lava rifts and scared the ravens from their nests.

Eric, too, stopped his charge and laughed aloud; then walked back to where Asmund stood, unarmed, to second him in the holmgang.

"I can get little honour from such champions as these," he said.

"Nay," answered Asmund, "thou hast got the greatest honour, and they, and Ospakar, such shame as may not be wiped out."

Now when Blacktooth saw what had come to pass, he well-nigh choked, and fell from his horse in fury. Still, he could find no stomach for fighting, but, mustering his company, rode straightway from the Thing home again to Swinefell. But he caused those two whom he had put up to do battle with Eric to be set upon with staves and driven from his following, and the end of it was that they might stay no more in Iceland, but took ship and sailed south, and now they are out of the story.

On the next day, Asmund, and with him Eric and all their men, rode back to Middalhof. Gudruda greeted Eric well, and for the first time since Swanhild went away she kissed him. Moreover, she wept bitterly when she learned that he must go into outlawry, while she must bide at home.

"How shall the days pass by, Eric?" she said, "when thou art far, and I know not where thou art, nor how it goes with thee, nor if thou livest or art already dead?"

"In sooth I cannot say, sweet," he answered; "but of this I am sure that, wheresoever I am, yet more weary shall be my hours."

"Three years," she went on—"three long, cold years, and no sight of thee, and perchance no tidings from thee, till mayhap I learn that thou art in that land whence tidings cannot come. Oh, it would be better to die than to part thus."

"Well I wot that it is better to die than to live, and better never to have been born than to live and die," answered Eric sadly. "Here, it would seem, is nothing but hate and strife, weariness and bitter envy to fret away our strength, and at last, if we come so far, sorrowful age and death, and thereafter we know not what. Little of good do we find to our hands, and much of evil; nor know I for what ill-doing these burdens are laid upon us. Yet must we needs breathe such an air as is blown about us, Gudruda, clasping at this happiness which is given, though we may not hold it. At the worst, the game will soon be played, and others will stand where we have stood, and strive as we have striven, and fail as we have failed, and so on, till man has worked out his doom, and the Gods cease from their wrath, or Ragnarrök come upon them, and they too are lost in the jaws of grey wolf Fenrir."

"Men may win one good thing, and that is fame, Eric."

"Nay, Gudruda, what is it to win fame? Is it not to raise up foes, as it were, from the very soil, who, made with secret hate, seek to stab us in the back? Is it not to lose peace, and toil on from height to height only to be hurled down at last? Happy, then, is the man whom fame flies from, for hers is a deadly gift."

"Yet there is one thing left that thou hast not numbered, Eric, and it is love—for love is to our life what the sun is to the world, and, though it seems to set in death, yet it may rise again. We are happy, then, in our love, for there are many who live their lives and do not find it."

So these two, Eric Brighteyes and Gudruda the Fair, talked sadly, for their hearts were heavy, and on them lay the shadow of sorrows that were to come.

"Say, sweet," said Eric at length, "wilt thou that I go not into banishment? Then I must fall into outlawry, and my life will be in the hands of him who may take it; yet I think that my foes will find it hard to come by while my strength remains, and at the worst I do but turn to meet the fate that dogs me."

"Nay, that I will not suffer, Brighteyes. Now we will go to my father, and he shall give thee his dragon of war—she is a good vessel—and thou shalt man her with the briskest men of our quarter: for there are many who will be glad to fare abroad with thee, Eric. Soon she shall be bound and thou shalt sail at once, Eric: for the sooner thou art gone the sooner the three years will be sped, and thou shalt come back to me. But, oh! that I might go with thee."

Now Gudruda and Eric went to Asmund and spoke of this matter.

"I desired," he answered, "that thou, Eric, shouldst bide here in Iceland till after harvest, for it is then that I would take Unna, Thorod's daughter, to wife, and it was meet that thou shouldst sit at the wedding-feast and give her to me."

"Nay, father, let Eric go," said Gudruda, "for well begun is, surely, half done. He must remain three years in outlawry: add thou no day to them, for, if he stays here for long, I know this: that I shall find no heart to let him go, and, if go he must, then I shall go with him."

"That may never be," said Asmund; "thou art too young and fair to sail a-viking down the sea-path. Hearken, Eric: I give thee the good ship, and now we will go about to find stout men to man her."

"That is a good gift," said Eric; and afterwards they rode to the seashore and overhauled the vessel as she lay in her shed. She was a great dragon of war, long and slender, and standing high at stem and prow. She was fashioned of oak, all bolted together with iron, and at her prow was a gilded dragon most wonderfully carved.

Eric looked on her and his eyes brightened.

"Here rests a wave-horse that shall bear a viking well," he said.

"Ay," answered Asmund, "of all the things I own this ship is the very best. She is so swift that none may catch her, and she can almost go about in her own length. That gale must be heavy that shall fill her, with thee to steer; yet I give her to thee freely, Eric, and thou shalt do great deeds with this my gift, and, if things go well, she shall come back to this shore at last, and thou in her."

"Now I will name this war-gift with a new name," said Eric. "'Gudruda,' I name her: for, as Gudruda here is the fairest of all women, so is this the fairest of all war-dragons."

"So be it," said Asmund.

Then they rode back to Middalhof, and now Eric Brighteyes let it be known that he needed men to sail the seas with him. Nor did he ask in vain, for, when it was told that Eric went a-viking, so great was his fame grown, that many a stout yeoman and many a great-limbed carle reached down sword and shield and came up to Middalhof to put their hands in his. For mate, he took a certain man named Hall of Lithdale, and this because Björn asked it, for Hall was a friend to Björn, and he had, moreover, great skill in all manner of seamanship, and had often sailed the Northern Seas—ay, and round England to the coast of France.

But when Gudruda saw this man, she did not like him, because of his sharp face, uncanny eyes, and smooth tongue, and she prayed Eric to have nothing to do with him.

"It is too late now to talk of that," said Eric. "Hall is a well-skilled man, and, for the rest, fear not: I will watch him."

"Then evil will come of it," said Gudruda.

Skallagrim also liked Hall little, nor did Hall love Skallagrim and his great axe.

At length all were gathered; they were fifty in number and it is said that no such band of men ever took ship from Iceland.

Now the great dragon was bound and her faring goods were aboard of her, for Eric must sail on the morrow, if the wind should be fair. All day long he stalked to and fro among his men; he would trust nothing to others, and there was no sword or shield in his company but he himself had proved it. All day long he stalked, and at his back went Skallagrim Lambstail, axe on shoulder, for he would never leave Eric if he had his will, and they were a mighty pair.

At length all was ready and men sat down to the faring-feast in the hall at Middalhof, and that was a great feast. Eric's folk were gathered on the side-benches, and by the high seat at Asmund's side sat Brighteyes, and near to him where Björn, Asmund's son, Gudruda, Unna, Asmund's betrothed, and Saevuna, Eric's mother. For this had been settled between Asmund and Eric, that his mother Saevuna, who was some somewhat sunk in age, should flit from Coldback and come with Unna to dwell at Middalhof. But Eric set a trusty grieve to dwell at Coldback and mind the farm.

When the faring-toasts had been drunk, Eric spoke to Asmund and said: "I fear one thing, lord, and it is that when I am gone Ospakar will trouble thee. Now, I pray you all to beware of Blacktooth, for, though the hound is whipped, he can still bite, and it seems that he has not yet put Gudruda from his mind."

Now Björn had sat silently, thinking much and drinking more, for he loved Eric less than ever on this day when he saw how all men did him honour and mourned his going, and his father not the least of them.

"Methinks it is thou, Eric," he said, "whom Ospakar hates, and thee on whom he would work his vengeance, and that for no light cause."

"When bad fortune sits in thy neighbour's house, she knocks upon thy door, Björn. Gudruda, thy sister, is my betrothed, and thou art a party to this feud," said Eric. "Therefore it becomes thee better to hold her honour and thy own against this Northlander, than to gird at me for that in which I have no blame."

Björn grew wroth at these words. "Prate not to me," he said. "Thou art an upstart who wouldst teach their duty to thy betters—ay, puffed up with light-won fame, like a feather on the breeze. But I say this: the breeze shall fail, and thou shalt fall upon the goose's back once more. And I say this also, that, had I my will, Gudruda should wed Ospakar: for he is a mighty chief, and not a long-legged carle, outlawed for man-slaying."

Now Eric sprang from his seat and laid hand upon the hilt of Whitefire, while men murmured in the hall, for they held this an ill speech of Björn's.

"In thee, it seems, I have no friend," said Eric, "and hadst thou been any other man than Gudruda's brother, forsooth thou shouldst answer for thy mocking words. This I tell thee, Björn, that, wert thou twice her brother, if thou plottest with Ospakar when I am gone, thou shalt pay dearly for it when I come back again. I know thy heart well: it is cunning and greedy of gain, and filled with envy as a cask with ale; yet, if thou lovest to feel it beating in thy breast, strive not to work me mischief and to put Gudruda from me."

Now Björn sprang up also and drew his sword, for he was white with rage; but Asmund his father cried, "Peace!" in a great voice.

"Peace!" he said. "Be seated, Eric, and take no heed of this foolish talk. And for thee, Björn, art thou the Priest of Middalhof, and Gudruda's father, or am I? It has pleased me to betroth Brighteyes to Gudruda, and it pleased me not to betroth her to Ospakar, and that is enough for thee. For the rest, Ospakar would have slain Eric, not he Ospakar, therefore Eric's hands are clean. Though thou art my son, I say this, that, if thou workest ill to Eric when he is over sea, thou shalt rightly learn the weight of Whitefire: it is a niddering deed to plot against an absent man."

Eric sat down, but Björn strode scowling from the hall, and, taking horse, rode south; nor did he and Eric meet again till three years had come and gone, and then they met but once.

"Maggots shall be bred of that fly, nor shall they lack flesh to feed on," said Skallagrim in Eric's ears as he watched Björn pass. But Eric bade him be silent, and turned to Gudruda.

"Look not so sad, sweet," he said, "for hasty words rise like the foam on mead and pass as soon. It vexes Björn that thy father has given me the good ship: but his anger will soon pass, or, at the very worst, I fear him not while thou art true to me."

"Then thou hast little to fear, Eric," she answered. "Look now on thy hair: it grows long as a woman's, and that is ill, for at sea the salt will hang to it. Say, shall I cut it for thee?"

"Yes, Gudruda."

So she cut his yellow locks, and one of them lay upon her heart for many a day.

"Now thou shalt swear to me," she whispered in his ear, "that no other man or woman shall cut thy hair till thou comest back to me and I clip it again."

"That I swear, and readily," he answered. "I will go long-haired like a girl for thy sake, Gudruda."

He spoke low, but Koll the Half-witted, Groa's thrall, heard this oath and kept it in his mind.

Very early on the morrow all men rose, and, taking horse, rode once more to the seaside, till they came to that shed where the Gudruda lay.

Then, when the tide was high, Eric's company took hold of the black ship's thwarts, and at his word dragged her with might and main. She ran down the greased blocks and sped on quivering to the sea, and as her dragon-prow dipped in the water people cheered aloud.

Now Eric must bid farewell to all, and this he did with a brave heart till at the last he came to Saevuna, his mother, and Gudruda, his dear love.

"Farewell, son," said the old dame; "I have little hope that these eyes shall look again upon that bonny face of thine, yet I am well paid for my birth-pains, for few have borne such a man as thou. Think of me at times, for without me thou hadst never been. Be not led astray of women, nor lead them astray, or ill shall overtake thee. Be not quarrelsome because of thy great might, for there is a stronger than the strongest. Spare a fallen foe, and take not a poor man's goods or a brave man's sword; but, when thou smitest, smite home. So shalt thou win honour, and, at the last, peace, that is more than honour."

Eric thanked her for her counsel, and kissed her, then turned to Gudruda, who stood, white and still, plucking at her golden girdle.

"What can I say to thee?" he asked.

"Say nothing, but go," she answered: "go before I weep."

"Weep not, Gudruda, or thou wilt unman me. Say, thou wilt think on me?"

"Ay, Eric, by day and by night."

"And thou wilt be true to me?"

"Ay, till death and after, for so long as thou cleavest to me I will cleave to thee. I will first die rather than betray thee. But of thee I am not so sure. Perchance thou mayest find Swanhild in thy journeyings and crave more kisses of her?"

"Anger me not, Gudruda! thou knowest well that I hate Swanhild more than any other woman. When I kiss her again, then thou mayst wed Ospakar."

"Speak not so rashly, Eric," she said, and as she spoke Skallagrim drew near.

"If thou lingerest here, lord, the tide will serve us little round Westmans," he said, eyeing Gudruda as it were with jealousy.

"I come," said Eric. "Gudruda, fare thee well!"

She kissed him and clung to him, but did not answer, for she could not speak.

XIII

HOW HALL THE MATE CUT THE GRAPNEL CHAIN

Gudruda bent her head like a drooping flower, and presently sank to earth, for her knees would bear her weight no more; but Eric marched to the lip of the sea, his head held high and laughing merrily to hide his pain of heart. Here stood Asmund, who gripped him by both hands, and kissed him on the brow, bidding him good luck.

"I know not whether we shall meet again," he said; "but, if my hours be sped before thou returnest, this I charge thee: that thou mindest Gudruda well, for she is the sweetest of all women that I have known, and I hold her the most dear."

"Fear not for that, lord," said Eric; "and I pray thee this, that, if I come back no more, as well may happen, do not force Gudruda into marriage, if she wills it not, and I think she will have little leaning that way. And I say this also: do not count overmuch on Björn thy son, for he has no loyal heart; and beware of Groa, who was thy housekeeper, for she loves not that Unna should take her place and more. And now I thank thee for many good things, and farewell."

"Farewell, my son," said Asmund, "for in this hour thou seemest as a son to me."

Eric turned to enter the sea and wade to the vessel, but Skallagrim caught him in his arms as though he were but a child, and, wading into the surf till the water covered his waistbelt, bore him to the vessel and lifted him up so that Eric reached the bulwarks with his hands.

Then they loosed the cable and got out the oars and soon were dancing over the sea. Presently the breeze caught them, and they set the great sail and sped away like a gull towards the Westman Isles. But Gudruda sat on the shore watching till, at length, the light faded from Eric's golden helm as he stood upon the poop, and the world grew dark to her.

Now Ospakar Blacktooth had news of this sailing and took counsel of Gizur his son, and the end of it was that they made ready two great ships, dragons of war, and, placing sixty fighting men in each of them, sailed round the Iceland coast to the Westmans and waited there to waylay Eric. They had spies on the land, and from them they learned of Brighteyes' coming, and sailed out to meet him in the channel between the greater and the lesser islands, where they knew that he must pass.

Now it drew towards evening when Eric rowed down this channel, for the wind had fallen and he desired to be clear at sea. Presently, as the Gudruda came near to the mouth of the channel, that had high cliffs on either hand, Eric saw two long dragons of war—for their bulwarks were shield-hung—glide from the cover of the island and take their station side by side between him and the open sea.

"Now here are vikings," said Eric to Skallagrim.

"Now here is Ospakar Blacktooth," answered Skallagrim, "for well I know that raven banner of his. This is a good voyage, for we must seek but a little while before we come to fighting."

Eric bade the men lay on their oars, and spoke:

"Before us is Ospakar Blacktooth in two great dragons, and he is here to cut us off. Now two choices are left to us: one is to bout ship and run before him, and the other to row on and give him battle. What say ye, comrades?"

Hall of Lithdale, the mate, answered, saying:

"Let us go back, lest we die. The odds are too great, Eric."

But a man among the crew cried out, "When thou didst go on holmgang at Thingvalla, Eric, Ospakar's two chosen champions stood before thee, yet at Whitefire's flash they skurried through the water like startled ducks. It was an omen, for so shall his great ships fly when we swoop on them." Then the others shouted:

"Ay, ay! Never let it be said that we fled from Ospakar—fie on thy woman's talk, Hall!"

"Then we are all of one mind, save Hall only," said Eric. "Let us put Ospakar to the proof." And while men shouted "Yea!" he turned to speak with Skallagrim. The Baresark was gone, for, wasting no breath in words, already he was fixing the long shields on the bulwark rail.

The men busked on their harness and made them fit for fight, and, when all was ready, Eric mounted the poop, and with him Skallagrim, and bade the rowers give way. The Gudruda leapt forward and rushed on towards Ospakar's ships. Now they saw that these were bound together with a cable and yet they must go betwixt them.

Eric ran forward to the prow, and with him Skallagrim, and called aloud to a great man who stood upon the ship to starboard, wearing a black helm with raven's wings:

"Who art thou that bars the sea against me?"

"I am named Ospakar Blacktooth," answered the great man.

"And what must we lose at thy hands, Ospakar?"

"But one thing—your lives!" answered Blacktooth.

"Thrice have we stood face to face, Ospakar," said Eric, "and it seems that hitherto thou hast won no great glory. Now it shall be proved if thy luck has bettered."

"Art yet healed, lord, of that prick in the shoulder which thou camest by on Horse-Head Heights?" roared Skallagrim.

For answer, Ospakar seized a spear and hurled it straight at Eric, and it had been his death had he not caught it in his hand as it flew. Then he cast it back, and that so mightily that it sped right through the shield of Ospakar and was the bane of a man who stood beside him.

"A gift for a gift!" laughed Eric. On rushed the Gudruda, but now the cable was strained six fathoms from her bow that held together the ships of Ospakar and it was too strong for breaking. Eric looked and saw. Then he drew Whitefire, and while all men wondered, leaped over the prow of the ship and, clasping the golden dragon's head with his arm, set his feet upon its claws and waited. On sped the ship and spears flew thick and fast about him, but there Brighteyes hung. Now the Gudruda's bow caught the great rope and strained it taut and, as it rose beneath her weight, Eric smote swift and strong with Whitefire and clove it in two, so that the severed ends fell with a splash into the quiet water.

Eric sprang back to deck while stones and spears hissed about him.

"That was well done, lord," said Skallagrim; "now we shall be snugly berthed."

"In oars and out grappling-irons," shouted Eric.

Up rose the rowers, and their war-gear rattled as they rose. They drew in the long oars, and not before it was time, for now the Gudruda forced her way between the two dragons of Ospakar and lay with her bow to their sterns. Then with a shout Eric's men cast the irons and soon the ships were locked fast and the fight began. The spears flew thick, and on either side some got their death before them. Then the men of that vessel, named the Raven, which was to larboard of the Gudruda, made ready to board. On they came with a rush, and were driven back, though hardly, for they were many, and those who stood against them few. Again they came, scrambling over the bulwarks, and this time a score of them leapt aboard. Eric turned from the fight against the dragon of Ospakar and saw it. Then, with Skallagrim, he rushed to meet the boarders as they swarmed along the hold, and naught might they withstand the axe and sword.

Through and through them swept the mighty pair, now Whitefire flashed, and now the great axe fell, and at every stroke a man lay dead or wounded. Six of the boarders turned to fly, but just then the grappling-iron broke and their ship drifted out with the tide towards the open sea, and presently no man of that twenty was left alive.

Now the men of the ship of Ospakar and of the Gudruda pressed each other hard. Thrice did Ospakar strive to come aboard and thrice he was pushed back. Eric was ever where he was most needed, and with him Skallagrim, for these two threw themselves from side to side, and were now here and now there, so that it seemed as though there were not one golden helm and one black, but rather four on board the Gudruda.

Eric looked and saw that the other ship was drawing round, though somewhat slowly, to come alongside of them once more.

"Now we must make an end of Ospakar, else our hands will be overfull," he said, and therewith sprang up upon the bulwarks and after him many men. Once they were driven back, but came on again, and now they thrust all Ospakar's men before them and passed up his ship on both boards. By the mast stood Ospakar and with him Gizur his son, and Eric strove to come to him. But many men were between them, and he could not do this.

Presently, while the fight yet went on hotly and men fell fast, Brighteyes felt the dragon of Ospakar strike, and, looking, saw that they had drifted with the send of the tide on to the rocks of the island. There was a great hole in the hull amidships and the water rushed in fast.

"Back! men; back!" he cried, and all his folk that were unhurt, ran, and leapt on board the Gudruda; but Ospakar and his men sprang into the sea and swam for the shore. Then Skallagrim cut loose the grappling-irons with his axe, and that not too soon, for, scarcely had they pushed clear with great toil when the long warship slipped from the rock and foundered, taking many dead and wounded men with her.

Now Ospakar and some of his people stood safe upon the rocks, and Eric called to him in mockery, bidding him come aboard the Gudruda.

Ospakar made no answer, but stood gnawing his hand, while the water ran from him. Only Gizur his son cursed them aloud.

Eric was greatly minded to follow them, and land and fight them there; but he might not do this, because of the rocks and of the other dragon, that hung about them, fearing to come on and yet not willing to go back.

"We will have her, at the least," said Eric, and bade the rowers get out their oars.

Now, when the men on board the other ship saw the Gudruda drawing on, they took to their oars at once and rowed swiftly for the sea, and at this a great roar of laughter went down Eric's ship.

"They shall not slip from us so easily," said Eric; "give way, comrades, and after them."

But the men were much wearied with fighting, and the decks were all cumbered with dead and wounded, so that by the time that the Gudruda had put about, and come to the mouth of the waterway, Ospakar's vessel had shaken out her sails and caught the wind, that now blew strong off shore, and sped away six furlongs or more from Eric's prow.

"Now we shall see how the Gudruda sails," said Eric, and they spread their canvas and gave chase.

Then Eric bade men clear the decks of the dead, and tend the wounded. He had lost seven men slain outright, and three were wounded, one to death. But on board the ship there lay of Ospakar's force twenty and three dead men.

When all were cast into the sea, men ate and rested.

"We have not done so badly," said Eric to Skallagrim.

"We shall do better yet," said Skallagrim to Eric; "rather had I seen Ospakar's head lying in the scuppers than those of all his carles; for he may get more men, but never another head!"

Now the wind freshened till by midnight it blew strongly. The mate Hall came to Eric and said:

"The Gudruda dips her nose deep in Ran's cup. Say, Eric, shall we shorten sail?"

"Nay," answered Eric, "keep her full and bail. Where yonder Raven flies, my Sea-stag must follow," and he pointed to the warship that rode the waves before them.

After midnight clouds came up, with rain, and hid the face of the night-sun and the ship they sought. The wind blew ever harder, till at length, when the rain had passed and the clouds lifted, there was much water in the hold and the bailers could hardly stand at their work.

Men murmured, and Hall the mate murmured most of all; but still Eric held on, for there, not two furlongs ahead of them, rode the dragon of Ospakar. But now, being afraid of the wind and sea, she had lowered her sail somewhat, and made as though she would put about and run for Iceland.

"That she may not do," called Eric to Skallagrim, "if once she rolls side on to those seas Ran has her, for she must fill and sink."

"So they hold, lord," answered Skallagrim; "see, once more she runs!"

"Ay, but we run faster—she is outsailed. Up, men, up: for presently the fight begins."

"It is bad to join battle in such a sea," quoth Hall.

"Good or bad," growled Skallagrim, "do thou thy lord's bidding," and he half lifted up his axe.

The mate said no more, for he misdoubted him of Skallagrim Lambstail and his axe.

Then men made ready for the fray as best they might, and stood, sword in hand and drenched with foam, clinging to the bulwarks of the Gudruda as she wallowed through the seas.

Eric went aft to the helm and seized it. Now but a length ahead Ospakar's ship laboured on beneath her small sail, but the Gudruda rushed towards her with all canvas set and at every leap plunged her golden dragon beneath the surf and shook the water from her foredeck.

"Make ready the grapnel!" shouted Eric through the storm. Skallagrim seized the iron and stood by. Now the Gudruda rushed alongside the Raven, and Eric steered so skilfully that there was a fathom space, and no more, between the ships.

Skallagrim cast the iron well and truly, so that it hooked and held. On sped the Gudruda and the cable tautened—now her stern kissed the bow of Ospakar's ship, as though she was towing her, and thus for a space they travelled through the seas.

Eric's folk shouted and strove to cast spears; but they did this but ill, because of the rocking of the vessel. As for Ospakar's men, they clung to their bulwarks and did nothing, for all the heart was out of them between fear of Eric and terror of the sea. Eric called to a man to hold the helm, and Skallagrim crept aft to where he stood.

"What counsel shall we take now?" said Eric, and as he spoke a sea broke over them—for the gale was strong.

"Board them and make an end," answered Skallagrim.

"Rough work; still, we will try it," said Eric, "for we may not lie thus for long, and I am loath to leave them."

Then Eric called for men to follow him, and many answered, creeping as best they might to where he stood.

"Thou art mad, Eric," said Hall the mate; "cut loose and let us drive, else we shall both founder, and that is a poor tale to tell."

Eric took no heed, but, watching his chance, leapt on to the bows of the Raven, and after him leapt Skallagrim. Even as he did so, a great sea came and swept past and over them, so that half the ship was hid for foam. Now, Hall the mate stood near to the grapnel cable, and, fearing lest they should sink, out of the cowardice of his heart, he let his axe fall upon the chain, and severed it so swiftly that no man saw him, except Skallagrim only. Forward sprang the Gudruda, freed from her burden, and rushed away before the wind, leaving Eric and Skallagrim alone upon the Raven's prow.

"Now we are in an evil plight," said Eric, "the cable has parted!"

"Ay," answered Skallagrim, "and that losel Hall hath parted it! I saw his axe fall."

XIV

HOW ERIC DREAMED A DREAM

Now, when the men of Ospakar, who were gathered on the poop of the Raven, saw what had come about, they shouted aloud and made ready to slay the pair. But Eric and Skallagrim clambered to the mast and got their backs against it, and swiftly made themselves fast with a rope, so that they might not fall with the rolling of the ship. Then the people of Ospakar came on to cut them down.

But this was no easy task, for they might scarcely stand, and they could not shoot with the bow. Moreover, Eric and Skallagrim, being bound to the mast, had the use of both hands and were minded to die hard. Therefore Ospakar's folks got but one thing by their onslaught, and that was death, for three of their number fell beneath the long sweep of Whitefire, and one bowed before the axe of Skallagrim. Then they drew back and strove to throw spears at these two, but they flew wide because of the rolling of the vessel. One spear struck the mast near the head of Skallagrim. He drew it out, and, waiting till the ship steadied herself in the trough of the sea, hurled it at a knot of Ospakar's thralls, and a man got his death from it. After that they threw no more spears.

Thence once more the crew came on with swords and axes, but faint-heartedly, and the end of it was that they lost some more men dead and wounded and fell back again.

Skallagrim mocked at them with bitter words, and one of them, made mad by his scoffing, cast a heavy ballast-stone at him. It fell upon his shoulder and numbed him.

"Now I am unmeet for fight, lord," said Skallagrim, "for my right arm is dead and I can scarcely hold my axe."

"That is ill, then," said Eric, "for we have little help, except from each other, and I, too, am well-nigh spent. Well, we have done a great deed and now it is time to rest."

"My left arm is yet whole, lord, and I can make shift for a while with it. Cut loose the cord before they bait us to death, and let us rush upon these wolves and fall fighting."

"A good counsel," said Eric, "and a quick end; but stay a while: what plan have they now?"

Now the men of Ospakar, having little heart left in them for such work as this, had taken thought together.

"We have got great hurt, and little honour," said the mate. "There are but nineteen of us left alive, and that is scarcely enough to work the ship, and it seems that we shall be fewer before Eric Brighteyes and Skallagrim Lambstail lie quiet by yonder mast. They are mighty men, indeed, and it would be better, methinks, to deal with them by craft, rather than by force."

The sailors said that this was a good word, for they were weary of the sight of Whitefire as he flamed on high and the sound of the axe of Skallagrim as it crashed through helm and byrnie; and as fear crept in valour fled out.

"This is my rede, then," said the mate: "that we go to them and give them peace, and lay them in bonds, swearing that we will put them ashore when we are come back to Iceland. But when we have them fast, as they sleep at night, we will creep on them and hurl them into the sea, and afterwards we will say that we slew them fighting."

"A shameful deed!" said a man.

"Then go thou up against them," answered the mate. "If we slay them not, then shall this tale be told against us throughout Iceland: that a ship's company were worsted by two men, and we may not live beneath that dishonour."

The man held his peace, and the mate, laying down his arms, crept forward alone, towards the mast, just as Eric and Skallagrim were about to cut themselves loose and rush on them.

"What wouldest thou?" shouted Eric. "Has it gone so well with you with arms that ye are minded to come up against us bearing none?"

"It has gone ill, Eric," said the mate, "for ye twain are too mighty for us. We have lost many men, and we shall lose more ere ye are laid low. Therefore we make you this offer: that you lay down your weapons and suffer yourselves to be bound till such time as we touch land, where we will set you ashore, and give you your arms again. Meanwhile, we will deal with you in friendly fashion, giving you of the best we have; nor will we set foot any suit against you for those of our number whom ye two have slain."

"Wherefore then should we be bound?" said Eric.

"For this reason only: that we dare not leave you free within our ship. Now choose, and, if ye will, take peace, which we swear by all the Gods we will keep towards you, and, if ye will not, then we will bear you down with beams and sails and stones, and slay you."

"What thinkest thou, Skallagrim?" said Eric beneath his breath.

"I think that I find little faith in yon carle's face," answered Skallagrim. "Still, I am unfit to fight, and thy strength is spent, so it seems that we must lie low if we would rise again. They can scarcely be so base as to do murder having handselled peace to us."

"I am not so sure of that," said Eric; "still, starving beggars must eat bones. Hearken thou: we take the terms, trusting to your honour; and I say this: that ye shall get shame and death if ye depart from them to harm us."

"Have no fear, lord," said the mate, "we are true men."

"That we shall look to your deeds to learn," said Eric, laying down his sword and shield.

Skallagrim did likewise, though with no good grace. Then men came with strong cords and bound them fast hand and foot, handling them fearsomely as men handle a live bear in a net. Then they led them forward to the prow.

As they went Eric looked up. Yonder, twenty furlongs and more away, sailed the Gudruda.

"This is good fellowship," said Skallagrim, "thus to leave us in the trap."

"Nay," answered Eric. "They cannot put about in such a sea, and doubtless also they think us dead. Nevertheless, if ever it comes about that Hall and I stand face to face again, there will be need for me to think of gentleness."

"I shall think little thereon," growled Skallagrim.

Now they were come to the prow, and there was a half deck under which they were set, out of reach of the wind and water. In the deck was a stout iron ring, and the men made them fast with ropes to it, so that they might move but little, and they set their helms and weapons behind them in such fashion that they could not come at them. Then they flung cloaks about them, and brought them food and drink, of which they stood much in need, and treated them well in every way. But for all this Skallagrim trusted them no more.

"We are new-hooked, lord," he said, "and they give us line. Presently they will haul us in."

"Evil comes soon enough," answered Eric, "no need to run to greet it," and he fell to thinking of Gudruda, and of the day's deeds, till presently he dropped asleep, for he was very weary.

Now it chanced that as Eric slept he dreamed a dream so strong and strange that it seemed to live within him. He dreamed that he slept there beneath the Raven's deck, and that a rat came and whispered spells into his ear. Then he dreamed that Swanhild glided towards him, walking on the stormy seas. He saw her afar, and she came swiftly, and ever the sea grew smooth before her feet, nor did the wind so much as stir her hair. Presently she stood by him in the ship, and, bending over him, touched him on the shoulder, saying:

"Awake, Eric Brighteyes! Awake! awake!"

It seemed to him that he awoke and said "What tidings, Swanhild?" and that she answered:

"Ill tidings, Eric—so ill that I am come hither from Straumey[*] to tell of them—ay, come walking on the seas. Had Gudruda done so much, thinkest thou?"

[*] Stroma, the southernmost of the Orkneys.

"Gudruda is no witch," he said in his dream.

"Nay, but I am a witch, and it is well for thee, Eric. Ay, I am a witch. Now do I seem to sleep at Atli's side, and lo! here I stand by thine, and I must journey back again many a league before another day be born—ay, many a league, and all for love of thee, Eric! Hearken, for not long may the spell endure. I have seen this by my magic: that these men who bound thee come even now to take thee, sleeping, and cast thee and thy thrall into the deep, there to drown."

"If it is fated it will befall," he said in his dream.

"Nay, it shall not befall. Put forth all thy might and burst thy bonds. Then fetch Whitefire; cut away the bonds of Skallagrim, and give him his axe and shield. This done, cover yourselves with your cloaks, and wait till ye hear the murderers come. Then rise and rush upon them, the two of you, and they shall melt before your might. I have journeyed over the great deep to tell thee this, Eric! Had Gudruda done as much, thinkest thou?"

And it seemed to him that the wraith of Swanhild kissed him on the brow, sighed and vanished, bearing the rat in her bosom.

Eric awoke suddenly, just as though he had never slept, and looked around. He knew by the lowness of the sun that it was far into the night, and that he had slept for many hours. They were alone beneath the deck, and far aft, beyond the mast, as the vessel rose upon the waves—for the sea was still rough, though the wind had fallen—Eric saw the mate of the Raven talking earnestly with some men of his crew. Skallagrim snored beside him.

"Awake!" Eric said in his ear, "awake and listen!"

He yawned and roused himself. "What now, lord?" he said.

"This," said Eric, and he told him the dream that he had dreamed.

"That was a fey dream," said Skallagrim, "and now we must do as the wraith bade thee."

"Easy to say, but hard to do," quoth Eric; "this is a great rope that holds us, and a strong."

"Yes, it is great and strong; still, we must burst it."

Now Eric and Skallagrim were made fast in this fashion: their hands were bound behind them, and their legs were lashed above the feet and above the knee. Moreover, a thick cord was fixed about the waist of each, and this cord was passed through the iron ring and knotted there. But it chanced that beneath the hollows of their knees ran an oaken beam, which held the forepart of the dragon together.

"We may try this," said Eric: "to set our feet against the beam and strain with all our strength upon the rope; though I think that no two men can part it."

"We shall know that presently," said Skallagrim, gathering up his legs.

Then they set their feet against the beam and pulled till it groaned; but, though the rope gave somewhat, it would not break. They rested a while, then strained again till the sweat burst out upon them and the rope cut into their flesh, but still it would not part.

"We have found our match," said Eric.

"That is not altogether proved yet," answered the Baresark. "Many a shield is riven at the third stroke."

So once again they set their feet against the beam, and put out all their strength.

"The ring bends," gasped Eric. "Now, when the roll of the ship throws our weight to leeward, in the name of Thor pull!"

They waited, then put out their might, and lo! though the rope did not break, the iron ring burst asunder and they rolled upon the deck.

"Well pulled, truly," said Skallagrim as he struggled to his haunches: "I am marked about the middle with rope-twists for many a day to come, that I will swear. What next, lord?"

"Whitefire," answered Eric.

Now, their arms were piled a fathom or more from where they sat, and right in the prow of the ship. Hither, then, they must crawl upon their knees, and this was weary work, for ever as the ship rolled they fell, and could in no wise save themselves from hurt. Eric was bleeding at the brow, and bloody was the hooked nose of Skallagrim, before they came to where Whitefire was. At length they reached the sword, and pushed aside the bucklers that were over it with their heads. The great war-blade was sheathed, and Eric must needs lie upon his breast and draw the weapon somewhat with his teeth.

"This is an ill razor to shave with," he said, rising, for the keen blade had cut his chin.

"So some have thought and perchance more shall think," answered Skallagrim. "Now set the rope on the edge and rub."

This they did, and presently the thick cord that bound them was in two. Then Eric knelt upon the deck and pressed the bonds that bound his legs upon the blade, and after him Skallagrim. They were free now, except for their hands, and it was no easy thing to cut away the bonds upon their wrists. It was done thus: Skallagrim sat upon the deck, and Eric pushed the sword between his fingers with his feet. Then the Baresark rose, holding the sword, and Eric, turning back to back with him, fretted the cords upon his wrists against the blade. Twice he cut himself, but the third time the cord parted and he was free. He stretched his arms, for they were stiff; then took Whitefire and cut away the bonds of Skallagrim.

"How goes it with that hurt of thine?" he asked.

"Better than I had thought," answered Skallagrim; "the soreness has come out with the bruise."

"That is good news," said Eric, "for methinks, unless Swanhild walked the seas for nothing, thou wilt soon need thine arms."

"They have never failed me yet," said Skallagrim and took his axe and shield. "What counsel now?"

"This, Skallagrim: that we lie down as we were, and put the cloaks about us as though we were yet in bonds. Then, if these knaves come, we can take them unawares as they think to take us."

So they went again to where they had been bound, and lay down upon their shields and weapons, drawing cloaks over them. Scarcely had they done this and rested a while, when they saw the mate and all the crew coming along both boards towards them. They bore no weapons in their hands.

"None too soon did Swanhild walk," said Eric; "now we shall learn their purpose. Be thou ready to leap forth when I give the word."

"Ay, lord," answered Skallagrim as he worked his stiff arms to and fro. "In such matters few have thought me backward."

"What news, friends?" cried Eric as the men drew near.

"Bad news for thee, Brighteyes," answered the mate, "and that Baresark thrall of thine, for we must loose your bands."

"That is good news, then," said Eric, "for our limbs are numb and dead because of the nipping of the cords. Is land in sight?"

"Nay, nor will be for thee, Eric."

"How now, friend? how now? Sure, having handselled peace to us, ye mean no harm towards two unarmed men?"

"We swore to do you no harm, nor will we, Eric; this only will we do: deliver you, bound, to Ran, and leave her to deal with you as she may."

"Bethink you, sirs," said Eric: "this is a cruel deed and most unmanly. We yielded to you in faith—will ye break your troth?"

"War has no troth," he answered, "ye are too great to let slip between our fingers. Shall it be said of us that two men overcame us all?"

"Mayhap!" murmured Skallagrim beneath his breath.

"Oh, sirs, I beseech you," said Eric; "I am young, and there is a maid who waits me out in Iceland, and it is hard to die," and he made as though he wept, while Skallagrim laughed within his sleeve, for it was strange to see Eric feigning fear.

But the men mocked aloud.

"This is the great man," they cried, "this is that Eric of whose deeds folk sing! Look! he weeps like a child when he sees the water. Drag him forth and away with him into the sea!"

"Little need for that," cried Eric, and lo! the cloaks about him and Skallagrim flew aside. Out they came with a roar; they came out as a she-bear from her cave, and high above Brighteyes' golden curls Whitefire shone in the pale light, and nigh to it shone the axe of Skallagrim. Whitefire flared aloft, then down he fell and sought the false heart of the mate. The great axe of Skallagrim shone and was lost in the breast of the carle who stood before him.

"Trolls!" shrieked one. "Here are trolls!" and turned to fly. But again Whitefire was up and that man flew not far—one pace, and no more. Then they fled screaming and after them came axe and sword. They fled, they fell, they leaped into the sea, till none were left to fall and leap, for they had no time or heart to find or draw their weapons, and presently Eric Brighteyes and Skallagrim Lambstail stood alone upon the deck—alone with the dead.

"Swanhild is a wise witch," gasped Eric, "and, whatever ill she has done, I will remember this to her honour."

"Little good comes of witchcraft," answered Skallagrim, wiping his brow: "to-day it works for our hands, to-morrow it shall work against them."

"To the helm," said Eric; "the ship yaws and comes side on to the seas."

Skallagrim sprang to the tiller and put his strength on it, and but just in time, for one big sea came aboard them and left much water in the hold.

"We owe this to thy Baresark ways," said Eric. "Hadst thou not slain the steersman we had not filled with water."

"True, lord," answered Skallagrim; "but when once my axe is aloft, it seems to fly of itself, till nothing is left before it. What course now?"

"The same on which the Gudruda was laid. Perhaps, if we may endure till we come to the Farey Isles,[*] we shall find her in harbour there."

[*] The Faroes.

"There is not much chance of that," said Skallagrim; "still, the wind is fair, and we fly fast before it."

Then they lashed the tiller and set to bailing. They bailed long, and it was heavy work, but they rid the ship of much water. After that they ate food, for it was now morning, and it came on to blow yet more strongly.

For three days and three nights it blew thus, and the Raven sped along before the gale. All this time, turn and turn about, Eric and Skallagrim stood at the helm and tended the sails. They had little time to eat, and none to sleep. They were so hard pressed also, and must harbour their strength so closely, that the bodies of the dead men yet cumbered the hold. Thus they grew very weary and like to fall from faintness, but still they held the Raven on her course. In the beginning of the fourth night a great sea struck the good ship so that she quivered from stem to stern.

"Methinks I hear water bubbling up," said Skallagrim in a hoarse voice.

Eric climbed down into the well and lifted the bottom planks, and there beneath them was a leak through which the water spouted in a thin stream. He stopped up the rent as best he might with garments from the dead men, and placed ballast stones upon them, then clambered on to the deck again.

"Our hours are short now," he said, "the water rushes in apace."

"Well, it is time to rest," said Skallagrim; "but see, lord!" and he pointed ahead. "What land is that?"

"It must be the Fareys," answered Eric; "now, if we can but keep afloat for three hours more, we may yet die ashore."

After this the wind began to fall, but still there was enough to drive the Raven on swiftly.

And ever the water gained in the hold.

Now they were not far from land, for ahead of them the bleak hills towered up, shining in the faint midnight light, and between the hills was a cleft that seemed to be a fjord. Another hour passed, and they were no more than ten furlongs from the mouth of the fjord, when suddenly the wind fell, and they were in calm water under shelter of the land. They went amidships and looked. The hold was half full of water, and in it floated the bodies of Ospakar's men.

"She has not long to live," said Skallagrim, "but we may still be saved if the boat is not broken."

Now aft, near the tiller, a small boat was bound on the half deck of the Raven. They went to it and looked; it was whole, with oars lashed in it, but half full of water, which they must bail out. This they did as swiftly as they might; then they cut the little boat loose, and, having made it fast with a rope, lifted it over the side-rail and let it fall into the sea, and that was no great way, for the Raven had sunk deep. It fell on an even keel, and Eric let himself down the rope into it and called to Skallagrim to follow.

"Bide a while, lord," he answered; "there is that which I would bring with me."

For a space Eric waited and then called aloud, "Swift! thou fool; swift! the ship sinks!"

And as he called, Skallagrim came, and his arms were full of swords and byrnies, and red rings of gold that he had found time to gather from the dead and out of the cabin.

"Throw all aside and come," said Eric, laying on to the oars, for the Raven wallowed before she sank.

"There is yet time, lord, and the gear is good," answered Skallagrim, and one by one he threw pieces down into the boat. As the last fell the Raven sank to her bulwarks. Then Skallagrim stepped from the sinking deck into the boat, and cut the cord, not too soon.

Eric gave way with all his strength, and, as he pulled, when he was no more than five fathoms from her, the Raven vanished with a huge swirl.

"Hold still," he said, "or we shall follow."

Round spun the boat in the eddy, she was sucked down till the water trickled over her gunwale, and for a moment they knew not if they were lost or saved. Eric held his breath and watched, then slowly the boat lifted her nose, and they were safe from the whirlpool of the lost dragon.

"Greed is many a man's bane," said Eric, "and it was nearly thine and mine, Skallagrim."

"I had no heart to leave the good gear," he answered; "and thou seest, lord, it is safe and we with it."

Then they got the boat's head round slowly into the mouth of the fjord, pausing now and again to rest, for their strength was spent. For two hours they rowed down a gulf, as it were, and on either side of them were barren hills. At length the waterway opened out into a great basin, and there, on the further side of the basin, they saw green slopes running down to the water's edge, strewn with white stock-fish set to dry in the wind and sun, and above the slopes a large hall, and about it booths. Moreover, they saw a long dragon of war at anchor near the shore. For a while they rowed on, easing now and again. Then Eric spoke to Skallagrim.

"What thinkest thou of yonder ship, Lambstail?"

"I think this, lord: that she is fashioned wondrous like to the Gudruda."

"That is in my mind also," said Eric, "and our fortune is good if it is she."

They rowed on again, and presently a ray from the sun came over the hills—for now it was three hours past midnight—and, the ship having swung a little with the tide, lit upon her prow, and lo! there gleamed the golden dragon of the Gudruda.

"This is a strange thing," said Eric.

"Ay, lord, a strange and a merry, for now I shall talk with Hall the mate," and the Baresark smiled grimly.

"Thou shalt do no hurt to Hall," said Eric. "I am lord here, and I must judge."

"Thy will is my will," said Skallagrim; "but if my will were thine, he would hang on the mast till sea-birds nested amidst his bones."

Now they were close to the ship, but they could see no man. Skallagrim would have called aloud, but Eric bade him hold his peace.

"Either they are dead, and thy calling cannot wake them, or perchance they sleep and will wake of themselves. We will row under the stern, and, having made fast, climb aboard and see with our own eyes."

This, then, they did as silently as might be, and saw that the Gudruda had not been handled gently by the winds and waves, for her shield rail was washed away. This they found also, that all men lay deep in sleep. Now, amidships a fire still burned, and by it was food. They came there and ate of the food, of which they had great need. Then they took two cloaks that lay on the deck, and, throwing them about them, warmed themselves over the fire: for they were cold and wet, ay, and utterly outworn.

As they sat thus warming themselves, a man of the crew awoke and saw them, and being amazed, at once called to his fellows, saying that two giants were aboard, warming themselves at the fire. Now men sprang up, and, seizing their weapons, ran towards them, and among them was Hall the mate.

Then suddenly Eric Brighteyes and Skallagrim Lambstail threw aside the cloaks and stood up. They were gaunt and grim to see. Their cheeks were hollow and their eyes stared wide with want of sleep. Thick was their harness with brine, and open wounds gaped upon their faces and their hands. Men saw and fell back in fear, for they held them to be wizards risen from the sea in the shapes of Eric and the Baresark.

Then Eric sang this song:
"Swift and sure across the Swan's Bath
Sped Sea-stag on Raven's track,

Heav'd Ran's breast in raging billows,
Stream'd gale-banners through the sky!
Yet did Eric the war-eager
Leap with Baresark-mate aboard,
Fierce their onset on the foemen!
Wherefore brake the grapnel-chain?"

Hall heard and slunk back, for now he saw that these were indeed Eric and Skallagrim come up alive from the sea, and that they knew his baseness.

Eric looked at him and sang again:
"Swift away sped ship Gudruda,
Left her lord in foeman's ring;
Brighteyes back to back with Baresark
Held his head 'gainst mighty odds.
Down amidst the ballast tumbling,
Ospakar's shield-carles were rolled.
Holy peace at length they handselled,
Eric must in bonds be laid!
"Came the Grey Rat, came the Earl's wife,
Came the witch-word from afar;
Cag'd wolves roused them, and with struggling
Tore their fetter from its hold.
Now they watch upon their weapons;
Now they weep and pray for life;
Now they leap forth like a torrent—
Swept away in foeman's strength!
"Then alone upon the Raven
Three long days they steer and sail,
Till the waters, welling upwards,
Wash dead men about their feet.
Fails the gale and sinks the dragon,
Barely may they win the boat:
Safe they stand on ship Gudruda—
Say, who cut the grapnel-chain?"

Men stood astonished, but Hall the mate slunk back.

"Hold, comrade," said Eric, "I have something to say that songs cannot carry. Hearken, my shield-mates: we swore to be true to each other, even to death: is it not so? What then shall be said of that man who cut loose the Gudruda and left us two to die at the foeman's hand?"

"Who was the man?" asked a voice.

"That man was Hall of Lithdale," said Eric.

"It is false!" said Hall, gathering up his courage; "the cable parted beneath the straining of the ship, and afterwards we could not put about because of the great sea."

"Thou art false!" roared Skallagrim. "With my eyes I saw thee let thine axe fall upon the cable. Liar art thou and dastard! Thou art jealous also of Brighteyes thy lord, and this was in thy mind: to let him die upon the Raven and then to bind his shoes upon thy cowardly feet. Though none else saw, I saw; and I say this: that if I may have my will, I will string thee, living, to the prow in that same cable till gulls tear out thy fox-heart!"

Now Hall grew very white and his knees trembled beneath him. "It is true," he said, "that I cut the chain, but not from any thought of evil. Had I not cut it the vessel must have sunk and all been lost."

"Did we not swear, Hall," said Eric sternly, "together to fight and together to fall—together to fare and, if need be, together to cease from faring, and dost thou read the oath thus? Say, mates, what reward shall be paid to this man for his good fellowship to us and his tenderness for your lives?"

As with one voice the men answered "Death!"

"Thou hearest, Hall?" said Eric. "Yet I would deal more gently with one to whom I swore fellowship so lately. Get thee gone from our company, and let us see thy cur's face no more. Get thee gone, I say, before I repent of my mercy."

Then amidst a loud hooting, Hall took his weapons and without a word slunk into the boat of the Raven that lay astern, and rowed ashore; nor did Eric see his face for many months.

"Thou hast done foolishly, lord, to let that weasel go," said Skallagrim, "for he will live to nip thy hand."

"For good or evil, he is gone," said Eric, "and now I am worn out and desire to sleep."

After this Eric and Skallagrim rested three full days, and they were so weary that they were awake for little of this time. But on the third day they rose up, strong and well, except for their hurts and soreness. Then they told the men of that which had come to pass, and all wondered at their might and hardihood. To them indeed Eric seemed as a God, for few such deeds as his had been told of since the God-kind were on earth.

But Brighteyes thought little of his deeds, and much of Gudruda. At times also he thought of Swanhild, and of that witch-dream she sent him: for it was wonderful to him that she should have saved him thus from Ran's net.

Eric was heartily welcomed by the Earl of the Farey Isles, for, when he heard his deeds, he made a feast in his honour, and set him in the high seat. It was a great feast, but Skallagrim became drunk at it and ran down the chamber, axe aloft, roaring for Hall of Lithdale.

This angered Eric much and he would scarcely speak to Skallagrim for many days, though the great Baresark slunk about after him like his shadow, or a whipped hound at its master's heel, and at length humbled his pride so far as to ask pardon for his fault.

"I grant it for thy deeds' sake," said Eric shortly; "but this is upon my mind: that thou wilt err thus again, and it shall be my cause of death—ay, and that of many more."

"First may my bones be white," said Skallagrim.

"They shall be white thereafter," answered Eric.

At Fareys Eric shipped twelve good men and true, to take the seats of those who had been slain by Ospakar's folk. Afterwards, when the wounded were well of their hurts (except one man who died), and the Gudruda was made fit to take the sea again, Brighteyes bade farewell to the Earl of those Isles, who gave him a good cloak and a gold ring at parting, and sailed away.

Now it were too long to tell of all the deeds that Eric and his men did. Never, so scalds sing, was there a viking like him for strength and skill and hardihood, and, in those days, no such war-dragon as the Gudruda had been known upon the sea. Wherever Eric joined battle, and that was in many places, he conquered, for none prevailed against him, till at last foes would fly before the terror of his name, and earls and kings would send from far craving the aid of his hands. Withal he was the best and gentlest of men. It is said of Eric that in all his days he did no base deed, nor hurt the weak, nor refused peace to him who prayed it, nor lifted sword against prisoner or wounded foe. From traders he would take a toll of their merchandise only and let them go, and whatever gains he won he would share equally, asking no larger part than the meanest of his band. All men loved Eric, and even his foes gave him honour and spoke well of him. Now that Hall of Lithdale was gone, there was no man among his mates who would not have passed to death for him, for they held him dearer than their lives. Women, too, loved him much; but his heart was set upon Gudruda, and he seldom turned to look on them.

The first summer of his outlawry Eric warred along the coast of Ireland, but in the winter he came to Dublin, and for a while served in the body-guard of the king of that town, who held him in honour, and would have had him stay there. But Eric would not bide there, and next spring, the Gudruda being ready for sea, he sailed for the shores of England. There he gave battle to two vikings' ships of war, and took them after a hard fight. It was in this fight that Skallagrim Lambstail was wounded almost to death. For when, having taken one ship, Eric boarded the other with but few men, he was driven back and fell over a beam, and would have been slain, had not Skallagrim thrown himself across his body, taking on his own back that blow of a battle-axe which was aimed at Eric's head. This was a great wound, for the axe shore through the steel of the byrnie and sank into the flesh. But when Eric's men saw their lord down, and Skallagrim, as they deemed, dead athwart him, they made so fierce a rush that the foemen fell before them like leaves before a winter gale, and the end of it was that the vikings prayed peace of Eric. Skallagrim lay sick for many days, but he was hard to kill, and Eric nursed him back to life. After this these two loved each other as brother loves twin brother, and they could scarcely bear to be apart. But other people did not love Skallagrim, nor he them.

Eric sailed on up the Thames to London, bringing the viking ships with him, and he delivered their captains bound to Edmund, Edward's son, the king who was called Edmund the Magnificent. These captains the King hung, for they had wrought damage to his ships.

Eric found much favour with the King, and, indeed, his fame had gone before him. So when he came into the court, bravely clad, with Skallagrim at his back, who was now almost recovered of his wound, the King called out to him to draw near, saying that he desired to look on the bravest viking and most beauteous man who sailed the seas, and on that fierce Baresark whom men called "Eric's Death-shadow."

So Eric came forward up the long hall that was adorned with things more splendid than ever his eyes had seen, and stood before the King. With him came Skallagrim, driving the two captive viking chiefs before him with his axe, as a flesher drives lambs. Now, during these many months Brighteyes had grown yet more great in girth and glorious to look on than he was before. Moreover, his hair was now so long that it flowed like a flood of gold down towards his girdle, for since Gudruda trimmed it no shears had come near his head, and his locks grew fast as a woman's. The King looked at him and was astonished.

"Of a truth," he said, "men have not lied about thee, Icelander, nor concerning that great wolf-hound of thine," and he pointed at Skallagrim with his sword of state. "Never saw I such a man;" and he bade all the mightiest men of his body-guard stand forward that he might measure them against Eric. But Brighteyes was an inch taller than the tallest, and measured half a span more round the chest than the biggest.

"What wouldest thou of me, Icelander?" asked the King.

"This, lord," said Eric: "to serve thee a while, and all my men with me."

"That is an offer that few would turn from," answered the King. "Thou shalt go into my body-guard, and, if I have my will, thou shalt be near me in battle, and thy wolf-dog also."

Eric said that he asked no better, and thereafter he went up with Edmund the King to make war on the Danes of Mercia, and he and Skallagrim did great deeds before the eyes of the Englishmen.

That winter Eric and his company came back to London, and abode with the King in much state and honour. Now, there was a certain lady of the court named Elfrida. She was both fair and wealthy, the sweetest of women, and of royal blood by her mother's side. So soon as her eyes fell on Eric she loved him, and no one thing did she desire more than to be his wife. But Brighteyes kept aloof from her, for he loved Gudruda alone; and so the winter wore away, and in the spring he went away warring, nor did he come back till autumn was at hand.

The Lady Elfrida sat at a window when Eric rode through London Town in the King's following, and as he passed she threw him a wreath of flowers. The King saw it and laughed.

"My cold kinswoman seems to melt before those bright eyes of thine, Icelander," he said, "as my foes melt before Whitefire's flame. Well, I could wish her a worse mate," and he looked on him strangely.

Eric bowed, but made no answer.

That night, as they sat at meat in the palace, the Lady Elfrida, being bidden in jest of Edmund the King to fill the cup of the bravest, passed down the board, and, before all men, poured wine into Eric's cup, and, as she did so, welcomed him back with short sweet words.

Eric grew red as dawn, and thanked her graciously; but after the feast he spoke with Skallagrim, asking him of the Gudruda, and when she could be ready to take the sea.

"In ten days, lord," said Skallagrim; "but stay we not here with the King this winter? It is late to sail."

"Nay," said Eric, "we bide not here. I would winter this year in Fareys, for they are the nighest place to Iceland that I may reach. Next summer my three years of outlawry are over, and I would fare back homewards."

"Now, I see the shadow of a woman's hand," said Skallagrim. "It is very late to face the northern seas, and we may sail to Iceland from London in the spring."

"It is my will that we should sail," answered Eric.

"Past Orkneys runs the road to Fareys," said Skallagrim, "and in Orkneys sits a hawk to whom the Lady Elfrida is but a dove. In faring from ill we may hap on worse."

"It is my will that we sail," said Eric stubbornly.

"As thou wilt, and as the King wills," answered Skallagrim.

On the morrow Eric went in before the King, and craved a boon.

"There is little that thou canst ask, Brighteyes," said the King, "that I will not give thee, for, by my troth, I hold thee dear."

"I am come back to seek no great thing, lord," answered Eric, "but this only: leave to bid thee farewell. I would wend homeward."

"Say, Eric," said the King, "have I not dealt well with thee?"

"Well, and overwell, lord."

"Why, then, wouldst thou leave me? I have this in my mind—to bring thee to great honour. See, now, there is a fair lady in this court, and in her veins runs blood that even an Iceland viking might be proud to mate with. She has great lands, and, mayhap, she shall have more. Canst thou not find a home on them, thinkest thou, Brighteyes?"

"In Iceland only I am at home, lord," said Eric.

Then the King was wroth, and bade him begone when it pleased him, and Eric bowed before him and went out.

Two days afterwards, while Eric was walking in the Palace gardens he met the Lady Elfrida face to face. She held white flowers in her hand, and she was fair to see and pale as the flowers she bore.

He greeted her, and, after a while, she spoke to him in a gentle voice: "They say that thou goest from England, Brighteyes?" she said.

"Yes, lady; I go," he answered.

She looked on him once and twice and then burst out weeping. "Why goest thou hence to that cold land of thine?" she sobbed—"that hateful land of snow and ice! Is not England good enough for thee?"

"I am at home there, lady, and there my mother waits me."

"'There thy mother waits thee,' Eric?—say, does a maid called Gudruda the Fair wait thee there also?"

"There is such a maid in Iceland," said Eric.

"Yes; I know it—I know it all," she answered, drying her tears, and of a sudden growing cold and proud; "Eric, thou art betrothed to this Gudruda; and, for thy welfare, somewhat overfaithful to thy troth. For hearken, Eric Brighteyes. I know this: that little luck shall come to thee from the maid Gudruda. It would become me ill to say more; nevertheless, this is true—that here, in England, good fortune waits thy hand, and there in Iceland such fortune as men mete to their foes. Knowest thou this?"

Eric looked at her and answered: "Lady," he said, "men are not born of their own will, they live and do little that they will, they do and go, perchance, whither they would not. Yet it may happen to a man that one meets him whose hand he fain would hold, if it be but for an hour's travel over icy ways; and it is better to hold that hand for this short hour than to wend his life through at a stranger's side."

"Perhaps there is wisdom in thy folly," said the Lady Elfrida. "Still, I tell thee this: that no good luck waits thee there in Iceland."

"It well may be," said Eric: "my days have been stormy, and the gale is still brewing. But it is a poor heart that fears the storm. Better to sink; for, coward or hero, all must sink at last."

"Say, Eric," said the lady, "if that hand thou dost desire to hold is lost to thee, what then?"

"If that hand is cold in death, then henceforth I wend my ways alone."

"And if it be held of another hand than thine?"

"Then I will journey back to England, lady, and here in this fair garden I may crave speech of thee again."

They looked one on another. "Fare thee well, Eric!" said the Lady Elfrida. "Here in this garden we may talk again; and, if we talk no more—why, fare thee well! Days come and go; the swallow takes flight at winter, and lo! at spring it twitters round the eaves. And if it come not again, then farewell to that swallow. The world is a great house, Eric, and there is room for many swallows. But alas! for her who is left desolate—alas, alas!" And she turned and went.

It is told of this lady Elfrida that she became very wealthy and was much honoured for her gentleness and wisdom, and that, when she was old, she built a great church and named it Ericskirk. It is also told that, though many sought her in marriage, she wedded none.

XVI

HOW SWANHILD WALKED THE SEAS

Within two days afterwards, the Gudruda being bound for sea, Eric went up to bid farewell to the King. But Edmund was so angry with him because of his going that he would not see him. Thereon Eric took horse and rode down sadly from the Palace to the river-bank where the Gudruda lay. But when he was about to give the word to get out the oars, the King himself rode up, and with him men bearing costly gifts. Eric went ashore to speak with him.

"I am angry with thee, Brighteyes," said Edmund, "yet it is not in my heart to let thee go without words and gifts of farewell. This only I ask of thee now, that, if things go not well with thee there, out in Iceland, thou wilt come back to me."

"I will—that I promise thee, King," said Eric, "for I shall never find a better lord."

"Nor I a braver servant," said the King. Then he gave him the gifts and kissed him before all men. To Skallagrim also he gave a good byrnie of Welsh steel coloured black.

Then Eric went aboard again and dropped down the river with the tide.

For five days all went well with them, the sea being calm and the winds light and favourable. But on the fifth night, as they sailed slowly along the coasts of East Anglia over against Yarmouth sands, the moon rose red and ringed and the sea fell dead calm.

"Yonder hangs a storm-lamp, lord," said Skallagrim, pointing to the angry moon. "We shall soon be bailing, for the autumn gales draw near."

"Wait till they come, then speak," said Eric. "Thou croakest ever like a raven."

"And ravens croak before foul weather," answered Skallagrim, and just as he spoke a sudden gust of wind came up from the south-east and laid the Gudruda over. After this it came on to blow, and so fiercely that for whole days and nights their clothes were scarcely dry. They ran northwards before the storm and still northward, sighting no land and seeing no stars. And ever as they scudded on the gale grew fiercer, till at length the men were worn out with bailing and starved with wet and cold. Three of their number also were washed away by the seas, and all were in sorry plight.

It was the fourth night of the gale. Eric stood at the helm, and by him Skallagrim. They were alone, for their comrades were spent and lay beneath decks, waiting for death. The ship was half full of water, but they had no more strength to bail. Eric seemed grim and gaunt in the white light of the moon, and his long hair streamed about him wildly. Grimmer yet was Skallagrim as he clung to the shield-rail and stared across the deep.

"She rolls heavily, lord," he shouted, "and the water gains fast."

"Can the men bail no more?" asked Eric.

"Nay, they are outworn and wait for death."

"They need not wait long," said Eric. "What do they say of me?"

"Nothing."

Then Eric groaned aloud. "It was my stubbornness that brought us to this pass," he said; "I care little for myself, but it is ill that all should die for one man's folly."

"Grieve not, lord," answered Skallagrim, "that is the world's way, and there are worse things than to drown. Listen! methinks I hear the roar of breakers yonder," and he pointed to the left.

"Breakers they surely are," said Eric. "Now the end is near. But see, is not that land looming up on the right, or is it cloud?"

"It is land," said Skallagrim, "and I am sure of this, that we run into a firth. Look, the seas boil like a hot spring. Hold on thy course, lord, perchance we may yet steer between rocks and land. Already the wind falls and the current lessens the seas."

"Ay," said Eric, "already the fog and rain come up," and he pointed ahead where dense clouds gathered in the shape of a giant, whose head reached to the skies and moved towards them, hiding the moon.

Skallagrim looked, then spoke: "Now here, it seems, is witchwork. Say, lord, hast thou ever seen mist travel against wind as it travels now?"

"Never before," said Eric, and as he spoke the light of the moon went out.

Swanhild, Atli's wife, sat in beauty in her bower on Straumey Isle and looked with wide eyes towards the sea. It was midnight. None stirred in Atli's hall, but still Swanhild looked out towards the sea.

Now she turned and spoke into the darkness, for there was no light in the bower save the light of her great eyes.

"Art thou there?" she said. "I have summoned thee thrice in the words thou knowest. Say, Toad, art there?"

"Ay, Swanhild the Fatherless! Swanhild, Groa's daughter! Witch-mother's witch-child! I am here. What is thy will with me?" piped a thin voice like the voice of a dying babe.

Swanhild shuddered a little and her eyes grew brighter—as bright as the eyes of a cat.

"This first," she said: "that thou show thyself. Hideous as thou art, I had rather see thee, than speak with thee seeing thee not."

"Mock not my form, lady," answered the thin voice, "for it is as thou dost fashion it in thy thought. To the good I am fair as day; to the evil, foul as their heart. Toad thou didst call me: look, now I come as a toad!"

Swanhild looked, and behold! a ring of the darkness grew white with light, and in it crouched a thing hideous to see. It was shaped as a great spotted toad, and on it was set a hag's face, with white locks hanging down on either side. Its eyes were blood-red and sunken, black were its fangs, and its skin was dead yellow. It grinned horribly as Swanhild shrank from it, then spoke again:

"Grey Wolf thou didst call me once, Swanhild, when thou wouldst have thrust Gudruda down Goldfoss gulf, and as a grey wolf I came, and gave thee counsel that thou tookest but ill. Rat didst thou call me once, when thou wouldst save Brighteyes from the carles of Ospakar, and as a rat I came and in thy shape I walked the seas. Toad thou callest me now, and as a toad I creep about thy feet. Name thy will, Swanhild, and I will name my price. But be swift, for there are other fair ladies whose wish I must do ere dawn."

"Thou art hideous to look on!" said Swanhild, placing her hand before her eyes.

"Say not so, lady; say not so. Look at this face of mine. Knowest thou it not? It is thy mother's—dead Groa lent it me. I took it from where she lies; and my toad's skin I drew from thy spotted heart, Swanhild, and more hideous than I am shalt thou be in a day to come, as once I was more fair than thou art to-day."

Swanhild opened her lips to shriek, but no sound came.

"Troll," she whispered, "mock me not with lies, but hearken to my bidding: where sails Eric now?"

"Look out into the night, lady, and thou shalt see."

Swanhild looked, and the ways of the darkness opened before her witch-sight. There at the mouth of Pentland Firth the Gudruda laboured heavily in the great seas, and by the tiller stood Eric, and with him Skallagrim.

"Seest thou thy love?" asked the Familiar.

"Yea," she answered, "full clearly; he is worn with wind and sea, but more glorious than aforetime, and his hair is long. Say, what shall befall him if thou aidest not?"

"This, that he shall safely pass the Firth, for the gale falls, and come safely to Fareys, and from Fareys isles to Gudruda's arms."

"And what canst thou do, Goblin?"

"This: I can lure Eric's ship to wreck, and give his comrades, all save Skallagrim, to Ran's net, and bring him to thy arms, Swanhild, witch-mother's witch-child!"

She hearkened. Her breast heaved and her eyes flashed.

"And thy price, Toad?"

"Thou art the price, lady," piped the goblin. "Thou shalt give thyself to me when thy day is done, and merrily will we sisters dwell in Hela's halls, and merrily for ever will we fare about the earth o' nights, doing such tasks as this task of thine, Swanhild, and working wicked woe till the last woe is worked on us. Art thou content?"

Swanhild thought. Twice her breath went from her lips in great sighs. Then she stood, pale and silent.

"Safely shall he sail the Firth," piped the thin voice. "Safely shall he sit in Fareys. Safely shall he lie in white Gudruda's arms—hee! hee! Think of it, lady!"

Then Swanhild shook like a birth-tree in the gale, and her face grew ashen.

"I am content," she said.

"Hee! hee! Brave lady! She is content! Ah, we sisters shall be merry. Hearken: if I aid thee thus I may do no more. Thrice has the night-owl come at thy call—now it must wing away. Yet things will be as I have said; thine own wisdom shall guide the rest. Ere morn Brighteyes shall stand in Atli's hall, ere spring he will be thy love, and ere autumn Gudruda shall sit on the high seat in the hall of Middalhof the bride of Ospakar. Draw nigh, give me thine arm, sister, that blood may seal our bargain."

Swanhild drew near the toad, and, shuddering, stretched out her arm, and then and there the red blood ran, and there they sealed their sisterhood. And as the nameless deed was wrought, it seemed to Swanhild as though fire shot through her veins, and fire surged before her eyes, and in the fire a shape passed up weeping.

"It is done, Blood-sister," piped the voice; "now I must away in thy form to be about thy tasks. Seat thee here before me—so. Now lay thy brow upon my brow—fear not, it was thy mother's—life on death! curling locks on corpse hair! See, so we change—we change. Now thou art the Death-toad and I am Swanhild, Atli's wife, who shall be Eric's love."

Then Swanhild knew that her beauty had entered into the foulness of the toad, and the foulness of the toad into her beauty, for there before her stood her own shape and here she crouched a toad upon the floor.

"Away to work, away!" said a soft low voice, her own voice speaking from her own body that stood before her, and lo! it was gone.

But Swanhild crouched, in the shape of a hag-headed toad, upon the ground in her bower of Atli's hall, and felt wickedness and evil longings and hate boil and seethe within her heart. She looked out through her sunken horny eyes and she seemed to see strange sights. She saw Atli, her lord, dead upon the grass. She saw a woman asleep, and above her flashed a sword. She saw the hall of Middalhof red with blood. She saw a great gulf in a mountain's heart, and men fell down it. And, last, she saw a war-ship sailing fast out on the sea, afire, and vanish there.

Now the witch-hag who wore Swanhild's loveliness stood upon the cliffs of Straumey and tossed her white arms towards the north.

"Come, fog! come, sleet!" she cried. "Come, fog! come, sleet! Put out the moon and blind the eyes of Eric!" And as she called, the fog rose up like a giant and stretched his arms from shore to shore.

"Move, fog! beat, rain!" she cried. "Move and beat against the gale, and blind the eyes of Eric!"

And the fog moved on against the wind, and with it sleet and rain.

"Now I am afeared," said Eric to Skallagrim, as they stood in darkness upon the ship: "the gale blows from behind us, and yet the mist drives fast in our faces. What comes now?"

"This is witch-work, lord," answered Skallagrim, "and in such things no counsel can avail. Hold the tiller straight and drive on, say I. Methinks the gale lessens more and more."

So they did for a little while, and all around them sounded the roar of breakers. Darker grew the sky and darker yet, till at the last, though they stood side by side, they could not see each other's shapes.

"This is strange sailing," said Eric. "I hear the roar of breakers as it were beneath the prow."

"Lash the helm, lord, and let us go forward. If there are breakers, perhaps we shall see their foam through the blackness," said Skallagrim.

Eric did so, and they crept forward on the starboard board right to the prow of the ship, and there Skallagrim peered into the fog and sleet.

"Lord," he whispered presently, and his voice shook strangely, "what is that yonder on the waters? Seest thou aught?"

Eric stared and said, "By Odin! I see a shape of light like to the shape of a woman; it walks upon the waters towards us and the mist melts before it, and the sea grows calm beneath its feet."

"I see that also!" said Skallagrim.

"She comes nigh!" gasped Eric. "See how swift she comes! By the dead, it is Swanhild's shape! Look, Skallagrim! look how her eyes flame!—look how her hair streams upon the wind!"

"It is Swanhild, and we are fey!" quoth Skallagrim, and they ran back to the helm, where Skallagrim sank upon the deck in fear.

"See, Skallagrim, she glides before the Gudruda's beak! she glides backwards and she points yonder—there to the right! Shall I put the helm down and follow her?"

"Nay, lord, nay; set no faith in witchcraft or evil will befall us."

As he spoke a great gust of wind shook the ship, the music of the breakers roared in their ears, and the gleaming shape upon the waters tossed its arms wildly and pointed to the right.

"The breakers call ahead," said Eric. "The shape points yonder, where I hear no sound of sea. Once before, thou mindest, Swanhild walked the waves to warn us and thereby saved us from the men of Ospakar. Ever she swore she loved me; now she is surely come in love to save us and all our comrades. Say, shall I put about? Look: once more she waves her arms and points," and as he spoke he gripped the helm.

"I have no rede, lord," said Skallagrim, "and I love not witch-work. We can die but once, and death is all around; be it as thou wilt."

Eric put down the helm with all his might. The good ship answered, and her timbers groaned loudly, as though in woe, when the strain of the sea struck her abeam. Then once more she flew fast across the waters, and fast before her glided the wraith of Swanhild. Now it pointed here and now there, and as it pointed so Eric shaped his course. For a while the noise of breakers lessened, but now again came a thunder, like the thunder of waves smiting on a cliff, and about the sides of the Gudruda the waves hissed like snakes.

Suddenly the Shape threw up its arms and seemed to sink beneath the waves, while a sound like the sound of a great laugh went up from sea to sky.

"Now here is the end," said Skallagrim, "and we are lured to doom."

Ere ever the words had passed his lips the ship struck, and so fiercely that they were rolled upon the deck. Suddenly the sky grew clear, the moon shone out, and before them were cliffs and rocks, and behind them a great wave rushed on. From the hold of the ship there came a cry, for now their comrades were awake and they knew that death was here.

Eric gripped Skallagrim round the middle and looked aft. On rushed the wave, no such wave had he ever seen. Now it struck and the Gudruda burst asunder beneath the blow.

But Eric Brighteyes and Skallagrim Lambstail were lifted on its crest and knew no more.

Swanhild, crouching in hideous guise upon the ground in the bower of Atli's hall, looked upon the visions that passed before her. Suddenly a woman's shape, her own shape, was there.

"It is done, Blood-sister," said a voice, her own voice. "Merrily I walked the waves, and oh, merry was the cry of Eric's folk when Ran caught them in her net! Be thyself, again, Blood-sister—be fair as thou art foul; then arise, wake Atli thy lord, and go down to the sea's lip by the southern cliffs and see what thou shalt find. We shall meet no more till all this game is played and another game is set," and the shape of Swanhild crouched upon the floor before the hag-headed toad muttering "Pass! pass!"

Then Swanhild felt her flesh come back to her, and as it grew upon her so the shape of the Death-headed toad faded away.

"Farewell, Blood-sister!" piped a voice; "make merry as thou mayest, but merrier shall be our nights when thou hast gone a-sailing with Eric on the sea. Farewell! farewell! Were-wolf thou didst call me once, and as a wolf I came. Rat thou didst call me once, and as a rat I came. Toad didst thou call me once, and as a toad I came. Say, at the last, what wilt thou call me and in what shape shall I come, Blood-sister? Till then farewell!"

And all was gone and all was still.

XVII

HOW ASMUND THE PRIEST WEDDED UNNA, THOROD'S DAUGHTER

Now the story goes back to Iceland.

When Brighteyes was gone, for a while Gudruda the Fair moved sadly about the stead, like one new-widowed. Then came tidings. Men told how Ospakar Blacktooth had waylaid Eric on the seas with two long ships, dragons of war, and how Eric had given him battle and sunk one dragon with great loss to Ospakar. They told also how Blacktooth's other dragon, the Raven, had sailed away before the wind, and Eric had sailed after it in a rising gale. But of what befell these ships no news came for many a month, and it was rumoured that this had befallen them—that both had sunk in the gale, and that Eric was dead.

But Gudruda would not believe this. When Asmund the Priest, her father, asked her why she did not believe it, she answered that, had Eric been dead, her heart would surely have spoken to her of it. To this Asmund said that it might be so.

Hay-harvest being done, Asmund made ready for his wedding with Unna, Thorod's daughter and Eric's cousin.

Now it was agreed that the marriage-feast should be held at Middalhof; for Asmund wished to ask a great company to the wedding, and there was no place at Coldback to hold so many. Also some of the kin of Thorod, Unna's father, were bidden to the feast from the east and north. At length all was prepared and the guests came in great companies, for no such feast had been made in this quarter for many years.

On the eve of the marriage Asmund spoke with Groa. The witch-wife had borne herself humbly since she was recovered from her sickness. She passed about the stead like a rat at night, speaking few words and with downcast eyes. She was busy also making all things ready for the feasting.

Now as Asmund went up the hall seeing that everything was in order, Groa drew near to him and touched him gently on the shoulder.

"Are things to thy mind, lord?" she said.

"Yes, Groa," he answered, "more to my mind than to thine I fear."

"Fear not, lord; thy will is my will."

"Say, Groa, is it thy wish to bide here in Middalhof when Unna is my housewife?"

"It is my wish to serve thee as aforetime," she answered softly, "if so be that Unna wills it."

"That is her desire," said Asmund and went his ways.

But Groa stood looking after him and her face was fierce and evil.

"While bane has virtue, while runes have power, and while hand has cunning, never, Unna, shalt thou take my place at Asmund's side! Out of the water I came to thee, Asmund; into the water I go again. Unquiet shall I lie there—unquiet shall I wend through Hela's halls; but Unna shall rest at Asmund's side—in Asmund's cairn!"

Then again she moved about the hall, making all things ready for the feast. But at midnight, when the light was low and folk slept, Groa rose, and, veiled in a black robe, with a basket in her hand, passed like a shadow through the mists that hang about the river's edge, and in silence, always looking behind her, like one who fears a hidden foe, culled flowers of noisome plants that grow in the marsh. Her basket being filled, she passed round the stead to a hidden dell upon the mountain side. Here a man stood waiting, and near him burned a fire of turf. In his hand he held an iron-pot. It was Koll the Half-witted, Groa's thrall.

"Are all things ready, Koll?" she said.

"Yes," he answered; "but I like not these tasks of thine, mistress. Say now, what wouldst thou do with the fire and the pot?"

"This, then, Koll. I would brew a love-potion for Asmund the Priest as he has bidden me to do."

"I have done many an ill deed for thee, mistress, but of all of them I love this the least," said the thrall, doubtfully.

"I have done many a good deed for thee, Koll. It was I who saved thee from the Doom-stone, seeming to prove thee innocent—ay, even when thy back was stretched on it, because thou hadst slain a man in his sleep. Is it not so?"

"Yea, mistress."

"And yet thou wast guilty, Koll. And I have given thee many good gifts, is it not so?"

"Yes, it is so."

"Listen then: serve me this once and I will give thee one last gift—thy freedom, and with it two hundred in silver."

Koll's eyes glistened. "What must I do, mistress?"

"To-day at the wedding-feast it will be thy part to pour the cups while Asmund calls the toasts. Last of all, when men are merry, thou wilt mix that cup in which Asmund shall pledge Unna his wife and Unna must pledge Asmund. Now, when thou hast poured, thou shalt pass the cup to me, as I stand at the foot of the high seat, waiting to give the bride greeting on behalf of the serving-women of the household. Thou shalt hand the cup to me as though in error, and that is but a little thing to ask of thee."

"A little thing indeed," said Koll, staring at her, and pulling with his hand at his red hair, "yet I like it not. What if I say no, mistress?"

"Say no or speak of this and I will promise thee one thing only, thou knave, and it is, before winter comes, that the crows shall pick thy bones! Now, brave me, if thou darest," and straightway Groa began to mutter some witch-words.

"Nay," said Koll, holding up his hand as though to ward away a blow. "Curse me not: I will do as thou wilt. But when shall I touch the two hundred in silver?"

"I will give thee half before the feast begins, and half when it is ended, and with it freedom to go where thou wilt. And now leave me, and on thy life see that thou fail me not."

"I have never failed thee yet," said Koll, and went his ways.

Now Groa set the pot upon the fire, and, placing in it the herbs that she had gathered, poured water on them. Presently they began to boil and as they boiled she stirred them with a peeled stick and muttered spells over them. For long she sat in that dim and lonely place stirring the pot and muttering spells, till at length the brew was done.

She lifted the pot from the fire and smelt at it. Then drawing a phial from her robe she poured out the liquor and held it to the sky. The witch-water was white as milk, but presently it grew clear. She looked at it, then smiled evilly.

"Here is a love-draught for a queen—ah, a love-draught for a queen!" she said, and, still smiling, she placed the phial in her breast.

Then, having scattered the fire with her foot, Groa took the pot and threw it into a deep pool of water, where it could not be found readily, and crept back to the stead before men were awake.

Now the day wore on and all the company were gathered at the marriage-feast to the number of nearly two hundred. Unna sat in the high seat, and men thought her a bonny bride, and by her side sat Asmund the Priest. He was a hale, strong man to look on, though he had seen some three-score winters; but his mien was sad, and his heart heavy. He drank cup after cup to cheer him, but all without avail. For his thought sped back across the years and once more he seemed to see the face of Gudruda the Gentle as she lay dying, and to hear her voice when she foretold evil to him if he had aught to do with Groa the Witch-wife. And now it seemed to him that the evil was at hand, though whence it should come he knew not. He looked up. There Groa moved along the hall, ministering to the guests; but he saw as she moved that her eyes were always fixed, now on him and now on Unna. He remembered that curse also which Groa had called down upon him when he had told her that he was betrothed to Unna, and his heart grew cold with fear. "Now I will change my counsel," Asmund said to himself: "Groa shall not stay here in this stead, for I will look no longer on that dark face of hers. She goes hence to-morrow."

Not far from Asmund sat Björn, his son. As Gudruda the Fair, his sister, brought him mead he caught her by the sleeve, whispering in her ear. "Methinks our father is sad. What weighs upon his heart?"

"I know not," said Gudruda, but as she spoke she looked first on Asmund, then at Groa.

"It is ill that Groa should stop here," whispered Björn again.

"It is ill," answered Gudruda, and glided away.

Asmund saw their talk and guessed its purport. Rousing himself he laughed aloud and called to Koll the Half-witted to pour the cups that he might name the toasts.

Koll filled, and, as Asmund called the toasts one by one, Koll handed the cups to him. Asmund drank deep of each, till at length his sorrow passed from him, and, together with all who sat there, he grew merry.

Last of all came the toast of the bride's cup. But before Asmund called it, the women of the household drew near the high seat to welcome Unna, when she should have drunk. Gudruda stood foremost, and Groa was next to her.

Now Koll filled as before, and it was a great cup of gold that he filled.

Asmund rose to call the toast, and with him all who were in the hall. Koll brought up the cup, and handed it, not to Asmund, but to Groa; but there were few who noted this, for all were listening to Asmund's toast and most of the guests were somewhat drunken.

"The cup," cried Asmund—"give me the cup that I may drink."

Then Groa started forward, and as she did so she seemed to stumble, so that for a moment her robe covered up the great bride-cup. Then she gathered herself together slowly, and, smiling, passed up the cup.

Asmund lifted it to his lips and drank deep. Then he turned and gave it to Unna his wife, but before she drank he kissed her on the lips.

Now while all men shouted such a welcome that the hall shook, and as Unna, smiling, drank from the cup, the eyes of Asmund fell upon Groa who stood beneath him, and lo! her eyes seemed to flame and her face was hideous as the face of a troll.

Asmund grew white and put his hand to his head, as though to think, then cried aloud:

"Drink not, Unna! the draught is drugged!" and he struck at the vessel with his hand.

He smote it indeed, and so hard that it flew from her hand far down the hall.

But Unna had already drunk deep.

"The draught is drugged!" Asmund cried, and pointed to Groa, while all men stood silent, not knowing what to do.

"The draught is drugged!" he cried a third time, "and that witch has drugged it!" And he began to tear at his breast.

Then Groa laughed so shrilly that men trembled to hear her.

"Yes, lord," she screamed, "the draught is drugged, and Groa the Witch-wife hath drugged it! Ay, tear thy heart out, Asmund, and Unna, grow thou white as snow—soon, if my medicine has virtue, thou shalt be whiter yet! Hearken all men. Asmund the Priest is Swanhild's father, and for many a year I have been Asmund's mate. What did I tell thee, lord?—that I would see the two of you dead ere Unna should take my place!—ay, and on Gudruda the Fair, thy daughter, and Björn thy son, and Eric Brighteyes, Gudruda's love, and many another man—on them too shall my curse fall! Tear thy heart out, Asmund! Unna, grow thou white as snow!

The draught is drugged and Groa, Ran's gift! Groa the Witch-Wife! Groa, Asmund's love! hath drugged it!"

And ere ever a man might lift a hand to stay her Groa glided past the high seat and was gone.

For a space all stood silent. Asmund ceased clutching at his breast. Rising he spoke heavily:

"Now I learn that sin is a stone to smite him who hurled it. Gudruda the Gentle spoke sooth when she warned me against this woman. New wed, new dead! Unna, fare thee well!"

And straightway Asmund fell down and died there by the high seat in his own hall.

Unna gazed at him with ashen face. Then, plucking at her bosom she sprang from the dais and rushed along the hall, screaming. Men made way for her, and at the door she also fell dead.

This then was the end of Asmund Asmundson the Priest, and Unna, Thorod's daughter, Eric's cousin, his new-made wife.

For a moment there was silence in the hall. But before the echoes of Unna's screams had died away, Björn cried aloud:

"The witch! where is the witch?"

Then with a yell of rage, men leaped to their feet, seizing their weapons, and rushed from the stead. Out they ran. There, on the hill-side far above them, a black shape climbed and leapt swiftly. They gave tongue like dogs set upon a wolf and sped up the hill.

They gained the crest of the hill, and now they were at Goldfoss brink. Lo! the witch-wife had crossed the bed of the torrent, for little rain had fallen and the river was low. She stood on Sheep-saddle, the water running from her robes. On Sheep-saddle she stood and cursed them.

Björn took a bow and set a shaft upon the string. He drew it and the arrow sung through the air and smote her, speeding through her heart. With a cry Groa threw up her arms.

Then down she plunged. She fell on Wolf's Fang, where Eric once had stood and, bouncing thence, rushed to the boiling deeps below and was no more seen for ever.

Thus, then, did Asmund the Priest wed Unna, Thorod's daughter, and this was the end of the feasting.

Thereafter Björn, Asmund's son, ruled at Middalhof, and was Priest in his place. He sought for Koll the Half-witted to kill him, but Koll took the fells, and after many months he found passage in a ship that was bound for Scotland.

Now Björn was a hard man and a greedy. He was no friend to Eric Brighteyes, and always pressed it on Gudruda that she should wed Ospakar Blacktooth. But to this counsel Gudruda would not listen, for day and night she thought upon her love. Next summer there came tidings that Eric was safe in Ireland, and men spoke of his deeds, and of how he and Skallagrim had swept the ship of Ospakar single-handed. Now after these tidings, for a while Gudruda walked singing through the meads, and no flower that grew in them was half so fair as she.

That summer also Ospakar Blacktooth met Björn, Asmund's son, at the Thing, and they talked much together in secret.

XVIII

HOW EARL ATLI FOUND ERIC AND SKALLAGRIM ON THE SOUTHERN ROCKS OF STRAUMEY ISLE

Swanhild, robed in white, as though new risen from sleep, stood, candle in hand, by the bed of Atli the Earl, her lord, crying "Awake!"

"What passes now?" said Atli, lifting himself upon his arm. "What passes, Swanhild, and why dost thou ever wander alone at nights, looking so strangely? I love not thy dark witch-ways, Swanhild, and I was wed to thee in an ill hour, wife who art no wife."

"In an ill hour indeed, Earl Atli," she answered, "an ill hour for thee and me, for, as thou hast said, eld and youth are strange yokefellows and pull different paths. Arise now, Earl, for I have dreamed a dream."

"Tell it to me on the morrow, then," quoth Atli; "there is small joyousness in thy dreams, that always point to evil, and I must bear enough evil of late."

"Nay, lord, my rede may not be put aside so. Listen now: I have dreamed that a great dragon of war has been cast away upon Straumey's south-western rocks. The cries of those who drowned rang in my ears. But I thought that some came living to the shore, and lie there senseless, to perish of the cold. Arise, therefore, take men and go down to the rocks."

"I will go at daybreak," said Atli, letting his head fall upon the pillow. "I have little faith in such visions, and it is too late for ships of war to try the passage of the Firth."

"Arise, I say," answered Swanhild sternly, "and do my bidding, else I will myself go to search the rocks."

Then Atli rose grumbling, and shook the heavy sleep from his eyes: for of all living folk he most feared Swanhild his wife. He donned his garments, threw a thick cloak about him, and, going to the hall where men snored around the dying fires, for the night was bitter, he awoke some of them. Now among those men whom he called was Hall of Lithdale, Hall the mate who had cut the grapnel-chain. For this Hall, fearing to return to Iceland, had come hither saying that he had been wounded off Fareys, in the great fight between Eric and Ospakar's men, and left there to grow well of his hurt or die. Then Atli, not knowing that the carle lied, had bid him welcome for Eric's sake, for he still loved Eric above all men.

But Hall loved not labour and nightfarings to search for shipwrecked men of whom the Lady Swanhild had chanced to dream. So he turned himself upon his side and slept again. Still, certain of Atli's folk rose at his bidding, and they went together down to the south-western rocks.

But Swanhild, a cloak thrown over her night-gear, sat herself in the high seat of the hall and fixing her eyes, now upon the dying fires and now upon the blood-marks in her arm, waited in silence. The night was cold and windy, but the moon shone bright, and by its light Atli and his people made their way to the south-western rocks, on which the sea beat madly.

"What lies yonder?" said Atli, pointing to some black things that lay beneath them upon the rock, cast there by the waves. A man climbed down the cliff's side that is here as though it were cut in steps, and then cried aloud:

"A ship's mast, new broken, lord."

"It seems that Swanhild dreams true," muttered Atli; "but I am sure of this: that none have come ashore alive in such a sea."

Presently the man who searched the rocks below cried aloud again:

"Here lie two great men, locked in each other's arms. They seem to be dead."

Now all the men climb down the slippery rocks as best they may, though the spray wets them, and with them goes Atli. The Earl is a brisk man, though old in years, and he comes first to where the two lie. He who was undermost lay upon his back, but his face is hid by the thick golden hair that flowed across it.

"Man's body indeed, but woman's locks," said Atli as he put out his hand and drew the hair away, so that the light of the moon fell on the face beneath.

He looked, then staggered back against the rock.

"By Thor!" he cried, "here lies the corpse of Eric Brighteyes!" and Atli wrung his hands and wept, for he loved Eric much.

"Be not so sure that the men are dead, Earl," said one, "I thought I saw yon great carle move but now."

"He is Skallagrim Lambstail, Eric's Death-shadow," said Atli again. "Up with them, lads—see, yonder lies a plank—and away to the hall. I will give twenty in silver to each of you if Eric lives," and he unclasped his cloak and threw it over both of them.

Then with much labour they loosed the grip of the two men one from the other, and they set Skallagrim on the plank. But eight men bore Eric up the cliff between them, and the task was not light, though the Earl held his head, from which the golden hair hung like seaweed from a rock.

At length they came to the hall and carried them in. Swanhild, seeing them come, moved down from the high seat.

"Bring lamps, and pile up the fires," cried Atli. "A strange thing has come to pass, Swanhild, and thou dost dream wisely, indeed, for here we have Eric Bright-eyes and Skallagrim Lambstail. They were locked like lovers in each other's arms, but I know not if they are dead or living."

Now Swanhild started and came on swiftly. Had the Familiar tricked her and had she paid the price for nothing? Was Eric taken from Gudruda and given to her indeed—but given dead? She bent over him, gazing keenly on his face. Then she spoke.

"He is not dead but senseless. Bring dry clothes, and make water hot," and, kneeling down, she loosed Eric's helm and harness and ungirded Whitefire from his side.

For long Swanhild and Atli tended Eric at one fire, and the serving women tended Skallagrim at the other. Presently there came a cry that Skallagrim stirred, and Atli with others ran to see. At this moment also the eyes of Eric were unsealed, and Swanhild saw them looking at her dimly from beneath. Moved to it by her passion and her joy that he yet lived, Swanhild let her face fall till his was hidden in her unbound hair, and kissed him upon the lips. Eric shut his eyes again, sighing heavily, and presently he was asleep. They bore him to a bed and heaped warm wrappings upon him. At daybreak he woke, and Atli, who sat watching at his side, gave him hot mead to drink.

"Do I dream?" said Eric, "or is it Earl Atli who tends me, and did I but now see the face of Swanhild bending over me?"

"It is no dream, Eric, but the truth. Thou hast been cast away here on my isle of Straumey."

"And Skallagrim—where is Skallagrim?"

"Skallagrim lives—fear not!"

"And my comrades, how went it with them?"

"But ill, Eric. Ran has them all. Now sleep!"

Eric groaned aloud. "I had rather died also than live to hear such heavy tidings," he said. "Witch-work! witch-work! and that fair witch-face wrought it." And once again he slept, nor did he wake till the sun was high. But Atli could make nothing of his words.

When Swanhild left the side of Eric she met Hall of Lithdale face to face and his looks were troubled.

"Say, lady," he asked, "will Brighteyes live?"

"Grieve not, Hall," she answered, "Eric will surely live and he will be glad to find a messmate here to greet him, having left so many yonder," and she pointed to the sea.

"I shall not be glad," said Hall, letting his eyes fall.

"Why not, Hall? Fearest thou Skallagrim? or hast thou done ill by Eric?"

"Ay, lady, I fear Skallagrim, for he swore to slay me, and that kind of promise he ever keeps. Also, if the truth must out, I have not dealt altogether well with Eric, and of all men I least wish to talk with him."

"Speak on," she said.

Then, being forced to it, Hall told her something of the tale of the cutting of the cable, being careful to put another colour on it.

"Now it seems that thou art a coward, Hall," Swanhild said when he had done, "and I scarcely looked for that in thee," for she had not been deceived by the glozing of his speech. "It will be bad for thee to meet Eric and Skallagrim, and this is my counsel: that thou goest hence before they wake, for they will sit this winter here in Atli's hall."

"And whither shall I go, lady?"

Swanhild gazed on him, and as she did so a dark thought came into her heart: here was a knave who might serve her ends.

"Hall," she said, "thou art an Icelander, and I have known of thee from a child, and therefore I wish to serve thee in thy strait, though thou deservest it little. See now, Atli the Earl has a farm on the mainland not two hours' ride from the sea. Thither thou shalt go, if thou art wise, and thou shalt sit there this winter and be hidden from Eric and Skallagrim. Nay, thank me not, but listen: it may chance that I shall have a service for thee to do before spring is come."

"Lady, I shall wait upon thy word," said Hall.

"Good. Now, so soon as it is light, I will find a man to sail with thee across the Firth, for the sea falls, and bear my message to the steward at Atli's farm. Also if thou needest faring-money thou shalt have it. Farewell."

Thus then did Hall fly before Eric and Skallagrim.

On the morrow Eric and Skallagrim arose, sick and bruised indeed, but not at all harmed, and went down to the shore. There they found many dead men of their company, but never a one in whom the breath of life remained.

Skallagrim looked at Eric and spoke: "Last night the mist came up against the wind: last night we saw Swanhild's wraith upon the waves, and there is the path it showed, and there"—and he pointed to the dead men—"is the witch-seed's flower. Now to-day we sit in Atli's hall and here we must stay this winter at Swanhild's side, and in all this there lies a riddle that I cannot read."

But Eric shook his head, making no answer. Then, leaving Skallagrim with the dead, he turned, and striding back alone towards the hall, sat down on a rock in the home meadows and, covering his face with his hands, wept for his comrades.

As he wept Swanhild came to him, for she had seen him from afar, and touched him gently on the arm.

"Why weepest thou, Eric?" she said.

"I weep for the dead, Swanhild," he answered.

"Weep not for the dead—they are at peace; if thou must weep, weep for the living. Nay, weep not at all; rejoice rather that thou art here to mourn. Hast thou no word of greeting for me who have not heard thy voice these many months?"

"How shall I greet thee, Swanhild, who would never have seen thy face again if I might have had my will? Knowest thou that yesternight, as we laboured in yonder Firth, we saw a shape walking the waters to lead us to our doom? How shall I greet thee, Swanhild, who art a witch and evil?"

"And knowest thou, Eric, that yesternight I woke from sleep, having dreamed that thou didst lie upon the shore, and thus I saved thee alive, as perchance I have saved thee aforetime? If thou didst see a shape walking the waters it was that shape which led thee here. Hadst thou sailed on, not only those thou mournest, but Skallagrim and thou thyself had now been numbered with the lost."

"Better so than thus," said Brighteyes. "Knowest thou also, Swanhild, that when last night my life came back again in Atli's hall, methought that Atli's wife leaned over me and kissed me on the lips? That was an ill dream, Swanhild."

"Some had found it none so ill, Eric," she made answer, looking on him strangely. "Still, it was but a dream. Thou didst dream that Atli's wife breathed back the breath of life into thy pale lips—be sure of it thou didst but dream. Ah, Eric, fear me no more; forget the evil that I have wrought in the blindness and folly of my youth. Now things are otherwise with me. Now I am a wedded wife and faithful hearted to my lord. Now, if I still love thee, it is with a sister's love. Therefore forget my sins, remember only that as children we played upon the Iceland fells. Remember that, as boy and girl, we rode along the marshes, while the sea-mews clamoured round our heads. The world is cold, Eric, and few are the friends we find in it; many are already gone, and soon the friendless dark draws near. So put me not away, my brother and my friend; but, for a little space, whilst thou art here in Atli's hall, let us walk hand in hand as we walked long years ago in Iceland, gathering up the fifa-bloom, and watching the midnight shadows creep up the icy jökul's crest."

Thus Swanhild spoke to him most sweetly, in a low voice of music, while the tears gathered in her eyes, talking ever of Iceland that he loved, and of days long dead, till Eric's heart softened in him.

"Almost do I believe thee, Swanhild," he said, stretching out his hand; "but I know thus: that thou art never twice in the same mood, and that is beyond my measuring. Thou hast done much evil and thou hast striven to do more; also I love not those who seem to walk the seas o' nights. Still, hold thou to this last saying of thine and there shall be peace between us while I bide here."

She touched his hand humbly and turned to go. But as she went Eric spoke again: "Say, Swanhild, hast thou tidings from Iceland yonder? I have heard no word of Asmund or of Gudruda for two long years and more."

She stood still, and a dark shadow that he could not see flitted across her face.

"I have few tidings, Eric," she said, turning, "and those few, if I may trust them, bad enough. For this is the rumour that I have heard: that Asmund the Priest, my father, is dead; that Groa, my mother, is dead—how, I know not; and, lastly, that Gudruda the Fair, thy love, is betrothed to Ospakar Blacktooth and weds him in the spring."

Now Eric sprang up with an oath and grasped the hilt of Whitefire. Then he sat down again upon the stone and covered his face with his hands.

"Grieve not, Eric," she said gently; "I put no faith in this news, for rumour, like the black-backed gull, often changes colour in its flight across the seas. Also I had it but at fifth hand. I am sure of this, at least, that Gudruda will never forsake thee without a cause."

"It shall go ill with Ospakar if this be true," said Eric, smiling grimly, "for Whitefire is yet left me and with it one true friend."

"Run not to meet the evil, Eric. Thou shalt come to Iceland with the summer flowers and find Gudruda faithful and yet fairer than of yore. Knowest thou that Hall of Lithdale, who was thy mate, has sat here these two months? He is gone but this morning, I know not whither, leaving a message that he returns no more."

"He did well to go," said Eric, and he told her how Hall had cut the cable.

"Ay, well indeed," answered Swanhild. "Had Atli known this he would have scourged Hall hence with rods of seaweed. And now, Eric, I desire to ask thee one more thing: why wearest thou thy hair long like a woman's? Indeed, few women have such hair as thine is now."

"For this cause, Swanhild: I swore to Gudruda that none should cut my hair till she cut it once more. It is a great burden to me surely, for never did hair grow so fast and strong as mine, and once in a fray I was held fast by it and went near to the losing of my life. Still, I will keep the oath even if it grows on to my feet," and he laughed a little and shook back his golden locks.

Swanhild smiled also and, turning, went. But when her face was hidden from him she smiled no more.

"As I live," she said in her heart, "before spring rains fall I again will cause thee to break this oath, Eric. Ay, I will cut a lock of that bright hair of thine and send it for a love-token to Gudruda."

But Eric still sat upon the rock thinking. Swanhild had set an evil seed of doubt in his heart, and already it put forth roots. What if the tale were true? What if Gudruda had given herself to Ospakar? Well, if so—she should soon be a widow, that he swore.

Then he rose, and stalked grimly towards the hall.

XIX

HOW KOLL THE HALF-WITTED BROUGHT TIDINGS FROM ICELAND

Presently as Eric walked he met Atli the Earl seeking him. Atli greeted him.

"I have seen strange things, Eric," he said, "but none more strange than this coming of thine and the manner of it. Swanhild is foresighted, and that was a doom-dream of hers."

"I think her foresighted also," said Eric. "And now, Earl, knowest thou this: that little good can come to thee at the hands of one whom thou hast saved from the sea."

"I set no faith in such old wives' tales," answered Atli. "Here thou art come, and it is my will that thou shouldest sit here. At the least, I will give thee no help to go hence."

"Then we must bide in Straumey, it seems," said Eric: "for of all my goods and gear this alone is left me," and he looked at Whitefire.

"Thou hast still a gold ring or two upon thy arm," answered the Earl, laughing. "But surely, Eric, thou wouldst not begone?"

"I know not, Earl. Listen: it is well that I should be plain with thee. Once, before thou didst wed Swanhild, she had another mind."

"I have heard something of that, and I have guessed more, Brighteyes; but methinks Swanhild is little given to gadding now. She is as cold as ice, and no good wife for any man," and Atli sighed, "'Snow melts not if sun shines not,' so runs the saw. Thou art an honest man, Eric, and no whisperer in the ears of others' wives."

"I am not minded indeed to do thee such harm, Earl, but this thou knowest: that woman's guile and beauty are swords few shields can brook. Now I have spoken—and they are hard words to speak—be it as thou wilt."

"It is my will that thou shouldest sit here this winter, Eric. Had I my way, indeed, never wouldest thou sit elsewhere. Listen: things have not gone well with me of late. Age hath a grip of me, and foes rise up against one who has no sons. That was an ill marriage, too, which I made with Swanhild yonder: for she loves me not, and I have found no luck since first I saw her face. Moreover, it is in my mind that my days are almost sped. Swanhild has already foretold my death, and, as thou knowest well, she is foresighted. So I pray thee, Eric, bide thou here while thou mayest, for I would have thee at my side."

"It shall be as thou wilt, Earl," said Eric.

So Eric Brighteyes and Skallagrim Lambstail sat that winter in the hall of Atli the Earl at Straumey. For many weeks all things went well and Eric forgot his fears. Swanhild was gentle to him and kindly. She loved much to talk with him, even of Gudruda her rival; but no word of love passed her lips. Nevertheless, she did but bide her time, for when she struck she determined to strike home. Atli and Eric were ever side by side, and Eric gave the Earl much good counsel. He promised to do this also, for now, being simple-minded, his doubts had passed and he had no more fear of Swanhild. On the mainland lived a certain chief who had seized large lands of Atli's, and held them for a year or more. Now Eric gave his word that, before he sailed for Iceland in the early summer, he would go up against this man and drive him from the lands, if he could. For Brighteyes might not come to Iceland till hard upon midsummer, when his three years of outlawry were spent.

The winter wore away and the spring came. Then Atli gathered his men and went with Eric in boats to where the chief dwelt who held his lands. There they fell on him and there was a fierce fight. But in the end the man was slain by Skallagrim, and Eric did great deeds, as was his wont. Now in this fray Eric was wounded in the foot by a spear, so that he must be borne back to Straumey, and he lay there in the hall for many days. Swanhild nursed him, and most days he sat talking with her in her bower.

When Eric was nearly healed of his hurt, the Earl went with all his people to a certain island of the Orkneys to gather scat[*] that was unpaid, and Skallagrim went with him. But Eric did not go, because of his hurt, fearing lest the wound should open if he walked overmuch. Thus it came to pass that, except for some women, he was left almost alone with Swanhild.

[*] Tribute.

Now, when Atli had been gone three days, it chanced on an afternoon that Swanhild heard how a man from Iceland sought speech with her. She bade them bring him in to where she was alone in her bower, for Eric was not there, having gone down to the sea to fish.

The man came and she knew him at once for Koll the Half-witted, who had been her mother Groa's thrall. On his shoulders was the cloak that Ospakar Blacktooth had given him; it was much torn now, and he had a worn and hungry look.

"Whence comest thou, Koll?" she asked, "and what are thy tidings?"

"From Scotland last, lady, where I sat this winter; before that, from Iceland. As for my tidings, they are heavy, if thou hast not heard them. Asmund the Priest is dead, and dead is Unna his wife, poisoned by thy mother, Groa, at their marriage-feast. Dead, too, is thy mother, Groa. Björn, Asmund's son, shot her with an arrow, and she lies in Goldfoss pool."

Now Swanhild hid her face for a while in her hands. Then she lifted it and it was white to see. "Speakest thou truth, fox? If thou liest, this I swear to thee—thy tongue shall be dragged from thee by the roots!"

"I speak the truth, lady," he answered. But still he spoke not all the truth, for he said nothing of the part which he had played in the deaths of Asmund and Unna. Then he told her of the manner of their end.

Swanhild listened silently—then said:

"What news of Gudruda, Asmund's daughter? Is she wed?"

"Nay, lady. Folk spoke of her and Ospakar, that was all."

"Hearken, Koll," said Swanhild, "bearing such heavy tidings, canst thou not weight the ship a little more? Eric Brighteyes is here. Canst thou not swear to him that, when thou didst leave Iceland it was said without question that Gudruda had betrothed herself to Ospakar, and that the wedding-feast was set for this last Yule? Thou hast a hungry look, Koll, and methinks that things have not gone altogether well with thee of late. Now, if thou canst so charge thy memory, thou shalt lose little by it. But, if thou canst not, then thou goest hence from Straumey with never a luck-penny in thy purse, and never a sup to stay thy stomach with."

Now of all things Koll least desired to be sent from Straumey; for, though Swanhild did not know it, he was sought for on the mainland as a thief.

"That I may do, lady," he said, looking at her cunningly. "Now I remember that Gudruda the Fair charged me with a certain message for Eric Brighteyes, if I should chance to see him as I journeyed."

Then Swanhild, Atli's wife, and Koll the Half-witted talked long and earnestly together.

At nightfall Eric came in from his fishing. His heart was light, for the time drew near when he should sail for home, and he did not think on evil. For now he feared Swanhild no longer, and, no fresh tidings having come from Iceland about Ospakar and Gudruda, he had almost put the matter from his mind. On he walked to the hall, limping somewhat from his wound, but singing as he came, and bearing his fish slung upon a pole.

At the men's door of the hall a woman stood waiting. She told Eric that the lady Swanhild would speak with him in her bower. Thither he went and knocked. Getting no answer he knocked again, then entered.

Swanhild sat on a couch. She was weeping, and her hair fell about her face.

"What now, Swanhild?" he said.

She looked up heavily. "Ill news for thee and me, Eric. Koll, who was my mother's thrall, has come hither from Iceland, and these are his tidings: that Asmund is dead, and Unna, thy cousin, Thorod of Greenfell's daughter, is dead, and my mother Groa is dead also."

"Heavy tidings, truly!" said Eric; "and what of Gudruda, is she also dead?"

"Nay, Eric she is wed—wed to Ospakar."

Now Eric reeled against the wall, clutching it, and for a space all things swam round him. "Where is this Koll?" he gasped. "Send me Koll hither."

Presently he came, and Eric questioned him coldly and calmly. But Koll could lie full well. It is said that in his day there was no one in Iceland who could lie so well as Koll the Half-witted. He told Eric how it was said that Gudruda was plighted to Ospakar, and how the match had been agreed on at the Althing in the summer that was gone (and indeed there had been some such talk), and how that the feast was to be at Middalhof on last Yule Day.

"Is that all thy tidings?" said Eric. "If so, I give no heed to them: for ever, Koll, I have known thee for a liar!"

"Nay, Eric, it is not all," answered Koll. "As it chanced, two days before the ship in which I sailed was bound, I saw Gudruda the Fair. Then she asked me whither I was going, and I told her that I would journey to London, where men said thou wert, and asked her if she would send a message. Then she alighted from her horse, Blackmane, and spoke with me apart. 'Koll,' she said, 'it well may happen that thou wilt see Eric Brighteyes in London town. Now, if thou seest him, I charge thee straightly tell him this. Tell him that my father is dead, and my brother Björn, who rules in his place, is a hard man, and has ever urged me on to wed Ospakar, till at last, having no choice, I have consented to it. And say to Eric that I grieve much and sorely, and that, though we twain should never meet more, yet I shall always hold his memory dear.'"

"It is not like Gudruda to speak thus," said Eric: "she had ever a stout heart and these are craven words. Koll, I hold that thou liest; and, if indeed I find it so, I'll wring the head from off thee!"

"Nay, Eric, I lie not. Wherefore should I lie? Hearken: thou hast not heard all my tale. When the lady Gudruda had made an end of speaking she drew something from her breast and gave it me, saying: 'Give this to Eric, in witness of my words.'"

"Show me the token," said Eric.

Now, many years ago, when they were yet boy and girl, it chanced that Eric had given to Gudruda the half of an ancient gold piece that he had found upon the shore. He had given her half, and half he had kept, wearing it next his heart. But he knew not this, for she feared to tell him, that Gudruda had lost her half. Nor indeed had she lost it, for Swanhild had taken the love-token and hidden it away. Now she brought it forth for Koll to build his lies upon.

Then Koll drew out the half-piece from a leather purse and passed it to him. Eric plunged his hand into his breast and found his half. He placed the two side by side, while Swanhild watched him. Lo! they fitted well.

Then Eric laughed aloud, a hard and bitter laugh. "There will be slaying," he cried, "before all this tale is told. Take thy fee and begone, thou messenger of ill," and he cast the broken piece at Koll. "For once thou hast spoken the truth."

Koll stooped, found the gold and went, leaving Brighteyes and Swanhild face to face.

He hid his brow in his arms and groaned aloud. Softly Swanhild crept up to him—softly she drew his hands away, holding them between her own.

"Heavy tidings, Eric," she said, "heavy tidings for thee and me! She is a murderess who gave me birth and she has slain my own father—my father and thy cousin Unna also. Gudruda is a traitress, a traitress fair and false. I did ill to be born of such a woman; thou didst ill to put thy faith in such a woman. Together let us weep, for our woe is equal."

"Ay, let us weep together," Eric answered. "Nay, why should we weep? Together let us be merry, for we know the worst. All words are said—all hopes are sped! Let us be merry, then, for now we have no more tidings to fear."

"Ay," Swanhild answered, looking on him darkly, "we will be merry and laugh our sorrows down. Ah! thou foolish Eric, under what unlucky star wast thou born that thou knewest not true from false?" and she called the serving-women, bidding them bring food and wine.

Now Eric sat alone with Swanhild in her bower and made pretence to eat. But he could eat little, though he drank deep of the southern wine. Close beside him sat Swanhild, filling his cup. She was wondrous fair that night, and it seemed to Eric that her eyes gleamed like stars. Sweetly she spoke also and wisely. She told strange tales and she sang strange songs, and ever her eyes shone more and more, and ever she crept closer to him. Eric's brain was afire, though his heart was cold and dead. He laughed loud and mightily, he told great tales of deeds that he had done, growing boastful in his folly, and still Swanhild's eyes shone more and more, and still she crept closer, wooing him in many ways.

Now of a sudden Eric thought of his friend, Earl Atli, and his mind grew clear.

"This may not be, Swanhild," he said. "Yet I would that I had loved thee from the first, and not the false Gudruda: for, with all thy dark ways, at least thou art better than she."

"Thou speakest wisely, Eric," Swanhild answered, though she meant not that he should go. "The Norns have appointed us an evil fate, giving me as wife to an old man whom I do not love, and thee for a lover to a woman who has betrayed thee. Ah, Eric Brighteyes, thou foolish Eric! why knewest thou not the false from the true while yet there was time? Now are all words said and all things done—nor can they be undone. Go hence, Eric, ere ill come of it; but, before thou goest, drink one cup of parting, and then farewell."

And she slipped from him and filled the cup, mixing in it a certain love-portion that she had made ready.

"Give it me that I may swear an oath on it," said Eric.

Swanhild gave him the cup and stood before him, watching him.

"Hearken," he said: "I swear this, that before snow falls again in Iceland I will see Ospakar dead at my feet or lie dead at the feet of Ospakar."

"Well spoken, Eric," Swanhild answered. "Now, before thou drinkest, grant me one little boon. It is but a woman's fancy, and thou canst scarce deny me. The years will be long when thou art gone, for from this night it is best that we should meet no more, and I would keep something of thee to call back thy memory and the memories of our youth when thou hast passed away and I grow old."

"What wouldst have then, Swanhild? I have nothing left to give, except Whitefire alone."

"I do not ask Whitefire, Eric, though Whitefire shall kiss the gift. I ask nothing but one tress of that golden hair of thine."

"Once I swore that none should touch my hair again except Gudruda's self."

"It will grow long, then, Eric, for now Gudruda tends black locks and thinks little on golden. Broken are all oaths."

Eric groaned. "All oaths are broken in sooth," he said. "Have then thy will;" and, loosing the peace-strings, he drew Whitefire from its sheath and gave her the great war-sword.

Swanhild took it by the hilt, and, lifting a tress of Eric's yellow hair, she shore through it deftly with Whitefire's razor-edge, smiling as she shore. With the same war-blade on which Eric and Gudruda had pledged their troth, did Swanhild cut the locks that Eric had sworn no hand should clip except Gudruda's.

He took back the sword and sheathed it, and, knotting the long tress, Swanhild hid it in her bosom.

"Now drink the cup, Eric," she said—"pledge me and go."

Eric drank to the dregs and cast the cup down, and lo! all things changed to him, for his blood was afire, and seas seemed to roll within his brain. Only before him stood Swanhild like a shape of light and glory, and he thought that she sang softly over him, always drawing nearer, and that with her came a scent of flowers like the scent of the Iceland meads in May.

"All oaths are broken, Eric," she murmured, "all oaths are broken indeed, and now must new oaths be sworn. For cut is thy golden hair, Brighteyes, and not by Gudruda's hand!"

XX

HOW ERIC WAS NAMED ANEW

Eric dreamed. He dreamed that Gudruda stood by him looking at him with soft, sad eyes, while with her hand she pointed to his hair, and spake.

"Thou hast done ill, Eric," she seemed to say. "Thou hast done ill to doubt me; and now thou art for ever shamed, for thou hast betrayed Atli, thy friend. Thou hast broken thy oath, and therefore hast thou fallen into this pit; for when Swanhild shore that lock of thine, my watching Spirit passed, leaving thee to Swanhild and thy fate. Now, I tell thee this: that shame shall lead to shame, and many lives shall pay forfeit for thy sin, Eric."

Eric awoke, thinking that this was indeed an evil dream which he had dreamed. He woke, and lo! by him was Swanhild, Atli's wife. He looked upon her beauty, and fear and shame crept into his heart, for now he knew that it was no dream, but he was lost indeed. He looked again at Swanhild, and hatred and loathing of her shook him. She had overcome him by her arts; that cup was drugged which he had drunk, and he was mad with grief. Yes, she had played upon his woe like a harper on a harp, and now he was ashamed—now he had betrayed his friend who loved him! Had Whitefire been to his hand at that moment, Eric had surely slain himself. But the great sword was not there, for it hung in Swanhild's bower. Eric groaned aloud, and Swanhild turned at the sound. But he sprang away and stood over her, cursing her.

"Thou witch!" he cried, "what hast thou done? What didst thou mix in that cup yestre'en? Thou hast brought me to this that I have betrayed Atli, my friend—Atli, thy lord, who left thee in my keeping!"

He seemed so terrible in his woe and rage that Swanhild shrank from him, and, throwing her hair about her face, peeped at him through its meshes as once she had peeped at Asmund.

"It is like a man," she said, gathering up her courage and her wit; "'tis like a man, having won my love, now to turn upon me and upbraid me. Fie upon thee, Eric! thou hast dealt ill with me to bring me to this."

Now Eric ceased his raving, and spoke more calmly.

"Well thou knowest the truth, Swanhild," he said.

"Hearken, Eric," she answered. "Let this be secret between us. Atli is old, and methinks that not for long shall he bide here in Straumey. Soon he will die; it is upon my mind that he soon will die, and, being childless, his lands and goods pass to me. Then, Eric, thou shalt sit in Atli's hall, and in all honour shall Atli's wife become thy bride."

Eric listened coldly. "I can well believe," he said, "that thou hast it in mind to slay thy lord, for all evil is in thy heart, Swanhild. Now know this: that if in honour or dishonour my lips touch that fair face of thine again, may the limbs rot from thy trunk, and may I lie a log for ever in the halls of Hela! If ever my eyes of their own will look again upon thy beauty, may I go blind and beg my meat from homestead to homestead! If ever my tongue whisper word of love into thy ears, may dumbness seize it, and may it wither to the root!"

Swanhild heard and sank upon the ground before him, her head bowed almost to her feet.

"Now, Swanhild, fare thee well," said Eric. "Living or dead, may I never see thy face again!"

She gazed up through her falling hair; her face was wild and white, and her eyes glowed in it as live embers glow in the ashes of burnt wood.

"We are not so easily parted, Eric," she said. "Not for this came I to witchcraft and to sin. Thou fool! hast thou never heard that, of all the foes a man may have, none is so terrible as the woman he has scorned? Thou shalt learn this lesson, Eric Brighteyes, Thorgrimur's son: for here we have but the beginning of the tale. For its end, I will write it in runes of blood."

"Write on," said Eric. "Thou canst do no worse than thou hast done," and he passed thence.

For a while Swanhild crouched upon the ground, brooding in silence. Then she rose, and, throwing up her arms, wept aloud.

"Is it for this that I have sold my soul to the Hell-hag?" she cried. "Is it for this that I have become a witch, and sunk so low as I sank last night—to be scorned, to be hated, to be betrayed? Now Eric will go to Atli and tell this tale. Nay, there I will be beforehand with him, and with another story—an ancient wile of women truly, but one that never yet has failed them, nor ever will. And then for vengeance! I will see thee dead, Eric, and dead will I see Gudruda at thy side! Afterwards let darkness come—ay, though the horror rides it! Swift!—I must be swift!"

Eric passed into Swanhild's bower, and, finding Whitefire, bore it thence. On the table was food. He took it. Then, going to the place where he was wont to sleep, he armed himself, girding his byrnie on his breast and his golden helm upon his head, and taking shield and spear in his hand. Then he passed out. By the men's door he found some women spreading fish in the sun. Eric greeted them, saying that when the Earl came back, for he was to come on that morning, he would find him on the south-western rocks nigh to where the Gudruda sank. This he begged of them to tell Atli, for he desired speech with him.

The women wondered that Brighteyes should go forth thus and fully armed, but, holding that he had some deed to do, they said nothing.

Eric came to the rocks, and there he sat all day long looking on the sea, and grieving so bitterly that he thought his heart would burst within him. For of all the days of Eric's life this was the heaviest, except one other only.

But Swanhild, going to her bower, caused Koll the Half-witted to be summoned. To him she spoke long and earnestly, and they made a shameful plot together. Then she bade Koll watch for Atli's coming and, when he saw the Earl leave his boats, to run to him and say that she would speak with him.

After this Swanhild sent a man across the firth to the stead where Hall of Lithdale sat, bidding him to come to her at speed.

When the afternoon grew towards the evening, Koll, watching, saw the boats of Atli draw to the landing-place. Then he went down, and, going to the Earl, bowed before him:

"What wouldst thou, fellow, and who art thou?" asked Atli.

"I am a man from Iceland; perchance, lord, thou sawest me in Asmund's hall at Middalhof. I am sent here by the Lady Swanhild to say that she desires speech with thee, and that at once." Then, seeing Skallagrim, Koll fled back to the house, for he feared Skallagrim.

Now Atli was uneasy in his mind, and, saying nothing, he hurried up to the hall, and through it into Swanhild's bower.

There she sat on a couch, her eyes red with weeping, and her curling hair unbound.

"What now, Swanhild?" he asked. "Why lookest thou thus?"

"Why look I thus, my lord?" she answered heavily. "Because I have to tell thee that which I cannot find words to fit," and she ceased.

"Speak on," he said. "Is aught wrong with Eric?"

Then Swanhild drew near and told him a false tale.

When it was done for a moment or so Atli stood still, and grew white beneath his ruddy skin, white as his beard. Then he staggered back against the wainscoting of the bower.

"Woman, thou liest!" he said. "Never will I believe so vile a thing of Eric Brighteyes, whom I have loved."

"Would that I could not believe it!" she answered. "Would that I could think it was but an evil dream! But alas! Nay, I will prove it. Suffer that I summon Koll, the Icelander, who was my mother's thrall—Groa who now is dead, for I have that tidings also. He saw something of this thing, and he will bear me witness."

"Call the man," said Atli sternly.

So Koll was summoned, and told his lies with a bold face. He was so well taught, and so closely did his story tally with that of Swanhild, that Atli could find no flaw in it.

"Now I am sure, Swanhild, that thou speakest truth," said the Earl when Koll had gone. "And now also I have somewhat to say to this Eric. For thee, rest thyself; that which cannot be mended must be borne," and he went out.

Now, when Skallagrim came to the house he asked for Eric. The women told him that Brighteyes had gone down to the sea, fully armed, in the morning, and had not returned.

"Then there must be fighting toward, and that I am loth to miss," said Skallagrim, and, axe aloft, he started for the south-western rocks at a run. Skallagrim came to the rocks. There he found Eric, sitting in his harness, looking out across the sea. The evening was wet and windy; the rain beat upon him as he sat, but Eric took no heed.

"What seekest thou, lord?" asked the Baresark.

"Rest," said Eric, "and I find none."

"Thou seekest rest helm on head and sword in hand? This is a strange thing, truly!"

"Stranger things have been Skallagrim. Wouldst thou hear a tale?" and he told him all.

"What said I?" asked Skallagrim. "We had fared better in London town. Flying from the dove thou hast found the falcon."

"I have found the falcon, comrade, and she has pecked out my eyes. Now I would speak with Atli, and then I go hence."

"Hence go the twain of us, lord. The Earl will be here presently and rough words will fly in this rough weather. Is Whitefire sharp, Brighteyes?"

"Whitefire was sharp enough to shear my hair, Skallagrim; but if Atli would strike let him lay on. Whitefire will not be aloft for him."

"That we shall see," said Skallagrim. "At least, if thou art harmed because of this loose quean, my axe will be aloft."

"Keep thou thine axe in its place," said Eric, and as he spoke Atli came, and with him many men.

Eric rose and turned to meet the Earl, looking on him with sad eyes. For Atli, his face was as the face of a trapped wolf, for he was mad with rage at the shame that had been put upon him and the ill tale that Swanhild had told of Eric's dealings with her.

"It seems that the Earl has heard of these tidings," said Skallagrim.

"Then I shall be spared the telling of them," answered Eric.

Now they stood face to face; Atli leaned upon his drawn sword, and his wrath was so fierce that for a while he could not speak. At length he found words.

"See ye that man, comrades?" he said, pointing at Eric with the sword. "He has been my guest these many months. He has sat in my hall and eaten of my bread, and I have loved him as a son. And wot ye how he has repaid me? He has put me to the greatest shame, me and my wife the Lady Swanhild, whom I left in his guard—to such shame, indeed, that I cannot speak it."

"True words, Earl," said Eric, while folk murmured and handled their swords.

"True, but not all the truth," growled Skallagrim. "Methinks the Earl has heard a garbled tale."

"True words, thyself thou sayest it," went on Atli "thou hound that I saved from the sea! 'Ran's gift, Hela's gift,' so runs the saw, and now from Ran to Hela thou shalt go, thou mishandler of defenceless women!"

"Here is somewhat of which I know nothing," said Eric.

"And here is something of which thou shalt know," answered Atli, and he shook his sword before Eric's eyes. "Guard thyself!"

"Nay, Earl; thou art old, and I have done the wrong—I may not fight with thee."

"Art thou a coward also?" said the Earl.

"Some have deemed otherwise," said Eric, "but it is true that heavy heart makes weak hand. Nevertheless this is my rede. With thee are ten men. Stand thou aside and let them fall on me till I am slain."

"The odds are too heavy even for thee," said Skallagrim. "Back to back, lord, as we have stood aforetime, and let us play this game together."

"Not so," cried Atli, "this shame is mine, and I have sworn to Swanhild that I will wipe it out in Eric's blood. Stand thou before me and draw!"

Then Eric drew Whitefire and raised his shield. Atli the Earl rushed at him and smote a great two-handed blow. Eric caught it on his shield and suffered no harm; but he would not smite back.

Atli dropped his point. "Niddering art thou, and coward to the last!" he cried. "See, men, Eric Brighteyes fears to fight. I am not come to this that I will cut down a man who is too faint-hearted to give blow for blow. This is my word: take ye your spear-shafts and push this coward to the shore. Then put him in a boat and drive him hence."

Now Eric grew red as the red light of sunset, for his manhood might not bear this.

"Take shield," he said, "and, Earl, on thine own head be thy blood, for none shall live to call Eric niddering and coward."

Atli laughed in his folly and his rage. He took a shield, and, once more springing on Brighteyes, struck a great blow.

Eric parried, then whirled Whitefire on high and smote—once and once only! Down rushed the bright blade like a star through the night. Sword and shield did Atli lift to catch the blow. Through shield it sheared, and arm that held the shield, through byrnie mail and deep into Earl Atli's side. He fell prone to earth, while men held their breath, wondering at the greatness of that stroke.

But Eric leaned on Whitefire and looked at the old Earl upon the rock.

"Now, Atli, thou hast had thy way," he said, "and methinks things are worse than they were before. But I will say this: would that I lay there and thou stoodest to watch me die, for as lief would I have slain my father as thee, Earl Atli. There lies Swanhild's work!"

Atli gazed upwards into Eric's sad eyes and, while he gazed so, his rage left him, and of a sudden a light brake upon his mind, as even then the light of the setting sun brake through the driving mist.

"Eric," he said, "draw near and speak with me ere I am sped. Methinks that I have been beguiled and that thou didst not do this thing that Swanhild said and Koll bore witness to."

"What did Swanhild say, then, Earl Atli?"

The Earl told him.

"It was to be looked for from her," said Eric, "though I never thought of it. Now hearken!" and he told him all.

Atli groaned aloud. "I know this now, Eric," he said: "that thou speakest truth, and once more I have been deceived. Eric, I forgive thee all, for no man may fight against woman's witchcraft, and witch's wine. Swanhild is evil to the heart. Yet, Eric, I lay this doom upon thee—I do not lay it of my own will, for I would not harm thee, whom I love, but because of the words that the Norns put in my mouth, for now I am fey in this the hour of my death. Thou hast sinned, and that thou didst sin against thy will shall avail thee nothing, for of thy sin fate shall fashion a handle to the spear which pierces thee. Henceforth thou art accursed. For I tell thee that this wicked woman Swanhild shall drag thee down to death, and worse than death, and with thee those thou lovest. By witchcraft she brought thee to Straumey, by lies she laid me here before thee. Now by hate and might and cruel deeds shall she bring thee to lie more low than I do. For, Eric, thou art bound to her, and thou shalt never loose the bond!"

Atli ceased a while, then spoke again more faintly:

"Hearken, comrades," he cried; "my strength is well-nigh spent. Ye shall swear four things to me—that ye will give Eric Brighteyes and Skallagrim Lambstail safe passage from Straumey. That ye will tell Swanhild the Fatherless, Groa's daughter and Atli's wife, that, at last, I know her for what she is—a murderess, a harlot, a witch and a liar; and that I forgive Eric whom she tricked, but that her I hate and spit upon. That ye will slay Koll the Half-witted, Groa's thrall, who came hither about two days gone, since by his lies he hath set an edge upon this sword of falsehood. That ye will raise no blood-feud against Eric for this my slaying, for I goaded him to the deed. Do ye swear?"

"We swear," said the men.

"Then farewell! And to thee farewell, also, Eric Brighteyes! Now take my hand and hold it while I die. Behold! I give thee a new name, and by that name thou shalt be called in story. I name thee Eric the Unlucky. Of all tales that are told, thine shall be the greatest. A mighty stroke that was of thine—a mighty stroke! Farewell!"

Then his head fell back upon the rock and Earl Atli died. And as he died the last rays of light went out of the sky.

XXI

HOW HALL OF LITHDALE TOOK TIDINGS TO ICELAND

Now on the same night that Atli died at the hand of Eric, Swanhild spake with Hall of Lithdale, whom she had summoned from the mainland. She bade him do this: take passage in a certain ship that should sail for Iceland on the morrow from the island that is called Westra, and there tell all these tidings of the ill-doings of Eric and of the slaying of Atli by his hand.

"Thou shalt say this," she went on, "that Eric had been my love for long, but that at length the matter came to the ears of Atli, the Earl. Then, holding this the greatest shame, he went on holmgang with Eric and was slain by him. This shalt thou add to thy tale also, that presently Eric and I will wed, and that Eric shall rule as Earl in Orkneys. Now these tidings must soon come to the ears of Gudruda the Fair, and she will send for thee, and question thee straightly concerning them, and thou shalt tell her the tale as thou toldest it at first. Then thou shalt give Gudruda this packet, which I send her as a gift, saying, that I bade her remember a certain oath which Eric took as to the cutting of his hair. And when she sees that which is within the packet is somewhat stained, tell her that is but the blood of Atli that is upon it, as his blood is upon Eric's hands. Now remember thou this, Hall, that if thou fail in the errand thy life shall pay forfeit, for presently I will also come to Iceland and hear how thou hast sped."

Then Swanhild gave him faring-money and gifts of wadmal and gold rings, promising that he should have so much again when she came to Iceland.

Hall said that he would do all these things, and went at once; nor did he fail in his tasks.

Atli being dead, Eric loosed his hand and called to the men to take up his body and bear it to the hall. This they did. Eric stood and watched them till they were lost in the darkness.

"Whither now, lord?" said Skallagrim.

"It matters little," said Eric. "What is thy counsel?"

"This is my counsel. That we take ship and sail back to the King in London. There we will tell all this tale. It is a far cry from Straumey to London town, and there we shall sit in peace, for the King will think little of the slaying of an Orkney Earl in a brawl about a woman. Mayhap, too, the Lady Elfrida will not set great store by it. Therefore, I say, let us fare back to London."

"In but one place am I at home, and that is Iceland," said Eric. "Thither I will go, Skallagrim, though it be but to miss friend from stead and bride from bed. At the least I shall find Ospakar there."

"Listen, lord!" said Skallagrim. "Was it not my rede that we should bide this winter through in London? Thou wouldst none of it, and what came about? Our ship is sunk, gone are our comrades, thine honour is tarnished, and dead is thy host at thine own hand. Yet I say all is not lost. Let us hence south, and see no more of Swanhild, of Gudruda, of Björn and Ospakar. So shall we break the spell. But if thou goest to Iceland, I am sure of this: that the evil fate which Atli foretold will fall on thee, and the days to come shall be even more unlucky than the days that have been."

"It may be so," said Eric. "Methinks, indeed, it will be so. Henceforth I am Eric the Unlucky. I will go back to Iceland and there play out the game. I care little if I live or am slain—I have no more joy in my life. I stand alone, like a fir upon a mountain-top, and every wind from heaven and every storm of hail and snow beats upon my head. But I say to thee, Skallagrim: go thy road, and leave a luckless man to his ill fate. Otherwise it shall be thine also. Good friend hast thou been to me; now let us part and wend south and north. The King will be glad to greet thee yonder in London, Lambstail."

"But one severing shall we know, lord," said Skallagrim, "and that shall be sword's work, nor will it be for long. It is ill to speak such words as these of the parting of lord and thrall. Bethink thee of the oath I swore on Mosfell. Let us go north, since it is thy will: in fifty years it will count for little which way we wended from the Isles."

So they went together down to the shore, and, finding a boat and men who as yet knew nothing of what had chanced to Atli, they sailed across the firth at the rising of the moon.

Two days afterwards they found a ship at Wick that was bound for Fareys, and sailed in her, Eric buying a passage with the half of a gold ring that the King had given him in London.

Here at Fareys they sat a month or more; but not in the Earl's hall as when Eric came with honour in the Gudruda, but in a farmer's stead. For the tale of Eric's dealings with Atli and Atli's wife had reached Fareys, and the Earl there had been a friend of Atli's. Moreover, Eric was now a poor man, having neither ship nor goods, nor friends. Therefore all looked coldly on him, though they wondered at his beauty and his might. Still, they dared not to speak ill or make a mock of him; for, two men having done so, were nearly slain of Skallagrim, who seized the twain by the throat, one in either hand, and dashed their heads together. After that men said little.

They sat there a month, till at length a chapman put in at Fareys, bound for Iceland, and they took passage with him, Eric paying the other half of his gold ring for ship-room. The chapman was not willing to give them place at first, for he, too, had heard the tale; but Skallagrim offered him choice, either to do so or to go on holmgang with him. Then the chapman gave them passage.

Now it is told that when his thralls and house-carles bore the corpse of Atli the Earl to his hall in Straumey, Swanhild met it and wept over it. And when the spokesman among them stood forward and told her those words that Atli had bidden them to say to her, sparing none, she spoke thus:

"My lord was distraught and weak with loss of blood when he spoke thus. The tale I told him was true, and now Eric has added to his sin by shedding the blood of him whom he wronged so sorely."

And thereafter she spoke so sweetly and with so much gentleness, craft, and wisdom that, though they still doubted them, all men held her words weighty. For

Swanhild had this art, that she could make the false sound true in the ears of men and the true sound false.

Still, being mindful of their oath, they hunted for Koll and found him. And when the thrall knew that they would slay him he ran thence screaming. Nor did Swanhild lift a hand to save his life, for she desired that Koll should die, lest he should bear witness against her. Away he ran towards the cliffs, and after him sped Atli's house-carles, till he came to the great cliffs that edge in the sea. Now they were close upon him and their swords were aloft. Then, sooner than know the kiss of steel, the liar leapt from the cliffs and was crushed, dying miserably on the rocks below. This was the end of Koll the Half-witted, Groa's thrall.

Swanhild sat in Straumey for a while, and took all Atli's heritage into her keeping, for he had no male kin; nor did any say her nay. Also she called in the moneys that he had out at interest, and that was a great sum, for Atli was a careful and a wealthy man. Then Swanhild made ready to go to Iceland. Atli had a great dragon of war, and she manned that ship and filled it with stores and all things needful. This done, she set stewards and grieves over the Orkney lands and farms, and, when the Earl was six weeks dead, she sailed for Iceland, giving out that she went thither to set a blood-suit on foot against Eric for the death of Atli, her lord. There she came in safety just as folk rode to the Thing.

Now Hall of Lithdale came to Iceland and told his tale of the doings of Eric and the death of Atli. Oft and loud he told it, and soon people gossiped of it in field and fair and stead. Björn, Asmund's son, heard this talk and sent for Hall. To him also Hall told the tale.

"Now," said Björn, "we will go to my sister Gudruda the Fair, and learn how she takes these tidings."

So they went in to where Gudruda sat spinning in the hall, singing as she span.

"Greeting, Gudruda," said Björn; "say, hast thou tidings of Eric Brighteyes, thy betrothed?"

"I have no tidings," said Gudruda.

"Then here is one who brings them."

Now for the first time Gudruda the Fair saw Hall of Lithdale. Up she sprang. "Thou hast tidings of Eric, Hall? Ah! thou art welcome, for no tidings have come of him for many a month. Speak on," and she pressed her hand against her heart and leaned towards him.

"My tidings are ill, lady."

"Is Eric dead? Say not that my love is dead!"

"He is worse than dead," said Hall. "He is shamed."

"There thou liest, Hall," she answered. "Shame and Eric are things apart."

"Mayst thou think so when thou hast heard my tale, lady," said Hall, "for I am sad at heart to speak it of one who was my mate."

"Speak on, I say," answered Gudruda, in such a voice that Hall shrank from her. "Speak on; but of this I warn thee: that if in one word thou liest, that shall be thy death when Eric comes."

Now Hall was afraid, thinking of the axe of Skallagrim. Still, he might not go back upon his word. So he began at the beginning, telling the story of how he was wounded in the fight with Ospakar's ships and left Farey isles, and how he came thence to Scotland and sat in Atli's hall on Orkneys. Then he told how the Gudruda was wrecked on Straumey, and, of all aboard, Eric and Skallagrim alone were saved because of Swanhild's dream.

"Herein I see witch-work," said Gudruda.

Then Hall told that Eric became Swanhild's love, but of the other tale which Swanhild had whispered to Atli he said nothing. For he knew that Gudruda would not believe this, and, moreover, if it were so, Swanhild had not sent the token which he should give.

"It may well be," said Gudruda, proudly; "Swanhild is fair and light of mind. Perchance she led Brighteyes into this snare." But, though she spoke thus, bitter jealousy and anger burned in her breast and she remembered the sight which she had seen when Eric and Swanhild met on the morn of Atli's wedding.

Then Hall told of the slaying of Atli the Good by Eric, but he said nothing of the Earl's dying words, nor of how he goaded Brighteyes with his bitter words.

"It was an ill deed in sooth," said Gudruda, "for Eric to slay an old man whom he had wronged. Still, it may chance that he was driven to it for his own life's sake."

Then Hall said that he had seen Swanhild after Atli's slaying, and that she had told him that she and Eric should wed shortly, and that Eric would rule in Orkneys by her side.

Gudruda asked if that was all his tale.

"Yes, lady," answered Hall, "that is all my tale, for after that I sailed and know not what happened. But I am charged to give something to thee, and that by the Lady Swanhild. She bade me say this also: that, when thou lookest on the gift, thou shouldst think on a certain oath which Eric took as to the cutting of his hair." And he drew a linen packet from his breast and gave it to her.

Thrice Gudruda looked on it, fearing to open it. Then, seeing the smile of mockery on Björn's cold face, she took the shears that hung at her side and cut the thread with them. And as she cut, a lock of golden hair rose from the packet, untwisting itself like a living snake. The lock was long, and its end was caked with gore.

"Whose hair is this?" said Gudruda, though she knew the hair well.

"Eric's hair," said Hall, "that Swanhild cut from his head with Eric's sword."

Now Gudruda put her hand to her bosom. She drew out a satchel, and from the satchel a lock of yellow hair. Side by side she placed the locks, looking first at one and then at the other.

"This is Eric's hair in sooth," she said—"Eric's hair that he swore none but I should cut! Eric's hair that Swanhild shore with Whitefire from Eric's head—Whitefire whereon we plighted troth! Say now, whose blood is this that stains the hair of Eric?"

"It is Atli's blood, whom Eric first dishonoured and then slew with his own hand," answered Hall.

Now there burned a fire on the hearth, for the day was cold. Gudruda the Fair stood over the fire and with either hand she let the two locks of Eric's hair fall upon

168

the embers. Slowly they twisted up and burned. She watched them burn, then she threw up her hands and with a great cry fled from the hall.

Björn and Hall of Lithdale looked on each other.

"Thou hadst best go hence!" said Björn; "and of this I warn thee, Hall, though I hold thy tidings good, that, if thou hast spoken one false word, that will be thy death. For then it would be better for thee to face all the wolves in Iceland than to stand before Eric in his rage."

Again Hall bethought himself of the axe of Skallagrim, and he went out heavily.

That day a messenger came from Gudruda to Björn, saying that she would speak with him. He went to where she sat alone upon her bed. Her face was white as death, and her dark eyes glowed.

"Eric has dealt badly with thee, sister, to bring thee to this sorrow," said Björn.

"Speak no evil of Eric to me," Gudruda answered. "The evil that he has done will be paid back to him; there is little need for thee to heap words upon his head. Hearken, Björn my brother: is it yet thy will that I should wed Ospakar Blacktooth?"

"That is my will, surely. There is no match in Iceland as this Ospakar, and I should win many friends by it."

"Do this then, Björn. Send messengers to Swinefell and say to Ospakar that if he would still wed Gudruda the Fair, Asmund's daughter, let him come to Middalhof when folk ride from the Thing and he shall not go hence alone. Nay, I have done. Now, I pray thee speak no more to me of Eric or of Ospakar. Of the one I have seen and heard enough, and of the other I shall hear and see enough in the years that are to come."

XXII

HOW ERIC CAME HOME AGAIN

Swanhild made a good passage from the Orkneys, and was in Iceland thirty-five days before Eric and Skallagrim set foot there. But she did not land by Westman Isles, for she had no wish to face Gudruda at that time, but by Reyjaness. Now she rode thence with her company to Thingvalla, for here all men were gathered for the Thing. At first people hung aloof from her, notwithstanding her wealth and beauty; but Swanhild knew well how to win the hearts of men. For now she told the same story of Eric that she had told to Atli, and there were none to say her nay. So it came to pass that she was believed, and Eric Brighteyes held to be shamed indeed. Now, too, she set a suit on foot against Eric for the death of Atli at his hand, claiming that sentence of the greater outlawry should be passed against him, and that his lands at Coldback in the Marsh on Ran River should be given, half to her in atonement for the Earl's death, and half to the men of Eric's quarter.

On the day of the opening of the Thing Ospakar Blacktooth came from the north, and with him his son Gizur and a great company of men. Ospakar was blithe, for from the Thing he should ride to Middalhof, there to wed Gudruda the Fair. Then Swanhild clad herself in beautiful attire, and, taking men with her, went to the booth of Ospakar.

Blacktooth sat in his booth and by him sat Gizur his son the Lawman. When he saw a beauteous lady, very richly clad, enter the booth he did not know who it might be. But Gizur knew her well, for he could never put Swanhild from his mind.

"Lo! here comes Swanhild the Fatherless, Atli's widow," said Gizur, flushing red with joy at the sight of her.

Then Ospakar greeted her heartily, and made place for her by him at the top of the booth.

"Ospakar Blacktooth," she said, "I am come to ask this of thee: that thou shalt befriend me in the suit which I have against Eric Brighteyes for the slaying of Earl Atli, my husband."

"Thou couldst have come to no man who is more willing," said Ospakar, "for, if thou hast something against Eric, I have yet more."

"I would ask this, too, Ospakar: that thy son Gizur should take up my suit and plead it; for I know well that he is the most skilful of all lawmen."

"I will do that," said Gizur, his eyes yet fixed upon her face.

"I looked for no less from thee," said Swanhild, "and be sure of this, that thou shalt not plead for nothing," and she glanced at him meaningly. Then she set out her case with a lying tongue, and afterwards went back to her booth, glad at heart. For now she learned that Hall had not failed in his errand, seeing that Gudruda was about to wed Ospakar.

Gizur gave warning of the blood-suit, and the end of it was that, though he had no notice and was not there to answer to the charge, against all right and custom Eric was declared outlaw and his lands were given, half to Swanhild and half to the men of his quarter. For now all held that Swanhild's was a true tale, and Eric the most shameful of men, and therefore they were willing to stretch the law against him. Also, being absent, he had few friends, and those men of small account; whereas Ospakar, who backed Swanhild's suit, was the most powerful of the northern chiefs, as Gizur was the most skilled lawman in Iceland. Moreover, Björn the Priest, Asmund's son, was among the judges, and, though Swanhild's tale seemed strange to him after that which he had heard from Hall of Lithdale, he loved Eric little. He feared also that if Eric came a free man to Iceland before Gudruda was wed to Ospakar, her love would conquer her anger, for he could see well that she still loved Brighteyes. Therefore he strove with might and main that Eric should be brought in guilty, nor did he fail in this.

So the end of it was that Eric Brighteyes was outlawed, his lands declared forfeit, and his head a wolf's head, to be taken by him who might, should he set foot in Iceland.

Thereafter, the Althing being ended, Björn, Gizur, and Ospakar, with all their company, rode away to Middalhof to sit at the marriage-feast. But Swanhild and her folk went by sea in the long war-ship to Westmans. For this was her plan: to seize on Coldback and to sit there for a while, till she saw if Eric came out to Iceland. Also she desired to see the wedding of Ospakar and Gudruda, for she had been bidden to it by Björn, her half-brother.

Now Ospakar came to Middalhof, and found Gudruda waiting his coming.

She stood in the great hall, pale and cold as April snow, and greeted him courteously. But when he would have kissed her, she shrank from him, for now he was more hideous in her sight than he had ever been, and she loathed him in her heart.

That night there was feasting in the hall, and at the feast Gudruda heard that Eric had been made outlaw. Then she spoke:

"This is an ill deed, thus to judge an absent man."

"Say, Gudruda," said Björn in her ear, "hast thou not also judged Eric who is absent?"

She turned her head and spoke no more of Eric; but Björn's words fixed themselves in her heart like arrows. The tale was strange to her, for it seemed that Eric had been made outlaw at Swanhild's suit, and yet Eric was Swanhild's love: for Swanhild's self had sent the lock of Brighteyes' hair by Hall, saying that he was her love and soon would wed her. How, then, did Swanhild bring a suit against him who should be her husband? Moreover, she heard that Swanhild sailed down to Coldback, and was bidden to the marriage-feast, that should be on the third day from now. Could it be, then, when all was said and done, that Eric was less faithless than she deemed? Gudruda's heart stood still and the blood rushed to her brow when she thought on it. Also, even if it were so, it was now too late. And surely it was not so, for had not Eric been made outlaw? Men were not made outlaw for a little thing. Nay, she would meet her fate, and ask no more of Eric and his doings.

On the morrow, as Gudruda sat in her chamber, it was told her that Saevuna, Thorgrimur's widow and Eric's mother, had come from Coldback to speak with her. For, after the death of Asmund and of Unna, Saevuna had moved back to Coldback on the Marsh.

"Nay, how can this be?" said Gudruda astonished, for she knew well that Saevuna was now both blind and bed-ridden.

"She has been borne here in a chair," said the woman who told her, "and that is a strange sight to see."

At first Gudruda was minded to say her nay; but her heart softened, and she bade them bring Saevuna in. Presently she came, being set in a chair upon the shoulders of four men. She was white to see, for sickness had aged her much, and she stared about her with sightless eyes. But she was still tall and straight, and her face was stern to look on. To Gudruda it seemed like that of Eric when he was angered.

"Am I nigh to Gudruda the Fair, Asmund's daughter?" asked Saevuna. "Methinks I hear her breathe."

"I am here, mother," said Gudruda. "What is thy will with me?"

"Set down, carles, and begone!" quoth Saevuna; "that which I have to say I would say alone. When I summon you, come."

The carles set down the chair upon the floor and went.

"Gudruda," said the dame, "I am risen from my deathbed, and I have caused myself to be borne on my last journey here across the meads, that I may speak with thee and warn thee. I hear that thou hast put away my son, Eric Brighteyes, to whom thou art sworn in marriage, and art about to give thyself to Ospakar Blacktooth. I hear also that thou hast done this deed because a certain man, Hall of Lithdale—whom from his youth up I have known for a liar and a knave, and whom thou thyself didst mistrust in years gone by—has come hither to Iceland from Orkneys, bearing a tale of Eric's dealings with thy half-sister Swanhild. This I hear, further: that Swanhild, Atli's widow, hath come out to Iceland and laid a suit against Eric for the slaying of Atli the Earl, her husband, and that Eric has been outlawed and his lands at Coldback are forfeit. Tell me now, Gudruda, Asmund's daughter, if these tales be true?"

"The tales are true, mother," said Gudruda.

"Then hearken to me, girl. Eric sprang from my womb, who of all living men is the best and first, as he is the bravest and most strong. I have reared this Eric from a babe and I know his heart well. Now I tell thee this, that, whatever Eric has done or left undone, naught of dishonour is on his hands. Mayhap Swanhild has deceived him—thou art a woman, and thou knowest well the arts which women have, and the strength that Freya gives them. Well thou knowest, also, of what breed this Swanhild came; and perchance thou canst remember how she dealt with thee, and with what mind she looked on Eric. Perchance thou canst remember how she plotted against thee and Eric—ay, how she thrust thee from Goldfoss brink. Say, then, wilt thou take her word? Wilt thou take the word of this witch-daughter of a witch? Wilt thou not think on Groa, her mother, and of Groa's dealings with thy father, and with Unna my kinswoman? As the mother is, so shall the daughter be. Wilt thou cast Eric aside, and that unheard?"

"There is no more room for doubt, mother," said Gudruda. "I have proof of this: that Eric has forsaken me."

"So thou thinkest, child; but I tell thee that thou art wrong! Eric loves thee now as he loved thee aforetime, and will love thee always."

"Would that I could believe it!" said Gudruda. "If I could believe that Eric still loved me—ay, even though he had been faithless to me—I would die ere I wed Ospakar!"

"Thou art foolish, Gudruda, and thou shalt rue thy folly bitterly. I am outworn, and death draws near to me—far from me now are hates and loves, hopes and fears; but I know this: that woman is mad who, loving a man, weds where she loves not. Shame shall be her portion and bitterness her bread. Unhappy shall she live, and when she comes to die, but as a wilderness—but as the desolate winter snow, shall be the record of her days!"

Now Gudruda wept aloud. "What is done is done," she cried; "the bridegroom sits within the hall—the bride awaits him in the bower. What is done is done—I may hope no more to be saved from Ospakar."

"What is done is done, yet it can be brought to nothing; but soon that shall be done which may never be undone! Gudruda, fare thee well! Never shall I listen to thy voice again. I hold thee shameless, thou unfaithful woman, who in thy foolish jealousy art ready to sell thyself to the arms of one thou hatest! Ho! carles; come hither. Bear me hence!"

Now the men came in and took up Saevuna's chair. Gudruda watched them bear her forth. Then suddenly she sprang from her seat and ran after her into the hall, weeping bitterly.

Now as Saevuna, Eric's mother, was carried out she was met by Ospakar and Björn.

"Stay," said Björn. "What does this carline here?—and why weeps Gudruda, my sister?"

The men halted. "Who calls me 'carline'?" said Saevuna. "Is the voice I hear the voice of Björn, Asmund's son?"

"It is my voice, truly," said Björn, "and I would know this—and this would Ospakar, who stands at my side, know also—why thou comest here, carline? and why Gudruda weeps?"

"Gudruda weeps because she has good cause to weep, Björn. She weeps because she has betrayed her love, Eric Brighteyes, my son, and is about to be sold in marriage—to be sold to thee, Ospakar Blacktooth, like a heifer at a fair."

Then Björn grew angry and cursed Saevuna, nor did Ospakar spare to add his ill words. But the old dame sat in her chair, listening silently till all their curses were spent.

"Ye are evil, the twain of you," she said, "and ye have told lies of Eric, my son; and ye have taken his bride for lust and greed, playing on the jealous folly of a maid like harpers on a harp. Now I tell you this, Björn and Ospakar! My blind eyes are opened and I see this hall of Middalhof, and lo! it is but a gore of blood! Blood flows upon the board—blood streams along the floor, and ye—ye twain!—lie dead thereon, and about your shapes are shrouds, and on her feet are Hell-shoon! Eric comes and Whitefire is aloft, and no more shall ye stand before him whom ye have slandered than stands the birch before the lightning stroke! Eric comes! I see his angry eyes—I see his helm flash in the door-place! Red was that marriage-feast at which sat Unna, my kinswoman, and Asmund, thy father—redder shall be the feast where sit Gudruda, thy sister, and Ospakar! The wolf howls at thy door, Björn! the grave-worm opens his mouth! trolls run to and fro upon thy threshold, and the ghosts of men speed Hellwards! Ill were the deeds of Groa—worse shall be the deeds of Groa's daughter! Red is thy hall with blood, Björn!—for Whitefire is aloft and—I tell thee Eric comes!"—and with one great cry she fell back—dead.

Now they stood amazed, and trembling in their fear.

"Saevuna hath spoken strange words," said Björn.

"Shall we be frightened by a dead hag?" quoth Ospakar, drawing his breath again. "Fellows, bear this carrion forth, or we fling it to the dogs."

Then the men tied the body of Saevuna, Thorgrimur's widow, Eric's mother, fast in the chair, and bore it thence. But when at length they came to Coldback, they found that Swanhild was there with all her following, and had driven Eric's grieve and his folk to the fells. But one old carline, who had been nurse to Eric, was left there, and she sat wailing in an outhouse, being too weak to move.

Then the men set down the corpse of Saevuna in the outhouse, and, having told all their tale to the carline, they fled also.

That night passed, and passed the morrow; but on the next day at dawn Eric Brighteyes and Skallagrim Lambstail landed near Westman Isles. They had made a bad passage from Fareys, having been beat about by contrary winds; but at length they came safe and well to land.

Now this was the day of the marriage-feast of Gudruda the Fair and Ospakar; but Eric knew nothing of these tidings.

"Where to now, lord?" said Skallagrim.

"To Coldback first, to see my mother, if she yet lives, and to learn tidings of Gudruda. Then as it may chance."

Near to the beach was a yeoman's house. Thither they went to hire horses; but none were in the house, for all had gone to Gudruda's marriage-feast. In the home meadow ran two good horses, and in the outhouses were saddles and bridles. They caught the horses, saddled them and rode for Coldback. When they had ridden for something over an hour they came to the crest of a height whence they could see Coldback in the Marsh.

Eric drew rein and looked, and his heart swelled within him at the sight of the place where he was born. But as he looked he saw a great train of people ride away from Coldback towards Middalhof—and in the company a woman wearing a purple cloak.

"Now what may this mean?" said Eric.

"Ride on and we shall learn," answered Skallagrim.

So they rode on, and as they rode Eric's breast grew heavy with fear. Now they passed up the banked way through the home meadows of the house, but they could see no one; and now they were at the door. Down sprang Eric and walked into the hall. But none were there to greet him, though a fire yet burned upon the earth. Only a gaunt hound wandered about the hall, and, seeing him, sprang towards him, growling. Eric knew him for his old wolf-hound, and called him by his name. The dog listened, then ran up and smelt his hands, and straightway howled with joy and leapt upon him. For a while he leapt thus, while Eric stared around him wondering and sad at heart. Then the dog ran to the door and stopped, whining. Eric followed after him. The hound passed through the entrance, and across the yard till he came to an outhouse. Here the dog stopped and scratched at the door, still whining. Eric thrust it open. Lo! there before him sat Saevuna, his mother, dead in a chair, and at her feet crouched the carline—she who had been Eric's nurse.

Now he grasped the door-posts to steady himself, and his shadow fell upon the white face of his mother and the old carline at her feet.

XXIII

HOW ERIC WAS A GUEST AT THE WEDDING-FEAST OF GUDRUDA THE FAIR

Eric looked, but said nothing.

"Who art thou?" whined the carline, gazing up at him with tear-blinded eyes. But Eric's face was in the shadow, and she only saw the glint of his golden hair and the flash of the golden helm. For Eric could not speak yet a while.

"Art thou one of the Swanhild's folk, come to drive me hence with the rest? Good sir, I cannot go to the fells, my limbs are too weak. Slay me, if thou wilt, but drive me not from this," and she pointed to the corpse. "Say now, will thou not help me to give it burial? It is unmeet that she who in her time had husband, and goods, and son, should lie unburied like a dead cow on the fells. I have still a hundred in silver, if I might but come at it. It is hidden, sir, and I will pay thee if thou wilt help me to bury her. These old hands are too feeble to dig a grave, nor could I bear her there alone if it were dug. Thou wilt not help me?—then may thine own mother's bones lie uncovered, and be picked of gulls and ravens. Oh, that Eric Brighteyes would come home again! Oh, that Eric was here! there is work to do and never a man to do it."

Now Eric gave a great sob and cried, "Nurse, nurse! knowest thou me not! I am Eric Brighteyes."

She uttered a loud cry, and, clasping him by the knees, looked up into his face.

"Thanks be to Odin! Thou art Eric—Eric come home again! But alas, thou hast come too late!"

"What has happened, then?" said Eric.

"What has happened? All evil things. Thou art outlawed, Eric, at the suit of Swanhild for the slaying of Atli the Earl. Swanhild sits here in Coldback, for she hath seized thy lands. Saevuna, thy mother, died two days ago in the hall of Middalhof, whither she went to speak with Gudruda."

"Gudruda! what of Gudruda?" cried Eric.

"This, Brighteyes: to-day she weds Ospakar Blacktooth."

Eric covered his face with his hand. Presently he lifted it.

"Thou art rich in evil tidings, nurse, though, it would seem, poor in all besides. Tell me at what hour is the wedding-feast?"

"An hour after noon, Eric; but now Swanhild has ridden thither with her company."

"Then room must be found at Middalhof for one more guest," said Eric, and laughed aloud. "Go on!—pour out thy evil news and spare me not!—for nothing has any more power to harm me now! Come hither, Skallagrim, and see and hearken."

Skallagrim came and looked on the face of dead Saevuna.

"I am outlawed at Swanhild's suit, Lambstail. My life lies in thy hand, if so be thou wouldst take it! Hew off my head, if thou wilt, and bear it to Gudruda the

Fair—she will thank thee for the gift. Lay on, Lambstail; lay on with that axe of thine."

"Child's talk!" said Skallagrim.

"Child's talk, but man's work! Thou hast not heard the tale out. Swanhild hath seized my lands and sits here at Coldback! And—what thinkest thou, Skallagrim?—but now she has ridden a-guesting to the marriage-feast of Ospakar Blacktooth with Gudruda the Fair! Swanhild at Gudruda's wedding!—the eagle in the wild swan's nest! But there will be another guest," and again he laughed aloud.

"Two other guests," said Skallagrim.

"More of thy tale, old nurse!—more of thy tale!" quoth Eric. "No better didst thou ever tell me when, as a lad, I sat by thee, in the ingle o' winter nights—and the company is fitting to the tale!" and he pointed to dead Saevuna.

Then the carline told on. She told how Hall of Lithdale had come out to Iceland, and of the story that he bore to Gudruda, and of the giving of the lock of hair.

"What did I say, lord?" broke in Skallagrim—"that in Hall thou hadst let a weasel go who would live to nip thee?"

"Him I will surely live to shorten by a head," quoth Eric.

"Nay, lord, this one for me—Ospakar for thee, Hall for me!"

"As thou wilt, Baresark. Among so many there is room to pick and choose. Tell on, nurse!"

Then she told how Swanhild came out to Iceland, and, having won Ospakar Blacktooth and Gizur to her side, had laid a suit against Eric at the Thing, and there bore false witness against him, so that Brighteyes was declared outlaw, being absent. She told, too, how Gudruda had betrothed herself to Ospakar, and how Swanhild had moved down to Coldback and seized the lands. Lastly she told of the rising of Saevuna from her deathbed, of her going to Middalhof, of the words she spoke to Björn and Ospakar, and of her death in the hall at Middalhof.

When all was told, Eric stooped and kissed the cold brow of his mother.

"There is little time to bury thee now, my mother," he said, "and perchance before six hours are sped there will be one to bury at thy side. Nevertheless, thou shalt sit in a better place than this."

Then he cut loose the cords that bound the body of Saevuna to the chair, and, lifting it in his arms, bore it to the hall. There he set the corpse in the high seat of the hall.

"We need not start yet a while, Skallagrim," said Eric, "if indeed thou wouldst go a-guesting with me to Middalhof. Therefore let us eat and drink, for there are deeds to do this day."

So they found meat and mead and ate and drank. Then Eric washed himself, combed out his golden locks, and looked well to his harness and to Whitefire's edge. Skallagrim also ground his great axe upon the whetstone in the yard, singing as he ground. When all was ready, the horses were caught, and Eric spoke to the carline:

"Hearken, nurse. If it may be that thou canst find any of our folk—and perchance now that they see that Swanhild has ridden to Middalhof some one of them will come down to spy—thou shalt say this to them. Thou shalt say that, if Eric Brighteyes yet lives, he will be at the foot of Mosfell to-morrow before midday, and if, for the sake of old days and fellowship, they are minded to befriend a friendless man, let them come thither with food, for by then food will be needed, and I will speak with them. And now farewell," and Eric kissed her and went, leaving her weeping.

As it chanced, before another hour was sped, Jon, Eric's thrall, who had stayed at home in Iceland, seeing Coldback empty, crept down from the fells and looked in. The carline saw him, and told him these tidings. Then he went thence to find the other men. Having found them he told them Eric's words, and a great gladness came upon them when they learned that Brighteyes still lived, and was in Iceland. Then they gathered food and gear, and rode away to the foot of Mosfell that is now called Ericsfell.

Ospakar sat in the hall at Middalhof, near to the high seat. He was fully armed, and a black helm with a raven's crest was on his head. For, though he said nothing of it, not a little did he fear that Saevuna spoke sooth—that her words would come true, and, before this day was done, he and Eric should once more stand face to face. At his side sat Gudruda the Fair, robed in white, a worked head-dress on her head, golden clasps upon her breast and golden rings about her arms. Never had she been more beautiful to see; but her face was whiter than her robes. She looked with loathing on Blacktooth at her side, rough like a bear, and hideous as a troll. But he looked on her with longing, and laughed from side to side of his great mouth when he thought that at last he had got her for his own.

"Ah, if Eric would but come, faithless though he be!—if Eric would but come!" thought Gudruda; but no Eric came to save her. The guests gathered fast, and presently Swanhild swept in with all her company, wrapped about in her purple cloak. She came up to the high seat where Gudruda sat, and bent the knee before her, looking on her with lovely mocking face and hate in her blue eyes.

"Greeting, Gudruda, my sister!" she said. "When last we met I sat, Atli's bride, where to-day thou sittest the bride of Ospakar. Then Eric Brighteyes held thy hand, and little thou didst think of wedding Ospakar. Now Eric is afar—so strangely do things come about—and Blacktooth, Brighteyes' foe, holds that fair hand of thine."

Gudruda looked on her and turned whiter yet in her pain, but she answered never a word.

"What! no word for me, sister?" said Swanhild. "And yet it is through me that thou comest to this glad hour. It is through me that thou art rid of Eric, and it is I who have given thee to the arms of mighty Ospakar. No word of thanks for so great a service!—fie on thee, Gudruda! fie!"

Then Gudruda spoke: "Strange tales are told of thee and Eric, Groa's daughter! I have done with Eric, but I have done with thee also. Thou hast thrust thyself here against my will and, if I may, I would see thy face no more."

"Wouldst thou see Eric's face, Gudruda?—say, wouldst see Eric's face? I tell thee it is fair!"

But Gudruda answered nothing, and Swanhild fell back, laughing.

Now the feast began, and men waxed merry. But ever Gudruda's heart grew heavier, for in it echoed those words that Saevuna had spoken. Her eyes were dim, and she seemed to see naught but the face of Eric as it had looked when he came back to her that day on the brink of Goldfoss Falls and she had thought him dead. Oh! what if he still loved her and were yet true at heart? Swanhild mocked her!—what if this was a plot of Swanhild's? Had not Swanhild plotted aforetime, and could a wolf cease from ravening or a witch from witch-work? Nay, she had seen Eric's hair—that he had sworn none save she should touch! Perchance he had been drugged, and the hair shorn from him in his sleep? Too late to think! Of what use was thought?—beside her sat Ospakar, in one short hour she would be his. Ah! that she could see him dead—the troll who had trafficked her to shame, the foe she had summoned in her wrath and jealousy! She had done ill—she had fallen into Swanhild's snare, and now Swanhild came to mock her!

The feast went on—cup followed cup. Now they poured the bride-cup! Before her heart beat two hundred times she would be the wife of Ospakar!

Blacktooth took the cup—pledged her in it, and drank deep. Then he turned and strove to kiss her. But Gudruda shrank from him with horror in her eyes, and all men wondered. Still she must drink the bridal cup. She took it. Dimly she saw the upturned faces, faintly she heard the murmur of a hundred voices.

What was that voice she caught above them all—there—without the hall?

Holding the cup in her hand, Gudruda bent forward, staring down the skali. Then she cried aloud, pointing to the door, and the cup fell clattering from her hand and rolled along the ground.

Men turned and looked. They saw this: there on the threshold stood a man, glorious to look at, and from his winged helm of gold the rays of light flashed through the dusky hall. The man was great and beautiful to see. He had long yellow hair bound in about his girdle, and in his left hand he held a pointed shield, in his right a spear, and at his thigh there hung a mighty sword. Nor was he alone, for by his side, a broad axe on his shoulder and shield in hand, stood another man, clad in black-hued mail—a man well-nigh as broad and big, with hawk's eyes, eagle beak, and black hair streaked with grey.

For a moment there was silence. Then a voice spoke:

"Lo! here be the Gods Baldur and Thor!—come from Valhalla to grace the marriage-feast!"

Then the man with golden hair cried aloud in a voice that made the rafters ring:

"Here are Eric Brighteyes and Skallagrim Lambstail, his thrall, come from over sea to grace the feast, indeed!"

"I could have looked for no worse guests," said Björn, beneath his breath, and rose to bid men thrust them out. But before he could speak, lo! gold-helmed Eric and black-helmed Skallagrim were stalking up the length of that great hall. Side by side they stalked, with faces fierce and cold; nor stayed they till they stood before the high seat. Eric looked up and round, and the light of his eyes was as the light of a sword. Men marvelled at his greatness and his wonderful beauty, and to Gudruda he seemed like a God.

"Here I see faces that are known to me," said Eric. "Greetings, comrades!"

"Greetings, Brighteyes!" shouted the Middalhof folk and the company of Swanhild; but the carles of Ospakar laid hand on sword—they too knew Eric. For still all men loved Eric, and the people of his quarter were proud of the deeds he had done oversea.

"Greeting, Björn, Asmund's son!" quoth Eric. "Greeting, Ospakar Blacktooth! Greeting, Swanhild the Fatherless, Atli's witch-wife—Groa's witch-bairn! Greeting, Hall of Lithdale, Hall the liar—Hall who cut the grapnel-chain! And to thee, sweet Bride, to thee Gudruda the Fair, greeting!"

Now Björn spoke: "I will take no greeting from a shamed and outlawed man. Get thee gone, Eric Brighteyes, and take thy wolf-hound with thee, lest thou bidest here stiff and cold."

"Speak not so loud, rat, lest hound's fang worry thee!" growled Skallagrim.

But Eric laughed aloud and cried—

"Words must be said, and perchance men shall die, ere ever I leave this hall, Björn!"

XXIV

HOW THE FEAST WENT

"Hearken all men!" said Eric.

"Thrust him out!" quoth Björn.

"Nay, cut him down!" said Ospakar, "he is an outlawed man."

"Words first, then deeds," answered Skallagrim. "Thou shalt have thy fill of both, Blacktooth, before day is done."

"Let Eric say his say," said Gudruda, lifting her head. "He has been doomed unheard, and it is my will that he shall say his say."

"What hast thou to do with Eric?" snarled Ospakar.

"The bride-cup is not yet drunk, lord," she answered.

"To thee, then, I will speak, lady," quoth Eric. "How comes it that, being betrothed to me, thou dost sit there the bride of Ospakar?"

"Ask of Swanhild," said Gudruda in a low voice. "Ask also of Hall of Lithdale yonder, who brought me Swanhild's gift from Straumey."

"I must ask much of Hall and he must answer much," said Eric. "What tale, then, did he bring thee from Straumey?"

"He said this, Eric," Gudruda answered: "that thou wast Swanhild's love; that for Swanhild's sake thou hadst basely killed Atli the Good, and that thou wast about to wed Swanhild's self and take the Earl's seat in Orkneys."

"And for what cause was I made outlaw at the Althing?"

"For this cause, Eric," said Björn, "that thou hadst dealt evilly with Swanhild, bringing her to shame against her will, and thereafter that thou hadst slain the Earl, her husband."

"Which, then, of these tales is true? for both cannot be true," said Brighteyes. "Speak, Swanhild."

"Thou knowest well that the last is true," said Swanhild boldly.

"How then comes it that thou didst charge Hall with that message to Gudruda? How then comes it that thou didst send her the lock of hair which thou didst cozen me to give thee?"

"I charged Hall with no message, and I sent no lock of hair," Swanhild answered.

"Stand thou forward, Hall!" said Eric, "and liar and coward though thou art, dare not to speak other than the truth! Nay, look not at the door: for, if thou stirrest, this spear shall find thee before thou hast gone a pace!"

Now Hall stood forward, trembling with fear, for he saw the eye of Skallagrim watching him close, and while Lambstail watched, his fingers toyed with the handle of his axe.

"It is true, lord, that Swanhild charged me with that message which I gave to the Lady Gudruda. Also she bade me give the lock of hair."

"And for this service thou didst take money, Hall?"

"Ay, lord, she gave me money for my faring."

"And all the while thou knewest the tidings false?"

Hall made no reply.

"Answer!" thundered Eric—"answer the truth, knave, or by every God that passes the hundred gates I will not spare thee twice!"

"It is so, lord," said Hall.

"Thou liest, fox!" cried Swanhild, white with wrath and casting a fierce look upon Hall. But men took no heed of Swanhild's words, for all eyes were bent on Eric.

"Is it now your pleasure, comrades, that I should tell you the truth?" said Brighteyes.

The most part of the company shouted "Yea!" but the men of Ospakar stood silent.

"Speak on, Eric," quoth Gudruda.

"This is the truth, then: Swanhild the Fatherless, Atli's wife, has always sought my love, and she has ever hated Gudruda whom I loved. From a child she has striven to work mischief between us. Ay, and she did this, though till now it has been hidden: she strove to murder Gudruda; it was on the day that Skallagrim and I overcame Ospakar and his band on Horse-Head Heights. She thrust Gudruda from the brink of Golden Falls while she sat looking on the waters, and as she hung there I dragged her back. Is it not so, Gudruda?"

"It is so," said Gudruda.

Now men murmured and looked at Swanhild. But she shrank back, plucking at her purple cloak.

"It was for this cause," said Eric, "that Asmund, Swanhild's father, gave her choice to wed Atli the Earl and pass over sea or to take her trial in the Doom-Ring. She wedded Atli and went away. Afterwards, by witchcraft, she brought my ship to wreck on Straumey's Isle—ay, she walked the waters like a shape of light and lured us on to ruin, so that all were drowned except Skallagrim and myself. Is it not so, Skallagrim?"

"It is so, lord. I saw her with my eyes."

Again folk murmured.

"Then we must sit in Atli's hall," said Eric, "and there we dwelt last winter. For a while Swanhild did no harm, till I feared her no more. But some three months ago, I was left with her: and a man called Koll, Groa's thrall, of whom ye know, came out from Iceland, bringing news of the death of Asmund the priest, of Unna my cousin, and of Groa the witch. To these ill-tidings Swanhild bribed him to add something. She bribed him to add this: that thou, Gudruda, wast betrothed to Ospakar, and wouldst wed him on last Yule Day. Moreover, he gave me a certain message from thee, Gudruda, and, in token of its truth, the half of that coin which I broke with thee long years ago. Say now, lady, didst thou send the coin?"

"Nay, never!" cried Gudruda; "many years ago I lost the half thou gavest me, though I feared to tell thee."

"Perchance one stands there who found it," said Eric, pointing with his spear at Swanhild. "At the least I was deceived by it. Now the tale is short. Swanhild mourned with me, and in my sorrow I mourned bitterly. Then it was she asked a boon, that lock of mine, Gudruda, and, thinking thee faithless, I gave it, holding all oaths broken. Then too, when I would have left her, she drugged me with a witch-draught—ay, she drugged me, and I woke to find myself false to my oath, false to Atli, and false to thee, Gudruda. I cursed her and I left her, waiting for the Earl, to tell him all. But Swanhild outwitted me. She told him that other tale of shame that ye have heard, and brought Koll to him as witness of the tale. Atli was deceived by her, and not until I had cut him down in anger at the bitter words he spoke, calling me coward and niddering, did he know the truth. But before he died he knew it; and he died, holding my hand and bidding those about him find Koll and slay him. Is it not so, ye who were Atli's men?"

"It is so, Eric!" they cried; "we heard it with our own ears, and we slew Koll. But afterwards Swanhild brought is to believe that Earl Atli was distraught when he spoke thus, and that things were indeed as she had said."

Again men murmured, and a strange light shone in Gudruda's eyes.

"Now, Gudruda, thou hast heard all my story," said Eric. "Say, dost thou believe me?"

"I believe thee, Eric."

"Say then, wilt thou still wed yon Ospakar?"

Gudruda looked on Blacktooth, then she looked at golden Eric and opened her lips to speak. But before a word could pass them Ospakar rose in wrath, laying his hand upon his sword.

"Thinkest thou thus to lure away my dove, outlaw? First I will see thee food for crows."

"Well spoken, Blacktooth," laughed Eric. "I waited for such words from thee. Thrice have we striven together—once out yonder in the snow, once on Horse-Head Heights, and once by Westman Isles—and still we live to tell the tale. Come down, Ospakar: come down from that soft seat of thine and here and now let us put it to the proof who is the better man. When we met before, the stake was Whitefire set against my eye. Now the stake is our lives and fair Gudruda's hand. Talk no more, Ospakar, but fall to it."

"Gudruda shall never wed thee, while I live!" said Björn; "thou art a landless loon, a brawler, and an outlaw. Get thee gone, Eric, with thy wolf-hound!"

"Squeak not so loud, rat—squeak not so loud, lest hound's fang worry thee!" said Skallagrim.

"Whether I wed Gudruda or whether I wed her not is a matter that shall be known in its season," said Eric. "For thy words, I say this: that it is risky to hurl names at such as I am, Björn, lest perchance I answer them with spear-thrusts. Thy answer, Ospakar! What need to wait? Thy answer!"

Now Ospakar looked at Brighteyes and grew afraid. He was a mighty man, but he knew the weight of Eric's arm.

"I will not fight with thee, carle," he said, "who hast naught to lose."

"Then thou art coward and niddering!" said Eric. "Ospakar Niddering I name thee here before all men! What! thou couldst plot against me—thou couldst waylay me, ten to one and two ships to one, but face to face with me alone thou dost not dare to stand? Comrades, look on your lord!—look at Ospakar the Niddering!"

Now the swarthy brow of Blacktooth grew red with rage, and his breath came in great gasps. "Ho, men!" he cried, "drive this knave away. Strip his harness off him and whip him hence with rods."

"Let but a man stir towards me and this spear flies through thy heart, Niddering," cried Eric. "Gudruda, what thinkest thou of thy lord?"

"I know this," said Gudruda, "that I will not wed a man who is named 'Niddering' in the face of all and lifts no sword."

Gudruda spoke thus, because she was mad with love and fear and shame, and she desired that Eric should stand face to face with Ospakar Blacktooth, for thus, alone, she might perhaps be rid of Ospakar.

"Such words do not come well from gentle lips," said Björn.

"Is it to be borne, brother," answered Gudruda, "that the man who would call me wife should be named Ospakar the Niddering? When that shame is washed away, and then only, can I think on marriage. I will never be Niddering's bride!"

"Thou hearest, Ospakar Niddering?" said Eric. Then he gave the spear in his hand to Skallagrim, and, gripping Whitefire's hilt, he burst the peace-strings, and tore it from the scabbard.

Now the great sword shone on high like lightning leaping from a cloud, and as it shone men shouted, "Ospakar! Ospakar Niddering! Come, win back Whitefire from Eric's hand, or be for ever shamed!"

Blacktooth could endure this no more. He snatched sword and shield, and, like a bear from a cave, like a wolf from his lair, rushed roaring from his seat. On he came, and the ground shook beneath his bulk.

"At last, Niddering!" cried Eric, and sprang to meet him.

"Back! all men, back!" shouted Skallagrim, "now we shall see blows."

As he spoke the great swords flashed aloft and clanged upon the iron shields. So heavy were the blows that fire leapt out from them. Ospakar reeled back beneath the shock, and Eric was beaten to his knee. Now he was up, but as he rushed, Ospakar struck again and swept away half of Brighteyen's pointed shield so that it fell upon the floor. Eric smote also, but Ospakar dropped his knee to earth and the sword hissed over him. Blacktooth cut at Eric's legs; but Brighteyes sprang from the ground and took no harm.

Now some cried, "Eric! Eric!" and some cried "Ospakar! Ospakar!" for no one knew how the fight would go.

Gudruda sat watching in the high seat, and as blows fell her colour came and went.

Swanhild drew near, watching also, and she desired in her fierce heart to see Eric brought to shame and death, for, should he win, then Gudruda would be rid of Ospakar. Now by her side stood Gizur, Ospakar's son, and near to her was Björn. These two held their breath, for, if Eric conquered, all their plans were brought to nothing.

Even as he sprang into the air, Eric smote down with all his strength. The blow fell on Ospakar's shield. It shore through the shield and struck on the shoulder beneath. But Blacktooth's byrnie was good, nor did the sword bite into it. Still the stroke was so heavy that Ospakar staggered back four paces beneath it, then fell upon the ground.

Now folk raised a shout of "Eric! Eric!" for it seemed that Ospakar was sped. Brighteyes, too, cried aloud, then rushed forward. Now, as he came, Swanhild whispered an eager word into the ear of Björn. By Björn's foot lay that half of Eric's shield which had been shorn away by the sword of Ospakar. Gudruda, watching, saw Björn push it with his shoe so that it slid before the feet of Brighteyes. His right foot caught on it, he stumbled heavily—stumbled again, then fell prone on his face, and, as he fell, stretched out his sword hand to save himself, so that Whitefire flew from his grasp. The blade struck its hilt against the ground, then circled in the air and fixed itself, point downwards, in the clay of the flooring. The hand of Ospakar rising from the ground smote against the hilt of Whitefire. He saw it, with a shout he cast his own sword away and clasped Whitefire.

Away circled the sword of Ospakar; and of that cast this strange thing is told, false or true. Far in the corner of the hall lurked Thorunna, she who had betrayed Skallagrim when he was named Ounound. She had come with a heavy heart to Middalhof in the company of Ospakar; but when she saw Skallagrim, her husband—whom she had betrayed, and who had turned Baresark because of her wickedness—shame smote her, and she crept away and hid herself behind the hangings of the hall. The sword sped along point first, it rushed like a spear through the air. It fell on the hangings, piercing them, piercing the heart of Thorunna, who cowered behind them, so that with one cry she sank dead to earth, slain by her lover's hand.

Now when men saw that Ospakar once more held Whitefire in his hand—Whitefire that Brighteyes had won from him—they called aloud that it was an omen. The sword of Blacktooth had come back to Blacktooth and now Eric would surely be slain of it!

Eric sprang from the ground. He heard the shouts and saw Whitefire blazing in Ospakar's hand.

"Now thou art weaponless, fly! Brighteyes; fly!" cried some.

Gudruda's cheek grew white with fear, and for a moment Eric's heart failed him.

"Fly not!" roared Skallagrim. "Björn tripped thee. Yet hast thou half a shield!"

Ospakar rushed on, and Whitefire flickered over Eric's helm. Down it came and shore one wing from the helm. Again it shone and fell, but Brighteyes caught the blow on his broken shield.

Then, while men waited to see him slain, Eric gave a great war-shout and sprang forward.

"Thou art mad!" shouted the folk.

"Ye shall see! Ye shall see!" screamed Skallagrim.

Again Ospakar smote and again Eric caught the blow; and behold! he struck back, thrusting with the point of the shorn shield straight at the face of Ospakar.

"Peck! Eagle; peck!" cried Skallagrim.

Once more Whitefire shone above him. Eric rushed in beneath the sword, and with all his mighty strength thrust the buckler-point at Blacktooth's face. It struck fair and full, and lo! the helm of Ospakar burst asunder. He threw wide his giant arms, then fell as a pine falls upon the mountain edge. He fell back, and he lay still.

But Eric, stooping over him, took Whitefire from his hand.

XXV: HOW THE FEAST ENDED

For a moment there was silence in the hall, for men had known no such fight as this.

"Why, then, do ye gape?" laughed Skallagrim, pointing with the spear. "Dead is Ospakar!—slain by the swordless man! Eric Brighteyes hath slain Ospakar Blacktooth!"

Then there went up such a shout as never was heard in the hall of Middalhof.

Now when Gudruda knew that Ospakar was sped, she looked at Eric as he rested, leaning on his sword, and her heart was filled with awe and love. She sprang from her seat, and, coming to where Brighteyes stood, she greeted him.

"Welcome to Iceland, Eric!" she said. "Welcome, thou glory of the south!"

Now Swanhild grew wild, for she saw that Eric was about to take Gudruda in his arms and kiss her before all men.

"Say, Björn," she cried; "wilt thou suffer that this outlaw, having slain Ospakar, should lead Gudruda hence as wife?"

"He shall never do so while I live," cried Björn, nearly mad with rage. "This is my command, sister: that thou dost see Eric no more."

"Say, Björn," answered Gudruda, "did I dream, or did I indeed see thee thrust the broken buckler before Eric's feet, so that he stumbled on it and fell?"

"That thou sawest, lady," said Skallagrim; "for I saw it also."

Now Björn grew white in his anger. He did not answer Gudruda, but called aloud to his men to slay Eric and Skallagrim. Gizur called also to the folk of Ospakar, and Swanhild to those who came with her.

Then Gudruda fled back to her seat.

But Eric cried aloud also: "Ye who love me, cleave to me. Suffer it not that Brighteyes be cut down of northerners and outland men. Hear me, Atli's folk; hear me, carles of Coldback and of Middalhof!"

And so greatly did many love Eric that half of the thralls of Björn, and almost all of the company of Swanhild who had been Atli's shield-men and Brighteyes' comrades, drew swords, shouting "Eric! Eric!" But the carles of Ospakar came on to make an end of him.

Björn saw, and, drawing sword, smote at Brighteyes, taking him unawares. But Skallagrim caught the blow upon his axe, and before Björn could smite again Whitefire was aloft and down fell Björn, dead!

That was the end of Björn, Asmund's son.

"Thou hast squeaked thy last, rat! What did I tell thee?" cried Skallagrim. "Take Björn's shield and back to back, lord, for here come foes."

"There goes one," answered Eric, pointing to the door.

Now Hall of Lithdale slunk through the doorway—Hall, the liar, who cut the grapnel-chain—for he wished to see the last of Skallagrim. But the Baresark still held Eric's spear in his hand. He whirled it aloft, and it hissed through the air. The aim was good, for, as he crept away, the spear struck Hall between neck and shoulder, pinning him to the doorpost, and there the liar died.

"Now the weasel is nailed to the beam," said Skallagrim. "Hall of Lithdale, what did I promise thee?"

"Guard thy head and my back," quoth Eric; "blows fall!"

Now men smote at Eric and Skallagrim, nor did they spare to smite in turn. And as foes fell before him, Eric stepped one pace forward towards the door, and Skallagrim, who, back to back with him, held off those who pressed behind, took one step rearwards. Thus, a foe for every step, they won their way down the long hall. Fierce raged the fray around them, for, made with hate and drink and the lust of fight, Swanhild's folk—Eric's friends—remembering the words of Atli, fell on Ospakar's; and the people of Björn fell on each other, brother on brother, and father on son—nor might the fray be stayed. The boards were overthrown, dead men lay among the meats and mead, and the blood of freeman, lord and thrall ran adown the floor. Everywhere through the dusky hall glittered the sheen of flashing swords and rose the clang of war. Darts clove the air like tongues of flame, and the clamour of battle beat against the roof.

Blinded of the Norns who brought these things to pass, men sought no mercy and they gave none, but smote and slew till few were left to slay.

And still Gudruda sat in her bride-seat, and, with eyes fixed in horror, watched the waxing of the war. Near to her stood Swanhild, marking all things with a fierce-set face, and calling down curses on her folk, who one and all cried "Eric! Eric!" and swept the thralls of Ospakar as corn is swept of the sickle.

And there, nigh to the door, pale of face and beautiful to see, golden Eric clove his way, and with him went black Skallagrim. Terrible was the flare of Whitefire as he flicked aloft like the levin in the cloud. Terrible was the flare of Whitefire; but more terrible was the light of Eric's eyes, for they seemed to flame in his head, and wherever that fire fell it lighted men the way to death. Whitefire sung and flickered, and crashed the axe of Skallagrim, and still through the press of war they won their way. Now Gizur stands before them, spear aloft, and Whitefire leaps up to meet him. Lo! he turns and flies. The coward son of Ospakar does not seek the fate of Ospakar!

The door is won. They stand without but little harmed, while women wail aloud.

"To horse!" cried Skallagrim; "to horse, ere our luck fail us!"

"There is no luck in this," gasped Eric; "for I have slain many men, and among them is Björn, the brother of her whom I would make my bride."

"Better one such fight than many brides," said Skallagrim, shaking his red axe. "We have won great glory this day, Brighteyes, and Ospakar is dead—slain by a swordless man!"

Now Eric and Skallagrim ran to their horses, none hindering them, and, mounting, rode towards Mosfell.

All that evening and all the night they rode, and at morning they came across the black sand to Mosfell slopes that are by the Hecla. Here they rested, and, taking off their armour, washed themselves in the stream: for they were very weary and foul with blood and wounds. When they had finished washing and had buckled on their harness again, Skallagrim, peering across the plain with his hawk's eyes, saw men riding fast towards them.

"Foes are soon afoot, lord," he said. "I thought we had stayed their hunger for a while."

"Would that I might stay mine," quoth Eric. "I am weary, and unfit for fight."

"I have still strength for one or two," said Skallagrim, "and then good-night! But these are no foes. They are of the Coldback folk. The carline has kept her word."

Then Eric was glad, and presently six men, headed by Jon his thrall, the same man who had watched on Mosfell when Eric went up to slay the Baresark, rode to them and greeted them. "Beggar women," said Jon, "whom they met at Ran River, had told them of the death of Ospakar, and of the great slaying at Middalhof, and they would know if the tidings were true."

"It is true, Jon," said Eric; "but first give us food, if ye have it, for we are hungered and spent. When we have eaten we will speak."

So they led up a pack-horse and from it took stockfish and smoked meat, of which Eric and Skallagrim ate heartily, till their strength came back to them.

Then Eric spoke. "Comrades," he said, "I am an outlawed man, and, though I have not sought it, much blood is on my head. Atli is dead at my hand; Ospakar is dead at my hand; Björn the Priest, Asmund's son, is dead at my hand, and with them many another man. Nor may the matter stay here, for Gizur, Blacktooth's son, yet lives, and Björn has kin in the south, and Swanhild will buy friends with gold, and all of these will set on me to slay me, so that at the last I die by the sword."

"No need for that," said Skallagrim. "Our vengeance is wrought, and now, as before, the sea is open, and I think that a welcome awaits us in London."

"Now Gudruda is widowed before she was fully wed," said Eric, "therefore I bide an outlawed man here in Iceland. I go hence no more, though it be death to stay, unless indeed Gudruda the Fair goes with me."

"It will be death, then," said Skallagrim, "and the swords are forged that we shall feel. The odds are too heavy, lord."

"Mayhap," answered Eric. "No man may flee his fate, and I shall not altogether grieve when mine finds me. Hearken, comrades: I go up to Mosfell height, and there I stay, till those be found who can drag me from my hole. But this is my counsel to you: that ye leave me to my doom, for I am an unlucky man who always chooses the wrong road."

"That will not I," said Skallagrim.

"Nor we," said Eric's folk; "Swanhild holds Coldback, and we are driven to the fells. To the fells then we will go with thee, Eric Brighteyes, and become cave-dwellers and outlaws for thy sake. Fear not, thou shalt still find many friends."

"I did not look for such a thing at your hands," said Eric; "but stormy waters show how the boat is built. May no bad luck come to you from your good fellowship. And now let us to our nest."

Then they caught the horses, and rode with Brighteyes up the steep side of Mosfell, till at length they came to that secret dell which Skallagrim had once shown to Eric. Here they turned the horses loose to feed, and, going forward on foot, reached the dark and narrow pass that Brighteyes had trod when he sought for the Baresark foe. Skallagrim led the way along it, then came Eric and the rest. One by one they stepped on to the giddy point of rock, and, catching at the birch-bush, entered the hole. So they gained the platform and the great cave beyond; and they found that no man had set foot there since the day when Eric had striven with Skallagrim. For there on the rock, rotten with the weather, lay that haft of wood which Brighteyes had hewed from the axe of Skallagrim, and in the cave were many things beside as the Baresark had left them.

So they took up their dwelling in the cave, Eric, Skallagrim, and the six Coldback men, and there they dwelt many months. But Eric sent out his men, one at a time, and got together food and a store of sheepskins, and other needful things. For he knew this well: that Gizur and Swanhild would before long come up against them, and, if they could not take them by force, would set themselves to watch the mountain-path and starve them out.

When Eric and Skallagrim rode away from Middalhof the fight still raged fiercely in the hall, and nothing but death might stay it. The minds of men were mad, and they smote one another, and slew each other, till at length of all that marriage company few were left unharmed, except Gizur, Swanhild, and Gudruda. For the serving thralls and womenfolk had fled the hall, and with them some peaceful men.

Then Gudruda spoke as one in a dream.

"Saevuna's prophecy was true," she said, "red was the marriage-feast of Asmund my father, redder has been the marriage-feast of Ospakar! She saw the hall of Middalhof one gore of blood, and lo! it is so; look upon thy work, Swanhild," and she pointed to the piled-up dead—"look upon thy work, witch-sister, and grow fearful: for all this death is on thy head!"

Swanhild laughed aloud. "I think it a merry sight," she cried. "The marriage-feast of Asmund our father was red, and thy marriage-feast, Gudruda, has been redder. Would that thy blood and the blood of Eric ran with the blood of Björn and Ospakar! That tale must yet be told, Gudruda. There shall be binding on of Hell-shoes at Middalhof, but I bind them not. My task is still to come: for I will live to fasten the Hell-shoes on the feet of Eric, and on thy feet, Gudruda! At the least, I have brought about this much, that thou canst scarcely wed Eric the outlaw: for with his own hand he slew Björn our brother, and because of this I count all that death as nothing. Thou canst not mate with Brighteyes, lest the wide wounds of Björn thy brother should take tongues and cry thy shame from sea to sea!"

Gudruda made no answer, but sat as one carved in stone. Then Swanhild spoke again:

"Let us away to the north, Gizur; there to gather strength to make an end of Eric. Say, wilt thou help us, Gudruda? The blood-feud for the death of Björn is thine."

"Ye are enough to bring about the fall of one unfriended man," Gudruda said. "Go, and leave me with my sorrow and the dead. Nay! before thou goest, listen, Swanhild, for there is that in my heart which tells me I shall never look again upon thy face. From evil to evil thou hast ever gone, Swanhild, and from evil to evil thou wilt go. It may well chance that thy wickedness will win. It may well chance that thou wilt crown thy crimes with my slaying and the slaying of the man who loves me. But I tell thee this, traitress—murderess, as thou art—that here the tale ends not. Not by death, Swanhild, shalt thou escape the deeds of life! There they shall rise up against thee, and there every shame that thou hast worked, every sin that thou hast sinned, and every soul that thou hast brought to Hela's halls, shall come to haunt thee and to drive thee on from age to age! That witchcraft which thou lovest shall mesh thee. Shadows shall bewilder thee; from the bowl of empty longings thou shalt drink and drink, and not be satisfied. Yea! lusts shall mock and madden thee. Thou shalt ride the winds, thou shalt sail the seas, but thou shalt find no harbour, and never shalt thou set foot upon a shore of peace.

"Go on, Swanhild—dye those hands in blood—wade through the river of shame! Seek thy desire, and finding, lose! Work thy evil, and winning, fail! I yet shall triumph—I yet shall trample thee; and, in a place to come, with Eric at my side, I shall make a mock of Swanhild the murderess! Swanhild the liar, and the wanton, and the witch! Now get thee gone!"

Swanhild heard. She looked up at Gudruda's face and it was alight as with a fire. She strove to answer, but no words came. Then Groa's daughter turned and went, and with her went Gizur.

Now women and thralls came in and drew out the wounded and those who still breathed from among the dead, taking them to the temple. They bore away the body of Ospakar also, but they left the rest.

All night long Gudruda sat in the bride's seat. There she sat in the silver summer midnight, looking on the slain who were strewn about the great hall. All night she sat alone in the bride's seat thinking—ever thinking.

How, then, would it end? There her brother Björn lay a-cold—Björn the justly slain of Brighteyes; yet how could she wed the man who slew her brother? From Ospakar she was divorced by death; from Eric she was divorced by the blood of Björn her brother! How might she unravel this tangled skein and float to weal upon this sea of death? All things went amiss! The doom was on her! She had lived to an ill purpose—her love had wrought evil! What availed it to have been born to be fair among women and to have desired that which might not be? And she herself had brought these things to pass—she had loosed the rock which crushed her! Why had she hearkened to that false tale?

Gudruda sat on high in the bride's seat, asking wisdom of the piled-up dead, while the cold blue shadows of the nightless night gathered over her and them—gathered, and waned, and grew at last to the glare of day.

XXVI

HOW ERIC VENTURED DOWN TO MIDDALHOF AND WHAT HE FOUND

Gizur went north to Swinefell, and Swanhild went with him. For now that Ospakar was dead at Eric's hand, Gizur ruled in his place at Swinefell, and was the greatest lord in all the north. He loved Swanhild, and desired to make her his wife; but she played with him, talking darkly of what might be. Swanhild was not minded to be the wife of any man, except of Eric; to all others she was cold as the winter earth. Still, she fooled Gizur as she had fooled Atli the Good, and he grew blind with love of her. For still the beauty of Swanhild waxed as the moon waxes in the sky, and her wicked eyes shone as the stars shine when the moon has set.

Now they came to Swinefell, and there Gizur buried Ospakar Blacktooth, his father, with much state. He set him in a chamber of rock and timbers on a mountain-top, whence he might see all the lands that once were his, and built up a great mound of earth above him. To this day people tell that here on Yule night black Ospakar bursts out, and golden Eric rides down the blast to meet him. Then come the clang of swords, and groans, and the sound of riven helms, till presently Brighteyes passes southward on the wind, bearing in his hand the half of a cloven shield.

So Gizur bound the Hell-shoes on his father, and swore that he would neither rest nor stay till Eric Brighteyes was dead and dead was Skallagrim Lambstail. Then he gathered a great force of men and rode south to Coldback, to the slaying of Eric, and with him went Swanhild.

Gudruda sat alone in the haunted hall of Middalhof and brooded on her love and on her fate. Eric, too, sat in Mosfell cave and brooded on his evil chance. His heart was sick with sorrow, and there was little that he could do except think about the past. He would not go to foray, after the fashion of outlaws, and there was no need of this. For the talk of his mighty deeds spread through the land, so that the people spoke of little else. And the men of his quarter were so proud of these deeds of Eric's that, though some of their kind had fallen at his hands in the great fight of Middalhof and some at the hands of Skallagrim, yet they spoke of him as men speak of a God. Moreover they brought him gifts of food and clothing and arms, as many as his people could carry away, and laid them in a booth that is on the plain near the foot of Mosfell, which thenceforth was named Ericsfell. Further, they bade his thralls tell him that, if he wished it, they would find him a good ship of war to take him from Iceland—ay, and man it with loyal men and true.

Eric thanked them through Jon his thrall, but answered that he wished to die here in Iceland.

Now, when Eric had sat two months and more in Mosfell cave and autumn was coming, he learned that Gizur and Swanhild had moved down to Coldback, and with them a great company of men who were sworn to slay him. He asked if Gudruda the Fair had also gathered men for his slaying. They told him no; that Gudruda stayed with her thralls and women at Middalhof, mourning for Björn her brother. From these tidings Eric took some heart of hope: at the least Gudruda laid no bloodfeud against him. For he waited, thinking, if indeed she yet loved him, that Gudruda would send him some word or token of her love. But no word came, since between them ran the blood of Björn. On the morrow of these tidings Skallagrim spoke to Eric.

"This is my counsel, lord," he said, "that we ride out by night and fall on the folk of Gizur at Coldback, and burn the stead over them, putting them to the sword. I am weary of sitting here like an eagle in a cage."

"Such is no counsel of mine, Skallagrim," answered Brighteyes. "I am weary of sitting here, indeed; but I am yet more weary of bringing men to their death. I will shed no more blood, unless it is to save my own head. When the people of Gizur came to seek me on Mosfell, they shall find me here; but I will not go to them."

"Thy heart is out of thee, lord," said Skallagrim; "thou wast not wont to speak thus."

"Ay, Skallagrim," said Eric, "the heart is out of me. Yet I ride from Mosfell today."

"Whither, lord?"

"To Middalhof, to have speech with Gudruda the Fair."

"Like enough, then, thou wilt be silent thereafter."

"It well may be," said Eric. "Yet I will ride. I can bear this doubt no longer."

"Then I shall come with thee," said Skallagrim.

"As thou wilt," answered Eric.

So at midday Eric and Skallagrim rode away from Mosfell in a storm of rain. The rain was so heavy that those of Gizur's spies who watched the mountain did not see them. All that day they rode and all the night, till by morning they came to Middalhof. Eric told Skallagrim to stay with the horses and let them feed, while he went on foot to see if by chance he might get speech with Gudruda. This the Baresark did, though he grumbled at the task, fearing lest Eric should be done to death, and he not there to die with him.

Now Eric walked to within two bowshots of the house, then sat down in a dell by the river, from the edge of which he could see those who passed in and out. Presently his heart gave a leap, for there came out from the woman's door a lady tall and beautiful to see, and with golden hair that flowed about her breast. It was Gudruda, and he saw that she bore a napkin in her hand. Then Eric knew, according to her custom on the warm mornings, that she came alone to bathe in the river, as she had always done from a child. It was her habit to bathe here in this place: for at the bottom of the dell was a spot where reeds and bushes grew thick, and the water lay in a basin of rock and was clear and still. For at this spot a hot spring ran into the river.

Eric went down the dell, hid himself close in the bushes and waited, for he feared to speak with Gudruda in the open field. A while passed, and presently the shadow of the lady crept over the edge of the dell, then she came herself in that beauty which since her day has not been known in Iceland. Her face was sad and sweet, her dark and lovely eyes were sad. On she came, till she stood within a spear's length of where Eric lay, crouched in the bush, and looking at her through the hedge of reeds. Here a flat rock overhung the water, and Gudruda sat herself on this rock, and, shaking off her shoes, dipped her white feet in the water. Then suddenly she threw aside her cloak, baring her arms, and, gazing upon the shadow of her beauty in the mirror of the water, sighed and sighed again, while Eric looked at her with a bursting heart, for as yet he could find no words to say.

Now she spoke aloud. "Of what use to be so fair?" she said. "Oh, wherefore was I born so fair to bring death to many and sorrow on myself and him I love?" And she shook her golden hair about her arms of snow, and, holding the napkin to her eyes, wept softly. But it seemed to Eric that between her sobs she called upon his name.

Now Eric could no longer bear the sight of Gudruda weeping. While she wept, hiding her eyes, he rose from behind the screen of reeds and stood beside her in such fashion that his shadow fell upon her. She felt the sunlight pass and looked up. Lo! it was no cloud, but the shape of Eric, and the sun glittered on his golden helm and hair.

"Eric!" Gudruda cried; "Eric!" Then, remembering how she was attired, snatching her cloak, she threw it about her arms and thrust her wet feet into her shoes. "Out upon thee!" she said; "is it not enough, then, that thou shouldst break thy troth for Swanhild's sake, that thou shouldst slay my brother and turn my hall to shambles? Wouldst now steal upon me thus!"

"Methought that thou didst weep and call upon my name, Gudruda," he said humbly.

"By what right art thou here to hearken to my words?" she answered. "Is it, then, strange that I should speak the name of him who slew my brother? Is it strange that I should weep over that brother whom thou didst slay? Get thee gone, Brighteyes, before I call my folk to kill thee!"

"Call on, Gudruda. I set little price upon my life. I laid it in the hands of chance when I came from Mosfell to speak with thee, and now I will pay it down if so it pleases thee. Fear not, thy thralls shall have an easy task: for I shall scarcely care to hold my own. Say, shall I call for thee?"

"Hush! Speak not so loud! Folk may hear thee, Eric, and then thou wilt be in danger—I would say that, then shall ill things be told of me, because I am found with him who slew my brother?"

"I slew Ospakar too, Gudruda. Surely the death of him by whose side thou didst sit as wife is more to thee than the death of Björn?"

"The bride-cup was not yet drunk, Eric; therefore I have no blood-feud for Ospakar."

"Is it, then, thy will that I should go, lady?"

"Yes, go!—go! Never let me see thy face again!"

Brighteyes turned without a word. He took three paces and Gudruda watched him as he went.

"Eric!" she called. "Eric! thou mayest not go yet: for at this hour the thralls bring down the kine to milk, and they will see thee. Liest thou hid here. I—I will go. For though, indeed, thou dost deserve to die, I am not willing to bring thee to thy end—because of old friendship I am not willing!"

"If thou goest, I will go also," said Eric. "Thralls or no thralls, I will go, Gudruda."

"Thou art cruel to drive me to such a choice, and I have a mind to give thee to thy fate."

"As thou wilt," said Eric; but she made as though she did not hear his words.

"Now," she said, "if we must stay here, it is better that we hide where thou didst hide, lest some come upon thee." And she passed through the screen of rushes and sat down in a grassy place beyond, and spoke again.

"Nay, sit not near me; sit yonder. I would not touch thee, nor look upon thee, who wast Swanhild's love, and didst slay Björn my brother."

"Say, Gudruda," said Eric, "did I not tell thee of the magic arts of Swanhild? Did I not tell thee before all men yonder in the hall, and didst thou not say that thou didst believe my words? Speak."

"That is true," said Gudruda.

"Wherefore, then, dost thou taunt me with being Swanhild's love—with being the love of her whom of all alive I hate the most—and whose wicked guile has brought these sorrows on us?"

But Gudruda did not answer.

"And for this matter of the death of Björn at my hands, think, Gudruda: was I to blame in it? Did not Björn thrust the cloven shield before my feet, and thus give me into the hand of Ospakar? Did he not afterwards smite at me from behind, and would he not have slain me if Skallagrim had not caught the blow? Was I, then, to blame if I smote back and if the sword flew home? Wilt thou let the needful deed rise up against our love? Speak, Gudruda!"

"Talk no more of love to me, Eric," she answered; "the blood of Björn has blotted out our love: it cries to me for vengeance. How may I speak of love with him who slew my brother? Listen!" she went on, looking on him sidelong, as one who wished to look and yet not seem to see: "here thou must hide an hour, and, since thou wilt not sit in silence, speak no tender words to me, for it is not fitting; but tell me of those deeds thou didst in the south lands over sea, before thou wentest to woo Swanhild and camest hither to kill my brother. For till then thou wast mine—till then I loved thee—who now love thee not. Therefore I would hear of the deeds of that Eric whom once I loved, before he became as one dead to me."

"Heavy words, lady," said Eric—"words to make death easy."

"Speak not so," she said; "it is unmanly thus to work upon my fears. Tell me those tidings of which I ask."

So Eric told her all his deeds, though he showed small boastfulness about them. He told her how he had smitten the war-dragons of Ospakar, how he had boarded the Raven and with Skallagrim slain those who sailed in her. He told her also of his deeds in Ireland, and of how he took the viking ships and came to London town.

And as he told, Gudruda listened as one who hung upon her lover's dying words, and there was but one light in the world for her, the light of Eric's eyes, and there was but one music, the music of his voice. Now she looked upon him sidelong no longer, but with open eyes and parted lips she drank in his words, and always, though she knew it not herself, she crept closer to his side.

Then he told her how he had been greatly honoured of the King of England, and of the battles he had fought in at his side. Lastly, Eric told her how the King would have given him a certain great lady of royal blood in marriage, and how Edmund had been angered because he would not stay in England.

"Tell me of this lady," said Gudruda, quickly. "Is she fair, and how is she named?"

"She is fair, and her name is Elfrida," said Eric.

"And didst thou have speech with her on this matter?"

"Somewhat."

Now Gudruda drew herself away from Eric's side.

"What was the purport of thy speech?" she said, looking down. "Speak truly, Eric."

"It came to little," he answered. "I told her that there was one in Iceland to whom I was betrothed, and to Iceland I must go."

"And what said this Elfrida, then?"

"She said that I should get little luck at the hands of Gudruda the Fair. Moreover, she asked, should my betrothed be faithless to me, or put me from her, if I should come again to England."

Now Gudruda looked him in the face and spoke. "Say, Eric, is it in thy mind to sail for England in the spring, if thou canst escape thy foes so long?"

Now Eric took counsel with himself, and in his love and doubt grew guileful as he had never been before. For he knew well that Gudruda had this weakness—she was a jealous woman.

"Since thou dost put me from thee, that is in my mind, lady," he answered.

Gudruda heard. She thought on the great and beauteous Lady Elfrida, far away in England, and of Eric walking at her side, and sorrow took hold of her. She said no word, but fixed her dark eyes on Brighteyes' face, and lo! they filled with tears.

Eric might not bear this sight, for his heart beat within him as though it would burst the byrnie over it. Suddenly he stretched out his arms and swept her to his breast. Soft and sweet he kissed her, again and yet again, and she struggled not, though she wept a little.

"It is small blame to me," she whispered, "if thou dost hold me on thy breast and kiss me, for thou art more strong than I. Björn must know this if his dead eyes see aught. Yet for thee, Eric, it is the greatest shame of all thy shames."

"Talk not, my sweet; talk not," said Eric, "but kiss thou me: for thou knowest well that thou lovest me yet as I love thee."

Now the end of it was that Gudruda yielded and kissed him whom she had not kissed for many years.

"Loose me, Eric," she said; "I would speak with thee," and he loosed her, though unwillingly.

"Hearken," she went on, hiding her fair face in her hands: "it is true that for life and death I love thee now as ever—how much thou mayest never know. Though Björn be dead at thy hands, yet I love thee; but how I may wed thee and not win the greatest shame, that I know not. I am sure of one thing, that we may not bide here in Iceland. Now if, indeed, thou lovest me, listen to my rede. Get thee back to Mosfell, Eric, and sit there in safety through this winter, for they may not come at thee yonder on Mosfell. Then, if thou art willing, in the spring I will make ready a ship, for I have no ship now, and, moreover, it is too late to sail. Then, perchance, leaving all my lands and goods, I will take thy hand, Eric, and we will fare together to England, seeking such fortune as the Norns may give us. What sayest thou?"

"I say it is a good rede, and would that the spring were come."

"Ay, Eric, would that the spring were come. Our lot has been hard, and I doubt much if things will go well with us at the last. And now thou must hence, for presently the serving-women will come to seek me. Guard thyself, Eric, as thou lovest me—guard thyself, and beware of Swanhild!" Then once more they kissed soft and long, and Eric went.

But Gudruda sat a while behind the screen of reeds, and was very happy for a space. For it was as though the winter were past and summer shone upon her heart again.

XXVII

HOW GUDRUDA WENT UP TO MOSFELL

Eric walked warily till he came to the dell where he had left Skallagrim and the horses. It was the same dell in which Groa had brewed the poison-draught for Asmund the Priest and Unna, Thorod's daughter.

"What news, lord?" said Skallagrim. "Thou wast gone so long that I thought of seeking thee. Hast thou seen Gudruda?"

"Ay," said Eric, "and this is the upshot of it, that in the spring we sail for England and bid farewell to Iceland and our ill luck."

"Would, then, that it were spring," said Skallagrim, speaking Brighteyes' own words. "Why not sail now and make an end?"

"Gudruda has no ship and it is late to take the sea. Also I think that she would let a time go by because of the blood-feud which she has against me for the death of Björn."

"I would rather risk these things than stay the winter through in Iceland," said Skallagrim, "it is long from now to spring, and yon wolf's den is cold-lying in the dark months, as I know well."

"There is light beyond the darkness," said Eric, and they rode away. Everything went well with them till late at night they came to the slopes of Mosfell. They were half asleep on their horses, being weary with much riding, and the horses were weary also. Suddenly, Skallagrim, looking up, caught the faint gleam of light from swords hidden behind some stones.

"Awake, lord!" he cried, "here are foes ahead."

Gizur's folk behind the stones heard his voice and came out from their ambush. There were six of them, and they formed in line before the pair. They were watching the mountain, for a rumour had reached them that Eric was abroad, and, seeing him, they had hidden hastily behind the stones.

"Now what counsel shall we take?" said Eric, drawing Whitefire.

"We have often stood against men more than six, and sometimes we have left more men than six to mark where we stood," answered Skallagrim. "It is my counsel that we ride at them!"

"So be it," said Eric, and he spurred his weary horse with his heels. Now when the six saw Eric and Skallagrim charge on them boldly, they wavered, and the end of it was that they broke and fled to either side before a blow was struck. For it had come to this pass, so great was the terror of the names of Eric Brighteyes and Skallagrim Lambstail, that no six men dared to stand before them in open fight.

So the path being clear they rode on up the slope. But when they had gone a little way, Skallagrim turned his horse, and mocked those who had lain in ambush, saying:

"Ye fight well, ye carles of Gizur, Ospakar's son! Ye are heroes, surely! Say now, mighty men, will ye stand there if I come down alone against you?"

At these words the men grew mad with wrath, and flung their spears. Skallagrim caught one on his shield and it fell to the earth, but another passed over his head and struck Eric on the left shoulder, near the neck, making a deep wound. Feeling the spear fast in him, Eric grasped it with his right hand, drew it forth, and turning, hurled it so hard, that the man before it got his death from the blow, for his shield did not serve to stay it. Then the rest fled.

Skallagrim bound up Eric's wound as well as he could, and they went on to the cave. But when Eric's folk, watching above, saw the fight they ran down and met him. Now the hurt was bad and Eric bled much; still, within ten days it healed up for the time.

But a little while after Eric's wound was skinned over, the snows set in on Mosfell, and the days grew short and the nights long. Once Gizur's men to the number of fifty came half way up the mountain to take it; but, when they saw how strong the place was, they feared, and went back, and after that returned no more, though they always watched the fell.

It was very dark and lonesome there upon the fell. For a while Eric kept in good heart, but as the days went by he grew troubled. For since he was wounded this had come upon him, that he feared the dark, and the death of Atli at his hand and Atli's words weighed more and more upon his mind. They had no candles on the fell, yet, rather than stay in the blackness of the cave, Eric would wrap sheepskins about him and sit by the edge of that gulf down which the head of the Baresark had foretold his fall, and look out at the wide plains and fells and ice-mountains, gleaming in the silver shine of the Northern lights or in the white beams of the stars.

It chanced that Eric had bidden the men who stayed with him to build a stone hut upon the flat space of rock before the cave, and to roof it with turves. He had done this that work might keep them in heart, also that they might have a place to store such goods as they had gathered. Now there was one stone lying near that no two men of their number could move, except Skallagrim and one other. One day, while it was light, Eric watched these two rolling the stone along to where it must stand, and it was slow work. Presently they stayed to rest. Then Eric came and putting his hands beneath the stone, lifted, and while men wondered, he rolled the mass alone, to where it should be set as the corner stone of the hut.

"Ye are all children," he said, and laughed merrily.

"Ay, when we set our strength against thine, lord," answered Skallagrim; "but look: the blood runs from thy neck—the spear-wound has broken out afresh."

"So it is, surely," said Eric. Then he washed the wound and bound it up, thinking little of the matter.

But that night, according to his custom, Eric sat on the edge of the gulf and looked at the winter lights as they played over Hecla's snows. He was sad and heavy at heart, for he thought of Gudruda and wondered much if they should live to wed. Remembering Atli's words, he had little faith in his good luck. Now as Eric sat and thought, the bandage on his neck slipped, so that the hurt bled, and the frost got hold of the wound and froze it, and froze his long hair to it also, in such fashion that when he went to the cave where all men slept, he could not loose his hair from the sore, but lay down with it frozen to him. On the morrow the hair was caked so fast about his neck that it could only be freed by shearing it. But this Eric would not suffer. None, he said, should shear his hair, except Gudruda. Thus he had sworn, and when he broke the oath misfortune had come of it. He would break that vow no more, if it cost him his life. For sorrow and his ill luck had taken so great a hold of Eric's mind that in some ways he was scarcely himself.

So it came to pass that he fell more and more sick, till at length he could not rise from his bed in the cave, but lay there all day and night, staring at the little light which pierced the gloom. Still, he would not suffer that anyone should touch his hair. And when one stole upon him sleeping, thinking so to cut it before he woke, and come at the wound, suddenly he sat up and dealt the man such a buffet on the head that he went near to death from it.

Then Skallagrim spoke.

"On this matter," he said, "it seems that Brighteyes is mad. He will not suffer that any touch his hair, except Gudruda, and yet, if his hair is not shorn, he must die, for the wound will fester under it. Nor may we cut it by strength, for then he will kill himself in struggling. It is come to this then: either Gudruda must be brought hither or Eric will shortly die."

"That may not be," they answered. "How can the lady Gudruda come here across the snows, even if she will come?"

"Come she can, if she has the heart," said Skallagrim, "though I put little trust in women's hearts. Still, I ride down to Middalhof, and thou, Jon, shalt go with me. For the rest, I charge you watch your lord; for, if I come back and find anything amiss, that shall be the death of some, and if I do not come back but perish on the road, yet I will haunt you."

Now Jon liked not this task; still, for love of Eric and fear of Skallagrim, he set out with the Baresark. They had a hard journey through the snow-drifts and the dark, but on the third day they came to Middalhof, knocked upon the door and entered.

Now it was supper-time, and people, sitting at meat, saw a great black man, covered with snow and rime, stalk up the hall, and after him another smaller man, who groaned with the cold, and they wondered at the sight. Gudruda sat on the high seat and the firelight beat upon her face.

"Who comes here?" she said.

"One who would speak with thee, lady," answered Skallagrim.

"Here is Skallagrim the Baresark," said a man. "He is an outlaw, let us kill him!"

"Ay, it is Skallagrim," he answered, "and if there is killing to be done, why here's that which shall do it," and he drew out his axe and smiled grimly.

Then all held their peace, for they feared the axe of Skallagrim.

"Lady," he said, "I do not come for slaying or such child's play, I come to speak a word in thine ear—but first I ask a cup of mead and a morsel of food, for we have spent three days in the snows."

So they ate and drank. Then Gudruda bade the Baresark draw near and tell her his tale.

"Lady," said he, "Eric, my lord, lies dying on Mosfell."

Gudruda turned white as the snow.

"Dying?—Eric lies dying?" she said. "Why, then, art thou here?"

"For this cause, lady: I think that thou canst save him, if he is not already sped." And he told her all the tale.

Now Gudruda thought a while.

"This is a hard journey," she said, "and it does not become a maid to visit outlaws in their caves. Yet I am come to this, that I will die before I shrink from anything that may save the life of Eric. When must we ride, Skallagrim?"

"This night," said the Baresark. "This night while the men sleep, for now night and day are almost the same. The snow is deep and we have no time to lose if we would find Brighteyes living."

"Then we will ride to-night," answered Gudruda.

Afterwards, when people slept, Gudruda the Fair summoned her women, and bade them say to all who asked for her that she lay sick in bed. But she called three trusty thralls, bidding them bring two pack-horses laden with hay, food, drugs, candles made of sheep's fat, and other goods, and ride with her. Then, all being ready, they rode away secretly up Stonefell, Gudruda on her horse Blackmane, and the others on good geldings that had been hay-fed in the yard, and by daylight they passed up Horse-Head Heights. They slept two nights in the snow, and on the second night almost perished there, for much soft snow fell. But afterwards came frost and a bitter northerly wind and they passed on. Gudruda was a strong woman and great of heart and will, and so it came about that on the third day she reached Mosfell, weary but little harmed, though the fingers of her left hand were frostbitten. They climbed the mountain, and when they came to the dell where the horses were kept, certain of Eric's men met them and their faces were sad.

"How goes it now with Brighteyes?" said Skallagrim, for Gudruda could scarcely speak because of doubt and cold. "Is he dead, then?"

"Nay," they answered, "but like to die, for he is beside himself and raves wildly."

"Push on," quoth Gudruda; "push on, lest it be too late."

So they climbed the mountain on foot, won the pass and came to that giddy point of rock where he must tread who would reach the platform that is before the cave. Now since she had hung by her hands over Goldfoss gulf, Gudruda had feared to tread upon a height with nothing to hold to. Skallagrim went first, then called to her to follow. Thrice she looked, and turned away, trembling, for the place was awful and the fall bottomless. Then she spoke aloud to herself:

"Eric did not fear to risk his life to save me when I hung over Golden Falls; less, then, should I fear to risk mine to save him," and she stepped boldly down upon the point. But when she stood there, over the giddy height, shivers ran along her body, and her mind grew dark. She clutched at the rock, gave one low cry and began to fall. Indeed she would have fallen and been lost, had not Skallagrim, lying on his breast in the narrow hole, stretched out his arms, caught her by the cloak and kirtle and dragged her to him. Presently her senses came back.

"I am safe!" she gasped, "but by a very little. Methinks that here in this place I must live and die, for I can never tread yonder rock again."

"Thou shalt pass it safe enough, lady, with a rope round thee," said Skallagrim, and led the way to the cave.

Gudruda entered, forgetting all things in her love of Eric. A great fire of turf burned in the mouth of the cave to temper the bitter wind and frost, and by its light Gudruda saw her love through the smoke-reek. He lay upon a bed of skins at the far end of the cave and his bright grey eyes were wild, his wan face was white, and now of a sudden it grew red with fever, and then was white again. He had thrown the sheepskins from his mighty chest, the bones of which stood out grimly. His long arms were thrust through the locks of his golden hair, and on one side of his neck the hair clung to him and it was but a black mass.

He raved loudly in his madness. "Touch me not, carles, touch me not; ye think me spent and weak, but, by Thor! if ye touch my hair, I will loosen the knees of some. Gudruda alone shall shear my hair: I have sworn and I will keep the oath that I once broke. Give me snow! snow! my throat burns! Heap snow on my head, I bid you. Ye will not? Ye mock me, thinking me weak! Where, then, is Whitefire?—I have yet a deed to do! Who comes yonder? Is it a woman's shape or is it but a smoke-wraith? 'Tis Swanhild the Fatherless who walks the waters. Begone, Swanhild, thou witch! thou hast worked evil enough upon me. Nay, it is not Swanhild, it is Elfrida; lady, here in England I may not stay. In Iceland I am at home. Yea, yea, things go crossly; perchance in this garden we may speak again!"

Now Gudruda could bear his words no longer, bur ran to him and knelt beside him.

"Peace, Eric!" she whispered. "Peace! It is I, thy love. It is Gudruda, who am come to thee."

He turned his head and looked upon her strangely.

"No, no," he said, "it is not Gudruda the Fair. She will have little to do with outlaws, and this is too rough a place for her to come to. It is dark also and Atli speaks in the darkness. If thou art Gudruda, give me a sign. Why comest thou here and where is Skallagrim? Ah! that was a good fight—

"Down among the ballast tumbling
Ospakar's shield-carles were rolled.

"But he should never have slain the steersman. The axe goes first and Skallagrim follows after. Ha, ha! Ay, Swanhild, we'll mingle tears. Give me the cup. Why, what is this? Thou art afire, a glory glows about thee, and from thee floats a scent like the scent of the Iceland meads in May."

"Eric! Eric!" cried Gudruda, "I am come to shear thy hair, as thou didst swear that I alone should do."

"Now I know that thou art Gudruda," said the crazed man. "Cut, cut; but let not those knaves touch my head, lest I should slay them."

Then Gudruda drew out her shears, and without more ado shore off Brighteyes' golden locks. It was no easy task, for they were thick as a horse's mane, and glued to the wound. Yet when she had cut them, she loosened the hair from the flesh with water which she heated upon the fire. The wound was in a bad state and blue, still Eric never winced while she dragged the hair from it. Then she washed the sore clean, and put sweet ointment on it and covered it with napkins.

This done, she gave Eric broth and he drank. Then, laying her hand upon his head, she looked into his eyes and bade him sleep. And presently he slept—which he had scarcely done for many days—slept like a little child.

Eric slept for a day and a night. But at that same hour of the evening, when he had fallen asleep, Gudruda, watching him by the light of a taper that was set upon a rock, saw him smile in his dreams. Presently he opened his eyes and stared at the fire which glowed in the mouth of the cave, and the great shadows that fell upon the rocks.

"Strange!" she heard him murmur, "it is very strange! but I dreamed I slept, and that Gudruda the Fair leaned over me as I slept. Where, then, is Skallagrim?

Perhaps I am dead and that is Hela's fire," and he tried to lift himself upon his arm, but fell back from faintness, for he was very weak. Then Gudruda took his hand, and, leaning over him, spoke:

"Hush, Eric!" she said; "that was no dream, for I am here. Thou hast been sick to death, Eric; but now, if thou wilt rest, things shall go well with thee."

"Thou art here?" said Eric, turning his white face towards her. "Do I still dream, or how comest thou here to Mosfell, Gudruda?"

"I came through the snows, Eric, to cut thy hair, which clung to the festering wound, for in thy madness thou wouldst not suffer anyone to touch it."

"Thou camest through the snows—over the snows—to nurse me, Gudruda? Thou must love me much then," and he was so weak that, as he spoke, the tears rolled down Eric's cheeks.

Then Gudruda kissed him, weeping also, and, laying her face by his, bade him be at peace, for she was there to watch him.

XXVIII

HOW SWANHILD WON TIDINGS OF ERIC

Now Eric's strength came back to him and his heart opened in the light of Gudruda's eyes like a flower in the sunshine. For all day long she sat at his side, holding his hand and talking to him, and they found much to say.

But on the fifth day from the day of his awakening she spoke thus:

"Eric, now I must go back to Middalhof. Thou art safe and it is not well that I should stay here."

"Not yet, Gudruda," he said; "leave me not yet."

"Yes, love, I must leave thee. The moon is bright, the sky has cleared, and the snow is hard with frost and fit for the hoofs of horses. I must go before more storms come. Listen now: in the second week of spring, if all is well, I will send thee a messenger with words of token, then shalt thou come down secretly to Middalhof, and there, Eric, we will be wed. Then, on the next day, we will sail for England in a trading-ship that I shall get ready, to seek our fortune there."

"It will be a good fortune if thou art by my side," said Eric, "so good that I doubt greatly if I may find it, for I am Eric the Unlucky. Swanhild must yet be reckoned with, Gudruda. Yes, thou art right: thou must go hence, Gudruda, and swiftly, though it grieves me much to part with thee."

Then Eric called Skallagrim and bade him make things ready to ride down to Middalhof with the Lady Gudruda.

This Skallagrim did swiftly, and afterwards Eric and Gudruda kissed and parted, and they were sad at heart to part.

Now on the fifth day after the going of Gudruda, Skallagrim came back to Mosfell somewhat cold and weary. And he told Eric, who could now walk and grew strong again, that he and Jon had ridden with Gudruda the Fair to Horse-Head Heights, seeing no man, and had left her there to go on with her thralls. He had come back also seeing no one, for the weather was too cold for the men of Gizur to watch the fell in the snows.

Now Gudruda came safely to Middalhof, having been eleven days gone, and found that few had visited the house, and that these had been told that she lay sick abed. Her secret had been well kept, and, though Swanhild had no lack of spies, many days went by before she learned that Gudruda had gone up to Mosfell to nurse Eric.

After this Gudruda began to make ready for her flight from Iceland. She called in the moneys that she had out at interest, and with them bought from a certain chapman a good trading-ship which lay in its shed under the shelter of Westman Isles. This ship she began to make ready for sea so soon as the heart of the winter was broken, putting it about that she intended to send her on a trading voyage to Scotland in the spring. And also to give colour to this tale she bought many pelts and other goods, such as chapmen deal in.

Thus the days passed on—not so badly for Gudruda, who strove to fill their emptiness in making ready for the full and happy time; but for Eric in his cave they were very heavy, for he could find nothing to do except to sleep and eat, and think of Gudruda, whom he might not see.

For Swanhild also, sitting at Coldback, the days did not go well. She was weary of the courting of Gizur, whom she played with as a cat plays with a rat, and her heart was sick with love, hate, and jealousy. For she well knew that Gudruda and Eric still clung to each other and found means of greeting, if not of speech. At that time she wished to kill Eric if she could, though she would rather kill Gudruda if she dared. Still, she could not come at Eric, for her men feared to try the narrow way of Mosfell, and when they met him in the open they fled before him.

Presently it came to her ears that Gudruda made a ship ready to sail to Scotland on a trading voyage, and she was perplexed by this tale, for she knew that Gudruda had no love of trading and never thought of gain. So she set spies to watch the ship. Still, the slow days drew on, and at length the air grew soft with spring, and flowers showed through the snow.

Eric sat in his mountain nest waiting for tidings, and watched the nesting eagles wheel about the cliffs. At length news came. For one morning, as he rose, Skallagrim told him that a man wanted to speak with him. He had come to the mountain in the darkness, and had lain in a dell till the breaking of the light, for, now that the snows were melting, the men of Gizur and Swanhild watched the ways.

Eric bade them bring the man to him. When he saw him he knew that he was a thrall of Gudruda's and welcomed him heartily.

"What tidings?" he asked.

"This, lord," said the thrall: "Gudruda the Fair bids me say that she is well and that the snows melt on the roof of Middalhof."

Now this was the signal word that had been agreed upon between Eric and Gudruda, that she should send him when all was ready.

"Good," said Eric, "ride back to Gudruda the Fair and say that Eric Brighteyes is well, but on Hecla the snows melt not."

By this answer he meant that he would be with her presently, though the thrall could make nothing of it. Then Skallagrim asked tidings of the man, and learned that Swanhild was still at Middalhof, and with her Gizur, and that they gave out that they wished to make an end of waiting and slay Eric.

"First snare your bird, then wring his neck," laughed Skallagrim.

Then Eric did this: among his men were some who he knew were not willing to sail from Iceland, and Jon, his thrall, was of them, for Jon did not love the angry sea. He bade these bide a while on Mosfell and make fires nightly on the platform of rock which is in front of the cave, that the spies of Gizur and Swanhild might be deceived by them, and think that Eric was still on the fell. Then, when they heard that he had sailed, they were to come down and hide themselves with friends till Gizur and his following rode north. But he told two of the men who would sail with him to make ready.

That night before the moon rose Eric said farewell to Jon and the others who stayed on Mosfell, and rode away with Skallagrim and the two who went with him. They passed the plain of black sand in safety, and so on to Horse-Head Heights. Now at length, as the afternoon drew on to evening, from Stonefell's crest they saw the Hall of Middalhof before them, and Eric's heart swelled in his breast. Yet they must wait till darkness fell before they dared enter the place, lest they should be seen and notice of their coming should be carried to Gizur and Swanhild. And this came into the mind of Eric, that of all the hours of his life that hour of waiting was the longest. Scarcely, indeed, could Skallagrim hold him back from going down the mountain side, he was so set on coming to Gudruda whom he should wed that night.

At length the darkness fell, and they went on. Eric rode swiftly down the rough mountain path, while Skallagrim and the two men followed grumbling, for they feared that their horses would fall. At length they came to the place, and riding into the yard, Eric sprang from his horse and strode to the women's door. Now Gudruda stood in the porch, listening; and while he was yet some way off, she heard the clang of Brighteyen's harness, and the colour came and went upon her cheek. Then she turned and fled to the high seat of the hall, and sat down there. Only two women were left in Middalhof with her, and some thralls who tended the kine and horses. But these slept, not in the hall, but in an outhouse. Gudruda had sent the rest of her people down to the ship to help in the lading, for it was given out that the vessel sailed on the morrow. She had done this that there might be no talk of the coming of Eric to Middalhof.

Now Brighteyes came to the porch, and, finding the door wide, walked in. But Skallagrim and the men stayed without a while, and tended the horses. A fire burned upon the centre hearth in the hall, and threw shadows on the panelling. Eric walked on by its light, looking to left and right, but seeing neither man nor woman. Then a great fear took him lest Gudruda should be gone, or perhaps slain of Swanhild, Groa's daughter, and he trembled at the thought. He stood by the fire, and Gudruda, watching from the shadow of the high seat, saw the dull light glow upon his golden helm, and a sigh of joy broke from her lips. Eric heard the sigh and looked, and as he looked a stick of pitchy driftwood fell into the fire and flared up fiercely. Then he saw. There, in the carved high seat, robed all in bridal white, sat Gudruda the Fair, his love. Her golden hair flowed about her breast, her white arms were stretched towards him, and on her sweet face shone such a look of love as he had never seen.

"Eric!" she whispered softly, and the breath of her voice ran down the empty panelled hall, that from all sides seemed to answer, "Eric."

Slowly he drew near to her. He saw nothing but the glory of Gudruda's face and the light shining on Gudruda's hair; he heard nothing save the sighing of her breath; he knew nothing except that before him sat his fair bride, won after many years.

Now he had climbed the high seat, and now, wrapped in each other's arms, they sat and gazed into each other's eyes, and lo! the air of the great hall rolled round them a sea of glory, and sweet voices whispered in their ears. Now Freya smiled upon them and led them through her gates of love, and they were glad that they had been born.

Thus then they were wed.

Now the story tells that Swanhild spoke with Gizur, Ospakar's son, in the house at Coldback.

"I tire of this slow play," she said. "We have tarried here for many weeks, and Atli's blood yet cries out for vengeance, and cries for vengeance the blood of black Ospakar, thy father, and the blood of many another, dead at great Eric's hand."

"I tire also," said Gizur, "and I am much needed in the north. I say this to thee, Swanhild, that, hadst thou not so strictly laid it on me that Eric must die ere thou weddest me, I had flitted back to Swinefell before now, and there bided my time to bring Brighteyes to his end."

"I will never wed thee, Gizur, till Eric is dead," said Swanhild fiercely.

"How shall we come at him then?" he answered. "We may not go up that mountain path, for two men can hold it against all our strength, and folk do not love to meet Eric and Skallagrim in a narrow way."

"The place has been badly watched," said Swanhild. "I am sure of this, that Eric has been down to Middalhof and seen Gudruda, my half-sister. She is shameless, who still holds commune with him who slew her brother and my husband. Death should be her reward, and I am minded to slay her because of the shame that she has brought upon our blood."

"That is a deed which thou wilt do alone, then," said Gizur, "for I will have no hand in the murder of that fair maid—no, nor will any who live in Iceland!"

Swanhild glanced at him strangely. "Hearken, Gizur!" she said: "Gudruda makes a ship ready to sail with goods to Scotland and bring a cargo thence before winter comes again. Now I find this strange, for never before did I know Gudruda turn her thoughts to trading. I think that she has it in her mind to sail from Iceland with this outlaw Eric, and seek a home over seas, and that I will not bear."

"It may be," said Gizur, "and I should not be sorry to see the last of Brighteyes, for I think that more men will die at his hand before he stiffens in his barrow."

"Thou art cowardly-hearted, thou son of Ospakar!" Swanhild said. "Thou sayest thou lovest me and wouldest win me to wife: I tell thee that there is but one road to my arms, and it leads over the corpse of Eric. Now this is my counsel: that we send the most of our men to watch that ship of Gudruda's, and, when she lifts anchor, to board her and search, for she is already bound for sea. Also among the peopeople here I have a carle who was born near Hecla, and he swears this to me, that, when he was a lad, searching for an eagle's eyrie, he found a path by which Mosfell might be climbed from the north, and that in the end he came to a large flat place, and, looking over, saw that platform where Eric dwells with his thralls. But he could not see the cave, because of the overhanging brow of the rock. Now we will do this: thou and I, and the carle alone—no more, for I do not wish that our search should be noised abroad—to-morrow at the dawn we will ride away for Mosfell, and, passing under Hecla, come round the mountain and see if this path may still be scaled. For, if so, we will return with men and make an end of Brighteyes."

This plan pleased Gizur, and he said that it should be so.

So very early on the following morning Swanhild, having sent many men to watch Gudruda's ship, rode away secretly with Gizur and the thrall, and before it was again dawn they were on the northern slopes of Mosfell. It was on this same night that Eric went down from the mountain to wed Gudruda.

For a while the climbing was easy, but at length they came to a great wall of rock, a hundred fathoms high, on which no fox might find a foothold, nor anything that had not wings.

"Here now is an end of our journey," said Gizur, "and I only pray this, that Eric may not ride round the mountain before we are down again." For he did not know that Brighteyes already rode hard for Middalhof.

"Not so," said the thrall, "if only I can find the place by which, some thirty summers ago, I won yonder rift, and through it the crest of the fell," and he pointed to a narrow cleft in the face of the rock high above their heads, that was clothed with grey moss.

Then he moved to the right and searched, peering behind stones and birchbushes, till presently he held up his hand and whistled. They passed along the slope and found him standing by a little stream of water which welled from beneath a great rock.

"Here is the place," the man said.

"I see no place," answered Swanhild.

"Still, it is there, lady," and he climbed on to the rock, drawing her after him. At the back of it was a hole, almost overgrown with moss. "Here is the path," he said again.

"Then it is one that I have no mind to follow," answered Swanhild. "Gizur, go thou with the man and see if his tale is true. I will stay here till ye come back."

Then the thrall let himself down into the hole and Gizur went after him. But Swanhild sat there in the shadow of the rock, her chin resting on her hand, and waited. Presently, as she sat, she saw two men ride round the base of the fell, and strike off to the right towards a turf-booth which stood the half of an hour's ride away. Now Swanhild was the keenest-sighted of all women of her day in Iceland, and when she looked at these two men she knew one of them for Jon, Eric's thrall, and she knew the horse also—it was a white horse with black patches, that Jon had ridden for many years. She watched them go till they came to the booth, and it seemed to her that they left their horses and entered.

Swanhild waited upon the side of the fell for nearly two hours in all. Then, hearing a noise above her, she looked up, and there, black with dirt and wet with water, was Gizur, and with him was the thrall.

"What luck, Gizur?" she asked.

"This, Swanhild: Eric may hold Mosfell no more, for we have found a way to bolt the fox."

"That is good news, then," said Swanhild. "Say on."

"Yonder hole, Swanhild, leads to the cleft above, having been cut through the cliff by fire, or perhaps by water. Now up that cleft a man may climb, though hardly, as by a difficult stair, till he comes to the flat crest of the fell. Then, crossing the crest, on the further side, perhaps six fathoms below him, he sees that space of rock where is Eric's cave; but he cannot see the cave itself, because the brow of the cliff hangs over. And so it is that, if any come from the cave on to the space of rock, it will be an easy matter to roll stones upon them from above and crush them."

Now when Swanhild heard this she laughed aloud.

"Eric shall mock us no more," she said, "and his might can avail nothing against rocks rolled on him from above. Let us go back to Coldback and summon men to make an end of Brighteyes."

So they went on down the mountain till they came to the place where they had hidden their horses. Then Swanhild remembered Jon and the other man whom she had seen riding to the booth, and she told Gizur of them.

"Now," she said, "we will snare these birds, and perchance they will twitter tidings when we squeeze them."

So they turned and rode for the booth, and drawing near, they saw two horses grazing without. Now they got off their horses, and creeping up to the booth, looked in through the door which was ajar. And they saw this, that one man sat on the ground with his back to the door, eating stock-fish, while Jon made bundles of fish and meal ready to tie on the horses. For it was here that those of his quarter who loved Eric brought food to be carried by his men to the cave on Mosfell.

Now Swanhild touched Gizur on the arm, pointing first to the man who sat eating the fish and then to the spear in Gizur's hand. Gizur thought a while, for he shrank from this deed.

Then Swanhild whispered in his ear, "Slay the man and seize the other; I would learn tidings from him."

So Gizur cast the spear, and it passed through the man's heart, and he was dead at once. Then he and the thrall leapt into the booth and threw themselves on Jon, hurling him to the ground, and holding swords over him. Now Jon was a man of small heart, and when he saw his plight and his fellow dead he was afraid, and prayed for mercy.

"If I spare thee, knave," said Swanhild, "thou shalt do this: thou shalt lead me up Mosfell to speak with Eric."

"I may not do that, lady," groaned Jon; "for Eric is not on Mosfell."

"Where is he, then?" asked Swanhild.

Now Jon saw that he had said an unlucky thing, and answered:

"Nay, I know not. Last night he rode from Mosfell with Skallagrim Lambstail."

"Thou liest, knave," said Swanhild. "Speak, or thou shalt be slain."

"Slay on," groaned Jon, glancing at the swords above him, and shutting his eyes. For, though he feared much to die, he had no will to make known Eric's plans.

"Look not at the swords; thou shalt not die so easily. Hearken: speak, and speak truly, or thou shalt seek Hela's lap after this fashion," and, bending down, she whispered in his ear, then laughed aloud.

Now Jon grew faint with fear; his lips turned blue, and his teeth chattered at the thought of how he should be made to die. Still, he would say nothing.

Then Swanhild spoke to Gizur and the thrall, and bade them bind him with a rope, tear the garments from him, and bring snow. They did this, and pushed the matter to the drawing of knives. But when he saw the steel Jon cried aloud that he would tell all.

"Now thou takest good counsel," said Swanhild.

Then in his fear Jon told how Eric had gone down to Middalhof to wed Gudruda, and thence to fly with her to England.

Now Swanhild was mad with wrath, for she had sooner died than that this should come about.

"Let us away," she said to Gizur. "But first kill this man."

"Nay," said Gizur, "I will not do that. He has told his tidings; let him go free."

"Thou art chicken-hearted," said Swanhild, who, after the fashion of witches, had no mercy in her. "At the least, he shall not go hence to warn Eric and Gudruda of our coming. If thou wilt not kill him, then bind him and leave him."

So Jon was bound, and there in the booth he sat two days before anyone came to loose him.

"Whither away?" said Gizur to Swanhild.

"To Middalhof first," Swanhild answered.

XXIX

HOW WENT THE BRIDAL NIGHT

Now Eric and Gudruda sat silent in the high seat of the hall at Middalhof till they heard Skallagrim enter by the women's door. Then they came down from the high seat, and stood hand in hand by the fire on the hearth. Skallagrim greeted Gudruda, looking at her askance, for Skallagrim stood in fear of women alone.

"What counsel now, lord?" said the Baresark.

"Tell us thy plans, Gudruda," said Eric, for as yet no word had passed between them of what they should do.

"This is my plan, Eric," she answered. "First, that we eat; then that thy men take horse and ride hence through the night to where the ship lies, bearing word that we will be there at dawn when the tide serves, and bidding the mate make everything ready for sailing. But thou and I and Skallagrim will stay here till to-morrow is three hours old, and this because I have tidings that Gizur's folk will search the ship to-night. Now, when they search and do not find us, they will go away. Then, at the dawning, thou and I and Skallagrim will row on board the ship as she lies at anchor, and, slipping the cable, put to sea before they know we are there, and so bid farewell to Swanhild and our woes."

"Yet it is a risk for us to sleep here alone," said Eric.

"There is little danger," said Gudruda. "Nearly all of Gizur's men watch the ship; and I have learned this from a spy, that, two days ago, Gizur, Swanhild, and one thrall rode from Coldback towards Mosfell, and they have not come back yet. Moreover, the place is strong, and thou and Skallagrim are here to guard it."

"So be it, then," answered Eric, for indeed he had little thought left for anything, except Gudruda.

After this the women came in and set meat on the board, and all ate.

Now, when they had eaten, Eric bade Skallagrim fill a cup, and bring it to him as he sat on the high seat with Gudruda. Skallagrim did so; and then, looking deep into each other's eyes, Eric Brighteyes and Gudruda the Fair, Asmund's daughter, drank the bride's cup.

"There are few guests to grace our marriage-feast, husband," said Gudruda.

"Yet shall our vows hold true, wife," said Eric.

"Ay, Brighteyes," she answered, "in life and in death, now and for ever!" and they kissed.

"It is time for us to be going, methinks," growled Skallagrim to those about him. "We are not wanted here."

Then the men who were to go on to the ship rose, fetched their horses, and rode away. Also they caught the horses of Skallagrim, Eric, and Gudruda, saddled them and, slipping their bridles, made them fast in a shed in the yard, giving them hay to eat. Afterwards Skallagrim barred the men's door and the women's door, and, going to Gudruda, asked where he should stay the night till it was time to ride for the sea.

"In the store-chamber," she answered, "for there is a shutter of which the latch has gone. See that thou watch it well, Skallagrim; though I think none will come to trouble thee."

"I know the place. It shall go badly with the head that looks through yonder hole," said Skallagrim, glancing at his axe.

Now Gudruda forgot this, that in the store-chamber were casks of strong ale.

Then Gudruda told him to wake them when the morrow was two hours old, for Eric had neither eyes nor words except for Gudruda alone, and Skallagrim went.

The women went also to their shut bed at the end of the hall, leaving Brighteyes and Gudruda alone. Eric looked at her.

"Where do I sleep to-night?" he asked.

"Thou sleepest with me, husband," she answered soft, "for nothing, except Death, shall come between us any more."

Now Skallagrim went to the store-room, and sat down with his back against a cask. His heart was heavy in him, for he boded no good of this marriage. Moreover, he was jealous. Skallagrim loved but one thing in the world truly, and that was Eric Brighteyes, his lord. Now he knew that henceforth he must take a second place, and that for one thought which Eric gave to him, he would give ten to Gudruda. Therefore Skallagrim was very sad at heart.

"A pest upon the women!" he said to himself, "for from them comes all evil. Brighteyes owes his ill luck to Swanhild and this fair wife of his, and that is scarcely done with yet. Well, well, 'tis nature; but would that we were safe at sea! Had I my will, we had not slept here to-night. But they are newly wed, and—well, 'tis nature! Better the bride loves to lie abed than to ride the cold wolds and seek the common deck."

Now, as Skallagrim grumbled, fear gathered in his heart, he knew not of what. He began to think on trolls and goblins. It was dark in the store-room, except for a little line of light that crept through the crack of the shutter. At length he could bear the darkness and his thoughts no longer, but, rising, threw the shutter wide and let the bright moonlight pour into the chamber, whence he could see the hillside behind, and watch the shadows of the clouds as they floated across it. Again Skallagrim sat down against his cask, and as he sat it moved, and he heard the wash of ale inside it.

"That is a good sound," said Skallagrim, and he turned and smelt at the cask; "aye, and a good smell, too! We tasted little ale yonder on Mosfell, and we shall find less at sea." Again he looked at the cask. There was a spigot in it, and lo! on the shelf stood horn cups.

"It surely is on draught," he said; "and now it will stand till it goes sour. 'Tis a pity; but I will not drink. I fear ale—ale is another man! No, I will not drink," and all the while his hand went up to the cups upon the shelf. "Eric is better lain yonder in Gudruda's chamber than I am here alone with evil thoughts and trolls," he said. "Why, what fish was that we ate at supper? My throat is cracked with thirst! If there were water now I'd drink it, but I see none. Well, one cup to wish them joy! There is no harm in a cup of ale," and he drew the spigot from the cask and watched the brown drink flow into the cup. Then he lifted it to his lips and drank, saying "Skoll! skoll!"[*] nor did he cease till the horn was drained. "This is wondrous good ale," said Skallagrim as he wiped his grizzled beard. "One more cup, and evil thoughts shall cease to haunt me."

[*] "Health! health!"

Again he filled, drank, sat down, and for a while was merry. But presently the black thoughts came back into his mind. He rose, looked through the shutter-hole to the hillside. He could see nothing on it except the shadows of the clouds.

"Trolls walk the winds to-night," he said. "I feel them pulling at my beard. One more cup to frighten them."

He drank another draught of ale and grew merry. Then ale called for ale, and Skallagrim drained cup on cup, singing as he drained, till at last heavy sleep overcame him, and he sank drunken on the ground there by the barrel, while the brown ale trickled round him.

Now Eric Brighteyes and Gudruda the Fair slept side by side, locked in each other's arms. Presently Gudruda was wide awake.

"Rouse thee, Eric," she said, "I have dreamed an evil dream."

He awoke and kissed her.

"What, then, was thy dream, sweet?" he said. "This is no hour for bad dreams."

"No hour for bad dreams, truly, husband; yet dreams do not weigh the hour of their coming. I dreamed this: that I lay dead beside thee and thou knewest it not, while Swanhild looked at thee and mocked."

"An evil dream, truly," said Eric; "but see, thou art not dead. Thou hast thought too much on Swanhild of late."

Now they slept once more, till presently Eric was wide awake.

"Rouse thee, Gudruda," he said, "I too have dreamed a dream, and it is full of evil."

"What, then, was thy dream, husband?" she asked.

"I dreamed that Atli the Earl, whom I slew, stood by the bed. His face was white, and white as snow was his beard, and blood from his great wound ran down his byrnie. 'Eric Brighteyes,' he said, 'I am he whom thou didst slay, and I come to tell thee this: that before the moon is young again thou shalt lie stiff, with Hell-shoes on thy feet. Thou art Eric the Unlucky! Take thy joy and say thy say to her who lies at thy side, for wet and cold is the bed that waits thee and soon shall thy white lips be dumb.' Then he was gone, and lo! in his place stood Asmund, thy father, and he also spoke to me, saying, 'Thou who dost lie in my bed and at my daughter's side, know this: the words of Atli are true; but I add these to them: ye shall die, yet is death but the gate of life and love and rest,' and he was gone."

Now Gudruda shivered with fear, and crept closer to Eric's side.

"We are surely fey, for the Norns speak with the voices of Atli and of Asmund," she said. "Oh, Eric! Eric! whither go we when we die? Will Valhalla take thee, being so mighty a man, and must I away to Hela's halls, where thou art not? Oh! that would be death indeed! Say, Eric, whither do we go?"

"What said the voice of Asmund?" answered Brighteyes. "That death is but the gate of life and love and rest. Hearken, Gudruda, my May! Odin does not reign over all the world, for when I sat out yonder in England, a certain holy man taught me of another God—a God who loves not slaughter, a God who died that men might live for ever in peace with those they love."

"How is this God named, Eric?"

"They name Him the White Christ, and there are many who cling to Him."

"Would that I knew this Christ, Eric. I am weary of death and blood and evil deeds, such as are pleasing to our Gods. Oh, Eric, if I am taken from thee, swear this to me: that thou wilt slay no more, save for thy life's sake only."

"I swear that, sweet," he made answer. "For I too am weary of death and blood, and desire peace most of all things. The world is sad, and sad have been our days. Yet it is well to have lived, for through many heavy days we have wandered to this happy night."

"Yea, Eric, it is well to have lived; though I think that death draws on. Now this is my counsel: that we rise, and that thou dost put on thy harness and summon Skallagrim, so that, if evil comes, thou mayst meet it armed. Surely I thought I heard a sound—yonder in the hall!"

"There is little use in that," said Eric, "for things will befall as they are fated. We may do nothing of our own will, I am sure of this, and it is no good to struggle with the Norns. Yet I will rise."

So he kissed her, and made ready to leave the bed, when suddenly, as he lingered, a great heaviness seized him.

"Gudruda," he said, "I am pressed down with sleep."

"That I am also, Eric," she said. "My eyes shut of themselves and I can scarcely stir my limbs. Ah, Eric, we are fey indeed, and this is—death that comes!"

"Perchance!" he said, speaking heavily.

"Eric!—wake, Eric! Thou canst not move? Yet hearken to me—ah! this weight of sleep! Thou lovest me, Eric!—is it not so?"

"Yea," he answered.

"Now and for ever thou lovest me—and wilt cleave to me always wherever we go?"

"Surely, sweet. Oh, sweet, farewell!" he said, and his voice sounded like the voice of one who speaks across the water.

"Farewell, Eric Brighteyes!—my love—my love, farewell!" she answered very slowly, and together they sank into a sleep that was heavy as death.

Now Gizur, Ospakar's son, and Swanhild, Atli's widow, rode fast and hard from Mosfell, giving no rest to their horses, and with them rode that thrall who had showed the secret path to Gizur. They stayed a while on Horse-Head Heights till the moon rose. Now one path led hence to the shore that is against the Westmans, where Gudruda's ship lay bound. Then Swanhild turned to the thrall. Her beautiful face was fierce and she had said few words all this while, but in her heart raged a fire of hate and jealousy which shone through her blue eyes.

"Listen," she said to the thrall. "Thou shalt ride hence to the bay where the ship of Gudruda the Fair lies at anchor. Thou knowest where our folk are in hiding. Thou shalt speak thus to them. Before it is dawn they must take boats and board Gudruda's ship and search her. And, if they find Eric, the outlaw, aboard, they shall slay him, if they may."

"That will be no easy task," said the thrall.

"And if they find Gudruda they shall keep her prisoner. But if they find neither the one nor the other, they shall do this: they shall drive the crew ashore, killing as few as may be, and burn the ship."

"It is an ill deed thus to burn another's ship," said Gizur.

"Good or ill, it shall be done," answered Swanhild fiercely. "Thou art a lawman, and well canst thou meet the suit; moreover Gudruda has wedded an outlaw and shall suffer for her sin. Now go, and see thou tarry not, or thy back shall pay the price."

The man rode away swiftly. Then Gizur turned to Swanhild, asking: "Whither, then, go we?"

"I have said to Middalhof."

"That is into the wolf's den, if Eric and Skallagrim are there," he answered: "I have little chance against the two of them."

"Nay, nor against the one, Gizur. Why, if Eric's right hand were hewn from him, and he stood unarmed, he would still slay thee with his left, as, swordless, he slew Ospakar thy father. Yet I shall find a way to come at him, if he is there."

Then they rode on, and Gizur's heart was heavy for fear of Eric and Skallagrim the Baresark. So fiercely did they ride that, within one hour after midnight, they were at the stead of Middalhof.

"We will leave the horses here in the field," said Swanhild.

So they leaped to earth and, tying the reins of the horses together, left them to feed on the growing grass. Then they crept into the yard and listened. Presently there came a sound of horses stamping in the far corner of the yard. They went thither, and there they found a horse and two geldings saddled, but with the bits slipped, and on the horse was such a saddle as women use.

"Eric Brighteyes, Skallagrim Lambstail, and Gudruda the Fair," whispered Swanhild, naming the horses and laughing evilly—"the birds are within! Now to snare them."

"Were it not best to meet them by the ship?" asked Gizur.

"Nay, thou fool; if once Eric and Skallagrim are back to back, and Whitefire is aloft, how many shall be dead before they are down, thinkest thou? We shall not find them sleeping twice."

"It is shameful to slay sleeping men," said Gizur.

"They are outlaws," she answered. "Hearken, Ospakar's son. Thou sayest thou dost love me and wouldst wed me: know this, that if thou dost fail me now, I will never look upon thy face again, but will name thee Niddering in all men's ears."

Now Gizur loved Swanhild much, for she had thrown her glamour on him as once she did on Atli, and he thought of her day and night. For there was this strange thing about Swanhild that, though she was a witch and wicked, being both fair and gentle she could lead all men, except Eric, to love her.

But of men she loved Eric alone.

Then Gizur held his peace; but Swanhild spoke again:

"It will be of no use to try the doors, for they are strong. Yet when I was a child before now I have passed in and out the house at night by the store-room casement. Follow me, Gizur." Then she crept along the shadow of the wall, for she knew it every stone, till she came to the store-room, and lo! the shutter stood open, and through it the moonlight poured into the chamber. Swanhild lifted her head above the sill and looked, then started back.

"Hush!" she said, "Skallagrim lies asleep within."

"Pray the Gods he wake not!" said Gizur beneath his breath, and turned to go. But Swanhild caught him by the arm; then gently raised her head and looked again, long and steadily. Presently she turned and laughed softly.

"Things go well for us," she said; "the sot lies drunk. We have nothing to fear from him. He lies drunk in a pool of ale."

Then Gizur looked. The moonlight poured into the little room, and by it he saw the great shape of Skallagrim. His head was thrown back, his mouth was wide. He snored loudly in his drunken sleep, and all about him ran the brown ale, for the spigot of the cask lay upon the floor. In his left hand was a horn cup, but in his right he still grasped his axe.

"Now we must enter," said Swanhild. Gizur hung back, but she sprang upon the sill lightly as a fox, and slid thence into the store-room. Then Gizur must follow, and presently he stood beside her in the room, and at their feet lay drunken Skallagrim. Gizur looked first at his sword, then on the Baresark, and lastly at Swanhild.

"Nay," she whispered, "touch him not. Perchance he would cry out—and we seek higher game. He has that within him which will hold him fast for a while. Follow where I shall lead."

She took his hand and, gliding through the doorway, passed along the passage till she came to the great hall. Swanhild could see well in the dark, and moreover she knew the road. Presently they stood in the empty hall. The fire had burnt down, but two embers yet glowed upon the hearth, like red and angry eyes.

For a while Swanhild stood still listening, but there was nothing to hear. Then she drew near to the shut bed where Gudruda slept, and, with her ear to the curtain, listened once more. Gizur came with her, and as he came his foot struck against a bench and stirred it. Now Swanhild heard murmured words and the sound of kisses. She started back, and fury filled her heart. Gizur also heard the voice of Eric, saying: "I will rise." Then he would have fled, but Swanhild caught him by the arm.

"Fear not," she whispered, "they shall soon sleep sound."

He felt her stretch out her arms and presently he saw this wonderful thing: the eyes of Swanhild glowing in the darkness as the embers glowed upon the hearth. Now they glowed brightly, so brightly that he could see the outstretched arms and the hard white face beneath them, and now they grew dim, of a sudden to shine bright again. And all the while she hissed words through her clenched teeth.

Thus she hissed, fierce and low:
"Gudruda, Sister mine, hearken and sleep!
By the bond of blood I bid thee sleep!—
By the strength that is in me I bid thee sleep!—
Sleep! sleep sound!

"Eric Brighteyes, hearken and sleep!
By the bond of sin I charge thee sleep!—
By the blood of Atli I charge thee, sleep!—
Sleep! sleep sound!"

Then thrice she tossed her hands aloft, saying:
"From love to sleep!
From sleep to death!

From death to Hela!
Say, lovers, where shall ye kiss again?"

Then the light went out of her eyes and she laughed low. And ever as she whispered, the spoken words of the two in the shut bed grew fainter and more faint, till at length they died away, and a silence fell upon the place.

"Thou hast no cause to fear the sword of Eric, Gizur," she said. "Nothing will wake him now till daylight comes."

"Thou art awesome!" answered Gizur, for he shook with fear. "Look not on me with those flaming eyes, I pray thee!"

"Fear not," she said, "the fire is out. Now to the work."

"What must we do, then?"

"Thou must do this. Thou must enter and slay Eric."

"That I can not—that I will not!" said Gizur.

She turned and looked at him, and lo! her eyes began to flame again—upon his eyes they seemed to burn.

"Thou wilt do as I bid thee," she said. "With Eric's sword thou shalt slay Eric, else I will curse thee where thou art, and bring such evil on thee as thou knowest not of."

"Look not so, Swanhild," he said. "Lead on—I come."

Now they creep into the shut chamber of Gudruda. It is so dark that they can see nothing, and nothing can they hear except the heavy breathing of the sleepers.

This is to be told, that at this time Swanhild had it in her mind to kill, not Eric but Gudruda, for thus she would smite the heart of Brighteyes. Moreover, she loved Eric, and while he lived she might yet win him; but Eric dead must be Eric lost. But on Gudruda she would be bitterly avenged—Gudruda, who, for all her scheming, had yet been a wife to Eric!

Now they stand by the bed. Swanhild puts out her hand, draws down the clothes, and feels the breast of Gudruda beneath, for Gudruda slept on the outside of the bed.

Then she searches by the head of the bed and finds Whitefire which hung there, and draws the sword.

"Here lies Eric, on the outside," she says to Gizur, "and here is Whitefire. Strike and strike home, leaving Whitefire in the wound."

Gizur takes the sword and lifts it. He is sore at heart that he must do such a coward deed; but the spell of Swanhild is upon him, and he may not flinch from it. Then a thought takes him and he also puts down his hand to feel. It lights upon Gudruda's golden hair, that hangs about her breast and falls from the bed to the ground.

"Here is woman's hair," he whispers.

"No," Swanhild answers, "it is Eric's hair. The hair of Eric is long, as thou hast seen."

Now neither of them knows that Gudruda cut Eric's locks when he lay sick on Mosfell, though Swanhild knows well that it is not Brighteyes whom she bids Gizur slay.

Then Gizur, Ospakar's son, lifts the sword, and the faint starlight struggling into the chamber gathers and gleams upon the blade. Thrice he lifts it, and thrice it draws it back. Then with an oath he strikes—and drives it home with all his strength!

From the bed beneath there comes one long sigh and a sound as of limbs trembling against the bed-gear. Then all is still.

"It is done!" he says faintly.

Swanhild puts down her hand once more. Lo! it is wet and warm. Then she bends herself and looks, and behold! the dead eyes of Gudruda glare up into her eyes. She can see them plainly, but none know what she read there. At the least it was something that she loved not, for she reels back against the panelling, then falls upon the floor.

Presently, while Gizur stands as one in a dream, she rises, saying: "I am avenged of the death of Atli. Let us hence!—ah! let us hence swiftly! Give me thy hand, Gizur, for I am faint!"

So Gizur gives her his hand and they pass thence. Presently they stand in the store-room, and there lies Skallagrim, still plunged in his drunken sleep.

"Must I do more murder?" asks Gizur hoarsely.

"Nay," Swanhild says. "I am sick with blood. Leave the knave."

They pass out by the casement into the yard and so on till they find their horses.

"Lift me, Gizur; I can no more," says Swanhild.

He lifts her to the saddle.

"Whither away?" he asks.

"To Coldback, Gizur, and thence to cold Death."

Thus did Gudruda, Eric's bride and Asmund's daughter, the fairest woman who ever lived in Iceland, die on her marriage night by the hand of Gizur, Ospakar's son, and through the hate and witchcraft of Swanhild the Fatherless, her half-sister.

XXX

HOW THE DAWN CAME

The dawn broke over Middalhof. Slowly the light gathered in the empty hall, it crept slowly into the little chamber where Eric slept, and Gudruda slept also with a deeper sleep.

Now the two women came from their chamber at the far end of the hall, and drew near the hearth, shivering, for the air was cold. They knelt by the fire, blowing at the embers till the sticks they cast upon them crackled to a blaze.

"It seems that Gudruda is not yet gone," said one to the other. "I thought she should ride away with Eric before the dawn."

"Newly wed lie long abed!" laughed the other.

"I am glad to see the blessed light," said the first woman, "for last night I dreamed that once again this hall ran red with blood, as at the marriage-feast of Ospakar."

"Ah," answered the other, "it will be well for the south when Eric Brighteyes and Gudruda are gone over sea, for their loves have brought much bloodshed upon the land."

"Well, indeed!" sighed the first. "Had Asmund the Priest never found Groa, Ran's gift, singing by the sea, Valhalla had not been so full to-day. Mindest thou the day he brought her here?"

"I remember it well," she answered, "though I was but a girl at the time. Still, when I saw those dark eyes of hers—just such eyes as Swanhild's!—I knew her for a witch, as all Finn women are. It is an evil world: my husband is dead by the sword; dead are both my sons, fighting for Eric; dead is Unna, Thorod's daughter; Asmund, my lord, is dead, and dead is Björn; and now Gudruda the Fair, whom I have rocked to sleep, leaves us to go over sea. I may not go with her, for my daughter's sake; yet I almost wish that I too were dead."

"That will come soon enough," said the other, who was young and fair.

Now the witch-sleep began to roll from Eric's heart, though his eyes were not yet open. But the talk of the women echoed in his ears, and the words "dead!" "dead!" "dead!" fell heavily on his slumbering sense. At length he opened his eyes, only to shut them again, because of a bright gleam of light that ran up and down something at his side. Heavily he wondered what this might be, that shone so keen and bright—that shone like a naked sword.

Now he looked again. Yes, it was a sword which stood by him upon the bed, and the golden hilt was like the hilt of Whitefire. He lifted up his hand to touch it, thinking that he dreamed. Lo! his hand and arm were red!

Then he remembered, and the thought of Gudruda flashed through his heart. He sat up, gazing down into the shadow at his side.

Presently the women at the fire heard a sound as of a great man falling to earth.

"What is that noise?" said one.

"Eric leaping from his bed," answered the other. "He has slept too long, as we have also."

As they spoke the curtain of the shut bed was pushed away, and through it staggered Eric in his night-gear, and lo! the left side of it was red. His eyes were wide with horror, his mouth was open, and his face was white as ice.

He stopped, looking at them, made as though to speak, and could not. Then, while they shrank from him in terror, he turned, and, walking like a drunken man, staggered from the hall down that passage which led to the store-chamber. The door stood wide, the shutter was wide, and on the floor, soaked in the dregs of ale, Skallagrim yet lay snoring, his axe in one hand and a cup in the other.

Eric looked and understood.

"Awake, drunkard!" he cried, in so terrible a voice that the room shook. "Awake, and look upon thy work!"

Skallagrim sat up, yawning.

"Forsooth, my head swims," he said. "Give me ale, I am thirsty."

"Never wilt thou look on ale again, Skallagrim, when thou hast seen that which I have to show!" said Eric, in the same dread voice.

Then Skallagrim rose to his feet and gaped upon him.

"What means this, lord? Is it time to ride? and say! why is thy shirt red with blood?"

"Follow me, drunkard, and look upon thy work!" Eric said again.

Then Skallagrim grew altogether sober, and grasping his axe, followed after Brighteyes, sore afraid of what he might see.

They went down the passage, past the high seat of the hall, till they came to the curtain of the shut bed; and after them followed the women. Eric seized the curtain in his hand, rent it from its fastenings, and cast it on the ground. Now the light flowed in and struck upon the bed. It fell upon the bed, it fell upon Whitefire's hilt and ran along the blade, it gleamed on a woman's snowy breast and golden hair, and shone in her staring eyes—a woman who lay stiff and cold upon the bed, the great sword fixed within her heart!

"Look upon thy work, drunkard!" Eric cried again, while the women who peeped behind sent their long wail of woe echoing down the panelled hall.

"Hearken!" said Eric: "while thou didst lie wallowing in thy swine's sleep, foes crept across thy carcase, and this is their handiwork:—yonder she lies who was my bride!—now is Gudruda the Fair a death-wife who last night was my bride! This is thy work, drunkard! and now what meed for thee?"

Skallagrim looked. Then he spoke in a hoarse slow voice:

"What meed, lord? But one—death!"

Then with one hand he covered his eyes and with the other held out his axe to Eric Brighteyes.

Eric took the axe, and while the women ran thence screaming, he whirled it thrice about his head. Then he smote down towards the skull of Skallagrim, but as he smote it seemed to him that a voice whispered in his ear: "Thy oath!"—and he remembered that he had sworn to slay no more, save for his own life's sake.

The mighty blow was falling and he might only do this—loose the axe before it clove Skallagrim in twain. He loosed and away the great axe flew. It passed over the head of Skallagrim, and sped like light across the wide hall, till it crashed through the panelling on the further side, and buried itself to the haft in the wall beyond.

"It is not for me to kill thee, drunkard! Go, die in thy drink!"

"Then I will kill myself!" cried the Baresark, and, rushing across the hall he tore the great axe from its bed.

"Hold!" said Eric; "perhaps there is yet a deed for thee to do. Then thou mayest die, if it pleases thee."

"Ay," said Skallagrim coming back, "perchance there is still a deed to do!"

And, flinging down the axe, Skallagrim Lambstail the Baresark fell upon the floor and wept.

But Eric did not weep. Only he drew Whitefire from the heart of Gudruda and looked at it.

"Thou art a strange sword, Whitefire," he said, "who slayest both friend and foe! Shame on thee, Whitefire! We swore our oath on thee, Whitefire, and thou hast cut its chain! Now I am minded to shatter thee." And as Eric looked on the great blade, lo! it hummed strangely in answer.

"'First must thou be the death of some,' thou sayest? Well, maybe, Whitefire! But never yet didst thou drink so sweet a life as hers who now lies dead, nor ever shalt again."

Then he sheathed the sword, but neither then nor afterwards did he wipe the blood of Gudruda from its blade.

"Last night a-marrying—to-day a-burying," said Eric, and he called to the women to bring spades. Then, having clothed himself, he went to the centre of the hall, and, brushing away the sand, broke the hard clay-flooring, dealing great blows on it with an axe. Now Skallagrim, seeing his purpose, came to him and took one of the spades, and together they laboured in silence till they had dug a grave a fathom deep.

"Here," said Eric, "here, in thine own hall where thou wast born and lived, Gudruda the Fair, thou shalt sleep at the last. And of Middalhof I say this: that none shall live there henceforth. It shall be haunted and accursed till the rafters rot and the walls fall in, making thy barrow, Gudruda."

Now this indeed came to pass, for none have lived in Middalhof since the days of Gudruda the Fair, Asmund's daughter. It has been ruined these many years, and now it is but a pile of stones.

When the grave was dug, Eric washed himself and ate some food. Then he went in to where Gudruda lay dead, and bade the women make her ready for burial. This they did. When she was washed and clad in a clean white robe, Eric came to her, and with his own hand bound the Hell-shoes on her feet and closed her eyes.

It was just then that a man came who said that the people of Gizur and of Swanhild had burned Gudruda's ship, driving the crew ashore.

"It is well," said Eric. "We need the ship no more; now hath she whom it should bear wings with which to fly." Then he went in and sat down on the bed by the body of Gudruda, while Skallagrim crouched on the ground without, tearing at his beard and muttering. For the fierce heart of Skallagrim was broken because of that evil which his drunkenness had brought about.

All day Eric sat thus, looking on his dead love's face, till the hour came round when he and Gudruda had drunk the bride-cup. Then he rose and kissed dead Gudruda on the lips, saying:

"I did not look to part with thee thus, sweet! It is sad that thou shouldst have gone and left me here. Natheless, I shall soon follow on thy path."

Then he called aloud:

"Art sober, drunkard?"

Skallagrim came and stood before him, saying nothing.

"Take thou the feet of her whom thou didst bring to death, and I will take her head."

So they lifted up Gudruda and bore her to the grave. Then Eric stood near the grave, and, taking dead Gudruda in his arms, looked upon her face by the light of the fire and of the candles that were set about.

He looked thrice, then sang aloud:
"Long ago, when swept the snow-blast,
Close we clung and plighted troth.
Many a year, through storm and sword-song,
Sore I strove to win thee, sweet!
But last night I held thee, Fairest,
Lock'd, a wife, in lover's arms.
Now, Gudruda, in thy death-rest,
Sleep thou soft till Eric come!

"Hence I go to wreak thy murder.
Hissing fire of flaming stead,
Groan of spear-carles, wail of women,
Soon shall startle through the night.
Then on Mosfell, Kirtle-Wearer,
Eric waits the face of Death.
Freed from weary life and sorrow,
Soon we'll kiss in Hela's halls!"

Then he laid her in the grave, and, having shrouded a sheet over her, they filled it in together, hiding Gudruda the Fair from the sight of men for ever.

Afterwards Eric armed himself, and this Skallagrim did also. Then he strode from the hall, and Skallagrim followed him. In the yard those horses were still tied that should have carried them to the ship, and on one was the saddle of Gudruda. She had ridden on this horse for many years, and loved it much, for it would follow her like a dog. Eric looked at him, then said aloud:

"Gudruda may need thee where she is, Blackmane," for so the horse was named. "At the least, none shall ride thee more!" And he snatched the axe from the hand of Skallagrim and slew the horse at a blow.

Then they rode away, heading for Coldback. The night was wild and windy, and the sky dark with scudding clouds, through which the moon peeped out at times. Eric looked up, then spoke to Skallagrim:

"A good night for burning, drunkard!"

"Ay, lord; the flames will fly briskly," answered Skallagrim.

"How many, thinkest thou, walked over thee, drunkard, when thou didst lie yonder in the ale?"

"I know not," groaned Skallagrim; "but I found this in the soft earth without: the print of a man's and a woman's feet; and this on the hill side: the track of two horses ridden hard."

"Gizur and Swanhild, drunkard," said Eric. "Swanhild cast us into deep sleep by witchcraft, and Gizur dealt the blow. Better for him that he had never been born than that he has lived to deal that coward's blow!"

Then they rode on, and when midnight was a little while gone they came to the stead at Coldback. Now this house was roofed with turves, and the windows were barred so that none could pass through them. Also in the yard were faggots of birch and a stack of hay.

Eric and Skallagrim tied their horses in a dell that is to the north of the stead and crept up to the house. All was still; but a fire burnt in the hall, and, looking through a crack, Eric could see many men sleeping about it. Then he made signs to Skallagrim and together, very silently, they fetched hay and faggots, piling them against the north door of the house, for the wind blew from the north. Now Eric spoke to Skallagrim, bidding him stand, axe in hand, by the south door, and slay those who came out when the reek began to smart them: but he went himself to fire the pile.

When Brighteyes had made all things ready for the burning, it came into his mind that, perhaps, Gizur and Swanhild were not in the house. But he would not hold his hand for this, for he was mad with grief and rage. So once more he prepared for the deed, when again he heard a voice in his ear—the voice of Gudruda, and it seemed to say:

"Thine oath, Eric! remember thine oath!"

Then he turned and the rage went out of his heart.

"Let them seek me on Mosfell," he said, "I will not slay them secretly and by reek, the innocent and the guilty together." And he strode round the house to where Skallagrim stood at the south door, axe aloft and watching.

"Does the fire burn, lord? I see no smoke," whispered Skallagrim.

"Nay, I have made none. I will shed no more blood, except to save my life. I leave vengeance to the Norns."

Now Skallagrim thought that Brighteyes was mad, but he dared say nothing. So they went to their horses, and when they found them, Eric rode back to the house. Presently they drew near, and Eric told Skallagrim to stay where he was, and riding on to the house, smote heavy blows upon the door, just as Skallagrim once had smitten, before Eric went up to Mosfell.

Now Swanhild lay in her shut bed; but she could not sleep, because of what she saw in the eyes of Gudruda. Little may she ever sleep again, for when she shuts her eyes once more she sees that which was written in the dead eyes of Gudruda. So, as she lay, she heard the blows upon the door, and sprang frightened from her bed. Now there was tumult in the hall, for every man rose to his feet in fear, searching for his weapons. Again the loud knocks came.

"It is the ghost of Eric!" cried one, for Gizur had given out that Eric was dead at his hand in fair fight.

"Open!" said Gizur, and they opened, and there, a little way from the door, sat Brighteyes on a horse, great and shadowy to see, and behind him was Skallagrim the Baresark.

"It is the ghost of Eric!" they cried again.

"I am no ghost," said Brighteyes. "I am no ghost, ye men of Swanhild. Tell me: is Gizur, the son of Ospakar, among you?"

"Gizur is here," said a voice; "but he swore he slew thee last night."

"Then he lied," quoth Eric. "Gizur did not slay me—he murdered Gudruda the Fair as she lay asleep at my side. See!" and he drew Whitefire from its scabbard and held it in the rays of the moon that now shone out between the cloud rifts. "Whitefire is red with Gudruda's blood—Gudruda slaughtered in her sleep by Gizur's cow-coward hand!"

Now men murmured, for this seemed to them the most shameful of all deeds. But Gizur, hearing, shrank back aghast.

"Listen again!" said Eric. "I was minded but now to burn you all as ye slept—ay, the firing is piled against the door. Still, I held my hand, for I have sworn to slay no more, except to save my life. Now I ride hence to Mosfell. Thither let Gizur come, Gizur the murderer, and Swanhild the witch, and with them all who will. There I will give them greeting, and wipe away the blood of Gudruda from Whitefire's blade."

"Fear not, Eric," cried Swanhild, "I will come, and there thou mayst kill me, if thou canst."

"Against thee, Swanhild," said Eric, "I lift no hand. Do thy worst, I leave thee to thy fate and the vengeance of the Norns. I am no woman-slayer. But to Gizur the murderer I say, come."

Then he turned and went, and Skallagrim went with him.

"Up, men, and cut Eric down!" cried Gizur, seeking to cover his shame.

But no man stirred.

XXXI: HOW ERIC SENT AWAY HIS MEN FROM MOSFELL

Now Eric and Skallagrim came to Mosfell in safety, and during all that ride Brighteyes spoke no word. He rode in silence, and in silence Skallagrim rode after him. The heart of Skallagrim was broken because of the sorrow which his drunkenness had brought about, and the heart of Eric was buried in Gudruda's grave.

On Mosfell Eric found four of his own men, two of whom had been among those that the people of Gizur and Swanhild had driven from Gudruda's ship before they fired her. For no fight had been made on the ship. There also he found Jon, who had been loosed from his bands in the booth by one who heard his cries as he rode past. Now when Jon saw Brighteyes, he told him all, and fell at Eric's feet and wept because he had betrayed him in his fear.

But Eric spoke no angry word to him. Stooping down he raised him, saying, "Thou wast never overstout of heart, Jon, and thou art scarcely to be blamed because thou didst speak rather than die in torment, though perhaps some had chosen so to die and not to speak. Now I am a luckless man, and all things happen as they are fated, and the words of Atli come true, as was to be looked for. The Norns, against whom none may stand, did but work their will through thy mouth, Jon; so grieve no more for that which cannot be undone."

Then he turned away, but Jon wept long and loudly.

That night Eric slept well and dreamed no dreams. But on the morrow he woke at dawn, and clothed himself and ate. Then he called his men together, and with them Skallagrim. They came and stood before him, and Eric, drawing Whitefire, leaned upon it and spoke:

"Hearken, mates," he said: "I know this, that my hours are short and death draws on. My years have been few and evil, and I cannot read the purpose of my life. She whom I loved has been slain by the witchcraft of Swanhild and the coward hand of Gizur the murderer, and I go to seek her where she waits. I am very glad to go, for now I have no more joy in life, being but a luckless man; it is an ill world, friends, and all the ways are red with blood. I have shed much blood, though but one life haunts me now at the last, and that is the life of Atli the Earl, for he was no match for my might and he is dead because of my sin. With my own blood I will wash away the blood of Atli, and then I seek another place, leaving nothing but a tale to be told in the ingle when fall the winter snows. For to this end we all come at the last, and it matters little if it find us at midday or at nightfall. We live in sorrow, we die in pain and darkness: for this is the curse that the Gods have laid upon men and each must taste it in his season. But I have sworn that no more men shall die for me. I will fight the last great fight alone; for I know this: I shall not easily be overcome, and with my fallen foes I will tread on Bifrost Bridge. Therefore, farewell! When the bones of Eric Brighteyes lie in their barrow, or are picked by ravens on the mountain side, Gizur will not trouble to hunt out those who clung to him, if indeed Gizur shall live to tell the tale. Nor need ye fear the hate of Swanhild, for she aims her spears at me alone. Go, therefore, and when I am dead, do not forget me, and do not seek to avenge me, for Death the avenger of all will find them also."

Now Eric's men heard and groaned aloud, saying that they would die with him, for they loved Eric one and all. Only Skallagrim said nothing.

Then Brighteyes spoke again: "Hear me, comrades. If ye will not go, my blood will be on your heads, for I will ride out alone, and meet the men of Gizur in the plain and fall there fighting."

Then one by one they crept away to seek their horses in the dell. And each man as he went came to Eric and kissed his hand, then passed thence weeping. Jon was the last to go, except Skallagrim only, and he was so moved that he could not speak at all.

It was this Jon who, in after years, when he was grown very old, wandered from stead to stead telling the deeds of Eric Brighteyes, and always finding a welcome because of his tale, till at length, as he journeyed, he was overtaken by a snowstorm and buried in a drift. For Jon, who lacked much, had this gift: he had a skald's tongue. Men have always held that it was to the honour of Jon that he told the tale thus, hiding nothing, seeing that some of it is against himself.

Now when all had gone, Eric looked at Skallagrim, who still stood near him, axe in hand.

"Wherefore goest thou not, drunkard?" he said. "Surely thou wilt find ale and mead in the vales or oversea. Here there is none. Hasten! I would be alone!"

Now the great body of Skallagrim shook with grief and shame, and the red blood poured up beneath his dark sin. Then he spoke in a thick voice:

"I did not think to live to hear such words from the lips of Eric Brighteyes. They are well earned, yet it is unmanly of thee, lord, thus to taunt one who loves thee. I would sooner die as Swanhild said yonder thrall should die than live to listen to such words. I have sinned against thee, indeed, and because of my sin my heart is broken. Hast thou, then, never sinned that thou wouldst tear it living from my breast as eagles tear a foundered horse? Think on thine own sins, Eric, and pity mine! Taunt me thus once more or bid me go once more and I will go indeed! I will go thus—on the edge of yonder gulf thou didst overcome me by thy naked might, and there I swore fealty to thee, Eric Brighteyes. Many a year have we wandered side by side, and, standing back to back, have struck many a blow. I am minded to do this: to stand by thee in the last great fight that draws on and to die there with thee. I have loved no other man save thee, and I am too old to seek new lords. Yet, if still thou biddest me, I will go thus. Where I swore my oath to thee, there I will end it. For I will lay me down on the brink of yonder gulf, as once I lay when thy hand was at my throat, and call out that thou art no more my lord and I am no more thy thrall. Then I will roll into the depths beneath, and by this death of shame thou shalt be freed of me, Eric Brighteyes."

Eric looked at the great man—he looked long and sadly. Then he spoke:

"Skallagrim Lambstail, thou hast a true heart. I too have sinned, and now I put away thy sin, although Gudruda is dead through thee and I must die because of thee. Stay by me if thou wilt and let us fall together."

Then Skallagrim came to Eric, and, kneeling before him, took his hands and kissed them.

"Now I am once more a man," he said, "and I know this: we two shall die such a great death that it will be well to have lived to die it!" and he arose and shouted:

"A! hai! A! hai! I see foes pass in pride!
A! hai! A! hai! Valkyries ride the wind!
Hear the song of the sword!
Whitefire is aloft—aloft!
Bare is the axe of the Baresark!
Croak, ye nesting ravens;
Flap your wings, ye eagles,
For bright is Mosfell's cave with blood!
Lap! lap! thou Grey Wolf,
Laugh aloud, Odin!

"Laugh till shake the golden doors;
Heroes' feet are set on Bifrost,
Open, ye hundred gates!
A! hai! A! hai! red runs the fray!
A! hai! A! hai! Valkyries ride the wind!"

Then Skallagrim turned and went to clean his harness and the golden helm of Eric.

Now at Coldback Gizur spoke with Swanhild.

"Thou hast brought the greatest shame upon me," he said, "for thou hast caused me to slay a sleeping woman. Knowest thou that my own men will scarcely speak with me? I have come to this evil pass, through love of thee, that I have slain a sleeping woman!"

"It was not my fault that thou didst kill Gudruda," answered Swanhild; "surely I thought it was Eric whom thy sword pierced! I have not sought thy love, Gizur, and I say this to thee: go, if thou wilt, and leave me alone!"

Now Gizur looked at her, and was minded to go; but, as Swanhild knew well, she held him too fast in the net of her witcheries.

"I would go, if I might go!" answered Gizur; "but I am bound to thee for good or evil, since it is fated that I shall wed thee."

"Thou wilt never wed me while Eric lives," said Swanhild.

Now she spoke thus truthfully, and by chance, as it were, not as driving Gizur on to slay Eric—for, now that Gudruda was dead, she was in two minds as to this matter, since, if she might, she still desired to take Eric to herself—but meaning that while Eric lived she would wed no other man. But Gizur took it otherwise.

"Eric shall certainly die if I may bring it about," he answered, and went to speak with his men.

Now all were gathered in the yard at Coldback, and that was a great company. But their looks were heavy because of the shame that Gizur, Ospakar's son, had brought upon them by the murder of Gudruda in her sleep.

"Hearken, comrades!" said Gizur: "great shame is come upon me because of a deed that I have done unwittingly, for I aimed at the eagle Eric and I have slain the swan Gudruda."

Then a certain old viking in the company, named Ketel, whom Gizur had hired for the slaying of Eric, spoke:

"Man or woman, it is a niddering deed to kill folk in their sleep, Gizur! It is murder, and no less, and small luck can be hoped for from the stroke."

Now Gizur felt that his people looked on him askance and heavily, and knew that it would be hard to show them that he was driven to this deed against his will, and by the witchcraft of Swanhild. So, as was his nature, he turned to guile for shelter, like a fox to his hole, and spoke to them with the tongue of a lawman; for Gizur had great skill in speech.

"That tale was not all true which Eric Brighteyes told you," he said. "He was mad with grief, and moreover it seems that he slept, and only woke to find Gudruda dead. It came about thus: I stood with the lady Swanhild, and was about to call aloud on Eric to arm himself and come forth and meet me face to face———"

"Then, lord, methinks thou hadst never met another foe," quoth the viking Ketel who had spoken first.

"When of a sudden," went on Gizur, taking no note of Ketel's words, "one clothed in white sprang from the bed and rushed on me. Then I, thinking that it was Eric, lifted sword, not to smite, but to ward him away; but the linen-wearer met the sword and fell down dead. Then I fled, fearing lest men should wake and trap us, and that is all the tale. It was no fault of mine if Gudruda died upon the sword."

Thus he spoke, but still men looked doubtfully upon him, for his eye was the eye of a liar—and Eric, as they knew, did not lie.

"It is hard to find the truth between lawman's brain and tongue," said the old viking Ketel. "Eric is no lawman, but a true man, and he sang another song. I would slay Eric indeed, for between him and me there is a blood-feud, since my brother died at his hand when, with Whitefire for a crook, Brighteyes drove armed men like sheep down the hall of Middalhof—ay and swordless, slew Ospakar. Yet I say that Eric is a true man, and, whether or no thou art true, Gizur the Lawman, that thou knowest best—thou and Swanhild the Fatherless, Groa's daughter. If thou didst slay Gudruda as thou tellest, say, how come Gudruda's blood on Whitefire's blade? How did it chance, Gizur, that thou heldest Whitefire in thy hand and not thine own sword? Now I tell thee this: either thou shalt go up against Eric and clear thyself by blows, or I leave thee; and methinks there are others among this company who will do the same, for we have no wish to be partners with murderers and their wickedness."

"Ay, a good word!" said many who stood by. "Let Gizur go up with us to Mosfell, and there stand face to face with Eric and clear himself by blows."

"I ask no more," said Gizur; "we will ride to-night."

"But much more shalt thou get, liar," quoth Ketel to himself, "for that hour when thou lookest once again on Whitefire shall be thy last!"

So Gizur and Swanhild made ready to go up against Eric. That day they rode away with a great company, a hundred and one in all, and this was their plan. They sent six men with that thrall who had shown them the secret path, bidding him guide them to the mountain-top. Then, when they were come thither, and heard the shouts of those who sought to gain the platform from the south, they were to watch till Eric and his folk came out from the cave, and shoot them with arrows from above or crush them with stones. But if perchance Eric left the platform and came to meet his foes in the narrow pass, then they must let themselves down with ropes from the height above, and, creeping after him round the rock, must smite him in the back. Moreover, in secret, Gizur promised a great reward of ten hundreds in silver to him who should kill Eric, for he did not long to stand face to face with him alone. Swanhild also in secret made promise of reward to those who should bring Eric to her, bound, but living; and she bade them do this—to bear him down with shields and tie him with ropes.

So they rode away, the seven who should climb the mountain from behind going first, and on the morrow morning they crossed the sand and came to Mosfell.

XXXII

HOW ERIC AND SKALLAGRIM GREW FEY

Now the night came down upon Mosfell, and of all nights this was the strangest. The air was quiet and heavy, yet no rain fell. It was so silent, moreover, that, did a stone slip upon the mountain side or a horse neigh far off on the plains, the sound of it crept up the fell and was echoed from the crags.

Eric and Skallagrim sat together on the open space of rock that is before the cave, and great heaviness and fear came into their hearts, so that they had no desire to sleep.

"Methinks the night is ghost-ridden," said Eric, "and I am fey, for I grow cold, and it seems to me that one strokes my hair."

"It is ghost-ridden, lord," answered Skallagrim. "Trolls are abroad, and the God-kind gather to see Eric die."

For a while they sat in silence, then suddenly the mountain heaved up gently beneath them. Thrice it seemed to heave like a woman's breast, and left them frightened.

"Now the dwarf-folk come from their caves," quoth Skallagrim, "and great deeds may be looked for, since they are not drawn to the upper earth by a little thing."

Then once more they sat silent; and thick darkness came down upon the mountain, hiding the stars.

"Look," said Eric of a sudden, and he pointed to Hecla.

Skallagrim looked, and lo! the snowy dome of Hecla was aglow with a rosy flame like the light of dawn.

"Winter lights," said Lambstail, shuddering.

"Death lights!" answered Eric. "Look again!"

They looked, and behold! in the rosy glow there sat three giant forms of fire, and their shapes were the shapes of women. Before them was a loom of blackness that stretched from earth to sky, and they wove at it with threads of flame. They were splendid and terrible to see. Their hair streamed behind them like meteor flames, their eyes shone like lightning, and their breasts gleamed like the polished bucklers of the gods. They wove fiercely at the loom of blackness, and as they wove they sang. The voice of the one was as the wind whistling through the pines; the voice of the other was as the sound of rain hissing on deep waters; and the voice of the third was as the moan of the sea. They wove fearfully and they sang loudly, but what they sang might not be known. Now the web grew and the woof grew, and a picture came upon the loom—a great picture written in fire.

Behold! it was the semblance of a storm-awakened sea, and a giant ship fled before the gale—a dragon of war, and in the ship were piled the corses of men, and on these lay another corse, as one lies upon a bed. They looked, and the face of the corse grew bright. It was the face of Eric, and his head rested upon the dead heart of Skallagrim.

Clinging to each other, Eric and Skallagrim saw the sight of fear that was written on the loom of the Norns. They saw it for a breath. Then, with a laugh like the wail of wolves, the shapes of fire sprang up and rent the web asunder. Then the first passed upward to the sky, the second southward towards Middalhof, but the third swept over Mosfell, so that the brightness of her flaming form shone on the rock where they sat by the cave, and the lightning of her eyes was mirrored in the byrnie of Skallagrim and on Eric's golden helm. She swept past, pointing downwards as she went, and lo! she was gone, and once more darkness and silence lay upon the earth.

Now this sight was seen of Jon the thrall also, and he told it in his story of the deeds of Eric. For Jon lay hid in a secret place on Mosfell, waiting for tidings of what came to pass.

For a while Eric and Skallagrim clung to each other. Then Skallagrim spoke.

"We have seen the Valkyries," he said.

"Nay," answered Eric, "we have seen the Norns—who are come to warn us of our doom! We shall die to-morrow."

"At the least," said Skallagrim, "we shall not die alone: we had a goodly bed on yonder goblin ship, and all of our own slaying methinks. It is not so ill to die thus, lord!"

"Not so ill!" said Eric; "and yet I am weary of blood and war, of glory and of my strength. Now I desire rest alone. Light fire—I can bear this darkness no longer; the marrow freezes in my bones."

"Fire can be seen of foes," said Skallagrim.

"It matters little now," said Eric, "we are feyfolk."

So Skallagrim lighted the fire, piling much brushwood and dry turf over it, till presently it burnt up brightly, throwing light on all the space of rock, and heavy shadows against the cliff behind. They sat thus a while in the light of the flames, looking towards the deep gulf, till suddenly there came a sound as of one who climbed the gulf.

"Who comes now, climbing where no man may pass?" cried Eric, seizing Whitefire and springing to his feet. Presently he sank down again with white face and staring eyes, and pointed at the edge of the cliff. And as he pointed, the neck of a man rose in the shadow above the brink, and the hands of a man grasped the rock. But there was no head on the neck. The shape of the headless man drew itself slowly over the brink, it walked slowly into the light towards the fire, then sat itself down in the glare of the flames, which shrank away from it as from a draught of wind. Pale with terror, Eric and Skallagrim looked on the headless thing and knew it. It was the wraith of the Baresark that Brighteyes had slain—the first of all the men he slew.

"It is my mate, Eric, whom thou didst kill years ago and whose severed head spoke with thee!" gasped Skallagrim.

"It is he, sure enough!" said Eric; "but where may his head be?"

"Perchance the head will come," answered Skallagrim. "He is an evil sight to see, surely. Say, lord, shall I fall upon him, though I love not the task?"

"Nay, Skallagrim, let him bide; he does but come to warn us of our fate. Moreover, ghosts can only be laid in one way—by the hewing off of the head and the laying of it at the thigh. But this one has no head to hew."

Now as he spoke the headless man turned his neck as though to look. Once more there came the sound of feet and lo! men marched in from the darkness on either side. Eric and Skallagrim looked up and knew them. They were those of Ospakar's folk whom they had slain on Horse-Head Heights; all their wounds were on them and in front of them marched Mord, Ospakar's son. The ghosts gazed upon Eric and Skallagrim with cold dead eyes, then they too sat down by the fire. Now once more there came the sound of feet, and from every side men poured in who had died at the hands of Eric and Skallagrim. First came those who fell on that ship of Ospakar's which Eric sank by Westmans; then the crew of the Raven who had perished upon the sea-path. Even as the man died, so did each ghost come. Some had been drowned and their harness dripped water! Some had died of spear-thrusts and the spears were yet fixed in their breasts! Some had fallen beneath the flash of Whitefire and the weight of the axe of Skallagrim, and there they sat, looking on their wide wounds!

Then came more and more. There were those whom Eric and Skallagrim had slain upon the seas, those who had fallen before them in the English wars, and all that company who had been drowned in the waters of the Pentland Firth when the witchcraft of Swanhild had brought the Gudruda to her wreck.

"Now here we have a goodly crew," said Eric at length. "Is it done, thinkest thou, or will Mosfell send forth more dead?"

As he spoke the wraith of a grey-headed man drew near. He had but one arm, for the other was hewn from him, and the byrnie on his left side was red with blood.

"Welcome, Earl Atli!" cried Eric. "Sit thou over against me, who to-morrow shall be with thee."

The ghost of the Earl seated itself and looked on Eric with sad eyes, but it spake never a word.

Then came another company, and at their head stalked black Ospakar.

"These be they who died at Middalhof," cried Eric. "Welcome, Ospakar! that marriage-feast of thine went ill!"

"Now methinks we are overdone with trolls," said Skallagrim; "but see! here come more."

As he spoke, Hall of Lithdale came, and with him Koll the Half-witted, and others. And so it went on till all the men whom Eric and Skallagrim had slain, or who had died because of them, or at their side, were gathered in deep ranks before them.

"Now it is surely done," said Eric.

"There is yet a space," said Skallagrim, pointing to the other side of the fire, "and Hell holds many dead."

Even as the words left his lips there came a noise of the galloping of horse's hoofs, and one clad in white rode up. It was a woman, for her golden hair flowed down about her white arms. Then she slid from the horse and stood in the light of the fire, and behold! her white robe was red with blood, a great sword was set in her heart, and the face and eyes were the face and eyes of Gudruda the Fair, and the horse she rode was Blackmane, that Eric had slain.

Now when Brighteyes saw her he gave a great cry.

"Greeting, sweet!" he said. "I am no longer afraid, since thou comest to bear me company. Thou art dear to my sight—ay even in yon death-sheet. Greeting, sweet, my May! I laid thee stiff and cold in the earth at Middalhof, but, like a loving wife, thou hast burst thy bonds, and art come to save me from the grip of trolls. Thou art welcome, Gudruda, Asmund's daughter! Come, wife, sit thou at my side."

The ghost of Gudruda spake no word. She walked through the fire towards him, and the flames went out beneath her feet, to burn up again when she had passed. Then she sat down over against Eric and looked on him with wide and tender eyes. Thrice he stretched out his arms to clasp her, but thrice their strength left them and they fell back to his side. It was as though they struck a wall of ice and were numbed by the bitter cold.

"Look, here are more," groaned Skallagrim.

Then Eric looked, and lo! the empty space to the left of the fire was filled with shadowy shapes like shapes of mist. Amongst them was Gizur, Ospakar's son, and many a man of his company. There, too, was Swanhild, Groa's daughter, and a toad nestled in her breast. She looked with wide eyes upon the eyes of dead Gudruda's ghost, that seemed not to see her, and a stare of fear was set on her lovely face. Nor was this all; for there, before that shadowy throng, stood two great shapes clad in their harness, and one was the shape of Eric and one the shape of Skallagrim.

Thus, being yet alive, did these two look upon their own wraiths!

Then Eric and Skallagrim cried out aloud and their brains swam and their senses left them, so that they swooned.

When they opened their eyes and life came back to them the fire was dead, and it was day. Nor was there any sign of that company which had been gathered on the rock before them.

"Skallagrim," quoth Eric, "it seems that I have dreamed a strange dream—a most strange dream of Norns and trolls!"

"Tell me thy dream, lord," said Skallagrim.

So Eric told all the vision, and the Baresark listened in silence.

"It was no dream, lord," said Skallagrim, "for I myself have seen the same things. Now this is in my mind, that yonder sun is the last that we shall see, for we have beheld the death-shadows. All those who were gathered here last night wait to welcome us on Bifrost Bridge. And the mist-shapes who sat there, amongst whom our wraiths were numbered, are the shapes of those who shall die in the great fight to-day. For days are fled and we are sped!"

"I would not have it otherwise," said Eric. "We have been greatly honoured of the Gods, and of the ghost-kind that are around us and above us. Now let us make ready to die as becomes men who have never turned back to blow, for the end of the story should fit the beginning, and of us there is a tale to tell."

"A good word, lord," answered Skallagrim: "I have struck few strokes to be shamed of, and I do not fear to tread Bifrost Bridge in thy company. Now we will wash ourselves and eat, so that our strength may be whole in us."

So they washed themselves with water, and ate merrily, and for the first time for many months Eric was merry. For now that the end was at hand his heart grew light within him. And when they had put the desire of food from them, and buckled on their harness, they looked out from their mountain height, and saw a cloud of dust rise in the desert plain of black sand beneath, and through it the sheen of spears.

"Here come those of whom, if there is truth in visions, some few shall never go back again," said Eric. "Now, what counsel hast thou, Skallagrim? Where shall we meet them? Here on the space of rock, or yonder in the deep way of the cliff?"

"My counsel is that we meet them here," said Skallagrim, "and cut them down one by one as they try to turn the rock. They can scarcely come at us to slay us here so long as our arms have strength to smite."

"Yet they will come, though I know not how," answered Eric, "for I am sure of this, that our death lies before us. Here, then, we will meet them."

Now the cloud of dust drew nearer, and they saw that this was a great company which came up against them. At the foot of the fell the men stayed and rested a while, and it was not till afternoon that they began to climb the mountain.

"Night will be at hand before the game is played," said Skallagrim. "See, they climb slowly, saving their strength, and yonder among them is Swanhild in a purple cloak."

"Ay, night will be at hand, Skallagrim—a last long night! A hundred to two—the odds are heavy; yet some shall wish them heavier. Now let us bind on our helms."

Meanwhile Gizur and his folk crept up the paths from below. Now that thrall who knew the secret way had gone on with six chosen men, and already they climbed the watercourse and drew near to the flat crest of the fell. But Eric and Skallagrim knew nothing of this. So they sat down by the turning place that is over the gulf and waited, singing of the taking of the Raven and of the slaying in the stead at Middalhof, and telling tales of deeds that they had done. And the thrall and his six men climbed on till at length they gained the crest of the fell, and, looking over, saw Eric and Skallagrim beneath them.

"The birds are in the snare, and hark! they sing," said the thrall; "now bring rocks and be silent."

But Gizur and his people, having learned that Eric and Skallagrim were alone upon the mountain, pushed on.

"We have not much to fear from two men," said Gizur.

"That we shall learn presently," answered Swanhild. "I tell thee this, that I saw strange sights last night, though I did not sleep. I may sleep little now that Gudruda is dead, for that which I saw in her eyes haunts me."

Then they went on, and the face of Gizur grew white with fear.

XXXIII

HOW ERIC AND SKALLAGRIM FOUGHT THEIR LAST GREAT FIGHT

Now the thrall and those with him on the crest of the fell heard the murmur of the company of Gizur and Swanhild as they won the mountain side, though they could not see them because of the rocks.

"Now it is time to begin and knock these birds from their perch," said the thrall, "for that is an awkward corner for our folk to turn with Whitefire and the axe of Skallagrim waiting on the farther side."

So he balanced a great stone, as heavy as three men could lift, on the brow of the rock, and aimed it. Then he pushed and let it go. It smote the platform beneath with a crash, two fathoms behind the spot where Eric and Skallagrim sat. Then it flew into the air, and, just as Brighteyes turned at the sound, it struck the wings of his helm, and, bursting the straps, tore the golden helm-piece from his head and carried it away into the gulf beneath.

Skallagrim looked up and saw what had come about.

"They have gained the crest of the fell," he cried. "Now we must fly into the cave or down the narrow way and hold it."

"Down the narrow way, then," said Eric, and while rocks, spears and arrows rushed between and around them, they stepped on to the stone and won the path beyond. It was clear, for Gizur's folk had not yet come, and they ran nearly to the mouth of it, where there was a bend in the way, and stood there side by side.

"Thou wast at death's door then, lord!" said Skallagrim.

"Head-piece is not head," answered Eric; "but I wonder how they won the crest of the fell. I have never heard tell of any path by which it might be gained."

"There they are at the least," said Skallagrim. "Now this is my will, that thou shouldst take my helm. I am Baresark and put little trust in harness, but rather in my axe and strength alone."

"I will not do that," said Eric. "Listen: I hear them come."

Presently the tumult of voices and the tramp of feet grew clearer, and after a while Gizur, Swanhild, and the men of their following turned the corner of the narrow way, and lo! there before them—ay within three paces of them—stood Eric and Skallagrim shoulder to shoulder, and the light poured down upon them from above.

They were terrible to see, and the light shone brightly on Eric's golden hair and Whitefire's flashing blade, and the shadows lay dark on the black helm of Skallagrim and in the fierce black eyes beneath.

Back surged Gizur and those with him. Skallagrim would have sprung upon them, but Eric caught him by the arm, saying: "A truce to thy Baresark ways. Rush not and move not! Let us stand here till they overwhelm us."

Now those behind Gizur cried out to know what ailed them that they pushed back.

"Only this," said Gizur, "that Eric Brighteyes and Skallagrim Lambstail stand like two grey wolves and hold the narrow way."

"Now we shall have fighting worth the telling of," quoth Ketel the viking. "On, Gizur, Ospakar's son, and cut them down!"

"Hold!" said Swanhild; "I will speak with Eric first," and, together with Gizur and Ketel, she passed round the corner of the path and came face to face with those who stood at bay there.

"Now yield, Eric," she cried. "Foes are behind and before thee. Thou art trapped, and hast little chance of life. Yield thee, I say, with thy black wolf-hound, so perchance thou mayest find mercy even at the hands of her whose husband thou didst wrong and slay."

"It is not my way to yield, lady," answered Eric, "and still less perchance is it the way of Skallagrim. Least of all will we yield to thee who, after working many ills, didst throw me in a witch-sleep, and to him who slew the wife sleeping at my side. Hearken, Swanhild: here we stand, awaiting death, nor will we take mercy from thy hand. For know this, we shall not die alone. Last night as we sat on Mosfell we saw the Norns weave our web of fate upon their loom of darkness. They sat on Helca's dome and wove their pictures in living flame, then rent the web and flew upward and southward and westward, crying our doom to sky and earth and sea. Last night as we sat by the fire on Mosfell all the company of the dead were gathered round us—ay! and all the company of those who shall die to-day. Thou wast there, Gizur the murderer, Ospakar's son! thou wast there, Swanhild the witch, Groa's daughter! thou wast there, Ketel Viking! with many another man; and there were we two also. Valkyries have kissed us and death draws near. Therefore, talk no more, but come and make an end. Greeting, Gizur, thou woman-murderer! Draw nigh! draw nigh! Out sword! up shield! and on, thou son of Ospakar!"

Swanhild spoke no more, and Gizur had no word.

"On, Gizur! Eric calls thee," quoth Ketel Viking; but Gizur slunk back, not forward.

Then Ketel grew mad with rage and shame. He called to the men, and they drew near, as many as might, and looked doubtfully at the pair who stood before them like rocks upon a plain. Eric laughed aloud and Skallagrim gnawed the edge of his shield. Eric laughed aloud and the sound of his laughter ran up the rocks.

"We are but two," he cried, "and ye are many! Is there never a pair among you will stand face to face with a Baresark and a helmless man?" and he tossed Whitefire high into the air and caught it by the hilt.

Then Ketel and another man of his following sprang forward with an oath, and their axes thundered loud on the shields of Eric and of Skallagrim. But Whitefire flickered up and the axe of Skallagrim crashed, and at once their knees were loosened, so that they sank down dead.

"More men! more men!" cried Eric. "These were brave, but their might was little. More men for the Grey Wolf's maw!"

Then Swanhild lashed the folk with bitter words, and two of them sprang on. They sprang on like hounds upon a deer at bay, and they rolled back as gored hounds roll from the deer's horns.

"More men! more men!" cried Eric. "Here lie but four and a hundred press behind. Now he shall win great honour who lays Brighteyes low and brings down the helm of Skallagrim."

Again two came on, but they found no luck, for presently they also were down upon the bodies of those who went before. Now none could be found to come up against the pair, for they fought like Baldur and Thor, and none could touch them, and no harness might withstand the weight of their blows that shore through shield and helm and byrnie, deep to the bone beneath. Then Eric and Skallagrim leaned upon their weapons and mocked their foes, while these cursed and tore their beards with rage and shame.

Now it is to be told that when the thrall and those with him saw Eric and Skallagrim had escaped their rocks and spears, they took counsel, and the end of it was that they slid down a rope to the platform that is under the crest of the fell.

Thence, though they could see nothing, they could hear the clang of blows and the shouts of those who fought and fell—ay! and the mocking of Eric and of Skallagrim.

"Now it goes thus," said the thrall, who was a cunning man: "Eric and Skallagrim hold the narrow way and none can stand against them. This, then, is my rede: that we turn the rock and take them in the back."

His fellows thought this a good saying, and one by one they stood upon the little rock and won the narrow way. They crept along this till they were near to Eric and Skallagrim. Now Swanhild, looking up, saw them and started. Skallagrim noted this and glanced over his shoulder, and that not too soon, for, as he looked, the thrall lifted sword to smite the head of Eric.

With a shout of "Back to back!" the Baresark swung round and ere ever the sword might fall his axe was buried deep in the thrall's breast.

"Now we must cut our path through them," said Skallagrim, "and, if it may be, win the space that is before the cave. Keep them off in front, and I will mind these mannikins."

Now Gizur's folk, seeing what had come about, took heart and fell upon Eric with a rush, and those who were with the dead thrall rushed at Skallagrim, and there began such a fight as has not been known in Iceland. But the way was so narrow that scarce more than one man could come to each of them at a time. And so fierce and true were the blows of Eric and Skallagrim that of those who came on few went back. Down they fell, and where they fell they died, and for every man who died Eric and Skallagrim won a pace towards the point of rock. Whitefire flamed so swift and swept so wide that it seemed to Swanhild, watching, as though three swords were aloft at once, and the axe of Skallagrim thundered down like the axe of a woodman against a tree, and those groaned on whom it fell as groans a falling tree. Now the shields of these twain were hewn through and through, and cast away, and their blood ran from many wounds. Still, their life was whole in them and they plied axe and sword with both hands. And ever men fell, and ever, fighting hard, they drew nearer to the point of rock.

Now it was won, and now all the company that came with the thrall from over the mountain brow were dead or sorely wounded at the hands of black Skallagrim. Lo! one springs on Eric, and Gizur creeps behind him. Whitefire leaps to meet the man and does not leap in vain; but Gizur smites a coward blow at Eric's uncovered head, and wounds him sorely, so that he falls to his knee.

"Now I am smitten to the death, Skallagrim," cries Eric. "Win the rock and leave me." Yet he rises from his knee.

Then Skallagrim turns, red with blood and terrible to see.

"'Tis but a scratch. Climb thou the rock—I follow," he says, and, screaming like a horse, with weapon aloft he leaps alone upon the foe. They break before the Baresark rush; they break, they fall—they are cloven by Baresark axe and trodden of Baresark feet! They roll back, leaving the way clear—save for the dead. Then Skallagrim follows Brighteyes to the rock.

Now Eric wipes the gore from his eyes and sees. Then, slowly, and with a reeling brain, he steps down upon the giddy point. He goes near to falling, yet does not fall, for now he lies upon the open space, and creeps on hands and knees to the rock-wall that is by the cave, and sits resting his back against it, Whitefire on his knee.

Before he is there, Skallagrim staggers to his side with a rush.

"Now we have time to breathe, lord," he gasps. "See, here is water," and he takes a pitcher that stands by, and gives Eric to drink from the pool, then drinks himself and pours the rest of the water on Eric's wound. Then new life comes to them, and they both stand on their feet and win back their breath.

"We have not done so badly!" says Skallagrim, "and we are still a match for one or two. See, they come! Say, where shall we meet them, lord?"

"Here," quoth Eric; "I cannot stand well upon my legs without the help of the rock. Now I am all unmeet for fight."

"Yet shall this last stand of thine be sung of!" says Skallagrim.

Now finding none to stay them, the men of Gizur climb one by one upon the rock and win the space that is beyond. Swanhild goes first of all, because she knows well that Eric will not harm her, and after her come Gizur and the others. But many do not come, for they will lift sword no more.

Now Swanhild draws near and looks on Eric and mocks him in the fierceness of her heart and the rage of her wolf-love.

"Now," she says, "now are Brighteyes dim eyes! What! weepest thou, Eric?"

"Ay, Swanhild," he answered, "I weep tears of blood for those whom thou hast brought to doom."

She draws nearer and speaks low to him: "Hearken, Eric. Yield thee! Thou hast done enough for honour, and thou art not smitten to the death of yonder cowardly hound. Yield and I will nurse thee back to health and bear thee hence, and together we will forget our hates and woes."

"Not twice may a man lie in a witch's bed," said Eric, "and my troth is plighted to other than thee, Swanhild."

"She is dead," says Swanhild.

"Yes, she is dead, Swanhild; and I go to seek her amongst the dead—I go to seek her and to find her!"

But the face of Swanhild grew fierce as the winter sea.

"Thou hast put me away for the last time, Eric! Now thou shalt die, as I have promised thee and as I promised Gudruda the Fair!"

"So shall I the more quickly find Gudruda and lose sight of thy evil face, Swanhild the harlot! Swanhild the murderess! Swanhild the witch! For I know this: thou shalt not escape!—thy doom draws on also!—and haunted and accursed shalt thou be for ever! Fare thee well, Swanhild; we shall meet no more, and the hour comes when thou shalt grieve that thou wast ever born!"

Now Swanhild turned and called to the folk: "Come, cut down these outlaw rogues and make an end. Come, cut them down, for night draws on."

Then once more the men of Gizur closed in upon them. Eric smote thrice and thrice the blow went home, then he could smite no more, for his strength was spent with toil and wounds, and he sank upon the ground. For a while Skallagrim stood over him like a she-bear o'er her young and held the mob at bay. Then Gizur, watching, cast a spear at Eric. It entered his side through a cleft in his byrnie and pierced him deep.

"I am sped, Skallagrim Lambstail," cried Eric in a loud voice, and all men drew back to see giant Brighteyes die. Now his head fell against the rock and his eyes closed.

Then Skallagrim, stooping, drew out the spear and kissed Eric on the forehead.

"Farewell, Eric Brighteyes!" he said. "Iceland shall never see such another man, and few have died so great a death. Tarry a while, lord; tarry a while—I come—I come!"

Then crying "Eric! Eric!" the Baresark fit took him, and once more and for the last time Skallagrim rushed screaming upon the foe, and once more they rolled to earth before him. To and fro he rushed, dealing great blows, and ever as he went they stabbed and cut and thrust at his side and back, for they dared not stand before him, till he bled from a hundred wounds. Now, having slain three more men, and wounded two others, Skallagrim might no more. He stood a moment swaying to and fro, then let his axe drop, threw his arms high above him, and with one loud cry of "Eric!" fell as a rock falls—dead upon the dead.

But Eric was not yet gone. He opened his eyes and saw the death of Skallagrim and smiled.

"Well ended, Lambstail!" he said in a faint voice.

"Lo!" cried Gizur, "yon outlawed hound still lives! Now I will do a needful task and make an end of him, and so shall Ospakar's sword come back to Ospakar's son."

"Thou art wondrous brave now that the bear lies dying!" said Swanhild.

Now it seemed that Eric heard the words, for suddenly his might came back to him, and he staggered to his knees and thence to his feet. Then, as folk fall from him, with all his strength he whirls Whitefire round his head till it shines like a wheel of fire. "Thy service is done and thou art clean of Gudruda's blood—go back to those who forged thee!" Brighteyes cries, and casts Whitefire from him towards the gulf.

Away speeds the great blade, flashing like lightning through the rays of the setting sun, and behold! as men watch it is gone—gone in mid-air!

Since that day no such sword as Whitefire has been known in Iceland.

"Now slay thou me, Gizur," says the dying Eric.

Gizur comes on with little eagerness, and Eric cries aloud:

"Swordless I slew thy father!—swordless, shieldless, and wounded to the death I will yet slay thee, Gizur the Murderer!" and with a loud cry he staggered towards him.

Gizur smites him with his sword, but Eric does not stay, and while men wait and wonder, Brighteyes sweeps him into his great arms—ay, sweeps him up, lifts him from the ground and reels on.

Eric reels on to the brink of the gulf. Gizur sees his purpose, struggles and shrieks aloud. But the strength of the dying Eric is more than the strength of Gizur. Now Brighteyes stands on the dizzy edge and the light of the passing sun flames about his head. And now, bearing Gizur with him, he hurls himself out into the gulf, and lo! the sun sinks!

Men stand wondering, but Swanhild cries aloud:

"Nobly done, Eric! nobly done! So I would have seen thee die who of all men wast the first!"

This then was the end of Eric Brighteyes the Unlucky, who of all warriors that have lived in Iceland was the mightiest, the goodliest, and the best beloved of women and of those who clung to him.

Now, on the morrow, Swanhild caused the body of Eric to be searched for in the cleft, and there they found it, floating in water and with the dead Gizur yet clasped in its bear-grip. Then she cleansed it and clothed it again in its rent armour, and bound on the Hell-shoes, and it was carried on horses to the sea-side, and with it were borne the bodies of Skallagrim Lambstail the Baresark, Eric's thrall, and of all those men whom they had slain in the last great fight on Mosfell, that is now named Ericsfell.

Then Swanhild drew her long dragon of war, in which she had come from Orkneys, from its shed over against Westman Isles, and in the centre of the ship, she piled the bodies of the slain in the shape of a bed, and lashed them fast. And on this bed she laid the corpse of Eric Brighteyes, and the breast of black Skallagrim the Baresark was his pillow, and the breast of Gizur, Ospakar's son, was his foot-rest.

Then she caused the sails to be hoisted, and went alone aboard the long ship, the rails of which were hung with the shields of the dead men.

And when at evening the breeze freshened to a gale that blew from the land, she cut the cable with her own hand, and the ship leapt forward like a thing alive, and rushed out in the red light of the sunset towards the open sea.

Now ever the gale freshened and folk, standing on Westman Heights, saw the long ship plunge past, dipping her prow beneath the waves and sending the water in a rain of spray over the living Swanhild, over the dead Eric and those he lay upon.

And by the head of Eric Brighteyes, her hair streaming on the wind, stood Swanhild the Witch, clad in her purple cloak, and with rings of gold about her throat and arms. She stood by Eric's head, swaying with the rush of the ship, and singing so sweet and wild a song that men grew weak who heard it.

Now, as the people watched, two white swans came down from the clouds and sped on wide wings side by side over the vessel's mast.

The ship rushed on through the glow of sunset into the gathering night. On sped the ship, but still Swanhild sung, and still the swans flew over her.

The gale grew fierce, and fiercer yet. The darkness gathered deep upon the raging sea.

Now that ship was seen no more, and the death-song of Swanhild as she passed to doom was never heard again.

For swans and ship, and Swanhild, and dead Eric and his dead foes, were lost in the wind and the night.

But far out on the sea a great flame of fire leapt up towards the sky.

Now this is the tale of Eric Brighteyes, Thorgrimur's son; of Gudruda the Fair, Asmund's daughter; of Swanhild the Fatherless, Atli's wife, and of Ounound, named

Skallagrim Lambstail, the Baresark, Eric's thrall, all of whom lived and died before Thangbrand, Wilibald's son, preached the White Christ in Iceland.

THE END

A Thane of Wessex by Charles W. Whistler

I: OUTLAWED!

The whole of my story seems to me to begin on the day when I stood, closely guarded, before my judges, in the great circle of the people at the Folk Moot of the men of Somerset gathered on the ancient hill of Brent. All my life before that seems to have been as nothing, so quiet and uneventful it was compared to what came after. I had grown from boyhood to manhood in my father's great hall, on the little hill of Cannington that looks out over the mouth of the river Parret to the blue hills beyond. And there, when I was but two-and-twenty and long motherless, I succeeded him as thane, and tried to govern my people as well and wisely as he, that I too might die loved and honoured as he died. And that life lasted but three years.

Maybe, being young and headstrong, I spoke at times, when the feasting was over and the ale cup went round, too boldly of the things that were beyond me, and dared, in my want of experience, to criticize the ways of the king and his ordering of matters -- thinking at the same time no thought of disloyalty; for had anyone disparaged the king to myself my sword would have been out to chastise the speaker in a moment. But, as it ever is, what seems wrong in another may be passed over in oneself.

However that may be, it came to pass that Matelgar, the thane of Stert, a rich and envious man, saw his way through this conceit of mine to his own profit. For Egbert, the wise king, was but a few years dead, and it was likely enough that some of the houses of the old seven kings might dare to make headway against Ethelwulf his successor, and for a time the words of men were watched, lest an insurrection might be made unawares. I thought nothing of this, nor indeed dreamt that such a thing might be, nor did one ever warn me.

My father and this Matelgar were never close friends, the open nature of the one fitting ill with the close and grasping ways of the other. Yet, when Matelgar spoke me fair at the rere-feast of my father's funeral, and thereafter would often ride over and sup with me, I was proud to think, in my foolishness, that I had won the friendship that my father could not win, and so set myself even above him from whom I had learnt all I knew of wisdom.

And that conceit of mine was my downfall. For Matelgar, as I was soon to find out, encouraged my foolishness, and, moreover, brought in friends and bought men of his, who, by flattering me, soon made themselves my boon companions, treasuring up every word that might tell against me when things were ripe.

Then at last, one day as I feasted after hunting the red deer on the Quantocks, my steward came into my hall announcing messengers from the king. They followed close on his heels, and I, who had seen nothing of courts, wondered that so many armed men should be needed in a peaceful hall, and yet watched them as one watches a gay show, till some fifty men of the king's household lined my hall and fifty more blocked the doorway. My people watched too, and I saw a smile cross from one of Matelgar's men to another, but thought no guile.

Then one came forward and arrested me in the king's name as a traitor, and I drew my sword on him, telling him he lied in giving me that name, calling too on my men to aid me. But they were overmatched, and dared not resist, for the swords of the king's men were out, and, moreover, I saw that Matelgar's men were weaponless. He himself was not with me, and still I had no thought of treachery.

So the end was that I was pinioned from behind and bound, and taken away that night to where I knew not. Only, wherever it was, I was kept in darkness and chains, maddened by the injustice of the thing and my own helplessness, till I lost count of days, and at last hope itself. And all that time the real reason for my arrest, and for the accusation that caused it, never entered my mind, and least of all did I suspect that Matelgar, my friend, was at the bottom of it. Indeed, I hoped at first that, hearing of my trouble, he would interfere and procure my release, till, as I say, hope was gone.

It was March when I was taken to prison. It was into broad May sunshine and greenness that I was brought out by my surly jailers at last, set, half blind with the darkness of the prison, on a good horse, and so, with my hands bound behind me, led off in the midst of a strong guard to the place of my trial.

Then, as mind and feeling came back to me with the fresh air and springtime warmth, I knew the place we were leaving: It was the castle of a friend of Matelgar -- and that seemed strange to me, for I had been hardly treated, seeing none save the men who fed me and saw that my chains were kept secure. Then I looked in the faces of my guards, but all were unknown to me. As I had not before been to that castle as a guest, I was not surprised, and I said nothing to them, for I had found the uselessness of question and entreaty when I spoke at the first to the jailers.

So, silently, we rode on, and the world looked very fair to me after the long grayness of the prison walls.

One who knows the west country, hunting through it as I have hunted, grows to love and recognize the changing shapes of every hill and coombe and spur of climbing forest on their sides, and so, before long, I knew we were making for the great hill of Brent, but why I could not tell. Then we crossed Parret river, and I watched a salmon leap as we did so; and then on over the level marshes till I could see that the wide circle on Brent top was black with swarming people. Often enough, as the cloud shadows passed from them, arms and bright armour sparkled in the sunlight among the crowd; and then I could have wept, having no arms or harness left me, for often when aforetime I rode free I would take a childish pleasure in seeing the churls blink and shade their eyes as I flashed on them, and would wonder, too, if my weapons shone as my father's shone as we rode side by side on some sunny upland.

Then, when we came under the hill of Brent, the hum of voices came down to us, for the day was still, and my guards straightened themselves in the saddle and set their ranks more orderly. But I, clad as I was in the rags of the finery I had worn at the feast whence I was taken, shrank within myself, ashamed to meet the gazes that must be turned on me presently, for I saw that we were going on up the steep ascent to mix with the crowd on the summit of the great knoll.

Now, by this time the long ride had brought back my senses to me, and I began to take more thought for myself and what might be meant by this journey. At first I had been so stunned and dazed by the release -- as my removal from the dungeon seemed to me --that I had been content to feel the light and air play about me once more; but that strangeness had worn off now, and the consciousness of being yet a prisoner took hold of me.

My guards had ridden silent, either in obedience to command, or because a Saxon is not often given to talk when under some responsibility, so that I had learnt nothing from them thus far. But as we turned our horses' heads up the steep, a longing at last came over me to speak, and I turned to a gray-bearded man who had ridden silently at my right hand all the morning and asked him plainly whither he was taking me, and for answer he pointed up the hill, saying nothing.

Then I asked him why I must be taken there, and, grimly enough, he replied in two words, "For trial", and so I knew that the Great Mooti was summoned, and that presently I should know the whole meaning of this thing that had befallen me. Then my spirits began to rise, for, being conscious of no wrongdoing, I looked forward to speedy release with full proof of innocence.

Then I began to look about me and to note the crowds of people whom the Moot had gathered. So many and various were these that I and my guards passed with little notice among those who toiled up the hill with us, the crowd growing thicker as we neared the edge of the first great square platform on the hilltop. And when we reached this, my guards reined up to breathe their horses, for Brent has from this first platform a yet steeper rise to the ancient circle on the very summit. Men say that both platform and circle are the work of the Welsh, whom our Saxon forefathers drove out and enslaved, but however this may be, they were no idle workmen who raised the great earthworks that are there.

All the many acres of that great platform were covered with wagons and carts, and everywhere were set booths and tents, and in them men and women were eating and drinking, having come from far. There were, too, shows of every kind to beguile the hours of waiting or to tempt the curious, for many of the people, thralls and unfree men, had taken holiday with their masters, and had come to see the Moot, though they had no part in the business thereof.

So there were many gaily-dressed tumblers and dancers, jugglers and gleemen, each with a crowd round them. But among these crowds were few freemen, so that I judged that the Moot was set, and that they were gathered on the higher circle that was yet before us to be climbed.

I had been on Brent once or twice before, but then it had been deserted, and my eyes had had time and inclination to look out over the wide view of hill and plain and sea and distant Welsh mountains beyond that. Now I thought nothing of these things, but looked up to where it seemed that I must be judged. I could make out one or two banners pitched and floating idly in the sunshine, and one seemed to have a golden cross at its stave head; but I could make out none of the devices on them, and so I looked idly back on the crowd again. And then men brought us food and ale, and at last, after some gruff talk among themselves, the guards untied my hands, though they left my feet bound under the saddle girths, and bade me help myself.

Nor was I loth to eat heartily, with the freshness of the ride on me, and with the hope of freedom strong in my heart.

Then we waited for an hour or more, and the sun began to slope westward, and my guards seemed to grow impatient. Still the crowds did not thin, and if one group of performers ceased another set began their antics.

At last a richly-clad messenger came towards us, the throng making hasty way for him, and spoke to the leader of our party. Then, following him, we rode to the foot of the great mound, and there dismounted. And now they bound my hands again, and if I asked them to forbear I cannot well remember, but I think I did so in vain. For my mind was in a great tumult as we climbed the hill, wondering and fearing and hoping all at once, and longing to see who were my judges, and to have this matter ended once for all.

We passed, I think, two groups coming down from some judgment given, and of these I know one contained a guarded and ironed man with a white, set face; and the other was made up of people who smiled and talked rapidly, leading one who had either gained a cause or had been acquitted. There were perhaps other people who met us or whom we passed, but these are the two I remember of them all. Then we gained the summit and stood there waiting for orders, as it seemed, and I could look round on all the ring.

And at first I seemed to be blinded by the brilliance of that assembly, for our Saxon folk love bright array and fair jewellery on arm and neck. Men sat four and six deep all round the great circle, leaving only the gap where we should enter; and right opposite that gap seemed the place of honour, for there were a score or more of chairs set, each with a thane thereon, and in the midst of them sat those behind whom the banners were raised. Near us at this end of the circle were the lesser freemen, and so round each bend of the ring to right and left in order of rank till those thanes were reached who were highest.

Before those stood some disputants, as it seemed, and I could not see the faces of the seated thanes clearly at first. But presently I knew the banners -- they were those of Eanulf the Ealdorman, and of Ealhstan the Bishop. And when I saw the first I feared, for the great ealdorman was a stern and pitiless man, from all I had ever heard; but when I knew that banner with the golden cross above it, my heart was lighter, for all men loved and spoke well of the bishop.

It seemed long before that trial was over; but at last the men ceased speaking, and the thanes seemed to take counsel upon it; and then Eanulf pronounced judgment, and the men sat down in their places in the ring, for it was, as one could tell, some civil dispute of boundary, or road, or the like which had been toward.

Then there was a silence for a space, until the ealdorman rose and spoke loudly, for all the great ring to hear.

"There is one more case this day that must come before this Moot, and that is one which brings shame on this land of ours. That one from among the men of Somerset should speak ill of Ethelwulf the King, and plot against him, is not to be borne. But that all men may know and fear the doom that shall be to such an one, he has been brought for trial by the Moot, with full proof of his guilt in this matter, that Somerset itself, as it were, should pronounce his sentence."

Now, when the assembly heard that, a murmur went round, and, as it seemed to me, of surprise mixed with wrath. And I myself felt the same for the moment -- but then the eyes of all turned in a flash upon me -- and I remembered the accusation that had been brought against me, and I knew that it was I of whom Eanulf spoke. Then shame fell on me, to give place at once to anger, and I think I should have spoken hotly, but that at some sign from the ealdorman, my guards laid hold of me, and led me across the open space and set me before him and the bishop.

But as he with the others laid hands on me, that gray-bearded man, who had answered me when I asked my one question, whispered hastily in my ear, "Be silent and keep cool."

I would he were alive now; but that might not be. And I knew not then why he thus spoke, unless he had known and loved my father.

So I stood before those two judges and looked them in the face; and then one moved uneasily in his seat to their left, and my eyes were drawn to him. It was Matelgar, and, as I saw him, I smiled for I thought him a friend at least; but he looked not at me. Then from him I turned to seek the face of some other whom I might know. And I saw thanes, friends of my father, whom I had not cared to seek; and of these some frowned on me, but some looked pityingly, as I thought, though it was but for a moment that my eyes might leave the faces of those two judges before me.

Now, were it not that when I go over what followed my heart still rises up again in a wrath and mad bitterness that I fain would feel no more, I would tell all of that trial, if trial one could call it, where there was none to speak for the accused, and every word was against him.

And in that trial I myself took little part by word or motion, standing there and listening as though the words spoken of me concerned another, as indeed, they might well have done.

But first Eanulf spoke to me, bending his brows as he did so, and frowning on me.

"Heregar, son of Herewulf the Thane, you are accused by honourable men of speaking evil of our Lord the King, Ethelwulf. What answer have you to make to this charge? And, moreover, you are further charged with conspiring against him -- can you answer to that charge?"

Then I was about to make loud and angry denial of these accusations, but that old guard of mine, who yet held my shoulder, gripped it tightly, and I remembered his words, so that in a flash it came to me that an innocent man need but deny frankly, as one who has no fear, and I looked Eanulf in the face and answered him.

"Neither of these charges are true, noble Eanulf; nor know I why they are brought against me, or by whom. Let them speak -- there are those here who will answer for my loyalty."

Now, as I spoke thus quietly, Eanulf's brows relaxed, and I saw, too, that the bishop looked more kindly on me. Eanulf spoke again.

"Know you not by whom these charges are brought?"

"Truly, I know not, Lord Eanulf," I answered, "for no man may say these things of me, save he lies."

"Have you enemies?" he asked.

"None known to me," I told him truthfully, for I had, as my father, lived at peace with all.

"Then is the testimony of those against you the heavier," said the ealdorman.

And with that he turned to the bishop before I could make reply; and they spoke together for a while in Latin, which I knew not.

So I looked to my friend Matelgar for comfort, but he seemed to see me not, looking away elsewhere. And I thought him plainly troubled for me, for his face was white, and the hand on which his chin rested was turning the ends of his beard between his teeth, so that he bit it -- as I had seen him do before when in doubt or perplexity.

As I watched him, the bishop spoke in Saxon, saying that it would be well to call the accusers first and hear them, that I might make such reply as was possible to me.

"For," said he, "it seems to me that this Heregar speaks truth in saying that he knows not his accusers."

Then Eanulf bowed gravely, and all the circle was hushed, for a little talk had murmured round as these two spoke in private.

And now I will forbear, lest the rage and shame of it should get the mastery of me again, and I should again think and speak things for which (as once before, at the bidding of the man I love best on earth) I must do long penance, if that may avail. For, truly, I forgave once, and I would not recall that forgiveness. Yet I must tell somewhat.

Eanulf bade the accusers stand forward and give their evidence; and slowly, and, as it were, unwillingly, rose Matelgar, my friend, as I had deemed him, and behind him a score of those friends of his who had kept me company for long days on moor and in forest, and had feasted in my hall.

Again that warning grasp on my shoulder, and I thought that surely either I or they had mistaken the summons, and that my defenders had come forward.

Then, as in a dream, I listened to words that I will not recall, making good those accusations. And through all that false witness there seemed to me to run, as it were, a thread of those foolish, boy-wise words of mine that had, and meant, no harm, but on which were now built mountains of seeming proof. So that, when at last all those men had spoken I was dumb, and knew that I had no defence. For no proof of loyalty had I to give -- for proof had never been required of me. And a man may live a quiet life, and yet conspire most foully.

As my accusers went back to their seats there ran a murmur among the folk, and then a silence fell. The level afternoon sun seemed to blaze on me alone, while to me the air seemed thick and close, and full of whispers.

Ealhstan the Bishop broke the silence.

"The proof is weighty, and Matelgar the Thane is an honourable man," he said, sadly enough; "but if a man conspires, there needs must be one other, at least, in the plot. Surely we have heard little of this."

Then was added more evidence. And men proved lonely journeys of mine, with evasion of notice thereof, and disavowal of the same. Yet I thought that Matelgar the Thane knew of my love for Alswythe, his daughter, whom I would meet, as lovers will meet, unobserved if they may, in all honour.

Yet, as I listened, it was of these meetings they spoke, saying only that I had been able to concord whom I met, and where, though Matelgar must have known it. When that was finished, Eanulf bade me call men to disprove these things. And I could not. For my accusers were my close companions, and of Alswythe I would not speak, and I must fain hold my peace.

Only, after a silence, I could forbear no longer, and cried:

"Will none speak for me?"

Then one by one my father's friends rose and told what they knew of my boyhood and training; but of these last few years of my manhood they, alas for my own folly could not speak. What they might they did, and my heart turned to them in gratitude for a little, though Matelgar's treachery had seemed to make it a stone within me.

They ended, and the silence came again. It seemed long, and weighed on me like a thunderstorm in the air, nor should I have started had the whole assembly broken into one thunderclap of hatred of me. But instead of that, came the calm voice of Ealhstan the Bishop:

"Eanulf and freemen of Somerset, there is one who witnesses for this Heregar more plainly than all these. That witness is himself, in his youth and inexperience. What are the wild words a boy will say? Who will plot against a mighty king with a boy for partner? What weight have his words? What help can come from his following? It seems to me that Matelgar the Thane and these friends of his might well have laughed away all these foolishnesses, rather than hoard them up to bring before this solemn council. This, too, I hold for injustice, that one should be kept in ward till his trial, unknowing of all that is against him, unhelped by the counsel of any freeman, and unable to send word to those who should stand by him at his trial. Indeed, this thing must be righted, I tell you, before England is a free land."

At that there went a sound of assent round the Moot, and it seems to me, looking back, that that trial of mine, hard as it was to bear, was yet the beginning of good to all the land, by reason of those words which it taught the bishop to say, and which found an abiding place in the hearts of the honest men who heard; so that in these days of Alfred, our wise king, they have borne fruit.

Then Eanulf signed to my guards, and they led me away and over the brow of the hill, that the Moot might speak its mind on me. There my guards bade me sit down, and I did so, resting head on hands, and thinking of nought, as it seemed to me, until suddenly rose up hate of Matelgar, and of Eanulf, and of all that great assembly, and of all the world.

There was an earthquake once when I was but a boy, and never could I forget how it was as though all things one had deemed solid and secure had suddenly become treacherous as Severn ooze. And now it was to me as though an earthquake had shaken my thoughts of men. For, till that day, never had I found cause to distrust anyone who was friend of mine. Now could I trust none.

Then rose up in my mind the image of Alswythe, fair, and blue eyed, and brown haired, smiling at me as she was wont. And I deemed her, too, false, as having tricked me to meet her that this might come upon me.

Well it was that they called me back into the ring to hear my doom, for such thoughts as these will drive a man to madness. Now must I think for myself again, and meet what must be. Yet I would look at no man as I went towards the place of my judges, and stood before them with my eyes cast down. For I was beaten, and cared no more for aught.

Eanulf spoke; but he had no anger in his voice and it seemed as though he repeated the words of others.

"Heregar, son of Herewulf," he said, "these things have been brought against you by honourable men, and you cannot disprove them -- hardly can you deny them. They may not be passed over; yet for the sake of your youth, and for the pleading of Ealhstan, our Bishop, your doom shall be lighter than some think fit. Death it might be; but that shall not pass now on you, or for this. But Thane you may be no longer, and we do confirm that sentence. Landless also you must be, as unworthy to hold it. Outlaw surely must he be who plots against the Head of law."

He paused a moment, and then said:

"This, then, is your doom. Outlawed you are from this day forward, but wolf's head ii you shall not be. None in all Wessex shalt harbour you or aid you, but none shall you harm, save you harm them. Go hence from this place and from this land, to some land where no man knows you; and so shall you rest again."

Now, had I not been blinded with rage and shame, I might have seen that there was mercy in this sentence, and hope also. For I had seen a man outlawed once, and given a day's start, like some wild beast, in which to fly from the hand of every man that would seek his life. But I was to be safe from such harm, and but that I must go hence, I was not to be hounded forth, nor was my shame to be published beyond Wessex. So that all the other kingdoms lay open and safe to me.

None of this I heeded; I only knew that my enemies had got the mastery, and that ruin was upon me. So I ground my teeth and was mute.

Then they cut my bonds and I stood free, but cared not. Nor did I stir from my place; and a look of surprise crossed Eanulf's face. But Ealhstan the Bishop, knowing well, I think, what was in my mind, rose from his seat, and came to me, laying his hands on my shoulders. I would have shaken them off; but be kept them there gently, and spoke to me.

"Heregar, my son," he said, and his words were like the cool of a shower after heat, to my burning brain, "be not cast down in the day of your trouble overmuch. There are yet things for you to do in this world of ours, and the ways of men are not all alike. Foolish you have been, Heregar, my son, but the Lord who gave wisdom to Solomon the youth, will give to you, if you will ask Him. Go your way in peace, and if you will heed my words, take your trouble to some wise man of God, and so be led by his counsel. And, Heregar," and here the bishop's voice was for me alone, "if you need forgiveness, forgive if there is aught by you to be forgiven."

Then I knew that the bishop, at least, believed in my innocence, and my hard heart bent before him, though my body would not. He laid his hand on my head for one moment, and so left me.

One of my father's old friends rose up and said:

"Ealdorman, he is unarmed. Give him that which will keep him from wanton attack, or from the wolves, even if it be but a thrall's weapons."

Eanulf signed assent.

On that they gave me a woodman's billhook, and a seax,iii such as the churls wear, and one thrust a good ash, iron-shod quarterstaff into my hands. Then my guards led me away from the assembly, and set my face towards the downward path. Once again the old man spoke to me with words of good counsel.

"Keep up heart, master. Make for Cornwall, and turn viking with the next Danes who come."

I would not answer him, but walked down the hill a little. Then the bitterness of my heart overcame me, and I turned, and shaking my staff up at the hill, cursed the Moot deeply.

So I went -- an outlaw.

II: THE FIGHT WITH TWO

Now whither I went for the next two hours I cannot tell, for my mind was heedless of time or place or direction -- only full of burning hate of all men, and of Matelgar most of all. And though that has long passed away from me, so that I may even think of him now as the pleasant comrade in field and feast that he once was, I wonder not at all I then felt; for this treachery had come on me so unawares, and was so deep.

Wherever it was I wandered it took me away from men, and at last, when I roused myself to a knowledge again of the land round me, I was hard on the borders of Sedgemoor Waste; and the sun was low down, and near setting.

Perhaps I had not roused even then; but it came into my mind that I was followed, and that for some time past I had heard, as in a dream, the noise of footsteps not far behind me. Now, since I was in the glade of a little wood, a snapping stick broke the dream, and I started and turned.

Where I stood was in the shadow, but twenty paces from me a red, level sunbeam came past the tree trunks, and made a bright patch of light on the new growing grass beneath the half-clad branches. And, even as I turned, into that patch of light came two of Matelgar's men, walking swiftly, as if here at last they would overtake me. And, moreover, that sunlight lit on drawn swords in their hands; so that in a moment I knew that his hate followed me yet, and that for him the Moot had been too merciful in not slaying me then and there, so that these were on that errand for him.

Then all earth and sky grew red before my eyes, for here seemed to me the beginning of my revenge; and before these two knew that I had turned, out of the dim shadow I leapt upon them, silent, with that quarterstaff aloft. Dazzled they were with the sunlight, and thinking least of all of my turning thus swiftly, if at all. And I was as one of the Berserks of whom men spoke -- caring not for death if only I might slay one of those who had wrought me wrong.

Into the face of that one to the left flew the iron-shod end of the heavy staff and he fell; and as the other gave back a pace, I whirled it round to strike his head. He raised his sword to guard the blow, and that fell in shivers as I smote it. Then a second blow laid him across his comrade, senseless.

Then I stood over them and rejoiced; and part of my anger and shame seemed to pass into the lust of revenge begun well. I knew the men as two of Matelgar's housecarles, and that made it the sweeter to see them lie thus helpless before me.

I knew not if they were dead yet, but I would make sure. So I leaned my staff against a tree, and drew the sharp seax from my belt.

Then came into my mind the words of my father, who would ever tell me that he is basest who would slay an unarmed foe, or smite a fallen man; and hastily I put back the seax again, lest I should be tempted to become base as men had said I was; for I hold treachery to be of the same nature as that of which my father warned me.

I took back my staff and leant on it, thinking, and looking at those men. They were the first I had ever met in earnest, and this was the first proof of the skill in arms my father had spent long years in giving me. So there crept over me a pride that I had met two and overcome them -- and I unarmed, as we count it, against mail-clad men. Then I thought that Herewulf, my father, would be proud of me could he see this.

And then, instantly, the shame of what had led to this swallowed up all my pride; and with that thought of my father's loved and honoured name, my hard heart was broken, and I leant my head against a tree, and wept bitterly.

One of the men stirred, and I sprang round hurriedly. It was the second man, whose sword I had broken. He had been but stunned, and now sat up as one barely awake, and unaware of what had happened. I might not slay him now, but quick as I could I took off my own broad leather belt and pinioned him from behind. He was yet too dazed to resist. And then I took his dagger from him, and bound his feet with his own belt, dragging him away from his comrade, and setting him against a tree. There he sat, blinking at me, but becoming more himself quickly.

Then I looked at the other man. He was dead, for the end of the quarterstaff had driven in his forehead, so madly had I struck at him with all my weight.

And now, seeing that I was cooler and might think more clearly, it seemed to me that it would be bitter to Matelgar that out of his wish to destroy me should come help to myself. I needed arms, and now I had but to take them from his own armoury, as it were. Well armed were all his housecarles, and this one I had slain was their captain, and his byrnie of linked mail was of the best Sussex steel, and his helm was crested with a golden boar, with linked mail tippet hanging to protect the neck. And his sword -- but as my eyes fell on that my heart gave a great leap of joy

-- for it was my own! Mine, too, was the baldric from which it hung, and mine was the seax that balanced it, close to the right hand in the belt.

As I saw that I began to know more of the plans of Matelgar -- for it must be that my hall and all my goods had fallen into his hands, and this was the reward his head man had asked and been given.

And now I minded that this man had been one of those who gave evidence of my lonely rides and secret meetings. So he had been bought thus, for my sword was a good one, and the hilt curiously wrought in ivory and silver.

Then I made no more delay, but stripped the man of his armour, and also of the stout leathern jerkin he wore beneath it, for I was clad in the rags of feasting garb, as I have said, and hated them even as I threw them aside. The man was of my own height and build, as it chanced, and his gear fitted me well. So I took his hide shoes also, casting away my frayed velvet foot coverings into the underwood.

Now once more I stood clad in the arms of a free man and how good it was to feel again the well known and loved weight of mail, and helm, and sword tugging at me I cannot say. But this I know, that, like the strong man of old our old priest told me of, as I shook myself, my strength and manhood came back to me.

But now, whereas I had been haled from my feasting a careless boy, and had stood before my judges as an angry man, as I look back, I see that from that arming I rose up a grim and desperate warrior with wrongs to right, and the will and strength to right them.

So I stood for a little, and the savage thoughts that went through my mind I may not write. Then I turned to my captive and looked at him, though I thought nothing concerning him. But what he saw written in my face as it glowered on him from under the helmet bade him cry aloud to me to spare him.

And at that I laughed. It was so good to feel that this enemy of mine feared me. At that laugh -- and it sounded not like my own, even to myself -- the man writhed, and besought me again for mercy. But I had no mind to kill him, and a thought crossed me.

"Matelgar bade you slay me," I said, "that I know. Tell me why he has sought my life and I will spare you."

"Master," said the man hastily, "I knew not whom I was to slay. Matelgar bade me follow Gurth yonder, and smite whom he smote."

"It would have mattered not -- you would have slain me as well as any other."

"Nay, master," the man said earnestly, "that would I not."

"You lie," I answered curtly enough; "like master like man. Tell me what I bade you."

"Truly I lie not, Heregar," cried he, "for I love my mistress over well to harm you."

Now at that mention of Alswythe the blood rushed into my face, for I had held her false with the rest, and this seemed to say otherwise, unless the plot had been hidden from such as this man. But I would fain learn more of that, for the sake of the hope of a love I had thought true.

"What is your mistress to me?" I asked. "Ye are all alike."

I think the man could see well at what I aimed, for he spoke of the Lady Alswythe more freely than he would have dared at other times, nor would I have let him name her lightly.

"Our mistress has gone sadly since the day you were taken, master; even asking me to tell her, if I could, where you were kept, thinking me one of those who guarded you, mayhap. But I knew not till today what had chanced to you. Men may know well from such tokens what is amiss."

Hearing that, my heart lightened within me, for I saw that the man spoke truth. However, I would not speak more of this to such as he, and I bade him cease his prating, and answer plainly my first question, laying my hand on my seax as if to draw it.

"Gurth could have told you; master," he cried, "but he is dead. Matelgar held no counsel with me. I can but tell you what the talk is among the men."

"Tell it."

"Because Matelgar had taken charge, as he said, of your lands while you were away, and knowing well that in your taking he had had some hand, men say it is to get possession thereof; and the women say that, while you were near, the Lady Alswythe would marry no other, so that he had had you removed."

The first I had guessed by the token of the sword that I had regained. That last was sweet to hear.

"Go on," I said. "How came Matelgar to have power to hold my lands?"

"There came one from the king, after you were taken, giving him papers with a great seal thereon, and these he read aloud in your hall, showing the king's own hand at the end. So men bowed thereto, and all your men he drove out if they would not serve him, and few remained. The rest have taken service elsewhere if they were free."

So Matelgar was in possession, and now would be confirmed in the same. What mattered that to an outlaw? But I could have borne anything better than to think of him sitting in my place as reward for his treachery. This was evidence of weakness, however, in his case, that he should have tried to have me slain.

Now I had learnt all I needed, and more, in the one thing next my heart, than I hoped, if that were true -- for still I could not but doubt the faith of all. Only one thing more I would ask, and that was if Matelgar bided in his own or my hall. The man told me that he kept in his own place.

"Now," said I, "I had a mind to leave you bound here for the wolves, but you shall take a message to your master."

On that the man swore to do my bidding, or, if I would, to follow me.

"Save your oaths," I said. "I have heard a many today, and I hold them as nothing. Take these cast rags of mine, and bear them back to your master. Give them to him, and then say to him whatsoever you will -- either that you have slain me and these are the tokens, but that Gurth was by me slain, and you must leave him and his arms here because of the wolves which you feared; or else you can tell him the truth, as it has happened, and see what he does to you. I mind how he hung up a thrall of his by the thumbs once for two days. He will surely take good care of one of two who were beaten by an unarmed man. But I think the lie will come easiest to your master's man."

Thus spoke I bitterly, and cut the belt which bound the man's arms, thinking all the while that he would never go back at all if he were wise. But he said he would go back and tell the lie, and I laughed at him.

It was dusk now, and though I feared not the man, I would play with him yet a little longer in my bitterness. So I bade him keep still, and stir not till I gave him leave. His feet were yet bound, and he would need an edge-tool to loose that binding. Telling him, then, that I would not run the chance of his falling on me from behind, I took his dagger and the seax they had given me, and stuck them in the ground a full hundred yards away, and then bade him, when I was out of sight, crawl thither as best he might and so loose himself.

The poor wretch was too glad to be spared to do aught but repeat that he would do my errand faithfully, and thank me; and, but for the sort of madness that was still on me, I must have been ashamed to torture him so. I am sorry now as I think of it, and many a man who has well deserved punishment have I let go since that day, fearing lest that old cruelty should be on me again, perhaps.

Then I turned and walked away, and even as I passed the weapons, I heard the low howl of a wolf from the swamp to my right. Far off it was, but at that sound the man cast himself on hands and knees and began to crawl in all haste to free himself.

Then I laughed again, and plunging deeper into the wood, lost sight of him.

III: BY BELL, BOOK, AND CANDLE

I had never been into Sedgemoor before, and so went straight on as I could, only turning aside from swampy places while the light lasted. Then I must wait for the moon to rise, and I sat me down under an old thorn tree on a little rise where I could see about me. I had come out of the woods, and all the moor was open to the west and south so far as I could see. I knew that the place was haunted of evil spirits, and shunned at night time by all: but now I was not afraid of them -- or indeed of anything, save the wolves. The terror of the man I had left had put that fear into my head, or I think that, desperate as I was, only the sound of a pack of them in full cry would have warned me. Still, I had heard no more since that one howled an hour ago.

Cold mists rose from the marsh, and in them I could see lights flitting. A month or two ago I should have feared them, thinking of Beowulf, son of Hygelac, and what befell him and his comrades from the marsh fiends, Grendel and his dam. Now I watched them, and half longed for a fight like Beowulf's.iv

At last the moon rose behind me, and I walked on. Once a vast shape rose up in the mist and walked beside me, and I half drew my sword on it. But that, too, drew sword, and I knew it for my own shadow on the thick vapour. Then a sheet of water stretched out almost under my feet, and thousands of wildfowl rose and fled noisily, to fall again into further pools with splash and mighty clatter. I must skirt this pool, and so came presently to a thicket of reeds, shoulder high, and out of these rose, looking larger than natural in the moonlight, a great wild boar that had his lair there, and stood staring at me before he too made off, grunting as he went.

So I went on aimless. The night was full of sounds, but whether earthly; from wildfowl and bittern and curlew, from fox, and badger, and otter; or from the evil spirits of the marsh, I knew not nor cared. For now the long imprisonment and the day's terrible doings, and the little food I had had since we halted on the hill of Brent, all began to get hold of me, and I stumbled on as a man in a bad dream.

But nothing harmed or offered to harm me. Only when some root or twisted tussock of grass would catch my foot and hinder me I cursed it for being in league with Matelgar, tearing my way fiercely over or through it. And at last, I think, my mind wandered.

Then I saw a red light that glowed close under the edge of some thick woodland, where the land rose, and that drew me. It was the hut of a charcoal burner, and the light came from the kiln close by, which was open, and the man himself was standing at it, even now taking out a glowing heap of the coal to cool, before he piled in fresh wood and closed it for the night.

When I saw the hut, it suddenly came on me that I was wearied out, and must sleep, and so went thither. The collier heard the clank of my armour, and turned round in the crimson light of the glowing coals to see what came. As he saw me standing he cried aloud in terror, and, throwing up his hands, fled into the dark beyond the kiln, calling on the saints to protect him.

For a moment I wondered that he should thus fly me; but I staggered to his hut, and I remember seeing his rush-made bed, and that is all.

When I woke again, at first I thought myself back in the dungeon, and groaned, but would not open my eyes. But I turned uneasily, and then a small voice spoke, saying:

"Ho, Grendel! are you awake?"

I sat up and looked round. Then I knew where I was -- but I had slept a great sleep, for out of the open door I saw the Quantock hills, blue across the moor, and the sun shone in almost level. It was late afternoon.

I looked for him who had spoken, and at first could see no one, for the sun shone in my face: but something stirred in a corner, and I looked there.

It was a small sturdy boy of some ten years old, red haired, and freckled all over where his woollen jerkin and leather hose did not cover him. He sat on a stool and stared at me with round eyes.

I stared back at him for a minute, and then, from habit, for I would always play with children, made a wry face at him, at which he smiled, pleased enough, and said:

"Spit fire, good Grendel, I want to see."

Now I was glad to be kept off my own fierce thoughts for a little, and so answered him back, wondering at the name he gave me, and at his request.

"So -- I am Grendel, am I?"

"Aye," said the urchin, "Dudda Collier ran into village in the night, saying that you had come out of the fen, all fire from head to foot, and so he fled. But I came to see."

"Where is the collier then?"

"He dare not come back, he says, without the priest, and has gone to get the hermit. So the other folk bided till he came too."

"Were not you afraid of me?"

"Maybe I was feared at first -- but I would see you spit fire before the holy man drives you away. So I looked in through a crack, and saw you asleep. Then I feared not, and bided your waking for a little time."

"What is your name, brave urchin?' I asked, for I was pleased with the child and his fearlessness.

"Turkil," he said.

"Well, Turkil -- I am not Grendel. He fled when I came in here."

"Did you beat him?" asked the boy, with a sort of disappointment.

"Nay; but he disappeared when the hot coals went out," I said. "And now I am hungry, can you find me aught to eat?" and, indeed, rested as I was with the long sleep, I had waked sound in mind and body again, and longed for food, and I think that finding this strange child here to turn my thoughts into a wholesome channel, when first they began to stir in me, was a mercy that I must ever be thankful for.

Turkil got up solemnly and went to the hearth. Thence he took an iron cauldron, and hoisted it on the great round of tree trunk that served as table in the midst of the hut.

"Dudda Collier left his supper when he fled. Wherefore if we eat it he will think Grendel got it -- and no blame to us," remarked the boy, chuckling.

And when I thought how I had not a copper sceatta left me in the world, I stopped before saying that I would pay him when he returned, and so laughed back at the boy and fell to.

When we had finished, the cauldron, which had been full of roe deer venison, was empty, and Turkil and I laughed at one another over it.

"Grendel or no Grendel," said the urchin, "Dudda will ask nought of his supper."

"Why not?"

"By reason of what it was made of."

Then I remembered that a thrall might by no means slay the deer, and that he would surely be in fear when he knew that one had found him out. So I said to the boy:

"Grendel ate it, doubtless. Nor you nor I know what was in the honest man's pot."

Turkil was ready to meet me in this matter, and looking roguishly at me, gathered up the bones and put them into the kilns.

"Now must I go home," he said, when this was done, "or I shall be beaten. But I would I had seen Grendel -- though I love warriors armed like you."

"Verily, Turkil, my friend," said I, "a stout warrior will you be if you go on as you have begun."

Thereupon something stirred within me, as it were, and I took the urchin and kissed him, for I had never thought to call one "friend" again.

Then I feared to let him go from me, lest the thoughts of yesterday should come back, as I knew they would, did I give way to them. So I told him to bide here with me till the village people came to drive away Grendel, and that I would make all right for him.

Then we went out of the little hut, and sat on the logs of timber, and he told me tales of the wood and stream and meres to which I must answer now and then, while I pondered over what I must do and where betake myself.

My outlawry would not be known till the people had got home from Brent, and then but by hearsay, till the sheriff's men had proclaimed me in the townships.

This place, too, where a man could slay roe deer fearless of discovery, must be far from notice, and I would bide here this next night, and so make my plans well, and grow fully rested. But always, whatever I thought, was revenge on Matelgar uppermost.

Now Turkil would see my sword, and then my seax, and try my helm on his head, laughing when it covered his eyes, and I had almost bade him come to my hall at Cannington and there try the little weapons I had when I was his size, so much his ways took from me the thought of my trouble. But that slip brought it all back again, and for a time I waxed moody, so that the child was silent, finding no answer to his prattle, and at last leant against me and slept. Presently, I leaned back and slept too, in the warm sun.

I woke with the sound of chanting in my ears, and the ringing of a little bell somewhere in the wood; but Turkil slept on, and I would not stir to wake him, sitting still and wondering.

Then out of the wood came towards the hut a little procession, and when I saw it I knew that I, as Grendel, was to be exorcised. But though I thought not of it, exorcism there had been already, and that of my evil spirit of yesterday, by the fearless hand of -- a little child.

There came first an old priest, fully vested, bearing a great service book in one hand, and in the other a crucifix, and reading as he went, but in Latin, so that I could not know what he read. And on either side of him were two youths, also vested, one bearing a great candle that flared and guttered in the wind, and the other a bell, which now and then he rang when the old priest ceased reading between the verses.

After these came the villagers. I saw the collier among the first, and his knees shook as he walked. Then some of the men were armed with bills and short swords, and a few with bows. All, I think, had staves. After them came some women, and I saw one who wept, looking about her eagerly.

They did not see me, for the timber pile was next the kiln and a little behind it; so that before they got near I was shut out from view for a time.

While they were thus hidden from me, they stopped and began to chant again, priest and people in turn. After that had gone on for a little time, Turkil woke and sat up, but I bade him in a whisper to be silent, and putting his finger in his mouth he obeyed, wide eyed.

Then the little bell gave a note or two, and the reading began, so near that I could hear the words, or seem to remember them as I know now what they were.

"Adjuro te maleficum Grendel vocatum diabolum --"

So far had the priest got when they turned the corner of the house, and I stood up. There came a shout from the men, and the exorcism went no further, for the old priest saw at once, as it seemed, that I was but a mortal. Not so some of his train, for several turned to fly, sorely fearing that the wrestle between the powers spiritual had begun, and, as one might think, lacking faith in their own side, for they showed little.

But Grendel or no Grendel, there was one who thought not of her own safety. That woman whom I had seen weeping gave a great cry and rushed at me, seizing my little comrade from my arms, for I had lifted him as I stood, and covering him with kisses, chided him and petted at the same time.

It was his mother, who hearing that her darling had wandered away from his playmates with the intention of "seeing Grendel" as he avowed, had dared to join the rest to learn what had been his end.

The old priest looked on this with something of a smile, and then turned to his people saying:

"Doubtless the fiend has fled, or this warrior and the child had not been here. Search, my children, and see if there be traces left of his presence, and I will speak to the stranger."

They scattered about the place in groups, for they yet feared to be alone, and the priest came up to me, scanning my arms as he did so, to guess my rank. My handsome sword and belt seemed to decide him, for though the armour and helm were plain, they were good enough for any thane who meant them for hard wear and not for show.

"Sir," he said, very courteously but without any servility, "I see you are a stranger, and you meet me on a strange errand. I am the priest whom they call the hermit, Leofwine -- should I name you thane?"

I was going to answer him as I would have replied but yesterday morning -- so hesitated a little, and then answered shortly.

"No thane, Father, but the next thing to it -- a masterless man."

"As you will, sir," he replied, thinking that I doubtless had my own reason for withholding whatever rank I had. "We meet few strangers in this wild."

"I lost my way, Father," I said, "and wandered here in the night, and, being sorely weary, slept in this empty hut till two hours ago, waking to find yon child here."

Now little Turkil, seeing that I looked towards him, got free from his mother and ran to me, saying that he must go home, and that I must speak for him, as his mother was wroth with him for playing truant.

The woman, who seemed to be the wife of some well-to-do freeman, followed him, and I spoke to her, begging her to forgive the boy, as he had been a pleasant comrade to me, and that, indeed, I had kept him, as he said some folk were coming from the village.

Whereon she thanked me for tending him, saying that she had feared the foul fiend whom the collier had seen would surely have devoured him. So I pleased her by saying that a boy who would face such a monster now would surely grow up a valiant man. Then Turkil must kiss me in going, bidding me come and see him again, and I knew not how to escape promising that, though it was a poor promise that could not be kept, seeing that I must fly the kingdom of Wessex as soon as I might. Then his mother took him away, he looking back often at me. With them went the most of the people, some wondering, but the greater part laughing at Dudda Collier's fright.

I asked the old priest where the village might be, and he told me that it lay in a clearing full two miles off, and that the father of Turkil was the chief franklin there, though of little account elsewhere. He had not yet come back from the great Moot at Brent, and that was good hearing for me, for though he must return next day, I should be far by that time.

While we talked, the collier and two or three men came to us, telling excitedly how that the kiln was raked out, and that the cauldron was empty -- doubtless the work of the fiend.

"Saw you aught of any fiend, good sir?" asked the priest of me.

Now I remembered the roe deer in time, and answered, "I saw nought worse than myself" -- but I think that, had the collier known my thoughts, he would have fled me as he fled that he took me for. But that he was sore terrified I have no doubt, for it seemed that he neither recognized me, nor remembered what he was doing at the kiln when I came. Maybe, as often happens, he had told some wild story to so many that he believed it himself.

"Then, my sons," said the hermit, "the fiend finding Dudda no prey of his, departed straightway, and he need fear no more."

However, they would have him sprinkle all the place with holy water, repeating the proper prayers the while, which he did willingly, knowing the fears of his people, and gladly trying to put them to rest.

Then the collier begged one after another to bide with him that night, but all refused, having other things to be done which they said might not he foregone. It was plain that they dared not stay; but this seemed to be my chance.

The men had many times looked hard at me, but as I was speaking with the priest, dared not question me as they would. So having seen this, I said:

"I am a stranger from beyond the Mendips, and lost my way last night coming back from Brent. Glad should I be of lodging here tonight, and guidance on the morrow, for it is over late for me to be on my way now."

That pleased the collier well enough, and he said he would take me in, and guide me where I would go next day. The other men wanted to ask me news of the Moot, but I put them off, saying that I had not sat thereon, but had passed there on my way from Sherborne. So they were content, and asking the hermit for his blessing, they went their way.

Then the old priest took off the vestments which were over his brown hermit garb, and giving them to the youths who had acted as his acolytes bade them depart also, having given them some directions, and so we three, the hermit, collier, and myself, were left alone by the hut.

The hermit bade the collier leave us, and he, evidently holding the old man in high veneration, bowed awkwardly, and went to fill and relight his kiln fires.

And then the old priest spoke to me.

"Sir, I was brought here, as you see, to drive away an evil spirit, which this poor thrall said had appeared to him last night, and from which he fled. Now all men know that these fens are haunted by fiends, even as holy Guthlac found in the land of the Gyrwa's,v being sorely troubled by them. But I have seen none, though I dwell in this fen much as he dwelt, though none so worthy, or maybe worth troubling as he. Know you what he saw? for I seem to see that your coming has to do with this --" and the old man smiled a little.

Then I told him how I had come unexpectedly into the firelight, and that the man had fled, adding that I was nigh worn out, and so, finding a resting place, slept without heeding him; and then how little Turkil had called me "Grendel", bidding me "spit fire for him to see".

At that the old man laughed a hearty laugh, looking sidewise to see that Dudda was at work and unheeding.

"Verily," he said, "it is as I deemed, but with more reason for the collier to fly than I had thought -- for truly mail-clad men are never seen here, and thy face, my son, is of the grimmest, for all you are so young. I marvel Turkil feared you not -- but children see below the outward mask of a man's face."

Now as he said that, the old man looked kindly, but searchingly, at me, and I rebelled against it: but he was so saintly looking that I might not be angry, so tried to turn it off.

"Turkil the Valiant called me Grendel, Father. Also I think you came out to exorcise the same by name, for I heard it in the Latin. But that was a heathen fiend."

The hermit sighed a little and answered me.

"They sing the song of Beowulf and love it, heathen though it be, better than aught else, and will till one rises up who will turn Holy Writ into their mother tongue, as Caedmon did for Northumbria. Howbeit, doubtless those who were fiends in the days of the false gods are fiends yet, and if Grendel then, so also Grendel now, though he may have many other names. And knowing that name from their songs, small wonder that the terror that came from the marsh must needs be he. And, no doubt," went on the good priest, though with a little twinkle in his eye, "he knew well enough whom I came to exorcise, even if the name were wrong, had he indeed been visibly here."

So he spoke: but my mind was wandering away to my own trouble; and when I spoke of Sherborne just now, the thought of Bishop Ealhstan and his words had come to me, and I wondered if I would tell my troubles to this old man as he bade me. But, though to think of it showed that I was again more myself, something of yesterday's bitterness rose up again as the scene at the Moot came back, and I would not.

The priest was silent for a while, and must have watched my face as these thoughts hardened it again.

"Be not wroth with an old man, my son," he said, very gently; "but there is some trouble on your mind, as one who has watched the faces of men as long as I may well see. And it is bitter trouble, I fear. Sometimes these troubles pass a little, by being told."

The kind words softened me somewhat, and I answered him quietly:

"Aye, Father -- there is trouble, but not to be told. I will take myself and it away in the morning, and so bear it by myself."

He looked wistfully at me as one who fain would help another, saying:

"Other men's troubles press lightly on such as I, my son, save that they add to my prayers."

And I was half-minded to tell him all and seek his counsel: but I would not. Still, I would answer him, and so feigning cheerfulness, said:

"One trouble, Father, I fear you cannot help me in. I have nought wherewith to reward this honest man for lodging and guidance -- nor for playing Grendel on him, and eating his food to boot."

"Surely you have honest hands by whom to send him somewhat? or he will lead you to friends who will willingly lend to you?"

And I had neither. I, who but a few weeks ago could have commanded both by scores -- and now none might aid me. None might call me friend -- I was alone. These words brought it home to me more clearly than before, and the loneliness of it sank into my heart, and my pride fled, and I told the good man all, looking to see him shrink from me.

But he did not, hearing me patiently to the end. I think if he had shrunk from me, the telling had left me worse than when I kept it hid from him.

When I ended, he laid his hand on my shoulder -- even as the bishop had laid his, and said:

"Vengeance is mine. I will repay, saith the Lord."

And I, who had never heard those words before, thought them a promise sent by the mouth of this prophet, as it were, to me, and wondered. Then he went on:

"Surely, my son, I believe you to be true, and that you suffer wrongfully, for never one who would lie told the evil of himself as you have told me. Foolish you have been, indeed, as is the way of youth, but disloyal you were not."

I was silent, and waited for him to speak such words again. And he, too, was silent for a little, looking out over the marsh, and rocking himself to and fro as he sat on the tree trunk beside me.

"Watching and praying and fasting alone, there has been given me some little gift of prophecy, my son; now and then it comes, but never with light cause. And now I will say what is given me to say. Cast out you are from the Wessex land, but before long Wessex shall be beholden to you. Not long shall Matelgar, the treacherous, hold your place -- but you shall be in honour again of all men. Only must you forego your vengeance and leave that to the hand of the Lord, who repays."

"What must I do now, Father?" I asked, in a low voice.

"Go your own way, my son, and, as you were bidden, depart from this kingdom as you will and whither; and what shall be, shall be. Fighting there is for you, both within and without: but the battle within will be the sorest: for I know that the longing for revenge will abide with you, and that is hard to overcome. Yet remember the message of forbearance."

Then I cried out that I must surely be revenged and the good man strove with me with many and sweet words, till he had quieted the thought within me again. Yet I longed for it.

So we talked till the sun sank, and he must go ere darkness fell. But at last he bade me kneel, and I knelt, who had thought in my pride never to humble myself before mortal man again, till one dealt me my death blow and I needs must fall before him.

So he blessed me and departed, bidding me remember that at sunrise and midday and sunset, Leofwine, the priest, and Turkil, the child, should remember me in their prayers. And, for he was very thoughtful, he told me that he would take such order with the collier that he would ask nought from me, nor must I offer him anything, save thanks. And he spoke to him in going.

I watched him go till I could see him no more, and then, calling my host, supped with him, and slept peacefully till the first morning light.

IV: THE SECRET MEETING

I woke before the collier, who slept across the doorway on some skins, and lay in his sleeping place for half an hour, thinking of what should be before me, and whither I would go this day.

And, thinking quietly enough now, I made the resolve to leave at all events my revenge that I had so longed for to sleep for a while -- for the words of the good priest had bided with me, and moreover, I had some hope from his words of prophecy. So I would see how that turned out, and then, if nought came of it, I would turn to my revenge again.

So having got thus far, the advice of the gray-haired warrior seemed as good as any, for it was easy to me to get into West Wales, and then take service with the under-king until such time as Danish or Norse vikings put in thither, as they would at times for provender, or to buy copper and tin from the miners.

But then a great longing came over me to see Alswythe once more, and learn the truth of her faith or falseness. The man I had bound seemed to speak truth, though she was the daughter of Matelgar. Yet if she were child of that false man, I had known her mother well, and loved her until she died a year ago. And she was a noble lady, and full of honesty.

Now as safe a way as any into the Westland would be over the Quantocks, and so into the wilds of Dartmoor and beyond, where no man would know or care for my outlawry -- if, indeed, I found not more proscribed men there than anywhere, who had fled, as I must fly, but with a price on them. And if I fled that way, it was but a step aside to pass close to Matelgar's hall.

It was the least safe path for me, it is true -- for I had had a taste of what sort of reception I should meet with at his hands did he catch me or meet with me. But love drew me, and I would venture and see at least the place where the one I loved dwelt.

Having made up my mind to that, I was all impatience to be going, and woke the collier, saying that I must be afoot. He, poor man, started up in affright, dreaming doubtless that the fiend had returned, but recovered himself, making a low obeisance to me, quickly.

Then he brought out bread of the coarsest and cheese of the best, grumbling that the fiend had devoured his better cheer. And I, being light hearted, having made up my mind, and being young enough not to look trouble in the face too long, asked him if he had none of the roe deer left over?

Whereat he started, and looked terrified at me. Then I laughed, and said that Grendel had told me what was in the pot, and the man, seeing that I was not angry, began to grin also, wondering. Then the meaning of the whole business seemed to come to him, and he sat down and began to laugh, looking at me from under his brows now and then, lest I should be wroth with him for the freedom. But I laughed also, and so in the end we two sat and laughed till the tears came, opposite one another, and that was a thing that I had never thought to do again. At last I stopped, and then he made haste to compose himself.

"Master," he said, "forgive me. But if you were Grendel, as I think now, there is a great fear off my mind."

"I was Grendel, Dudda," said I; "but you must have a sorely evil conscience to be so easily frighted."

"Nay, master; but from week to week I see none, least of all at midnight, and mail-clad men never at all. I think I am the only man who fears not this marsh and what may haunt it."

"That you may never boast again," said I; "for scared you were, and that badly!"

"It is between you and me, master," said he, with much cunning in his look; "as I pray the matter of what was in the cauldron may be also --"

"Well, as for that," I answered, "I ate it, and was glad of it, so I will not inquire how it came there."

But I was glad to have this secret as a sort of hold over this man, for thralls are not to be trusted far, nor was I in a mood to put much faith in any.

After that we ate in silence, and when we had finished, he put a loaf and a half cheese into a wallet, and took a staff, and asked me to command him. I knew not what the hermit had told him, so asked how much he had learned of my errand.

"That you are on king's business, master, and in haste. Moreover that your errand is secret, so that you would not be seen in town or village on your way."

"That is right," I said, thanking in my mind the good hermit, whose ready wit had made things so easy for me; moreover it was truthful enough, for outlawry is king's business in all earnest, though not the honour this poor thrall doubtless thought was put on me.

Then I told him that I need ask him but to guide me beyond Parret river, on this side of Bridgwater, for after that the long line of the Quantocks would guide me well enough. It was all I needed, for once out of this fenland I knew the country well -- aye, every furlong of it -- but I was willing enough to let him guide me through land I knew, that if ever he were questioned -- as he might well be when my outlawry was known -- his tale of my little knowledge of the country would make men think me some stranger, and so no blame would come on him for harbouring me.

So we started in the bright early morning, and he guided me well. There is little to say of that journey, but finding from the man's talk that the Moot rose not until the next day, I thought, with a lifting of my heart, how Matelgar would likely enough be yet there, and that I might almost in safety, unless he had sent word back concerning me to his men, go and try to gain speech of Alswythe.

Now it chanced presently that, looking about me, I seemed to know the lie of a woodland through which we passed, and in a little was sure we were in that glade where I fought my fight. And next, I saw my quarterstaff still resting against the tree where I had left it. The collier saw it too, and said that some forester was doubtless resting close by, seeming uneasy about the same. But I said that no question should be made of his presence in the wood, if it were so, and we came up to it. Then he started, and cried to me to look around.

My billhook, covered with new rust from the dew, lay where I had thrown it in stripping off my own garments to arm myself; but of the man I had slain only scattered bones were left. The wolves had devoured him.

When I saw that, I thought that this dead man might as well pass for myself -- Heregar, the outlaw. So I examined billhook and quarterstaff, and at last said I knew them. They had been given to one Heregar, who had been outlawed and driven from the Moot even as I stood to watch the gathering as I passed by.

"Then his outlawry has ended here," said the collier. "The wolves have devoured him."

"Just as well," I said carelessly. "Shall you take his staff and bill? They are good enough."

"Not I," said the man. "It is ill meddling with strange men's weapons, most of all an outlaw's."

"Mayhap you are wise," I said, and, casting down the things alongside the bones, went on.

Now I had looked all round, and saw that my old garments were gone, so that the man I had let go had at all events started away with them. But now I knew that the news of my death would soon spread, hard on the publishing of the sentence of outlawry, for the doings of an outlaw are of the first interest to those among whom he may wander. As it was, indeed, to my guide, who spoke so much thereof that I knew he would be full of it, and tell it to all whom he met. And when he told me he should go back through the town I was glad, for so Matelgar would have news of the same, confirming the tale of his man, though not accounting for his captain. Whereby he would be puzzled, and his life would be none the easier, for I knew he would dread my vengeance, though it might be hard for me to compass.

At last we crossed the river, and went a little way together into the woods beyond, till we came to the road which should lead the collier back to Bridgwater town. And there I made him give me directions for crossing the Quantocks, as though I would go by Triscombe -- which I feigned to know not, save by name given for my guidance on my way.

I looked for him to ask reward, but he did not, and what the hermit had told him I could not say, unless he had promised him reward on his return. He made a low salutation before me, cap in hand, and I thanked him for his pains, saying that I would not forget him, as I was sure he would not forget "Grendel". And so we laughed, and he went away pleased enough, giving me the wallet of food.

Then was I left alone in the woodlands that had been mine to hunt through, for, holding our land from the king himself, I had many rights that stretched far and wide, which doubtless that Matelgar coveted for himself, and would now enjoy. And hard it was, and bitter exceedingly, not to turn my steps straight through the town, where men had saluted me reverently, to my own hall where it nestles under the great rock that looks out over my low meadows, and away towards Brent across the wide river. But that might not be. So I tried to stay myself with the thought of the hermit's prophecy, and plunging deep into the woods, crossed far back of my own place, until I could circle round towards Matelgar's hall.

And there I must go carefully, lest I should be seen and known by any; but the woods were thick, and none knew them better than I. These things come by nature to a man, and so I should not be proud that the very woodmen would own that I was their master in all the craft of the forest, as my father had been before me.

Now Matelgar's hall, smaller than mine, though as well built, or better, lay in that glen which runs down towards the level meadows of Stert point between Severn and Parret, north of the little hills of Combwich and Stockland, and almost under that last. And there the forest came down the valley -- for it is not enough for me to call a combe -- almost to the rear of the hall and the quickset inclosure around it.

It was afternoon and towards evening when I came here, and I bided in the woods a mile from the hall, in a safe place where none ever came, until I heard the horn which called all men in to sup. Then, when I judged that they had gathered, I struck towards the path that leads down to the hall, keeping yet under cover. One ran in haste towards his supper as I neared it, so I knew that perhaps he was the last to take his place, and that for an hour or two I was secure.

Now in this wood, and not so far from where I was, is a little nook with a fallen tree, and here Alswythe and her mother were wont to come in the warm evenings, and sit while the feeding in hall went on, so soon as they could leave the board. And there, too, I had met Alswythe often lately, sitting and taking pleasure in her company, till she knew that I would want no better companion for all my life.

This was just such an evening as might tempt her there, and I would at least have the sorrow of biding there alone for the last time. So I crept to that place very softly, and sat me down to think.

Maybe I had sat there a quarter of an hour when I heard a step coming, and that step set my heart beating fast, for it was the one I longed for. Then I feared to frighten her with sight of an armed man in her retreat, but before I could move, she came round the bend of the path that made the place private, and saw me.

She gave a little scream, and half turned to fly, for she was alarmed, not knowing me in my arms. And all I could do was to take off my helm and hold out my hands to her, for I could not speak her name in my joy.

Then she laid her hand to her heart, and paused and looked; and before I could step towards her, she was in my arms of her own will; so I was content.

Now how we two found ourselves sitting side by side presently, in the old place, I may hardly say, but so it was. And I forgot all about her father and the evil he had wrought, knowing that she had no part in it, or indeed knowledge thereof.

For when we came to talk quietly, I found that she had thought me dead, and mourned for me: for Matelgar had told her that he knew nought of me. And I would not tell her of his treachery, for he was her father, and so for her sake I made such a tale as I knew he was like to tell her, though maybe the truth would come sooner or later: how that secret enemies had trapped me, and had brought false charges against me, which none of my friends could combat, so skilfully were they wrought, and then how that I was outlawed, and must fly.

And hearing this she wept bitterly, fearing, and with reason, that I should not return.

Then I comforted her with the hermit's prophecy, saying nought of her father. And she, sweet soul, promised that Matelgar should tend my lands and hall well till the words of the holy man came true, and I might take them back from him. And then she added that sorely cast down and troubled had her father seemed when he rode back from the Moot that day, and doubtless it was from this. But how glad would he be to know me living, and even now would take me in and set me on my way, notwithstanding the order of the ealdorman!

Now when I heard that Matelgar was indeed returned, and so close to me, I knew not what to do or say: for all my plans that he should think me dead were like to be overthrown by the talk of this innocent daughter of his.

And she, seeing me troubled, would have me say what it was, and I found it hard to answer her.

At last I told her how even Matelgar dared not harbour or assist me, and cried out on my folly in bringing blame even on her, were my presence known. But she stopped my mouth, telling me most lovingly that the risk was worth the running, so that she knew me living again.

Then I said that, lest harm should come to her father, it were better to keep secret that I had been here. And that, moreover, those enemies of mine would doubtless track me till they knew me gone from the kingdom, so that were a whisper to go abroad that I had been seen here, it might be death for me.

"And for this," I added, "it is likely that Matelgar, your father, will have it spread abroad that I am dead, in his care for my safety. For so will question about me and where I am cease."

This I said lest she should deny when the news came, as it must, that this was so.

Yet she longed to tell her father that I was here; but at last I overpersuaded her, and she promised to tell none, not even him, that she had seen me, and for my sake to feign to believe that I was dead.

Then we must part. I told her my plans for going still westward to make myself a name, if that might be; and promised to let her have news of me, if and when I might, and in all to be true to her.

And she, brave girl, would try not to weep as I kissed her for the last time; and gave me the little silver cross from her neck to keep for her sake, telling me that she would pray for me night and day, and that surely her prayers, and those of the holy man and the innocent child would be heard for me, so that the prophecy would come true. And more she said, which I may not write. Then footsteps came up the main path, and I must go.

I heard her singing as she went back to the hall in the evening light, and knew that that was for my sake, and not for lightness of heart; and so, when her voice died away, I plunged again into the woods, making westward while light lasted.

V: THE VIKINGS ARRIVE

Now after I had parted from Alswythe, my true love, I could not forbear a little heaviness at first, because I knew not when I should see her again. But there is a wonderful magic in youth, and good health, and strength, and yet more in true love requited, which will charm a man from any long heaviness. So before long, as I went through the twilight woodlands towards the mighty Quantock hills, my heart grew light within me; and I even dared to weave histories in my mind of how I would make a name for myself, and so return in high honour by very force of brave deeds done, deeds that should be spoken of through all the land. It is a strange heart in a youth that cannot, or will not, do the like for his future, and surely want of such thoughts will lead him to nothing great, even if it does not bid him sink to the level of his own thralls, as I have known men fall.

However, my heart was full of brave dreamings, always with the thought of Alswythe as my reward at the end; so that I began to long to start my new life, and went on swiftly that I might the sooner leave behind the land that was to be closed to me.

Night fell as I came to the mouth of the long combe that runs up under Triscombe where the road crosses, and to south of it, and I began to wonder how I should lodge for the night. Then I remembered a woodman's hut, deep in the combe, that would serve for shelter, keeping the wolves from me, as it kept them from the woodmen, who made it for the purpose -- the place being far from any village, so that at times they would bide there for nights when much work was on hand. None would be there in Maytime, for the season for felling was long past.

So I found my way to the hut, and there built a fire, and then must, in the dark, grope for a flint wherewith to strike light on steel, but could not find one among the thick herbage. So I sat in the dark, eating my bread and cheese, and thinking how that I was like to make a poor wanderer if I thought not of things such as this. However, I thought my wanderings would last no long time, and as the moon rose soon I was content enough, dreaming of her from whom I had parted so lately.

I will not say that the wish for revenge on Matelgar had clean gone, for him I hated sorely. But for me to strike the blow that I had longed for would be to lose Alswythe, and so I must long for the words of sooth to come true, that I might see revenge by other hands than mine. Then again must I think of hurt to Matelgar as of hurt to Alswythe, so that I dared not ponder much on the matter; but at last was fain to be minded to wait and let the hermit's words work themselves out, and again fall to my dreaming of great deeds to come.

Out of those dreams I had a rough waking, that told me that I was not all a cool warrior yet.

Something brushed by the door of the hut with clatter of dry chips, and snarl, as it went, and my heart stopped, and then beat furiously, while a cold chill went over me with the start, and I sprang up and back, drawing my sword. And it was but a gray badger pattering past the hut, which he feared not, it having been deserted for so long, on his search for food.

Then I was angry with myself, for I could not have been more feared had it been a full pack of wolves; but at last I laughed at my fears, and began to look round the hut in the moonlight. Soon I had shut and barred the heavy door, and laid myself down to sleep, with a log for pillow.

Though sleep seemed long in coming, it came at last, and it was heavy and dreamless, until the sun shone through the chinks between the logs whereof the hut was built, and I woke.

Then I rose up, opened the door, and looked out on the morning. The level sunbeams crept through the trees and made everything very fresh and fair, and a little light frost hung over twigs and young fern fronds everywhere, so that I seemed in the land of fairy instead of the Quantocks. The birds were singing loudly, and a squirrel came and chattered at me, and then, running up a bough, sat up, still as if carved from the wood it was resting on, and watched me seemingly without fear. Then I went down the combe and sought a pool, and bathed, and ate the last of the food the collier had given me. Where I should get more I knew not, nor cared just then, for it was enough to carry me on for the next day and night, if need be, seeing that I had been bred to a hunter's life in the open, and a Saxon should need but one full meal in the day, whether first or last.

Now while I ate and thought, it seemed harder to me to leave these hills and combes that I loved than it had seemed overnight; and at last I thought I would traverse them once again, and so make to the headland, above Watchet and Quantoxhead on either side, and then down along the shore, always deserted there, to the hills above Minehead, by skirting round Watchet, and so on into the great and lonely moors beyond, where I could go into house or hamlet without fear of being known.

Then I remembered that to seek help in the villages must be to ask charity. That would be freely given, doubtless, but would lead to questions, and, moreover, my pride forbade me to ask in that way. Then, again, for a man so subsisting it might be hard to win a way to a great man's favour, though, indeed, a stout warrior was always sure to find welcome with him who had lands to protect, but not so certainly with the other housecarles among whom he would come.

So I began to see that my plight was worse than I thought, and sat there, with my back to an ash tree, while the birds sang round me, and was downcast for a while.

Then suddenly, as I traced the course that I had laid out in my mind, going over the hunts of the old days, when I rode beside my father and since, I bethought me of one day when the stag, a great one of twelve points, took to the sea just this side of Watchet town, swimming out bravely into Severn tide, so that we might hardly see him from the strand. There went out three men in a little skiff to take him, having with them the young son of the owner of the boat. And in some way the boat was overturned, as they came back towing the stag after them, when some hundred or more yards from shore, and in deep water where a swift current ran. Two men clung to the upturned boat; but the other must swim, holding up his son, who, though a big boy of fourteen, was helpless in the water. And I saw that it was like to go hard with both of them, for the current bore them away from shore and boat alike.

So I rode in, and my horse swam well, and we reached them in time, so that I took the boy by his long hair and raised him above the water, while the man, his father, swam beside us, and we got safely back to the beach, they exhausted enough but safe, and I pleased that my good horse did so well.

But the man would have it that I and not the horse saved his son, and was most grateful, bidding me command him in anything all his life long, even to life itself, saying that he owed me both his own and the boy's. And that made me fain to laugh it away, being uneasy at his praise, which seemed overmuch. However, as we rode home, my father said I had made a friend for life, and that one never knew when such would be wanted.

Now this man was a franklin, and by no means a poor one, so now at last I remembered my father's words, and knew that I was glad to have one friend whom I knew well enough would not turn away from me, for I had seen him many times since, and liked him well.

I would go to him, tell him all -- if he had not yet heard it, which was possible -- and so ask him to lend me a few silver pieces in my need. I knew he would welcome the chance of showing the honesty of his words, and might well afford it. Thus would I go, after dark lest I should be seen and he blamed, and so make onward with a lighter heart and freer hand.

So I waited a little longer in the safe recesses of the deep combe until a great gray cloud covered all the tops of the hills above me, and I thought it well to cross the open under its shelter to Holford Coombe, which I did.

There I loitered again, hearing the stags belling at times across the hollows to one another, but hardly wishful to meet with them in their anger. I saw no man, for once I had crossed the highroad none was likely to seek the heights in Maytime. And I think that no one would have known me. For in my captivity my beard had grown, and my hair was longer than its wont; and when I had seen my face in the little pool that morning, I myself had started back from the older, bearded, and stern face that met me, instead of the fine, smooth, young looks that had been mine on the night of my last feast. But there were many at the Moot, which was even now dispersing, who had seen only this new face of mine, and I could not trust to remaining long unrecognized. None might harm me, that was true; but to be driven on, like a stray dog, from place to place, man to man, for fear of what should be done to him who aided me in word or deed, was worse, to my thought, than open enmity.

Now as night fell the clouds thickened up overhead, but it was still and clear below, if dark; and by the time the night fairly closed in, I stood on the heights above Watchet, and, looking down over the broad channel and to my left, saw the glimmering lights of the little town.

There I waited a little, pondering the safest way and time for reaching the franklin's house, for I would not bring trouble on him by being seen. All the while I looked out over the sea, and then I saw something else that I could not at first make out.

Somewhere on the sea, right off the mouth of the Watchet haven, and seemingly close under me, there flashed brightly a light for a moment and instantly, far out in the open water another such flash answered it -- seen and gone in an instant. Then came four more such flashes, each a little nearer than the second, and from different places. Then I found that the first and one other near it were not quite vanished, but that I could see a spark of them still glowing.

Now while I wondered what this might mean, those two nearer lights began to creep in towards the haven, closer and closer, and as they did so, flashed up again, and answering flashes came from the other places.

The night was still, and I sat down to see more or this, knowing that they who made these signals must be in ships or boats; but not knowing why they were made, or why so many ships should be gathered off the haven. Anyway there would be many people about to meet them if they came in, and that would not suit me.

Then all of a sudden the light from the nearest ship flamed up, bright and strong, and moved very fast towards the haven, and the others followed, for first one light and then another came into sight like the first two as they drew near. I knew not much about ships, but it seemed to me as if lanterns were on deck, and hidden from the shore by the bulwarks, perhaps, but that being so high above, I could look down on them.

"If they be honest vessels," thought I, all of a sudden, "why do they hide their lights?" for often had I seen the trading busses pass up our Parret river at night with bright torches burning on deck.

What was that?

Very faint and far away there came up to me in the still air, for what breeze there was set from the sea to me, a chant sung by many rough voices -- a chant that set my blood spinning through me, and that started me to my feet, running with all the speed I could make in the darkness to warn Watchet town that the vikings were on them! For now I knew. I had heard the "Heysaa", the war song of the Danes.

But before I could cover in the dark more than two miles I stopped, for I was too late. There shot up a tongue of flame from Watchet town, and then another and another, and the ringing of the church bell came to me for a little, and then that stopped, and up on Minehead height burnt out a war beacon that soon paled to nothing in the glare of the burning houses in the town. I could fancy I heard yells and shrieks from thence, but maybe that was fancy, though I know they were there for me to hear truly enough.

But I could do nothing. The town was too evidently in the hands of the enemy, and I could only climb up the hill again, and watch where the ships went, perhaps, as I had seen them come.

As I clomb the hill the heavy smell of the smoke caught me up and bided with me, making me wild with fury against the plunderers, and against Matelgar, in that now I might not call out my own men and ride to the sheriff's levy with them, and fight for Wessex as was my right.

And these Danes, or Northmen, whichever they might be -- but we called them all Danes without much distinction -- were the very men with whom I had thought to join when I won down to Cornwall.

One thing I could do, I could fire the beacon on the Quantocks. That was a good thought; and I hurried to the point where I knew it was ever piled, ready, since the day of Charnmouth fight two years agone.

I found it, and, hammering with the flint I had found in case of such a necessity as last night's, I kindled the dry fern at its foot to windward, and up it blazed. Then in a quarter hour's time it was answered from Brent, and from a score of hills around.

Now, as I stood by the fire, I heard the sound of running footsteps, far off yet, and knew they were the messengers who were bidden to fire the beacon. So I slipped aside into cover of its smoke, and lay down in a little hollow under some bushes, where I could both see and hear them when they came.

They were four in all, and were panting from their run.

"Who fired the beacon?" said one, looking round.

"Never mind," said another; "we shall have credit for mighty diligence in doing it."

"But," said the first, "he should be here."

Then they forgot that in the greater interest they had left, or escaped from, and began to talk of the vikings.

The men from two ships had landed, I learned, and had surprised the place; scarce had any time to flee; none to save goods. They mentioned certain names of the slain whom they had seen fall, and of these one was the franklin whom I was going to seek. There was no help for me thence now.

One man said he had heard there were more ships lying off; but they did not know how many, and I could see they had been in too great haste to care to learn.

Soon fugitives -- men, women, and children -- began to straggle in wretched little groups up the hill, weeping and groaning, and I knew there would soon be too many there for my liking. So I crept away, easily enough, and went out to the headland.

But I could see nothing on the sea now; and so, very sad at heart, I sought a bushy hollow and laid me down and slept, while the smoke of Watchet hung round me, and now and then a brighter glare flashed over the low clouds, as the roof of some building fell in and fed the flames afresh.

I woke in the light of the gray dawn, and the smell of burning was gone, and the sea I looked out on was clear again, for a fresh breeze from the eastward was sweeping the smoke, as I could see, away to the other hills, westward. But the town was gone -- only a smoke was left for all there was for me to look down on, instead of the red-tiled and gray-thatched roofs that I had so often seen before from that place or near it.

Next I saw the ships of the vikings. They lay out in the channel at anchor, for the tide was failing. I suppose they had gone into the little haven as soon as there was water enough, and that those lights I saw were signs made from one to the other when that was so. There were specks near them -- moving -- their boats, no doubt, from the shore, bringing off plunder. The long ships themselves looked like barley corns from so high above, or so I thought them to look, if they were larger to sight than that, for that was their shape.

Now I had not thought that they would have bided when the beacons were lit; but would have gone out westward with this tide. And therefore I wondered what their next move would be, but expected to see them up anchor and go soon.

Waiting so, I waxed hungry, for nought had I tasted, save a few birds' eggs that I had found in Holford Coombe, since that time yesterday. Birds' eggs, thought I, were better than nought, so I wandered among the bushes seeking more. As I did so, by and by, I came in sight of the beacon on the hilltop, and looking up at it, rather blaming my carelessness, saw that but two men were there, tending it, and from their silver collars I knew that they were thralls. They were putting on green bushes to make a smother and black smoke that would warn men that the enemy were yet at hand.

When I saw that both the men were strange to me, I went up to them, as though come to find out news of the business. And they saluted me, evidently not knowing me. I talked with them awhile, and then shared their breakfast with them, glad enough of it. They had, however, no more to tell me than I had already learnt, beyond tales of horror brought by the fugitives of last night, which I will not write.

Those people had soon passed on, fearing, as each new group came up, that the enemy was on their heels. They had doubtless scattered into the villages beyond.

So the time went idly, and the sun rose, while yet the tide fell and the ships lay beneath us. Smoke, as of cooking fires, rose from their decks, and they were evidently in no hurry. Nor need they be. In those days we had no warships such as our wise king has made us since then, and none could harm them on the open water.

In an hour's time, however, there came a change over the sea. Little waves began to curl over it, and when the sun broke out it flashed bright where the wind came over in flaws here and there. Then from each ship were unfurled great sails, striped in bright colours, and one by one they got under way, and headed over towards the Welsh coast, beyond channel. The tide had turned.

"They are going," said I, with much gladness.

One of the men shook his head.

"They do but slant across the wind, master. Presently they will go about and so fetch the Wessex shore again, and so on till they reach where they will up channel."

We watched them, and while we watched, a man came up from the west, heated and tired out, and limping with long running as it seemed. And when he saw me he ran straight to me, and thrusting a splinter of wood into my hand, cried in a panting voice:

267

"I can no more -- In the king's name to Matelgar of Stert -- the levy is at Bridgwater Cross. In all haste."

It was the war arrow. viNo man might refuse to bear that onward. Yet -- to Matelgar -- and by an outlaw! But the man was beat, and the thralls might not bear it.

"Look at me; know you who I am?" I said to the man, who had cast himself down on the grass, panting again.

"No -- nor care," he said, glancing at me sharply. "On, and tarry not."

"I am an outlaw," I said simply.

"Armed?" he said, with a laugh. "Outlaw in truth you will be, an you speed not."

"I am Heregar," I said again.

"Curse you!" said the man; "go on, and prate not. If you were Ealhstan himself, with his forked hat on, you must go."

"Heregar -- my master's friend," cried one of the two thralls, "if it be true you are outlawed, as I heard yesterday, go and win yourself inlawed again by this."

Then I turned, and wasted no more time, running swiftly down the hill and away towards the spot where my enemy lay at Stert, and that honest thrall of my friend, the slain franklin's, shouted after me for good speed.

"Well," I thought, as I went on at a loping pace, "I can prove my loyalty maybe -- but I have to bear this into the wolf's den -- and much the proof will serve me!"

Then I thought that presently I would feign lameness, and send on some other. And so I ran on.

I struck a path soon, and kept it, knowing that, if one met and recognized me, the token I bore was pass enough -- moreover, none might harm me, if they would, so that I was doing no wrong in being turned back, as it were, by emergency, from leaving the kingdom. Now, as I trotted swiftly along the track, there lay in my way what I thought was a stone till I neared it. Then I saw that it was a bag, and so picked it up, hardly pausing, shaking it as I did so.

It was full of money! Doubtless some one of the fugitives dropped it last night as they went in haste, hardly knowing they had it, perhaps. Well, better with me than with the Danes, I thought, and so bestowed the bag inside my mail shirt, and thanked the man who sent me on this errand. For now I felt as if free once more; for with sword and mail and money what more does man need?

When next I came to a place that looked out over sea, I could no more spy the ships. They must have stretched far across to the Welsh coast. Only the two holms broke the line of water to the north and east up channel.

Then the thought came to me that the Danes were gone, and what use going further with this errand? But that was not my business; the war arrow must go round, and the bearer must not fail, or else "nidring"vii should he be from henceforward. So I went on.

Now, at last, was I but a mile or two from Stert, and began to wish to meet one to whom to give the arrow -- but saw no man. I turned aside to a little cluster of thralls' and churls' huts I knew. There were no people there, and one hut was burnt down. Afterwards I heard that they had been deserted by reason of some pestilence that had been there; but now it seemed like a warning to do the duty that had been thrust on me.

Then at last I remembered the prophecy of the old hermit -- and my heart bounded within me -- for, indeed, unlooked for as this was, surely it was like the beginning of its working out.

Now would I go through with it, and on the head of Matelgar be the blame were I slain. Known was I by name to the messenger who gave me the arrow, and to those thralls, and known therefore would my going to Matelgar be.

Nevertheless, when I went down that path that I have spoken of, toward the hall, looking to meet with one at every turn, my heart beat thick enough for a time, till a great coolness came over me and I feared nought.

Yet must I turn aside one moment to lock into that nook where Alswythe and I had met, but it was empty. I knew that it must be so at that hour, but I was of my love constrained to go there.

Then I ran boldly round the outer palisade and came to the great gate.

VI: IN THE WOLF'S DEN

There was only one man near it, and he sat on the settle inside, so that he could see out and in as he wished. Him I knew at once, and was glad, for it was that old warrior who had showed some liking for me at Brent.

He got up slowly as he saw a stranger stand in the gateway and came out towards me. Then he started a little and frowned.

"Rash -- master, rash," he said, but not loudly. "This is no safe place for you," and he motioned me to fly.

Then I beckoned him out a little further and showed him what I bore in my hand. And he was fairly amazed and knew not what to say, that I, an outlaw, should have been sent on this errand, and more, that I should have come.

I told him, speaking quickly and shortly, how it had come about, and he understood that the man who gave me the arrow neither knew nor believed me.

"Master," he said, when I had done, "verily I believe that you are true, and wronged by him I have served this past two months. But of this I know not for certain, being a stranger here and little knowing of place or people. But this I know, from the man you sent back, that our thane sought your life against the word of the ealdorman, and, moreover, believes that you are dead. But by the arms you wear I can learn how that matter really went. Now, give me the arrow, and I will see to this -- do you fly."

But I was bent on ending the errand, and said I would carry out the task, as was my duty, to the end. I would put the arrow with its message into Matelgar's hand, and bide what might come.

He tried to dissuade me, but at last said that he would not stand by and see me harmed, and for that I thanked him.

"Well then," he told me, "you have come in a good hour. Most of the men have gone out here and there to spy what they may of the Danes and their plans -- if gone or not. Others are in the stables, and but one man sits at the door of the great hall, and he is of no account."

"Where is Matelgar?" I asked.

"I know not exactly; but do as I say and all will be well."

Then I said that his advice had saved me, I thought, when before the Moot, and I would follow it here.

"Then," he went on, "come you to the hall door and bide there while I go in and call the thane thither. He will stay by his great chair to hear your message, and I will stand by the man who keeps the door. Then, when you have given up the arrow, tarry not, but come out at once, and get out of this gate, lest he should raise some alarm. Then must you take to the woods quickly."

So he turned and went in before me. There were some twenty yards of courtyard to be crossed before we came to the great timber-built hall, round which the other buildings clustered inside the palisades. But there were no men about, though I could hear them whistling at their morning's work in the stables, for the idle time of the day was yet to come. Only a boy crossed from one side to the other on some errand, behind us, and paid no attention beyond pausing a little to stare, as I could judge by his footsteps. At any other time I should not have noticed even that, but now that I was in the very jaws of the wolf, as it were, I saw and heard everything. And all the while my heart beat fast -- but that was not from fear, but for thinking I might by chance see Alswythe.

Yet I will say it truly, that thought of her had no share in bringing me on this mad errand, which might have ending in such fashion as would break her heart.

One man, as my guide had said, sat just inside the hall, but I knew him not. Since he had my hall and his own to tend, Matelgar must have hired more and new housecarles. This man was trimming a bow at the hearth, and did not rise, seeing that, whoever I might be, I was brought in by his comrade. The great hall looked wide and empty, for the long tables were cleared away, and only the settle by the hearth in the centre remained, beside the thane's own carved seat on the dais at the far end.

"Bide by the fire till he comes," said my guide, seeing that the man did not know me, and leaving me there, he went through a door beyond the thane's chair to seek him.

So I stood where the smoke rose between me and that door, waiting and warming my hands quietly, and as unconcernedly to all seeing as I could.

"Ho, friend," said the man, so suddenly that he made me start; "look at your sword hilt before the thane comes," and he pointed and grinned.

Sure enough, my sword hilt was not fastened to the sheath as it should be in a peaceful hall, but the thong hung loose, as if ready for me to thrust wrist through before drawing the blade. So I grinned back, without a word, lest Matelgar should hear my voice and know it, and began to pretend to knot the thong round the scabbard. All the same, I was not going to fasten it so that I could not draw if need were, and only kept on plaiting and twisting.

Then I heard Matelgar's voice and footstep, and I desisted, and, taking the arrow from my belt, stood up and ready.

He came in, looking round, but not seeing me at first through the blue smoke, for as I knew he would, he entered by the door through which my guide had gone just now. So I waited till he stood with his hand on his chair, while the old warrior came down towards me.

Then I strode forward boldly up to the foot of the dais, and looking steadily a Matelgar, cast the arrow at his feet, saying:

"In the king's name. The levy is at Bridgwater Cross. In all haste."

He threw up his hands as one too terrified to draw sword -- who would ward off some sudden terror -- giving back a pace or two, and staring at me with wild eyes. His face grew white as milk, and drawn, and his breath went in between his teeth with a long hissing sound. But he spoke no word, and as he stood there, I turned and walked out into the courtyard and to the gate, going steadily and without looking round, like a man who has nothing either to keep or hurry him.

Three grooms, whom I knew, stood with an unbridled horse on one side, but they were busy and minded me not till I was just at the gate.

Then one said to the other, "Yonder goes Heregar, as I live!"

Then there came a cry like a howl of rage from the hall, but no word of command as yet, nor did either housecarle come out that I could hear.

Then I was at the gate, and as I passed it, turning sharp to the right, for that was the nearest way to the woods, I heard one running across the court.

When I heard that, instead of keeping straight on, I doubled quickly round the angle of the palisade. By the time I had turned it the man may have been at the gate, and would think me vanished. But now I ran and got to cover in a thicket close to the rear of the house. A bad place enough, but I must chance it.

I could hear shouts now from the courtyard. I looked round for a way to escape, but to reach the woods I had now a long bit of open ground to cover, and was puzzled. Then overhead I heard a bird rustle, and I looked up, and at once a thought came to me. The tree was an old, gnarled ash, and the leaves on it were thick for the time of year. Moreover, the branches were so large that surely in the fork I could find a hiding place. And being so close to the hall, search would be with little, if any, care.

So with a little difficulty I climbed up, and there, sure enough, found the tree hollow in the fork, so that if I crouched down none could see me from below, while, lying flat against a great branch, I could safely see something of what might be on hand.

I was hardly sure of this when men began to spread here and there about the place, but mostly going in the direction of the woods. I heard Matelgar's voice, harsh and loud, promising reward to him who should bring in the outlaw, dead or alive, and presently saw him stand clear of the palisading, about a bowshot from me.

He was red enough now, but his hand played nervously with his sword hilt, and once when men shouted in the wood, he clutched it. Clearly I had terrified him, and if he deemed me, as it seemed, a ghost at first sight, the token of the arrow had undeceived him, and little rest would he have now, night or day, while I was yet at large.

So I laughed to myself, and watched him till he went back.

Presently the men straggled in, too. One party, having made a circle, came close by me, and they were laughing and saying that the thane had seen a ghost.

"Moreover," said another, "we saw him cross the court slowly enough, and when we got to the gate -- lo! he was gone."

Then one said that he had heard the like before, and their voices died away as he told the story.

Soon after this the horns were blown to recall all the men, and I knew that Matelgar must needs, even were it a ghost who brought the war arrow, lead his following to the sheriff's levy.

Aye, and the following that should be mine as well. The message I had brought should have been to me as a king's thane, and I myself should have sent one to Matelgar to bid him come to the levy, even as he would now send to the other lesser thanes and the franklins round about, in my place. The men were running out even now, north and west and east, as I thought of this in my bitterness, and I watched them, knowing well to whom this one and that must go in each quarter.

This was hard to think of. Yet I had stood in Matelgar's presence, and had him in my power for a minute, while I might have struck him down, and had not done so. And all that long night in Sedgemoor I had promised myself just such a moment, and had pictured him falling at my feet, my revenge taken.

But how long ago that seemed. Truly I was like another man then. And since that night there had been the wise counsel of the hermit, the prattle of the child, the touch and voice of my loved one, the thought of a true friend, and now the sore need of the country I loved. And, for the sake of all those things, I do not wonder that, as I saw Matelgar pale and tremble before me, the thought of slaying him never entered my head.

I will not say that I was much conscious of all these things moulding my conduct; but I know that since I took this message on me, and it seemed to me that the prophecy was on its way to fulfilment, I had, as it were, stood by to see another avenger then myself at work in a way that should unfold itself presently -- so sure was I that all would come out as the hermit foretold. So it was with a sort of confidence, and a boy's love of adventure, too, that I had run into danger thus, while now that I had come off so well, my confidence was yet stronger. However, it would not make me foolhardy, for my father was wont to tell me that one may only trust to luck after all care taken to be well off without it.

Men came trooping in from the nearer houses and farms very soon, armed and excited. Often some passed under me, not ten paces off, and then I shrank down into the hollow. All spoke of the Danes as gone, but at last one said he thought he could see them, away by Steepholme Island, half an hour agone. Though it might be fancy, he added, for their ships were very low, and hard to see if no sail were spread.

But from all I gathered, the Danes were over on the other coast, and out of our way for the time at least.

Then I grew very stiff in the tree: but so many were about that I dared not come down. They were, however, mostly gathered in the open in front of the great gate, and only passers by came near me. It was some three hours after noon before they gathered into ranks at last, and the roll was called over by Matelgar himself, as he rode along the line fully armed.

When that was done, he put himself at the head, and they filed off up the road towards Bridgwater. I remembered that, when I was quite little, my father once had to call out a levy against the West Welsh, and then there was great cheering as the men started. There was none now -- only the loud voice of the thane as he chided loiterers and those who seemed to straggle.

I began to think of coming down when the last had gone, but a few men from far off came running past to catch them up, and I kept still yet. Then a great longing came upon me to join the levy and fight the Danes, if fight there should be, and I began to plan to do it in some way, yet could not see how to disguise myself, or think to whose company to pretend to belong.

The place seemed very quiet after all the loud talk and shouting that had been going on. My father's levy had had ale in casks, and food brought out to them while they waited. But I had seen none of that here. Maybe, however, it was in the courtyard, I thought, and this I might see, if I climbed higher, above the palisading.

So I left my sword in the hollow, lest it should hamper me, and went up a big branch until I could see over just enough to look across to the great gate, which still stood open. Then I forgot all about that which had made me curious, for I saw two figures in the gateway.

Alswythe stood there, talking with my friend, as I will call him ever, the old housecarle, and no one else was near them.

My first thought was to come down and run to her; but I remembered that I could but see one corner of the court, and that many more housecarles might be at hand, and waited, not daring to take my eyes from Alswythe lest I should lose her.

They were too far off for me to hear their voices, nor did they make sign or movement that would let me guess that which they spoke of; but presently the old man saluted, and Alswythe went out of the gate.

Then my heart leaped within me, for I thought, and rightly, that she sought her bower in the wood. And so she passed close by me in going there, and I must not speak or move for fear of terrifying her.

But when she had gone up the path, I looked round carefully once or twice, and came down, and then, buckling on my sword again, looked warily out of the thicket, and seeing that none was near, crossed the open and followed her.

There I found her in her place as she had found me the other day, and soon once more we were side by side on the old seat; and she was blaming me, tenderly, for my rashness. Yet she knew not that it was I who had brought the arrow, and her one fear was that I had joined those Danes. And when I looked at her, I saw that she had been sorely troubled, and this was the cause, for she said:

"I knew that you, my Heregar, would not fight against your own land, and so they would surely slay you."

So will a woman see the truth of things often more clearly than a man. For that the vikings might call on me to fight my Saxon kin had, till last night, never crossed my mind, yet after Charnmouth fight it was like enough.

Then she asked what brought me here, and I told her that, seeing the burning of Watchet, I had a mind to join the levy, if I could, and so fight both for country and for her. That was true enough as my thoughts ran now -- and surely I was not wrong in leaving out the story of the errand with the war arrow, for that would have told her of her father's lust for my destruction.

Then she wept lest I should fall, but being brave and thoughtful for my honour, and for my winning back name and lands, bade me do so if I could, cheering me with many fond and noble words, so that I wondered that such a man as I could have won the love of such a woman as she.

Now the time was all too short for me to tarry long: but before I went, Alswythe would bring me out food and drink that I might go well strengthened and provided. And as I let her go back to the hall, I asked her the name of that old warrior to whom she spoke, for it was he, I told her, who had tried to help me before the Moot.

And then I was sorry I had told her that, for she might ask him of the matter and hear more than was good for her peace of mind; but it was done, and nothing could recall it.

Yet she did not notice it then, but said his name was Wulfhere, and that he was a stranger from Glastonbury, as she thought, lately come into her father's service. She was going then, and I asked her to let me have speech with him, as I thought it safe, if he were to be trusted, for I needed his advice in some things.

She said she would sound him first, not knowing how he had seen me already, of course, and so went quickly away towards the hall.

What I needed the old man for was but to try to repair my slip of the tongue, and warn him of my love's ignorance of her father's unfaith to me; but as it fell out, it was well I asked to see him.

Presently he came to me. I had to slip into the bushes and lie quiet till I knew who it was, and when I came out he smiled gravely at me, shaking his head, yet as one not displeased altogether.

"Well managed, master," he said, still smiling, "but I knew not that you had so strong a rope to draw you hither."

Then I told him the trouble I was like to bring on Alswythe if he told her all that passed at Brent; letting him have his own thoughts about my reason for coming to Matelgar's hall, which were wrong enough, though natural at first sight, maybe.

He promised to be most wary, and I was content. Then I asked him how I should join the levy.

"Master," he said, very gravely, "this is like to be a matter of which we have not seen the end. Yon Danes are up channel, and, as I believe, lying at anchor by the Holms. It will not be their way, if, having gone so far up, they sack not every town on their way back - unless they are beaten off on their first landing. Now the country is raised against them, sure enough; but our levy is a weak crowd when it is first raised, and they are tried warriors, every one. Now they may go on up tide to the higher towns, or else they will be back here, like a kite on a chicken, before men think, and Bridgwater town will see a great fight, and maybe a burning, before tomorrow."

Then I said that the levy would beat them off easily enough; but the old warrior shook his head.

"I was at Charnmouth," he said, "when King Ethelwulf himself led the charge. And our men fought well; but it was like charging a wall bristling with spears. Again and again our men charged, but the Danes stood in a great ring which never broke, although it wavered once or twice, until we were wearied out, and then they swung into line and swept us off the field. Until we learn to fight as they fight, we are weaker."

Then I began to fear for Alswythe, and asked him what guard was left for the hall, and again he shook his head.

"Myself, and five others -- not the strongest -- and a dozen women, and three boys, thralls."

I knew not what to say to this; but the wise old man had already thought of a plan in case of danger. And in this, he said, I could advise him, for he was a stranger.

"Horses enough are left," he told me, "and if the Danes come to Bridgwater, and are not beaten off, I shall mount the Lady Alswythe and the women, and take them to a safer place. But whither?"

I told him at once of the house of a great thane beyond the Quantocks, easily reached by safe roads through the forest land, where Danes would not care to follow, and he thanked me.

Then he said that I might well try to join the levy; but that it was possible that it would be hard for me. And I told him that if I could not manage it I would join in the fight when no man would question me, and that seemed possible to both of us. But if the Danes yet kept away I knew I could wait in hiding, having money now, safely enough till they had gone and the levy dispersed.

Then came Alswythe back, bearing with her the things I needed. And Wulfhere begged her not to bide alone in the wood now, since robbers might be overbold now that the men were drawn off to the levy. That was good advice in itself; but I knew that he would have her near the hall, lest there should be sudden need for fleeing. She promised him, thanking him for the warning, and he left us.

Then she tended me as I ate, carefully, and never had there been for me so sweet a meal as that, outlawed and homeless though I was to the world. For her word was my law now, and my home was all in her love for me.

I think no man can rightly be held an outlaw who has kept law and has home such as that. For while he has, and loves those, wrong will he do to none.

It was Alswythe who bade me go at last, not for her own sake, but for mine, that I might go on my way to win my fair name back again.

VII: OSRIC THE SHERIFF

Through the woods I reached Bridgwater town before the sun set, and looking down from the steep hill that overhangs the houses, I could see the market square full of men, shining in arms and armour, and noisy enough, as I could hear. But every one of the townsfolk knew me, and by this time also knew what had befallen me, so that as I stood there it seemed not quite so easy to win a way to the levy as before. The highways were yet full of men coming in, for from where I stood on the edge of the cover I could see the bend of one road, and straight down another. If I went on them I must walk like a leper, alone and shunned by all, with maybe hard words to hear as well.

While I thought of all this, there crept out from among the woods an old crone, doubled up under the weight of a faggot of dry sticks, who stayed to stare at me. I did not mind her, but of a sudden she dropped her bundle of wood, and I saw that it was like to be a heavy task for her to raise it again. So I turned and laid hold of it, for she was but six paces from me, saying:

"Let me help you, Mother, to get it hoisted again. Truly would I carry it for you for a while, but I must bide here."

"That must you, Heregar the outlaw," said the old woman coolly, without a word of thanks, and I thought my story and face were better known than I deemed. Therefore I must make the best of it.

"Well, Mother," said I, "you know me, and if you know me, so also must many others. But I want to join the levy, and fight if need be."

"Thereby knew I you to be Heregar," said she; "for none but he must stand here with the light of battle in his eyes and his hand clutched on his sword hilt and not go down to the Cross yonder, as the summons is."

Then I marvelled at the old dame's wisdom, though maybe it was but a guess, and asked her what I should do, seeing that she was wise, and the words of such as she are often to be hearkened to.

"It is a wise man," she answered, "who will take advice; but never a word should you have had from old Gundred, save you had helped her, as a true man should."

"Truly, Mother Gundred," I said, "I have no rede of my own, and am minded to take yours."

"Then, fool," she said curtly, "link up that tippet of mail across your face, go down to Osric the Sheriff himself, beg to be allowed to fight, and see what he will tell you."

I had forgotten that I could hook the hanging chain mail of my helmet across, in such manner that little but my eyes could be seen; but then that was never done but in battle -- and I had never seen that yet.

"Thanks, Mother," said I, with truth, for I saw that I might do this. "This is help indeed."

"Not so fast, young sir," answered the crone; "Osric will not have you."

"How know you that?"

"How does an old woman of ninety years know many things? When you tell me that, I will say how I know that Osric will send you about your business; and that will be the best day's work he ever did."

Now I was nearly angry at that, for it seemed to set light store on my valour; but there seemed something more in the old woman's tone than her taunting words would convey, so I said plainly:

"Then shall I go to him?"

"Aye, fool, did I not tell you so?"

"But if it is no good?"

"Is it no good for a man who is accused of disloyalty to have witness that he wished, at least, to spend his life for his country? Moreover, there is work for you to do which fighting will hinder for this turn -- go to, Heregar, I will tell you no more. Now do my bidding and go, and never will you forget that you helped an old witch with her burden."

"Well, then, Mother," I said, hooking up the mail tippet across my face, "if I must go down into the town, surely I will carry that bundle."

"That shall you not," she answered, dropping it again, and sitting down on it. "Heregar the king's thane -- the standard bearer -- shall bend to no humbler burden than the Dragon of Wessex. Go; and Thor and Odin strike with you."

And then she covered up her face, and would look no more at me. I thought her crazed, maybe, but a sort of chill came over me as I heard her name the old heathen gods, and I thought of the Valas of old time, and knew how here and there some of the old worship lingered yet.

However, good advice had she given, showing me the way to try my fortune in the way I wished, and after that heathenish blessing I had no mind to stay longer, for such like are apt to prove unlucky; so I bid her good even, and went my way towards the town. After all, I thought, king's thane I was once, and may be again; and to bear the standard must be won by valour, so that, too, may come to pass. Whereupon I remembered the badger that scared me in the moonlight, and was less confident in myself.

Many were the questions put me as I passed into the marketplace of Bridgwater, but I answered none, pushing on to where I saw Osric the Sheriff's banner over a great house. Mostly the men scoffed at me for thinking that I should win more renown in disguise; but some thought me a messenger, and clustered after me, to hear what they might.

When I came to the house door, where Osric lay, it was guarded, and the guards asked me my business. I said I would see the sheriff and then they demanded name and errand. Now, I could give neither, and was at a loss for a moment. Then I said that I was one of the bearers of the war arrow, and though that was but a chance shot, as it were, it passed me in at once, for often a bearer would return to give account of some thane ill, or absent, or the like.

They took me to a great oaken-walled hall where sat many thanes along great tables, eating and drinking, and at the highest seat was Osric, and next him, Matelgar. This assembly, and most of all that my enemy should be present, was against me in making my plea; but as the old crone had said, I should be no loser by witness.

I waited till a thrall had told Osric that one of his messengers was here, and then they beckoned me to go to him. He shifted round in his chair to speak to me, but I was watching Matelgar, and saw his glance light on my sword hilt. Recognizing it, he grew pale, and then red, half-rising from his seat to speak to Osric, but thinking better thereof.

"Well; what news and whence?" said the sheriff, who was a small, wiry man, with a sour look, as I thought. Men spoke well of him though.

"The Danes lie off the Holms, sir," I said, for I would gain time.

"I know that," he answered testily; "pull that mail off your face, man; they are not here yet, and your voice is muffled behind it."

I suppose that the coming and going of messengers was constant, and indeed there came another even then, so the other thanes paid little attention after they heard my stale news, except Matelgar; who went on watching me closely.

I was just about to ask the sheriff to hear me privately, when Matelgar plucked him by the sleeve, having made up his mind at last, and drawing him down a little, spoke to him a few words, among which I caught my own name.

The sheriff looked sharply at me, twitching his sleeve away, and I saw that there was to be no more concealment; so I dropped the tippet and let him see who I was, saying at the same time:

"Safe conduct I crave, Osric the Sheriff."

Then a silence came over the thanes who saw and knew me, looking up to see what this new freak of mine was. And Osric frowned at me, but said nothing, so I spoke first.

"Outlaw I am, Osric, but I can fight; today I bore the war arrow --that one who neither knew nor believed me gave me -- faithfully to Matelgar the Thane, who is here in obedience to that summons. And when I took it I was on my way out of the kingdom as I was bidden, but I turned back because of the need for a trusty messenger. Now I ask only to be allowed to fight alongside your men in this levy, and after that it is over -- if I live -- I will go my way again."

That was all I had to say, and when I ceased a talk buzzed up among the thanes. But Matelgar looked black, and Osric made no answer, frowning, indeed, but more I think at the doubt he was in than with anger at me.

I saw that Matelgar longed to speak, but dared not as yet, and then he cast his eye down the hall, and seemed to make some sign.

Presently Osric said in a doubtful way, "Never heard I the like. Now I myself know not why an outlaw should not fight if he wills to do so.

"What say you, thanes?" he cried loudly, turning to those down the hall.

Instantly one rose up and shouted, "We will have no traitors in our ranks."

Then I knew what Matelgar's sign meant, for this was a close friend of his. On that, too, several others said the same, and one cried that I should be hounded out of the hall and town. Osric frowned when he heard that, and looked at me; but I stood with my arms folded, lest I should be tempted to lay hand on sword, and so give my enemies a hold on me. Matelgar himself said nothing, as keeping up his part of friend bound by loyalty to accuse me against his will.

As for the other thanes, they talked, but all the outcry was against my being allowed to join, and at last Osric seemed to be overborne by them, for voices in my favour were few heard, if many thought little harm of my request. But then the offer of the help of one man was, anyway, a little thing, and if he were doubted it would be ill. And I could see, as Osric would also see, that the matter would be spread through the levy by those against me.

Now as I thought of the likelihood of one of Matelgar's men spearing me during the heat of fight, I wondered if he feared the same of me, for I have often heard tales of the like.

Then Osric answered me, kindly enough, but decidedly:

"Nay, Heregar, you hear that this must not be. Outlaw is outlaw, and must count for naught. I may not go against the word of the Moot, and inlaw you again by giving you a place. Go hence in peace, and take your way; yet we thank you for bearing the message to Matelgar. Link up your mail again, and tell any man that you bear messages from me; the watchword is 'Wessex' for the guards are set by now, and you will need it."

As he spoke thus kindly Matelgar's face grew black as night; but he dared say no word. So I bowed to the sheriff and, linking up my mail, went sadly enough down the hall. It was crowded at one place, and there some friendly hand patted me softly on the shoulder, though most shrank from me; but yet I would not turn to see who it was, that helped me.

Now I have often wondered that no inquiry was made about my arms, and how I came by them; but what I believe is, that even then men began to know that Matelgar and his friends had played me false, but that they would not, and Matelgar's people dared not, say much. As for Osric, his mind was full of greater troubles, and I suppose he never thought thereof.

I passed out into the street, but now it was falling dark, and few noticed me. The men sat about along the house walls on settles, eating and drinking and singing. And I, coming to a dark place, sat down among a few and ate and drank as well for half an hour, and then passing the guards at the entrance to the town on the road to Cannington, struck out for Stert, that I might be near Alswythe, and wait for the possible coming of the Danes, and the battle in which I might join.

CHAPTER VIII: THE FIRES OF STERT

I went along the highroad now, for it was dark, and few were about. Only now and then I met a little party of men hurrying to the gathering place, and mostly they spoke to me, asking for news. And from them I learned, too, that nothing had been seen, while daylight served, of the Danes. Once, I had to say I was on Osric's errand, as he bade me, being questioned as to why I was heading away from the town.

I could not see my hall as I passed close by its place, for the lights that ever shone thence in the old days, so lately, yet seeming so long, gone, were quenched. But I thought of a safe place whence to watch if the Danes came, where were trees in which I might hide if need were, as I had hidden this morning. This was on the little spur of hill men call by the name of the fisher's village below it, Combwich. It looked on all the windings of Parret river, and there would I soon know if landing was to be made for attack on Bridgwater. But I thought it likely that there would be an outpost of our men there for the same reason, and going thither went carefully.

Sure enough there was a little watchfire and half a dozen men round it on the best outlook, and so I passed on still further, following round the spur of hill till I came to where the land overlooks the whole long tongue of Stert Point. That would do as well for me, I thought, and choosing, as best I could in the dark, a tree into which I knew by remembrance that I might easily get, I sat down at its foot, looking seaward.

Now by this time the tide, which runs very strong and swiftly, must be flowing again, and I thought that most likely the Danes, having anchored during the ebb, would go on up channel with it, and that therefore I might have to hang about here for days before they landed, even were they to land at all. And this I had heard said many times by the men of the levy, some, indeed, saying that they might as well go home again.

But I should do as well here as anywhere, or better, since, while Matelgar was away, I might yet see Alswythe again; though that, after my repulse by the sheriff, or perhaps I should rather say by his advisers, I thought not of trying yet. It would but be another parting. Still, I might find old Wulfhere, and send her messages by him before setting out westward again.

Almost was I dozing, for the day had been very long, when from close to Stert came that which roused me completely, setting my heart beating.

It was a bright flash of light from close inshore, on the Severn side of the tongue, followed by answering flashes, just as I had seen them at Watchet. But now the flashes came and went out instantly, for I was no longer looking down on the ship's decks as then.

Well was it that I had seen this before from Quantock heights; for I knew that once again the Danes were landing, and that the peril was close at hand.

Then at once I knew the terrible danger of Alswythe, for Matelgar's was the first hall that would be burnt.

My first thought was to hasten thither and alarm Wulfhere, and then to hurry back to that outpost I had passed half a mile away, for the country danger must be thought of too.

Then a better thought than either came to me. If it was, as it must be, barely half tide, the Danes would find mud between them and shore, too deep to cross, and must wait till the ships could come up to land, or until there was water enough to float their boats. I had an hour or more yet before they set foot on shore.

Moreover, I would find out if landing was indeed meant, or if these were but signals for keeping channel on the outward course.

So across the level meadows of Stert I ran my best, right towards the place where I had seen the light, which was at the top, as it were, of the wedge that Stert makes between the waters of Parret and the greater Severn Sea. There are high banks along the shore to keep out the spring tides, and under these I could watch in safety, unseen. Three fishers' huts were there only; but these I knew would be deserted for fear of the Danes.

So I found them, and then, creeping up the bank, I stood still and peered out into the darkness. Yet it was not so dark on the water (which gleamed a little in the tide swirls here and there beyond half a mile of mud, black as pitch in contrast) but that I could make out at last six long black ships, lying as it seemed on the edge of the ooze. And I could hear, too, hoarse voices crying out on board of them, and now and then the rattle of anchor chains or the like, when the wind blew from them to me.

And ever those ships crept nearer to me, so that I knew they were edging up to the land as the tide rose.

That learnt, I knew what to do. I ran to the nearest fishers' hut, and pulled handfuls of the thatch from under the eaves, piling it to windward against the wooden walls. Then I fired the heap, and it blazed up bright and strong, and at once came a great howl of rage from the ships, plain to be heard, for they knew that now they might not land unknown.

So had I warned Osric the Sheriff, and that matter was out of my hands. And, moreover, Wulfhere, being an old and tried warrior, would be warned as well. That, however, I would see to myself, and, if I could, I would aid him in getting Alswythe into a place of safety. So I ran back, bending my steps now towards her father's hall, up the roadway, if one might so call the track through the marshland that led thither.

Just at the foot of the hill I met three men of the outpost, who were hurrying down to see what my fire meant. They challenged me, halting with levelled spears across the track. Then was I glad of the password, and answered by giving it.

"Right!" said the man who seemed to be the leader. "What news?"

I told him quickly, bidding him waste no time, but hurry back and tell the sheriff that the Danes would be ashore in half an hour. I spoke as I was wont to speak when I was a thane, forgetting in the dire need of the moment that I was an outlaw now, and the man was offended thereat.

"Who are you to command me thus?" he said shortly.

"Heregar, the thane of Cannington." said I, still only anxious that he should go quickly.

"Heard one ever the like!" said the man, and then I remembered.

I looked round at my fire. Two huts were burning now, very brightly, for the wind fanned the flames.

"Saw you ever the like?" I said, and pointed. "Now, will you go?"

The bright light shone on a row of flashing, gilded dragon heads on the ships' stems -- on lines of starlike specks beyond them, which were helms and mail coats -- and on lines again of smaller stars above, which were spear points.

"Holy saints!" cried the man, adding a greater oath yet; "be you Heregar the outlaw or no, truth you tell, and well have you done. Let us begone, men!"

And with that those three leapt away into the darkness up the hill, leaving me to follow if I listed.

That was not my way, however, and I ran on to Matelgar's hall.

One stood at the gate. It was Wulfhere. Inside I heard the trampling of horses, and knew that they would be ready in time. Wulfhere laid hand on sword as I came up, doubting if I were not a Dane, but I cried to him who I was, and he came out a step or two to me, asking for news.

And when I told him what I had seen and done, he, too, said I had done well, and that I had saved Alswythe, if not many more. Also, that he had sent a man to tell Matelgar of his plans. Then he told me that even now the horses were ready, and that he was about to abandon the place, going to the house of that thane of whom I had told him. And I said that I would go some way with him, and then return to join the levy, making known my ill-luck with Osric.

"Ho!" said he; "it was well he sent you away, as it seems to me."

That was the word of the old crone, I remembered, that it should be so.

Then came a soft touch on my arm, and on turning I saw Alswythe standing by me, wrapped in a long cloak, and ready. And neither I nor she thought shame that I should lay my arm round her, and kiss her there, with the grim old housecarle standing by and pretending to look out over Stert, where the light of my fires shone above the trees.

"Heregar, my loved one, what does it all mean?" she said, trembling a little. "Have they come?"

I folded my arm more closely round her, and would have answered, but that Wulfhere did so for me.

"Aye, lady, and it is to Heregar that we owe our safety, for he has been down to Stert and warned us all."

At that my love crept closer to me, as it were to thank me. Then she said:

"Will there be fighting? And will my father have to fight?"

"Aye, lady," said Wulfhere again, "as a good Saxon should."

"Must I go from here?" she asked again; and I told her that the house would be burnt, maybe, in an hour or so.

At that she shivered, and tried not to weep, being very brave.

"Where must we go?" she said, with a little tremble in her voice.

I told her where we would take her, and then she cried out that she must bide near at hand lest her father should be hurt, and none to tend him.

And Wulfhere and I tried a little to overpersuade her, but then a groom came to say that all was ready.

And, truly, no time must be lost, if we would get off safely.

Then I said that it would be safe to go to Bridgwater, for then we should be behind the levy, and that the Danes must cut through that before reaching us. And to that Wulfhere agreed, for I knew he would rather be swinging his sword against the Danes at Stert than flying through the woods of the Quantocks.

Alswythe thanked me, without words indeed, and then in a few minutes she was mounted, and we were going up towards the high road to Bridgwater. We had twelve horses, and on them were the women of the house, bearing what valuables they might, as Wulfhere had bade them. One horse carried two women, but they were a light burden, and we had no such terrible haste to make, seeing that every moment brought us nearer the levy. There were the men and boys as well, but they led the beasts.

Now when we reached the high road, some half mile away, suddenly Alswythe reined up her horse, by which I walked, giving a little cry, and I asked what it was.

Then she said, sobbing a little, that she would her cows were driven out into the forest where they were wont to feed, lest the cruel Danes should get them. And to please her I think I should myself have gone back, but that Wulfhere called one of the men, who, it seemed, was the cowherd, bidding him return and do this, if the Danes were not coming yet. Glad enough was I to hear the man say that he had done it already -- "for no Dane should grow fat on beasts of his tending, and they were a mile off by now."

So we went on, and every minute I looked to meet our levy advancing. But the moon rose, and shone on no line of glancing armour that I longed for, and Wulfhere growled to himself as he went. I would have asked him many questions, but would not leave Alswythe, lest she should be alarmed. And all the way, as we went, I told her of what had befallen me with Osric, saying only that her father was there, but had not been able to speak for me. And I told her of the old crone's words, which she thought would surely come true, all of them, as they had begun to do so.

It is a long five miles from Matelgar's place to the town, and we could only travel at a foot's pace. But still we met no force. Indeed, until we were just a half mile thence, we saw no one. Then we met a picket, who, seeing we were fugitives, let us go on unchallenged.

But Wulfhere stopped and questioned the men, and got no pleasant answer as it seemed, for he caught us up growling, coming alongside of me, and saying -- for Alswythe could not know the ways of war -- that they would attack with morning light. But I felt only too keenly, though I knew so little, that to fight the Danes when they had their foot firmly ashore, was a harder matter than to meet them but just landed.

We were so close to the town now that I asked Alswythe where she would be taken. Already we were passing groups of fugitives from the nearer country, and the town would be full of them, to say nothing of the men of the levy.

She thought a little, and then asked me if she might not go to her father, wherever he was. But I told her that he was but a guest of Osric, as it seemed. Then she said that she would go to her aunt, who was the prioress of the White Nuns, and bide in the nunnery walls till all was safe. And that seemed a good plan, both to me and Wulfhere, for it would -- though this we said not to Alswythe -- set us free to fight, as there we might not come, and she would be safe without us.

Then I told Wulfhere how we could reach that house without going through the crowded town, and so turned to the right, skirting round in the quiet lanes.

The gray dawn began to break as we saw the nunnery before us, and it was very cold. But Alswythe pointed to a crimson glow behind us, as we topped the last rise, saying that the sun would be up soon.

Wulfhere and I looked at each other. That glow was not in the east, but shone from Matelgar's hall -- in flames.

And then we feigned cheerfulness, and said that it would be so; and Alswythe smiled on me, though she was pale and overwrought with the terror she would not show, and the long, dark, and cold journey.

We came to the nunnery gate and knocked; and the old portress looked out of the wicket and asked our business, frightened at the glint of mail she saw. But Alswythe's voice she knew well, as she answered, begging lodging for herself and her maidens, till this trouble was over.

It was no new thing for a lady of rank to come into that quiet retreat with her train when on a journey; and after a little time, while the portress told the prioress, the doors were thrown open, and we rode into the great courtyard, where torches burnt in the dim gray morning light.

Then came the prioress, mother's sister to Alswythe, a tall and noble-looking lady, greeting her and us kindly, and so promising safe tending to her niece so long as she needed.

Here Alswythe must part from me, giving me but her hand to kiss, as also to Wulfhere, but there was a warm pressure on my hand for myself alone that bided with me. And the prioress thanked us for our care, not knowing me in the half light, and in mail, and so were we left in the courtyard, where an old lay brother, brought from the near monastery, showed us the stabling and provender for our horses, and the loft where the men should sleep, outside the walls of the inclosed building.

Here Wulfhere bade the men and boys remain, tending their horses until he should return, or until orders came from their master himself or from the lady Alswythe; for they were thralls, and not men who should be with the levy.

Then he and I went out into the roadway and walked away until we were alone.

"What now?" I asked.

"I must join my master, telling him what I have done, and that the lady is safe. So shall I march with the rest most likely. What shall I say of your part in this?"

"Nought," I answered.

"Maybe that is best -- just now," he agreed.

We had come to the town streets now, and they seemed empty. The light was strong enough by this time, and there came a sound of shouting from the place of the market cross, and then we heard the bray of war horns, and Wulfhere quickened his pace, saying that the men were mustering, or maybe on the march.

Then I longed to go with him, but that might not be. So I left him at last, saying that I should surely join in the fight.

I had not gone six paces from him when he called me, and I could see that he looked anxious.

"Master," he said, "this is going to be a doubtful fight as it seems to me. Yon Danes know that the country is raised, but yet they have come back, and they mean to fight. Now our levy is raw, and has no discipline, and I doubt it will be as it was at Charnmouth. If that is so, Bridgwater will be no safe place for the lady Alswythe. She must be got hence with all speed."

"Shall you not return and hide with her?" I asked.

"That is as the master bids," said he, and then he added, looking at me doubtfully, "I would you were not so bent on this fight."

Then was I torn two ways -- by my longing to strike a blow for Wessex, and by my love for my Alswythe and care for her safety. And I knew not what to say. Wulfhere understood my silence, and then decided for me.

"You have hearkened to me before, master, and now I will speak again. Get you to your place of last night on Combwich Hill, and there look on the fight; or, if it be nearer this, find such a place as you know. Then, if there is victory for us, all is well: but if not, you could not aid with your one strength to regain it. Then will Alswythe need you."

"I would fain fight," I said, still doubting.

"Aye, master; but already have you done well, and deserved well of the sheriff, and of all. He bade you fight not today -- let it be so. There is loyalty also in obedience, and ever must some bide with the things one holds dear."

"I will do as you say," said I shortly, and so I turned and went.

He stood and looked after me for a little, and then he too hurried away towards the cross. Then I skirted round the town, and waited at that place where I had met with the old woman, until I saw the van of our forces marching down the road towards Cannington. These I kept up with by hurrying from point to point alongside the road, as best I might.

They were a gallant show to look on, gay with banners and bright armour. Yet I had heard of the ways of armies, and thought to see them marching in close order and in silence. But they were in a long line with many gaps, and here and there the mounted thanes rode to and fro, seemingly trying to make them close up. And they sang and shouted as they went.

When we came to the steep rise of Cannington hill, some of those thanes spurred on and rode to the summit, and there waited a little, till the men joined them. There was silence, and a closing up as they breasted the steep pitch; and then I must go through woods, and so lost sight of them for a while. I passed close to my own hall -- closed and deserted. Every soul in all the countryside had fled into the town, though after the levy came a great mixed crowd of thralls and the like to see the fray.

Now here I thought to cross in the rear of the force that I might reach Combwich hill. But that was not to be.

When I saw the array again it was halted, and the men were closing up. And between the levy and that crowd of followers was a great gap, and some of these last were making for the shelter of swamp and wood. I myself was on a little rise of heathy land and could see plainly before me the road going up over the neck of Combwich hill in the steep-sided notch there is there, where the ascent is easiest.

And that road was barred halfway up the hillside by a close-ranked company, on which the sun shone brightly, showing scarlet cloaks and gilded helms not only on the roadway, but flanking the hills on either side. These were the Danes, and behind them, over the hill, rose the smoke from Matelgar's burnt home.

Even as I looked, a great roar of defiance came from our men; but the Danes made no answer, standing still and silent. And that seemed terrible to me. So for a moment they stood, and then, as at some signal, from them broke out that deep chant with its terrible swinging melody, that had come faintly to me from Watchet haven.

Then our men rushed forward, and even where I stood I could hear the crash of arms on shields as the lines met -- the ringing of the chime of war -- and our men fought uphill.

And now it needed all my force to keep myself, for Alswythe's sake, from joining in that fray, and presently, when I would take my hand from my sword hilt, it was stiff and cramped from clutching hard upon it, as I watched those two lines swaying, and heard the yells of the fighters.

And indeed I should surely have joined, but there came a voice to me:

"Bide here in patience, Heregar, the king's thane! There is work for you yet that fighting will hinder."

And the old crone, Gundred, who had come I know not how, laid her hand on my arm.

"Look at the tide, Heregar, look at the tide!" she said, pointing to Parret river, where the mud banks lay bare and glistening with the falling water. "Let them drive these Danes back to their stranded ships, and how many will go home again to Denmark, think you?"

And I prayed that this might be so: for I knew she spoke truth. If they might not reach their ships, and became penned in on Stert, they were lost -- every one, for none might cross the deep ooze.

"Not this time, Heregar. Remember, when the time comes," she said.

And I paid no heed to her. For now horses were galloping riderless along the road and into the fields. And men were crawling back from the fight, to fall exhausted in the rear, and then -- then the steadfast line of the scarlet-cloaked Danes charged down the hill, driving our men like sheep before them.

"Up and to your work!" said the crone, pointing towards Bridgwater; and I, who had already made two steps, with drawn sword, towards that broken, flying rabble, remembered Alswythe, and turned away, groaning, to hasten to her rescue. For it was, as Wulfhere had said, all that I could do.

Swiftly I went, turning neither to right nor left along the road, hearing always behind me the cries of those who fled, and the savage shouts of the pursuing vikings. I was in the midst of that crowd of thralls once, but they thinned, taking to the woods whence I had come; while I kept on.

Then I saw one of those horses, a great white steed, standing, snorting, by the wayside where he had stopped, and I spoke to him, and he let me catch and mount him, and so I rode on.

Yet when I came to the top of Cannington Hill I looked back. All the road was full of our men, flying; and a thought came into my head, and I dared to draw rein and wait for them, linking my mail again across my face.

They came up, panting, and wild with panic, and there with voice and hand I bade them stand on that vantage ground and block the way against the Danes; bidding them remember the helpless ones in the town, who must have time to fly, and how the Danes must needs shrink from a second fight after hot pursuit.

And there is that in a Saxon's stubborn heart which bade them heed me, and there they formed up again, wild with rage and desperate, and the line grew thicker and firmer as more came up, with the sheriff himself, till the foremost pursuing Danes recoiled, and some were slain, and I knew that the flight was over.

Then I slipped from my horse and made my way on foot, lest men should notice my going, but the horse followed me, and soon I mounted him again and galloped on.

Then I found that though I had not noticed it, my mail had fallen apart: but I knew not if any had known me, or even had noted who I might be.

So I came to Bridgwater, bringing terror with me, as men gathered what had befallen from my haste. Yet I stayed for none; but went on to the nunnery.

IX: IN BRIDGWATER

Two of Wulfhere's men were by the gate, lounging against the sunny wall; but they roused into life as they heard the clatter of my horse's hoofs, and came to meet me and take the bridle, as was their duty. They knew who I was well enough; but thralls may not question the ways of a thane, as I was yet in their eyes, though outlawed. Yet they asked me for news of the fight, and I told them -- lest they should raise a panic, or maybe leave us themselves -- only that our men stood against the Danes on Cannington Hill, and that beyond them the invaders could not come. And that satisfied them.

I was doubtful whether to go in at once and seek audience with the prioress, or wait until some fresh news came in; for now I began to have a hope that our men would sweep down the hill on the Danes and scatter them in turn, even as they had themselves been overborne. So for half an hour I waited, pacing the road before the nunnery, while I bade the men see to my horse; but the place was very quiet, being on that side the town away from the fight, so that any coming thence would stay their flight when the shelter of the houses was reached.

At last came one, running at a steady pace, and I sprang to meet him, for it was Wulfhere. His face was hard and set, his armour was covered with blood, and he had a bandage round his head instead of helmet; but he was not hurt much, as one might see by the way he came.

He grasped my hand without a word, and threw himself on the bank by the road side to get breath, and I stood by him, silent for a while.

"Heregar," he said at last, "it is well for Bridgwater town, and these here in this nunnery, that you obeyed and fought not."

"Wherefore?" I said. "Must we fly?"

"I saw you rally the men on Cannington Hill, and that was the best thing done in all this evil day."

"Then," I asked, "do they yet stand?"

"Aye; for the Danes have drawn off, and our men bar the way here."

I told him what I had hoped from a charge of our levy; but he shook his head and told me that, even had our men the skill to see their advantage, the Danes had formed up again on seeing that this might be, and had gone back in good order to their first post at Combwich.

"But our levy will not bide a second fight," he said sadly. "Already the men are making off home, in twos and threes, saying that the Danes will depart, and the like. Tomorrow the way here will be open, for there will be no force left to Osric by the morning. I have seen such things before."

"Then must the Lady Alswythe fly," I said: "but where is Matelgar?"

"Struck down as he fled," said Wulfhere grimly. "I saw Osric and twenty of his men close round him and beat back the Danes for a moment: but I could not win to them, and so came back to you as you rallied us. That was well done," he said again.

"I left when Osric came up. Matelgar I saw not," I said.

"Osric saw you, though," answered Wulfhere, "and, moreover, knew you. And I heard him cry out when he saw the white horse riderless; for the arrows were still flying, and he thought you slain, I think."

Now I wondered if Osric would be wroth with me, thinking I had fought against his orders; but I had little time to think of myself, all my care being for Alswythe, who had lost home and father in one day; being left to Wulfhere, and me -- an outlaw.

Then Wulfhere and I took counsel about flight, being troubled also about the holy women in this place; for the heathen would not respect the walls of a nunnery. But for them we thought Osric would surely care.

Now there came to us as we stood and talked, a housecarle in a green cloak, and asked us if we had seen a warrior, wounded maybe, riding a great white horse, which, he added, had been Edred the Thane's, who was killed.

"Aye, that have I," said Wulfhere, "what of him?"

"Osric the Sheriff seeks him. Tell me quickly where I may find him."

"Is Osric back in the town?" asked Wulfhere in surprise.

"Aye, man, and half the levy with him. The Danes will go away now. Enough are left to mind them."

Then Wulfhere stamped on the ground in rage, cursing the folly of every man of the levy. And the housecarle stared at him as at one gone suddenly mad; but I knew only too well that his worst fears were on the way to be realized, and that soon there would be no force left on Cannington Hill.

Suddenly he turned on the messenger and asked if he knew the name of the man he sought.

"No; but men say that it was one Heregar -- an outlawed thane. And some say that it was one of the saints."

"Will Osric string him up, think you, if he can catch him, and it be Heregar only, and no saint?"

The man stared again.

"Surely not," he said, "for he was sore cast down once, on the hill, thinking him slain. But men had seen him remount and ride on, And Osric bid me, and all of us who seek him, pray Heregar -- if Heregar it be -- to come to him in all honour. Let me go and seek him."

Then Wulfhere turned to me and asked if I would go. And at that the man made reverence to me, giving his message again.

Then I said "Is Matelgar the Thane with him?" and he answered that Matelgar was slain before the stand was made.

Then I said I would go, if only to ask Osric for a guard to keep the Lady Alswythe safe in her flight. And Wulfhere agreed, but doubtfully, saying that nevertheless he would make ready the horses and provisions for a journey, biding till I came back, or sent a messenger.

So I went with the housecarle, who led me again through the marketplace to that same great house whence I had been sent forth overnight. All the square was full of men, drinking deeply, some boasting of their deeds, and some of deeds to be done yet. But many sat silent and gloomy, and more cried out with pain as their wounds were dressed by the leeches or the womenfolk. All was confusion, and, indeed, one might not know if this turmoil was after victory or defeat.

None noticed me or my guide, but, indeed, I saw few men I knew in all the crowd, for the men of Bridgwater and those of Matelgar's following had fought most fiercely on their own land, and even now stayed to guard what they might on the hill.

Osric again sat in the great chair in the hall, as I could see through the open door, and round him were the thanes; but far fewer than last night. And presently a housecarle spoke to him, and he rose up and left the hall. Then they led me to a smaller chamber, and there he was alone, and waiting for me.

Now I knew not what his wish to see me might mean, but from him I looked for no harm, remembering how he had seemed to favour me even in refusing my request. But, least of all did I look for him to come forward to meet me, taking both my hands, and grasping them, while he thanked me for the day's work.

"Lightly I let you go last night, Heregar," he said, "setting little store on the matter among all the trouble of the gathering. But when I sent you away and forgot you, surely the saints guided me. For I have heard how you dared to go down to Stert and warn us all, and I saw you stay the flight, even now. Much praise, and more than that, is due to you. Were you in the fight?"

Then I could answer him to a plain question; for all this praise, though it was good to hear, abashed me.

"Nay, Sheriff," I answered. "Fain would I have been there, but a wiser head than mine advised me, and bade me do your bidding, and forbear. Else should I surely have fought."

"Loyalty has brought good to us all, Heregar," he said, looking squarely at me. "Yet should I have hardly blamed you had you disobeyed me."

Then I flushed red, thinking shame not to have done so, and went to excuse myself for obedience.

"Yet had I the safety of a lady who must die, if the battle went wrongly for us, laid on me in a way," I said.

"Matelgar's fair daughter?" he asked.

"Aye, Sheriff," And I told him of the flight from the hall, and where she was now, wondering how he guessed this. But I had come from Stert, and therefore the guess was no wonder. He looked at me gravely, and then sat down, motioning me to be seated also. He treated me not as an outlaw, I thought.

"Matelgar is dead," he said. "I saw him fall, and tried to bring him off. He was not yet sped when we beat off the Danes. And he had time to speak to me."

I bowed in silence, not knowing what to say. Strange that, now my enemy was dead, I had no joy in it; but I thought of Alswythe only.

The sheriff went on, looking at me closely.

"He bade me find Heregar, the outlawed thane who spoke last night to me, and bid him forgive. Then he died, and I must needs leave him, for the Danes came on in force."

Still I was silent, for many thoughts came up in my heart and choked me. How I had hated him, and yet how he had wronged me -- even to seeking my life. Yet was I beginning to think of him but as a bad father to my Alswythe, but a man to be held in some regard, for the sake of her love to him. And it seems to me that shaping my words to this end so often had gradually turned my utter bitterness away: for one has to make one's thoughts go the way one speaks, if one would seem to speak true.

"I may not make out all this, Heregar, my friend," said the sheriff; "but that you were disloyal ever, no man may say in my hearing after this day's work. And I know that Matelgar was the foremost in accusing you. Wherefore it seems to me that there was work there to be forgiven by you. Is that so?"

The thing was so plain that I could but bow my head in assent.

"Now," he went on, "I have heard private talk of this sort before now; but never mind. I cannot inlaw you again, Heregar; for that must needs be done in full Moot, as was the outlawry. Yet shall all my power be bent to help you back to your own, if only for the sake of today."

Then would I thank him, but he stopped me.

"To the man who lit the fire of Stert, who checked the panic on Cannington Hill, thanks are due, not gratitude from him. And to him justice and reward."

Now I knew not what to say; but at that moment came a hurried rapping on the door and the sound of voices, speaking together. Then the door was thrown open and a man entered, heated and breathless, crying:

"The Danes -- they are on our men again!"

Then Osric flushed red, and his eyes sparkled, and he bid the thanes who crowded after the messenger get to horse and sound the assembly at once to go to the assistance of those who were yet on the hill.

And yet he turned to me when this was said, and took my hand again.

"Get your lady in safety to Glastonbury, where Ealhstan the Bishop is. I will care for the nuns if need be. Take this ring of mine and show it to him, and then ride with it to Eanulf the Ealdorman and tell him of our straits. The words I leave to you, who have done better than all of us today."

Then he took helm and sword from one who brought them in haste, and armed himself, while I, putting the ring he had given me on my finger, yet stood beside him. When he was armed he turned sharply to me.

"You want to fight again," he said. "Well, I will not blame you; but believe me, you will do more for us in going to Eanulf than in spending your life here for nought."

Then he saw he had said too much, perhaps, and motioning his man out of the room, so that we were alone, he went on quickly: "I say for nought, because all I can do is to hold back the Danes for a little; you have seen how it is. We are evenly matched in numbers, or thereabout; but they are trained and hardened warriors, and our poor men are all unused to war. Moreover, Heregar, these Danes come to fight, and our men do but fight because they must. Now I will send one after you to Glastonbury to let you know how this matter goes; but it will be, I fear, no pleasant message."

Then would I not ask him for men as I had been minded to do, knowing what a strait he was in, and that his words were only too true. Those two differences between Dane and Saxon in those days of the first fighting left the victory too plainly on the side of the newcomers. And they sum up all the reasons for the headway they made against us till Alfred, our wise king, taught us to meet them in their own way.

So once more I felt the grip of Osric's hand on mine, and I left him, with a heavy heart indeed, but with a new hope for myself and for Alswythe, in the end.

I stood for a moment before I turned out of the marketplace, eating a loaf I had taken from the table as I passed, and watching the men gather, spiritless, for this new fight. On many, too, the strong ale had told, and it was a sorry force that Osric could take with him.

But I might not stay, and was turning to go, when I saw one standing like myself and watching, close by. It was my host of Sedgemoor, Dudda the Collier. And never was face more welcome than his grimy countenance, for now I knew that I had found one who, in an hour, would take Alswythe into paths where none might follow, and that, too, on the nearest road to Glastonbury. There is no safer place for those who would fly, than the wastes of Sedgemoor to those who know, or have guide to them, and there no Danes would ever come.

So I stepped up to him and touched him, and he grinned at seeing a known face, muttering to himself, "Grendel, the king's messenger."

And as I beckoned he willingly followed me towards my destination, asking me of the fight, and what was on hand now so suddenly.

I told him shortly, finding that he had been drawn from his own neighbourhood by curiosity, which must be satisfied before he went back. And I told him that now the Danes were close on Bridgwater, and that I must bear messages to Eanulf the Ealdorman. Would he earn a good reward by getting me and some others across Sedgemoor by the paths along which he had led me?

And at that he grinned, delighted, saying, "Aye, that will I, master," seeming to forget all else in prospect of gain.

So I bade him follow me closely, and soon we were back at the nunnery gates.

They were open, and inside I could see the horses standing. Wulfhere was waiting for me, looking anxious; but his brow cleared as he saw me, and he asked for the news, saying that he feared I had fallen into the wrong hands.

Then I told him I had, as I thought, no more to fear, showing him the sheriff's ring and telling him of my errand.

"That is nigh as good as inlawed again," he said gladly. "Anyway, you ride as the sheriff's man now."

Then his face clouded a little, and he added, "But Glastonbury is a far cry, master, for the roads are none so direct."

Then I called the collier, and Wulfhere questioned him, and soon was glad as I that I had met with him, saying that in an hour we should be in safety. But he would that the prioress and her ladies would come also, for he knew that Osric's fears would be only too true. Then must we go and tell Alswythe of the journey she must make; and how to tell of her father's death I knew not, nor did Wulfhere. And there we two men were helpless, looking at one another in the courtyard, and burning with impatience to get off.

"Let us go first, and tell her on the way" said he.

But I reminded him that we were here even now, and not on the far side of the Quantocks, because she would by no means leave her father.

Now while we debated this, the old sister who was portress, opened the wicket and asked us through it why these horses stood in the yard, and what we armed men did there. And that decided me. I would ask for speech with the prioress, and tell her the trouble.

That pleased Wulfhere: and I did so. Then the portress asked who I might be, and lest my name should but prove a bar to speech with the lady, I showed her Osric's ring, which she knew as one he was wont to give to men as surety that they came from him on his errand. And that was enough, for in a few minutes she came back, taking me to the guest chamber.

There I unhelmed and waited, while those minutes seemed very long, though they were but few before the lady came in.

She started a little when she saw who I was, for she had known me well, and knew now in what case I had been. But Alswythe had told her also of what I had been able to do for her last night, if she had heard no more, for news gets inside even closed walls, in one way or another, from the lay people who serve the place.

I bent my knee to her, and she looked at me very sadly, saying: "I knew and loved your mother, Heregar, my son, and sorely have I grieved for you -- not believing all the things brought against you. How come you here now?"

Then I held out my hand and showed her Osric's ring, only saying that as the good sheriff trusted me I would ask her to do so. And at that she looked glad, and said that she would hold Osric's trust as against any word she had heard of me in dispraise.

So I bowed, and then, thinking it foolish to waste time, begged her to forgive bluntness, and told her of the death of Matelgar and of the sore danger of the town, and of how Osric had bidden me take Alswythe to Glastonbury to the bishop, and how he would himself care for her own safety.

She was a brave lady, and worthy of the race of Offa from which she sprung. And she heard me to the end, only growing very pale, while her hand that rested on the table grew yet whiter as she clenched it.

"Can we not recover the body of the thane?" she asked, speaking very low.

I could but shake my head, for I knew that where he lay was now in the hands of the Danes. True, if Osric could beat them off again he might gain truce for such recovery on both sides; but that seemed hopeless to me. Then I was bold to add:

"Now, lady, this matter is pressing, and in your hands I must leave it. Trust the Lady Alswythe to me and her faithful servant, Wulfhere, and I will be answerable for her with my life. But of her father's death I dare not tell her."

Then she bowed her head a little, and, I think, was praying. For when she looked at me again her face was very calm though so pale.

"Alswythe has told me of you, Heregar, my son," she said, "and to you will I trust her. Moreover I will bid her go at once, and I will tell her that heavy news you bring. You will not have long to wait, for in truth we are ready, fearing such as this."

Then I kissed her hand, and she blessed me, and went from the room. And, taught by her example, I prayed that I might not fail in this trust, but find safety for her I loved.

Now came the sister who had charge of such things, and set before me a good meal with wine, saying no word, but signing the cross over all in token that I might eat, and glad enough was I to do so, though in haste. Yet before I would begin I asked that sister to let Wulfhere know that all was going right, and to bid him be ready. She said no word, as must have been their rule, but went out, and I knew afterwards that she sent one to tell him.

In a quarter hour or so, and when I, refreshed with the good food I so needed, was waxing restless and impatient, the prioress came back, and signed me to follow her, and taking my helm, I did so, till we came to the great door leading to the courtyard. There stood Alswythe, very pale, and trying to stop her weeping very bravely, and she gave me her hand for a moment, without a word, and it was cold as ice, and shook a little; yet it had a lingering grasp on mine, as though it would fain rest with me for a little help.

There were but two of her maidens with her, and the prioress saw that I was surprised, and said: "The rest bide with us, Heregar, and here they will surely be safe. Alswythe will take no more than these, lest you are hindered on the journey."

And I was glad of that, though I should have loved to see her better attended, as befitted her; yet need was pressing, and this was best. Then the prioress kissed Alswythe and the maidens, and Wulfhere set them on their horses, for though I would fain help Alswythe myself, the lady had more to say to me, and kept me.

She told me to take my charge to the abbess of her own order at Glastonbury, where they would be tended in all honour as here with herself, and she gave me a letter also to the abbess to tell her what was needed and why they came, and then she gave me a bag with gold in it, knowing that I might have to buy help on the way. For all this I thanked her; but she said that rather it was I who should be thanked, and from henceforward, if her word should in any way have weight, it should go with that of Osric the Sheriff for my welfare.

And this seemed to me to be much said before my task was done, but afterwards I knew that she had talked with Wulfhere, who had told her all -- even to the treachery of Matelgar. That would I have prevented, had I known, but so it was to be, and I had no knowledge of it till long after. Wulfhere had been called in to give her news while I was with Osric, yet he had not dared to tell her of the thane's death.

All being ready, I mounted that white steed that had been the dead thane's, knowing that in war and haste these things must be taken as they come, and that he was better in Saxon hands than Danish. Then I gave the word, and we started, Dudda the Collier going by my side, and staring at the prioress and all things round him.

Alswythe turned and looked hard at her aunt as we passed the gates, and I also. She stood very still on the steps before the great door, with the portress beside her. There was only the old lay brother in the court beside, and so we left her. And what my fears were for her and hers I could not tell Alswythe. For, as we left the gates, something in the sky over towards the battleground caught my eyes, and I turned cold with dread. It was the smoke from burning houses at Cannington.

CHAPTER X: FLIGHT THROUGH SEDGEMOOR

I was glad we had not to go through the town, for the sights there were such as Alswythe could not bear to look on. And if that smoke meant aught, it meant that our men were beaten back, and would even now be flying into the place with perhaps the Danes at their heels.

I rode alongside Wulfhere, and motioned to him to look, and as he did so he groaned. Then he spoke quite cheerfully to his lady, saying that we had better push on and make a good start; and so we broke into a steady trot and covered the ground rapidly enough, ever away from danger.

I rode next Alswythe, but I would not dare speak to her as yet. She had her veil down, and was quite silent, and I felt that it would be best for me to wait for her wish.

Beside me trotted the collier, Wulfhere was leading, and next to Alswythe and me came the two maidens. After them came the three men and two boys, all mounted, and leading with them the other three horses of the twelve we had brought from Stert. They were laden with things for the journey given by the prioress, and with what they had saved from Matelgar's hall, though that was little enough.

Wulfhere would fain have made the collier ride one of these spare horses; but the strange man had refused, saying that his own legs he could trust, but not those of a four-footed beast.

It was seven in the bright May morning when Dane and Saxon met on Combwich Hill. It was midday when I met Wulfhere at the nunnery, and now it was three hours and more past. But I thought there was yet light enough left for us to find our way across Sedgemoor, and lodge that night in safety in the village near the collier's hut; and so, too, thought Wulfhere when I, thinking that perhaps Alswythe's grief might find its own solace in tears when I was not by her, rode on beside him for a while.

"Once set me on Polden hills, master," said Wulfhere, "I can do well enough, knowing that country from my youth. But this is a good chance that has sent you your friend the collier."

So he spoke, and then I fell to wondering, if it was all chance, as we say, that led my feet in that night of wandering to Dudda's hut, that now I might find help in sorer need than that. For few there are who could serve as guide over that waste of fen and swamp, and but for him we must needs have kept the main roads, far longer in their way to Glastonbury, as skirting Sedgemoor, and now to be choked with flying people.

Presently Wulfhere asked me if in that village we might find one good house where to lodge the Lady Alswythe. And I told him that there I had not been, but at least knew of one substantial franklin, for my playfellow, Turkil, had been the son of such an one, as I was told. The collier, who ran, holding my stirrup leather, tireless on his lean limbs as a deerhound, heard this, and told me that the man's house was good and strong -- not like those in Bridgwater -- but a great house for these parts. So I was satisfied enough.

Then this man Dudda, finding I listened to him in that matter, began to talk, asking me questions of the fighting, and presently "if I had seen the saint?"

I asked him what he meant; and as I did so I heard Wulfhere chuckle to himself. Then he told me a wild story that was going round the town. How that, when all seemed lost, there came suddenly a wondrous vision, rising up before the men, of a saint clad in armour and riding a white horse, having his face covered lest men should be blinded by the light thereof, who, standing with drawn sword on Cannington Hill, so bade the men take courage that they turned and beat the Danes back. Whereupon he vanished, though the white horse yet remained for a little, before it, too, was gone.

Well, thought I, Grendel the fiend was I but the other day, and now I am to be a saint. And with that I could not restrain myself, but laughed as once before I had laughed at this same man, for the very foolishness of the thing. Yet I might not let Alswythe know that I laughed, and so could not let it go as I would, and I saw that Wulfhere was laughing likewise, silently.

Now this is not to be wondered at, though it was but a little thing maybe. For we had been like a long-bent bow, overstrained with doubt and anxiety, and, now that we were in safety with the lady, it needed but like this to slacken the tension, and bid our minds relieve themselves. So that laugh did us both good, and moreover took away some of the downcast look from our faces when next we spoke to our charge.

When he could speak again, Wulfhere answered the man, still smiling.

"Aye, man, I saw him. And he was wondrous like Heregar, our master, here."

And at that the collier stared at me, and then said: "There be painted saints in our church. But they be not like mortal men, being no wise so well-favoured as the master."

And that set Wulfhere laughing again, for the good monks who paint these things are seldom good limners, but make up for bad drawing by bright colour. So that one may only know saint from fiend by the gold, or the want of it, round his head.

Then fell I to thinking again about myself, and what it takes to make man a saint or a fiend. And that thought was a long thought.

Now were we come across Parret, and began our journey into the fens. And presently we must ride in single file along a narrow pathway which I could barely trace, and indeed in places could not make out at all. And here the collier led, going warily, then came Wulfhere, and then Alswythe, with myself next behind her to help if need were. After us the maidens, and then the rest.

So we were in safety, for half a mile of this ground was safer than a wall behind us. We went silently for a little while, save for a few words of caution here and there. But at last Alswythe turned to me, and lifted her veil, smiling a little to me at last, and asking why we left the good roads for this wild place, for though we men were used to the like in hunting, she knew not that such places and paths could be, brought up as she was in the wooded uplands of our own corner of the country.

I told her how I was to make all speed to Glastonbury, and that this was the nearest road: and she was content, being very trustful in both her protectors. But then she asked if that place should be reached before dark, having little knowledge of places or distances.

Then I must needs tell how we were bound for that village where the hermit was, and Turkil of whom I had told her, seeing that it was over late to reach the town, but that there we hoped to come next day. And she said she would fain see those two, "and maybe Grendel also," smiling again a little to please me. And I knew how much that little jest cost her to make, and loved her the more for her thought for me. Then she was silent for a while.

Presently one of the men in the rear shouted, and there was a great splashing and snorting of horses, and we looked round. One of the led horses had gone off the path and was in a bog, and that had set the rest rearing with fright.

So we had to halt, and Wulfhere gave his horse to Dudda to hold while he went back. And that kept us for a while waiting, and then I could stand beside Alswythe for a little.

"I have seen the last of my outlaw, they tell me," she said, wanting to learn how things were with me.

Yet I was still that, if only for loss of lands and place. Though as Osric's chosen messenger I had that last again for a little, because of his need.

So I told her that that matter must be settled by the Moot, but that Osric was my friend, and that while I bore his ring at least none might call me "outlaw". And at that she was glad, and told me that if she saw Leofwine the hermit she would tell him that his words were coming true. Then she looked hard at me, and said that she had heard from her aunt why Osric so trusted me, and that she was proud of Heregar. And I said that I had but done the things that someone had to do, and which came in my way, as it seemed to me, wherein I was fortunate.

At that she smiled at me, seeming to think more of the matter than that, and so talked of other things. Yet she must needs at last come to that which lay nearest her heart, and so asked me if I had seen her father fall.

And I was glad to say that I had not; adding that it was near Combwich Hill, as I had heard, and close to where Osric the Sheriff fought.

So I think that all her life long she believed him to have fallen fighting in the first line, where Osric was, with his face to the enemy; for all men spoke well of the sheriff's valour that day, and none would say more than I told her. Yet it may have been that the thane fought well, unobserved, in that press, and there is perhaps little blame to many who fly in a panic.

Now, that spoken of and passed over, she became more like her brave self, and from that time on would speak cheerfully both to Wulfhere and myself, as, the horses set in order again, we once more went on our winding way, following our guide.

Glad was I when, just before sunset, we saw the woodland under which his hut was set, and heard the vesper bell ringing far off from the village church. Soon we were on hard ground again, and then I could show Alswythe where I had played Grendel unwittingly, and point the way I had wandered from Brent.

There we rested the horses, for we had yet two miles to go, and they were weary with the long and heavy travelling of the fens. And Alswythe would go into the hut, and there her maidens brought her food and wine, and we stayed for half an hour.

Wulfhere and I looked out towards Bridgwater town, now seeming under the very hills, in the last sunlight. Smoke rose from behind it, but that was doubtless from Cannington; yet there were other clouds of smoke rising against the sun, and as he looked at these the old warrior said that he feared the worst, for surely the Danes were spreading over the country and that need for them to keep together was gone.

"If we see not Bridgwater on fire by tomorrow," he said, "it will be a wonder."

But we knew that we could bide here for this night safe as if no Danes were nearer than the Scaw.

After that rest we rode on through the woodland path, down which they had come to exorcise me, till we saw before us in the gray twilight the church and houses of the village, pleasant with light from door and window, and noise of barking dogs, as we crossed the open mark.viii

Dudda the Collier led us to the largest house which stood on the little central green round which the buildings clustered, and there the door stood open, and a tall man with a small boy beside him looked out to see what was disturbing the dogs. Behind them the firelight shone red on a pleasant and large room where we could see men at supper.

And the light shone out on me, for the boy sprang out from his father's side, shouting that it was "Grendel come back again", and running to me to greet me.

So we found a welcome in that quiet place, and soon the good franklin's wife came out, bustling and pitiful in her care for Alswythe and sorrow for her need to fly from her lost home, for it took but few words to explain what had befallen.

They brought us in, and the thralls left supper to tend our horses, though Wulfhere would go with them to see that done before he joined us in the wide oak-built room that made all the lower floor of the house. Overhead was the place where Alswythe and her maidens should be, and built against the walls outside were the thralls' quarters, save for a few who slept in the lower room round the great fire.

Now, how they treated us it needs not to be told, for it was in the way of a good Somerset franklin, and that is saying much. But that night he would talk little, seeing that I and Wulfhere were overdone with want of sleep. Indeed it was but the need of caution that had kept me from falling asleep on my horse more than once on the road. So very soon they brought us skins and cloaks, and we stretched ourselves before the fire, and warmed, and cleansed, and well refreshed with food and drink, fell to sleep on the instant.

Yet not so soundly could I sleep at first, but that I woke once, thinking I heard the yells of the Danes close on us: but it was some farmyard sound from without, and peaceful.

Then I slept again until, towards dawning I think, I awoke, shivering, and with a great untellable fear on me, and saw a tall, gray figure standing by my couch. And I looked, and lo it was Matelgar the Thane.

Then I went to rouse Wulfhere, but my hand would not be stretched out, and the other men slept heavily, so that I lay still and looked in the dead thane's face and grew calmer.

For his face was set with a look of sorrow such as I had never seen there, and he gazed steadfastly at me and I at him, and the grief in his face did but deepen. And at last he spoke, and the voice was his own, and yet not his own.

"Heregar, sorely have I wronged you," he said, "and my rest is troubled therefor. Yet, when I heard what you had done for mine last night, my heart was sore within me, and I repented of all, and would surely have made amends. And now it is too late, and my body lies dishonoured on Parret side while I am here. Yet do you forgive, and mayhap I shall rest."

Then I strove to speak, bidding him know that I forgave, but I could not, and he seemed to grow more sad, watching me yet. And when I saw that, I made a great effort, and stretching my hand towards him signed the blessed sign in token that that should bid me forgive him, so leaving my hand outstretched towards him.

And then his face changed and grew brighter, and he took my hand in his, as I might see, though I could feel nought but a chill pass on it, as it were, and spoke again, saying:

"It is well, and shall be, both with you and me. And when you need me I shall stand by you once again and make amends."

Then he was gone, and my hand fell from where his had been, and straightway I slept again in a dreamless sleep till Wulfhere roused me in the full morning light.

And in that light this matter seemed to me but a dream that had come to me. Yet even as I should have wished to speak to Alswythe's father, had I done, and I would not have had it otherwise. Then the dream in a way comforted me, being good to think on, for I would not willingly be at enmity with any man, or living or dead. But that it was only a dream seemed more sure, because in it Matelgar had said he knew of my saving Alswythe. And Wulfhere and I had agreed not to tell him that. Also I had little need of Matelgar living, in good truth, and surely less need of him now that he was gone past making amends.

Down into the great chamber to break her fast with us came Alswythe, bright and fresh, and with her grief put on one side, for our sakes who served her. And Turkil talked gaily with both Alswythe and me and Wulfhere, and would fain tell all the story of how he sought the fire-spitting fiend and was disappointed.

Then I missed the collier, and asked where he was. He had gone to bring the good hermit the franklin told me, and would be back shortly.

Now, when we had broken our fast it was yet very early, and the villagers must needs hear all the news of the great fight and terror beyond the fens, and as they heard, a growl of wrath went round, and the men grasped spade and staff and fork fiercely, bidding the franklin lead them at once to join the levy.

But Wulfhere told them that they needs must now wait a second raising, and that I was even now on my way to Eanulf the Ealdorman to tell him of the need. Then the franklin asked that he and his might go with me, but I, seeing that for an outlaw to take a following with him was not to be thought of, bade them wait for word and sure tidings of the gathering place.

While we talked thus the little bell in the church turret began to ring, and we knew that the hermit, Leofwine the priest, had come, and would say mass for us. Then, perhaps, was such a gathering to pray for relief for their land, as had not been since those days, far off now, when the British prayed, in that same place, the like prayers for deliverance from my own forbears. And as I prayed, looking on the calm face of the old man who had bidden me take heart and forgive, I knew that last night's dream was true in this, that I had forgiven.

So when the mass was over, and Wulfhere had begged Alswythe to take order at once for our going on our journey, I found the old man, and could greet him with a light heart. And he, looking on me, could read, as he had read the trouble, how that that had passed, and asked me if all was well, as my face seemed to say.

I told him how I had fared, and how my outlawry, though still in force, was now light on me as the sheriff's messenger -- though this I thought was but because, flying with Alswythe, I might as well take the message as one who could be less easily spared.

Then he said that already he deemed the prophecy that had been given him was coming true, and spoke many good and loving words to me to strengthen my thoughts of peace withal.

Presently he looked at our horses, now standing ready at the franklin's door, and would have me go back with him into his own chamber in the little timber-walled church. And there he found writing things in a chest, and wrote on a slip of parchment a letter which he bade me give to the bishop when I came to him, signing it with his name at the end, as he told me, though I could not read it, for one who has been bred a hunter and warrior has no need for the arts of the clerk. Indeed, I had seen but two men write before, and one was our old priest at Cannington, and the other was Matelgar, and I ever wondered that this latter should be able to do so, and why of late he was often sending men with letters. Yet it seems to me now that surely they had to do with his schemes that had so come to nought.

Then the old man blessed me, telling me again that I should surely prosper unless that I failed by my own fault, and that it seemed to him that there was yet work for me to do that should set me again in my place, and maybe higher.

So talking with him, Wulfhere called me, and I must needs say farewell to Turkil and his father, and they bade us return, when the time came, by this way back to our own place. And Turkil wept, and would fain have gone with us, but I promised to see him again, and waved hand to him before the broad meadows of the mark were passed, and the woods hid the village from us.

Then did Alswythe, in her kindness, fall into a like mistake as that I had made with the boy; for she turned to me, smiling, and said that she would surely take him into her service at Stert, and see to his training hereafter, but then remembered that she had no longer home, and her smile faded into tears.

My heart ached for her, knowing I could give her no comfort. After that we rode in silence, and quickly, for the track was good.

Now there is little to tell of that ride till we reached the hilltop that Wulfhere knew, and where we could look down on the land we were to cross, and fancy we could see Glastonbury far away. Here Dudda the Collier's task was ended, and I called him to me, pulling out the purse the good prioress had given me, that I might give him a gold piece for his faithful service.

He stood before me, cap in hand, and I gave him a bright new coin, and he took it, turning it over curiously.

"Take it, Dudda," I said, "you have earned it well."

Then he grinned in his way, and answered: "It is no good to me, master. I pray you give me silver instead. Like were I to starve if life lay in the changing of this among our poor folk."

So I turned over the money to find silver, but there was not enough, and so I took out that bag which I had found in the roadway, and had not opened since, having almost forgotten it. There was silver and copper only in that, and I began to give him his reward.

But still the man hesitated, and seemed anxious to ask me something, and, while I counted out the money, he spoke: "Master, the men call you Heregar, and that is an outlaw's name."

"Well." said I, fearing no reproach from that just now, and being sure that by this time the man knew all about me from our thralls with us. "Heregar, the outlawed thane I was, and am, except that the sheriff has bid me ride on his business."

"Then, master," said he, "give me no reward but to serve you. No man's man am I, either free or unfree, but son of escaped thralls who are dead long ago. Therefore am I outlaw also by all rights, and would fain follow you. And it seems to me that you will need one to mind your steed."

Now this was a long speech for the collier, who, as I had learnt, could hold his tongue: and we were short-handed also, with all these horses. Therefore I told him that it should be as he would, for service offered freely in this way was like to be faithful, seeing that there had been trial on both sides. But I gave him four silver pennies, which he would have refused, but that I bade him think of them as fasten pennies, which contented him well.

This, too, pleased both Alswythe and Wulfhere, who were glad of the addition to our party. So we rode on. But many were the far-off columns of smoke we looked back on beyond Parret, before the hills rose behind us and hid them.

XI: EALHSTAN THE BISHOP

It was in the late afternoon when we rode into Glastonbury town, past the palisadings of the outer works, and then among cottages, and here and there a timber house of the better sort, till we came to the great abbey. It was not so great then as now, nor is it now as it will be, for ever have pious hands built so that those who come after may have room to add if they will. But it was the greatest building that I had ever seen, and, moreover, of stone throughout, which seemed wonderful to me. And there, too, Wulfhere showed me the thorn tree which sprang from the staff of the blessed Joseph of Arimathea, which flowers on Christmas Day, ever.

Then we came to the nunnery where we should leave Alswythe, and I, for my part, was sorry that the journey was over, sad though it had been in many ways, for when I must leave her I knew not how long it should be, if ever, before I saw her again.

And I think the same thought was in her heart, for, when Wulfhere showed her the great house, she sighed, looking at me a little, and I could say nothing. But she began to thank us two for our care of her, as though we could have borne to take less than we had. And her words were so sweet and gracious that even the old warrior could not find wherewith to answer her, and we both bowed our heads in thanks, and rode, one on each side of her, in silence.

Then she must ask Wulfhere what he would do when she was safely bestowed. And that was a plain question he could answer well.

"Truly, lady, if you will give me leave, I would see Heregar, our master, through whatever comes of his messages."

Then was I very glad, and the more that, though I might not think myself such, the old warrior would call me his master, for that told me that he had full belief in me.

Yet I could but say: "Friend should you call me, Wulfhere, my good counsellor, not master."

And I reached out my hand to him, bowing to Alswythe, whose horse's neck I must cross. And Wulfhere took it, and on our two rough hands Alswythe laid her white fingers, pressing them, and, looking from one to the other, said:

"Two such friends I think no woman ever had, or wiser, or braver. Go on together as you will, and yet forget not me here in Glastonbury."

Then we loosed our hands, looking, maybe, a little askance, for our Saxon nature will oft be ashamed, if one may call it so, of a good impulse acted on, and Wulfhere said that we must think of those things hereafter.

When we came to the gate there was a little crowd following us, for word had gone round in some way that we were fugitives from Parret side. But Wulfhere had bade the men answer no questions till we had seen the bishop, lest false reports should go about the place. So the crowd melted away soon, and we knocked, asking admission, and showing the letter from the prioress of Bridgwater.

Now here there was much state, as it seemed, and we must wait for a little, but then the gates were thrown open, and we rode through them into the courtyard, which was large and open. Then opened a great door on the left, and there was the abbess with many sisters, and one asked me for the letter we bore. So I gave it, and, standing there, the abbess read it while we waited.

As she read she grew pale, and then flushed again, and at last, after twice reading, came down the steps, all her state forgotten, and with tears embraced Alswythe, giving thanks for her safety. And then, leaving her, she came to me where I sat, unhelmed, and gave me her hand, thanking me for all I had done, and, as she said, perhaps for the safety of the Bridgwater sisters also.

Then all of a sudden she went back up the steps, where the sisters were whispering together, and became cold and stately again, so that I wondered if I had offended her in not speaking, which I dared not.

When she was back again in her place, she bade Alswythe and her maidens welcome, and added that all her sister prioress asked her she would do. Also, that one would come and show us lodging for men and horses, which should be at the expense of the nunnery.

So Alswythe must needs part from us coldly, even as she had joined us at Bridgwater, as a noble lady from her attendants, giving us her hand to kiss only. But I went back to my horse well content, knowing that her love and thoughts went out to me.

She went through the great door, but it closed not so fast but that I might see the abbess put her arm around her very tenderly, her state forgotten again, and I knew that she was in good hands.

Now when the horses were stabled, and our men knew where they should bide in the strangers' lodgings -- set apart for the trains of guests to the nunnery, which were very spacious -- Wulfhere and I must needs find the way to get audience of the bishop. As far as the doors of the abbey where he abode was easy enough, but there, waiting for alms and broken meats, were crowds of beggars, sitting and lying about in the sun, with their eyes ever on the latch to be first when it was lifted for the daily dole. And again, round the gate were many men of all sorts, suitors, as we deemed for some favour at the hands of bishop or abbot -- for the Abbot of Glastonbury was nigh as powerful as Ealhstan himself, in his own town at least.

When we came among these we were told that we must bide our time, for audience was not given but at stated hours. And one man, grumbling, said that that was not Ealhstan's way in his own place at Sherborne, for there the doors were open ever.

But I knew that my business might not wait, and so, after a little of this talk, went up to the gate and thundered thereon in such sort that the wicket opened, and the porter's face looked through it angrily enough, and he would have bidden us begone, for war and travel had stained us both, so that doubtless we were in no better case, as to looks, than the crowd that pressed after us -- very quietly, indeed -- to hear the parley.

One difference in our looks there was, however, which made the porter silent -- we wore mail and swords, and at that he seemed to stare in wonder.

Then I held up the ring and said, "Messages from Osric the Sheriff."

Whereupon the wicket closed suddenly, and there was a sound of unbarring, and the door opened and we were let in, the rest, who must wait, grumbling loudly at the preference shown to us, while the beggars, who had roused at the sound of the hinges creaking, went back whining in their disappointment.

Then one came and bade us follow him, and we were led into the abbey hall and there waited for a little. There were a few monks about, passing and repassing, but they paid no attention to us, and we, too, were silent in that quiet place. Only a great fire crackled at one end of the hall, else there would have been no noise at all. It was, I thought, a strangely peaceful place into which to bring news of war and tumult.

Then I thought of Ealhstan the Bishop, as he had seemed to me when he judged me, and that seemed years ago, nor could I think of myself as the same who had stood a prisoner before him. So I wondered if I should seem the same to him.

Now it is strange that of Eanulf, the mighty ealdorman who had pronounced my doom, I thought little at all, but as of one who was by the bishop. All that day's doings seemed to have been as a dream, wherein I and Wulfhere had living part with this bishop, while the rest, Eanulf and Matelgar and the others, were but phantoms standing by.

Maybe this is not so wonderful, for the doom was the doom of the Moot, and spoken by Eanulf as its mouthpiece, and that passed on my body only. And Matelgar had found a new place in my thoughts, but Wulfhere was my friend, and the bishop had spoken to my heart, so that his words and looks abode there.

Then the servant cut short my thoughts, and led us to the bishop, bidding me unhelm first.

He sat in a wide chamber, with another most venerable-looking man at the same table. And all the walls were covered with books, and on the table, too, lay one or two great ones, open, and bright with gold and crimson borderings, and great litters on the pages. But those things I saw presently, only the bishop first of all, sitting quietly and very upright in his great chair, dressed in a long purple robe, and with a golden cross hanging on his breast.

And for a moment as I looked at him, I remembered the day of the Moot, and my heart rose up, and I was ready to hide my face for minding the shame thereof.

But he looked at me curiously, and then all of a sudden smiled very kindly and said:

"Heregar, my son, are you the messenger?"

And I knelt before him on one knee, and held out the ring for him to take, and he did so, laying it on the table before him -- for my errand was in hand yet.

"Then," he said, "things are none so ill with you, my son," and he smiled gravely; "but do your errand first, and afterwards we will speak of that."

So I rose up, and standing before him, told him plainly all that had befallen, though there was no need for me to say aught of myself in the matter, except that, flying with the lady, Osric had chosen me to bear the message of defeat and danger.

And the while I spoke the bishop's face grew very grave, but he said nothing till I ended by saying that Wulfhere could tell him of the fight.

Then he bade Wulfhere speak, being anxious to know the worst, as it seemed to me. But the old man with him was weeping, and his hands shook sorely.

Now into what Wulfhere told, my name seemed to come often, for he began with the first landing at Watchet, and my bearing the war arrow, and so forward to the firing of the huts at Stert, to the rallying on Cannington Hill, and our flight, and how Osric sent for me.

Then said the bishop, "Is that the worst?"

And Wulfhere was fain to answer that he feared not, telling of the smoke clouds we had seen, and what he judged therefrom.

"Aye," said the bishop, as it were to himself and looking before him as one who sees that which he is told of, "we saw the like after Charnmouth, and let them have their way. Now must we wait, trembling, for Osric's next messenger."

But as for me, though the old man was sorely terrified, as one might see, I thought there was little trembling on the bishop's part, though he spoke of it. Rather did he seem to speak in scorn of such as would so wait.

"Tell me now," he went on presently, "how the men rallied, and with what spirit, on the hill where Heregar stayed them?"

"Well and bravely," answered Wulfhere, "so that the Danes drew back, forming up hastily lest there should be an attack on them; but none was made."

Then the bishop's eyes flashed, and I thought to myself that I would he had been there. Surely he would have swept the Danes back to their ships, and I think that was in Wulfhere's mind also, for he said:

"We want a leader who can see these things. No blame to Osric therein, for it was his first fight."

Then the bishop laughed softly in a strange way, though his eyes still flashed, and he seemed to put the matter by.

"Truly," said he, "with you, Wulfhere, to advise, and myself to ask questions, and Heregar to prevent our running away, I think we might do great things. Well, there is Eanulf, who fought at Charnmouth."

So saying he rose up, and clapped his hands loudly. The old man had fallen to telling his beads, and paid no attention to him or us any longer, doubtless dreaming of the burning of his abbey over his head, unless some stronger help was at hand than that of the three men before him.

A lay brother came in to answer the bishop's summons.

"Take these thanes to the refectory," he said, "and care for them with all honour. In two hours I will speak with them again, or sooner, if Osric's messenger comes."

"I am no thane," said Wulfhere, not willing to be mistaken.

"I am Bishop of Sherborne," said he, smiling in an absent way, and waving his hand for us to go.

So we went, and thereafter were splendidly treated as most honoured guests, even to the replacing of the broad hat which Wulfhere had gotten from the franklin by a plain steel helm, with other changes of garment, for which we were most glad.

Now as we bathed and changed, I found that letter which Leofwine the hermit priest had given me, and I prayed the brother to give it to the bishop at some proper moment, and he took it away with him. I had forgotten it in the greater business.

While we ate and drank, and talked of how to reach Eanulf the Ealdorman, the brother came back and brought us a message, saying:

"The bishop bids you rest here in peace. He has sent messengers to Eanulf, bidding him come here in all haste to speak with him and you."

So I asked where he was, and the brother said that he lay at Wells, which pleased Wulfhere, who said that he would be here shortly, and that we were in luck, seeing that he wanted another good night's rest; and indeed so did I, sorely, though that I might yet stay near Alswythe was better still.

Before the two hours the bishop had set, there was a clamour in the great yard, and we thought the messenger from Osric had surely come. And so it was, for almost directly the bishop sent for us, and we were taken back to the same chamber. But he was alone now, and motioned us to seats beside him to one side.

Then they brought in a thane whom I did not know, and he said he was a messenger from Osric, laying a letter on the table at the same time. I saw that his armour was battle stained, and that he looked sorely downcast.

Not so the bishop as he read, for that which was written he had already expected, and he never changed his set look. Once he read the letter through, and then again aloud for us to hear. Thus it ran after fit greeting:

"Now what befell in the first fight you know or shall know shortly from our trusty messenger Heregar, by whom the flight was stayed from that field, on the Hill of Cannington. And this was well done. So, seeing that the Danes had drawn off, I myself, foolishly deeming the matter at an end, left three hundred men on that hill to watch the Danes back to their ships, and returned to the town, there to muster again the men who were sound, and, if it were possible, to lead them on the Danes as they went on board again to depart. For the men, save those of Bridgwater, would not bide on the hill, but came back, saving the Danes would surely depart. And, indeed, I also thought so; but wrongly. For even as I talked with Heregar of his own affairs, news came of a fresh attack, whereon I sent him to you, fearing the worst, for the men on the hill were few, and those in the town seeming of little spirit.

"Now when I came three parts of the way to Cannington, our men there were sped and driven back on us. Whereupon I could no longer hold together any force, and whither the men are scattered I know not. Scarcely could I save the holy women and the monks, for even as they fled under guard into the Quantock woods, and so to go beyond the hills, the houses of Bridgwater next the Danes were burning.

"Now am I with two hundred men on Brent, and wait either for the Danes to depart, or for orders from yourself or the Ealdorman Eanulf, to whom I pray you let this letter be sent in haste after that you have read it."

So it ended with salutations, and when he had read it, the bishop folded it slowly and looked at the thane, who shrugged his broad shoulders and said:

"True words, Lord Bishop, and all told."

"It is what I expected," said Ealhstan, "these two thanes told me it was like to be thus."

"Surely," answered the thane. "What else?"

The bishop looked at him and asked him his name.

"Wislac, the Thane of Gatehampton by the Thames, am I," he said. "A stranger here, having come on my own affairs to Bridgwater, and so joining in the fight. Also, Osric's thanes having trouble enough on hand, I rode with this letter."

"Thanks therefor," said the bishop. "I see that you fought also in a place where blows were thick."

"Aye, in the first fight," said Wislac. "As for the second, being with Osric, I never saw that."

"Did you stay on the hill where men rallied?"

"That did I, as any man would when the saints came to stay us. Otherwise I had surely halted at Bridgwater, or this side thereof," answered the strange thane, with a smile that was bitter enough.

Now the bishop had not heard that tale of the saint on a white horse; but he was quick enough, and glanced aside at me. Whereupon Wislac the Thane looked also, and straightway his mouth opened, and he stared at me. Then, being nowise afraid of the bishop, or, as it seemed, of saints, he said aloud, seemingly to himself:

"Never saw I bishop before. Still, I knew that they were blessed with visions; but that live saints should sit below their seat, I dreamt not!" and so he went on staring at me.

So the bishop, for all his trouble, could but smile, and asked him if he saw a vision.

"Surely," he said, "this is the saint who stayed us on yonder hill."

"Nay, that is Heregar the Thane, messenger of Osric."

"Then," said Wislac, "let me tell you, Heregar the Thane, that one of the saints, and I think a valiant one, is mightily like you. Whereby you are the more fortunate."

Now for all the mistake I could not find a word to say, and was fain to thank him for the good word on my looks. Yet he went on looking at me now and then in a puzzled sort of way. And the bishop seemed to enjoy his wonderment, but was in no mind to enlighten him.

Presently the bishop bade Wislac sit down, and then he took up Osric's ring that I had given him, and also another which lay beside it on the table -- silver also, with some device on it, like that I had worn.

"See, thanes," he said, "have you three a mind to stay with me for a while and be my council in this matter? For I am here without a fighting man of my own to speak with."

Now this was what I would most wish, and I said so, eagerly and with thanks.

And Wislac said that he was surely in good company, and having nought to call him home would gladly stay also.

Then said the bishop, "Stranger you are, friend Wislac, and therefore wear this ring of Osric's, that men may pay heed to you as his friend and mine; and do you, Heregar, wear this of mine that men may know you for bishop's man, and so respect your word."

So was I put under the bishop's protection, and he would answer for my presence in Wessex to all and any. That was good, and I felt a free man again in truth, for here was no errand that would end, as Osric's was ended, when I had seen Eanulf.

Now Wulfhere had not spoken, and the bishop asked him if he too would not stay.

"Ay, lord," answered Wulfhere, "gladly; but you spoke of thanes only."

"When the Bishop of Sherborne names one as a thane," said Ealhstan, smiling, "men are apt to hold him as such. But only to the worthy are such words spoken. Now, friend Wulfhere, I have heard of you at Charnmouth fight, and also there is more in Osric's letter than I have read to you. So if you will be but a bishop's landless thane, surely you shall be one"

Then Wulfhere grew red with pleasure, and rising up, did obeisance to the bishop for the honour, and the bishop called us two others to witness that the same was given.

"Now is my council set," he said, "I to ask questions, and you to advise."

So for a long two hours we sat and told him all we knew of those Danes, I of the ships, and Wulfhere and Wislac of numbers, and Wulfhere of their ways in raiding a country, for this he had seen before, in Dorset, and also in Ireland, as he told us, in years gone by.

That night we were treated as most honoured guests of the bishop's own following, and early in the morning the bishop sent for me, before mass. Once again I found him alone in that room of his, and all he said to me I cannot write down. But I found that Leofwine the hermit had told him of how I had taken counsel of him and abided by it, even as Ealhstan himself had bidden me; and, moreover, that Osric had written in his letter of what I had been able to do against the Danes, and of Matelgar's last words concerning me. And for that remembrance of me, according to his promise, even when writing of far greater matters, I am ever grateful to the good sheriff.

So, because of these things known, Ealhstan spoke to me as a most loving father, praising me where it seemed that praise was due, and reproving me for the many things of deed and thought that were evil. And I told him freely and fully all that had passed from the time I left the hill of Brent till when I had seen the signals of the vikings from above Watchet, and bore the war arrow to Matelgar. The rest he knew in a way; but I opened all my heart to him, he drawing all from me most gently, till at last I came to my dream of Matelgar, and my wish that for me he might rest in peace.

"It is not all forgiveness, Heregar, my son," he said presently. "There is love for Alsywthe, and pride in yourself, and thought of Matelgar's failure, which have at least brought you to a beginning of it. But true forgiveness comes slowly, and many a long day shall it be before that has truly come."

And I knew that maybe he was right, and asked his help; whereupon that was freely given, and in such sort that all my life long I must mind the words he said, and love him in the memory.

When all that was said he would have me hear mass with him, as though I needed urging. And there, too, were Wulfhere and Wislac; and that mass in the great abbey was the most wonderful I ever heard.

After that we three went out into the town, and Wislac and I marvelled at everything. Then we went to the nunnery gates and asked how our charges fared, and then saw to our steeds. There was the collier, working as a groom with the other men, and he told me that he was learning his new trade fast, but would fain walk ever, rather than ride, having fallen many times from the abbess' mule, which he had bestridden in anxiety to learn. Whether the mule was the better for this lesson I doubt.

When we went back to the abbey Eanulf had come, and with him many thanes. And I feared to meet these somewhat, for they might have been among the Moot, and would know me. Yet Ealhstan had foreseen this, and one was posted at the door to meet me, bidding me aside privately, since the bishop needed me.

Wulfhere and Wislac went into the hall and left me, therefore, and I was taken to a chamber where were six or seven lay brethren, who asked me many things about the fight, and specially at last about the saint who had appeared. And that was likely to be a troublesome question for me, as I could not claim to have been the one so mistaken; but another struck in, saying that there were many strange portents about, for that a fiend had appeared bodily from the marsh and had devoured a child, in Sedgemoor. Now it seems that fiends are rarer than saints among these holy men, and they forgot the first wonder and ran on about the second, not thinking that I could have told them of that also. And at last one fetched a great book, as I thought in some secrecy, and made thereout nothing more nor less than parts of the song of Beowulf itself, and all about Grendel, which pleased us all well, and so we were quiet enough, listening.

And it happened that while we were all intent on this reading (and I never heard one read as brother Guthlac read to us) the sub-prior came in to call me, and pulling back the hangings of the doorway, stood listening, where I could see him.

First of all he looked pleased to find his people so employed. Then when the crash of the fighting verses came to his ears he started a little, and looked round. The good brothers were like to forget their frocks, for their fists were clenched and their eyes sparkled, and their teeth were set, and verily I believe each man of them thought himself one of Beowulf's comrades, if not the hero himself.

Whereupon the sub-prior and I were presently grinning at one another.

"Ho!" said he, all of a sudden. "Now were I Swithun, where would you heathens spend tonight? Surely in the cells!"

Then for a moment they thought Grendel had indeed come, such power has verse like this in the mouth of a good reader, and they started up, one and all.

And the reader saw who it was, and that there was no hiding the book from him, so they stood agape and terrified, for by this time the good man had managed to look mighty stern.

"Good Father," said I, seeing that someone must needs speak, "I am but a fighting man, and the brothers were considering my weakness."

"H'm," said the sub-prior, seeming in great wrath. "Is there no fighting to be read from Holy Writ that you must take these pagan vanities from where you ought not? Go to! Yet, by reason of your care for the bishop's thane, your penance shall be light now and not heavy hereafter. Brother Guthlac shall read aloud in refectory today the story of David and Goliath, and you brother," pointing to one, "that of Ahab at Ramoth, and you, of Joshua at Jericho," and so he went on till each had a chapter of war assigned him, and I thought it an easy penance.

"But," he added, "and until all these are read, your meals shall be untasted before you."

Then the brothers looked at one another, for it was certain that all this reading would last till the meal must be left for vespers.

Then the sub-prior bade the reader take back the book and go to his own cell, and beckoning me, we passed out and left the brothers in much dismay, not knowing what should befall them from the abbot when he heard.

So I ventured to tell the sub-prior how this came about, and he smiled, saying that he should not tell Tatwine the Abbot, for the brothers were seldom in much fault, and that maybe it was laudable to search even pagan books for the manners of fiends, seeing that forewarned was forearmed.

Then he said that surely he wished (but this I need tell none else) that he had been there in my place to hear Guthlac read it. Also that he was minded to make the old rhyme more Christian-like, if he could, writing parts of it afresh. And this he has done since, so that any man may read it; but it is not so good as the old one.ix

Now we came to the bishop's chamber, and he went in, calling me after him in a minute or so. I could hear Ealhstan's voice and that of another as I waited outside.

The other was Eanulf the Ealdorman, and as I entered he rose up and faced me.

"So, Heregar," he said, "you are bishop's man now, and out of my power. I am glad of it," and so saying he reached me out his hand and wrung mine, and looked very friendly as he did so.

"I have heard of your doings," he said, "and thank you for them. And I will see this matter of yours looked into, for I think, as the bishop believes, that there has been a plot against you for plain reasons enough. However, that must stand over as yet. But come with me to the hall and I will right you with the thanes there."

At that I thanked him, knowing that things were going right with me, and the bishop smiled, as well pleased, but said nothing, as Eanulf took me by the arm, and we went together to the great hall, where the thanes, some twenty of them, were talking together. At once I saw several whose faces had burnt themselves, as it were, into my mind at the Moot; but none of Matelgar's friends among them.

They were quiet when their leader went in, and he wasted no time, but spoke in his own direct way.

"See here, thanes; here is Heregar, whom we outlawed but the other day. Take my word and Ealhstan's and Osric's for it that there was a mistake. We know now that there is no truer man, for he has proved it, as some of you know - he being the man who lit the huts at Stert in face of the Danes, and being likewise the Saint of Cannington --"

"Aye, it is so," said several voices, and others laughed. Then, like honest Saxons as they were, they came crowding and laughing to shake hands with an outlawed saint, as one said; so that I was overdone almost with their kindness, and knew not what to say or do.

But Eanulf pushed me forward among them, saying that I, being bishop's man, was no more concern of his, outlaw or no outlaw, and that saints were beyond him. So he too laughed, and went back to the bishop; and I found Wulfhere and Wislac, and soon I was one of my own sort again, and the bad past seemed very far away.

But Wislac looked at me and said: "You have spoilt a fine tale I had to take home with me; but maybe I need not tell the ending. Howbeit, I always did hold that there was none so much difference between a fighting saint and one of ourselves."

And that seemed to satisfy him.

XII: THE GREAT LEVY

It was not long before Eanulf made up his mind to action, and he was closeted with the bishop all that morning. Then, after the midday meal, he called a council of all who were there, and we sat in the great hall to hear his plans.

Ealhstan came with him, and these two sat at the upper end of the hall, and we on the benches round the walls, for the long tables had been cleared.

When all was ready, Eanulf stood up and told the thanes, for some were men who had had no part in Osric's levy, all about the fighting, and how it had ended. And having done that, he asked for the advice of such as would have aught to say.

Very soon an old thane rose up and said that he thought all would be well if forces were so posted as to prevent the Danes coming beyond the land they then held.

And several growled assent to that; and one said that Danes bided in one place no long time, but would take ship again and go elsewhere.

That, too, seemed to please most, and I saw Eanulf bite his lip, for he was a man who loved action. And Wulfhere, too, shifted in his seat, as if impatient.

Then they went back to the first proposal, and began to name places where men might be posted to keep the Danes in Parret valley at least, till they went away.

Then at last Wulfhere grew angry, and rose up, looking very red.

"And what think you will Parret valley be like when they have done their will therein? Does no man remember the going back to his place when these strangers had bided in it for a while, after they beat us in Dorset?"

There were two thanes who had lands in that part, and they flushed, so that one might easily know they remembered; but they said naught.

Then Eanulf spake, very plainly:

"I am for raising the levy of Somerset again, and stronger, and driving them out; but I cannot do it without your help."

Then there was silence, and the thanes looked at one another for so long that I waxed impatient, and being headstrong, maybe, got up and spoke:

"Landless I am, and maybe not to be hearkened to, but nevertheless I will say what it seems to me that a man should say. Into this land of peace these men from over seas have come wantonly, slaying our friends, burning our houses, driving our cattle, making such as escape them take to the woods like hunted wild beasts. Where is Edred the Thane? Where is Matelgar? Where twenty others you called friends? Dead by Combwich, and none to bury them. The Danes have their arms, the wolves their bodies. Is no vengeance to be taken for this? Or shall the Danes sail away laughing, saying that the hearts of the Saxons are as water?"

Then there rose an angry growl at that, and I was glad to hear it. So was Eanulf, as it seemed. And Wulfhere got up and stood beside me and spoke.

"This is good talk, and now I will add a word. Why came back the Danes here? Because after we were beaten before, we let them do their worst, and hindered them not; therefore come they back even now -- aye, and if we drive them not from us, hither will they come yet again, till we may not call the land our own from year to year. I say with the ealdorman, let us up and drive them out, showing them what Saxons are made of. What? Are we done fighting after they have scattered one hastily gathered levy? Shame there is none to us in being so beaten once, but I hold it shame to let them so easily have the mastery."

Then there was a murmur, but not all of assent; though I could see that many would side with us. Whereon Wislac rose up slowly, and looking round, said:

"I am a stranger, but having been present at the beating the other day, yonder, am minded to see if I may yet go home on the winning side. And it would be shame, even as these two thanes have said, not to give a guest a chance to have his pleasure. I pray you, thanes, pluck up spirit, and follow the ealdorman."

Now, though Wislac's words seemed idle at the beginning, there was that in his last words which brought several of the younger thanes to their feet, looking angrily at him, and one asked if he meant to call that assembly "nidring".

"Not I," said Wislac, smiling peacefully, "seeing that you have done naught to deserve that foul name; but being a beaten man, as I said, I need a chance to prove that I am not 'nidring' myself, so please you."

And they could not take offence at his tone, yet they saw well what he meant; and this in the end touched them very closely, for they were in the same case as he, but with more right, being of Somerset, to wipe out their defeat. But maybe there would have been a quarrel if Eanulf had not spoken.

"Peace, thanes," he said. "Heregar is right, and we must avenge our dead. Wulfhere is right, and for the land's sake we must give these Danes a lesson to bide at home. Wislac is right, and this defeat must be wiped out. Now say if you will help me to raise the levy afresh?"

"Aye, we will," said the thanes, but there was not that heartiness in their tones that one might have looked for.

In truth, though, it was no want of courage, but the thought of the easier plan of waiting, that held them back.

Then Ealhstan the Bishop rose up and faced us all, with his eyes shining, and his right hand gripping his crosier so tightly that his knuckles shone white.

"What, my sons, shall it be said of you, as it is said of us Dorset folk, that you let the Danes bide in your land and work their worst on you and yours? I tell you that since we went back and saw, as we still see, their track over our homes, our folk burn to take revenge on them; and I, being what I am, think no wrong of counselling revenge on heathen folk. Listen, for ye are men."

And then he told us in burning words such a tale of what must be were these heathen to have their way, such things that he himself had seen and known after Charnmouth fight, that we would fain at last be up and drive them away without waiting for the levy.

And at last he said:

"Eanulf, this will I do. I will gather the Dorset levy and lead them to your help, and so will we make short work of these heathen."

Then all the thanes shouted that they would not be behind in the matter; and so their cool Saxon blood was fired to that white rage which is quenched but in victory or death.

Now after that there was talk of nothing but of making the levy as soon as might be, and Eanulf, thanking everyone, and most of all the bishop, straightway gave his orders; and before that night the war arrow was speeding through all Somerset and Dorset likewise, and word was sent to Osric and the other sheriffs that the gathering place named was at the hill of Brent.

Now of those days that followed there is little to say. The other thanes left, each to gather his own men, vowing vengeance on the Danes; but before they went there was hardly one who did not seek out Wulfhere, Wislac, and myself, and in some way or another tell us that we had spoken right. One fiery young thane, indeed, was minded to fight Wislac, but the Mercian turned the quarrel very skilfully, and in the end agreed with the thane that the matter should be settled by the number of Danes each should slay, "which," said Wislac, "will be as good sport and more profitable than pounding one another, and quite as good proof that neither of us may be held nidring."

So that ended very well.

But every day came in reports, brought by fugitives, of the Danes and their doings, which made our blood boil. At last came one who brought a message for myself, could I be found. It was from the aunt of Alswythe, the Prioress of Bridgwater, telling of her safety and that of her nuns, at Taunton. And I begged the bishop to let me tell this good news to Alswythe, and so gained speech with her once more. Yet would the abbess be present, reading the while; but I might tell my love all that had befallen me, and she rejoiced, bidding me go fight and win myself renown in the good cause of my own country.

And when I left her I felt that I must indeed be strong for the sake of her, and by reason of her words, which would be in my mind ever.

Now one day when I went to see the horses and ride out with Wulfhere and Wislac, the collier came and hung about, seeming to wish to ask somewhat. And when I noticed this and bade him speak, he prayed me that I would give him arms, and let him follow me to the coming fighting. Arms, save those I wore, I had none, but I promised him such as I could buy him with what remained of the money I had found, which might be enough, seeing that we lived at free quarters with the bishop, and had little expense. As for the other money, I left that with the abbess after I had seen Alswythe, for it was less mine than hers.

But I asked Dudda if he were able to use a sword. Whereupon he grinned, and said that Brother Guthlac tended the abbot's mule, and had taught him much when he came to the stables daily. He also showed me a bruised arm and broken head in token of hard play with the ash plant between them.

"Here is the said Guthlac," said Wulfhere; and there was the reader of Beowulf coming, with frock and sleeves tucked up, from out the stables. So I called him, and asked him to try a bout with the collier, telling him why.

At first he denied all knowledge of carnal warfare, but I reminded him of his reading of Beowulf, saying that, if he knew naught of fighting, the verses would have had none of that fire in them. So, in the end, they went to it, and I saw that Guthlac was well used to sword play, and was satisfied also with his pupil.

Then I asked Guthlac whence he got his skill in arms, and why he was shut up thus inside four walls.

"Laziness, Thane," he answered, telling me nothing of the first matter at all. Nor would he. But I found afterwards that he had been lamed once, and tended by the monks, and so had bided in the abbey, liking the life, though he had been a stout housecarle to some thane or other.

Then Wislac must ask him if there were any more of his sort in the abbey, and seeing that we meant no harm, and looking on me as an ally in that matter of the reading, he said there were five more, "whom Heregar the Thane knew, if he would remember, reading certain Scriptures at supper time."

And I found that these six kindred spirits had managed to get themselves told off to amuse me while I waited that day, so that they might hear of the fighting.

So we laughed and rode out, and I thought no more of Guthlac and his brethren till the time came when I remembered them gladly.

All day long during that week came pouring in the Dorset levies in answer to the bishop's summons. Hard and wiry men they were, and as I could well see, a very much harder set than Osric's first levy, for these were veterans. Ealhstan's word had gone out that all men who would wipe out the defeat of Charnmouth should gather to him, and these were the men who had fought there, and only longed to try their strength again against their conquerors of that disastrous day.

Day by day, also, would Ealhstan go out into the marketplace, and there speak burning words to them, bidding them remember the days gone by, and the valour of their fathers who won the land for them, and to have ever in mind that this war was not of Christian against Christian, but against heathen men who were profaning the houses of God wherever they came.

Many more things did he say, ever finding something fresh wherewith to stir their courage, but ever, also, did he bid them remember how the Danes had won by discipline more than courage, and to pay heed to that as their leaders bade them.

Also, day by day, he bade the thanes who had seen fighting, train their men as well as they might, and they worked well at that. Moreover, he could teach them much, reading to us at times from a great Latin book of the wars of Caesar such things as seemed like to be useful, putting it into good Saxon as he went on.

Then, as the week drew to an end, there began to be questions as to who should be leader of the Dorset men. And many said that Osric should be the man, for he was an Ealdorman of Dorset. But when the bishop sent to Brent for him, and asked him to lead his men, Osric doubted; and what he said to the other thanes, and to us three, made them send us to the bishop with somewhat to ask.

So we, finding him ever ready to hear what was wanted, put the question to him plainly as they had bidden us. And that was, that he himself should lead the levy of Dorset.

Now Tatwine, the old abbot, sat with him and heard this, and straightway he began to tremble, and cry out that such work was unfit for a bishop.

So the bishop said to me, very quietly, but with a look in his eyes which seemed to show that this was what he longed for:

"Heregar, my son, go and tell the thanes what the abbot says, and ask if they will go without me."

All the thanes were waiting to hear the bishop's answer to our request, and I told them this, and they knew at once what answer to give, for they said, or Osric said for them, while all applauded:

"We will not go against these heathens unless the bishop leads us. Else must Somerset fight her own battles."

So with that word I went back to the bishop, and told him.

"So, Tatwine, my brother, you see how it is. Needs must that I go, else were it shame to us that heathen men should have freedom in a Christian land."

But Tatwine groaned, and, maybe knowing the bishop well, said no more.

Then Ealhstan bade him remember all the saints who had warred against the heathen, and were held blameless -- nay, rather, the holier.

"Therefore," said he, "I am in good company, and will surely go."

Whereupon Tatwine rose up and went out, saying that he should go to the abbey and seek protection for the bishop, and men say he bided there almost night and day, praying until all was past. Certainly I saw him no more in his accustomed places, save at mass.

When he had gone the bishop smiled a little, looking after him, and then spoke to us.

"I may tell my council that this is what I should love. Nevertheless, it will not be I who lead, but you three. For the counsel must be Wulfhere's, and the coolness Wislac's, and the rest Heregar's, who will by no means bide that we run away. Now, I think that you three will make a good leader of me."

On that we thanked him for his words, and we followed him out to the hall. And there the thanes shouted and cheered as he came, and still more when he prayed them to follow him to victory or a warrior's death. And that they swore to do, not loudly, but in such sort that none could mistake that they would surely do so.

Then he bade them muster their men by the first light in the morning, and so he would lead them first of all to Brent, to join the ealdorman. And Osric should be his second in command.

That pleased all, and soon we were left alone with him again, but we could hear outside the cheering of men now and then, as some thane gathered his following and told them the name of their leader.

So we three went out presently and saw to our horses, and then I was wondering about arms for Dudda, for I had left the matter too long, and it seemed there were few weapons remaining for sale in the town by reason of men of the levy buying or borrowing what they lacked in equipment. And the poor fellow hung about sadly, thinking he should find none in the end, and swearing he would follow me even had he naught but a quarterstaff in his hand.

But when we went back to the abbey, the bishop sent for us, and we were taken into a room we had not seen before, and there on the table were laid out three suits of mail, helmets, and arms.

"Now," said Ealhstan, as he saw our eyes go, as a man's eyes will, straight to these things, "if you thanes are not too proud to accept such as I can give, let me arm you, and tell you where you shall bear these arms."

And that was what we longed for, for as yet we had no post in the levy, and we told him as much.

"That is well," he answered. "See, Wislac, here is bright steel armour and helm and shield for you. Sword also, if you need it, for maybe you will scarce part from your own tried weapon?"

But Wislac smiled at that, and took hold of his sword hilt, loosening the strings which bound it to the sheath. There were but eight inches of blade left, and these were sorely notched.

"Aha!" quoth the bishop, "now know I why Wislac thought well to stop fighting the other day," which pleased the Mercian well enough.

"Then, Wulfhere," went on Ealhstan, "here is this black armour and helm and shield for you, and sword or axe as you will."

And Wulfhere thanked him, taking the axe, as his own sword was good.

"Now, Heregar, my son, this is yours," said the bishop, looking kindly at me.

And as I looked I thought I had never seen more beautiful arms. No better were they than the other two suits, for all three were of good Sussex ring mail as to the byrnies,x while the boar-crested helms were of hammered steel.

But mine was silver white, with gold collar and gold circles round the arms. Gold, too, was the boar-crest of the helm, and gold the circle round the head, and to me it seemed as I looked that this was too good. And Ealhstan knew my thoughts and answered them.

"Black for the man of dark counsel, bright steel for the warrior, and silver-bright armour for the man who brings back hope when all seems lost."

"That is good," said Wislac. "Now read us the meaning of the gold thereon also," for he seemed to see that the bishop had some meaning in that, whereat the bishop smiled.

"Gold for trust," he said, "and for the man who shall be honoured."

"That is well also," said Wulfhere, and Wislac nodded gravely.

"Now," said the bishop, "I will put Heregar out of my council for a minute, so that he may not speak nor hear. Tell me, Thanes both, if it will be well to give Heregar the place whereto men shall rally in need?"

"Aye, surely," they said. "We know he can fill that place."

"Then shall he bear my standard," said the bishop, "and none will gainsay it," and so he turned to me.

"Now, Heregar, may you hear this decision. Standard bearer to me shall you be, and I know you will bear it well and bravely. And these two, your friends and mine, shall stand to right and left of you, and six stout carles may you choose from the levy to stand before and behind you. And whom you choose I will arm alike, that all may know them."

Now knew I not what to say or do, but I knelt before the bishop and kissed his hand, and so he laid it on my head and blessed me, bidding me speak no words of thanks, but only deserve them from him.

Now there was a little silence after this, and Wislac, being ever ready, broke it for us,

"Much do I marvel," he said, "that these suits of armour should be so exactly fitting to each of us. Surely there is some magic in it."

"Only the magic of a wearied man's sleep, and of a good weapon smith," said the bishop, laughing. "One measured your mail, byrnie and helm both, as you slept. We have lay brethren apt for every craft."

And that reminded me of Brother Guthlac, and a thought came to me.

"Father," I said, "six men have you bidden me choose, and I know none of the Dorset men. Yet there are six lay brethren here who have been warriors, of whom brother Guthlac is one, and if they may march against heathen men, I pray you let me have them."

Now that the Bishop seemed to find pleasant, as though he knew something of those lovers of war songs, and answered that he wot not if Tatwine would let them go. But, in any case, he would choose men for me of the best, and that we all thought well, knowing in what spirit he would put those men whom he should choose.

So he bade us go, taking our arms with us, and we, thanking him, went out. But I found my collier, and showed him the arms I had been wearing, saying they should be his, and then took him, rejoicing, into the town. There I bought him, after some search, a plain, good sword and target, which he bore to his lodgings to scour and gaze at for the rest of the day.

XIII: A MESSAGE FROM THE DEAD

How shall I tell what it was like when the bishop, standing aloft at the head of the abbey steps with all the monks round him, gave into my hands, as I knelt, his standard to bear at the head of his men?

Very early in the morning it was, and all the roofs were golden in bright sunlight, and the men, drawn up in a hollow square fronting the abbey, were silent and attentive as mass was sung in the great church, so that the sound of the chanting came out to them through the open doors. And when the sacring xi bell rang, as though a wave went along the ranks, all knelt, and there was a clash and ring of steel, and then silence for a space, very wonderful.

Then came out, when mass was said, bishop, and thanes, and monks, and there gave me the banner, Wulfhere and Wislac kneeling on either side of me, and behind us those six stout housecarles whom the bishop had chosen and armed for me. So the banner was given and blessed, and I rose up, grasping the golden-hafted cross from which it hung, and lifted it that all might see.

Then was a great shout from all the men, and swords were drawn and brandished on every side, and, without need of command, all the Dorset host swore to follow it even to the death. And that was good to hear.

But as for me, my thoughts were more than I may write, but it seems to me that they were as those of Saint George when he rode out to slay the dragon in the old days, so great were they.

After that a little wait, and then the horses; and the bishop mounted a great bay charger, managing him as a master. And to me was brought my white horse by the collier, looking a grim fighting man enough in his arms, and to Wulfhere and Wislac black and gray steeds given by Ealhstan himself.

Now the bishop rode, followed by us, to the centre of the levy, and again a great shout rose up even mightier than that first, and when it ended he spoke to the men as he was wont to speak but even yet more freely, and then put himself at their head, and so began the march to Brent. And all the town was out to see us go, never doubting of our victory, nor thinking of how few might return of all that long line of sturdy and valiant fighting men.

When we were clear of the town at last, and went, the men singing as they marched, down the ancient green lanes that had seen our forefathers' levies and the Roman legions alike, I had time to look around me at my own following, being conscious in some way that, mixed up as it were with the war song, there had been the sound of the droning of a chant as by monks close by me. And I could see no monks near. The thanes were riding round and after the bishop, who came next me as I led the way with the standard, and Ealhstan indeed had on his robes; but there was a stiffness about him, and a glint of steel also, when a breeze shifted the loose fold of his garments, that seemed to say that his was not all peaceful gear.

Just behind me, as I rode with Wulfhere and Wislac to right and left, came my six men, big powerful housecarles, all in black armour and carrying red and black shields, and with a red cross on their helms' fronts. And the squarest of these six, he who seemed to be their leader, looked up at me, when I turned again, with a grin that I seemed to know. So I took closer notice of him, and lo! it was Guthlac, the reader of Beowulf, and the other five were his brethren. Small wonder that I had not recognized the holy men in their war gear, so little looked they like the peaceful brethren who had walked in the abbey cloisters.

With them was my collier, keeping step and holding himself with the best of them, and I thought that they would be seven hardy Danes who should overmatch my standard guard. So I was well content with the bishop's choice for me.

Now of that march to Brent, and the meeting there with the Somerset levy, there is no need to tell. But by the time we marched from thence against the Danes, there were five hundred men of Dorset, and near nine hundred of Somerset. Of the Danes some judged that there would be eight hundred or more, but if that was so, they were tried men, and our numbers were none too great. Moreover, we must separate, so as to drive them down to their ships, for they were spread over the country, burning and destroying on every side.

We lay but one night on Brent, while the leaders held counsel, and even as we sat gathered, we could see plainly the fires the Danes had lit, of burning hamlet and homestead, far and wide across the marshes of Parret. And the end of that council was that Eanulf should take his Somerset men up Parret valley, and so drive down the Danes, while Ealhstan should fall on them by Bridgwater as they came down, and so scatter them.

Therefore would the Somerset levy march very early, before light; while we should wait till the next night, unless word should come beforehand.

So we went to sleep. And as I slept in my place, with the standard flapping above me, and my comrades on either side and behind, it seemed to me that one came and waked me. And when I sat up and looked, thinking it was a messenger from the bishop, I saw that it was Matelgar.

Now this time I had no fear of him, and I waited for him to speak, just as though he had been before me in the flesh, for there seemed naught uncanny about the matter to me. And yet even at the moment that seemed strange, though it was so.

But for a while he looked not at me, but out over the low lands towards Parret mouth and Stert, shading his eyes with his hand as though it were broad noonday. And then he turned back to me and spoke.

"Heregar; I promised to stand by you again when the time came. Now I bid you go to Combwich hill, there to wait what betides. So, if you will do the bidding of the dead who has wronged you, but would now make amends, shall you thank me for this hereafter -- aye, and not you only."

Then out over Parret he gazed again and faded from beside me, so that I could ask him nothing. Then knew I that I was awake, and that this had been no dream; for a great fear came on me for a little, knowing what I had seen to be not of this world. Yet all around me my comrades slept, and only round the rim of the trenched hill went the wakeful sentries, too far for speech -- for we leaders were in the centre of the camp.

But presently I began to think less of the vision, and more of the words. And at first they seemed vain, for Combwich hill was over near to Stert; nor did I see how I could reach the place without cutting through the Danes (who would doubtless leave a strong guard with the ships, and were also in and about Bridgwater), seeing that the river must be crossed.

Then as I turned over the matter, not doubting but that a message so given was sooth, and by no means lightly to be disregarded, I seemed to wake to a resolve concerning the meaning of the whole thing. What if I could win there under cover of darkness, and so fall on the Danish host as Eanulf drove them back and the bishop and Osric chased them to the ships?

That seemed possible, if only I could cross Parret with men enough, and unseen. I would ask Wulfhere and Wislac, when morning came, and so, if they could help, lay the matter before the bishop himself. So thinking I fell asleep again, peacefully enough, nor dreamt I aught.

With morning light that vision and the bidding to Combwich, and what I had thought thereon, seemed yet stronger. Very early the Somerset men went with Eanulf, and we of the bishop's levy only remained on Brent after the morning meal.

Then as we three stood on the edge of the hill, and looked out where Matelgar had looked, I told my two friends of his coming and of his words.

"Three things there are," said Wislac, "that hinder this ghost's business; namely, want of wings, uncertainty of darkness, and ignorance of the time when the Danes shall come."

"There are also three things that make for it, brother," said Wulfhere. "Namely: that men can swim, that there is no moon, and that the Danes are careless in their watch of the waste they leave behind them."

318

"Think you that the hill will be unguarded?" asked I, glad that Wulfhere did not put away the plan at once.

"Why should they guard it? There are Danes at the ships -- though few, I expect, for we have been well beaten. And more in plenty from Parret to Quantocks, and no Saxon left between the two forces."

"Why not burn the ships then?" asked Wislac.

"Doubtless that could we, once over Parret," answered Wulfhere, "but what then? Away go the Danes through Somerset, burning and plundering even to Cornwall, and there bide till ships come, and then can be gone in safety. That is not what we need. We have to trap them and beat them here."

"So then, Wulfhere," I said, "think you that the plan is good?"

"Aye," he answered, "good enough; but not easy. Moreover, I doubt if the bishop would let his standard bearer part from him."

That was likely enough to stop all the plan; but yet I would lay it before Ealhstan, for it seemed to us that such a message might by no means go untold at least.

So we sought him, and asked for speech with him; and at that he laughed, saying that surely his council had the best right to that. Osric was with him, and the bishop told him how that we three had been his first advisers in this matter.

Then we sat down and I told Ealhstan all, asking nothing.

When I had ended, Osric looked at me, and said that the plan was venturesome; but no doubt possible to be carried out, and if so, by none better than myself, who knew every inch of that country. Then, thinking over it, as it were, he added that the woods beyond Matelgar's hall would shelter any force that must needs seek cover, so that, even were Combwich hill unsafe, there was yet a refuge whence attack could again be made.

Then Ealhstan, who had listened quietly, said that such messages were rare, but all the less to be despised. Therefore would he think thereof more fully.

"What," he asked, "is the main difficulty?"

I said that the crossing of Parret was like to be hard in any case; but at night and unobserved yet more so. But that, could we reach the farther bank, I could find places where we might lie in wait for a day, if need were, with many men.

Thereupon the bishop took that great book of Caesar's wars, and looked into it. But he seemed long in finding aught to meet that case, while we talked of one thing or another concerning it among ourselves.

At last he shut the book and said, very gravely: "I would that I could swim."

"I also, Father," said Wislac, "and why I cannot, save for sheer cowardice, I know not, having been brought up on Thames side, and never daring to go out of depth."

At that we were fain to laugh, so dismally did the broad-shouldered Mercian blame himself. But the bishop said that if I went, needs must that he came also. But he did not dissuade me in any way.

"Wulfhere the Counsellor," he said then, "have you no plan?"

"To cross the river?" answered the veteran. "Aye, many, if they may be managed. Rafts for those who cannot swim, surely."

Now I bethought me of the many boats that ever lay in the creek under Combwich, and wondered if any were yet whole. For if they were, surely one might swim over and bring one back. And that I said.

Then of a sudden, the bishop rose up, and seemed to have come to a decision, saying:

"See here, thanes; ever as we march to Bridgwater, we draw nearer Parret. Now by this evening, we shall be close over against this place Combwich, so that one may go thither and spy what there is to be done, and come back in good time and tell us if crossing may be made by raft or boat. Let this rest till then. But if it may be so, then I, and Heregar and his following, and two hundred men will surely cross, and wait for what may betide. For I think this plan is good."

So he would say no more of it then. And presently all his men were mustered, and we marched from Brent slowly along the way to Bridgwater.

XIV: ELGAH THE FISHER

Now men have said that this plan of mine needed no ghost to set it forth, but is such that would enter the mind of any good leader. That might be so had there been one there who knew the country as I knew it, but there was not. And I was no general as was Eanulf. However that might be, I tell what happened to me in the matter, and sure am I that but for Matelgar's bidding I had never thought of this place or plan.

But once Ealhstan had heard thereof, the thought of it seemed ever better to him. And when we were fairly marching along the level towards Bridgwater he called me, and began to talk of that business of spying out the crossing place.

Now I too had been thinking of that same, and asked him to let me go at once, taking one man with me. Then would I rejoin him as best I might, and close to the place where I might fix on means of getting over.

Now there seemed little danger in the matter, for our spies had reported no Danes on this side of Parret, for they kept the water between us and them, doubtless knowing that Osric had gone to Brent at first, and thinking it likely that another levy might be made. So the bishop, not very willingly, as it seemed to me, let me go, as there was none else who could go direct to the point as I could without loss of time, even as Osric told him.

Then I gave the standard into Wulfhere's hand, and must seek one to go with me. First I thought of Wislac, but he was a stranger, and then my eyes lit on my collier, and I knew that I need go no further. So I called him, and taking him aside -- while the men streamed past us, looking at my silver arms and speaking thereof to one another -- told him what we had to do.

Whereat his eyes sparkled, and he said that it was good hearing.

"But, master," he went on, "take off those bright arms of yours and let us go as marshmen. Then will be no suspicion if the Danes see us from across the water."

That was wise counsel, and we left our arms in a baggage wagon, borrowing frocks from the churls who followed us, and only keeping our seaxes in our belts.

Then Dudda found a horse that was led with the wagons, and I bade the man whose it was lend it to him, promising good hire for its use. And so we two rode off together across the marshland, away by Burnham, while the levy held on steadily by the main road.

Then was I glad that I had brought the collier, for the marsh was treacherous and hard to pass in places. But he knew the firm ground, as it were, by nature, and we went on quickly enough. Now and then we passed huts, but they were empty; for away across the wide river mouth at Burnham, though we rode not into that village, we could see the six long black ships as they lay at Stert, and the smoke of the fires their guard had made on shore.

But on this side of the river they had been, for Burnham was but a heap of ashes. They had crossed in their small boats, doubtless, and found the place empty.

Then at last we came to a hut some two miles off in the marshes from Combwich, and in that we left our horses, giving them hay from the little rick that stood thereby. To that poor place, at least, the Danes had not come, for the remains of food left on the table showed that the owners had fled hastily, but in panic, and that none had been near the place since.

Now Dudda would have us take poles and a net we found left, on our shoulders, that we might seem fishers daring to return, or maybe driven by hunger to our work. For we must go unhidden soon, where the marshland lay open and bare down to the river, the alder and willow holts ceasing when their roots felt the salt water of the spring tides. But we had been able to keep under their cover as far as the hut.

So we went towards the river, as I had many a time seen the fishers go in the quiet days that were past; and we said little, but kept our eyes strained both up and down the river for sign of the Danes.

But all we saw was once, far off on Stert, the flash of bright arms or helm; and there we knew before that men must be.

On Combwich hill was no smoke wreath of the outpost fires I had feared, nor could I see aught moving among the trees. Then at last we stood on the river bank and looked across at the little haven. All the huts were burnt and silent. There were many crows and ravens among the trees above where they had stood, and a great osprey wheeled over our heads as we looked.

"No men here," said my comrade, "else would not yon birds be so quiet."

But I could see no boat, and my heart sank somewhat; for nothing was there on this bank wherewith to make the raft of which Wulfhere spake.

Then said I: "Let us swim over and see what we can find."

Now it was three hours after noon, or thereabouts, and the tide was running out very swiftly, and it was a long passage over. Nevertheless we agreed to try it, and so, going higher up the stream, we cast ourselves in, and swam quartering across the tide.

A long and heavy swim it was, but no more than two strong men could well manage. All the time, however, I looked to see some red-cloaked Dane come out from the trees and spy us; but there was none.

Then we reached the other bank, and stood to gain breath, for now we were in the enemy's country, and tired as we were, we threw ourselves down in the shelter of a broad-stemmed willow tree, on the side away from the hill and village.

In a moment the collier touched my arm and pointed. On the crest of the hill stood a man, looking down towards us, but he was unarmed, as well as I could see, and, moreover, his figure seemed familiar. We watched him closely, for he began to come down towards us, and as he came nearer I knew him. It was one of the Combwich villeins -- a fisher of the name of Elgar.

Now I would speak with him, for he could tell me all I needed; yet I knew not if he had made friends with the Danes, being here and seeming careless.

We lost sight of him among the trees, and the birds flew up, croaking, from them, marking his path as yet towards us; and at last he came from behind a half-burnt hut close to us. Then I called him by name.

He started, and whipped out a long knife, and in a moment was behind the hut wall again. So I knew that he was not in league with the enemy, but feared them. Therefore I rose up and called him again, adding that I was Heregar, and needed him.

Then he came out, staring at me with his knife yet ready. But when he saw that it was really myself he ran to meet me with a cry of joy and knelt before me, kissing my hands and weeping; so that it was a while before I could ask him anything. Very starved and wretched he looked, and I judged rightly that he had taken to the woods from the first.

Presently he was quiet enough to answer my questions, and he told me that at first the Danes had had a strong post on the hill above us; but that, growing confident, they had left it these two days. But there were many passing and repassing along the road, bringing plunder back to the ships. He had watched them from the woods, he said.

Also he told me that even now mounted men had ridden past swiftly, going to the ships, and from that I guessed that Eanulf's force had been seen at least, and tidings sent thereof.

Then I asked him if any boats were left unburnt, and at that a cunning look came into his thin face, and he answered:

"Aye, master. Three of us were minded to save ours, and we sank them with stones in the creek before we fled. But the other two are slain, and I only am left to recover them."

Now that was good hearing, and I bade the men show me where they lay, and going with him found that now the water was low, we could see them and reach them easily. There were two small boats that might hold three men each, and one larger.

Then I told Elgar how I needed them for this night's work, and at first he was terrified, fearing nothing more than that his boats should be lost to him after all. But I promised him full amends if harm came to them, and that in the name of Osric, which he knew well. And with that he was satisfied.

So with a little labour we got the two small boats afloat, and then cast about where to hide them; for though Elgar said that the Danes came not nigh the place, it was likely that patrols would be sent out after the alarm of Eanulf's approach, and might come on them.

At last Elgar said that there was a creek half a mile or less up the river, and on the far side, where they might lie unseen perhaps. And that would suit us well if we could get them there. And the time was drawing on, so that we could make no delay.

Then out of a hollow tree Elgar drew oars for both boats, and we got them out into the river, and Dudda rowing one, and Elgar the other, in which I sat, we went to the place where they should be, keeping under the bank next the Danes. And it was well for us that the tide was so low, for else we should surely have been spied.

Yet we got them into the creek, Elgar making them fast so that they would rise as the water rose. Then he said he would swim back, and if he could manage it would raise the large boat and bring that also.

So without climbing out from under the high banks of the creek he splashed out into the tideway, and started back.

Now Dudda and I must make our way along to the horses, and so we began to get out of the creek, which was very deep, at this low ebb of the water, below the level of the meadows. Dudda was up the bank first, and looked towards Combwich. Then he dropped back suddenly, and bade me creep up warily and look also, through the grass.

So I did, and then knew how near an escape we had had, for there was a party of Danes, idlers as it seemed, among the burnt huts, turning over the ashes with their spears and throwing stones into the water.

Then I saw Elgar's head halfway across the river, and knew he could not see the Danes over the high bank. He was swimming straight for them, and unless he caught sight of one who stood nearest, surely he was lost. It was all that I could do to keep myself from crying out to him; but that would have betrayed us also, and, with us, the hope of our ambush. So we must set our teeth and watch him go.

Then a Dane came to the edge of the high bank and saw him, and at the same moment was himself seen. The Dane shouted, and Elgar stopped paddling with his hands and keeping his head above water.

Now we looked to see him swim back to this bank, and began to wonder if the enemy would follow him and so find us. And for one moment I believe he meant to do so, and then, brave man as he was, gave himself away to save us; for he stretched himself out once more and began to swim leisurely downstream, never looking at the Danes again; for now half a dozen were there and watching him, calling, too, that he should come ashore, as one might guess. But Elgar paid no heed to them, and swam on.

They began to throw stones, and one cast a spear at him, but that fell short. Then the bank hid him from us; but we saw a Dane fixing arrow to bowstring, and saw him shoot; but he missed, surely, for he took another arrow and ran on down the bank.

Then Dudda pulled me by the arm, and motioned me to follow him, and I saw no more.

Now the creek wherein we were ran inland for a quarter mile that we could see, ever bending round so that our boats were hidden from the side where the Danes were. Up that creek we ran, or rather paddled, therefore, knee deep in mud, but quite unseen by any but the great erne that fled over us crying.

Hard work it was, but before the creek ended we had covered half a mile away from danger, and looking back through the grass along the bank could see the Danes no longer. Yet we had no surety that they could not see us, and therefore crawled yet among grass and thistles, along such hollows as we could find.

At last we dared stand up, and still we could see no Danes as we looked back. And then we grew bolder and walked leisurely, as fishers might, not daring to run, across to that hut where the horses were. And reaching that our adventure was ended, for we were safe, and believed ourselves unnoticed if not unseen, for there was no reason why the Danes should think aught of two thralls, as we seemed, crossing the marsh a mile away, and quietly, even if they spied us.

After we reached our horses, there is nothing to tell of our ride back to the bishop. We overtook him before dark, where his men were halted two miles from Bridgwater, on the road, waiting for word from Eanulf.

Much praise gave he to me and the collier for what we had done, as also did Osric. And we, getting our arms again, went back to our own places well content; eager also was I to tell Wulfhere and Wislac of all that had befallen, and how I had boats for the crossing.

And when they heard how Elgar the fisher had swam on, rather than draw attention to the place where we two lay, Wulfhere nodded and said: "That was well done," and Wislac said: "Truly I would I could do the like of that. Much courage is there in the man who will face a host with comrades beside him against odds; but more is there in the man who will go alone to certain death because thereby he will save others."

Even as we talked there came riding a man from Bridgwater, going fast, yet in no great hurry as it seemed. He rode up to us, for there was the standard, and asked for the bishop, having word from Eanulf for him; and Guthlac told Ealhstan, who came up to speak to him, bidding us bide and listen.

What the man had to tell was this. That the Danes had, in some way, had word of the march of our levies, and had straightway gathered together, or were yet gathering from their raidings here and there, on the steep hill above Bridgwater, having passed through the town, or such as was left thereof after many burnings. And it was Eanulf's plan to attack them there with the first light, if the bishop would join him with his levy.

Then the bishop asked if there had been any fighting. And the man said that there had been some between the van of our force, and the rear of the Danish host; but that neither side had lost many men, nor had there been any advantage gained except to clear the town of the heathen.

Having heard that, Ealhstan bade me go aside with him, and called Osric and some more of the thanes to hold a council. And in the end it was decided that Osric should take on the bulk of the levy to join the ealdorman, while the bishop and I, and two hundred of the men, should try that crossing at Combwich.

"For thus," said Ealhstan, "we can fall on the Danes from behind if they stand or in flank if they retreat."

And except that the bishop would go with me, this pleased them well enough; but they tried to dissuade him from leaving the levy. But he laughed and said that indeed he was only going on before it, for to reach him they would have to go clear through the Danes where they stood thickest, and when they reached the standard, victory would be theirs.

Then they cried that they would surely not fail to reach him, and so the matter was settled, and the thanes told this to their men, who shouted and cheered, so that this seemed to be a good plan after all.

Now the bishop rode among the men, calling out those whom he knew well, and bidding the thanes give him their best, or if they had no best, such as could swim, and very shortly we had full two hundred men ranged on one side of the road, waiting with us, while the rest went off towards Bridgwater, the bishop blessing them ere they started. And as they went they shouted that we should meet again across the ranks of Danes.

When they were gone the bishop bade us rest. And while we lay along the roadside he went up and down, sorting out men who could swim well, and there were more than half who could do so, and more yet who said they were swimmers though poor at it.

Then he told me his plan. How that the men who could not swim must go over first in the boats, and then the arms of the rest should be ferried over while they swam, and so little time would be lost: but all must be done in silence and without lights. So we ate and slept a little, and then, when it grew dark, started off across the meadows. And there the collier guided us well, having taken note of all the ground we had crossed in the morning, as a marshman can.

It was dark, and a white creeping mist was over the open land when we reached it. But over the mists to our left we could see the twinkle of Danish watch-fires, where they kept the height over Bridgwater; and again to the right we could see lights of fires at Stert, where the ships lay. But at Combwich were no lights at all, and that was well.

Presently we reached a winding stretch of deep water, and though it was far different when I saw it last, I knew it was the creek in which our boats lay, and up which Dudda and I had fled, full now with the rising tide.

We held on down its course until Dudda told me in a low voice that we were but a bowshot from the boats, and that now it were well for the men to lie down that they might be less easily noticed.

So the word was passed in a whisper down the line, and immediately it seemed as if the force had vanished, as the white mist crept over where they had stood.

Now Dudda and I went down to the boats and there found, not the two we had left only, but a third and larger one beside them. And at first this frightened us, and we stood looking at them, almost expecting armed men to rise from the dark hollows of the boats and fall on us.

Then I would see if such were there, and stepped softly into the nearest. It was empty, and so was the next, and these were our two. Dudda came after me, and he hissed to me under his breath. The oars had been muffled with sacking.

Now none but a friend would have done this, unless it was a most crafty trap to take us withal; and yet to leave the boats as they were had been surer than to meddle with them, if such was meant.

Now Dudda, perplexed as I, though in my heart was a thought that after all Elgar had escaped, stepped into the large boat, and there he started back so suddenly as almost to overturn it, smothering a cry. Then was silence for a moment, while I for my part drew my dagger. Then I saw him stoop down, and again he hissed to me. The boats were afloat, and I drew that I was in up to the big boat.

"Oh, master," said Dudda, whispering, "surely this is Elgar the fisher!"

And I, peering into the dark bottom of the boat could see a dark still form, lying doubled over a thwart, that seemed to me to bear likeness to him.

"Is he dead?" I asked.

"Aye, master, but not long," answered the collier; feeling about.

"Ah!" he said, with a sort of groan, "here is a broken arrow in his shoulder, and in his hand somewhat to muffle the oars withal. Well done, brave Elgar -- well done!"

Then I climbed softly over the gunwale, and so it was. Wounded to death as he had been by the arrow shot, he had yet in some way contrived to get this boat here, and afterwards to use his last strength in muffling the oars, and so died, spent, before he could end his task!

And for him I was not ashamed of weeping, thinking there in the darkness, as we bore him hastily to the bank and laid him beyond the reach of hurrying feet to come, of how he must have been shot, and so at once feigning death have floated, or perhaps stranded on the mud, till the Danes were gone, and then returned in spite of pain and growing weakness to do what he had set himself for the sake of his country.

But there was no time for more than thought, and now that we knew the boats safe, I went back to the bishop, and told him that all was ready. And he, ever thoughtful, had told off skilful men to row the boats over, and though now we must have enough for three, he had found six or eight oarsmen, and there was no delay, though they must work with less change, and the tide was still making, so that the pull to Combwich creek would be hard.

Then ten men went softly to the boats, and at the last I bade them pull across to where they might, not making for the creek, and in a minute or two they were gone into the mist and darkness.

Then came crawling to the river bank some six or eight men, strong swimmers, and would have tried to cross; but I bade them wait till the next boatloads went over, so that they might cross beside them, and cling to the gunwale if the stream was too strong. However, though most knew that was good counsel, two must needs try it, and one got across, nearly spent, and the other came back, clinging to the first boat to return, else had he been drowned, and it was a lucky chance that the boat met him.

Now the man who rowed this first boat reported that there was silence, and no sign of Danes, on the other side, and so also did the rest as they came. After that the crossing went on quickly, men swimming beside the boats, and in an hour and a half all were over.

When we found that all was safe, the bishop bade me cross with the standard, and so keep the men together. He himself came last of all.

When Wulfhere came, swimming beside the boat in which sat Wislac, he took three men and went quietly to Combwich, which was nearly half a mile from where we landed, and was back presently, reporting all quiet.

Then Dudda and the other rowers sank the boats, lest they should be seen by chance, and so betray us and our crossing.

Now we went -- I leading through this place I knew so well -- round the head of the little creek, and so on up the hill, walking in single file almost, and very silently. And when we topped the hill -- there before us, among the tree trunks, glowed a little fire, and round that sat six Danes, wrapped in their red cloaks, and, as I could see, all or most of them asleep.

At that I stopped, and the line behind me stopped also, making a clatter of arms as men ran against one another in the dark.

One of the Danes stirred at that, and looked up and round; but he could see nothing, and so folded himself up again. Then I saw that they had an ale cask.

Now I knew that this post must be surrounded and taken, and whispered to Wulfhere, who was next me, what to do. And he answered that he would manage it, bidding me stand still. Then he went down the line, whispering in each man's ear, till he had told off twenty men, and them he sent off right and left into the darkness and I was left with Wislac standing alone, watching the Danes.

I kept my eyes fixed on them till they seemed to waver and grow dim, so intently did I watch them; and then all of a sudden there was the sound of a raven's croak, and into the firelight and on those careless watchers leapt Wulfhere and his men from all around.

There was one choked cry, and that was all, and Wulfhere beckoned to me. I advanced, and the line closed up and followed.

Now we stood on Combwich hill, and all was well so far. Ealhstan came up to me, unknowing of what had caused the halt, being over the brow of the hill, and when he knew, said it was well done, and that now we might rest safely for a time.

So we bade the men sit down, and those who were wet made up the fire afresh: for there was no need to put it out, but rather reason for allowing the Danes to see it burning, as if in safety.

When we three sat by the bishop, Wislac asked what we were to wait for, and, indeed, that must be the next thought.

Then said the bishop that after a while he would take the force to the woods that overhung the roadway, and so wait for the Danes as Eanulf and Osric drove them back; but that it was not more than midnight yet.

Then came a little silence, and in that I seemed to hear the sound of footsteps coming up the hill from Combwich, and bade the others listen. And at the same time some of the men heard the sound, and started up to see who came. But they were the steps of one man only, walking carelessly.

Into the light of the fire stepped one, at the sight of whom the men stared, though Wislac laughed quietly. It was that young thane who had wanted to fight my friend Wislac on the day of the council. He was very wet, and tired, throwing himself down beside us when he saw where we sat.

Ealhstan asked him who bade him come, and how he had followed us.

"Nearly had I forgotten a dispute I have with Wislac the Thane here. Wherefore I asked no man's leave, but followed you just too late for the crossing. So needs must swim. And here am I to see that Wislac counts fairly, and that he may have the same surety of me."

Whereat we were obliged to laugh, and most of all the bishop, because he would fain have been angry, and could not. Then the thane, whose name was Aldhelm, asked who was the slain man over whose body he had well-nigh fallen on the other side of the river. So I told them of Elgar the fisher and of his brave deeds, and they were silent, thinking of what his worth was; too great indeed for praise. Only the bishop said he should surely have a mound raised over him as over a warrior, charging us three, or whichever lived after this fight, to see to that.

Now we slept a little, posting sentries at many points, and giving those next the Danes on either side the red cloaks of the picket we had slain, lest daylight should betray them. It was in all our minds that at daybreak our men would attack from Bridgwater, driving the Danes back on us, and so we should fall on them while they were retreating, and complete the victory. So we had men on the hill overlooking the road to Bridgwater through Cannington that they might give us the first warning.

Therefore I slept quietly, and all with me. And as I slept I dreamed.

It seemed that I was standing alone on Brent Hill and from that I could look all over the land of Somerset, as an eagle might look, but being close to everything that I would see. And I saw all that I had done since I stood there as a prisoner, watching myself curiously in all that I did, and yet knowing all the thoughts that drove me to deed after deed.

And so through the mirk wood till I turned and slew, and armed myself, and tormented my prisoner; then to the collier's hut, and my talking with the child; then on till I saw the lights of the viking ships and so thereafter bore the war arrow -- everything, till at last I saw myself sleeping under the trees, on the top of this hill of Combwich, and there I thought my dream would surely end; but it did not.

For now out of the shadows came Matelgar and stood beside me and waked me, and he told me that when the tide was out I must be up and doing. And so he passed. And the old crone, Gundred, came out of the shadows, and sat on her bundle of sticks and looked at me, and she too bade me be up and doing when the tide was low. And she looked at the standard that lay beside me, and said, "Aye, a standard; but not yet the Dragon of Wessex"; and so she, too, faded away.

And then came Alswythe, and as she came, it seemed, as I looked, that I stretched my arms to her; but she smiled and said, "Love, when the tide is out, I shall be praying in the abbey for you and your men."

And then from beside her came Turkil, the little child, smiling also, but hanging to Alswythe's dress as he said, "Warrior, when the water falls low, my father will call me from the hill, and I will pray for you and for him."

So these two were gone. And at that I seemed to see our men lie in Bridgwater, and there was Turkil's father, the franklin, sleeping with the rest. But up and down among them went Eanulf the Ealdorman, watching ever.

Then fled I, as it were, to that hill where lay the Danes, and on the road thither I saw Osric and twenty men, looking up at the fires that burnt where the enemy lay.

And then I looked on those fires, and there were no men round them. One shook me by the shoulder, and my dream went. It was Dudda, and his eyes were bright in the firelight.

And over Brent the first streaks of dawn were broadening, and the mists were gone.

"Master, master," he said, "come with me to the roadway. Something is afoot."

Then I woke Wulfhere, asking him to wait for me, guarding the standard, and followed my man swiftly to the place where the road cuts the hill. And there was a knot of the men, standing and listening.

I listened also, and far off towards Cannington I could hear the sound of the tread of many feet, for the morning was still and quiet; and the men said that this was growing nearer.

Then knew I that the Danes were falling back to the ships without risking battle, and my dream came back to me, with its vision of unguarded watch fires, and it seemed to me that surely, unless we could stay them, they would depart with the tide as it fell.

"How is the tide?" asked I of the men round me.

"Failing now," said one who knew, "but not fast."

Then I remembered things I had hardly noted in years gone by. How the tide hung around Stert Point, as though Severn and Parret warred for a while, before the mighty Severn ebb sucked Parret dry, and how the ebb at last came swift and sudden.

"When the tide is low," said they whom I had seen in my dream.

And in a moment I recalled the first fight, and the words of Gundred, and I knew that we had the Danes in a trap.

They were marching now in time to gain their ships and be off as the last man stepped on board, with the full draft of the ebb to set them out to sea beyond Lundy Isle, into open water. Nor had they left their post till the last moment, lest our levy should be on their heels, or else some more distant marauding party had not come in till late.

I went back to Wulfhere and told him this, and in it all he agreed.

And, as we whispered together, Ealhstan sat up, asking quickly, "Who spoke to me?" and looking round for one near him, as it seemed.

"None spoke, Father," said I, "or none but Wulfhere to me, whispering."

"What said Wulfhere?"

"That the tide was failing," I answered.

The bishop was silent for a moment, and then he said:

"I heard a voice, plainly, that cried to me, 'Up! for the Lord has delivered these heathen into your hands'."

"We heard no such voice, Father," I said, "but I think it spoke true."

Now the light was broadening, making all things cold and gray as it came. And quickly I told Ealhstan what I had heard, and what both I and Wulfhere thought of the matter.

"Can we let them pass us, and so fall on them as they gain the level land of Stert?" asked Ealhstan, saying nothing more.

"That can we," I answered. "They will keep to the road, and we can draw back to the edge of the hill, so taking them in flank as they leave it."

For the hills bend round a little beyond the place where the road falls into the level below Matelgar's hall.

"So be it," said the bishop. "Go you, Wulfhere, and see how near the host is, and come back quickly."

When he was gone the bishop bade me wake the men. And at first I was for going round, but by this thane Wislac had waked, and had been listening to us: and he said that if I would let him wake the men he could do it without alarm or undue noise. Only I must raise the standard and bid them be silent. At that the bishop smiled and nodded, and I raised the standard, and waited.

Then Wislac stood up and crowed like a cock, and instantly the men began to turn and sit up, and as their eyes lit on the standard raised in their midst, became broad awake, each man rousing the next sleeper if one lay near him. And there was the bishop, finger on lip, and they were silent.

"Verily I thought on the hard chapel stones," muttered Guthlac, the lay brother, behind me.

"It is the war chime, not the matin bell, you shall hear this morning," said one of his brethren.

"That is better -- mea culpa," said Guthlac, clapping his hand on his mouth to stop his own warlike ejaculation.

Then came Wulfhere back, swiftly. Barely a mile were they from the hill, he said, and coming on quickly in loose order. Moreover, a horseman had passed, riding hard to the ships, doubtless to bid them be ready. But that would take little time, for these vikings are ever ready for flight, keeping their ships prepared from day to day.

XV: THE GREAT FIGHT AT PARRET MOUTH

Now very silently we drew off from that place to the edge of the hill which looks across the road to Stert. And there the bishop drew us up in line, four deep, and told the men what we must do, bidding them be silent till we charged, though that could not prevent a hum of stern approval going down the line.

One man the bishop called out by name, and when he stood before him, bade him, as a swift runner, hasten back to Eanulf or Osric, and bid them on here with all speed. And, when the man's face fell, the bishop bade him cheer up and go, for the swifter he went the sooner would he be back at the sword play. Whereat the man bowed, and, leaving his mail at a tree foot, started at a steady run over the ground we had covered already, and was lost in the trees.

Then we waited, and the light grew stronger every moment. As we lay in line among the bushes we could see without much fear of being ourselves seen, and by and by we could make out the ships. They had their masts raised, and the sails were plain to be seen, ready for hoisting. The men were busy about their decks, and on shore as well, while the vessels were yet close up to the land.

They must haul off soon, little by little, or they would be aground, as doubtless they had been with every tide till this, for rocks are none, only soft mud on which a ship may lie safely, but through which no man may go, save on such a "horse" as the fishers use to reach their nets withal, sledge-like contrivances of flat boards which sink not.

The wait seemed long, but at last we heard the hum of voices, and the tramp of feet, and our hearts beat fast and thick, for the time was coming.

Over the hill and down it they streamed in a long, loose line, laughing and shouting as the ships came in sight. A long breath came from us, and there was a little stir among the men; but the time was not yet, and we crouched low, waiting to make our spring.

Then ran up a long red forked flag, with a black raven on it, from the largest ship, and that seemed to be a signal for haste, for the tide was failing, so that some of the foremost men began to stream away from their comrades. And then I saw that many carried packs full of plunder, and also that the last of them were on the level.

So also saw the bishop, and he rose to his feet, pointing with the great mace he bore (for he might not wield sword) to the Danes, and saying:

"For the honour of Dorset -- for the holy cross -- charge!"

With a mighty shout we rose up, each in his place, and down the hill we rushed sword and axe aloft, on that straggling line.

Then from the Danes came a howl of wrath and terror, and, for a moment, dropping their burdens, they fled in a panic towards the ships.

Yet that was not the way of Danish men and vikings, and that flight stayed almost before it had gone fifty yards. Up rose amidst the throng a mighty double axe, and a great voice was heard shouting, and round their chief began to form a great ring of tried warriors, shoulder to shoulder as well as might be. But that ring might not be perfect all at once -- too close were we upon them, having already cut down many of the last to fly.

And then the battle began in earnest, and I will tell what I saw of it. For I was in the centre of our line, as befitted, and on either side of me were Wulfhere and Wislac, and on either side of them again, my collier next to Wulfhere, and next to Wislac his young thane. Before me were Guthlac and two brethren, and the other three behind me. That was the standard's shield wall. Behind that came Ealhstan the Bishop, hemmed in by twelve of his own best men.

So, with voice, and gesture of arm and mace the bishop swung our line in a half circle round the face of that grim ring of vikings, and as they closed up we closed, and faced them. Then saw I that we were outnumbered by three to one, but we were fresh, and they tired with a long march, quickly made, and under burdens.

Now began the spears to fly from one side to the other, and men began to fall. And yet there was no great attack made on either side. Then grew I impatient, for it seemed to me that as we were the weaker side the first charge might do all for us. So I spoke to Wulfhere, saying:

"We must charge before they. Let us break into that circle."

"Aye!" said the veteran, and "Aye!" shouted Wislac; and so I pointed the banner forward and shouted for my shield men to charge.

And that, with a great roar, they did; and down before the brawny arms of those foremost three lay brethren went three of the heathen, and we were pressing into the circle. Then a brother fell, dragging a Dane with him, and Wislac took his place, and three more Danes fell. Then went Aldhelm to Wislac's side, and Lo! the circle was broken, and our standard stood in the midst.

Yet was not that ring destroyed, and in a moment it closed after us, and now were we ten in the midst of a crowd of foes, while again outside them raged Ealhstan and his men, striving to break through to us.

Then knew I that our case was hard, and I struck the spear that held the standard into the ground, and round it we stood, back to back, Wulfhere and Wislac once more to right and left of me. And it would seem that so grim looked we in our desperation, that they feared us a little, or, at least, that each feared to be the first to fall on us, for the Danes drew back and let us stand for a breathing space, until that great chief who rallied the men -- leaving the care of the outer ring for a moment -- came and faced me, speaking in fair Saxon enough, and bidding us surrender.

And for answer I threw my seax at him, and as he raised shield to stop it, for it flew straight and hard as a forester can throw, I leapt at him, going in under his shield, and he fell heavily, moving not, for my blow went home. Well it was that Wulfhere came after me, for he warded blow of axe that would have slain me. And then the Danes howled and fell on us.

Hard fighting it was, but round us grew a ring of dead, and no man had laid hands on the standard. Guthlac was down, and Aldhelm, two lay brethren also, and we were all but sped when I was ware of a Saxon shout, and the crash of a great mace on a helmet before me, and then, "Well done, my sons!" cried Ealhstan the Bishop, as he came and ringed us round with his own men, and we might breathe again.

Now was the ring of Danes parted, and the ring was of our men; yet round it raged the vikings, as we had raged round their ring but a short space before. Yet, every man of us knew that we had won, for, even if each one of us fell before Eanulf came, the ships would not sail that tide. For the tall masts were listing over as two ships took the ground unheeded, and four were hauling out as the tide fell.

And I thought of my vision last night, and of those I had seen, and of what they had bid me think of them; and the roar of battle went on unheeded by me as I leant against the standard staff while I might, and found my strength again.

"See," cried Wislac, pointing. And I looked over to the hill where the road came down. It was full of horsemen, charging with levelled spears, and surely that was Osric at their head! Then near me a voice cried thrice "Victory!" but it seemed not as one of our men's rough voices, but very strange.

Over the level the spearmen swept, and a cry broke from the Danes as they saw the fresh foe upon them, and again they fell back from us quickly, and, spite of our charge on them, and the spears of the leading horsemen, once more closed up into their iron ring. But now it was not motionless, but moved ever towards the ships, going backward steadily.

Round it went Osric and his men: but into it they could not break. For the Danes hewed the ash shafts of the spears, and near them no horse might live, for their axes would shear through man and horse alike.

Then Ealhstan shouted to Osric, bidding us stand. And right glad were we to do this, while ever the Danes shrank away from us.

"Trapped they are, Sheriff," said Ealhstan, when Osric rode up to him, bearing still a headless spear. "Let them bide till Eanulf comes. None can reach the ships."

"He is hard behind me with all the levy," said Osric. "Let us finish this without him."

But Ealhstan shook his head, pointing to our men. And when he looked more coolly, he saw that barely half of us were left, and those worn out. So must we stand and wait; but we had done what we went to do, and had trapped the heathen when the tide was low. Yet the Danes went steadily back towards their ships, having yet half a mile to cover, but they left a line of wounded men to mark where they had gone, as one after another dropped.

Now were we who were left safe, and knew we had done a deed which would he told and sung till other tales of victory blotted out its remembrance if they might.

Then Ealhstan bade us sit down, for our horsemen were between us and the foe, and thereon he raised his voice, and with one accord his lay brethren and his own housecarles joined in singing a psalm of victory. And it was just at the matin time -- yet that psalm ended not as it was wont, for ere the last verses were sung, it was drowned in a great and thundering war song of Wessex, old as the days of Ceawlin or beyond him. And if I mistake not, in that song bishop and lay brethren joined, leaving the chant for their own native and well-loved tongue, else would they have been the only men of all the host unstirred thereby and silent.

Now, from that war song came a strange thing. It caused two great Danes to go berserk in their rage, and back they flew on us, their shields cast aside, and their broad axes overhead, howling and foaming as they came.

One of Osric's men tried to stop them. But he and his horse fell, for (I say truth) one leapt high above the horse, smiting downwards with his axe, so that the man was swept in twain under that blow, and the berserk Dane came on unhindered, straight for the standard, for his comrade had hewed off the horse's head.

Now I rested, by the standard, a long spear's length in front of our line. But by this I had leapt to my feet; and it was time, for he was almost on me. Spear had I none; so I dragged out the standard shaft from the ground where I had struck it, and levelled that sharp butt end full at his chest. Overhead was his axe again, and I had no shield to stop the blow; but I must leap aside from it.

He paid no heed to the spear-ended shaft, but rushed straight on it, spitting himself through and through, while his axe fell; but I had wrenched myself and the shaft at once to one side, and he fell over, burying the axe head in the ground but an inch from the collier's foot. Yet had he not done with me, for, leaving the axe, he clawed the ashen shaft and dragged himself up along it, howling, not with the pain, but with madness, and I must needs smite him with my sword, for his dagger was already at my throat.

Then looked I round for the other, but at first could not see him, for he was dead also, pinned to the ground by another of the horsemen, from behind. And all our men were on their feet, and the ring of Danes were shouting, and cheering their two mad men, yet keeping close order.

This seems long in telling; but it was all done in a flash, as it were, for the first I knew of the coming of these men was by the wheeling of the horse and the leaping of the berserk above it.

Then my men came and rid the standard of its burden, not easily, while Ealhstan stood with his arm on my shoulder, looking white and scared: for that had been the greatest danger he had seen that day, as he told me, which, indeed, it must have been, for else he had never changed countenance.

"Gratias Domino," he said, "verily into these heathen evil spirits enter, driving them to death. Now have you fought the evil one, both spiritually and bodily, my son, and have won the victory!"

Even as he spoke, the men, being sure of no more of such comings, began to crowd round me, shouting and cheering as though I had done some great deed. Which, if it were such, it seems to me that great deeds are forced on men at times; for what else I could have done I know not, unless, as Wislac says, I had run away, even as he was minded to do. But I had no time for that, nor do I believe his saying concerning himself.

When the Danes were nigh their ships Ealhstan bade us tend our wounded. And the first man tended was myself, for Wulfhere came to me, looking me over, and at last binding a wound on my left shoulder, of which I knew not, saying that my good mail had surely saved me. He himself had a gash across his face, and Wislac one on the leg, but none of us was much hurt.

Then Wislac sought Aldhelm, whom he found sitting up, dazed, from a blow across the helm that had stunned him, but he was soon able to walk, though dizzy and sick. But Guthlac was slain outright, and two others of the brethren.

Well, so might I go on, for of all our two hundred men there were left but ninety fit to go on with the fight, the rest being slain or sore wounded by the Danish axes. Ealhstan was unhurt; for, save that once when he had broken the ring to reach us when we were hemmed in, his men had kept before him.

Now what befell after that will not bear telling; for it was not long before Eanulf and all the Somerset and the rest of the Dorset levy came down and fell on the Danes as they fought their last fight as brave men should, with a quarter mile of deep mud between them and their ships.

Into that fight none of us bishop's men went, for we had done our part. But we lay and saw the Danes charge again and again against odds, their line growing thinner each time, until our men swept the last of them from the bank into the ooze, and there was an end.

Yet a few managed, I know not how, to reach the ships, and there they were safe; but thence they constantly shot their arrows into our men, harmless enough, but yet showing their mettle.

So was a full end made of that host, for none but those few were left alive from Stert field, and Somerset and Dorset had taken their fill of vengeance.

But, for all the victory, down sat Ealhstan the Bishop, and hiding his face in his hands wept that such things could be, and must be till war is no more.

XVI: AT GLASTONBURY

On that hard-won field we lay all that day, for we knew not if more Danes were left up country, or if by chance the ships might fall into our hands with the rising tide. And I think we might have taken them had not our men, in their fury, broken the boats which lay along the bank; so that we could not put off to them. Therefore, as the tide rose again and they floated, the men on board hauled out, and setting sail with much labour, for there were very few in each ship, stood off into mid channel. Out of Severn they could not get, for the wind was westerly, and the tide setting eastward, so at last they brought up in the lee of the two holms, and there furled sail and lay at anchor.

Very stiff and sore were we when we had rested for a little, and there fell a sadness on the levy, now that the joy of battle had gone, and the cost of victory must be counted. And that was heavy, for so manfully and steadily had the vikings fought that they had accounted for man to man as nearly as one might count, either slain or maimed.

Now on this matter I heard Wislac speak to Aldhelm, who sat facing him, and holding his aching head with both hands.

"So, friend," quoth Wislac, "as touching that matter of dispute we had. How stands the account?"

"I know not, nor care," said Aldhelm. "All I wot is that my head is like to split."

"Nay, that will it not, having stood such a stout blow," said Wislac, laughing. "Cheer up, and count our score of heads."

"I can count but one head, and that my own. Let it bide."

"So, that is better," said Wislac. "I should surely have been slain five times by my own count, but it seems I am wrong. Wherefore I must have escaped somehow. And that is all I know about it."

Then he turned to me, and asked if I had noted any doings at all.

And when I thought, all I could remember plainly were the fall of the tall chief I slew, and the coming of Ealhstan, and the attack of the berserk, and no more; all the rest was confused, and like a dream. So I said that it seemed to me that we had had no time to do more than mind ourselves, but that withal my shield wall had kept the standard. And that kept, there need be no question as to who had done best.

Then Wislac nodded, after his wont, and said that if Aldhelm was content so was he.

Whereupon Aldhelm held out his hand, and said that Wislac was wise and he foolish. And Wislac, grasping it, answered that it was a lucky foolishness that had brought so stout a comrade to his side, for had it not been for Aldhelm putting his thick head betwixt him and an axe, slain he would have been.

"Aye, brother," he said, "deny it not, for I saw you thrust yourself forward and save me by yourself, which doubtless is your way of settling a grudge, brother, and a good one."

So those two were sworn friends from that day forward, as were many another couple who met on that field for the first time, fighting side by side for Wessex.

Thus wore away the day and the next night, and with the morning those ships were yet under the holms, swinging at their anchors, for the westerly breeze held.

Then said Eanulf: "Let them be; harm can they do none, being so few. They will go with the shift of wind."

But the shift of wind came not for days and days, and there they lay, never putting out from shelter. And they are out of my story, so that I will say what befell them.

One night it freshened up to a gale, and in the morning there were five ships where six had been. One had sunk at her moorings. Then men said that the Danes had made a hut on the flat holm, plain to be seen from the nearest shore. And at last a shift of wind came, and they put not out.

So certain fishers dared to sail across and spy what was amiss, and finding no man in the ships, nor seeing any about the hut, went ashore, none hindering them.

Ships and hut and shore were but the resting place of the dead, for after a while they had no food left, and were too few and weak even to man one ship and go.

Many a long year it was before the king of their land, Norse or Dane, whichever he was, learned what had befallen his host, and how their bones lay on the Wessex shore and islands, for not one of all that had sailed that spring returned to give the news, or to tell how his comrades died on Stert fighting to the last, and on the island wishing they had fallen with the slain.

Now must I tell how we went back to Glastonbury town, marching proudly as became conquerors, while on every side was shouting of men, and at the same time weeping of women for those who had fallen.

When we came to the great square there stood Tatwine the Abbot and all his monks; but I had no eyes for them. For there, with abbess and nuns, stood Alswythe, smiling on me through tears of joy, and though her cheeks were thinner and paler by reason of fasting and prayer for us all, looking most beautiful, and to me like a vision of some saint.

That was all I could see of her then, for we must kneel, while a great Te Deum was sung, and then crowd into the abbey to hear mass once more.

Then after that was over, there was a great feast in the wide hall of the abbey, where Ealhstan and Eanulf sat side by side in the high seats, and on their right,

Osric and myself, and on the left, Wulfhere and Wislac, none grudging those chief places to the men who had kept the standard and broken the Danish ring.

When the feasting was done, then came the telling of great deeds over the ale cup, and that lasted long, and many were the brave men praised; nor were the deeds of the vikings, as brave foes, forgotten, for men praised them also. Moreover, the gleemen sang of the fight, and in those songs my name came so often, as needs it must, seeing that I bore the standard, that I will not set them down. Nor is there need, for the housecarles sing them even yet.

Now before we went to rest, Eanulf bade me wait on him early in the morning, and so, being refreshed by a long, quiet night, I went to him as he had bidden me.

There he thanked me as man to man for that crossing of Parret, and for staying the going of the Danes, saying that a greater man than he should add to the thanks. For needs must that one took word of all that had befallen to Ethelwulf the King, and that to be such a messenger was most honourable. Therefore should I myself bear the news, taking with me my two friends and such men as I chose, and should bear, written down, the reports of both Osric and Ealhstan, besides his own.

"Else," said he, "there are perhaps some to whom credit is due whose names may pass unmentioned."

And thanking him, I said that that was likely, for I knew few in the levy, which came from far and wide.

Whereat he laughed, saying that I was either very modest or very simple. So I knew that he spoke of myself, and thanked him again.

"Nay," he said, "small thanks to me, for if I did you not justice the men would."

Then all of a sudden he asked me about the business of my trial, and what I thought of it, bidding me tell him as a friend, thinking naught of the judge.

And that I was able to do now without passion, so far off and small a thing it seemed after all these stirring doings. And I knew that but for it I had been only a foolish thane, and slain maybe over my feasting in my own hall, or on Combwich hill, with my back to the foe, beside Matelgar.

Now when I had ended my tale and my thoughts concerning it, he told me that he had found out much of late, as he and the thanes spoke together here while waiting for the levy, and that word should go to the king of the whole matter, so that without waiting for the Moot, he should inlaw me again.

Then I knew not enough to say; but he clapped me on the shoulder, saying that he had been an unjust judge for once, and that I must be heedful if ever I sat in his place, and so bid me go and find my friends -- and get ready to ride to Salisbury, where the king lay, having moved from Winchester nearer to us.

That went I to do with a light heart, and only sorry that I might not see Alswythe before I went.

And this I told Wislac, who looked oddly at me, and then laughed, saying that he believed I feared an old nun more than a wild berserk. And true it was that I was afraid of that stately abbess, though not in the same way as one fears a raging madman flying on one.

"Pluck up courage," said he, "and go and ask the old dame to let you have speech with your lady; and if she grants it not, I am mistaken, for the lady is not one of her nuns, and there is a guest chamber for such folk as bishop's right-hand men, surely!"

That was good counsel, and so I went to the nunnery, trembling first because I was afraid, and next lest I might not see Alswythe.

Now that wondrous silver mail of mine was too easily known, and so soon as I got out into the street, the beggar men began to shout and crawl towards me. And then others looked, and ran, and then more, till there was a crowd of men of the levy pressing round me, stretching hands to pat me and the like.

Then one stood in front of me, hands on hips, and stared at me, and all at once he shouted: "Ho, comrades, this is the saint of Cannington hill! I saw him there, and soundly did he rate me for running, even as I deserved."

And at that there was a mighty shouting and crowding, so that I could in no wise go on my way, and I began to wax wroth.

My back was to the abbey gates, which were closed after me by the porter, and just then I saw some of the men look up over my head and point, and laugh; so I turned round, and there were Eanulf and Osric on the gateway battlements, looking on, as drawn thither by the noise. And just then Eanulf, laughing, made some sign or speech which I could not hear, to the men, who cheered; and soon they brought a great shield and on that set me, in spite of myself, raising me up shoulder high and saluting me as the man who had gained all the honour and victory. There must I lie still, lest I should fall and be made to look more foolish yet, and when I sat up, crosslegged thereon, they stopped shouting and stared at me.

"Let me down, ye pigs!" said I, very cross, and unmindful of the honour they would do me.

"Speak to us, Thane; speak to us," they cried; and one -- he who knew me at Cannington after the first fight -- added:

"Aye, Thane, you made us strong again on the hill the other day -- blaming us rightly. Praise us now if that may be."

Then I cast about for what to say, not being a great hand at speaking, though maybe, when real occasion is, the words have come fast enough. Howbeit, this was in coolness. But I knew that they were worthy of praise, so I said:

"Well have ye done, every man of you, even as I knew ye would when once ye turned to bay. And if the Danes come again, as I think they will not speedily, fight as ye fought at Stert, and there will be victory again."

Then they cheered and shouted again, louder than before; and I made to leap down, but they would not suffer me.

Then said I: "Let me go, for I have an errand."

Whereupon the men who held the shield, and could hear me amid the slackening uproar, asked where I would go, and being dazed by the noise and tumult, like an owl in daylight, I must needs answer, without thinking; "To the great nunnery."

And the end of that foolishness was that they bore me thither, for it was not far, with a great crowd of all sorts following and shouting. And there must I stand with all that tail after me while they beat on the gates in such sort that the poor nuns must have thought the Danes at their doorstep.

But I held up my hand for silence, not thinking it would come; but as it were by nature longing for it. And instantly all the crowd was hushed, and that surprised me, though when I told Wulfhere thereof he said it was no wonder.

Seeing which I begged them all to go away and not scare the holy women, who were used to quiet in the place. And then I remembered the honour the honest warriors had meant this for, and thanked them, bidding them make allowances for my being put out at first.

Then took they off their helms and shouted thrice; and then fled rapidly, for the gates opened behind me, and there was the abbess herself, with her cheeks red, and her eyes burning bright in anger, as I thought, while behind her peeped all her nuns at the crowded street, and at myself standing shamefaced on the steps, doffing my helm as I saw her.

But instead of being angry, she held out both her hands, and spoke kindly, saying; "Never has our quiet place heard such clamour before; but we women will not be behind the men in welcoming Heregar;" and so she bade the nuns come forward, laying her hands on my shoulder, and adding; "See, daughters, this is he who dared to warn the land of its danger, saving the lives of our sisters of Bridgwater, and many others, and who has even now led the host and conquered, giving us safety and peaceful rest again."

But I knelt and kissed her hand, while there went a little murmur among the nuns.

Then the lady abbess touched gently my bound shoulder, and said that the hurt was but rudely tended and that she must bind it afresh; so should she show her gratitude to one who had bled for the land. And they led me into the courtyard; and thence to the guest chamber, and there waited Alswythe.

Now when I looked to see her greet me formally, as in the presence of the abbess, she ran into my arms, and I found that we were alone.

Then must she hear and I tell all that had happened to me since we parted; but that was too long for the telling then, for very soon the abbess came with clatter of vessels along the passage, bringing warm water and salves to bind my small wound afresh.

And in that Alswythe helped her, with many pitying words and soft touches, so that I thought it good to be hurt if such tendance might ever be had. And many things they asked, as of Wulfhere's safety, and the collier's, and of how I got that wound, and the like. And that last I could not tell them, marvelling myself when it came, and more that it was the only one; but I know I smote flatwise once or twice myself in the heat of fight, so doubtless it was so with others, else would Aldhelm have been in halves or thereabouts.

Then I told them of my message to the king, and at that Alswythe rejoiced. And the abbess said that doubtless the king would reward the messenger, and what reward would I ask an he did so?

Now there was only one reward to me in all the world, and for answer I took Alswythe's hand, all wet with the water she bathed my hurt with, and kissed it. On which the maiden blushed, and looked down, but the abbess laughed softly, saying, "Verily, I thought so," and then seemed to choke a little, turning away from us. And Alswythe did not draw away her hand from mine, but let her cheek rest for a moment against my head, and so there was a little silence.

Then the abbess turned round again, and her eyes were bright, but the shine was of tears in them, and she spoke briskly.

"Now must you get hence, Heregar, my son, and go your way to the king with all haste, so shall you be back the sooner. Give him a scarf to bind that wound, Alswythe; so shall it seem an honour and not a scar."

So there was a little leave taking, but not much, though enough, and I went from the nunnery with Alswythe's white and red and gold scarf over my shoulder; gay enough to look at, but no gayer than the heart beneath it.

And there, waiting for me in the street, was my tail, armed and drawn up in line of fours to see me back to the abbey. So I went there at the head of them, with more shouting of people.

There was Wulfhere sitting on the doorsteps of the great door, having a bag in his hand, and when I got up to him, he thrust it out to me, saying "largess", and that I was glad enough to understand.

So I put my hand into the bag, and crying, "Here is withal to drink to Somerset and Dorset shoulder to shoulder," scattered the silver pennies among them, and so left them without any order among them at all, though shoulder to shoulder certainly.

"Ho, master!" said Wulfhere, "you looked mighty angry when you were carried aloft an hour ago."

"Aye," said I, "'tis pity a thane cannot walk abroad quietly on his own business."

"Well, well, they thought that you were their business, doubtless."

"Whence came all those pennies?" I asked, for we had no store at all to cast away.

"From Eanulf and Ealhstan," said Wulfhere, laughing. "They came to me, and saying that they were sore jealous, and minded to have good cause therefor, gave me this that you might carry off all well to the end."

And that was good of them, for else I know not how I should have left the men without more speech making.

Just then came the ealdorman into the hall where we were, and laughing, asked me if I meant to take all that following to Salisbury. But I only wanted the standard guards who were left, and Aldhelm, as one who had fought as such. This I had told Wulfhere before, so that I was not surprised when I heard that all were ready, and but waiting for me to set off.

Then Eanulf and Osric took me to the bishop, and there gave me writings to deliver to the king, and also bade me tell all that he asked, in my own way.

And those three saw us set forth, all well mounted, and a goodly company to look at, the bishop blessing us before we went, and the people and warriors following and cheering us on our way through the town, and even some way beyond the walls.

XVII: ALFRED THE ATHELING

Of our long ride to the king's place there is little to tell. Only that everywhere the news seemed to have flown before us, and men knew who we were and what our errand, crowding round us to hear all about the fighting, and to be assured that the Danes had truly gone. And great cheer made they for us everywhere, so that we were treated as princes almost.

Therefore, that was a merry ride and a pleasant in the early June weather, and we were ever cheerful, for it so happened, as may have been already seen, that no one of us had lost close friend or kin in the battles, but had the rather gained much. Yet maybe we were the only ones of whom that might be said; for mixed with the joy was mourning over all the land. And of all my company, I had the most cause to be lighthearted; so that for all I had gained I thought the hard things I had gone through were well worth the bearing. Ever, therefore, have I judged him the happiest who out of hardship gains rest; for he best knows its worth.

So at last we came to Salisbury town, and that was full of a brilliant company: the courtiers of the king, and their following again. Yet, for all their magnificence, thanks to our good bishop's gifts, we showed well as we rode into the streets, and I think were envied by many because the marks of honourable war were yet on us; so that the men spoke of Aldhelm's crushed headpiece, or Wulfhere's gashed shield that bore the mark of the axe that he stopped from me, or my riven mail that Alswythe's scarf would scarcely hide, and Wislac's broken crest.

And if they looked from us to our men, there was yet more of the like to speak about; for not one of the standard guard had been scatheless from heavy weapon play.

Being thus marked we were easy to be known, and hardly had we drawn rein at the great hostelry where we should wait till the king summoned us, when a thane came to me, asking if we were from bishop or ealdorman. And when I said we were so, bearing letters from them, he bade us to the king's presence at once, tarrying for nothing, as we were waited for.

Fain would we have washed away the stains of travel; but he was urgent, saying that the king's word brooked no delay. Therefore, leaving our horses with the people of the inn, we followed him, marching in order, to the great house where Ethelwulf was.

Here were guards and many thanes, and I must show the tokens given me, before we might enter, while our thane stood by, impatient at the formalities.

Those over, we came to a greet hall high-ceiled with oak, and carved everywhere, and strewn with sweet sedges, and on the high place sat the king and queen and one of the athelings.

Now I had never seen the king before, but I thought him like all that I had heard of in stories. For he sat in his purple robes, ermine-trimmed, having on a little gold crown over his long, curling hair, and his gloves and shoes were of cloth of gold, curiously wrought with pearls, while at his feet sat a page, holding a cushion whereon lay sceptre and orb.

But I looked to see the face of a warrior under the gold circle of the king, and therein was disappointed; for his face was kind and gentle, as many a good warrior's has been in time of peace, but lacked those lines which a man might know would harden into grimness and strength in time of need. And I thought that Ealhstan was like a king, and Ethelwulf like a bishop rather.

Yet by the king's side, leaning on his chair, was one whom I then noted not, having eyes only for his father -- Alfred the Atheling, who, to my mind, is both warrior and saint, as though Ethelwulf, his father, and Ealhstan, his teacher, had each taught him the properties of the other, making a perfect king.

Now, while I looked, our guide went and made obeisance before the king, telling him of our coming, and at that the face of Ethelwulf lighted up, and he called to us to come near and give our message. And I saw the queen clasp her hands, as preparing to hear things all too heavy for a lady's ear, while the atheling stood up and gazed eagerly at us. Then, too, over all the court was deep silence, as they made a lane through which we must pass to reach the throne, and our feet seemed to make all the sound there was.

So we tramped up, and bowed low before the king, who ran his eyes over us, though not as a captain: but as one who knows men of all sorts well, and is accustomed to judge their faces.

Then he said to me; "You are Heregar, the bishop's standard bearer. We have heard of you as such, and welcome you, knowing you must bring good news, as your face tells me."

"I am Heregar, Lord King," I answered, "and I bring good news -- written in these which I am to give into your own hand."

Then the king smiled a little, and signed the atheling to take the letters, and give them him.

But I, not knowing court ways, must needs think this beside my duty, and said quickly, not knowing to whom I spoke; "Pardon me, Thane, I am to give these into the king's own hand," and so stepped past him, holding out the letters to Ethelwulf.

And at that the atheling laughed outright, which was strange to me in the king's presence, saying, "Not so far wrong, standard bearer, if not very polite;" and so stepped back to his place, still laughing.

But Ethelwulf did not notice this, having taken the letters eagerly from me, and broken open the first that came.

Now when he had read the first few lines, he looked up, and reading from the letter, which doubtless told him the names of the bearers -- "Heregar I know," he said; "which is Wulfhere?"

Then Wulfhere bowed, and the king asked for Wislac and Aldhelm, and then for each of the men in turn. And when each had answered, he looked hard at us, still holding the letter open, but saying nothing, and then fell to reading again. So we must stand still till all those letters were read.

Presently he took one, and reading the outside, gave it to the atheling, saying it was to him, and went on reading. That the atheling took, and as he read, looked at us, and it seemed particularly at me, though I thought nothing of that.

At last the king finished, and turned to a tall, noble-looking warrior who stood very near the dais, bidding him treat us with all honour, and see to our lodging near him while we were at court. Shortly, he said, he would speak to us of all we could tell him.

Then he held out his ungloved hand to us, which the atheling made a smiling sign for me to kiss, and that we all did, and then he looked pleasantly at us, and went his way from the hall, followed by his close attendants, with the queen and the atheling.

So soon as the king was gone, the talk began all over the hall, and most of all they crowded round us to learn what we could tell them; but that tall thane, whose name was Ceorle, came and took us away, telling the rest jestingly that they should have the second telling of the news, but that the king must have the first. And so he took us to guest chambers in his own house, and there left us in charge of his steward, treating us four thanes with all honour, and our men, as became their standing, among his own best men.

At least, this last was but for a short time, for the lay brethren came to me, looking oddly at me, and saying that they were in a strait; for, being lay brethren first, and warriors after, they knew not how to join in the talk and idle jests of the servants and housecarles. Moreover, they said that their vows obliged them to certain duties of prayer. And this I thought was honest of them, for many a lay brother would, when he found that I noted not their state, have broken out of bounds gladly, for the time.

So I sent for the steward, and asked him where they might be bestowed, and after a little thought, he said that the abbot, who had a following of honest housecarles, would take them in; and that he managed for us, and afterwards told me that Ealhstan's men had gained great praise, both for themselves and the bishop, by their ways in the abbey.

This is a little thing: but I tell it because it shows what sort of man Bishop Ealhstan was. For even over these rough warriors he had gained such a power for good that he had made of them all he wished -- sturdy champions of the faith, both bodily and spiritually.

So when those three were gone elsewhere our only serving man was my collier, and well was he treated in Ceorle's house.

We bided quietly there all the rest of that day and that night, and then in the morning were bidden to speak with the king, Ceorle taking us four himself and sending one to find the lay brethren and Dudda.

The king sat with Alfred the Atheling in a private chamber, no other but Ceorle being beside him while we were there. And I was a little frightened about my putting aside the young prince now, for I knew who he was from Ceorle. But he had a pleasant look and greeting for us as we came in. So also had Ethelwulf himself, who seemed less stately than yesterday when he sat in his royal attire in full court.

Richly dressed he was now, with a gold circlet on his head and great gold bracelets on his arms; but he was in no high place, only sitting easily in a carved and cushioned chair, while the atheling sat on a settle by the window.

The letters I had brought lay open on the table at the king's elbow, and his hand was on them, and there were other writings scattered about; great ones with red seals hanging thereto -- made no doubt by the gold signet which stood close by in its open casket.

"Come near, Thanes," the king said in his deep, quiet voice. "Let us talk together of this matter as friends, for a useless king were I but for such as you who keep my throne from the blows of enemies."

"Stay, Father," said Alfred the Atheling, starting up. "Let me write while the thanes speak," and he gathered up pens and such, and a roll of parchment, sitting down at the table and then holding pen ready, and looking at us.

The king smiled at him and his haste, and said, "Verily, Thanes, you must mind your words if Alfred writes them down, for he will ever keep records of tales such as yours, saying that they are for men to read hereafter."

But that had no terrors for us, seeing that we had a plain tale to tell, truth and nothing more. So, as Ceorle bid us, we four sat down by the window, and the king asked me to tell my story from the first.

So I began by saying that I had seen the landing of the Danes at Stert, and warned the watchmen of the levy.

There Alfred stopped me, holding up his pen suddenly.

"Tell us, Thane, of the Watchet landing," he said.

And when I began to tell of that he looked up again, with his eyes dancing, and asked me how I came on Quantock hill.

Thereat the king laughed a little, saying that Alfred should have been a lawman, and the atheling said that, with his father's help, he meant to be such, and a good one.

And that he has become, for the laws he has given us will last, as it seems to me, till the name of Saxon has departed.

Then I was a little in doubt what to say, and the king saw this. So he told me kindly that he had had very full accounts written by the bishop and ealdormen; but now both he and the atheling would fain hear about myself; that is, if my friends already knew all, and if I would not heed Ceorle.

Now I saw that I must speak more of myself than I wished, and would fain have been excused, saying something of that sort. But the atheling asked me to think of them as friends who would feel for me, saying, too, that of my own history he would not write, and so kindly did he urge me, drawing me on, that at last I had told him all from the beginning of my troubles, even to the time when I rode with Alswythe into Glastonbury and sought the bishop.

"That is well told," said Alfred, when I had finished so far, and the king sighed a little, but left all the speaking to his son.

"Now, Wulfhere," he went on, "it is your turn," and so made the old warrior take up the tale; but he bade him begin at the first fight.

However, Wulfhere must needs go back to the war arrow business, and then to the staying of the flight at Cannington, and in this Alfred did not stop him, though I thought it more than needed.

So he told all his tale, even to the slaying of the berserk, and things like that. And as he told of the breaking of the ring, and our stand inside of it, Alfred the Atheling wrote fast, and presently he bade Wulfhere cease, and going to a corner took down a harp, while his father smiled on him, and tuning it, broke out into a wondrous war song that made our hearts beat fast, for we seemed to feel that it was full of the very shout and ring of battle inside our circle of foes, and we were as men who looked on and saw our own deeds over again, only made more glorious by the hand of the poet and the voice of the singer.

So that when he ended the king's eyes flashed, and Ceorle's face was red and good to look at with a war light on it, and Wislac shouted, as I had nearly done.

But at that sound, strange in the king's presence, we all started, and Wislac seemed abashed.

"Truly, Lord King," he said humbly, "I could not help it."

"Almost had I done as you did," said the kindly king. "Alfred must bear the blame. Now shall you tell your story."

But Wislac said he had nought to add to Wulfhere's tale, save that Aldhelm here had saved him at his own cost, and that he had had, moreover, as much fighting as he was like ever to want.

But even from him Alfred gained many things about the fighting, and from Aldhelm also, and these he wrote down.

Thus we all told our tales, and they were long in the telling, so that when Aldhelm had finished, the king rose up, blaming Alfred gently for the long sitting, saying, however, that he had feared somewhat of the sort, but that doubtless the thanes were more wearied than either of the other three who had listened.

"Now," he said, "well have you four thanes deserved of me and of all, and you shall not say that the king is ungrateful. And I think that each of you has said less of your own selves than might be said, or, indeed, than is said in these letters. Now have Ceorle and I and my council spoken of this matter, and we have thought of rewards fitting for the shield wall of the standard."

Then would we thank the king; but he bade us wait for a little, putting his hand on those great parchments with the seals. One of these he took and gave to Aldhelm.

"This is to your father, confirming his rights of the land he holds of me to him and his heirs for ever, by reason of your good service. Yet is there a little blame to you from the way in which you found a foremost place, though much praise for the holding thereof and in your manner of ending that quarrel."

So Aldhelm took the deed and kissed the king's hand in token of homage, going to his place very glad, for this was what his father desired most of all.

Then the king beckoned Wislac and gave him also a deed like Aldhelm's, granting him the lordship of the manor of Goring on the Thames, and that was a good reward to the stout Mercian, who thanked the king, saying that he wotted not how his majesty knew what he would have most wished. Whereupon the king laughed, saying that kings knew more than men gave them credit for, and so Wislac did homage, and sat down.

Then Ethelwulf looked at Wulfhere, and said; "Wulfhere, my old warrior, I know not rightly what to do with you, for you are a lonely man, and I think that a place in my court would not suit you. Nor would you care to hold a manor in a strange place. Wait a little, and we will think it over."

Now at that Wulfhere looked glad, for I think he feared rather than desired reward.

Now came my turn, and my face flushed, and I was a little frightened, for there was but one thing I wanted, and I feared that that might not be.

But the king made a step towards me and took me by the hand, looking hard at me.

"Heregar," he said, "yours has been a strange story, and from beginning to end you have been first in this victory that will gain us peace for many years to come. Moreover you have suffered wrong, being punished for evil falsely laid to your charge on my account. And that I must show all men to be untrue, and that I, the king, hold it so. Now shall you choose your own reward."

Then was I sorely abashed, not knowing how to say what I longed for, and the king stood waiting a little. And maybe I should never have got it out, but the atheling looked up, and said:

"May I speak for you, Heregar?"

And so plainly did I see that he knew all, that I asked him to do so, and he came beside me and said; "Heregar needs but one thing, my father, and that is the hand of the maiden he loves -- Alswythe the daughter of Matelgar, and your ward since her father was slain."

"Are you so foolish as to ask no more than that?" said the king, smiling.

And on that my tongue was loosed, and I answered; "Aye my Lord the King. If foolish it be to long for the one whom a man loves, and who loves him, so that he holds her beyond all other reward."

"Then is your request granted," said the king very kindly. "Yet must you have withal to keep so great a treasure rightly."

Now I had forgotten that I was landless, and well it was for me that the king went on quickly; "So I give you the lands that were Matelgar's, and your own lands again; and my men, and at my cost, shall build your halls afresh that the Danes have burnt. And whatever rights were Matelgar's or your father's shall be confirmed to you and yours for ever. Yet these things are but justice, and no reward."

So he paused a little, and I found courage to speak.

"My Lord the King, I need no more than you have given, for love and honour and lands have come back to me, and withal friendship of these three here, and of Ealhstan the Bishop, and of the noble ealdormen; while but for what has befallen I might have been still a careless thane, living at ease and for naught; but now, having heard Your good words, it is enough, and reward fit for any man."

And this I meant from my heart, for no more could I see that any man should need than this: honour of his fellows and of the king, and love and lands, and friends. Surely is a man rich in these things.

Yet must Alfred the Atheling add a word.

"Call me your friend also, Heregar, if you will, for fain would I be so," and he held out his strong white hand to take mine.

And it is good to think that, as it were, the grasp of his has never slackened from that day to this, but that he is my friend still.

Then Ceorle must say likewise, and last of all the king said; "Friend to all my people would I be, and to none more than to those who have risked life for the land. Therefore, to you and yours am I friend always, so that you shall ever think of me as friend first and king after. Nor is it to everyone that I dare say that, Heregar, my friend."

And he took my hand also, as the atheling and Ceorle had taken it.

So was I fain to weep for very joy at all this that had come to me, and must turn away for a little lest it should be seen.

Then the king spoke cheerfully, as on business.

"Now, Heregar, I have work for you to do in your home; for I would have no man idle. Here is Watchet town burnt up, and no man left -- for its lord is slain -- to see that it is built aright, and that each man, or family, has his own again. Now, you knew that place well, nor is it very far from you. Therefore shall you see to all that, and you shall have writings from me to back you. But men must know that you yourself have power there, and, therefore, I make you lord of all Quantock side, from Watchet stream to Parret, and from the borders of your own land at Cannington to Severn shore between those two. And this shall you render in return for those rights: that you shall be ready at all times to bear the standard of Wessex, against all comers from over seas, at my bidding."

Now that was the Dragon of Wessex of which the old witch spoke. And lo! those things that had been foretold of me were sooth, and I knelt before the king, and swore to bear him this service faithfully.

So the rest bore witness of that oath gladly, rejoicing in the honour, which was in truth to them as well as to me, for I could not have gone through aught without them, and if mine was the grip on Ealhstan's banner shaft, theirs were the hands that had kept it there.

Then said Ethelwulf; "Choose now one who shall have charge under you of the watchings and beacons on your shore."

And straightway I turned to Wulfhere, and begged him to do this for me, and it was good to see the warrior's face light up with gladness as he promised to give me his help. Doubtless that was what the king had in store for him, for at once he gave him the manor of the Watchet thane who had been slain, for as it chanced he had no heirs, and the land came back to the king.

That was the end of a long morning's work, and very kindly did Ethelwulf take his leave of us, saying that we must have these matters confirmed when the Witanxii met in two days' time.

So we went out, landed men and noble, and with us went the atheling, who took us to his own lodgings at the abbey, where he would see and speak to our men that he might write yet more from their lips, for he said that often it was good to hear what the common sort thought.

And my collier must needs tell him -- for he was very pleasant, so that none need fear his rank -- of Grendel, and also of the saint, which mightily pleased the atheling. So that often would he call me "Grendel" in sport thereafter, for we grew close friends in the time we bided at Salisbury.

And that seemed long to me, for now would I fain be back at Glastonbury with Alswythe.

Soon Wislac, also, grew tired of the court, and said that he longed for the deep meadows and lofty trees, and green downs along the clear river in this June time, and must seek his own home again. But it seemed that Alfred over-persuaded him, for reasons which he told me not, and he stayed.

We went to the great meeting of the Witan, taking our seats there when our rights were confirmed to us. And into my hands was put the standard of Wessex by the king himself, and I bore it to the great church, there to be blessed in the bearing thereof.

And there stood Ealhstan himself in his robes, having come even that morning for this very purpose. And that was pleasant, and even as I should have most wished. Moreover, my friends, and Alfred, and Ceorle stood by me as if for shield wall at that time, and I was well attended.

Now betimes, in the afternoon, came Alfred the Atheling to me as I sat with Ceorle, talking of the arms of the vikings, and asked me to come and speak with friends of his, who would not see him save he brought me.

And at that Ceorle laughed, saying that they must be of importance if they would deny the prince an audience, making conditions. And Alfred said very gravely that they were so, and maybe the only people, save the king and queen, who might delay seeing him.

So I was curious to know who these were. But we left Ceorle still laughing. Then Alfred took me to the abbey, and sent one of his men to say we had come, who, when he returned, bade us into the presence of these people.

When we came to a great door, in a part of the abbey where I had not before been, he took my arm, and pushed me in first, saying that he would ensure himself a good reception; and there sat Ealhstan, and beside him stood Alswythe, smiling at me, and with a little colour in her face.

XVIII: PEACE IN THE LAND

Now of the wedding in the great church I knew very little, save that I had Alswythe beside me, and that Ealhstan married us. And that was all I cared for, heeding naught of the rest.

But the king and the queen were there, and many thanes, while the atheling must needs be a groomsman with my friends, and Ceorle gave away the bride on the king's behalf. There, too, was Eanulf, looking very noble in his court array, beside the king. And the little page in blue and silver who held Alswythe's dress was none other than Turkil, "Grendel's friend" as Alfred called him, whom Alswythe had begged the bishop to bring with him.

There also was Dudda the Collier, clad beyond knowledge by Wislac, holding my helm and sword, and the lay brethren, mail clad for the last time, with the white cross painted on their shields and helms. Lustily did they join in the chanting.

Osric only was not there, but on Alswythe's neck and arms shone presently wonderfully-wrought collar and bracelets of gold that he had sent, having had them made from the spoils of that tall viking chief that I had slain.

Then was there feasting, and songs of gleemen, and, better still, that song of Stert fight sung by Alfred the Atheling himself in full hall. And then had Wislac full excuse for what he did in the king's presence, for at the end all the hall joined in a mighty Wessex war shout. And that, said the atheling, was a poet's greatest praise, to have stirred the hearts of men to forgetfulness of aught but the song.

Now, when we must needs ride away westward, with Wulfhere and Aldhelm for attendants, and the collier and my lay brethren again for guards, the king gave Alswythe a ring, praying her to spare me to him if need should be; and she, half weeping, yet proudly, told him that she would be the first to arm me for his service. And the queen kissed her, but the atheling said that soon he should see us again, for he would ride with me over the battle-ground, and learn it all, when our hall was ready for a guest.

Then Wislac took leave of us last of all, even as we started, for he said he would have no long leave taking. Nor did he know if he must not come with Alfred to fight the battle over again. And we prayed him to do so, for I loved the quaint sayings and cool valour of the broad-shouldered thane.

But Eanulf and Ceorle rode with many of the thanes a mile or more with us on our way from the town, and there, having set us fairly off, left us with hearty good-speeds. But they left one behind, who joined himself to our little company. And that was Turkil, clad like myself in silver mail, and on a white pony, but with flame-coloured cloak and scarf. For that was the atheling's doing, when he knew that "Grendel's friend" was to be brought up in our hall, to grow into the stout warrior I had boded him to be.

Now should my story be ended were it a fairy tale, but it is not that. Well I knew that, happy as I was, the day must come when I must bear forward to battle the golden dragon banner of Wessex, and I cannot rightly tell if I dreaded or longed for that day. Maybe there was a mixture of both dread and longing in my thoughts thereof.

But when we came over Brent Knoll, on our way back to my place and Alswythe's at Cannington, there lay the black ships under the holms yet, and there, too, were the burnt walls of our houses, though these were rising up again as the king's men wrought at them. And all the land lay waste and neglected, and, as we rode over Cannington hill, a broken helm rolled from my horse's hoof from among the grass of the roadside. Those things brought back to us the memory of war and trouble even in our new happiness; and there, over the river, was the new-made mound over Elgar, the man who had died for his land, and not in vain.

It was many days since we started from Salisbury town, however, before we came to Cannington, and in that time we had sought the house of Turkil's father, the franklin, lodging with him for a day and night, that we might seek Leofwine the hermit. But him we might not find, for he was dead, and that grieved me sorely, for I would fain have seen him again, aye, and if it might be, taken him to live with us.

But he died as the tide went out on the day of Stert fight, and those who stood by him say that he had visions of all that befell there.

For many times he called to me as exhorting me; and once, after long silence, in the gray of early dawn, he rose up, crying, "Up, Ealhstan, up, for the Lord has delivered these heathen into your hands!"

And that was at the time when the bishop had heard those words spoken to him. And again, once more he roused, even at the time when the Danes drew off from us at the coming of Osric. He lifted his hands, crying "Victory!" thrice, and then saying very softly, "Heregar, my son," was silent thereafter till he died at the time of the lowest ebb, only his lips moving as if in prayer. And I remembered the strange voice I had heard crying round me, and I wept, for I thought how much more was wrought by the prayers of feeble ones than men wot of.

But his prophecy had indeed come true, and though I might not see him more, the memory of Leofwine is with me always, with his words of wise counsel that he had spoken to me.

Now of that other one who prophesied in her strange way to me I know no more, nor did I ever see her again. Gundred the witch, men called her, knowing her well, and fearing her. But she was never seen after the Danes swept over our land, and how she ended none ever knew. I sought her carefully that I might give her shelter and ease for the rest of her days, but without avail.

All his life long has Dudda the Collier bided with me, serving well and roughly, but in all most faithfully, as is his wont. And not many days after we came homewards he brought me the berserk's axe to hang in hall, for he had taken it and hidden it when we left the battlefield on the day after the fight. So there it is now, and beside it hangs the raven flag of the largest ship, for he must needs go with the fishers across to the holms, and bring me back the tale of how the last of the Danes had perished.

And now what am I to say of the years since our hall was built again? Long have they been, and not all happy, for many a time have I had to bear the standard of Wessex against the Danes. Yet Stert fight won us six years of peace, and after that the Earl Ceorle and I led our levies and conquered at Wenbury. But that was Wulfhere's last fight, for of his wounds he might not recover, though we bore him back and tended him carefully for a month or more. So he lies in God's Acre at Cannington, and is at rest.

Then came long years of fighting, and ever I bore the banner, and ever Alswythe set me forth most lovingly, with brave words that should bide with me till I came back to her. And all the time our hall was safe, for beyond Parret the Danes came not again.

And to tell of all those fights were too long, or of how Wislac and Aldhelm would ever fight beside me as of old, and at last Turkil in Aldhelm's place, when that brave thane fell at Wilton, fighting for Alfred the King.

Then were we in Athelney with Alfred, and it was the collier who found us that place of safety. And thence we went at last to victory again, and now once more the land has rest.

Yet Wislac is with us in Wulfhere's place, for his own land is in Danish hands, and we know not what wars may be yet with them, though we have stood by the king's side when the greatest victory of all was won, and Guthrum the heathen became Athelstan the Christian, and peaceful division of the land was made.

So I and Alswythe grow old here in Cannington, seeing our children grow up around us. And Alfred the king has our eldest in his court, there training him in all things well and wisely. And Turkil is thane of Watchet, and our son-in-law, much loved by all, well and faithfully tending all my shore as Wulfhere tended it in his time.

So to me and mine after storm has come peace, and with us and the land all is well.

THE END

The Valkyrs by Hélène Adeline Guerber

The Battle Maidens

Odin's special attendants, the Valkyrs, or battle maidens, were either his daughters, like Brunhild, or the offspring of mortal kings, maidens who were privileged to remain immortal and invulnerable as long as they implicitly obeyed the god and remained virgins. They and their steeds were the personification of the clouds, their glittering weapons being the lightning flashes. The ancients imagined that they swept down to earth at Valfather's command, to choose among the slain in battle heroes worthy to taste the joys of Valhalla, and brave enough to lend aid to the gods when the great battle should be fought.

"There through some battlefield, where men fall fast,
Their horses fetlock-deep in blood, they ride,
And pick the bravest warriors out for death,
Whom they bring back with them at night to Heaven
To glad the gods and feast in Odin's hall."

Balder Dead (Matthew Arnold).

These maidens were pictured as young and beautiful, with dazzling white arms and flowing golden hair. They wore helmets of silver or gold, and blood-red corselets, and with spears and shields glittering, they boldly charged through the fray on their mettlesome white steeds. These horses galloped through the realms of air and over the quivering Bifröst, bearing not only their fair riders, but the heroes slain, who after having received the Valkyrs' kiss of death, were thus immediately transported to Valhalla.

The Cloud Steeds

As the Valkyrs' steeds were personifications of the clouds, it was natural to fancy that the hoar frost and dew dropped down upon earth from their glittering manes as they rapidly dashed to and fro through the air. They were therefore held in high honour and regard, for the people ascribed to their beneficent influence much of the fruitfulness of the earth, the sweetness of dale and mountain-slope, the glory of the pines, and the nourishment of the meadow-land.

Choosers of the Slain

The mission of the Valkyrs was not only to battlefields upon earth, but they often rode over the sea, snatching the dying Vikings from their sinking dragon-ships.

Sometimes they stood upon the strand to beckon them thither, an infallible warning that the coming struggle would be their last, and one which every Northland hero received with joy.

> "Slowly they moved to the billow side;
> And the forms, as they grew more clear,
> Seem'd each on a tall pale steed to ride,
> And a shadowy crest to rear,
> And to beckon with faint hand
> From the dark and rocky strand,
> And to point a gleaming spear.
>
> "Then a stillness on his spirit fell,
> Before th' unearthly train;
> For he knew Valhalla's daughters well,
> The chooser of the slain!"

Valkyriur Song (Mrs. Hemans).

Their Numbers and Duties

The numbers of the Valkyrs differ greatly according to various mythologists, ranging from three to sixteen, most authorities, however, naming only nine. The Valkyrs were considered as divinities of the air; they were also called Norns, or wish maidens. It was said that Freya and Skuld led them on to the fray.

> "She saw Valkyries
> Come from afar,
> Ready to ride
> To the tribes of god;
> Skuld held the shield,
> Skaugul came next,
> Gunnr, Hildr, Gaundul,
> And Geir-skaugul.
> Thus now are told
> The Warrior's Norns."

Sæmund's Edda (Henderson's tr.).

The Valkyrs, as we have seen, had important duties in Valhalla, when, their bloody weapons laid aside, they poured out the heavenly mead for the Einheriar. This beverage delighted the souls of the new-comers, and they welcomed the fair maidens as warmly as when they had first seen them on the battlefield and realised that they had come to transport them where they fain would be.

> "In the shade now tall forms are advancing,
> And their wan hands like snowflakes in the moonlight are gleaming;
> They beckon, they whisper, 'Oh! strong Armed in Valour,
> The pale guests await thee—mead foams in Valhalla.'"

Finn's Saga (Hewitt).

Wayland and the Valkyrs

The Valkyrs were supposed to take frequent flights to earth in swan plumage, which they would throw off when they came to a secluded stream, that they might indulge in a bath. Any mortal surprising them thus, and securing their plumage, could prevent them from leaving the earth, and could even force these proud maidens to mate with him if such were his pleasure.

It is related that three of the Valkyrs, Olrun, Alvit, and Svanhvit, were once sporting in the waters, when suddenly the three brothers Egil, Slagfinn, and Völund, or Wayland the smith, came upon them, and securing their swan plumage, the young men forced them to remain upon earth and become their wives. The Valkyrs, thus detained, remained with their husbands nine years, but at the end of that time, recovering their plumage, or the spell being broken in some other way, they effected their escape.

> "There they stayed
> Seven winters through;
> But all the eighth
> Were with longing seized;
> And in the ninth
> Fate parted them.
> The maidens yearned
> For the murky wood,
> The young Alvit,
> Fate to fulfil."

Lay of Völund (Thorpe's tr.).

The brothers felt the loss of their wives extremely, and two of them, Egil and Slagfinn, putting on their snow shoes, went in search of their loved ones, disappearing in the cold and foggy regions of the North. The third brother, Völund, however, remained at home, knowing all search would be of no avail, and he found solace in the contemplation of a ring which Alvit had given him as a love-token, and he indulged the constant hope that she would return. As he was a very clever smith, and could manufacture the most dainty ornaments of silver and gold, as well as magic weapons which no blow could break, he now employed his leisure in making seven hundred rings exactly like the one which his wife had given him. These, when finished, he bound together; but one night, on coming home from the hunt, he found that some one had carried away one ring, leaving the others behind, and his hopes received fresh inspiration, for he told himself that his wife had been there and would soon return for good.

That selfsame night, however, he was surprised in his sleep, and bound and made prisoner by Nidud, King of Sweden, who took possession of his sword, a choice weapon invested with magic powers, which he reserved for his own use, and of the love ring made of pure Rhine gold, which latter he gave to his only daughter, Bodvild. As for the unhappy Völund himself, he was led captive to a neighbouring island, where, after being hamstrung, in order that he should not escape, the king put him to the incessant task of forging weapons and ornaments for his use. He also compelled him to build an intricate labyrinth, and to this day a maze in Iceland is known as "Völund's house."

Völund's rage and despair increased with every new insult offered him by Nidud, and night and day he thought upon how he might obtain revenge. Nor did he forget to provide for his escape, and during the pauses of his labour he fashioned a pair of wings similar to those his wife had used as a Valkyr, which he intended to don as soon as his vengeance had been accomplished. One day the king came to visit his captive, and brought him the stolen sword that he might repair it; but Völund cleverly substituted another weapon so exactly like the magic sword as to deceive the king when he came again to claim it. A few days later, Völund enticed the king's sons into his smithy and slew them, after which he cunningly fashioned drinking vessels out of their skulls, and jewels out of their eyes and teeth, bestowing these upon their parents and sister.

> "But their skulls
> Beneath the hair
> He in silver set,
> And to Nidud gave;
> And of their eyes
> Precious stones he formed,
> Which to Nidud's
> Wily wife he sent.
> But of the teeth
> Of the two
> Breast ornaments he made,
> And to Bödvild sent."
>
> *Lay of Völund* (Thorpe's tr.).

The royal family did not suspect whence they came; and so these gifts were joyfully accepted. As for the poor youths, it was believed that they had drifted out to sea and had been drowned.

Some time after this, Bodvild, wishing to have her ring repaired, also visited the smith's hut, where, while waiting, she unsuspectingly partook of a magic drug, which sent her to sleep and left her in Völund's power. His last act of vengeance accomplished, Völund immediately donned the wings which he had made in readiness for this day, and grasping his sword and ring he rose slowly in the air. Directing his flight to the palace, he perched there out of reach, and proclaimed his crimes to Nidud. The king, beside himself with rage, summoned Egil, Völund's brother, who had also fallen into his power, and bade him use his marvellous skill as an archer to bring down the impudent bird. Obeying a signal from Völund, Egil aimed for a protuberance under his wing where a bladder full of the young princes' blood was concealed, and the smith flew triumphantly away without hurt, declaring that Odin would give his sword to Sigmund—a prediction which was duly fulfilled.

Völund then went to Alf-heim, where, if the legend is to be believed, he found his beloved wife, and lived happily again with her until the twilight of the gods.

But, even in Alf-heim, this clever smith continued to ply his craft, and various suits of impenetrable armour, which he is said to have fashioned, are described in later heroic poems. Besides Balmung and Joyeuse, Sigmund's and Charlemagne's celebrated swords, he is reported to have fashioned Miming for his son Heime, and many other remarkable blades.

> "It is the mate of Miming
> Of all swerdes it is king,
> And Weland it wrought,
> Bitterfer it is hight."

Anglo-Saxon Poetry (Coneybeare's tr.).

There are countless other tales of swan maidens or Valkyrs, who are said to have consorted with mortals; but the most popular of all is that of Brunhild, the wife of Sigurd, a descendant of Sigmund and the most renowned of Northern heroes.

William Morris, in *The Land East of the Sun and West of the Moon*, gives a fascinating version of another of these Norse legends. The story is amongst the most charming of the collection in *The Earthly Paradise*.

Brunhild

The story of Brunhild is to be found in many forms. Some versions describe the heroine as the daughter of a king taken by Odin to serve in his Valkyr band, others as chief of the Valkyrs and daughter of Odin himself. In Richard Wagner's story, The Ring of the Nibelung, the great musician presents a particularly attractive, albeit a more modern conception of the chief Battle-Maiden, and her disobedience to the command of Odin when sent to summon the youthful Siegmund from the side of his beloved Sieglinde to the Halls of the Blessed.

The Elves by Hélène Adeline Guerber

The Realm of Faery

Besides the dwarfs there was another numerous class of tiny creatures called Lios-alfar, light or white elves, who inhabited the realms of air between heaven and earth, and were gently governed by the genial god Frey from his palace in Alf-heim. They were lovely, beneficent beings, so pure and innocent that, according to some authorities, their name was derived from the same root as the Latin word "white" (albus), which, in a modified form, was given to the snow-covered Alps, and to Albion (England), because of her white chalk cliffs which could be seen afar.

The elves were so small that they could flit about unseen while they tended the flowers, birds, and butterflies; and as they were passionately fond of dancing, they often glided down to earth on a moonbeam, to dance on the green. Holding one another by the hand, they would dance in circles, thereby making the "fairy rings," which were to be discerned by the deeper green and greater luxuriance of the grass which their little feet had pressed.

"Merry elves, their morrice pacing
To aërial minstrelsy,
Emerald rings on brown heath tracing,
Trip it deft and merrily."

Sir Walter Scott.

If any mortal stood in the middle of one of these fairy rings he could, according to popular belief in England, see the fairies and enjoy their favour; but the Scandinavians and Teutons vowed that the unhappy man must die. In illustration of this superstition, a story is told of how Sir Olaf, riding off to his wedding, was enticed by the fairies into their ring. On the morrow, instead of a merry marriage, his friends witnessed a triple funeral, for his mother and bride also died when they beheld his lifeless corpse.

"Master Olof rode forth ere dawn of the day
And came where the Elf-folk were dancing away.
The dance is so merry,
So merry in the greenwood.
"And on the next morn, ere the daylight was red,
In Master Olof's house lay three corpses dead.
The dance is so merry,
So merry in the greenwood.

"First Master Olof, and next his young bride,
And third his old mother—for sorrow she died.
The dance is so merry,
So merry in the greenwood."

Master Olof at the Elfin Dance (Howitt's tr.).

The Elf-dance

These elves, who in England were called fairies or fays, were also enthusiastic musicians, and delighted especially in a certain air known as the elf-dance, which was so irresistible that no one who heard it could refrain from dancing. If a mortal, overhearing the air, ventured to reproduce it, he suddenly found himself incapable of stopping and was forced to play on and on until he died of exhaustion, unless he were deft enough to play the tune backwards, or some one charitably cut the strings of his violin. His hearers, who were forced to dance as long as the tones continued, could only stop when they ceased.

The Will-o'-the-wisps

In medival times, the will-o'-the-wisps were known in the North as elf lights, for these tiny sprites were supposed to mislead travellers; and popular superstition held that the Jack-o'-lanterns were the restless spirits of murderers forced against their will to return to the scene of their crimes. As they nightly walked thither, it is said that they doggedly repeated with every step, "It is right;" but as they returned they sadly reiterated, "It is wrong."

Oberon and Titania

In later times the fairies or elves were said to be ruled by the king of the dwarfs, who, being an underground spirit, was considered a demon, and allowed to retain the magic power which the missionaries had wrested from the god Frey. In England and France the king of the fairies was known by the name of Oberon; he governed fairyland with his queen Titania, and the highest revels on earth were held on Midsummer night. It was then that the fairies all congregated around him and danced most merrily.

"Every elf and fairy sprite
Hop as light as bird from brier;
And this ditty after me
Sing, and dance it trippingly."

Midsummer Night's Dream (Shakespeare).

These elves, like the brownies, Huldra folk, kobolds, etc., were also supposed to visit human dwellings, and it was said that they took mischievous pleasure in tangling and knotting horses' manes and tails. These tangles were known as elf-locks, and whenever a farmer descried them he declared that his steeds had been elf-ridden during the night.

Alf-blot

In Scandinavia and Germany sacrifices were offered to the elves to make them propitious. These sacrifices consisted of some small animal, or of a bowl of honey and milk, and were known as Alf-blot. They were quite common until the missionaries taught the people that the elves were mere demons, when they were transferred to the angels, who were long entreated to befriend mortals, and propitiated by the same gifts.

Many of the elves were supposed to live and die with the trees and plants which they tended, but these moss, wood, or tree maidens, while remarkably beautiful when seen in front, were hollow like a trough when viewed from behind. They appear in many of the popular tales, but almost always as benevolent and helpful spirits, for they were anxious to do good to mortals and to cultivate friendly relations with them.

Images on Doorposts

In Scandinavia the elves, both light and dark, were worshipped as household divinities, and their images were carved on the doorposts. The Norsemen, who were driven from home by the tyranny of Harald Harfager in 874, took their carved doorposts with them upon their ships. Similar carvings, including images of the gods and heroes, decorated the pillars of their high seats which they also carried away. The exiles showed their trust in their gods by throwing these wooden images overboard when they neared the Icelandic shores and settling where the waves carried the posts, even if the spot scarcely seemed the most desirable. "Thus they carried with them the religion, the poetry, and the laws of their race, and on this desolate volcanic island they kept these records unchanged for hundreds of years, while other Teutonic nations gradually became affected by their intercourse with Roman and Byzantine Christianity." These records, carefully collected by Sæmund the learned, form the Elder Edda, the most precious relic of ancient Northern literature, without which we should know comparatively little of the religion of our forefathers.

The sagas relate that the first settlements in Greenland and Vinland were made in the same way,—the Norsemen piously landing wherever their household gods drifted ashore.

Canute the Great by Laurence Marcellus Larson

The Rise of Danish Imperialism during the Viking Age

Among the many gigantic though somewhat shadowy personalities of the Viking age, two stand forth with undisputed pre-eminence: Rolf the founder of Normandy and Canute the Emperor of the North. Both were sea-kings; each represents the culmination and the close of a great migratory movement,—Rolf of the earlier Viking period, Canute of its later and more restricted phase. The early history of each is uncertain and obscure; both come suddenly forth upon the stage of action, eager and trained for conquest. Rolf is said to have been the outlawed son of a Norse earl; Canute was the younger son of a Danish king: neither had the promise of sovereignty or of landed inheritance. Still, in the end, both became rulers of important states—the pirate became a constructive statesman. The work of Rolf as founder of Normandy was perhaps the more enduring; but far more brilliant was the career of Canute.

Few great conquerors have had a less promising future. In the early years of the eleventh century, he seems to have been serving a military apprenticeship in a Viking fraternity on the Pomeranian coast, preparatory, no doubt, to the profession of a sea-king, the usual career of Northern princes who were not seniors in birth. His only tangible inheritance seems to have been the prestige of royal blood which meant so much when the chief called for recruits.

But it was not the will of the Norns that Canute should live and die a common pirate, like his grand-uncle Canute, for instance, who fought and fell in Ireland: his heritage was to be greater than what had fallen to any of his dynasty, more than the throne of his ancestors, which was also to be his. In a vague way he inherited the widening ambitions of the Northern peoples who were once more engaged in a fierce attack on the West. To him fell also the ancient claim of the Danish kingdom to the hegemony of the North. But more specifically Canute inherited the extensive plans, the restless dreams, the imperialistic policy, and the ancient feuds of the Knytling dynasty. Canute's career is the history of Danish imperialism carried to a swift realisation. What had proved a task too great for his forbears Canute in a great measure achieved. In England and in Norway, in Sleswick and in Wendland, he carried the plans of his dynasty to a successful issue. It will, therefore, be necessary to sketch with some care the background of Canute's career and to trace to their origins the threads of policy that Canute took up and wove into the web of empire. Some of these can be followed back at least three generations to the reign of Gorm in the beginning of the tenth century.

In that century Denmark was easily the greatest power in the North. From the Scanian frontiers to the confines of modern Sleswick it extended over "belts" and islands, closing completely the entrance to the Baltic. There were Danish outposts on the Slavic shores of modern Prussia; the larger part of Norway came for some years to be a vassal state under the great earl, Hakon the Bad; the Wick, which comprised the shores of the great inlet that is now known as the Christiania Firth, was regarded as a component part of the Danish monarchy, though in fact the obedience rendered anywhere in Norway was very slight.

In the legendary age a famous dynasty known as the Shieldings appears to have ruled over Danes and Jutes. The family took its name from a mythical ancestor, King Shield, whose coming to the Daneland is told in the opening lines of the Old English epic Beowulf. The Shieldings were worthy descendants of their splendid progenitor: they possessed in full measure the royal virtues of valour, courage, and munificent hospitality. How far their exploits are to be regarded as historic is a problem that does not concern us at present; though it seems likely that the Danish foreworld is not without its historic realities.

Whether the kings of Denmark in the tenth century were of Shielding ancestry is a matter of doubt; the probabilities are that they sprang from a different stem. The century opened with Gorm the Aged, the great-grandfather of Canute, on the throne of Shield, ruling all the traditional regions of Denmark,—Scania, the Isles, and Jutland—but apparently residing at Jelling near the south-east corner of the peninsula, not far from the Saxon frontier. Tradition remembers him as a tall and stately man, but a dull and indolent king, wanting in all the elements of greatness. In this case, however, tradition is not to be trusted. Though we have little real knowledge of Danish history in Gorm's day, it is evident that his reign was a notable one. At the close of the ninth century, the monarchy seems to have faced dissolution; the sources tell of rebellious vassals, of a rival kingdom in South Jutland, of German interference in other parts of the Jutish peninsula. Gorm's great task and achievement were to reunite the realm and to secure the old frontiers.

Though legend has not dealt kindly with the King himself, it has honoured the memory of his masterful Queen. Thyra was clearly a superior woman. Her nationality is unknown, but it seems likely that she was of Danish blood, the daughter of an earl in the Holstein country. To this day she is known as Thyra Daneboot (Danes' defence)—a term that first appears on the memorial stone that her husband raised at Jelling soon after her death. In those days Henry the Fowler ruled in Germany and showed hostile designs on Jutland. In 934, he attacked the viking chiefs in South Jutland and reduced their state to the position of a vassal realm. Apparently he also encouraged them to seek compensation in Gorm's kingdom. To protect the peninsula from these dangers a wall was built across its neck between the Schley inlet and the Treene River. This was the celebrated Danework, fragments of which can still be seen. In this undertaking the Queen was evidently the moving force and spirit. Three years, it is said, were required to complete Thyra's great fortification. The material character of the Queen's achievement doubtless did much to preserve a fame that was highly deserved; at the same time, it may have suggested comparisons that were not to the advantage of her less fortunate consort. The Danework, however, proved only a temporary frontier; a century later Thyra's great descendant Canute pushed the boundary to the Eider River and the border problem found a fairly permanent solution.

In the Shielding age, the favourite seat of royalty was at Lethra (Leire) in Zealand, at the head of Roeskild Firth. Here, no doubt, was located the famous hall Heorot, of which we read in Beowulf. There were also king's garths elsewhere; the one at Jelling has already been mentioned as the residence of Gorm and Thyra. After the Queen's death her husband raised at Jelling, after heathen fashion, a high mound in her honour, on the top of which a rock was placed with a brief runic inscription:

Gorm the king raised this stone in memory of Thyra his wife, Denmark's defence.

The runologist Ludvig Wimmer believes that the inscription on the older Jelling stone dates from the period 935-940; a later date is scarcely probable. The Queen evidently did not long survive the famous "defence."

A generation later, perhaps about the year 980, Harold Bluetooth, Gorm's son and successor, raised another mound at Jelling, this one, apparently, in honour of his father. The two mounds stand about two hundred feet apart; at present each is about sixty feet high, though the original height must have been considerably greater. Midway between them the King placed a large rock as a monument to both his parents, which in addition to its runic dedication bears a peculiar blending of Christian symbols and heathen ornamentation. The inscription is also more elaborate than that on the lesser stone:

Harold the king ordered this memorial to be raised in honour of Gorm his father and Thyra his mother, the Harold who won all Denmark and Norway and made the Danes Christians.

In one sense the larger stone is King Harold's own memorial. It is to be observed that the inscription credits the King with three notable achievements: the unification of Denmark, the conquest of Norway, and the introduction of Christianity. The allusion to the winning of Denmark doubtless refers to the suppression of revolts, perhaps more specifically to the annihilation of the viking realm and dynasty south of the Danework (about 950). In his attitude toward his southern neighbours Harold continued the policy of Gorm and Thyra: wars for defence rather than for territorial conquest.

It is said that King Harold became a Christian (about 960) as the result of a successful appeal to the judgment of God by a zealous clerk named Poppo. The heated iron (or iron gauntlet, as Saxo has it) was carried the required distance, but Poppo's hand sustained no injury. Whatever be the truth about Poppo's ordeal, it seems evident that some such test was actually made, as the earliest account of it, that of Widukind of Corvey, was written not more than a decade after the event. The importance of the ordeal is manifest: up to this time the faith had made but small headway in the Northern countries. With the conversion of a king, however, a new situation was created: Christianity still had to continue its warfare against the old gods, but signs of victory were multiplying. One of the first fruits of Harold Bluetooth's conversion was the Church of the Holy Trinity, built at Roeskild by royal command,—a church that long held an honoured place in the Danish establishment. In various ways the history of this church closely touches that of the dynasty itself:

here the bones of the founder were laid; here, too, his ungrateful son Sweyn found quiet for his restless spirit; and it was in this church where Harold's grandson, Canute the Great, stained and violated sanctuary by ordering the murder of Ulf, his sister's husband.

In the wider activities of the tenth century, Harold Bluetooth played a large and important part. About the time he accepted Christianity, he visited the Slavic regions on the south Baltic coasts and established his authority over the lands about the mouth of the Oder River. Here he founded the stronghold of Jomburg, the earls and garrisons of which played an important part in Northern history for more than two generations. The object of this expansion into Wendland was no doubt principally to secure the Slavic trade which was of considerable importance and which had interested the Danes for more than two centuries. As the Wendish tribes had practically no cities or recognised markets, the new establishment on the banks of the Oder soon grew to be of great commercial as well as of military importance.

During the same period Harold's attention was turned to Norway where a difficult situation had arisen. Harold Fairhair, the founder of the Norse monarchy, left the sovereignty to his son Eric (later named Bloodax); but the jealousies of Eric's many brothers combined with his own cruel régime soon called forth a reaction in favour of a younger brother, Hakon the Good, whose youth had been spent under Christian influences at the English court. King Hakon was an excellent ruler, but the raids of his nephews, the sons of Eric, caused a great deal of confusion. The young exiles finally found a friend in Harold Bluetooth who even adopted one of them, Harold Grayfell, as his own son.

The fostering of Harold Grayfell had important consequences continuing for two generations till the invasion of Norway by Canute the Great. With a force largely recruited in Denmark, the sons of Eric attacked Norway and came upon King Hakon on the island of Stord where a battle was fought in which the King fell (961). But the men who had slain their royal kinsman found it difficult to secure recognition as kings: the result of the battle was that Norway was broken up into a number of petty kingdoms and earldoms, each aiming at practical independence.

A few years later there appeared at the Danish court a young, handsome, talented chief, the famous Earl Hakon whose father, Sigurd, earl in the Throndelaw, the sons of Eric had treacherously slain. The King of Denmark had finally discovered that his foster-son was anything but an obedient vassal, and doubtless rejoiced in an opportunity to interfere in Norwegian affairs. Harold Grayfell was lured down into Jutland and slain. With a large fleet the Danish King then proceeded to Norway. The whole country submitted: the southern shores from the Naze eastward were added to the Danish crown; the Throndelaw and the regions to the north were apparently granted to Earl Hakon in full sovereignty; the rest was created into an earldom which he was to govern as vassal of the King of Denmark.

A decade passed without serious difficulties between vassal and overlord, when events on the German border brought demands on the earl's fidelity to which the proud Norseman would not submit. It seems probable that King Harold in a vague way had recognised the overlordship of the Emperor; at any rate, in 973, when the great Otto was celebrating his last Easter at Quedlingburg, the Danish

King sent embassies and gifts. A few weeks later the Emperor died and almost immediately war broke out between Danes and Saxons.

Hostilities soon ceased, but the terms of peace are said to have included a promise on Harold's part to introduce the Christian faith among his Norwegian subjects. Earl Hakon had come to assist his overlord; he was known to be a zealous heathen; but King Harold seized him and forced him to receive baptism. The earl felt the humiliation keenly and as soon as he had left Denmark he repudiated the Danish connection and for a number of years ruled in Norway as an independent sovereign. King Harold made an attempt to restore his power but with small success. However, the claim to Norway was not surrendered; it was successfully revived by Harold's son Sweyn and later still by his grandson Canute.

Earl Hakon's revolt probably dates from 974 or 975; King Harold's raid along the Norse coasts must have followed within the next few years. The succeeding decade is memorable for two notable expeditions, the one directed against King Eric of Sweden, the second against Hakon of Norway. In neither of these ventures was Harold directly interested; both were undertaken by the vikings of Jom, though probably with the Danish King's approval and support. The Jomvikings were in the service of Denmark and the defeat that they suffered in both instances had important results for future history. The exact dates cannot be determined; but the battles must have been fought during the period 980-986.

In those days the command at Jomburg was held by Styrbjörn, a nephew of the Swedish King. Harold Bluetooth is said to have given him the earl's title and his daughter Thyra to wife; but this did not satisfy the ambitious prince, whose desire was to succeed his uncle in Sweden. Having induced his father-in-law to permit an expedition, he sailed to Uppland with a strong force. The battle was joined on the banks of the Fyris River where King Eric won a complete victory. From that day he was known as Eric the Victorious.

Styrbjörn fell in the battle and Sigvaldi, the son of a Scanian earl, succeeded to the command at Jomburg. In some way he was induced to attack the Norwegian earl. Late in the year the fleet from the Oder stole northwards along the Norse coast hoping to catch the earl unawares. But Hakon's son Eric had learned what the vikings were planning and a strong fleet carefully hid in Hjörunga Bay lay ready to welcome the invader.

The encounter at Hjörunga Bay is one of the most famous battles in Old Norse history. During the fight, says the saga, Earl Hakon landed and sacrificed his young son Erling to the gods. The divine powers promptly responded: a terrific hailstorm that struck the Danes in their faces helped to turn the tide of battle, and soon Sigvaldi was in swift flight southwards.

As to the date of the battle we have no certain knowledge; but Munch places it, for apparently good reasons, in 986. Saxo is probably correct in surmising that the expedition was inspired by King Harold. As to the significance of the two defeats of the Jomvikings, there can be but one opinion: northward expansion of Danish power had received a decisive check; Danish ambition must find other fields.

The closing years of Harold's life were embittered by rebellious movements in which his son Sweyn took a leading part. It is not possible from the conflicting accounts that have come down to us to determine just why the Danes showed such restlessness at this time. It has been thought that the revolts represented a heathen reaction against the new faith, or a nationalistic protest against German influences; these factors may have entered in, but it is more likely that a general dissatisfaction with Harold's rule caused by the ill success of his operations against Germans, Swedes, and Norwegians was at the bottom of the hostilities. The virile personality of the young prince was doubtless also a factor. To later writers his conduct recalled the career of Absalom; but in this instance disobedience and rebellion had the victory. Forces were collected on both sides; battles were fought both on land and on sea. Finally during a truce, the aged King was wounded by an arrow, shot, according to saga, from the bow of Toki, the foster-father of Sweyn. Faithful Henchmen carried the dying King across the sea to Jomburg where he expired on All Saints' Day (November 1), probably in 986, the year of the defeat at Hjörunga Bay. His remains were carried to Roeskild and interred in the Church of the Holy Trinity.

Of Harold's family not much is known. According to Adam of Bremen his queen was named Gunhild, a name that points to Scandinavian ancestry. Saxo speaks of a Queen Gyrith, the sister of Styrbjörn. On a runic monument at Sönder Vissing, not far from the garth at Jelling, we read that

> Tova raised this memorial,
> Mistiwi's daughter,
> In memory of her mother,
> Harold the Good
> Gorm's son's wife.

Tova might be a Danish name, but Mistiwi seems clearly Slavic. It may be that Harold was thrice married; it is also possible that Tova in baptism received the name Gunhild. Gyrith was most likely the wife of his old age. The question is important as it concerns the ancestry of Canute the Great. If Tova was Canute's grandmother (as she probably was) three of his grandparents were of Slavic blood.

Of Harold's children four are known to history. His daughter Thyra has already been mentioned as the wife of the ill-fated Styrbjörn. Another daughter, Gunhild, was the wife of an Anglo-Danish chief, the ealdorman Pallig. Two sons are also mentioned, Sweyn and Hakon. Of these Sweyn, as the successor to the kingship, is the more important.

The accession of Sweyn Forkbeard to the Danish throne marks an era in the history of Denmark. Harold Bluetooth had not been a weak king: he had enlarged his territories; he had promoted the cause of the Christian faith; he had striven for order and organised life. But his efforts in this direction had brought him into collision with a set of forces that believed in the old order of things. In Harold's old age the Danish viking spirit had awakened to new life; soon the dragons were sailing the seas as of old. With a king of the Shielding type now in the high-seat at Roeskild, these lawless though energetic elements found not only further freedom but royal favour and leadership.

It would seem that the time had come to wipe away the stain that had come upon the Danish arms at Hjörunga Bay; but no immediate move was made in that direction. Earl Hakon was still too strong, and for a decade longer he enjoyed undisputed possession of the Norwegian sovereignty. Sweyn did not forget the claims of his dynasty, but he bided his time. Furthermore, this same decade saw larger plans developing at the Danish court. Norway was indeed desirable, but as a field of wider activities it gave no great promise. Such a field, however, seemed to be in sight: the British Isles with their numerous kingdoms, their large Scandinavian colonies, and their consequent lack of unifying interests seemed to offer opportunities that the restless Dane could not afford to neglect.

The three Scandinavian kingdoms did not comprise the entire North: in many respects, greater Scandinavia was fully as important as the home lands. It is not necessary for present purposes to follow the eastward stream of colonisation that transformed the Slavic East and laid the foundations of the Russian monarchy. The southward movement of the Danes into the regions about the mouth of the Oder will be discussed more in detail later. The story of Sweyn and Canute is far more concerned with colonising movements and colonial foundations in the West. Without the preparatory work of two centuries, Canute's conquest of the Anglo-Saxon kingdom would have been impossible.

The same generation that saw the consolidation of the Norse tribes into the Norwegian kingdom also saw the colonisation of the Faroe Islands and Iceland. A century later Norsemen were building homes on the bleak shores of Greenland. Less than a generation later, in the year 1000, Vineland was reached by Leif the Lucky. Earlier still, perhaps a century or more before the Icelandic migration, the Northmen had begun to occupy parts of the British Isles. The ships that first sought and reached North Britain probably sailed from two folklands (or shires) in Southwestern Norway, Hordaland and Rogaland, the territories about the modern ports of Bergen and Stavanger. Due west from the former city lie the Shetland Islands; in the same direction from Stavanger are the Orkneys. It has been conjectured that the earliest Scandinavian settlements in these parts were made on the shores of Pentland Firth, on the Orkneys and on the coast of Caithness. Thence the journey went along the north-western coast of Scotland to the Hebrides group, across the narrow straits to Ireland, and down to the Isle of Man.

The Emerald Isle attracted the sea-kings and the period of pillage was soon followed by an age of settlement. The earliest Norse colony in Ireland seems to have been founded about 826, on the banks of the Liffey, where the city of Dublin grew up a little later, and for centuries remained the centre of Norse power and influence on the island. Other settlements were established at various points on the east coast, notably at Wicklow, Wexford, and Waterford, which names show clearly their Norse origin. About 860 a stronghold was built at Cork.

Toward the close of the eighth century the vikings appeared in large numbers on the coasts of Northern England. Two generations later they had destroyed three of the four English kingdoms and were organising the Danelaw on their ruins. Still later Rolf appeared with his host of Northmen in the Seine Valley and founded the Norman duchy.

It must not be assumed that in these colonies the population was exclusively Scandinavian. The native elements persisted and seem, as a rule, to have lived on fairly good terms with the invaders. It is likely that wherever these energetic Northerners settled they became the dominant social force; but no feeling of contempt or aloofness appears to have been felt on either side after the races had learned to know each other. Intermarriage was frequent, not only between Dane and Angle, but between Celt and Norseman as well. In time the alien was wholly absorbed into the native population; but in the process the victorious element underwent a profound transformation which extended to social conventions as well as to race.

The largest of these colonies was the Danelaw, a series of Danish and Norse settlements extending from the Thames to the north of England. According to an English writer of the twelfth century, it comprised York and fourteen shires to the south. The area controlled was evidently considerably larger than the region actually settled; and in some of the shires the Scandinavian population was probably not numerous. Five cities in the Danelaw enjoyed a peculiar pre-eminence. These were Lincoln, Nottingham, Derby, Leicester, and Stamford. It has been conjectured that these were garrison towns held and organised with a view to securing the obedience of the surrounding country. If this be correct, we should infer that the population beyond the walls was largely Anglian. The Five Boroughs seem to have had a common organisation of a republican type: they formed "the first federation of boroughs known in this island, and in fact the earliest federation of towns known outside of Italy." Part of the Danelaw must have contained a large Scandinavian element, especially the shires of Lincoln and York. There were also Danish and Norwegian settlements in England outside the Danelaw in its narrower sense: in the north-western shires and in the Severn Valley, perhaps as high up as Worcestershire.

Danish power in England seems to have centered about the ancient city of York. It would be more nearly correct to speak of Northumbria in the ninth and tenth centuries as a Norse than as a Danish colony; but the Angles made no such distinction. The population must also have contained a large English element. A native ecclesiastic who wrote toward the close of the tenth century speaks with enthusiasm of the wealth and grandeur of York.

The city rejoices in a multitude of inhabitants; not fewer than 30,000 men and women (children and youths not counted) are numbered in this city. It is also filled with the riches of merchants who come from everywhere, especially from the Danish nation.

In some respects the Danelaw is the most important fact in the history of the Anglo-Saxon monarchy: it was the rock on which Old English nationality foundered. By the middle of the tenth century, Saxon England was practically confined to the country south of the Thames River and the western half of the Midlands, a comparatively small area surrounded by Scandinavian and Celtic settlements. If this fact is fully appreciated, there should be little difficulty in understanding the loss of English national freedom in the days of Sweyn and Canute. The English kings did, indeed, exercise some sort of suzerain authority over most of the neighbouring colonies, but this authority was probably never so complete as historians would have us believe.

It is worth noting that the scribe whom we have quoted above speaks of the Danes, not as pirates but as merchants. The tenth century was, on the whole, so far as piratical expeditions are concerned, an age of peace in the North. The word viking is old in the mediæval dialects, and Scandinavian pirates doubtless visited the shores of Christian Europe at a very early date. But the great viking age was the ninth century, when the field of piratical operations covered nearly half of Europe and extended from Iceland to Byzantium. The movement culminated in the last quarter of the century and was followed by a constructive period of nearly one hundred years, when society was being reorganised or built anew in the conquered lands. The Icelandic republic was taking form. The Norman duchy was being organised. The Northmen in the Danelaw were being forced into political relations with the Saxon kings. Trade began to follow new routes and find new harbours. The older Scandinavian cities acquired an added fame and importance, while new towns were being founded both in the home lands and in the western islands.

This lull in the activities of the sea-kings gave the western rulers an opportunity to regain much that had been lost. In England the expansion of Wessex which had begun in the days of Alfred was continued under his successors, until in Edgar's day one lord was recognised from the Channel to the Forth. But with Edgar died both majesty and peace. About 980 the viking spirit was reawakened in the North. The raven banner reappeared in the western seas, and soon the annals of the West began to recount their direful tales. Among all the chiefs of this new age, one stands forth pre-eminent, Sweyn with the Forked Beard, whose remarkable achievement it was to enlist all this lawless energy for a definite purpose, the conquest of Wessex.

In 979 Ethelred the Ill-counselled was crowned king of England and began his long disastrous reign. If we may trust the Abingdon chronicler, who, as a monk, should be truthful, England was duly warned of the sorrows to come. For "in that same year blood-red clouds resembling fire were frequently seen; usually they appeared at midnight hanging like moving pillars painted upon the sky." The King was a mere boy of ten summers; later writers could tell us that signs of degeneracy were discovered in the prince as early as the day of his baptism. On some of his contemporaries, however, he seems to have made a favourable impression. We cannot depend much on the praises of a Norse scald who sang in the King's presence; but perhaps we can trust the English writer who describes him as a youth of "elegant manners, handsome features, and comely appearance."

That Ethelred proved an incompetent king is beyond dispute. Still, it is doubtful whether any ruler with capabilities less than those of an Alfred could have saved England in the early years of the eleventh century. For Ethelred had succeeded to a perilous inheritance. In the new territorial additions to Wessex there were two chief elements, neither of which was distinctly pro-Saxon: the Dane or the half-Danish colonist was naturally hostile to the Saxon régime; his Anglian neighbour recalled the former independence of his region as Mercia, East Anglia, or Northumbria, and was weak in his loyalty to the southern dynasty. The spirit of particularism asserted itself repeatedly, for it seems unlikely that the many revolts in the tenth century were Danish uprisings merely.

It seems possible that Ethelred's government might have been able to maintain itself after a fashion and perhaps would have satisfied the demands of the age, had it not been that vast hostile forces were just then released in the North. These attacked Wessex from two directions: fleets from the Irish Sea ravaged the Southwest; vikings from the East entered the Channel and plundered the southern shores. It is likely that in the advance-guard of the renewed piracy, Sweyn Forkbeard was a prominent leader. We have seen that during the last years of Harold's reign, there were trouble and ill-feeling between father and son. These years, it seems, the undutiful prince spent in exile and piratical raids. As the Baltic would scarcely be a safe refuge under the circumstances, we may assume that those seven years were spent in the West.

In the second year of Ethelred's reign the incursions began: "the great chief Behemoth rose against him with all his companions and engines of war." In that year Chester was plundered by the Norsemen; Thanet and Southampton were devastated by the Danes. The troubles at Chester are of slight significance; they were doubtless merely the continuation of desultory warfare in the upper Irish Sea. But the attack on Southampton, the port of the capital city of Winchester, was ominous: though clearly a private undertaking it was significant in revealing the weakness of English resistance. The vikings probably wintered among their countrymen on the shores of the Irish Sea, for South-western England was again visited and harried during the two succeeding years.

For a few years (983-986) there was a lull in the operations against England. The energies of the North were employed elsewhere: this was evidently the period of Styrbjörn's invasion of Sweden and Sigvaldi's attack on Norway with the desperate battles of Fyris River and Hjörunga Bay. But, in 986, viking ships in great numbers appeared in the Irish Sea. Two years later a fleet visited Devon and entered Bristol Channel. It is probable that Norman ships took part in this raid; at any rate the Danes sold English plunder in Normandy.

In 991, the attack entered upon a new phase. Earlier the country had suffered from raids in which no great number of vikings had taken part in any instance; now they came in armies and the attack became almost an invasion. That year a fierce battle was fought near Maldon in Essex where one of the chief leaders of the vikings was an exiled Norwegian prince, Olaf Trygvesson, who four years later restored the Norwegian throne. It is likely, therefore, that the host was not exclusively Danish but gathered from the entire North.

The fight at Maldon was a crushing defeat for the English and consternation ruled in the councils of the irresolute King. Siric, the Archbishop of Canterbury, and two ealdormen were sent as an embassy to the viking camp to sue for peace. A treaty was agreed to which seems to imply that the host was to be permitted to remain in East Anglia for an undefined time. The vikings promised to defend England against any other piratical bands, thus virtually becoming mercenaries for the time being. In return Ethelred agreed to pay a heavy tribute and to furnish provisions "the while that they remain among us." Thus began the Danegeld which seems to have developed into a permanent tax in the reign of Canute.

The next year King Ethelred collected a fleet in the Thames in the hope of entrapping his new allies; but treason was abroad in England and the plan failed. The following year the pirates appeared in the Humber country; here, too, the English defence melted away. After relating the flight of the Anglian leaders, Florence of Worcester adds significantly, "because they were Danes on the paternal side."

The next year (994) King Sweyn of Denmark joined the fleet of Olaf and his associates and new purposes began to appear. Instead of seeking promiscuous plunder, the invaders attempted to reduce cities and strongholds. Once more the English sued for peace on the basis of tribute. Sweyn evidently returned to Denmark where his presence seems to have been sorely needed. For two years England enjoyed comparative peace. The energies of the North found other employment: we read of raids on the Welsh coast and of piratical expeditions into Saxony; interesting events also occurred in the home lands. To these years belong the revolt of the Norsemen against Earl Hakon, and perhaps also the invasion of Denmark by Eric the Victorious.

Thirty years of power had developed tyrannical passions in the Norwegian Earl. According to the sagas he was cruel, treacherous, and licentious. Every year he became more overbearing and despotic; every year added to the total of discontent. Here was Sweyn Forkbeard's opportunity; but he had other irons in the fire, and the opportunity fell to another. About 995 a pretender to the Norse throne arrived from the West,—Olaf Trygvesson, the great-grandson of Harold Fairhair.

Our earliest reliable information as to Olaf's career comes from English sources; they tell of his operations in Britain in 991 and 994 and the circumstances indicate that the intervening years were also spent on these islands. While in England he was attracted to the Christian faith, a fact that evidently came to be known to the English, for, in the negotiations of 994, particular attention was paid to the princely chieftain. An embassy was sent to him with Bishop Alphege as leading member, and the outcome was that Olaf came to visit King Ethelred at Andover, where he was formally admitted to the Christian communion, Ethelred acting as godfather.

At Andover, Olaf promised never to come again to England "with unpeace"; the Chronicler adds that he kept his word. With the coming of spring he set out for Norway and never again saw England as friend or foe. We do not know what induced him at this time to take up the fight with Hakon the Bad; but doubtless it was in large measure due to urging on the part of the Church. For Olaf the Viking had become a zealous believer; when he landed in Norway he came provided with priests and all the other necessaries of Christian worship. It is not necessary to tell the story of the Earl's downfall,—how he was hounded into a pig-sty where he died at the hands of a thrall. Olaf was soon universally recognised as king and proceeded at once to carry out his great and difficult purpose: to christianise a strong and stubborn people (995).

As to the second event, the invasion of Sweyn's dominions by the King of Sweden, we cannot be so sure, as most of the accounts that have come down to us are late and difficult to harmonise. Historians agree that, some time toward the close of his reign, King Eric sought revenge for the assistance that the Danish King had given his nephew Styrbjörn in his attempt to seize the Swedish throne. The invasion must have come after Sweyn's accession (986?) and before Eric's death, the date of which is variously given as 993, 995, 996. If Eric was still ruling in 994 when Sweyn was absent in England, it is extremely probable that he made use of a splendid opportunity to seize the lands of his enemy. This would explain Sweyn's readiness to accept Ethelred's terms in the winter of 994-995.

After the death of King Eric, new interests and new plans began to germinate in the fertile mind of Sweyn the Viking. Late in life the Swedish King seems to have married a young Swedish woman who is known to history as Sigrid the Haughty. Sigrid belonged to a family of great wealth and prominence; her father Tosti was a famous viking who had harvested his treasures on an alien shore. Eric had not long been dead before wooers in plenty came to seek the hand of the rich dowager. So importunate did they become that the Queen to get rid of them is said to have set fire to the house where two of them slept. Olaf Trygvesson was acceptable, but he imposed an impossible condition: Sigrid must become a Christian. When she finally refused to surrender her faith, the King is said to have stricken her in the face with his gauntlet. The proud Queen never forgave him.

Soon afterwards Sigrid married Sweyn Forkbeard who had dismissed his earlier consort, Queen Gunhild, probably to make room for the Swedish dowager. We do not know what motives prompted this act, but it was no doubt urged by state-craft. In this way the wily Dane cemented an alliance with a neighbouring state which had but recently been hostile.

The divorced Queen was a Polish princess of an eminent Slavic family; she was the sister of Boleslav Chrobri, the mighty Polish duke who later assumed the royal title. When Gunhild retired to her native Poland, she may have taken with her a small boy who can at that time scarcely have been more than two or three years old, perhaps even younger. The boy was Canute, the King's younger son, though the one who finally succeeded to all his father's power and policies. The only information that we have of Canute's childhood comes from late and not very reliable sources: it is merely this, that he was not brought up at the Danish court, but was fostered by Thurkil the Tall, one of the chiefs at Jomburg and brother of Earl Sigvaldi. The probabilities favour the accuracy of this report. It was customary in those days to place boys with foster-fathers; prominent nobles or even plain franklins received princes into their households and regarded the charge as an honoured trust. Perhaps, too, a royal child would be safer among the warriors of Jomburg than at the court of a stepmother who had employed such drastic means to get rid of undesirable wooers. The character of his early impressions and instruction can readily be imagined: Canute was trained for warfare.

When the young prince became king of England Thurkil was exalted to a position next to that of the ruler himself. After the old chief's death, Canute seems to have heaped high honours on Thurkil's son Harold in Denmark. We cannot be sure, but it seems likely that this favour is to be ascribed, in part, at least, to Canute's affection for his foster-father and his foster-brother.

In those same years another important marriage was formed in Sweyn's household: the fugitive Eric, the son of Earl Hakon whose power was now wielded by the viking Olaf, had come to Denmark, where Sweyn Forkbeard received him kindly and gave him his daughter Gytha in marriage. Thus there was formed a hostile alliance against King Olaf with its directing centre at the Danish court. In addition to his own resources and those of his stepson in Sweden, Sweyn could now count on the assistance of the dissatisfied elements in Norway who looked to Eric as their natural leader.

It was not long before a pretext was found for an attack. Thyra, Sweyn's sister, the widow of Styrbjörn, had been married to Mieczislav, the Duke of Poland. In 992, she was widowed the second time. After a few years, perhaps in 998, Olaf Trygvesson made her queen of Norway. Later events would indicate that this marriage, which Olaf seems to have contracted without consulting the bride's brother, was part of a plan to unite against Sweyn all the forces that were presumably hostile,—Poles, Jomvikings, and Norsemen.

The saga writers, keenly alive to the influence of human passion on the affairs of men, emphasise Sigrid's hatred for Olaf and Thyra's anxiety to secure certain possessions of hers in Wendland as important causes of the war that followed. Each is said to have egged her husband to the venture, though little urging can have been needed in either case. In the summer of 1000, a large and splendid Norwegian fleet appeared in the Baltic. In his negotiations with Poles and Jomvikings, Olaf was apparently successful: Sigvaldi joined the expedition and Slavic ships were added to the Norse armament. Halldor the Unchristian tells us that these took part in the battle that followed: "The Wendish ships spread over the bay, and the thin beaks gaped with iron mouths upon the warriors."

Sweyn's opportunity had come and it was not permitted to pass. He mustered the Danish forces and sent messages to his stepson in Sweden and to his son-in-law Eric. Sigvaldi was also in the alliance. Plans were made to ambush the Norse King on his way northward. The confederates gathered their forces in the harbour of Swald, a river mouth on the Pomeranian coast a little to the west of the isle of Rügen. Sigvaldi's part was to feign friendship for Olaf and to lead him into the prepared trap. The plan was successfully carried out. A small part of King Olaf's fleet was lured into the harbour and attacked from all sides. The fight was severe but numbers prevailed. Olaf's own ship, the famous Long Serpent, was boarded by Eric Hakonsson's men, and the King in the face of sure capture leaped into the Baltic.

The victors had agreed to divide up Norway and the agreement was carried out. Most of the coast lands from the Naze northwards were given to Earl Eric. The southern shores, the land from the Naze eastwards, fell to King Sweyn. Seven shires in the Throndhjem country and a single shire in the extreme Southeast were assigned to the Swedish King; but only the last-mentioned shire was joined directly to Sweden; the northern regions were given as a fief to Eric's younger brother Sweyn who had married the Swede-king's daughter. Similarly Sweyn Forkbeard enfeoffed his son-in-law Eric, but the larger part he kept as his own direct possession.

The battle of Swald was of great importance to the policies of the Knytlings. The rival Norse kingdom was destroyed. Once more the Danish King had almost complete control of both shores of the waterways leading into the Baltic. Danish hegemony in the North was a recognised fact. But all of Norway was not yet a Danish possession—that ambition was not realised before the reign of Canute. And England was still unconquered.

Made in the USA
Middletown, DE
27 October 2023

41454127R00209